The BEST of MEN

The BEST of MEN

CLAIRE LETEMENDIA

Jonathan Cape
London

Published by Jonathan Cape 2009

2 4 6 8 10 9 7 5 3 1

First published in Great Britain in 2009 by
Jonathan Cape
Random House, 20 Vauxhall Bridge Road,
London SW1V 2SA

Addresses for companies within The Random House Group Limited
can be found at: www.randomhouse.co.uk/offices.htm

The Random House Group Limited Reg. No. 954009

A CIP catalogue record for this book is available from the British Library

ISBN 9780224089371 (Hardback)
ISBN 9780224089388 (Trade paperback)

The Random House Group Limited makes every effort to ensure that
the papers used in its books are made from trees that have been legally
sourced from well-managed and credibly certified forests.
Our paper procurement policy can be found at:
www.randomhouse.co.uk/paper.htm

Printed and bound in Great Britain by
Clays Ltd, St Ives Plc

To Emily and Felix

He that weareth his heart in his fore-head, and is of an overt and
transparent nature, through whose words, as through cristall,
ye may see into every corner of his thoughts: That man is fitter
for a table of good-fellowship, then a Councell table.

Upon the Theater of public employment, either in peace or warre,
the actors must of necessity weare vizards, and change them in
evarie scene.

Wherefore a Prince may pretend a desire of friendship with the
weaker, when he meanes, and must, contract it with the stronger.

From Robert Dallington's 1613 translation of the *Civil and
Military Aphorisms of Guicciardini* which he dedicated to the
"High and Mightie Charles, Prince of Great Britain," the future
King Charles I.

PROLOGUE
Cadiz, Spain, July 1642

At a sharp bend on the road to Cadiz, Laurence heard a strangled cry pierce the air, as of a man being choked.

"God damn," he muttered, reining in his horse. If there was trouble up ahead, he could not circumvent it. To his left, sheer cliff descended to the sea miles below, and to his right, the barren, rocky hillside rose up too steeply for his horse to negotiate a path. Yet what did he care, anyway, he thought; he had no fear for himself.

Urging his mount forward again, he rounded the bend. Some twenty yards from him, a couple of men were assaulting an elderly fellow: one held a knife to his throat while the other searched him roughly. Both thieves were barefoot and scrawny, dressed in rags. They were jeering at their victim, doubtless pleased to have hit upon such easy prey, and so intent on their work that they did not notice Laurence. Nearby, indifferent to the spectacle, a pack mule stood nosing at the dusty earth.

Heaving a sigh, Laurence drew out his pistols. Empty as they were, he levelled them at the thieves. "*Déjale*," he yelled resignedly.

They turned, clearly taken by surprise. One bolted off immediately and scrambled up the hill, agile as a mountain goat.

Laurence watched him disappear before addressing his accomplice, who still had his blade tight to the old man's neck. "I said, leave him alone! And get lost before I shoot you."

"Get lost yourself, you son of a whore," the thief retorted with impressive bravado. "I was here first."

Laurence could not help smiling. "I'm not in your trade, and I have money. I'll give it to you, if you release him." He tossed the pistols some distance from his horse, catching as he did so an anguished flicker in the old man's eyes. Wary but curious, the thief squinted at Laurence as he dismounted and reached into his saddlebag. He withdrew his purse and poured from it a few coins, letting them slide through his fingers. Next he shook the purse, which emitted an unmistakable clinking sound, and threw it on the ground. "You can have the horse as well. In fact, you can have everything." The thief's confusion was so obvious that Laurence nearly laughed; no sane person would freely surrender his horse and weapons in such desolate countryside. "So, what are you waiting for?" he demanded, becoming impatient.

The thief stepped away from his victim to approach the purse, staring at it greedily. As he was about to snatch it, Laurence moved faster, kicking him in the shoulder. He howled, though he did not drop his knife. Grabbing Laurence by the knees, he brought him down, and they wrestled together in the dirt, rolling dangerously close to the edge of the precipice. The thief was all muscle, his grip on the weapon like a vice. He fought harder than Laurence, who only wished to allow the old man time to escape, and then let it all end quickly.

At length Laurence stopped struggling altogether. The thief was on top of him, aiming the steel point at his heart. Laurence gazed straight into his eyes and knew: the thief was afraid. "What's wrong with you, never killed a man before?" he taunted him contemptuously.

The thief scowled and bore down with the knife. But as the tip of the blade pricked Laurence's flesh, he smelt the thief's rotten breath full in his face and the stink of it roused his disgust: he was not prepared to die like this. He struck at the knife, which flew from the man's hand, and they began to wrestle again. He was unconscious of his actions, relying on instinct honed by long practice, the blood pounding in his ears and seething in his veins as if he were in the midst of battle. Suddenly he heard the thief shriek, and felt him grow limp and heavy. He thrust aside the body and lay back, panting; he must have managed to fish out the slim dagger that he always kept in his doublet, for it was driven to the hilt into the thief's chest, and his left hand was wet and sticky with gore.

He looked over at the old man, who was still beside the mule, his expression a mixture of puzzlement and awe. "You're safe," said Laurence. "You can be on your way."

"Bless you, sir." The man's face, brown and wrinkled like a cured olive, broke into a wide grin. He picked up the purse, the scattered coins, and the pistols and set them down neatly beside Laurence. Then he went over to the corpse and, without a hint of distaste, pulled out the dagger and cleaned it on the thief's rags. "You took a wild risk, in letting him have the advantage. To bluff with one's life is true courage." He frowned at Laurence thoughtfully. "Or else madness."

"It wasn't courage," Laurence said, sitting up to accept the knife from him.

"Whichever the case, you saved *my* life." The man produced a flask from a pocket in his travelling cloak and offered it to Laurence; it contained cool water, more reviving to Laurence's parched mouth than any spirits. "Are you bound for Cadiz, as I am?" Laurence nodded, drinking. "In return for what you have done, you must come to my house there, as my guest. I insist!"

Laurence hesitated. He would have preferred to refuse, but more thieves might be lurking about, and he did not want to leave the fellow unprotected. "Very well," he said, as he rose, wiping his hands on his already stained breeches.

"God is great," the man exclaimed, patting him on the shoulder. "God is great."

As they proceeded together on foot, walking their beasts, the man explained that he was a merchant returning from Tarifa. "I had to collect a bolt of silk, and while I was waiting to receive it, my two servants fell ill. They could not escort me back, but I was in a hurry to get home, so I set out alone. What a fool – and I could have been a dead fool had you not chanced by and rescued me. My name is José Moreno, sir. What is yours, and where are you from?" When Laurence told him, he seemed bemused. "An Englishman, are you? You don't look like a foreigner – and you speak with no accent. Indeed, at first I confess I thought the same as the thief – that you were another brigand," he remarked, surveying Laurence's garments. "Yet with this handsome black stallion – not to mention your gold, and your expensive arms – you are more of a target for robbery than I."

Dusk had fallen by the time they arrived at Cadiz. José guided him through winding streets to a passageway between high, forbidding walls. They reached a door upon which José knocked several times, in a distinct pattern. A servant as brown-skinned as he admitted them into a large torch-lit courtyard where fruit trees and flowers bloomed; the house was constructed in a square around it, with covered galleries on all sides.

While Laurence peered around, amazed that such beauty and luxuriant growth could be so perfectly concealed from the street beyond, the servant bowed to him, handed him down his saddlebags, and led away his horse and the mule. Then José took him beneath one of the galleries, saying, "We should not eat until we have cleansed ourselves." He paused a moment before calling out, "Khadija!"

A most extraordinary woman emerged from the shadows: she was an African, her skin not black but a ruddy copper hue. She wore indigo robes, with a cloth of the same colour wound about her temples, and her ears were pierced with gold rings from the top to the bottom of both lobes. Her hair was dressed in tiny plaits, sticking out from beneath the cloth like so many spiders' legs. At the corner of each eye there were three short scars, as though to simulate the lines of a smiling person, and her nose was long and fine, like José's. Her age could have been anywhere between thirty and fifty years old. José addressed her in what Laurence recognised as Arabic, and she went away, head held high as if she were a princess rather than the slave that he presumed she was.

"Khadija will bring us fresh linen and make food while we perform our ablutions," José told him.

In a separate room off the courtyard was the bath, wide and deep, like a rectangular pond, filled with scented water. José paused once more, regarding Laurence intently as if to gauge his reaction, and then began to undress. Laurence held back, embarrassed by the layers of grime beneath his clothes; he had not been able to wash properly more than once or twice in the past few months.

"What is it, sir?" José inquired, as he sank into the water. "Are you not accustomed to bathing? Or is it that you have never seen a circumcised man?" he added, in a low voice.

"But I have. I knew a Jew in The Hague."

José considered this carefully. "Could he practise his faith, where he was?"

"I believe so. I hope so, at any rate."

Again, José appeared surprised. "But you are a Christian, no?"

"I am . . . nothing," Laurence said, as he bent to rinse the thief's blood from his hands.

"You are not nothing in the eyes of God. Remember that. I shall be frank with you, sir," José continued. "My birth name is not José. It is Yusuf."

"Were you a Muslim?"

"I still am." There was a silence. "Do you regret now that you saved me?" asked Yusuf.

"Not at all – though isn't it forbidden for *you* to worship?"

"It is forbidden these days even to have infidel ancestry. As you may know, more than thirty years ago the *conversos* were almost all expelled, and amongst those of us left, few are brave enough to cling to our true religion. I could bring the Inquisition down upon me just for taking this bath."

So Yusuf had risked his own life, Laurence realised, in inviting him here.

After they had dried themselves, Yusuf gave Laurence a clean shirt. "My son's," he said. "He is away doing business on the Guinea Coast, where I bought my Khadija. She is now the lady of the house. My first wife died when I was still captain of a ship. I have five sons who are grown and gone to sea – they inherited my passion for it."

At table they were served by Khadija. Yusuf took no wine himself but filled Laurence's cup generously. When the plates were cleared, he brought out a pipe and lit it. After inhaling, he passed it to Laurence, who was familiar with the smell: he had smoked hashish as a youth with his tutor Seward in Venice, and on a few occasions since. Relaxed by the drug, he listened more than he talked, yet he began to suspect, from something in Yusuf's manner, that his host was deliberating over an unspoken question.

Finally Yusuf put down the pipe. "I must ask – why do you claim to be an Englishman? I am sure that you have Barbary blood. I should call you a Moor like myself, if it would not insult you."

"Oh no, I'm used to being called many things," said Laurence, amused. "I'm only half English, though. My mother is a Spaniard."

"Ah, that explains your facility with the language. Is she in Cadiz?"

"She's in England. I haven't seen her in six years."

"You have been away a while. As a soldier?"

"For most of the time."

"So what brings you to my city?"

Laurence laughed shortly. "No good reason."

"Are you by yourself?"

"Yes."

"Where will you go next?" Laurence shrugged. "You are welcome to stay with me however long you wish," Yusuf said, "or I could find you passage to Africa, or to the Indies, should that strike your fancy. There is also a ship in harbour bound for the English coast. She leaves within the week. Or would you prefer to travel by land?" Laurence shrugged again; he had absolutely no answer. "Khadija!" cried Yusuf. "Our guest is in need of advice."

Khadija came bearing a small woven basket. She tipped it on to the table and about a dozen small, shiny, oval-shaped shells fell out, smooth on one side and etched with what resembled little teeth on the other. "Pick them up and put them in my hands," she told Laurence, in accented Spanish. "Then I shall let them fall where they will, and read them for you. They will speak of your future."

"I'm sorry, but I don't believe they can," Laurence said, forcing a smile.

"Then what have you to worry about?" asked Yusuf.

It would be churlish to decline, so Laurence did as she bade. He must pretend interest, he reminded himself, as she surveyed the shells, her broad lips parted in concentration.

"You tried to kill yourself today," she began, her tone clear and certain.

Laurence betrayed no reaction. Privately, he was unsettled. Even if his host had described to her what had happened on the road to Cadiz, there was an earlier event about which Yusuf could not be aware.

"A woman has poisoned you," she went on, sending a shiver down his spine. "Now you are in hiding, from the world and from yourself. Yet soon you will cross paths with another woman, who will deserve your love. She has the name of a great queen and she will give birth to your child, if you are ready for her. But if you do not spit out the poison, you will lose her."

His scepticism returned: it was the sort of vague, trite prophecy that Juana might have invented, assuming that everyone wanted to hear about love and fertility. In his case, this could not be further from the truth. The strange apprehension that he had just felt was probably the hashish working on his troubled mind.

"Again," Khadija ordered. Obediently he gathered up the shells. This time when she released them they jumped apart and scattered as though possessed of their own force. She absorbed their arrangement and said with the same certainty, "You alone can prevent a tragedy in your land, and what you have that was stolen holds the key."

"What is it that I have?" Laurence demanded, his pulse quickening. "Can you tell me?"

Khadija made no sign that she had heard, putting the shells back in their basket one by one. She was too astute to spoil the impact of her guesswork by elaborating on it, he thought wryly. Remarkable, however, that she should have been quite so fortunate.

She gestured to him to give her his hands; hers were soft, her fingers slender and pliable as those of a girl. Was he meant to thank her, he wondered, or was she offering him some kind of blessing? Her expression at once tender and severe, she inspected his palms, calloused from riding, and his nails, broken from months of living rough; and she rolled up his sleeves to the elbow, palpating the lean flesh of his forearms with her fingertips. "You earn your way with your hands," she commented.

"He is a soldier, Khadija," Yusuf informed her.

"Not any more. He makes his living through games of chance." Laurence blinked at her, astonished. "And the night this was done to you," she said, touching the scar on his left wrist, "you played a game that changed your fate." He gasped, shuddering as she caressed it.

"Khadija, now you are scaring him," said Yusuf. "He'll think you are a witch."

She dropped Laurence's hands and leant forward to murmur in his ear. "You must go home."

"Why?" he whispered, his voice as tremulous as the rest of him.

"That is for you to learn." She slipped from her arm a thin leather bracelet, which seemed to contain something stitched inside. "Here – it will protect you on the journey, and remove the worst of the poison," she said, looping it about his scarred wrist. "Wear it until it falls off of its own accord." As she fastened it, uttering words in another, incomprehensible language, he felt every nerve in his body tense and he could not avert his gaze from hers. Then she ran her hands over his face, as if to release him from her spell, and smiled sadly.

He bowed his head, trying to comprehend what had passed through him, and when he looked up, he was half relieved to see that she had vanished.

Yusuf was refilling the pipe. Apparently oblivious to his guest's unease, he started to talk about the many ports he had visited, and the many occasions that he had braved death when his ships had been overrun by pirates, or swept into storms or wrecked on hostile shores; and he spoke of his love for the ocean, as whimsical a mistress as the goddess Fortune herself. "There is no life without her," he concluded, "and maybe one day I shall set sail for a last time." He fell silent, regarding Laurence with his dark, hooded eyes, before asking, "Which course will you choose tomorrow?"

"I don't know," Laurence said. "I honestly don't know."

"Not so," Yusuf told him quietly. "In your heart, you have already decided."

Part One

England, July–August 1642

CHAPTER ONE

I.

"How is it for you, Beaumont, to be in England again?" Ingram asked.

Beaumont glanced around as if he might find an answer somewhere in the dank atmosphere of the taproom. "Strange," he replied.

"Well, you look much the same," Ingram said, although this was not completely true.

"But look at *you*, Ingram. You've lost some hair."

Ingram ran a hand over his scalp. "Kind of you to mention it."

Beaumont, he observed, had not lost any of his hair, which was as black as ever, wavy and unkempt, tied back with a piece of string. As always, he appeared conspicuously foreign beside his fellow countrymen with their red and pink complexions, even when he was not burned to his present dark brown by a harsher sun than theirs; indeed, his colouring had earned him the derogatory Latin nickname of *Niger* when they were at university together. He still possessed his attitude of relaxed grace, leaning back against the wall so that he did not have to sit up straight on the wooden bench. He was clean-shaven, though not very well, and not very recently. He wore no jewellery save the plain gold earring that had a special significance for Ingram: on the night Beaumont had got his ear pierced, he himself had lost his virginity at an Oxford brothel. While waiting for him, Beaumont had submitted to this small operation, performed by his favourite girl. When she wanted to give Ingram the same treatment, he had refused, blushing after what he had just done, and anxious to return to the safety of their college.

It amused him to see that Beaumont's clothes were in typical disarray: his collar was missing, the front of his shirt hung open, and his doublet lacked most of its buttons. Apart from his shirt, which seemed reasonably fresh, everything was stained and torn. His dishevelled state could not be taken as an indication of his material circumstances. Ingram had known him to have his pockets full of money and be no better dressed.

Yet he had changed, Ingram thought. Though lanky as ever, he was broader in the shoulders: life in the army must have forced him into some more strenuous physical activities than drinking and bedding women. The shadowy skin around his pale green eyes had deepened in hue. His face was thinner, the lines on either side of his mouth now more pronounced, as were his high cheekbones, and he had acquired a small scar across his lower lip on the left side. His expression was not quite so mischievous as Ingram remembered; perhaps he even had a guarded look about him.

"You hardly acquired that blackamoor colour fighting in the Low Countries," Ingram remarked.

"I was in Spain for the last two or three months."

"In Spain! To see your mother's family?"

"No."

"Why, then?" Beaumont shifted in his seat. "Let me guess," Ingram said. "It was for a woman. Am I right?"

"Yes."

"Were you in love?" Beaumont squinted at him. "Tell me about her. Was she some Spanish duchess bored by an inattentive husband? A courtesan more skilled in the arts of seduction than you?"

"Enough, Ingram."

"It ended badly, I assume."

"Very badly."

"I'm sorry. Did you sail here straight from Spain?"

"No, I flew," said Beaumont sarcastically. "Let's get some more wine."

He gestured at the serving woman, who approached at once with a new jug. He asked her name, at which she blushed and answered, giggling, and hovered by their table until summoned by another drinker.

"Ever prodigal with your charm, aren't you," Ingram commented, when she had gone.

"It doesn't cost anything to be pleasant."

"Speaking of pleasant, this is the lowest tavern in Newbury. I wouldn't have set foot in it if you hadn't insisted. Why didn't you come to my brother's house, half a mile off? We serve much better wine."

"I'm sure you do," said Beaumont, availing himself of the inferior liquid, "but I didn't think Richard would be happy to see me. And I like low taverns."

"As well I recall. Oh, Beaumont, *I'm* overjoyed to see you. I kept wondering if you were alive, hoping you were."

Beaumont responded with one of the beautiful flashing smiles that Ingram had never managed to resist no matter how much his friend might irritate him, and reached out to pat Ingram's hand. As he did so, Ingram saw that he bore another much longer scar on the underside of his left wrist, a jagged white line that contrasted painfully with the skin around it and ran from some point hidden beneath his sleeve all the way down to the base of his thumb. About the same wrist was tied a curious leather band that he now pushed back beneath his sleeve as though he did not want Ingram to notice it.

"How did you get the scar?" Ingram asked.

"A game of cards," he said, dismissively.

"Still playing the tables, are you?"

"If the need arises."

They were silent for a while; then Ingram said, "I'm glad you caught me when you did. I was about to leave for Oxford to join my troop."

"Your *troop?*"

"I know – you'd think I'd be the last man to take up arms. But then *you* weren't exactly full of martial spirit six years ago."

"I wasn't, and I'm still not," Beaumont said, with a laugh.

"We may have no choice in the matter soon," Ingram said, lowering his voice. "War is very likely."

"What brought it all about, Ingram – politics or religion?" Beaumont inquired, pouring for them both.

Ingram sighed and considered. "As much the one as the other, I'd say. Parliament had its grievances over the King levying taxes without its consent, and imposing his prayer book, here and in Scotland. But there's been rioting everywhere. You may not have heard yet – Parliament has accused His Majesty of being seduced by evil counsellors, Lord Digby above all, and Queen Henrietta Maria herself. Can you imagine – the radicals in the House of Commons were threatening to impeach her, to bring her to trial! They believed she was scheming to import Catholic troops from Ireland to stamp out the dissent in London. His Majesty had to send her to The Hague, they were both in such fear of her life. Hard to believe their own subjects would show such disrespect for her – and for a king who ruled in peace for so many years."

"For over ten of which he couldn't even be bothered to hold a Parliament," Beaumont said, in his ironic way. "He only summoned it back because he was short of money. That doesn't show much respect for his subjects."

"I see you're more informed than you pretend to be. Why did you ask for my opinion of events?" Beaumont merely shrugged. "I think you enjoy playing devil's advocate. You always have."

"Don't be annoyed with me, Ingram. All I'm suggesting is that there seems to be wrong on both sides, and that the differences between King and Parliament could be negotiated –"

"He'd have to surrender his royal authority to Parliament!"

"Isn't that better than a civil war?"

"Good God. You sound as if you'd favour a republic!"

"There might be worse things," Beaumont murmured, still smiling slightly. "But aren't there some people left who want to avoid bloodshed?"

"There are, though at present they're all crying in the wilderness. Look, man," Ingram went on, feeling that he must set his friend straight, "Parliament has seized control of the Royal Navy, as well as London and most of our ports. It demanded that the King surrender the militias, an outrageous request which His Majesty refused in no uncertain terms. I believe the time for negotiation has passed. If the King raises his standard, I'll be with him, and I trust you will be too." An uncomfortable look crossed Beaumont's face, and Ingram felt uncomfortable himself, trying to guess where his friend's loyalties might lie. "Beaumont," he said, "I'd like to introduce you to the man who's raising my troop, Sir Bernard Radcliff. He served in the foreign war, as you did. He's a fine fellow and an excellent soldier."

"A rare combination."

"How's that?"

"The military life abroad did tend to corrupt," Beaumont said delicately.

Ingram stood up, wobbling a little on his feet. "I have to piss."

Beaumont grinned at him. "What, *again*?"

"Yes, and don't you finish my wine for me," Ingram told him, grinning back.

When Ingram returned from the yard, the taproom was almost empty save for a group of newcomers drinking ale in a corner. They wore bright cockades in their hats and swords at their sides; local fellows, taking advantage of a coming war and a hot summer night to prowl the neighbourhood in search of trouble. Beaumont, meanwhile, was idly making patterns on the table with tallow drippings from a candle. The men were watching him, talking amongst themselves.

"You're not from these parts, are you?" one of them barked out suddenly, from across the room. Beaumont paid no attention to him. "He's a foreigner," the man announced to his companions. "Like as not a papist mercenary sent over by our papist queen to cut our throats. Is that so?" He took a few steps closer to Beaumont. "Haven't you got the manners to address me? Or don't you talk my language?"

In former days Ingram had witnessed Beaumont engage in many altercations, more often than not leading to brawls, so he hastily intervened. "My friend is as English as you are," he said, in a conciliatory tone. "And he's no papist. He was away serving with the Protestant armies."

"Can't he speak for himself?"

Ingram frowned at Beaumont. "I think we should be on our way."

"He's not ready to leave yet," said the man. "He's still got half a jug in front of him. I think we should have a chat, me and your friend."

"About what?" Beaumont asked equably, raising his eyes at last to inspect the man.

"About you, you son of a papist whore." The man's companions were waiting in smug anticipation, Ingram realised, as if they had witnessed such a scene before and knew how it would end. "Didn't you hear me?" the man inquired, clearly nettled that his insult had elicited no reaction.

"I don't have any quarrel with you," Beaumont said, much to Ingram's relief, but the man was not pacified.

"By Jesus, you're asking for one," he declared, striding over. "I've a mind to tan your arse with the back of my sword."

"Beaumont, let's be off," Ingram said.

"Because of this gentleman?" Beaumont was pouring himself a fresh cup. "Don't worry about him. He's just had a bit too much to drink."

"Say that again, you filthy cur," the man growled.

Beaumont seemed oblivious until the man reached for the hilt of his sword. In the same moment Beaumont jumped up, overturning the bench with a crash, and caught him with two neat blows, to the nose and on the jaw. The man's head snapped back and he fell, his sword still stuck in its scabbard. Blood trickled from his nostrils, and he lay without moving, a stupefied look on his face. It had happened with such speed that everyone was stunned into silence; then murmurs of indignation issued from the man's companions.

"Beaumont, out!" said Ingram.

"All right, all right." Beaumont took up his saddlebag, threw it over his shoulder, paused to empty his cup, walked past the enraged audience with an amicable nod, and followed Ingram into the yard.

Ingram grabbed his sleeve. "We'd better run, or they'll make quick work of us."

"No, no – he was the only one who wanted to pick a fight," said Beaumont, moving at an unhurried pace.

"Beaumont," Ingram said anxiously, "if you'll allow me, I'd like to give you a piece of advice. Things aren't what they were over here. Tempers have grown very hot, and it would serve you to be more careful. He was armed, for God's sake."

"Well thank you for that piece of advice, Ingram, but so was I." Beaumont showed him a pair of pistols tucked into his saddlebag.

Ingram eyed them, feeling still more anxious: he had never shot a man, nor seen a man shot. "Good that it went no further. It might have if he'd seen them, or if you'd been wearing a sword."

"That's exactly why I kept them hidden, and why I left my sword behind where I stabled my horse. I've no desire to fight anyone at all," Beaumont said, with an air of outraged innocence.

"You broke his nose!"

"Purely in self-defence."

Ingram started to laugh. "And we didn't even pay for that last round."

"That's unforgivable. Should we go back?"

"Certainly not. I should be off to bed."

"Is someone waiting there for you?" Beaumont asked slyly.

"I wish!" said Ingram, still laughing.

They had arrived at a churchyard. Beaumont pushed him through the gate, and they sat down on the grass. After hunting about in his saddlebag, Beaumont produced a flask. He offered it to Ingram, who had a swig of the contents.

"That would put hair on anyone's chest!" he spluttered, as the fierce liquor burnt its way down his insides.

"Not on mine," said Beaumont, taking back the flask.

"Still smooth as a baby's bum, is it? Well, at least you have plenty on your scalp." Ingram chuckled. "Remember when we were up at Merton, how we had a bet as to who would start shaving first?"

"Which you won."

"And now I'm paying for it! Kate's always after me with one thing or another that she promises will restore my locks to their former glory."

"How is your sister, by the way?" Beaumont asked, stretching out his long legs.

"Very well. She's getting married next month, to Sir Bernard Radcliff."

"Radcliff? Ah – your excellent soldier."

"One of the best men I've ever met." Ingram paused to stifle a belch. "Thank heaven she had the sense to accept him. We were at the end of our tether trying to find a match for her. She's not so young any more. Twenty-two on her last birthday."

Beaumont made a shocked sound through his teeth. "Ancient! What about him?"

"He's somewhat older than she is, I grant you, but he's never been married. He fell madly in love with her. He came all the way back from service in Holland just to make his proposal. Wasn't even bothered that she had such a small dowry," Ingram added, stifling another belch.

"Then how *could* she refuse him! What about you, Ingram, have you thought of marrying again?" Beaumont inquired, more gently.

Ingram recalled his wife as he had last seen her, in death, her face ruined from the smallpox and her jaw tied up with a band of linen so that it would not fall open. It upset him that eight years later he remembered so little of her when she was alive. "I did consider it once," he said, "but I couldn't bring myself to speak to the woman. I've no property, and no great prospects, and now, with the war . . ."

"Oh yes, the war."

Emboldened by alcohol, Ingram ventured, "Your family were at their wits' end, not hearing from you all this time, apart from a couple of brief letters you sent. I'd like to see their faces when you appear at their door tomorrow. I'd like to see your face, too."

"Please – let's not talk about them." Beaumont handed him the flask again, then got up and turned away to unlace.

"Families are splitting over their politics," Ingram said, while his friend was relieving himself. "If there's a war, they'll have to face killing their own flesh and blood."

"Not a happy prospect."

"No, it isn't. Beaumont," Ingram went on, "I met your brother when I was last in Oxford."

"What was he doing there?"

"The same as Radcliff. Raising a troop for the King."

"Tom always enjoyed ordering people about," Beaumont said, as he fastened the front of his breeches and sat back down.

"That's unfair, man."

"Why – has he improved with age?"

"He may have. And you mustn't fall to arguing as soon as you see him. This is no time to air your private differences."

"I'd say it's the perfect time. War provides a cover for all sorts of differences, private and public."

"I'm serious. You must look to your duty, as he is doing. There's more than duty at stake, especially for you, as heir to your father's estate. Isn't it worth fighting to protect? And you were ready to defend your religion abroad –"

"Come on, Ingram," Beaumont said, laughing. "I wasn't defending my religion. You know I've no religion to defend."

"Shush, not so loud," Ingram said uneasily.

"We're in a graveyard!"

"All the same, we're on consecrated ground."

"Have another drink. Those are the only spirits I believe in."

"I wish you would change your mind about – about that issue. No one can live without faith. It's inconceivable."

"For you it may be. But if I ever had any doubts, what I saw while I was away confirmed to me that there's no God in heaven. Though hell exists, right here on earth."

"You sided with the Protestants, didn't you? You must have had some attachment to their cause."

"I hate to deceive you, but our friend in the taproom wasn't so far from the truth. When I arrived, I served with the Spanish infantry. Papists to a man."

Ingram hesitated, as the information sank in. "You mean – you mean you fought for the Hapsburg Emperor?"

"Yes, but not for long. At the siege of Breda I discovered I was on the losing side, and probably wouldn't come out of it alive. So I went over to the Dutch."

"Sweet Jesus – you were a turncoat," Ingram whispered.

"I wasn't the only one."

"But – I don't understand – what made you join up in the first place, if you couldn't care less why you were risking your life?"

Beaumont took a moment to answer, grabbing the flask from Ingram and tipping it to his lips. "I suppose I wanted to test myself," he said, after wiping his mouth on his sleeve. "I'd led such a soft, useless life until then."

"I won't dispute that. But how could you throw your lot in with an emperor who stole the Palatinate from the brother-in-law of our own king, and has sent his dearest sister and her family into exile?" Ingram demanded reproachfully.

"The Spanish happened to be the first troops I encountered. And I wanted to go where I wouldn't be seen as what I am here: heir to my father's estate, as you put it. They didn't give a shit whether I was born in a castle or a pigsty. And they taught me a lot," Beaumont added, passing over the flask again.

"Such as?"

"How to go without sleep for weeks and march day after day with my feet bleeding into my boots. They humbled me. They have great endurance and a sense of humour even in the worst of circumstances."

Ingram quaffed from the flask, his head spinning. "Dear God! But weren't you under suspicion after your abrupt change of allegiance?"

"Yes, mostly from the other Englishmen over there, though I made some friends amongst them in the Dutch service. Then you'll be glad to hear that I *did* end up with a number of English and a mixed contingent of Germans and Swedes who'd been sent to help Charles Louis win back the Palatinate. Not a wise choice of mine, in retrospect."

"Why? You were finally fighting for a noble cause."

"Noble, perhaps, but doomed to failure, and partly by His Majesty our king, who wasn't prepared to give his nephew enough funds to succeed. Poor Charles Louis lost hope of ever reclaiming his lands after his army was wiped out at Vlotho. You should have seen it, man. The fields were red with blood."

"And then what did you do?"

Beaumont shrugged. "I fell in with another cavalry regiment under Bernard of Weimar. When he died, we were sold over to French command and pushed all the way south down the Rhine, taking town after town, and then across the river . . ." He tailed off, as if remembering, then shook himself. "Look, Ingram," he said, gazing straight at his friend, "as you well know, there aren't just Protestants fighting the Emperor – the French are as Catholic as the Spanish. And of those that are Protestant, there's a host of little German states that shift alliances constantly, and of course the Swedes, who are still the most feared of the mercenaries. The destruction they wrought was incredible – most unchristian, you might say. It's not a religious war any longer, if ever it was," he concluded, in a bitter tone. "It's a struggle for power – an obscene game played out all the way from the Alps to the Baltic Sea. So please don't talk to me about causes. They make no sense to me."

Ingram belched more loudly, gagging as the oily taste of the liquor came back up into his throat. "I feel ill."

"Has our little talk upset your stomach?" Beaumont inquired, jokingly, but with an edge to his voice. Ingram did not answer, busy attempting to stand. His legs buckled and he nearly toppled over. "Let me help," Beaumont said, grasping his shoulders to steady him.

Together they negotiated a circuitous route over holy ground, finding at last the gate through which they had entered the churchyard. They had not gone far when Ingram was violently sick, though it made him no soberer, and he had to lean on Beaumont for the rest of the way. Some time afterwards he was vaguely conscious of a voice raised in argument, and an icy weight crashed over his head, depriving him of breath. Then he was lifted up bodily, and he knew that he was being carried upstairs to his bed.

II.

Stretched out on his narrow pallet at the Lamb Inn, in Oxford, Sir Bernard Radcliff was too hot to sleep, and too uncomfortable, for the blankets were alive with vermin. He was also troubled by an irrational foreboding. He had hoped to see Walter Ingram in the city that day, but Ingram had sent a message to explain that he would not be coming until the following afternoon. An old friend of his had got back from the war abroad and they were to meet for the first time in years.

Radcliff recollected Ingram talking about the friend, whom he had known since he was up at university. Heir to a wealthy lord, Beaumont was apparently a heavy drinker with an eye for women. In all likelihood some insolent, red-faced nobleman, Radcliff thought; just the type he had always envied bitterly for the ease with which they could pay for their vices and escape moral disapprobation, quite apart from punishment under the law. To enjoy their freedom and exalted rank in society he must see his plans come to fruition and meanwhile put up with his lowly status as a country squire, owner of a few boggy acres near Cambridge that he could not even afford to drain and make productive, and that he was half ashamed to show to his future bride. He would have to put up with Ingram's friend, too: Ingram had insisted they be introduced, and was even hoping that the fellow might join their troop.

Radcliff turned onto his side, trying to avoid the worst lumps in the mattress. It was true, he acknowledged, that he was in need of experienced recruits who had the money to equip themselves. Nevertheless, he disliked the possibility that this friend, with all the privileges of birth and a longer history with Ingram, might supplant him in Ingram's affections. He had grown more and more fond of Ingram, and not only because they were soon to be related by marriage; he appreciated Ingram's warm, open nature and valued his admiration.

What a peculiar coincidence that the man should be called Beaumont, though of course the name was not uncommon. Radcliff had heard of a John Beaumont enlisted in the King's army, and then there was the famous playwright, Francis Beaumont, so popular with the Royal Court. In France, it was not an unusual name at all. But it dredged up the nagging worry that had plagued him ever since his fateful night in The Hague.

Scratching at his chest where he sensed the tickle of fleas, he thought how very unfair it was that such a trivial error, a last bachelorhood indulgence in an expensive Dutch house of pleasure, had drawn such trouble upon him. If only, he had mused countless times; if only he had left his servant to guard his possessions; if only he had not drawn the curtain when he took the whore to bed. He might have seen that other woman creep into the chamber and with quick, adroit fingers steal his purse, snatch his sword, and slip out as silently as she had entered. Lying afterwards to his great patron, the Earl of Pembroke, had filled Radcliff with dread. He had admitted that the thief had taken the beautiful Toledo sword that Pembroke had given him, and all the money that he had been carrying to buy arms for the earl's personal security. But he could not reveal that she had also made off with something yet more valuable to him, though she would never have known it: the coded correspondence between him and Pembroke, which he had preserved in case their association turned to enmity or some unanticipated event frustrated their plans. If Pembroke ever found out, Radcliff would not be long for this world.

Yet it seemed impossible. The thief was thousands of miles away. As Radcliff knew from the brothel-keeper's grooms, she was an ignorant gypsy paired up with a cardsharp, *Monsieur Beaumont*, as he had been called at the house, so no doubt a Frenchman, perhaps illiterate too. And even had they discovered the letters tucked inside the lining of Radcliff's purse, they would have been unable to make head or tail of the code.

No, surely he was safe, Radcliff comforted himself, as safe as was his reputation with Pembroke, who believed in and depended upon his arcane knowledge and skills to negotiate the complex twists and turns of the road ahead. For in the coming war, he and Pembroke would appear to be on opposite sides, Pembroke on Parliament's and Radcliff on the King's, while all along working towards a change of rule that would appall His Majesty's most virulent opponents. The boldness, the vaunting ambition of it, still dazzled Radcliff, but it was written in the stars, as he had foreseen.

Again he reflected on the irony that although he could draw up the horoscopes of other men and women, he could not chart his own: his birth had been a lengthy and difficult process costing his mother her life, and no record had been kept of when exactly he had emerged. Pembroke, however, was a different case: his eminent family had set down all the essential details of time and place. And he, as Radcliff had already assured him, would live through the war to a prosperous dotage, so there seemed no reason to believe that he could fail in his political aims.

Hearing the college bells chime two of the clock, Radcliff began to dwell, more happily, upon Kate. Without her knowledge, he had also cast her horoscope, so that he could at least catch a glimpse of his future from hers. Their union would be fruitful, he had discovered, and her life, like Pembroke's, would last into old age.

He had not cared for any woman as much before. He remembered proposing to her last year at Richard Ingram's house in Newbury, and how, when she accepted, her blue eyes had returned his gaze without coquetry or shyness.

"I must go abroad again, Kate, to arrange to free myself from my commission with the Dutch," he had said, expecting some feminine anxiety on his behalf. She had merely nodded and allowed him to kiss her cheek: their first kiss.

Back in England after the theft, still smarting from Pembroke's angry disappointment, Radcliff had gone to see her again. He had kissed her once more, on the lips, and she had been equally undemonstrative. "She's an odd girl, always was," Ingram had told him. "The ice queen, we used to call her. Doesn't even gossip with Richard's wife."

"I like that," Radcliff had said, confident of winning her affection slowly and patiently, in the same way that he hoped to lay the foundations for his own success. She was superior to other women, pure and self-contained, in every way fitted for the honours that he wished to confer upon her. And it was her very iciness that made him yearn to stir her to passion, as soon as they were wed.

III.

Ingram's older brother, Richard, begrudgingly allowed Laurence to stay the night, on two strict conditions: that he share his unconscious friend's chamber, to keep an eye on him, and leave at once the next day. Laurence agreed. He was himself drunker than he had thought, and ready to sleep.

Yawning as he took off his doublet, he touched the scar at his right side, a deep trough in the flesh that ached occasionally in damp weather. He could still remember the impact, the intense shock rather than pain, of being shot, and then the stupid sense of injustice, as if his luck should have held indefinitely.

It happened by the banks of the Rhine during a brief skirmish with the enemy. The musket ball came from nowhere, shattering the edge of Laurence's light breastplate, almost blasting him from his saddle. He clung to the reins with one hand but would have fallen and been trampled instantly had someone not pulled him out of the fray. Eventually he was thrown with a pile of other groaning men into a cart, the bouncing of which, as it bore him over the torn and broken earth, sent him into oblivion.

At a nearby village some barns and stables, now emptied of livestock and fodder, had been commandeered as a makeshift hospital for

the wounded French and German troops. After regaining consciousness, he waited there, on a floor puddled with blood and human waste,
beside a man already dead, until a surgeon could be found to extract the
ball. His breastplate had slowed its pace, preventing it from passing
cleanly through him and leaving small pieces of metal embedded so
deep that they could only be removed by repeated incisions. By the time
the surgeon had finished, Laurence was hoarse from screaming. The
surgeon stuffed ash into his wound to staunch the bleeding; then he
was bandaged inadequately with the remnants of his shirt, fed a cup of
sour wine, and abandoned to the clouds of flies.

Delirious, he lost all awareness of time. Days must have passed
before he could walk a few steps, hunched over to protect the hole in
his side. He learnt that since the army could not afford to have its
progress slowed, it had marched on, taking most of the supplies and all
but the most decrepit of horses and oxen. As to the men left behind,
scant provision had been made for their comfort. With bowels loosened by rotten food and tainted water, they froze at night, having been
robbed long ago of any decent clothing or valuable possessions. Many
who might have survived their wounds succumbed to the flux or the
ague, while others went more quickly, their injuries putrid and gan-
grenous in a matter of hours.

Laurence was fortunate. At last his wound stopped leaking yellow
fluid and dried over in a thick scab that itched unbearably. He increased
his perambulations to the courtyard and fields beyond, where he would
watch the bodies being taken out for burial in a common pit and listen
to the dark jokes of those fit enough to perform that unsavoury chore.
As the local population began to starve, there was talk of cannibalism.
He had witnessed evidence of this after long sieges, once every dog and
cat and rat had been hunted down: corpses with hunks of meat neatly
removed from the thigh or the buttock. Yet in the hospital there were
still victuals, and women came each day to prostitute themselves or their

offspring in exchange for food. This, too, was not a new sight, but he found himself in a powerless rage against the men who deliberately chose to copulate with small children, in order to avoid being poxed by their mothers. He was laughed at for his sensitivity, and nor were the children grateful, for he was interfering in their livelihood. After the soldiers were done with them, they would limp away, uncomplaining, blood between their legs, clutching some precious morsel.

Perhaps he was wrong, he had thought then. In such a place, there was no room for moral indignation: brute survival dictated all. Yet he could not reconcile himself to life on such terms and so, although growing physically stronger, he had felt as though his mind were slowly becoming unhinged.

IV.

Laurence woke to the sound of snoring, from Ingram, in the bed beside him. Ingram seemed older in the morning light: small crow's feet marked the corners of his eyes, and his moustache was threaded with grey. The little tuft of beard between lower lip and chin that had become so fashionable of late gave him a rakish air that belied his true nature.

"Ingram, I have to go," Laurence said, shaking him.

He sighed drowsily. "What a night. I remember something wet on my head."

"Your brother threw a bucket of water over you."

"He must have given us hell."

"He gave me hell. You weren't in any condition to listen."

"Beaumont, your shirt," Ingram said, indicating the pinkish stains that speckled the front of it. "I'll lend you another, though it may be a bit short for you in the sleeves. Over there, in the clothes press." Laurence accepted the offer, and had just stripped off and was about to dress when Ingram pointed to his side and exclaimed, "What on earth did that to you?"

"A musket ball," Laurence said, hurrying to pull on the clean garment.

"How long ago?"

"About three years."

"Let me see."

"No."

"Why not? Most men are proud of their battle scars."

"What's there to be proud of? The surgeon was worse than a butcher's apprentice."

Ingram sighed again, heavily. "I owe you an apology for last night."

"For puking on me?"

"I'm sorry for that, yes – but what I mean is, I shouldn't judge you for what you did abroad, when in your situation I might have acted no differently myself."

"You would have acted very differently, my friend," Laurence said, thinking to himself that Ingram did not know the half of it. "Thanks, though, all the same."

"Where will you go now, to your family?"

"I must." Laurence felt in his doublet for the coded letters he had tucked away there and was relieved to find them safe. "Oh – I meant to ask, do you know if William Seward is still at Merton?"

"Yes, I believe he is, although he was very old for a tutor even when we had him."

"Must be the sight of those fresh-faced boys that's keeping him alive."

"What made you think of him?"

"Er . . . no special reason. He was always good to me."

"Because he wanted to bugger you. He wasn't as well disposed to *me*, but then I wasn't as pretty as you were, nor as clever. I was rather afraid of him, in fact, with his magical alembics and jars full of concoctions. And those cats he kept, like a witch's familiars – disgusting!"

"Too true – his rooms stank of cat piss." Laurence picked up his saddlebag, about to leave. "When shall I see you next?"

"I'll come by Chipping Campden in a few days, to find out how you're bearing up. I could take you back to Oxford with me, to meet my brother-in-law." Ingram propped himself up on one elbow and smiled at Laurence. "Are you a little nervous about going home?"

"As the Pope is Catholic," Laurence replied, laughing. "Goodbye, Ingram."

When he went to fetch his horse from the stables, the ostler could not praise it enough. "Never seen a crossbreed come out so nicely, sir! Tall, yet with the daintiness and sturdiness of a Barbary. Odd for it to be black, sir. Most beasts of that blood tend to white or grey. And the workmanship on this sword," he added, handing it back to Laurence. "Spanish, I'd guess."

"That's right," Laurence said, thinking suddenly of Juana; how surprised she would be, if she knew how far the sword had travelled from its native land.

On the ride northwards out of Newbury, he saw no signs of war. Crops flourished in the fields and the sheep grazed in their pasture undisturbed. Yet approaching the outskirts of Oxford he began to encounter groups of armed men on the road, so he took a longer, rarely travelled route around the prosperous market towns of Woodstock and Chipping Norton, into the Cotswold hills. It seemed to him as though he had never been away, as he recognised the old markers on his journey: the rising of church spires, the farmhouses, the copses and spinneys, the low dry-stone walls, and the River Evenlode gleaming between green banks.

By early evening, he arrived at his father's property. He chose to avoid the gatehouse, and went around to a lower part of the surrounding wall that his horse could jump easily. The sun still gave out surprising warmth, drying his mud-splattered clothes. He reined in, and looked over the expanse of the park. Some of the older trees had been cut down or polled, and others that had been saplings when he left had matured and filled out their boughs. In the distance he could hear the cooing of wood pigeons, while the air around him was heavy with the monotonous chirrup of crickets.

Gradually he was overwhelmed by a sickening apprehension: all this was his birthright. If he could not accept it, with the responsibilities it entailed, he should never have come back to England. He knew, far better than before, that he was no more suited to be his father's heir than he was to military life, though not for the reasons he might have given six years ago. Then, his natural indolence and a blithe spirit of rebellion against authority had caused him to reject the world into which he was born. Now, he feared that he had witnessed too much to settle within its confines, and had done too many sordid things to be worthy of its respect. But he had to think of his father, whom he had missed terribly and often, in self-reproach after committing the basest of deeds, and in sorrow when he had been most lonely or miserable.

Lord Beaumont's mansion might have been unremarkable beside a Venetian canal or on some Umbrian slope, yet it obtruded amongst these English hills like an exotic beast at a country fair. It impressed Laurence as larger and more extravagant than he recalled, with stables and outbuildings grander than most other men's dwellings. As he rode up the elegant, winding path that led to the courtyard, he saw liveried grooms unharnessing a pair of horses from the family coach, while a small boy vigorously polished the Beaumont coat of arms emblazoned on its door.

The boy glimpsed Laurence first, and shouted, "Who's he?"

One of the men silenced him with a cuff on the ear. Then an old, dignified fellow emerged from the stables: Lord Beaumont's Master of the Horse.

"Why, it's Master Beaumont, back from the wars!" he cried. "We never thought we'd see you again, sir. What a great day for us all, and a blessing for his lordship your father. Praise God you're whole!"

"And you too, Jacob," Laurence said warmly, dismounting to clasp the man's hand.

"Glad you haven't forgotten my name, sir, though that's as should be," Jacob affirmed. "I gave you your first riding lessons, when you could scarcely walk."

Laurence would have taken his horse into the stables, but the grooms insisted on doing this for him, and as one of them unloaded his belongings, Jacob accompanied him to the house, talking all the way.

"We had the coach out for your brother's wife, sir. She went to visit her mother at Winchcombe. Her ladyship wasn't pleased at all, but the girl was pining for her own folk, with Master Thomas off in Oxford. You didn't get a wife while you were in those foreign parts, did you, sir?"

"Oh no," Laurence replied, somewhat amused as he thought again of Juana; what a scandal it would have caused had he brought her back with him.

At the top of the flight of stone steps stood a manservant whom Laurence did not recognise. He was dressed in a suit of velvet, his hair pomaded and curled, his expression curious beneath a veneer of professional haughtiness. "Welcome home, sir," he said, bowing. "You will find his lordship and her ladyship in the great hall, with Mistress Elizabeth and Mistress Anne."

Laurence thanked him, climbed the stairs, and went in. The entrance to the hall was flanked by two marble statues that his father must have acquired while he was away. They were as tall as he: a naked youth wrestling with a serpent and a nymph clad in a light vestment, her perfectly shaped breasts exposed, her sculpted hand holding out a cluster of grapes. He stood gazing at them dumbly until the servant came up behind him.

"Is something amiss, sir?" Laurence shook his head. "Allow me to announce your arrival, if it please you," the man said, with a friendlier air. "It might be as well to prepare them."

"I wish you could prepare *me*," Laurence muttered.

The man gave him a quick grin before resuming his previous demeanour and entering the hall. Walking more slowly behind, Laurence had a view of his two sisters poring over a book, his father in a padded armchair, and his mother at the window, half turned, looking out towards the gardens. For a moment he wished he could leave them precisely as they were. But before the servant had finished speaking, Lord Beaumont leapt up and came hurrying towards Laurence, arms outstretched. He wept openly as they embraced, and Laurence found himself blinking away tears. When his mother greeted him, however, she merely brushed his cheek with her lips, not quite touching him. She had not aged, apart from a hint of grey in her hair. As for the girls, they had grown into women, and they hung back from Laurence shyly until he gave them both a hug.

Once Lord Beaumont had recovered his composure, he called for his special Malaga to be brought out, and ordered a barrel of ale for the servants, in celebration of his son's return. As they were served, he kept grabbing Laurence's hand and squeezing it forcefully, exclaiming, "It is no dream – you are truly here."

The Malaga was finer than any wine Laurence had tasted in months, yet it did not alleviate the sinking in his guts. He felt oppressed, as much by his father's generous affection as by his mother's reserve. Meanwhile, his sisters were absorbing every detail of him with fascinated eyes.

"I hear you're getting married," he said to Elizabeth.

"Who told you that?" Lady Beaumont interjected, before her daughter could respond.

"Ingram."

"When?"

"Yesterday. I passed through Newbury on my way here."

"Did you," she said. He caught the rebuke: he should have come straight home. "Elizabeth is to marry at Christmas," she went on. "I trust you will attend. That is, if you are better disposed to the institution of matrimony than you were six years ago. Don't rush to his defence," she told her husband, who was about to interrupt. "In all that time we had almost no communication from him. Here he sits, without a word of apology for the distress he caused us, as if he has forgotten that he stole out of the house like some petty thief, on the eve of his own wedding. Are you not ashamed of it, Laurence?"

"I should be," Laurence said, hiding a smile. He had genuinely detested the girl to whom he had been betrothed, though Lady Beaumont was right that he could have exited more gracefully from the arrangement.

"Have pity on him, my dear," Lord Beaumont said. "By a miracle he has been restored to us. Let the matter pass."

"I shall hope for some future explanation," she murmured.

Lord Beaumont turned to his son. "Walter Ingram must have given you an account of our country's desperate ills. Some think that war cannot be prevented, though many are still trying to settle affairs peacefully. Thank God there are moderates on both sides – in Parliament, the Earls of Holland, Northumberland, and Pembroke, and on the King's side, the lawyer Edward Hyde and Lord Falkland, of course. Did you hear that his lordship has been made His Majesty's chief Secretary of State?"

"Falkland is Secretary of State?" Laurence repeated, surprised. Falkland's house at Great Tew was not far away, and he had been a frequent guest at Chipping Campden, as Lord Beaumont's close friend and not Laurence's, although he and Falkland were only a couple of years apart in age. They had met on just a few occasions, for after finishing his university studies Laurence had been living mostly in London. "Isn't he too virtuous for public office?" Laurence added, on reflection.

"What is wrong with virtue in public office?" Lady Beaumont queried.

"Nothing in theory, but everything in practice."

"Would His Majesty do better to choose self-serving rogues as his ministers?"

How little she had changed, Laurence noted; she was as sharp as ever. "No," he said, "although he may already have plenty of those in his Council. What I meant is that it's more difficult for men like Falkland to reconcile their consciences with political necessity."

"Falkland did not seek out the honour," Lord Beaumont said. "And in truth, I believe he may be somewhat torn between his conscience and his devotion to the King."

"His conscience should inform him of his duty, which *is* to the King," Lady Beaumont retorted, to her husband.

"Yes, though we must admit, His Majesty has made errors, as a result of bad advice, naturally. Not to excuse the treasonous behaviour of the radicals, but the country was ruled too long without a Parliament. All manner of resentment was bound to emerge, over religious differences and taxation and God knows what else. Parliament would reset the limits of royal power, and His Majesty is unwilling to bend on that issue."

"He bent on others, my lord. He let one of his most faithful ministers go to the scaffold."

"So he did," Lord Beaumont acknowledged, turning to Laurence. "I attended the Earl of Strafford's trial, and he defeated every charge Parliament laid against him."

"As well he would!" said Lady Beaumont. "What crime did he commit, in urging a stern response to the disorder breaking out in this kingdom?"

"Strafford was too much hated by the people to survive. The King had no option, though I know it tore at his heart and he bears the pain still. Laurence, has Ingram enlisted yet in His Majesty's service?" Lord Beaumont asked next.

"He has, yes," Laurence said.

"He visited us often while you were away, hoping for some news of you. Thomas saw him in Oxford not a week past."

"Thomas is raising a troop under the family colours," said Lady Beaumont. "You will be eager to join him, Laurence."

Laurence made no comment, fidgeting with the glass in his hand.

"My dear son," Lord Beaumont said, perhaps reading his discomfort, "what terrible things you must have seen happen abroad. I have been blessed to live thus far in a time of peace, and the thought of bloodshed appalls me no end. It has been nigh on two hundred years since this country was last devastated by civil war, though we came close in the past century. But if some violence cannot be avoided, at least we can anticipate a short engagement, an affair of gentleman. We shall not suffer here the atrocities you doubtless witnessed in the Low Countries. And now, no more talk of war."

"And no more wine, my lord," said Lady Beaumont, as her husband was about to call for another round. "I must insist that you go to your chamber and bathe before supper, Laurence, and make yourself presentable."

"Please excuse me, then," he said, and obeyed, feeling their eyes upon him as he walked from the hall. On his way upstairs, other eyes followed him, painted and inscrutable: those of his ancestors whose portraits lined the walls. As he reached the door to his chamber, the same manservant was there to open it for him, also regarding him intently, ready to set out clean clothes for the evening. Laurence had to confess that he had brought with him only a dirty shirt. When the bath had been drawn the man lingered, waiting in attendance rather like one of Lord Beaumont's statues, with a pile of towels draped over his arm. Laurence wanted to laugh at the absurd luxury of it all. Instead he asked the man to leave him, not out of modesty, but because he wanted to be alone.

V.

The second day after Laurence's return proved sunny and humid, so Lord Beaumont had retreated to the cool of his library, where he sat over a volume of Petrarch. From the garden directly beneath his window came the sound of voices, those of his son and daughters; and as he listened, it occurred to him that Laurence was spending most of his time with them and very little with his parents, as though he were wishing to avoid any serious discussion of his years abroad, or of his future plans.

"Tom will arrive tomorrow," Lord Beaumont heard Elizabeth declare. "Geoffrey went to Oxford this morning to fetch him. Laurence, will you join his troop?"

Lord Beaumont sat forward, to listen more keenly.

"Not if I have a choice," Laurence said, after a small pause.

"Why would anyone choose to fight!" she said. "I am so weary of politics. Ormiston talks of nothing else when he visits."

"John Ormiston is her betrothed," Anne explained.

"I hope he knows how lucky he is," Laurence remarked, in such a protective, brotherly tone that Lord Beaumont felt touched to the heart. "So tell me all about him."

"Where to begin," sighed Elizabeth. "He's eight years older than I am, and was married before but his first wife died in childbirth. His father left him property near Hereford, where his mother lives with his two spinster sisters. Mrs. Ormiston is a shrew blessed with unnatural good health."

"Isn't that always the case. What about Tom's wife? What sort of person is she?"

"She brought in a huge dowry," said Anne. "And she worships Tom."

"She does indeed," Elizabeth giggled. "I must admit she irritates me no end. She keeps making such tiresome comments to me about my wedding night, as if it is all a complete mystery to me."

Lord Beaumont caught his son laughing. "*Is* it?"

"Not entirely, but I do have a few questions that you might be able to answer."

"You can ask me whatever you want. The less of a mystery it is, the more you might enjoy it."

Lord Beaumont set aside Petrarch and rose from his chair, alarmed lest his wife might also be within earshot of the garden. He was about to call down an admonition, when there came a knock at the library door. A servant had arrived bearing his afternoon glass of fruit cordial.

"Please summon my son," Lord Beaumont told the man, and waited, pacing up and down, until Laurence strolled in.

"Sit down, sir." Lord Beaumont regarded him sternly. "Laurence, you must be more prudent in what you discuss with Elizabeth and Anne. They are innocent creatures."

"Ah, so you overheard us," he said, with a smile.

"They may be upset by your candour on certain subjects." Lord Beaumont hesitated. "Marriage, for example."

"On the subject of marriage, I'm quite ignorant myself."

"You know what I mean," said Lord Beaumont, suppressing his own amusement. "Now why are you so unwilling to join your brother?" Laurence's smile hardened slightly, and he looked away with a hint of impatience. Pondering whether to press him further, Lord Beaumont observed not the changes in his son's appearance but what was the same: his rangy physique, his untidiness, the animation in his features, and his eyes, so much his mother's. It was the colour and set of her eyes that had captivated Lord Beaumont over thirty years ago in Seville: celadon, fringed with long dark lashes, they were almond-shaped and slanted like those of an Oriental. He remained utterly hostage to their charm.

"Ingram told me that Seward is still at Merton," Laurence said abruptly, leaving his father's query unanswered.

"He is," said Lord Beaumont, allowing it to pass, gratified that Laurence should ask after their former tutor. "He has given up most of his teaching and pursues his esoteric studies, which I pray will not get him into the same trouble he once faced in King James' reign, when I was up at College."

"Ah yes. He was suspected of witchcraft, or something of the kind, wasn't he."

"It was all nonsense, of course, and he defended himself admirably, but academics have long memories. He wrote to me during your absence assuring me that you would return, although at the time I believed it was just to comfort me. He was so attached to you when you were a lad. Indeed, your mother often worried that he might be . . . overly attached."

"She shouldn't have worried," Laurence said, laughing. "I really must call on him."

"He would be delighted. Oh, and while you are there, you might do me a small favour." From the book he had been reading, Lord Beaumont pulled out a sheet of paper. "This is from John Earle, a fellow of Merton for some years whom Seward no doubt knows. Earle and I have been playing a game together, an exchange of letters in cipher to test our wits, although in this case, I fear Earle has tested mine too greatly, for I cannot unscramble what he has put down here. Perhaps I might beg your assistance with it. You studied such things with Seward, did you not, and had quite a talent for them?" Laurence nodded, a peculiar wariness in his eyes. "You might have better luck than I, and you could then leave our transcription at the College, for Earle to collect at his convenience." As his son began to read the letter, Lord Beaumont went on, "Earle belonged to Lord Falkland's circle of friends at Great Tew. He was also chaplain to the Earl of Pembroke, then chancellor of Oxford. It was a shock to me, by the bye, that Pembroke sided with Parliament."

"But you never liked him," Laurence commented. "You called him an ambitious, foul-mouthed boor."

"Did I! Yet he is a patron of the arts, like his brother before him. He no doubt held a grudge against the King after his dismissal last summer from the office of Lord Chamberlain. Hoping to appease the radicals, and please Her Majesty who always detested him, the King had him replaced by the Earl of Essex. Essex sided with Parliament anyway, and so the King only ended by making an enemy out of his former ally."

"Too late for appeasement, as with the execution of Strafford. Still, I thought you said that Pembroke was one of the moderates in Parliament."

"He is, and as a figure in the Lords he can exert his influence in favour of a peaceful settlement."

"He'd have much to lose if the King won victory in battle, and he was caught on the wrong side."

"From what I hear, he claims he would not take up arms against His Majesty."

"Ah, so he's merely hedging his bets."

"I trust principle still has some role in his actions," Lord Beaumont said, discomfited by Laurence's cynicism. "At any rate, let us return to John Earle. He has lately been appointed tutor to the young Prince Charles and may be too busy for games, but I should like to answer him nonetheless. What do you make of it?"

Laurence inspected the passage again and asked for a quill. Lord Beaumont waited, watching him as he scribbled various numbers below the original characters, matched them with alphabetical letters, and at length produced groups of syllables, then words, and finally full lines. "It's a substitution cipher with suppressed vowels," he said, and showed his father the result.

"Pray read it aloud for me, sir." Laurence obliged him, after which he exclaimed triumphantly, "A passage from Herodotus – how excellent! You must explain how you unravelled the cipher. And could you write me a better one, to confound Dr. Earle?"

"I think so," said Laurence, wiping an inky forefinger and thumb on his breeches.

"Laurence," Lord Beaumont said, an idea surfacing in his mind, "you should not waste your gifts. Why not put them to some nobler purpose? You might work for Lord Falkland. The concerns of state security fall under his charge, as does the collection of intelligence. You could be useful to him."

"What are you suggesting?" Laurence asked, a tension audible in his voice that puzzled Lord Beaumont.

"You could decipher messages for him and invent codes, as you are doing for me. I meant no more than that – perish the thought of you being a mole! That is not an occupation for gentlemen."

"It certainly isn't," Laurence murmured.

Lord Beaumont felt a shade fearful, wondering what his son had done while abroad, and he realised that he did not actually want to find out. "Falkland would never use you so," he said. "Yet to allay any concerns you might have, it can be made clear to him which duties you will accept, and which you will not."

"How would that be made clear?"

"Through a letter of introduction. I could set out precisely –"

"I haven't depended on your name for some years," Laurence interrupted. "But that's not the point. Falkland can't assure you that he'll keep my nose clean, and it would be unfair to ask it of him."

"He is my good friend! He is also a man of honour, the best and most scrupulous of His Majesty's advisors, which is why he was selected –"

"That he may be. But there is such a thing as *raison d'état*."

"Yes, I admit –"

"And it takes precedence over anyone's scruples, in peace as in war – especially in war. And if war breaks out, I don't think it will be a short engagement, nor will it be an affair of gentlemen. Though I could be wrong," Laurence concluded sardonically. "The atrocities I witnessed abroad may have tainted my view of matters here."

Good God, thought Lord Beaumont, shaken by the force of his son's reaction and deliberate choice of words. "Nevertheless," he said, "we must not forget that our King did rule these seventeen years over a prosperous realm, the envy of many other crowned heads."

"And now the money is spent, and he's had to call a Parliament that won't vote him what he wants. And his Queen, who's been run out of England by his own subjects, must pawn the crown jewels for arms so that he can afford to wage a war."

"We may still hope that cooler tempers will prevail. I have the greatest faith in Falkland and his allies. My son, you too could have some voice in all this. You have so much to offer – your swift intelligence, your academic learning, as well as your experience of conflict, which has taught you the value of peace. To act upon the stage of politics would befit a man of your rank." *A role I never played myself*, Lord Beaumont mused regretfully. Then he hurried on, "I do not wish you to be compromised in any way, if you believe that is what might happen. Yet you should visit Falkland, if only to pay your respects."

There was a silence, during which he saw a kind of weary distaste in his son's face, and afterwards a more calculating expression, which he did not altogether like.

"All right," Laurence said, "I'll go. Though I don't need a letter of introduction."

"Your mother will be proud of you."

"For the first time."

"Well, sir," said Lord Beaumont, "there is a first time for everything."

VI.

Upon leaving the library, Laurence went to his chamber, sat down on the edge of his bed, and put his head in his hands. He stayed motionless for some minutes, lost in contemplation, before searching inside his doublet and producing the folded letters, now grubby from much handling and far more inscrutable than Dr. Earle's missive, proof even against his own gifts. He had not needed Khadija to tell him of their value, just as he had not needed her to comfort him with promises of a future love. And what tragedy could these flimsy sheets of paper prevent? They could not stop a war: the conflict between King and Parliament had been fomenting too long and had too many causes. But if they had a bearing on it, as he strongly suspected, the Secretary of State might take an interest in them. At the same time, he remembered Ingram's reaction to a few mere details of his own past. He was one of many hundreds of returning veterans, and rumour had a way of spreading. If Lord Falkland were to hear anything discreditable about his activities abroad, so also might Lord Beaumont. And the truth would hurt him, Laurence knew.

VII.

Laurence had to admit that if not for Captain von Mansfeld, he would have abandoned his sanity altogether, stuck in that vile field hospital, still weak from his wound and with no hope of escape. On the bleak night that they first met, he was squatting to defecate in a corner of the yard when a group of officers rode in on glossy, well-fed horses. Behind them, moving more slowly, was a mule dragging a stretcher with a body tied up on it. The officers dismounted and led the mule and its awkward burden into a barn, now vacant, where prisoners of war had been kept. As he pulled up his breeches, Laurence considered stealing one of the horses, trying to calculate whether he had the strength to mount on his own, let alone ride any distance. Then he heard a voice cry out in a familiar tongue. Squelching through the thick mud towards the barn, he peered around the door.

The officers were standing over the man on the stretcher, volleying questions at him in their native German. As the man panted out a reply, Laurence realised that he was a Spaniard, and the officers' visible confusion suggested that they could not speak his tongue.

Laurence stepped forward, so that they could see him in the glow of their single lantern. "I can translate for you," he told them.

They surveyed him derisively, and no wonder: he was half naked, unshaven and filthy, with a repulsive scab below his ribs.

"Are you another Spanish prisoner of war?" asked one of them.

"No, I'm an Englishman," said Laurence, "and I was wounded fighting on *your* side."

"An Englishman?"

"Hard to see what he is under all that dirt," scoffed a second officer.

"Well, whatever you are, help us quickly," said the first. "This bastard won't last long. Got caught in crossfire, and had both his legs blown off. But he's a known courier and had a package of coded messages on him. We must find out what they are about, before he dies."

"I'll do nothing until you tell me what it's worth to you," said Laurence, at which they hooted with laughter.

"You've got balls, attempting to bargain with us," exclaimed the first officer. He extended his hand, which Laurence was too shamed to sully by grasping in his own. "I am Captain Franz von Mansfeld, no kin, alas, to Wallenstein's famous adversary, slain when I was a youth. And what is your name?" Laurence told him. "How little there is of you, Herr Beaumont, you're skin and bone. Help us question the Spaniard and we'll give you enough to buy a meal and put some clothes on your back."

"That's not what I want," Laurence said, struggling to hide his desperation. "I want you to get me out of this place."

"Fair enough, if you can do us good service," the Captain said. "We haven't a spare horse, but you are welcome to the mule. Come, to work."

Laurence knelt beside the pallet, his appetite aroused, despite himself, at the familiar bacon-like odour of singed flesh. The Spaniard's legs had been shredded by cannon fire, and he would soon be dead. "*Amigo*," Laurence began, "*no tienes mucho más tiempo en este mundo.*" The Spaniard started to writhe about, moaning that he would die unshriven. Laurence thought quickly, and whispered in his ear, "That's why the Germans brought me to you. I am a priest, also a captive here. I've come to take your last confession." Leaning in still closer, he hissed, "They can't understand a word we're saying. They have your package, which will go undelivered, but I can pass on what intelligence you give me. God willing, I intend to escape tonight."

"First save my soul," the man responded, a faint suspicion in his eyes.

After his years in the Spanish army, Laurence had witnessed so many priests officiating that he could rattle off a convincing version of the last sacrament. Making fast work of the man's sins, he pronounced him absolved. Only then did the man begin to provide a more interesting confession, but eventually he wearied, and in a barely audible voice he murmured, "*Gracías, padre, y que Díos te bendiga.*" A spume of blood bubbled forth from his lips, and he was gone.

The officers threw a sack over the body and strode out into the dull morning light, and Laurence followed. "Well, Herr Beaumont, did all that mumbling between the two of you bear any fruit?" von Mansfeld inquired impatiently.

"I know who these were for." Laurence pointed at the blood-splattered documents in von Mansfeld's hand, and explained what he had found out.

Von Mansfeld looked astonished. "How in the devil's name did you persuade him to talk?"

"In *God's* name," Laurence replied. "I told him I was a priest."

"Nice work, Herr Beaumont!" von Mansfeld congratulated him. "But that information is of little use to us if we cannot learn what is in these papers he was carrying."

"Let me see them," Laurence begged. Von Mansfeld passed them over to him, and he scanned the lines of densely packed numbers. "I know this cipher," he said, feigning confidence. "I can break it. Give me a chance and I'll show you."

The Captain glanced at his companions, who appeared dubious, then shrugged and nodded. "Very well, sir, we shall give you your chance."

And so, after a journey of some twenty miles, Laurence was found quarters, nourishing food, hot water to wash, and clean clothes. By the next evening, he managed to complete his task for von Mansfeld, who was duly impressed. His rescue could not have been better timed. He heard subsequently that the hospital was razed to the ground by a mob of villagers furious at the depredations of the mercenary troops. Any wounded who had not perished in the flames were hacked to death.

Other work arrived for him while he recovered his full health, for von Mansfeld discovered that Herr Beaumont had an unusual aptitude with codes and ciphers. And since the prospect of facing gunfire again filled Laurence with the utmost panic, he did not object when, later on, some new duties were added to his conditions of employment. He travelled regularly throughout the Low Countries, the German states, and even into France to deliver messages. He frequented taverns and alehouses listening for gossip, and made tongues wag with alcohol. He bribed, he told lies, and he bedded women to learn their husbands' secrets. He hung about alleys tracking down and sometimes dispatching enemy spies. More reluctantly, he assisted in the interrogation of prisoners, after which he suffered from nightmares and bouts of profound self-loathing that he tried in vain to banish with drink. He was good at his work, using finesse rather than torture to extract the truth. Over time, however, those around him began to gossip that he treated his subjects gently because he was working under cover for the Hapsburg Emperor, and that he had only pretended to turn coat at the siege of Breda. The slander spread, and he was shunned and vilified. He would have been in more serious danger had not von Mansfeld come yet again to the rescue, offering him a place in his troop of horse.

VIII.

In his quarters at Leicester, Lord Falkland was sorting through his correspondence in preparation for a meeting of Council. "Yet another begging letter, Stephens," he complained to his servant.

"From whom, my lord?" Stephens asked.

"A fellow of my acquaintance named Charles Danvers, likeable enough but dissolute in his habits. No surprise that he says he has money troubles. He wants some kind of employment. He has a great ear for gossip, he tells me. What a recommendation!"

"Colonel Hoare is always interested in gossip, my lord."

Falkland sighed. "Whenever I hear that man's name, I am reminded of those duties necessitated by my office that I would rather not contemplate."

"Every Secretary of State must have his spymaster. And he is a most capable manager of your agents."

"That may be, but he takes too much pleasure in extorting confessions from anyone he has occasion to arrest."

"He's a military man, my lord," Stephens observed, "and hence accustomed to the use of force where no other means will suffice."

"So he is." *And I know he frowns upon my scant experience in that regard*, Falkland nearly added. But if it came to war here, all might soon be remedied, he thought sorrowfully. He looked down again at the note, penned in an elegant hand with bold flourishes. Danvers might be too unreliable for clandestine work, though Hoare could be the judge of that. They were in need of new agents, since some of their valued men had chosen to side with Parliament.

"My lord, if you please." Stephens indicated the tray waiting by the fire. "Her ladyship would be concerned if you did not eat."

"You are right, Stephens," agreed Falkland, with a smile. "Dear Lettice would give me a thorough scolding. Burn these." He passed a sheaf of letters to Stephens, who obediently consigned them to the flames; their wax seals gave out spitting sounds, as if protesting their own destruction. "I do not look forward to tonight," Falkland went on, more to himself than to his servant, as he sat down to his food. "There seem to be few good tidings for His Majesty since he came to the north. The local gentry welcome him with declarations of loyalty, but they are hanging back from any more commitment than mere words. And the surrender of Hull to Parliament was a blow. Yet another port lost. With some diplomacy, it could have been avoided."

Stephens coughed dryly as he filled Falkland's glass, suggesting to Falkland that he had an opinion to express. "With all respect, my lord," he said, "you cannot deny that His Majesty had cause to be affronted by the demands of Parliament's Commissioners at Hull. They sought to bargain with their sovereign in exchange for delivering up to him one of his own cities."

"They asked him to return in peace to London and negotiate with them. It was not such an outrageous request." Falkland took a small sip of wine to chase down a morsel of roast fowl and wiped his mouth on the edge of the tablecloth. "I had better set out, Stephens. It would not do for me to be late."

With a disapproving glance at the platter that Falkland had barely touched, Stephens went to fetch their cloaks and hats, and accompanied his master over the short distance to the royal apartments.

In the end Falkland was early. He found His Majesty alone with Lord Digby. This immediately set Falkland's nerves on edge: if he had to pick a single man he could hold responsible for the widening chasm between King and Parliament it would be George Digby, who seemed to change political colour as readily as a chameleon. Over the past year Falkland had been noting apprehensively the ease with which Digby had managed to insinuate himself more and more into the King's favour.

"As I said at the g-gates of Hull," the King was remarking in his soft Scottish accent, punctuated with a mild stammer, "let all the world now judge who b-began this war."

"Your Majesty," Digby said, "no one could honestly accuse you of sparing any effort to prevent armed conflict. You have been provoked beyond measure, and yet still you hold out the olive branch to your unworthy subjects." He broke off on seeing Falkland, who bowed to them both. "How are you, Lucius?" Digby cried, addressing Falkland as ever by his Christian name. Such unusual familiarity irked Falkland, even though he guessed this was Digby's intention.

"I am in good health, thank you, my lord," he said, feeling awkward beside Digby's suave and graceful presence. "And I am gratified to learn that the olive branch remains on offer, Your Majesty," he continued, which the King acknowledged with a benign smile.

"I wonder what Prince Rupert will think of that when he arrives," Digby said, playing with one of his blond lovelocks.

"Have you news of your nephew from Holland, Your Majesty?" Falkland inquired.

The King's face instantly brightened. "Yes, indeed. We may expect him and his brother Prince Maurice to land here any day – that is, if they are not stopped by Parliament."

"Such a bold young man will outstrip any attempt of the rebels to seize his ship," declared Digby.

"Then he will have better fortune than you did on your late return from Holland," Falkland said, at which the King began to laugh.

"My fate was cruel indeed!" Digby lamented. "First to be caught sailing in so humble a vessel as a fishing ketch, and then the sheer indignity of being taken in chains as a prisoner of Parliament to Hull! But you must admit that I did good business there," he concluded, smiling again. "I almost had the Governor hand me the keys to the city."

"Almost but not quite," said Falkland. "Once the effect of your silver tongue wore off, he did not long remain persuaded that he should surrender the port to us."

"It crossed his mind, however – and he *was* persuaded to release *me*."

A fate less cruel than would have befallen you, had he surrendered you to Parliament, Falkland was tempted to rejoin.

"As for his Royal Highness Prince Rupert," Digby went on, "it was such a delight, all that time we spent together with Her Majesty in The Hague – nigh on six months."

"You must have got to know him well," the King said eagerly; he had not seen his beloved nephew since the prince visited England as a youth, Falkland remembered.

"I should say so, Your Majesty. He is very forthright in his manners, as one might imagine, since he has spent most of his twenty-three years in army service, and very handsome, too. He will make a splendid commanding officer, an inspiration to all those other bold young men who are flocking to the royal cause."

And an irritation to the older ones, Falkland thought. "His Highness the Prince will not appreciate, then, that we intend to continue in our peace talks," he said.

A haughty expression came over the King's face. "My Lord Falkland, we do share in your eagerness to avert a war, but how many times must we s-suffer to be insulted by Parliament's Commissioners? I am afraid there is in London a faction that will yield only to a drawn sword."

"You have many staunch supporters in the upper House –"

"Such as Lord Holland, who lately confronted me at Hull, and the Earl of Pembroke, with his demands that I render up control of my m-militias? And Lord Essex, who refused to join me at York? And they are called the moderates!" Although the King still spoke softly, his words were an unmistakeable reproach to Falkland, who sensed that Digby was enjoying his discomfiture. "You have worked long and hard to win over those misguided souls," His Majesty said more amiably, laying his hand on Falkland's shoulder. "Do not for a moment believe that my desire for peace is insincere. Yet we must ready for the worst." At this he left them, to greet some other members of Council who had entered the chamber.

Digby was regarding Falkland, his round blue eyes apologetic. "I am sorry, Lucius, that I was amongst those who urged your appointment to the Secretaryship. Yet I could conceive of no wiser a person, nor yet more learned, nor of more impartial disposition, to advise His Majesty at this critical juncture. I, and others, have placed a heavy burden upon you, and you must curse us for it."

"I do not curse you. I am only puzzled, my lord, that *you* should have foregone this burden yourself," Falkland said, although he knew that Digby's shifts of allegiance had made him too unpopular a candidate for the office.

"I could not do it justice," Digby responded smoothly. "I lack your nobility of character." Then he burst into laughter, as if at his own performance. That he was genuinely amused by it, Falkland realised, was why for all his slipperiness he was hard to dislike. "Lucius," he said, "on the next occasion we meet, please remind me that you are one of the few men I know who is not susceptible to flattery. Otherwise I shall continue to waste my breath as I have just now."

"Why should I remind you," Falkland said, "when I have so little to entertain me these days."

Digby appeared pensive for a moment. "What you are lacking, Lucius, is the sweet influence of female company."

"I know, I cannot bear so long a separation from my wife," Falkland admitted, touched that Digby should have thought of her. "You must feel much the same."

"Oh, Anne and I understand these things very well," Digby said, with a shrug. "I am soon to be comforted, in any event, by the arrival of my lovely ward, Mistress Isabella Savage. She has decided to quit London – a most uncongenial place to anyone associated with my name – and is travelling north to join me."

"Your ward? Is she still a child?"

"Dear me, no! She is a woman of some twenty-five years, and as yet unmarried, though one of the most ravishing creatures in all England. She was presented at Court upon her eighteenth birthday, and has been capturing hearts ever since. I am amazed that you should not have been introduced. But you did tend to hide away in the country with your academic friends, when not occupied with Parliamentary affairs."

"They were my happiest times," said Falkland.

"You have never heard of Mistress Savage, even by reputation?" Digby insisted, with a purposive curiosity.

"No, my lord," replied Falkland, wondering that Digby should ask him. Why should he, as a devoted husband, have any special interest in this ravishing creature, or in Digby's relations with her, whatever they might be?

CHAPTER TWO

I.

In the comfort of his feather bed, Laurence drifted between slumber and full consciousness. He must have pushed aside the bedclothes during the night, for he felt warmth on his skin from the sun streaming through the open curtains. Gradually he became aware that he was not alone in the chamber: he could hear the swish of a woman's skirts. His immediate thought was of Juana and the usual dull sorrow flooded through him, although while half asleep he could almost conjure up her presence like the ghost of a lost limb.

On opening his eyes a fraction, he was bemused to see his mother inspecting his saddlebag and the clothes he had left strewn on the floor as if she were hunting for something. With furtive care, she picked up his sword, which he had propped against a wall, and unsheathed it. For some time she examined the blade, frowning, before sheathing it again and replacing it quietly. He watched, yet more puzzled: what on earth did she expect to find? As she straightened herself to turn towards him, he quickly shut his eyes. He heard her approach the bed, and sensed that she was gazing down at him. He waited a long while for her to move, or to speak. At length she heaved a deep sigh, and muttered low under her breath a word, perhaps a name, that he did not catch. Her behaviour was beginning to unnerve him. He sat up in bed and noticed her wince at the sight of his scar, which he quickly covered.

She retreated a step, flushing. "Laurence, do you not own a night-shirt?"

"I'm afraid I don't," he said.

"And what have you been doing, to get so very black?" she demanded, in an accusatory tone. "As if you have been labouring naked!" He did not reply, but pulled the sheets up to his chin; she was the intruder, after all. "It is past ten of the clock," she said. "You cannot lie abed all morning. I want to speak with you. You may find me in my chamber." And she walked out, slamming the door behind her.

Conquering his irritation, he rose and dressed.

When he entered the little office that she kept on the upper floor of the house, he found her sitting at her desk, quill in hand, examining her account book. She ignored him, not even inviting him to sit, and so he stood, leaning against the wall, arms folded across his chest, until she deigned to address him.

At length, setting aside her quill, she glanced up. "Tomorrow you must be measured for a suit of clothes. Yours are in a terrible state. It is not appropriate for a man of your rank to be so unconcerned as to how you go about. And it is high time for you to make amends for the anguish you caused us."

"Is that still possible?" he asked lightly, smiling at her.

"Indeed it is. You know what a war could mean to our family. You are thirty years of age, Laurence. You must marry, and give his lord-ship an heir. Oh sit, will you!" He obeyed, crossing his legs. "We have a match in mind," she continued. "If you thoroughly dislike the girl, as I presume you did the last, there will be others to choose from. But it must be done. Can you not see how his lordship has grown old, for fretting about you?"

"I'm sorry," he said, more seriously.

"You should be." Closing the account book, she got up to lock it away in her enamelled cabinet. "Are you not curious about this new prospect?"

"I haven't had the opportunity to consider my feelings, one way or the other," he responded, still smiling.

"You shall, once we arrange for you to meet her. And if I may beg another favour, keep your distance from the servants," she said, as she settled back at her desk. "They won't respect you if you treat them as equals. I don't know why you persist in that."

"A bad habit I must have picked up abroad," he murmured.

"No, sir, you have always done so," she corrected him. There fell a silence, and he had the impression that she was steeling herself to broach a more difficult subject. "I gather you sustained some wounds abroad." Laurence merely nodded, unwilling to make things easier for her. "I trust that you . . . that you are not damaged permanently from any of them?"

"Damaged?" he repeated. What a word to use, he thought to himself.

"Oh, for heaven's sake, don't pretend you misunderstand me," she snapped, blushing again. "Are you capable of fathering a child?"

He hesitated a little, enjoying her embarrassment. "I gave you the answer to that question some years ago, if I remember."

"Then I take it there is no impediment?"

"Not as far as I'm aware."

"Laurence, I can only assume that you have led a rather loose life in the past. Were you ever infected?"

He laughed, genuinely amused; he might as well be a prize bull for breeding, which in fact he supposed he was. "Not that I've ever noticed, though my good luck amazes me."

"I beg of you to put an end to such debauchery, in view of what is to come."

"*Casar, casar, que bien, que mal,*" he remarked, knowing that she hated to hear her mother tongue and that the old Spanish proverb, a wry comment on matrimony, would annoy her just as much.

She frowned at him severely. "You shall marry, sir, for my peace of mind and for that of his lordship. And one more thing."

"Yes?"

"Elizabeth also told us that you do not want to serve in Thomas' troop. If this is because of some foolish past rivalry between you, remember that he was a boy of nineteen when you last saw him. You will find him altered. He has been a most dutiful son to us, in your absence. He and his wife, Mary, stayed here at Chipping Campden after their wedding last year, though they would no doubt have preferred to establish their own household. Your father granted them a manor and some acreage near Gloucester, but as we had begun to lose all hope that you would return, we thought it best that he become acquainted with the business of the estate."

"Of course," Laurence said. Poor Tom, he reflected; the prize had just been snatched away.

"It will comfort his lordship to know that you and Thomas are together, if circumstances require you to fight. That is all," she concluded. "You may go now, and break your fast."

"Thank you," he said, forgetting to bow to her as he left. He was still thinking of his brother.

II.

He had been fifteen, and Tom almost ten. One afternoon in very late summer when rain prevented him from going to the river to bathe, he had escaped to his other favourite place, for both contemplation and a solitary, forbidden pleasure to which youths of his age were much addicted. The tall barn had been built for storing grain but was dilapidated and empty; he liked to sit on the topmost level, from which a platform extended so that men could toss sacks of corn down into the waiting carts. It provided an excellent view of the fields beyond, stacked with bales of fresh hay.

As he arrived, the sky cleared and rays of sunshine began to filter through the disappearing clouds. He went onto the platform, took off his doublet and shirt and lay back to bask in the heat; and he had just slipped a hand lazily below the waist of his breeches when he saw Tom clamber out of the barn.

"So this is where you hide!" Tom exclaimed.

"Go away," Laurence said, snatching out his hand and sitting up. Tom was forever tagging after him, being more and more of a nuisance with his incessant questions and his desire to ape everything that his older brother did.

Tom peered over the edge of the platform. "Would it kill you if you fell? I'll bet it would, unless you landed over in that haystack."

He chattered on and on in his grating childish voice, so to silence it Laurence asked, "Shall we see?"

"You wouldn't dare," Tom said.

As though a powerful drug had been released into his system, Laurence strode to the edge, feeling a weightlessness in his body that convinced him he could fly or float in the air.

"No!" shouted Tom, but Laurence had already sailed off.

He fell, squarely, in the midst of the nearby haystack and rolled down, laughing and exhilarated until he glimpsed his brother's silhouette against the sky. Horrified, he jumped up and ran to catch Tom as he leapt, and they both collapsed together in a panting heap. Tom suffered a broken ankle and a few scrapes and scratches. Laurence was unharmed, though ridden with guilt at his own heedlessness. As punishment, he was thrashed so hard that he could not sit down for days, though he deserved worse. They could both have broken their necks. Afterwards, Tom shied away from him whenever he tried to apologise, and eventually he gave up.

That September he left for his first term at Oxford, and when he returned to the house for the Christmastide holiday, the distance between him and his brother seemed even greater: he had made new friends, such as Ingram, and found himself bored by Tom's company. He took to teasing Tom, and they would end up in fights that he won, since he was bigger and stronger. Over the years his brother grew almost as tall, and stockier in build, so the physical sparring ceased and they fought with words. These battles Laurence also won, sending Tom into speechless rage. By the time that Tom started at Merton College, at the age of seventeen, Laurence was off in London and visited home infrequently. If they chanced to encounter one another alone, Tom barely addressed him.

III.

"When did you hear?" Ingram asked Tom, as they rode towards Chipping Campden.

"My father sent his valet two days ago with the news. I'm glad you came to find me before I set out – I was in need of some company," Tom confessed, at which Ingram guessed that he must have mixed feelings about Beaumont's reappearance. "Ingram, is my brother any different?"

"I'm sure he is," Ingram replied cautiously. "He saw some awful things while he was away. And he was wounded over there, almost killed."

"I can't imagine him as a soldier, he was so poor at fencing. He used to hate any form of discipline. He always did exactly as he pleased." Ingram smiled at the truth of this. "You know," Tom went on, "I wanted to fight abroad, too, but my father wouldn't allow it."

"He couldn't afford to risk both of his sons in a foreign conflict."

"It will be different here."

"Yes, it will," Ingram said, looking at him. He had Lord Beaumont's good features and colouring, his hair and beard dark blond as his father's would once have been. Save for a hint of his brother in the fine lines of his jaw and high cheekbones, nothing else betrayed their kinship.

Certainly not his manner, Ingram thought: Tom carried himself with all the poise and authority of a handsome young nobleman, in his well-cut clothes and expensive calfskin boots. Yet he had a sober, martial air about him these days that Ingram had not observed in him before. "How's the troop?" Ingram asked.

"I'm proud of the men, to be honest, though we're still too few in number. I can't wait to see them tested in the field."

"Soon enough," Ingram said, unable to hide his own pessimism.

"You're not afraid of a war, are you?" Tom said, as though no one should be.

"I *am* afraid, of what it will do to this country."

"Those scoundrels in Parliament should get what they're asking for!"

Tom spurred on his horse, and they passed the rest of their journey in silence. Upon galloping into the courtyard, he dismounted, flung his reins to the groom, and marched up to the house with his head held high, which made Ingram wonder if he was still angry from their brief political discussion. Ignoring the manservant who offered to take his hat and cloak, he entered the hall, with Ingram on his heels.

Beaumont was installed in an armchair, slouched back, a glass of wine in one hand and a book in the other. He looked up at them and then slowly extricated himself from the chair.

"Home at last, eh?" Tom said, in a brusque tone. "How are you, Laurence?"

"I'm well, thanks," Beaumont said, sounding formally polite. "And you?"

"Never better."

Ingram started to laugh. "Is that all you have to say to each other after six years? How about a fraternal hug?"

Tom approached rather awkwardly, his arms wide.

"Oh, Tom – you don't have to embrace me if you don't want to," Beaumont said, relaxing into a laugh also. Tom flushed and dropped his arms. "Here, have some wine," Beaumont offered, perhaps aware that he had been ungracious.

"Fond of the grape, as ever," remarked Tom, still eyeing him as he served it out.

"Of this wine, yes, especially after what I've been drinking for the past months."

"Lord Beaumont does keep a wonderful cellar," Ingram said, raising his glass.

At that moment Lord Beaumont himself entered, and they all bowed to him.

"Ingram, how happy I am to see you!" he exclaimed. "And Thomas, I thank you for coming home so quickly. Are we not blessed that Laurence is here safe and sound again?" He accepted a glass and sipped at it, saying afterwards, "The ladies have abandoned us. They are on a visit to the almshouses. And, Thomas, your darling Mary departed a couple of days ago to pay her respects to her family at Winchcombe."

Tom looked disappointed. "I may miss her, then. We can only stay for the night."

"Ah, that's a pity. So, what news have you from Oxford?"

"It's said that His Majesty will soon raise the royal standard, and his nephew Prince Rupert should have arrived in England by now," Tom told him more cheerfully. "He's to be one of the chief commanders of the horse. I only pray our troop will serve under him. I've heard he's a formidable soldier, and he's been trained in all the most advanced cavalry manoeuvres."

"It is war, then," murmured Lord Beaumont, becoming grave.

"But His Majesty is still very short of recruits," Ingram said. "My friend Radcliff's troop, woefully so. And the infantry are a disaster. None of them know their right foot from their left."

"We can always console ourselves that the rebels are much worse off," Tom asserted.

"How so?" inquired Lord Beaumont.

"They're mostly weavers or tailors, or apprentices. They haven't been bred to fight. They'll desert in droves at the first engagement."

"What about the Earl of Essex?" Ingram put in. "And Russell? And Mandeville? Or Lord Fairfax, in the north? Many men of quality have sided with Parliament, seasoned veterans amongst them."

"But not you, I trust?" Tom asked his brother.

"No, not me," Beaumont replied evenly.

"Tell me, who did you serve with in the Low Countries? The Dutch, I presume."

"Er . . . I was with the Germans for most of the time," Beaumont said, casting Ingram a warning glance.

"In the cavalry?"

"Yes."

"Then you must have been drilled in the new Swedish fashion."

"The what?"

"You must know of it – the style favoured by King Gustavus. His Highness Prince Rupert will no doubt introduce it here. Three ranks of horsemen in loose formation and then a charge with the sword. No pistol fire until you meet the enemy."

"Don't the Germans use the six-rank formation, Tom?" Ingram pointed out.

Tom gave a little shrug and turned to his father. "I shall have to ask you for more money to cover bills for the troop. The Oxford merchants have all raised their prices on us. The colleges are no better. When they were asked to contribute to the war effort, some of them began hiding away their plate."

"As I can understand," Lord Beaumont said. "To see such beautiful things melted down, for such an unhappy purpose! My cousin

Stratton came recently to consult me on that issue. He was reluctant to part with some silver plate from the family, yet he felt it was his duty to do so."

"As you must have advised him."

"Oh no. I told him he must follow his own conscience, but that the plate was as nothing compared to his greatest treasure, which neither King nor Parliament could ask him to surrender. I refer to his wife," Lord Beaumont added, smiling. "Did you ever meet her, Laurence?"

"I forget," Beaumont said, at which Ingram heard Tom stifle a snigger.

"If you had met her, you would surely remember her. She and a friend of hers, a dark-haired lady whose name now escapes me, were judged two of the greatest beauties at Court. Stratton told me that Van Dyke had begged them to sit for him together, before his untimely death last year. Stratton considered it an unnecessary expense and so only her friend was painted, at the request of Lord Digby." Lord Beaumont's eyes took on a rather wicked glint. "I saw the finished work at Van Dyke's studio, and I confess, I was most struck by it – she was in a classical costume that left little to the imagination. Stratton said he was relieved, at the time, that Diana had avoided such an immodest display of her charms. But I suspect he must since regret that she was not painted at all. When he visited, he could not stop admiring my own portrait by the late master."

Ingram surveyed the huge canvas over the fireplace, of Lord Beaumont seated in his library gazing pensively into the distance, a volume of poetry resting on the table before him. "It's a remarkable likeness."

"A trifle flattering," Lord Beaumont said, modestly. "At any rate, Stratton is almost a neighbour now. He left the capital this winter to take up residence at Wytham. With all the rioting, he was afraid for his family. He has children, Laurence, two young sons. I expect that he may call here again; I asked Geoffrey to stop by his house on the way to Oxford, to tell him of your return."

Tom was watching his brother, Ingram noticed; then he shot a question at him, as though delivering an order. "Will you come back to town with us tomorrow?"

"Yes, I think I shall," said Beaumont.

"He wishes to pay a visit on Dr. Seward," Lord Beaumont told Tom.

"What do you want from him, Laurence, more lessons in Greek?" Tom joked.

"No, I just want to see him again, as a friend."

"That reminds me," said Lord Beaumont, setting down his glass. "I must go and copy out the transcription for my letter to Earle. Laurence, do me the favour of reading it over, once I've completed it, and then you can take it with you to Merton. Until later, gentlemen."

As soon as he had gone, Tom refilled his own glass, and Ingram's. "So," he said to his brother, "you *do* intend to join up with me, don't you."

Beaumont's eyes were on the wine jug, which was now empty. "I haven't decided yet."

"Do you think you're too good for us because you have some practice under your belt?"

"Oh no."

"I hear you and Ingram got thoroughly soused the other night in Newbury," Tom said next. "A shame I wasn't with you."

Beaumont only shrugged his shoulders. Dear God, Ingram thought; he could at least say that he was sorry, too.

Tom's jaw tightened. Then he began to laugh. "You're still such a liar! Wasn't Stratton's wife your mistress, before you left?"

"Who told you that?"

"Someone in a position to know."

"Since we're discussing married women," Beaumont said, with a provoking smile, "tell me all about your wife, Tom."

"Oh, for Christ's sake," Tom responded, his face reddening. "You should try marriage. It has its benefits."

"Really? I think I'd be liable to stray. But then perhaps that's the difference between us."

"Well, we're all human," Ingram said, seeing Tom scowl. "We must struggle to overcome our faults as best we can."

"How right you are," Beaumont said, getting up. "Excuse me – I should help my father with that letter."

"You mustn't press him too hard about serving again," Ingram said to Tom, after Beaumont had disappeared. "He's been home such a short time. He may be more inclined to join you when he's had a chance to catch his breath. Although have you ever thought –" Ingram stopped, and took a drink from his glass. "You know, Tom, it might be easier on you both if he were in another troop."

Tom gaped at this. "We're riding under the family colours! What would people say?"

"What will people say if you end up snipping at each other, as you did just now?" Tom gave a little nod. "He's less quick to argue than he used to be, however," Ingram went on. "While we were out drinking, some local piss-pot started to harass him. Called him some choice names. When we were young, he would have answered back with as good as he got."

"He might not be as fast with his fists as he once was."

"On the contrary – he's faster, and stronger. The fellow came at him anyway, and was sent to the floor with two punches."

"If he's willing to fight local piss-pots, then why is he trying to avoid army service?"

"I can't speak for him. But he might listen to someone who knows how it was, in the other war. I've promised to introduce him to my future brother-in-law, who certainly paid his military dues with the

Dutch. What if your brother were to join up with his troop instead?"

Tom did not speak, evidently mulling over the idea. "I suppose I might accept it," he said, at last, "even if our father wouldn't be at all pleased. These days, we must think beyond ourselves."

IV.

After the family had taken supper, Laurence repaired with Ingram to his father's library and lit a fire, although Ingram protested that it was a waste of firewood in early August.

"I still find it so cold over here," Laurence said, throwing himself down by the hearth.

"You will let me take you to meet Sir Bernard Radcliff tomorrow?" Ingram asked, as he filled his pipe. Laurence nodded; he had forgotten about Radcliff. "By the way, I had a talk with Tom. He said he'd understand if you didn't accept his offer."

"What offer? Oh, to join his merry little band of men."

Ingram puffed out a cloud of smoke. "I wish you'd make an effort with him."

"I *was* making an effort."

"With that snide inquiry about his wife? Beaumont, can't you see how galling it must have been for him, when without a care in the world you walked out on everything you were born to – a station in life that would turn most men green with envy? I've some sympathy for him. I'm a second son, too."

"He would have been the fourth if all of my brothers had survived infancy. But if I could have us put back in the womb and pulled out in the opposite order, I wouldn't hesitate to do it."

"Since you can't, try to be easier on him."

Laurence smiled affectionately at Ingram. "Always the peacemaker, aren't you."

"He used to adore you," Ingram muttered.

"Thank God he grew out of *that*." Conscious of Ingram's disapproval, Laurence changed the subject. "My mother gave me some news today. She's arranging another marriage for me. And she has a candidate picked out."

"So quickly!"

"Don't underestimate her. If she were His Majesty, she'd have subdued Parliament long ago."

"Who's the girl?"

"I didn't ask."

"She might appeal to you more than the other prospect you rejected."

"Ha! That wouldn't be difficult."

"I've always wondered, Beaumont," Ingram said, "why didn't you just choose someone else?"

"It was a matter of land. Both families were set on it. I assume land is at issue again. No," Laurence corrected himself, stirring up the fire, although it was blazing quite well by itself. "This time, the main issue *is* issue." He glanced back at Ingram. "Why are you frowning at me like that? Don't you appreciate my views on marriage?"

"Were you and Lady Stratton lovers?"

"I wouldn't say lovers, exactly."

"So you were. You must have been mad! She's your father's cousin!"

"Only by marriage."

"All the same, you could have caused a proper scandal if you'd been found out," Ingram persisted.

Laurence shrugged, mildly ashamed that he had not thought of Diana at all until his father had mentioned her. Now he began to remember how attractive she was, and how enthusiastic in bed. "She seemed so bored with that prig of a husband," he said. "Do you know how many women get no joy out of marriage? *That's* a proper scandal, if you ask me."

"Ah," said Ingram. "Then it was a mission of mercy on your part." Laurence could not help laughing, and even Ingram began to smile. "Let's talk of something else, Beaumont. What's your opinion on those training manoeuvres – with cavalry, I mean. You are familiar with them, aren't you?"

"Yes. And we *were* taught the German formation, not the Swedish."

"So which is best?"

"It depends on the situation. But no commander should be so prejudiced against either one that he won't adapt to suit the moment. They both share a major disadvantage, however, and I don't understand why it hasn't been corrected."

"What's that?"

"The horses aren't taught to jump."

Ingram blew out more tobacco smoke. "In an enclosed place that would be a problem."

"Once they're cornered, they start to panic. The men who are thrown get trampled to death, and it doesn't take much to finish off the rest."

"Why didn't you say any of this to Tom?"

"Because my years in the army were hardly glorious, as I tried to explain to you the other night."

"From what I heard from your father, you may not have to engage in active duty. He confided to me over supper that he believes Lord Falkland might take you into his service. That would be a piece of luck, to work for the Secretary of State."

"I'm not so sure," Laurence said darkly, alarmed that Lord Beaumont should have spoken of it to Ingram. Yet why should he not, when he had no notion as to what such work might entail?

Ingram was now staring at him as though struck by an unpleasant thought. "Beaumont, did you . . . did you do anything of the sort while you were abroad?" Laurence was silent. "Who for?"

"My German mercenary friends – or should I say, whoever happened to be paying them at the time," Laurence answered, wishing that Ingram would not probe him any further.

Ingram lowered his eyes. "Forgive me again. You must think I'm judging you."

"Well, aren't you?"

It was Ingram's turn to hesitate. "Your father said you weren't keen on his suggestion, that you feared you might be forced into some objectionable duties. I don't know that you'd have to worry. Falkland is a family friend. And this is not the Low Countries. You've become jaded and now think all wars are the same, but we're Englishmen here, and, God willing, we shall treat each other with respect."

"My father said almost the same thing. Are you going to shake hands with your enemy before you fire on him?"

"Oh come, Beaumont, wouldn't you prefer a position with Falkland to joining up?"

"I prefer neither."

"Then what will you do?"

"As I said to Tom, I haven't decided. I might discuss it with Seward when I go to see him tomorrow."

Ingram drew on his pipe, examining Laurence all the while. Finally he asked, "How long were you in the business of espionage?"

"About a year."

"Then you went back into service?" Laurence nodded. "But you must have left again, if you ended up in Spain. Why?"

"Too many questions, Ingram," Laurence said, grabbing the poker again, to adjust a smouldering log.

"I should hope you weren't discharged for some offence."

Laurence tossed aside the poker and faced his friend. "If you must know, I was never discharged. I deserted. After one last barbarity I was involved in, I couldn't go on. And I don't want to talk about it," he added, suddenly angry. "But take my word: hanging would have been a small price to pay, for some of the things I've done."

"I can't believe that of you!"

"You should. I've become worse than jaded, man. I've lost my honour, in the truest sense, and I'm not sure if I can get it back."

Ingram blinked and bit his lip. "So," he said, at length, "where did you go, after you deserted?"

"To The Hague. I would have stayed there, if it had been possible. But once the armies were mustering for the spring campaign, I had to escape. I went south, into France – and then to Spain."

Ingram sighed and got up to tamp out his pipe in the fireplace. "We're starting out early tomorrow. I should get my rest. What about you? Not tired?"

"No."

"I'm afraid I raised some ghosts for you."

"They're not ghosts to me yet. Good night, Ingram, and sleep well."

"You too, my friend," said Ingram, with a tremor in his voice. He stopped at the door for a moment as if he would add something else, but then left quietly.

Laurence rose to put more wood on the fire. He was annoyed with himself now. He should not have been ill-tempered with a friend who had always been so faithful to him, and who wanted to have faith in him still. But what most upset him was that he had not warned Ingram explicitly to keep quiet about all that they had talked about. Tomorrow morning he must remedy his error.

Settling at his father's desk, he took the coded letters from his doublet, determined to make a last attempt to understand their secret language before he showed them to Seward. There were three pages of very fine yet durable parchment; two bore the writing of a measured hand, while one was in a different, more aggressive style. Laboriously he copied out the script onto fresh paper, underlining each symbol and counting the frequency with which it reappeared. He could recall the tables he had memorised during his studies with Seward, detailing how many times certain vowels and consonants most commonly occurred in various languages, and he tried to match the figures with the frequencies of English, French, German, Spanish, Italian, Latin, Greek, and even Arabic. No pattern emerged. By now his candles had dwindled to molten stumps, and his hand was beginning to cramp.

As he pushed back his chair to stretch, he heard a knock at the door, and went to answer.

Elizabeth was hovering outside wearing an embroidered dressing gown, her hair loose beneath her nightcap, her feet bare. "I couldn't sleep, and then I saw your light under the door," she whispered. "May I come in?"

"Of course," he said, and made way for her, shutting the door behind them.

"You're busy." She indicated the papers. "Is it another one of our father's games?"

"Something like that."

"May I sit with you, while you work?"

"If you can find me some candles."

He set a chair for her next to his; and when she had accomplished her task, she sat down, close to him. She smelt of roses, and her presence was as sweet and comforting. Yet as he picked up his quill and began to ink it, he was shocked to feel her hand on his side.

"It's here, isn't it," she said. "Ingram told me." He did not move as she pulled his clothing up at the waist, nor did he help her, disturbed by the intimacy of her actions. She examined the scar with awed fascination. "I could put my fingers inside, as doubting Thomas did with Jesus' wound." He must have given her a peculiar look, for as if to reassure him, she tucked his shirt back neatly. "Laurence, I have so much to learn about you. I was so young when you left us."

"And now you're not?"

"I am nineteen this year. Do I have to remind you that I'll be married at Christmas? Isn't it strange that Tom and I should be married before *you* are!"

"I hope everyone is."

She screwed up her nose at him. "But you must have been in love. Who's the one you loved most?"

"A woman who told fortunes," he said; *and other lies*, he added mutely.

"Did she ever tell you your fortune?"

"No, and I wouldn't have believed a word of it if she had."

"Would I have liked her?"

He had to laugh. "You'd find her rather different from yourself."

"Why?"

He gazed at Elizabeth, in whose face he read the confidence of youth, looks and noble birth, and who, in the whole course of her existence, had probably known not a single serious hardship. "She was a gypsy," he said, at which Elizabeth's mouth dropped open.

"How did you meet?"

"It's a long story. And you," he went on quickly, "are you in love with Ormiston?"

She smiled and nodded. "I think you will like him, Laurence."

"What matters is that you do," he said. She leant towards him and kissed him on the cheek, and he heard what sounded like a hiccup. Then he realised that she had started to cry. "What's wrong, Liz?" he asked, putting his arms around her.

"The dreadful war, how it scares me! What if Ormiston is killed before we are even married? Or if I'm left a – a widow!"

"You know there's still a chance it won't break out. A great many people don't want it."

"But you don't believe that, do you." He said nothing, unable to contradict her. "I'm afraid for you, too." She looked up at him, her blue eyes solemn. "You can't tempt fate twice. Or more than twice," she murmured, stroking the scar on his wrist.

"Oh, that wasn't from any war."

"How did it happen, then?"

"I'll tell you some other time."

"And what's this?" she said, fingering the leather bracelet.

He drew his hand away. "You should go to bed, my dear."

"I shall." She gave him another kiss on the cheek. "Thank you, Laurence," she told him, without explaining what for, and tiptoed out.

He could not work any longer. Instead he went over to the dying fire, seized the poker, and smashed every glowing ember into dust.

V.

After deserting from the German cavalry, Laurence was hiding out, passing the short, dark days of early December playing at cards or dice in the worst taverns The Hague could provide, where he thought no officers would set foot. He was wrong, as it turned out, for one evening as he was gaming with some drunken Dutch, von Mansfeld himself strolled in, sleek and well-groomed, and evidently perturbed to see him.

"Herr Beaumont," he said, in a low voice, after they had greeted each other, "when you went missing from my troop, I assumed you had sailed for home."

"Are you here to arrest me?" Laurence asked, with a nervous smile.

"Not now, my friend, but come spring you must make yourself scarce or else return to duty, otherwise I won't be able to save you from a hanging. Why waste your skill on these idiots?" von Mansfeld continued more jocularly, indicating the Dutchmen. "I can take you to a place where it will be appreciated. The best brothel in town, run, most unusually, by a young Israelite named Simeon. He's a dealer in precious stones, and his tables are as rich as he is. All the dignitaries in town are his customers."

"I know, I've heard of him. But he wouldn't let me through the door," Laurence said, gesturing at his own worn clothes.

The Captain laughed and stroked his moustache. "For that, you may rely upon my name."

They were admitted, just as he had said, and Laurence felt a thrill of pleasure as he looked about the main room, elegantly appointed with tables for gaming and sideboards decked out with refreshments. Simeon's subtle taste in décor reminded him of a similarly fine establishment that he used to frequent in London, and the women were alluring and graceful, rather than of the blowsy, full-figured type common amongst the Dutch. From the amount of money tossed about the gaming tables, he saw that he could have made a small fortune, had he not promised von Mansfeld half his winnings for the privilege of entry.

They prospered steadily until the early hours, then Simeon himself came by, ostensibly to congratulate them. He more resembled an honourable burgher in his sober, fur-trimmed garments than a brothel-keeper. "Captain," he said, "who is your companion?"

"May I introduce you to Herr Beaumont," von Mansfeld said, "an Englishman whom I met some time ago when he was in adverse circumstances."

"An Englishman? He told you that and expected you to believe him?" Wearily, Laurence explained his heritage. "Is that so, sir," Simeon remarked. "My own mother still calls herself a Spaniard though my family has been in The Hague one hundred and fifty years. Yet what does it signify? Here we have no past and live only in the moment, for God knows what the future will bring us." He paused to study Laurence, who waited, knowing that he would be accused of cheating.

"How goes your business these days, Simeon?" von Mansfeld inquired.

"Not as I would like. The overseer of my tables was an oaf and my ladies could not abide his clumsy advances. I dismissed the fellow, but since then I have been plagued by cardsharps, who can play their tricks and rob me with impunity," he concluded, his eyes still fixed on Laurence.

"Herr Beaumont is not one of them or I would not have brought him here."

"Then what accounts for his extraordinary success?"

"A perfect memory. He could recite to you the sequence of every card we played tonight, and the odds against it."

"Is that true, sir?" Simeon asked Laurence.

"Yes," Laurence said. "Though I can always be surprised by luck."

"Is he honest with you, von Mansfeld?"

"Thus far, Simeon."

Simeon regarded Laurence more thoughtfully. "I suppose you are familiar with all the tricks of the trade, and what you don't know you learn quickly?"

"I try."

"What were your takings tonight between the two of you?" Von Mansfeld chuckled and told him. "Herr Beaumont, if you did not come so highly recommended, I would order my guards to rifle your pockets," said Simeon, laughing too.

They sat together and discussed politics for a while, and von Mansfeld happened to mention that Laurence was seeking a respite from army service. Laurence worried that his friend might have revealed too much, for Simeon was listening intently, and questioned afterwards, "Will you return to England, Herr Beaumont? There are disturbances brewing, and those of you who have fighting experience will be much in demand."

"No," said Laurence. "I had thought to go to France."

"Why? France is no better than here." Simeon hesitated. "I am about to do something I trust I shall not regret. Herr Beaumont, you are safe enough from service for a couple of months while the armies are resting, and this is my busiest time. Would you care to stay and supervise my tables? We can negotiate a fee. If you play me foul, I shall have you turned in to your regiment. If you are honest with me, I shall protect you and treat you as a friend."

Laurence considered only briefly; he was in need of both a refuge and a ready source of income. "I accept."

"*Herr Beaumont.* I don't like the ring of it. From now on we shall call you *Monsieur Beaumont*," Simeon said, using the French pronunciation. "It will lend you a more distinguished air."

"You can call me whatever you like."

"You'll have no regrets," von Mansfeld assured Simeon.

Almost a month passed, during which Laurence had no regrets himself.

One late night around Christmastide after all the customers had departed, Simeon announced to his women, "My darlings, as you are aware, I am having an outstandingly lucrative season, largely thanks to our Monsieur Beaumont. Yet since we live in a republic, I must put all matters that concern our house to a vote. Let us decide: should we keep him?"

"Well," said Marie, "he's nice to look at, and he has lovely manners."

"And he has all his own teeth," said Pascale.

"He's teaching me English," added Cecilia.

Marie smiled at her archly. "Oh yes, he's awfully clever with his tongue."

"And he never farts in bed," Marguerite said. "He doesn't even snore."

The other women were giggling, to Laurence's dismay, for the expression on Simeon's face now suggested to him that he had overstepped his privileges at the house.

"Are you so dedicated to your work that you would toil after hours?" Simeon asked them, in his driest tone. "And Monsieur, I thought I hired you to look after my tables. I got rid of your predecessor for just such a breach of discipline as you appear to have committed."

"It's not his fault, Simeon," Cecilia declared. "It's ours."

"Pray explain."

"Well, we were discussing the nature of men recently, and we had all arrived at the conclusion that the uglier a man is, the greater the effort he generally makes to please a woman, and that, as a consequence, handsome men must be the worst lovers. Then Marie said, could we think of any exception to the rule. We were at a loss until Monsieur Beaumont came in, so we put the proposition to him. And he gave us a most satisfactory answer."

"Why did you not request my permission before conducting your little experiment?"

"As you once told us yourself, you do not own our bodies after hours," said Pascale, with a haughty toss of her head.

"Well, Monsieur Beaumont," Simeon said, "von Mansfeld sold you short, in failing to mention you were a courtesan as well as a cardsharp. I believe I must review the terms of our initial agreement."

"It's not necessary," Laurence said, abashed. "I'll leave tonight."

"I won't allow it, Monsieur – you are far too useful an employee. What I mean," Simeon continued, in the same admonitory tone, "is that from henceforth you must exercise whatever weapons you have in your arsenal to please my beloved ladies, on the condition that you don't spoil them for their trade. And for as long as you wish to be with us, we shall indeed keep you." The women burst out cheering and clapping. "I take it that you are willing to abide by my new regulations," Simeon inquired, "or have you lost that clever tongue of yours?"

"I am," Laurence said, heaving a sigh of relief, for this respite at the house had worked upon him like a soothing opiate, dulling his livid memories of warfare and giving him hope that there were still some vestiges of courtesy left in the world, and in himself.

"Then the matter is settled. Let us drink to it."

They were about to raise their glasses when from the courtyard there came a series of high-pitched shrieks answered by hoarse shouts, and a male voice swearing volubly in French.

"Monsieur, should we investigate?" Simeon suggested. "Excuse us, ladies."

He and Laurence hurried to the front entrance, which had already been barred for the night, and opened the door to a gust of snow. His grooms were standing about in a circle watching as a gentleman in a fur cape delivered a thrashing to some child in rags.

Laurence grabbed the man's arm in mid-blow. "What do you think you're doing?" he demanded, and to the grooms, "Why didn't you stop him?"

"The gypsy picked my pocket!" yelled the man in French.

"Them gypsies are all bloody thieves," one of the grooms put in.

"And who the hell are you?" the man said to Laurence, his breath smoking in the chill air. "Some kin of the Jew's?"

"He is my associate," said Simeon. "And I'll thank you to treat him with respect."

"Tell him to get his hands off me! I want my money back. I came here to play."

"We are closed, sir, and you would be wise to go home."

"Do you know who I am? Seigneur Louis de Saint-Etienne!"

Simeon gestured for Laurence to release the Frenchman. "Your reputation precedes you, sir."

"As well it should. And now I'm going to strip that little felon bare."

Laurence glanced at the child cowering in the snow, whimpering, and then at Saint-Etienne, tall and arrogant in his rich furs. "How much money did he steal?" he asked the Frenchman, who named an impressive sum. "All right, then. I'll give you the same amount, if you'll wager it all against the house."

Saint-Etienne looked amazed, and very pleased. "It's a bargain!"

"What on earth are you playing at," Simeon hissed to Laurence. "Let him wager his own coin."

Laurence pretended not to hear. "And the child's coming in with us," he insisted, helping the boy up, over Simeon's objections.

Inside, he asked a maidservant to take charge of the boy, while Saint-Etienne commanded that a table be cleared for the proceedings.

As they sat down, he ordered Laurence, "Roll up your sleeves. I won't have any fancy moves tried on me."

"Then you must do the same," Laurence said, "once you've surrendered your sword."

"No weapons are allowed here, sir – a policy of the house to which all customers are subject," Simeon explained.

Saint-Etienne had to accede. With a pile of gold before him, he became calmer, and the opening hands were his. And as his pile grew, Laurence's shrank.

"Monsieur Beaumont, I don't like this," Simeon murmured, in between rounds.

"Don't worry," Laurence murmured back. "Keep him well served."

Marie brought forth some strong burnt wine in a crystal bottle, and they continued. At length Saint-Etienne pushed most of his winnings to the centre of the table. "Match that if you can!" he said.

Laurence had to request a loan from Simeon. Then they laid down their cards.

"By Christ," exclaimed Saint-Etienne.

"Every dog will have his day," Laurence said, sweeping up his gains. "Another hand?"

"Not with these poxy cards." Saint-Etienne withdrew a deck of his own from the fur cape and tossed it on the table.

"Forgive us, but rules are rules," Simeon intervened. "House cards only, sir."

Laurence took the deck, shuffling it to see how the cards were marked. "Now, Simeon," he said, "for such a distinguished guest, we can make an exception. Your deal," he told Saint-Etienne.

His confidence fully restored, the Frenchman wagered nearly all of his remaining money. But after the next hand, he groaned in disbelief.

"What's wrong?" Laurence asked.

"I don't like your luck."

"They're *your* cards."

Saint-Etienne sat back, screwing up his eyes suspiciously. "One more round."

"The wager's too small. It doesn't interest me."

"It interests *me*, so you shall play."

"Seigneur de Saint-Etienne," said Simeon, "it has been an honour, but I must ask you to leave us to our rest."

"One more round, I say! His run of fortune won't last."

"I can give you no credit here."

"I don't need it, usurer." Saint-Etienne reached deep into his cloak again and plucked out a stone that flashed in the candlelight. "You should know the worth of this diamond. I'll wager it for twice the money I lost."

Simeon examined the stone and laid it on the table. "Your choice, Monsieur Beaumont."

"One more," Laurence told Saint-Etienne, "but I hope you haven't forgotten that it's my turn to deal." The Frenchman obviously still trusted his marked cards, for he nodded, though he watched closely as Laurence shuffled. "What brings you to The Hague?" Laurence inquired, to distract him. "I suspect you're here for the same reason as most of the French – to buy arms."

Laurence's comment had the requisite effect: Saint-Etienne looked at him rather than the deck, and he managed to slip a card under his elbow, whereupon Marie, who was behind him, concealed it in her sleeve.

"As if I'd answer you, you whoreson," Saint-Etienne said, and he smirked as he saw his cards.

Marie craned forward, offering Saint-Etienne an irresistible view of her cleavage. "Oh, Monsieur Beaumont," she gasped, slipping back to Laurence the hidden card, "you are undone!"

For the last time they lay down their hands. "By God's wounds," Saint-Etienne said slowly, staring at them.

"What a twist of fate!" remarked Simeon.

"Not so." Saint-Etienne banged a fist on the table. "He cheated me, and I won't leave without my money, Jew, if I have to cut the thieving monkey a new arsehole and make him shit it out!"

"Why don't you try," said Laurence, delighted by his own victory.

Saint-Etienne leapt up, feeling for his absent sword. Even more furious, he overturned the table, spilling coins everywhere.

"Fetch the men!" Simeon shouted to Marie, as Laurence snatched the diamond and threw it to him.

He caught it deftly just as Saint-Etienne seized the bottle and smashed it in half. With a dueller's agility he aimed the jagged edge at Laurence's face, and out of instinct, Laurence put up his left hand as a shield. The glass sliced into the exposed flesh of his wrist, though he hardly felt it, reaching for the knife in his doublet with his other hand. But Simeon was ahead of him, pointing a stiletto at the Frenchman's chest.

"Drop the bottle," he said. Saint-Etienne hesitated, then threw it aside. "Now please leave, unless you wish me to draw blood."

"The gypsy has my money," the Frenchman responded, his tone menacing. "Give me back what's mine and I shall go, or on my honour as a gentleman, I'll make sure that this house is closed down within the month. If you have friends in The Hague, so do I."

At this, Simeon relented. "Fetch the boy and search his clothes," he told the grooms, who had rushed in, panting.

The gypsy was dragged up and had his cloak ripped away. In the bright candlelight he seemed more a youth than a boy, though delicate in feature and still beardless. He wore a tight cap on his head that the men also stripped off; and as they did so, a cascade of long black hair fell out.

"Saints alive!" cried Marguerite. "It's a woman."

"I don't care if it has a cunt or a cock between its legs," said Saint-Etienne. "I want my money."

The gypsy had been clutching her chest. Now she bent over and shook out half a dozen coins from the front of her shirt, glaring at him with wild, defiant eyes.

"Is that everything you stole?" Laurence asked her, though he could not have cared less if she had kept all of it.

She nodded vigorously.

"Not even close to the sum you mentioned, Seigneur de Saint-Etienne," Simeon commented, as a groom picked up the coins. "So much for your honour as a gentleman. Pray take your money and relieve us of your presence – and don't return."

Saint-Etienne swung about, to face Laurence. "I *will* return, and as God is my witness, on that day I'll slit you from stem to stern."

"Why don't you go and fuck yourself," sneered Laurence, and the grooms hustled Saint-Etienne out.

"You could not have made a worse foe, Monsieur Beaumont," Simeon told Laurence grimly afterwards. "He's one of the most talented duellers in France."

"And one of the most conceited pricks, which is some achievement in his country."

"So you went to all this trouble to teach him a lesson in humility?" Laurence shrugged, somewhat less elated as he noticed the pool of blood accumulating at his feet. "You crazy fellow," Simeon said. "I can't believe you've survived as long as you have – you must be as lucky in life as you are at cards. Sit down, before you fall over, and let me attend to that cut."

Laurence obeyed. His vision was beginning to fog and his ears were ringing. Just then he felt someone tug at his good arm, and looked, as through a mist, to see the gypsy crouched beside him. "Thank you, kind sir," she mumbled, in oddly inflected Dutch. "I am forever in your debt."

CHAPTER THREE

I.

Since seven of the morning Radcliff had been at drill with his troop in the meadows outside Oxford, and as the sun reached its zenith he decided that they should break for their noonday meal. They were growing increasingly listless, though on hearing the drummer beat out Radcliff's command, they let out a cheer and dispersed with great alacrity to receive their rations from the quartermaster. Radcliff was also in need of refreshment, his throat sore from yelling orders. He had arranged to meet Walter Ingram at the Lamb Inn, where he was staying, and he invited two of his men, Blunt and Fuller, to come along.

"There's a garden at the back that should provide some relief from this heat," he said. They accepted gratefully; both of them had sweated damp half-moons at the armpits of their buff jackets, and Blunt's face was burnt to a raw pink.

They walked their horses into town, where the traffic was so dense that they could scarcely pass, and the stench of ordure, human and animal, forced Radcliff to cover his nose.

"Some effort must be made to clean up after the troops," he remarked, "or else they'll be falling like ninepins from the foul air."

"That one's just falling from strong drink," said Blunt, as an inebriated recruit weaved across their path.

"It's as well there's talk of imposing a curfew soon," Fuller added. "Too many tossers like him. Bad for morale."

The Lamb, when they reached it, was as crowded as every other tavern in Oxford. While its reputation as a superior establishment attracted the higher ranks and other gentlemen of quality, Radcliff had chosen it mainly because he could have a private chamber upstairs to himself, however small, in case he had to send out or receive any messages for Pembroke.

"Well now, this makes a change," Fuller commented, as they strolled into the shady garden after leaving their mounts with a groom to be rubbed down.

Trestle tables and benches were set up amongst the trees, and an aroma of roasted meat drifted out from the inn's kitchen. As they were settling in, a new party of men arrived, splendidly attired, with colourful silk sashes about their waists. They seemed to have had a table reserved for them by the Lamb's proprietor, and they received prompt service, flagons and bottles appearing before them at once, as if by magic.

"Important folk," Blunt said, eyeing them with jealous disgust.

"Yes, that's Henry Wilmot, with the blue sash," Radcliff said, "and the man beside him is Charles Danvers. I know them from the Dutch cavalry. The others I don't recognise."

"Henry Wilmot," Fuller repeated, in an awed tone. "Wasn't it he who led the charge against the Scots, at the battle of Newburn two years ago?"

"And got captured by them afterwards, for his valour. He was Commissioner General of the King's Horse in that war, so he's sure to be given a similar command here."

Radcliff observed Ingram coming in, and stood to catch his attention. A pitcher of ale arrived just in time, for Ingram looked as hot and sweaty as they were, and as thirsty. They exchanged a quick greeting, and gulped down their ale.

"Nothing better than that, after a long ride," Ingram said, licking the foam from his lips.

"Where did you come from?" Blunt asked.

"I was at Chipping Campden in Gloucestershire where my friend's father, Lord Beaumont, has his seat. Beaumont and I rode in together, but he had some errand to do before meeting us. He should be here soon."

"Have you spoken to him yet about our troop?" Radcliff inquired, picturing again a bluff country nobleman.

"Yes, though it turns out he may have other plans. There's a chance he might be employed by the Secretary of State, who is a neighbour of Lord Beaumont's."

How very convenient, Radcliff thought. "Employed in what capacity?"

Ingram seemed to hesitate. "I believe he has some experience with ciphers, from his time in the German army. At any rate, Radcliff," he went on hastily, "you'll have a lot in common. At least, I hope you will."

A girl came bearing their plates of capon and pork, and cheese and onion pasties. Blunt and Fuller pounced on the food, chewing noisily.

"How are the men at drill?" Ingram asked Radcliff, who had selected a drumstick and was about to bite into it, careful not to spill grease on the front of his doublet.

"We're making progress," he said, "though this weather tends to sap the men's energy. Oh, and I've purchased twenty new pistols. Some fellows will still be without but I haven't the funds to buy more. Nonetheless, I'd like to train them all properly in the use of their weapons before the month is up. We can't have any lives lost through accidents, and they must learn to load and fire more speedily."

"They must," agreed Fuller, "or they'll be finished off in no time if it comes to an engagement."

Ingram flushed; at practice recently he had failed to hit a target, sending the ball way overhead. "We're not hunting ducks on the wing," Blunt had teased him, and he had been visibly offended.

"So, Ingram, did you enjoy your reunion with Beaumont?" Radcliff asked.

"What I remember of it. He brought me back to Richard's house in a sorry state. Richard was not pleased."

"Your brother could forgive a little excess. You hadn't seen Beaumont in years."

"Richard's never been very forgiving of Beaumont. He thinks Beaumont's had a bad influence on me ever since we were students up at university."

"And is Richard correct?"

"In some ways, yes," Ingram said, laughing, as the girl set a fresh round of ale before them.

Radcliff now saw another man arrive at Wilmot's table. He was tall and spare, his skin very dark, and his hair so black that it had almost a blue sheen to it, like a crow's plumage. He wore no hat nor armour, nor even a sword. He looked, in fact, rather shabby. Wilmot got up and clapped him on the shoulder, as did Charles Danvers.

"There he is – that's Beaumont," exclaimed Ingram.

Radcliff was surprised: this did not fit his image of Beaumont at all. Ingram called out to his friend, who waved back, and after a brief word to Wilmot, approached. Radcliff was amazed not only by the colour of his eyes but by his whole appearance. It could not be, Radcliff told himself.

"Beaumont," Ingram said, "may I introduce Sir Bernard Radcliff, and Corporals Fuller and Blunt." Too upset to rise, Radcliff extended his hand, which Beaumont grasped politely; his palm, unlike Radcliff's, was dry. "Some ale?" Ingram asked him, as he took a seat.

"Yes, thanks."

"We meet at last, sir," said Radcliff, exerting the utmost control to hide his shock. "Ingram told me you served six years abroad. We're looking for men of your calibre. You would be most welcome to ride as an officer in our troop." Beaumont inclined his head minimally, as if to acknowledge the offer. "Although you may have a prior commitment," Radcliff continued, curiosity getting the better of him. "To my Lord Falkland, or so Ingram mentioned."

This time Beaumont made no response. He cast Ingram a sidelong glance, at which Ingram winced back at him with an air of mute apology.

"Here's to the King," Radcliff said, distributing ale amongst them.

"To the King," chorused Blunt and Fuller.

About to reach for his cup, Beaumont pushed back his sleeve with a casual movement, exposing his wrist. Radcliff tried not to stare. Sweat broke out on his brow, and a while passed before he could speak. "A war wound, is it?" he said, pointing at the scar.

Beaumont smiled and shook his head, his face lighting up in a charming manner. "I got into an argument over some cards," he replied. He had an undistinguished accent, lacking the crisp intonation typical of an aristocrat.

Radcliff swallowed, his mouth parched in spite of the ale. "When did it happen?"

"Oh, last winter."

"And where were you then?" Radcliff said, aware from the slight impatience in Beaumont's eyes that he was pressing too far. But he was now almost certain.

"In The Hague."

"Knife, was it?" Fuller put in.

"No. Someone cut me with a broken bottle."

"Nasty, that," Blunt said.

Radcliff picked up his cup to raise it to his mouth, then quickly set it down again; he was feeling sick to his stomach.

"What's the matter, Radcliff?" Ingram asked. "You don't seem well."

Radcliff essayed a smile. "Must be the heat."

"You're white as a ghost, sir," Fuller said. "You should rest. We'll see to the drill this afternoon."

"I do thank you," Radcliff said, through his teeth, as they all got up. "A short sleep is probably what I need."

"You have to leave, too?" Beaumont asked Ingram.

"Duty calls." Ingram gestured in the direction of Wilmot. "You can always rejoin the Commissioner General, Beaumont. He seems to be a great friend of yours."

"When it suits him," remarked Beaumont, with a laugh. "But no, I've something else to do. I hope you feel better soon," he said to Radcliff.

"Thank you, sir." Radcliff bowed to him, and the party broke up.

Radcliff waited until the others were out of sight before heading inside and upstairs to his chamber. He went in, shut the door, and lay down on his pallet, taking deep breaths to calm the fluttering in his chest. What a calamitous stroke of fate! He could not have predicted it. Blinded to his own future, he was like a man fighting with one arm tied behind his back.

Gradually, however, his nausea abated. He was looking at things from the wrong perspective, he realised, as if from the wrong end of a spyglass. There must be a design behind it all: he and Beaumont had met so that he could regain what was rightfully his.

More optimistic, he descended to the taproom and paid a boy to deliver a message for him. Half an hour later, he heard three raps at the door to his chamber.

"Come in," he said.

Tyler entered, ducking so as not to hit his head against the door-frame; as always, he wore his wide-brimmed hat tipped low, perhaps to hide the fact that one of his eyes was askew, lending his face a permanently sinister quality.

"Did you avoid the garden on your way in, as I told you?" Radcliff asked at once.

"Aye," Tyler said. There was nowhere for him to sit, so he squatted on his haunches, resting his massive forearms on his thighs. "Wouldn't do for us to be seen together."

"Indeed it wouldn't. And now we must be particularly vigilant. Remember the cardsharp at the brothel? *Monsieur Beaumont*, as they called him?"

"How could I not, after you had me chase him and his slut across France."

"Well, he's here in Oxford. I was introduced to him this afternoon in the garden."

"By the very devil!" Tyler removed his hat, which left an indentation in his thick hair that would normally have provoked Radcliff's mirth. "How in hell –"

"It came about through Walter Ingram, who was badgering me to meet a friend of his, lately returned from the Low Countries, a nobleman's son by the name of Beaumont. Not for the life of me would I have expected it, but he is the same Beaumont."

"You must be mistaken!"

"You couldn't mistake a man like him. He is exactly as the Jew's grooms described him to us, scar and all."

"Might he have recognised you?"

"Certainly not. Neither he nor the gypsy saw me that night. Tyler, we have been given a wonderful opportunity. If Beaumont still has my correspondence, I may be able to retrieve it. Of course he'll have spent the gold, but the letters –"

"Why would he bother keeping them?" said Tyler, scratching at the stubble on his chin. Radcliff frowned, for it was a good question. Still, he had not forgotten what Ingram had let slip about Beaumont's experience with ciphers. "And if he did, what could it matter?"

Tyler went on. "You said the code couldn't be broken, so why worry?"

"I am not worried, Tyler – I just want the letters for my own satisfaction," Radcliff answered shortly.

"Oh, I see now." Tyler grinned. "Whatever I didn't do abroad, I'll do here."

Radcliff let out a harsh sigh. "Listen to me. We are in England. Beaumont is not some Jew's minion whose throat you can slit in a dark alleyway without any consequences. His father is a respected peer."

"I shall make it look clean."

"I forbid you to try it yet. We could lose any chance we might have of getting back the letters. Is that understood?"

Tyler assumed a sulky expression. "When have I disobeyed you?"

"Not once, and rest assured, I shall reward you for that in time." Radcliff paused, then said more quietly, "I know from Ingram where Beaumont's family estate lies, in the Cotswolds, and can easily ask when he might next be there. We shall confront him on his father's territory, which will come as something of a jolt to him, I believe. I shall send Poole to demand that he surrender the letters for a reasonable sum."

"You said his father was a peer! Why would he need money? Even if he spent your gold, his dad must be rich enough to keep him."

"I have thought of that. If the money doesn't spark his interest, Poole will suggest what the letters could cost him should he refuse to hand them over. The mere hint of menace to his noble family could be enough, though if he fails to bend, you might be allowed to demonstrate to him that our threats are far from idle." Radcliff smiled at Tyler. "Only play your highest card when it is imperative for victory: a rule of gaming with which Beaumont must be very familiar."

"Poole can't game."

"He's a lawyer. He games with words."

"Words," murmured Tyler disdainfully, yet Radcliff could see that he was flattered to be held in reserve.

"Beaumont won't be hard to keep track of around here, and I can also provide you with information about his movements from Ingram. I want you to stay on his tail, as you did in France. But if he catches sight of you, we are both finished – *you* above all. Is that clear?"

Tyler nodded and stood up, his head grazing the beamed ceiling; he was fingering the brim of his hat. "Why won't you tell me what's in those letters? I risked my neck to get them for you."

"You were paid generously, even though you were unsuccessful."

"If I hadn't fallen sick in Paris, I wouldn't have lost him."

"And you found him, and lost him *again*."

"I did my best. I wanted him and the slut dead as much as you. He may be the son of a lord, but I know him for a canny rogue. He could still do you mischief. Let me take him down!"

"Not until I know about the letters. After that, we shall see. Good day to you, Tyler."

When his servant had gone, Radcliff sat back down on his pallet and heaved another sigh. How to raise enough money to tempt Beaumont into handing over the letters, if he still had them? Radcliff's own scant funds were almost spent in outfitting the troop. He had no choice: he would have to sell some of the jewels that Pembroke had given him for Kate as a wedding present.

II.

What a nuisance, Laurence thought, on his way out of Oxford. As soon as he had arrived at the Lamb Inn, he had run into Wilmot and Danvers, both of whom he had known abroad. They had asked if there was any truth to the rumour that he had narrowly escaped being hanged for desertion last winter. He had laughed it off, and was called away conveniently by Ingram, but the question would be posed again. Danvers had insisted on meeting up with him at a different tavern, towards early evening.

As for Ingram's new friends, Laurence recognised in Corporals Blunt and Fuller a certain cast of soldier: brave, simple, and slavishly loyal to their senior officers. Sir Bernard Radcliff he read less easily, though he was puzzled that Ingram could be so fond of the man, with his inquisitorial grey eyes and chilly demeanour. Yet Radcliff might be well suited to Kate Ingram. Laurence had only met her once when she was sixteen, and while undeniably beautiful, she had seemed to him a proud, spoilt girl. He had taken no more to Radcliff today, and the needling reference to a prior commitment to the Secretary of State still bothered him. He had scolded Ingram afterwards for being so indiscreet, and Ingram had sworn it would not happen again.

With some hours to spare in the afternoon, Laurence decided to visit Diana Stratton, to learn how she was faring, as an old and dear friend, and to see if she had changed over the years; any more than that, he did not admit to himself. If Sir Robert were home, which might preclude any frank conversation with her, Laurence would say he had come to present his father's greetings and leave as soon as he could. Then he would return to town and share a jug with Danvers, and call on Seward late, when he would be sure to find him at Merton.

Northwest of the city, on the border of Wytham Wood, Laurence asked a girl picking berries in a hedgerow for directions to the house. She stammered them out so fearfully that he had to strain to understand her. Annoyed, he rode on. Just a few weeks back in England, he was already beginning to tire of the effect his looks had on most people.

Stratton's house was an old, timbered mansion, standing in an apple orchard surrounded by a wall of weathered Cotswold stone. As Laurence approached, he heard the shrill cries of children at play. He reined in his horse and peered over the wall. A fat, cheerful woman was sitting in the shade of a tree with two small boys playing about her, picking daisies and tossing them into her lap, while she threaded them into chains. When she observed Laurence, she gave a start, and the boys clung to her, regarding him with wide eyes.

"What do you want?" she shouted, struggling up and pressing them to her side as if he were about to snatch them from her and devour them whole.

Such concrete evidence of Diana's motherhood stirred in Laurence a vague apprehension: she might not welcome his visit at all. "Is Sir Robert Stratton at home, madam?" he inquired.

"And who are you to ask?" When Laurence gave his name, she said sharply, "Stay here," and herded the children from the orchard and through the front door of the house, shutting it firmly behind her.

He dismounted and waited, kicking a pebble about in the dust, tempted to disappear. Then the door opened again to reveal another woman, younger than the nurse, and pretty. She dropped a curtsey, examining him from beneath her eyelashes. "Mr. Beaumont," she said, "the master is away, I am afraid, but the mistress will see you. Pray come in."

The woman guided him into a parlour where he found Diana arranging some flowers in a vase. She had on a gown of blue that matched the colour of her eyes and set off her fair skin and blonde hair; and she looked to him as lovely as before. She bade him good day and gave him her hand to kiss as though he were, as indeed he was, a distant relative. "Such a long time since we have seen you, sir," she said, in such a way that he could not guess whether she was being cautious or genuinely indifferent. "His lordship your father and her ladyship must be so very grateful for your safe return."

"Are you in good health, Lady Stratton?" he asked.

"Excellently well, thank you."

"And Sir Robert?"

"He is well, also, though preoccupied these days with the war, and how it might affect his trade. He is in town, negotiating a contract.

I do not expect him home early. Thank you, Margaret," she told the other woman. "You may go."

Margaret obeyed, closing the parlour door.

Immediately Diana threw her arms about Laurence. "Beaumont," she whispered, "why did you leave me without even a note, nothing to explain your absence! I cried for weeks and weeks afterwards! And now I can't believe my eyes! Here you are, my sweet lover, come to find me!"

"Diana," he began, taken aback as much by this wave of emotion as by her eagerness to rekindle their affair, "I only came to see how –"

But she would not let him speak, kissing him with violent force. Then she rushed over to the window and drew the curtains. "Make love to me," she said, hurrying back to him. "Margaret will keep guard for us."

"We can't," he said.

"Why not?" Her expression altered. "Don't tell me – are you – were you *hurt* in that terrible war?"

"No!" he replied, nearly laughing; was this everyone's concern?

"Do I not please you any more? Have I lost my looks?"

"Far from it."

"So make love to me," she urged, searching beneath his doublet to caress him.

For the briefest moment he forgot himself, enjoying her touch. But as she started to unbutton the doublet and unlace his breeches, he moved away and took her hands in his. "Diana, I'm here on a friendly visit. I wanted to find out how you were." She gazed up at him, frowning. "Look," he persisted, "I'm sorry, all those years ago, that I couldn't tell you I was leaving. Even if I'd stayed, it wouldn't have been wise for us to continue our . . . our meetings." Remembering his conversation with Ingram, he added, "I wasn't thinking of the consequences for *you*. It was very selfish of me."

"As though I hadn't a mind of my own! I desired you, Beaumont, and I desire you now." She grabbed his arm, trying to drag him to the door. "We can go into the woods, if you're afraid we'll be discovered!"

"No," he told her, gently detaching her fingers. "You must understand, it's finished. But I was hoping we could still be friends."

"We were *always* friends, Beaumont," she said desperately. "Loving friends! Why should that change?" And she kissed him again.

Suddenly they heard Margaret's panicked voice outside the door. "Sir Robert is home, my lady! He's riding into the courtyard!"

Thank God, Laurence thought, as Diana at last released him. "I do apologise most sincerely for everything," he said, aware that this was an inadequate parting speech. "Goodbye, Diana."

She did not speak, but only stared at him, so he bowed to her and walked out.

III.

After a tiring day in the city, Sir Robert Stratton desired only a quiet meal with his wife. He was therefore irritated to ascertain, upon dismounting in the courtyard, that they must have a visitor, for an unfamiliar black stallion was tethered there, twitching its withers and stamping its slender hind legs. Then the front door opened and a man exited hastily, though he stopped short when he saw Stratton.

"Mr. Beaumont, such an unexpected pleasure!" Stratton declared, with a bow. "It has been many years since we last met. I must thank you for calling on us, sir. Surely you are not about to leave just as I arrive?"

"Yes, you must excuse me, Sir Robert," Beaumont said, in a subdued tone, fumbling with a lower button on his doublet. "I have an appointment in town."

"But you must be late for it and share a glass of wine with us," Stratton said, thinking what a contrast there was between this new

Beaumont and the lounging, impudent rascal who had once graced
their London house. Those years abroad had taken their toll on him:
the sauciness of privileged youth was altogether gone from his manner,
and instead he had the air of a fox run to ground.

"No, I – er – I can't, I'm afraid."

"Then I pray you will come back on another occasion."

"Yes, indeed," Beaumont said, untethering his horse.

"And do me the favour of greeting his lordship and her ladyship,
when you are next at Chipping Campden."

"I shall, sir. Good day."

And with that, Beaumont mounted and galloped off.

"Well, well," murmured Stratton.

When he entered the house, Margaret greeted him in a high, flustered voice.

"Would you be so kind as to bring me a light repast," he told her,
taking off his cloak and handing it over. "I have not eaten since breakfast and cannot wait for supper. Where is her ladyship?"

Margaret hesitated. "In . . . in the parlour," she said eventually, as
though revealing some dread secret.

Stratton was perturbed to find his wife collapsed in a chair, her
shoulders quivering. "What is the matter?" he asked, as she rose to face
him. "It's not about Lord Beaumont? Has he come to some mishap? Is
that why his son was here?"

Like Margaret, she did not answer at once; and he had a sinful
thought, about Lord Beaumont's will, and how he might benefit from
it. "No, Sir Robert," she said tremulously. "Mr. Beaumont was merely
paying us his respects."

"I see. My dear, you have been crying. Is it your time of the month?"
She shook her head. "Come to table with me."

He ushered her over, and they sat in silence until Margaret arrived with a dish of pickled artichokes decorated with little slices of fried bread. She set it before them, along with a pitcher of barley water and glasses, and left.

"Have a morsel with me," he suggested to his wife. "It will put the colour back in your cheeks."

"I am not hungry," she said, inspecting the vegetables as though they were laced with poison.

"Then I shall eat for you." Between mouthfuls, he commented, "How remarkable to see Mr. Beaumont again. Though I hardly exchanged a word with him, I think he is greatly altered, would you not agree?" She did not respond. "He must have got his just deserts while in the army," Stratton went on. "The rigours of such a life would prove a severe test for someone like him."

"Why do you say that?" Diana inquired faintly, serving him barley water.

"Because he was no more than a pampered brat when he left. He had all the fortune in the world before him and an excellent marriage prospect, yet he tossed it aside. All he cared for at the time was to game, drink, and fornicate with whoever would have him."

"Sir Robert!" she gasped. "What do you really know of him except idle gossip?"

Stratton speared an artichoke with his knife. "I am sad to inform you that it is not *idle gossip*, my dear. So often you do not see people for what they truly are. At Court, for example, some of your friends were very ill chosen. That scheming, conniving Isabella Savage for one. And did you know that bets were openly exchanged amongst the men as to how many of the younger wives they could seduce? Beaumont was probably one of the worst of those blackguards." Diana's mouth began to wobble as he finished speaking. "What is wrong with you?" he demanded, setting aside the knife.

"Nothing," she said, as tears welled up in her eyes.

"If it's not your health that ails you, there must be some other cause! My poor girl, perhaps you should rest for a while, and we shall speak when you are calmer. Margaret!" he called out. "Help your mistress upstairs."

As he watched Margaret take his wife from the room, he remarked to himself how like little children women were, with their mysterious moods and fits of weeping. He must write to Lord Beaumont about his heir's return, he mused next. It might provide another excuse to visit Chipping Campden. He was rather intrigued to talk to the son again, and discover whether the changes in him were as much internal as external. But such a look on Beaumont's face when they had met, as furtive as that of a thief caught red-handed! And the fellow could not wait to escape.

Stratton froze, an artichoke halfway to his mouth. What if Beaumont had not changed? Could he have made some impertinent advance upon Diana? Stratton knew that many men admired her beauty, though she was always oblivious to the attention of others when he pointed it out to her. Sweet creature that she was, she had not a guileful bone in her body. In her very innocence, however, she might have encouraged Beaumont unwittingly. And how insulted she would have been by him, how utterly aggrieved, exactly as she had appeared today. Stratton felt disinclined to raise the issue, lest he insult her more. He would talk to Margaret, instead.

IV.

"Oh, Margaret," said Diana, as her gentlewoman applied a cooling cucumber poultice to her swollen eyelids, "I know you disapprove. You think me a bad woman and a dishonest wife."

"My lady, it's *he* who is to blame. And when you first told me about him, you said you wouldn't forgive him for vanishing as he did. What happened to your resolve? Think of your family, of your position in society! Would you jeopardise everything again, just for a tumble?"

Diana sighed and reclined on her bed. "It is not just that."

"It would be no more for him. I could tell by the way he looked at me that he considers all women fair game. He has a most degenerate face, and those eyes of his made my skin crawl. If I were you, I should never have let him near me. But my lady," Margaret said, in a lower voice, "are you sure that Sir Robert never guessed about him?"

"If Sir Robert had, he would have confronted me," Diana assured her, sniffing. "You know how he fears the slightest hint of scandal and is always so keen to impress others. Indeed," she concluded, beginning to weep again, "it was his very eagerness to flaunt his noble connections that first brought Beaumont to our door."

V.

In the summer of 1635, after she and Sir Robert had been married some eleven months, he expressed a wish to call on Lord Beaumont, a kinsman whom he had mentioned with pride on many occasions. "I have heard that some sketches by the artist Van Dyke, to whom his lordship is most partial, have just come up for sale," he went on. "I should be doing his lordship a favour if I alerted him." They would pass a day or so at Lord Beaumont's house in Chipping Campden, he told her, and then travel south to their property at Wytham.

Towards the end of their journey, as they drove up through the park, Diana was awed by the palatial dimensions of Lord Beaumont's residence, built in a style far more modern than their London home, and when they were welcomed in, its owner charmed her instantly with his warmth and utter lack of affectation. She had to wonder whether he or his Spanish wife was most responsible for the continental atmosphere of the house, from the grandiose canvases and statues that decorated it, to the silver forks with which they ate their food at dinner.

And as they ate, she tried not to stare at Lady Beaumont, with her chiselled profile and those extraordinarily luminous eyes; and such a graceful figure, clad in a tailored gown that made Diana's seem positively unfashionable in comparison. Her skin was not sallow, as Diana had expected, but golden in sheen, and her natural expression, enhanced by her long, straight nose and the slight flare to her nostrils, betrayed all the proud disdain for which her countrymen were celebrated. In her speech, however, no discernible foreignness could be heard, except for the odd soft consonant.

Her eldest son, Laurence, was apparently away in London. The younger boy, Thomas, a youth of about eighteen, greeted Diana bashfully, while the two little daughters were less shy, and chattered away to her until they were sent up to bed. On the following morning, Robert discussed the sale of Van Dyke's work with Lord Beaumont, who had already commissioned a portrait from the artist and was most anxious to buy the sketches. Robert, pleased to act as agent, insisted on putting up the money himself upon receipt of the art, to be reimbursed at his lordship's convenience.

Diana heard no more of it for a number of months. They retired to Wytham, where she moped about the dark, timbered rooms, dreaming of the Palladian splendour of the Beaumont house and yearning for city life. Then Robert announced an alteration in plan to suit them both: they would move back to London in late August. Lord Beaumont's sketches were about to be sent, and the man selling them must be paid.

"I really don't see the value of such unfinished studies," Robert said, as they were unwrapped in the parlour of their London home. "Van Dyke will prove merely a passing fashion, as is so frequently the case with popular artists." Diana wished to contradict him, for she hoped to be painted by the Dutch master, who had complimented her and her friend Isabella Savage at Court. "Why did I turn down that letter of credit when his lordship offered it to me," Robert added, and she was tempted to laugh. He had wanted to appear gracious and offhand about a sum that staggered him and left him short.

A few days later, they were entertaining friends to a light supper of winkles, ale, and a joint of beef when the servant told her that there was someone calling for Sir Robert. "I didn't let him in, my lady, because the fellow looks a rough sort," the servant explained. She said that she would go with him to attend to the visitor and excused herself, glad to escape a boring conversation.

As she opened the door to the half-light of dusk, she saw a tall man slouched against the wall outside. He turned, and she gasped at his uncanny resemblance to Lady Beaumont. In his face, however, she read a different expression, indolent and sensual. He had dark circles under his eyes, as if he slept very little, and he was unshaven and carelessly dressed. No wonder the servant had been suspicious of him.

"You must be Lord Beaumont's son," she exclaimed. "How can you forgive us our rudeness? The servant – oh dear – he did not know."

Mr. Beaumont smiled at her, and she no longer saw his mother in him, for the smile wrinkled the corners of his mouth and lent the sweep of his brows an impish air. "Oh, it's not his fault – you weren't expecting me," he said, as if he had known her for years. "I came with some money, from my father."

"Have you eaten, sir? We are just sitting down at table."

"Thank you, but I can't stay."

She found herself searching for a reason to delay his departure. "Sir Robert will scold me for my lack of manners if you do not at least take a glass of wine with us."

"Well, then," he said, with the same engaging smile, "I better had."

She admitted him as she might some unpredictable animal, with no idea as to how he would behave, and led him to the chamber where they were eating, conscious of his gaze on her as she went ahead. Robert made introductions and had his best wine fetched, while his friends ogled the new arrival. After handing Robert a leather purse, which was received with profuse thanks, Mr. Beaumont seemed disinclined to talk, sitting back in his chair and giving such monosyllabic answers that Robert was forced to resume chatting with the other guests. And all along, she felt Mr. Beaumont watching her with his captivating feline eyes.

When he rose to leave, she offered to see him to the door. "I'm so sorry," she said. "Robert's friends weren't to your taste."

"They aren't to yours, either," he said.

His comment threw her for a moment. But before he could disappear into the night, she amazed herself by asking, "Are you ever at Court?"

"No, not often."

"We shall be attending the reception at Whitehall in early September, for the Spanish ambassador. I expect you speak Spanish, Mr. Beaumont?"

"I do, yes."

"Then you could translate for us."

He laughed and shrugged. "I don't like receptions – too much ceremony. Good night, Lady Stratton," he said; and then he was gone.

When she rejoined the others, they were talking about him: how badly turned out he was, and what a trial to his family, and how he had debauched habits. This only fascinated her all the more.

The night of the reception was very humid, and Robert was nursing a headache. "You cannot miss such an important event," he told her, and he arranged an escort of friends for her. She had a premonition that everything was unfolding, or unravelling, as if fated. She made her toilette with special care, hoping that her efforts would not go to waste, though she did not know for what, precisely, she was preparing herself.

At the Banqueting House there was hardly space to stand in the galleries overlooking the King's dais, and the combined perfumes and bodily odours of the crowd began to stifle her. Then she caught sight of Mr. Beaumont in the gallery on the opposite side. He saw her too, and signalled that she should go towards the doors. She whispered to her companions that she needed fresh air, and after refusing their offers of assistance and eluding her maidservant, she met him on the stairs.

"It stinks in here," he said. "Why don't we go out for a walk?"

"Mr. Beaumont, that would not be appropriate. I should fetch my maid."

"Are you afraid to be alone with me?" he inquired, with his playful smile.

"No," she said, though she was, deliciously so.

He took her down towards the river, not touching her except to steer her away from messes on the street as they walked, and he recounted to her what the ambassador's delegation had said amongst themselves of the English court and its French queen Henrietta Maria. His salacious comments made her laugh despite her nerves, and his volubility was in marked contrast to his silence at Robert's party.

"Please, sir, let's not go any further," she said, after a while. "My friends will be anxious if I am away too long."

They had reached the bank of the Thames, where it was peaceful except for the cries of the watermen in the distance. He sat down on the grass and motioned for her to do the same, and so she did. "Now tell me about yourself," he said.

"You would find it dull," she said, but on his encouragement she described how she had grown up in the country with an oppressive father and a weak-willed mother, and how she had married Robert at nineteen, although he was not her first suitor.

"Why *him?*" asked Mr. Beaumont, and she guessed what he thought about Robert.

"Because he has a house in London, and he promised to have me presented at Court," she answered, with more honesty than she knew was proper.

"Two very sound reasons." He stretched out and rested his head on his arm, surveying her. "What next? Should we go back?"

"No," she whispered. "I want you to kiss me."

"Are you sure?" he said, though he did not look particularly surprised.

"Yes."

His mouth tasted of wine. She had not been kissed so before, attentively and without hurry. Slipping her dress down to bare her shoulders, he continued to kiss her, lower and lower, until she felt his tongue circle a nipple. She was trembling from the excitement and the danger. Then he stopped and asked again, "Are you still sure?"

"Yes, quite sure," she said.

His hand shifted to beneath her skirts, then up to her knees, and parted her legs. She tensed at first, embarrassed; yet his fingers were provoking in her a most marvellous and unaccustomed sensation. She could not concentrate on anything else. Moments later, hot potent waves broke within her, and she opened her eyes, which she had not realised were closed.

"Did you like that?" he inquired, his hand still between her thighs, evidently at home there.

"Yes," she admitted.

"Would you like more?"

"Yes," she said, hungering for him, blocking from her mind every other thought.

He lifted her skirts, and in the next second, it seemed, he entered her smoothly, without any of Robert's fumbling. She was liquid around him as he moved. He did not moan, as Robert did, or weigh her down, as his hands came to her buttocks, raising her up so that his groin massaged again that sensitive part of hers. He understood her body better than she did herself, and he made love to her until she was weak, shaking in every limb. Then he propped himself up on one elbow and gave her an amicable smile, as if they had just enjoyed some decorous conversation, and she smiled back, thinking that had she been told an hour before that she would find herself blasted heavenwards, committing adultery with a man who was almost her cousin, she would not have believed it.

As they walked back to the Banqueting House, she felt the moisture trickling out of her, down to the tops of her stockings; and she was filled with a languid passion, clinging to his arm. "Do you have other mistresses?" she asked.

"I'd rather call you my friend," he said. "We can be friends, can't we?"

"I suppose," she agreed, unsure of what he meant, teetering on the edge of disappointment.

"Come and see me, then." He told her where he had rooms, in Southwark, and they parted outside the House, to which, she observed, he did not return. This both flattered and frightened her: he had attended the reception for only one purpose.

As she pushed through the crowd towards her companions, she felt that she must reek of sex and that her sin must somehow be written on her face. They were too intent on the celebrations to notice. She was able to say she had been ill, and wished to go home. That night she lay awake in bed next to Robert, and thought of Beaumont and the new pleasure he had awakened in her.

The next day, however, she was haunted by guilt and fear of discovery: what if he were to boast publicly of seducing her? He had, several times, given her the opportunity to resist him, and she had urged him on. She would have to make him swear on his honour as a gentleman to keep private an incident that must not be repeated. She sent her servant with a note requesting that she might visit briefly to discuss an urgent matter, and received a reply, in untidy writing, that she could come the following afternoon if it suited. She told Robert that she was going on a charitable call, and he congratulated her on her benevolence.

Mr. Beaumont lived down an unsavoury street, in a house that he apparently shared with several other people, amongst them a bright young lady in a low-cut gown who curtseyed to Diana as they passed each other on the stairs. After she knocked on Mr. Beaumont's door, she had to wait, and wondered if he was indeed in. Then it opened. He looked sleepy, dressed only in a rumpled shirt and breeches, and he was rubbing his eyes, but he beamed at her disarmingly and invited her in. After the opulence of his family home, she had not expected such impoverished quarters, barely furnished save for a bed and a mountain of books piled up beside it. The bed was unmade, and she nearly trod on some garments lying about on the floor.

"Mr. Beaumont," she began. "I must –"

"A glass of wine?" he interrupted. "I think I have some left from last night, unless I drank it all." As he hunted about, she felt so overwrought that she had to sit, on the bed, since there was no alternative place. At length, he brought her wine. "So," he said, "what's this urgent matter?"

"It is, that I – that *we* –" But she could not say what she had intended.

Her charitable calls became regular. She could never stay with Beaumont much above an hour or two, yet as she got to know him, she came to like him more and more, and not just for the physical gratification he gave her, with seemingly boundless energy and inventiveness. He had a remarkably cheerful disposition, taking everything as a joke, and she discovered that he held outrageous opinions about politics, religion, the relation between the sexes, and the world in general. He was also strangely sensitive to her moods, asking questions that Robert would never put to her.

Although unconcerned with many social niceties, he paid great heed to personal cleanliness. She noticed that his sheets were always fresh and as sweet-smelling as he, and this was, indirectly, the cause of their sole argument. Once, arriving early, she heard female laughter as she climbed the stairs to his room. The door stood open, and so she looked in. A woman was with him, comely though flashily dressed, presumably a laundress since she was holding his bundled-up sheets.

"You *are* keeping me busy these days," she was saying. "You naughty boy, don't you ever get tired?" He did not answer, but pulled her to him, the sheets crushed between their bodies, and kissed her full on the mouth. He had not observed Diana, though the laundress did as she turned to go. "Good day, madam," she said pertly, and to him, "I believe I shall be seeing you again very soon, my dear."

Diana was aghast. "Are you – are you *familiar* with her?" she cried to him, once they were alone. "Do you make love with her?"

"I wouldn't call it that. But yes, now and again. I don't see that you have any right to object," he added, with a disparaging laugh. "After all, you sleep with your husband every night."

"Would you have me leave him?" she asked, almost wishing Beaumont to say yes.

"Of course not. You must know me by now. If I'm making you unhappy, you should stop coming here."

"No," she said quickly. She did not question him again, nor did she see him with another woman.

Their affair lasted for almost a year. Then one day Robert received a letter, which he opened over breakfast. "They will get him married at last," he announced, when he had finished reading.

"Who's to be married?" she asked.

"Lord Beaumont's eldest son. Poor girl, he will lead her a dance. Though heaven knows, if I were a woman I'd marry him myself, to become mistress of that estate."

When she next saw Beaumont, he told her he did not want to talk about it, and his insouciance lulled her into believing that nothing would change between them. That afternoon, he got her tipsy, removed every stitch of her clothing with the proficiency of a well-trained maid-servant, and sent her into such ecstasy that she thought she would die. The following week, she went to his lodgings and found an empty room, not even a book in sight. The bright lady downstairs said that the contents of his chamber had been sold to pay off rent that he owed; he had disappeared a few days earlier and no one knew where he had gone. Diana collapsed at the news. At home she waited, hoping he might have sent some message that had perhaps been delayed. But none came. A fortnight later, nausea rose in her stomach, her breasts grew tender, and she knew that she was pregnant. The consequences of her folly now appalled her: what if the child was Beaumont's? Those distinctive looks that had so seduced her could be her very undoing. Tormented by the prospect of giving birth to a dark infant with telltale green eyes, she allowed her health to suffer; and whether luckily or unluckily, she miscarried in her second month.

VI.

"Beaumont, did I mention to you a certain lady who has stolen my heart? A Mrs. Sterne?"

"I don't believe you did," said Laurence, as Charles Danvers filled his cup. At first he had found Danvers' company a relief after his awkward encounter with Diana, but now he felt restless: it must be nine or ten o'clock, time for him to visit Seward.

"Well," Danvers said, with the air of settling into his story, "I asked Mistress Savage, her best friend, to arrange a tryst for us yesterday in the meadows. It was laid out when we arrived – cushions on the grass, wine, and sweetmeats – perfection. Then Mistress Savage and her maidservant gave some excuse to depart, leaving Mrs. Sterne to my tender wooing. I had to promise that I would get a chamber for us tomorrow."

"And where was Mr. Sterne, during all this?"

"Oh, he's an elderly fellow, you see, and keeps to his bed most of the day. But what can he expect, if he marries a woman young enough to be his granddaughter. And in his state of health he is, alas –" Danvers held up his hand and let it flop at the wrist.

"How unfortunate for him. Does she know that you're married, too?"

"No, and I am not about to tell her. I seem to remember you and I had a few such adventures with the fair sex while we were in the Dutch service together, and you never objected to my being married."

"I still have not the slightest objection," Laurence said, laughing, and Danvers joined in.

"Thank Christ for that. I heard you were dealing cards in some fancy house in The Hague last winter, but judging by your colour, you must have been in some warmer clime more recently."

"I had to get away from the cold."

"Or from a rope," Danvers joked. "Such a bother that I must leave Oxford soon," he continued, with a sigh. "It was going so swimmingly with Mrs. Sterne. But Wilmot has orders for us to ride north."

"You never know, she might follow you."

"By God, you're right. Women can do the rashest things when they're smitten. But they can also be damned tricky. Isabella Savage, for example. Not that I'd be interested in her, despite her attractions. She's up her to neck in politics, with her friend Lord Digby. Too sharp-witted by far."

"A terrible disadvantage in a woman," Laurence remarked, though Danvers did not pick up the irony. "In this case, however, she seems to be using her wits to your benefit."

"Yes, she is, though I'd wager she has her own motives for doing so. Beaumont," Danvers went on, "are you going to ride with Wilmot? He swears there'll be rich pickings off those bastards in Parliament once we've thrashed their arses in the field. Think of the sport we could have together. You've got to join us."

"We'll see," Laurence said, bored with the same old question.

Danvers cocked his head to one side and squinted at him. "I suppose you've no need to fret about money, now that you're home. It must have been different for you over there – you must have done a lot of things just to get by. As a matter of fact, I even heard that you were a mole for the Germans."

"Who said that?"

"I can't reveal my sources," Danvers replied smugly. "I also heard a rumour that you were playing on both sides of the game. Not that I'd give it any credit."

Laurence yawned and stood up. "Thanks for a most enjoyable evening."

"Stay," Danvers said. "If you run off now, you'll make me think my sources were correct." Laurence ignored him, counting out some coins. "I might find a use for your talents. Aren't you curious to know who I'm working for?"

"Will this be enough?" Laurence inquired, of the money.

Danvers eyed it appreciatively. "More than enough. Most generous of you. My turn next."

"It's never your turn," Laurence said, smiling. "Your pockets are always empty. Good night, man."

He felt glad to breathe clean night air after the fug of the Blue Boar's taproom. How quickly his past had caught up with him, he thought, as he walked over to Merton. Yet Danvers deserved his thanks for all that careless talk: better to know what was being said than not.

Once at the College, Laurence passed through the front quad-rangle and beneath the Fitzjames Arch into the newer quadrangle, built just a few years before his birth, to house the Fellows. He could recall as a youth sitting out late there, his breeches getting damp with dew, making ambitious plans for his own future that usually involved faraway places and exotic women. And now, miles from Spain and from Juana, he found himself where he had been on the day before he left England: paying a call on Seward.

He was encouraged to see light glimmer from Seward's windows. "Who's there?" came a thin, quavering voice, as he knocked at the door.

"It's me, Seward, open up," he said, smelling the familiar odour of cat's urine, acrid as gunpowder.

The door swung wide to reveal a large striped tom with tail erect and fluffed up, hissing at him. Then Seward came forward, dressed in his faded black cap and gown, and shoved the beast aside with his foot so that Laurence could cross the threshold. "By all the saints, my dear fellow!" cried Seward, embracing him, and then holding him back. "Let me have a look at you, Beaumont. A little sharpened about the edges, aren't you. And you've some new muscles." He squeezed Laurence's arm with his bony fingers. "Very impressive!"

Laurence examined him, in return; he was as gaunt and desiccated as ever, the skin stretched tight over his craggy features, yet he appeared unchanged, as if preserved from the ravages of time by some mysterious alchemical process.

"Where were you all these years, my boy?"

"In the Low Countries, fighting, for most of them."

"When I last saw your father, he said he'd given you up for dead. I told him not to despair, that I knew you were still amongst the living. But I'm afraid it was scant comfort to him," Seward said, severely, ushering Laurence in and shutting the door. "I cannot believe you spent so long in the army. You'd be egregiously unfit for it."

"I was."

"Hmm. What have you to show for your travels?" Laurence took from his doublet a small package wrapped in oily sackcloth and tossed it to Seward, who uncovered a hard, dark brown square, sticky yet crumbled at the edges, like dried fruit comfit. He began to chuckle, a wheezy sound rising from his hollow chest. "I've a pipe," he muttered, searching amidst the piles of books and manuscripts. "Aha! Here it is. Wherever did you obtain this fruit of dreamers?"

"From a Moor in Spain."

"A Moor in Spain!" repeated Seward reverently. "Was he handsome?"

"No, he was old and wrinkled just like you."

Seward broke off a piece of the brown substance, held it over a candle flame until it smoked gently, then filtered it through his fingers into the bowl of his long pipe, blended it with a pinch of coarse tobacco from a pouch within his gown, lit it, and inhaled. "Very pure," he declared, snorting slightly as he exhaled an aromatic cloud. "Have a taste yourself," he added, and passed over the pipe.

"Seward," said Laurence, after they had exchanged and answered many questions, "there's something else I brought back that I've been waiting to show you." He reached into his doublet again and pulled out the letters. "Even with all you taught me, I can't make sense of these."

Seward took them to his desk, where the candlelight was brighter. Watching him peruse them, Laurence fancied that his expression altered, and his hands trembled a little more noticeably.

"Have you ever seen anything like this code?" Laurence asked.

Seward was still studying the sheets of paper. "How did you acquire them?" he said, after a while.

"They were stolen. The thief gave them to me."

"Stolen from whom?"

"I don't know. If you can break the code, we might be able to find out."

"They are certainly interesting." Seward flicked his gaze from one page to another. "We have two correspondents, both educated, judging by their hand. This author must be a man of violent passion. Witness the large strokes and bold pressure upon the parchment. And the parchment itself is of particularly good quality." He laid them on his desk and went to his cupboard, from which he produced a bottle covered in mould and a couple of stained glasses. "I've kept this since we last drank together, hoping to drink with you again," he said, as he poured for them. "Now, what were the circumstances of the theft?"

"It happened in February, around the time I had to get out of The Hague. There was a man threatening to kill me. I'd come close to losing an arm because of him, so I wasn't taking any chances."

"You were always into one scrape or another." Seward sat down, drew the cat onto his lap, and began to stroke it rhythmically. "Well, go on, Beaumont, I'm listening."

VII.

The day after Saint-Etienne had been banished from Simeon's house, Laurence became feverish. The cuts he had sustained were oozing pus, and the surrounding skin was swollen and discoloured. Simeon said that they should be cleaned out properly and summoned the woman who tended to his household's medical needs; an experienced abortionist, he assured Laurence, though he did not say whether her skills extended to other operations. She dosed him with a poppy and cannabis tincture, and unwrapped a bowl she had brought with her which contained several fat white maggots. "My beauties here will make short work of this infected flesh – it is their favourite meal," she informed him, and dropped them neatly into the gaping incisions. He lost consciousness temporarily, but when he regained it and had the courage to look, her beauties were back in the bowl and she had sewn him up tidily with catgut.

"Whatever next, good lady?" Simeon asked weakly.

"A paste of spiders' webs, honey, dried sage, and rock alum. The stitches can be plucked out if he heals, but if the wound festers again, call me. And don't wait too long, or the poison will spread. I know a surgeon who can hack off a leg at the thigh in twenty seconds, so an arm will take him no time at all."

"I thank you, madam, but if by some happy chance Monsieur Beaumont were to survive, he'd be worse than maimed without his left hand. His skill at cards depends on it. You must get well, Monsieur, or you'll be short of a livelihood," Simeon told Laurence.

Laurence was frankly terrified; he had witnessed more amputations than he could count. But the circumstances of his convalescence were very different to those of an army hospital, and gradually he started to mend.

"You look bored, Monsieur," Simeon said, visiting a few days later.

"I am. What happened to the gypsy? I haven't seen her since the night she arrived. Is she still here?"

"Alas for us all, yes. She refused to leave until you were out of peril, so I consigned her to the kitchen to chop vegetables. She's too high and mighty to earn her keep like the rest of the women. She said she'd rather suffer a hundred lashes than be fondled by a *gadjo*."

"What's her name?"

"Juana, but I call her the little minx, it suits her better," Simeon said, rolling his eyes comically. "Why, that first night, when we gave her a bath, she fought like a demon, biting and scratching. She had never washed from head to toe in her life before, and thought it would be the death of her. I had to make her a present of some gold earrings, just to shut her up. All she did was stick her tongue out at me, and say that we *gadje* could scrub ourselves with soap and water for as long as we wanted, but that we'd never get clean, with all our dirty habits. She can't believe we allow cats in the kitchen. 'You let them lick the plates you eat off, when they have just licked their own bums,' she keeps complaining. 'I wouldn't be surprised to catch you eating out of the privy.' In short, Monsieur, she's an ingrate, and I shall soon send her packing. Now," Simeon added, "I can see that your hand is out of action, but do you think you might be well enough to keep an eye on the tables?"

Laurence said that he was, and so Simeon had a daybed made up for him downstairs.

In her idle hours, Juana would sometimes sit with him. She was constantly eating, with the air of a stray animal expecting to be chased away from its meal. He too knew what it was to starve and did not blame her for making the most of her opportunities. Although she remained thin and grey-complexioned from want, her long, heavy black hair shone from repeated brushings, and the women had given her a dress to replace her boy's attire. In her face he saw a quick intelligence and a singular beauty, particularly in her large eyes and expressive mouth. It was difficult to judge how old she might be: perhaps twenty, perhaps less. She had no clue herself, when he inquired.

"Have you a wife in your country?" she asked him one day.

"No," he replied.

"I had a husband, but he died of the plague," she confided, with a shade of sorrow. "Monsieur," she went on, "Simeon says you come from a good family. Why, then, are you just a whore's whore, lying with these disgusting trollops after they have opened their legs all night for other men?"

"They're honest in what they do, and they do it well," he answered, obliquely.

"But when are you going to marry a decent woman, and father sons to look after you in your old age?" He shrugged, smiling. "Let me read your palm and I'll tell you how many children you will have. Which hand do you use most?" He held out his left, wrapped in bandages. "*La mano izqierda. Qué mala suerte,*" she declared, in a portentous tone.

"You're wasting your time," he told her, in the same language. "I don't believe in that nonsense about bad luck. And your fortune telling is only a trick for you gypsies to make money."

"*Oye, hombre,* so you're no Englishman!" she retorted. "Simeon told me your mother was a Spaniard, and I bet every last drop of your blood is from Spain. That I could see by your face, and now I hear you talk, I am certain of it."

"I'm only speaking Spanish to you because I can't understand your horrible Dutch."

"Well, as for us gypsies, you can't hold yourself above us, when you cheat at cards!"

"Should I regret cheating Saint-Etienne?" Laurence said, still smiling at her.

She did not smile back, appraising him with the utmost gravity. "I know what is wrong with you, Monsieur. You don't respect yourself." And with that she swept off to the kitchen.

As the winter snow melted and the ground thawed, giving way to a sea of mud, the house received alarming news: Saint-Etienne was back in The Hague and had announced publicly that he had come to wreak his revenge on Monsieur Beaumont.

"A pity you haven't recovered your full strength," Simeon remarked to Laurence. "It might at least narrow the odds between you."

"No it wouldn't," Laurence said. "I'm the worst swordsman that I know."

"Then buy yourself a fast horse and have your bags ready," Simeon counselled. "I shall be sad to see you go, yet I should be sadder still to see the Frenchman fulfil his threat. And I cannot shelter you any more, now that the armies are reassembling for the spring campaign."

"I'd never ask that of you, my friend," Laurence assured him. "You've done so much for me as it is."

In low spirits, Laurence retired to his chamber to practise dealing with his wounded hand. It was a humiliating experience, interrupted by Juana.

"Monsieur," she said, entering hesitantly and closing the door behind her, "Simeon told me that you have to leave, because of the

Frenchman. If the Frenchman comes here and finds you gone, he will take his wrath out on me. So I would like you to take me with you."

"Would you, now," he said.

She started to cry, which rather moved him; he had not yet seen her shed a single tear. "If I travel without anyone to protect me," she wailed, "I shall be raped and murdered, and my body will become carrion."

"You've defended yourself thus far."

"I am only alive because you rescued me."

"It's Simeon you should thank. He could have kicked you out that night."

"You know he detests my kind, and I am so tired of living with strangers, Monsieur. I want to find my people."

"And where would they be?"

"To the south of the mountains which the Jew calls 'Pyrenees,'" she said, blowing her nose on her skirt.

"Ah. Then you should have no problem at all."

"Of course not, I'll see their signs," she insisted, his sarcasm lost on her. "It will be easy for us, I promise."

"For you, you mean. I'm going no further than Paris. On my own."

"Oh, Monsieur, would you just travel with me to Paris?"

"How would you reach the Pyrenees from there? Have you any idea of the distance?" She shook her head, gazing at him with wet, imploring eyes; no one now could mistake her for a boy, he thought. "How did you come to be here in the first place, Juana, and why are you alone?"

"I was not, at the beginning." She paused, as if wondering whether to trust him with her story. "I was with several big families who had followed the Spanish armies north, to cadge a living off their scraps. The soldiers said we were like fleas on a dog, but we were useful to them in our way, fetching wood and water, and so forth. Then plague broke out in the camp and we were blamed for bringing it, though it killed more of us than it did them. That is when my husband died. Not long after, while we were still nursing our sick, the Spanish surrounded our tents and butchered every man, woman, and child. I was the only one to escape. I drenched myself in spilt blood and kept from moving. Finally those bastards tired of their sport and went away. So, now you must understand why we fear and hate the *gadje*, Monsieur."

He examined her, trying to remind himself that her tale of woe was as likely a complete or part fabrication as the truth. "There are many other gypsies hereabouts. Can't you seek refuge with them?"

"No. They are not from my tribe. They are *marime*."

"What's that?"

"They are impure, as polluted as the *gadje*."

"As I am, then."

"Monsieur, I can see inside you, and you are a gentleman with a heart of gold," she said, switching to a humble, wheedling tone.

"Save your flattery for someone who'll be deceived by it. I've seen *your* act a thousand times, and it always makes me laugh."

"But will you take me?" He shrugged, which she clearly interpreted as an affirmative. "Thank you, Monsieur, thank you!"

He picked up the cards, anticipating that she would depart since she had achieved her object, yet she stayed. "What else?" he asked brusquely.

"I must tell you before we set out, Monsieur, that I will not be your whore."

"How peculiar you should mention that," he said. "I was just about to tell you the same thing."

She seemed confused, then gave him a wary smile. "What will you do in Paris, Monsieur?"

"What I do here, if I have the opportunity."

"You should choose a different path." He paid no attention, shuffling the cards, but he was clumsy, and they shot from his hand to the floor. "It is an omen," she said, in her fortune-telling voice. "You must take another path, before it is too late."

"Oh, please. You've got what you came for. Now leave me in peace."

She bent to gather up the fallen cards and placed them back in his hand. "I'll provide for myself on the journey. I won't be a burden to you."

"If you are, you'll find yourself alone again."

To this she merely nodded, and hurried from the room.

Not a week later, early in the evening, a boy from the nearest tavern came to warn Simeon that Saint-Etienne was drinking there with a party of his fellow officers. They had ordered wine, and were talking of a trip to the brothel once it was finished.

In a chill sweat, Laurence raced upstairs to collect his saddlebag and pistols, hoping to slip away without Juana. But on descending, he found her in loud altercation with Simeon, watched nervously by the other women.

"Don't tell me you have agreed to travel with her, Monsieur!" cried Simeon. "Has she bewitched you? Don't you see that she will slow you down, and Saint-Etienne will catch you both?"

"That's not true," Juana protested. "I am more used to running in fear of my life than either of you! Every day since I was born, I have been driven from place to place, cursed at, spat upon, treated worse than a mad dog."

Simeon grabbed her by the arm and shook her hard. "You silly girl, don't you remember who I am? The gypsies are not the only ones cursed at and spat upon in this world."

"We are all refuse to the *gadje*," she yelled back, "but it was you Jews who crucified the Lord Jesus. We gypsies only made the nails!"

"For Christ's sake, we don't have time for this," Laurence snapped at her. "Shut up, or I'll leave you behind."

Suddenly Marie called out from the window. "Two riders have just come in! One of them might be Saint-Etienne."

Simeon rushed to look. "No, it's your English customer, Marie, with his servant. You can tell by the cut of their clothes."

"So it is," she said, breathing a sigh of relief. "He hasn't been here in months, that nice gentleman."

Simeon turned back to Laurence. "Saint-Etienne and his louts won't have left the tavern yet. I gave the boy some coin and told him to keep serving them as much as they could drink. They won't refuse, if it costs them nothing. But, Monsieur, you must be off." As Laurence paid him for Juana to take one of his horses, Simeon added, "I pray you don't regret your kindness to her."

Laurence did not see Juana as he ran out through the kitchen, and he did not intend to wait long for her in the stables as he saddled the horses. He was about to mount when she appeared, clutching her bundle of belongings and a sword, which she thrust towards him. "From Simeon," she panted.

"He must have lost his mind! I can't even handle a deck of cards."

"Take it," she urged.

With a deep sense of foreboding, Laurence helped her clamber into her saddle. "I hope to God you can ride fast," he told her, "or we'll both end up dead."

VIII.

"She'd robbed this Englishman, just before we left." Laurence passed Seward back the pipe. "She took his sword as well as his purse, which is where I discovered these documents, and over four hundred pounds in gold coin. He sent his servant after us, and we were followed all the way through France. I didn't know why, until she confessed to the theft when we got to Paris. That was the first time I saw the letters."

"What of the Englishman?"

"He may have been in the market for arms, for the war here. The Hague was full of dealers."

"Or he was a spy or a courier. Or all three. You never had a glimpse of him?"

"No, nor did she. While she was in his chamber, the curtains of the bed were drawn. Seward, your wine tastes like vinegar."

"Thank you, Beaumont. I distilled it myself, from elderflowers." Seward sampled a mouthful from his own cup and wrinkled his nose. "But it has perhaps been sitting too long," he agreed. "Tell me about the servant."

"He always kept far behind us on the road. I never saw him at close quarters, though she once did. He was a large man, apparently, and he had – what was it she said? – the evil eye."

"How curious. Did she elaborate?"

"No. We finally lost him at the Spanish border."

"What happened to the money?"

"What do you think? We lived off it, though I brought some back with me, and the sword."

"And what happened to her?"

Laurence lowered his eyes. "I'd prefer not to talk about that."

"You poor fool," Seward murmured. "Now replenish the pipe, my boy, while I concentrate on the letters."

At first it seemed that he might bring forth some speedy results, for he was scribbling away on another sheet various figures and calculations. But as the night wore on, Laurence stopped watching. Fatigued by the wine and hashish, he yawned and stretched out on the floor. All that he could hear was the scratch of Seward's nib.

He was with Juana in the plains. She sat before him on the sandy ground, knees drawn up and apart; and he noticed to his horror that her belly was swelling, slowly, like an inflated pig's bladder. Repulsed by this monstrosity, he exclaimed, "For God's sake, get rid of it!" In the same instant, as though he had wrought some spell upon her, she let out a shriek of pain, grabbing her stomach. Blood soaked her skirts, and she screamed and screamed.

He jolted awake as something landed on his chest. He opened his eyes to see the striped cat glowering at him with a malign intelligence that he did not appreciate; it had its paw upon his cheek.

"Pusskins," said Seward, "refrain from scratching my friend." He picked up the cat and deposited it some distance away while Laurence struggled up, his head throbbing. "You're right, Beaumont," Seward told him, "that wine I had was sour. It did not mix well with what we smoked. Now go out and wash. You can't have forgotten your way about College."

Afterwards he poured Laurence a small measure of dark, syrupy liquid that must have contained some potent remedy, for his headache rapidly dissipated. As they turned their attention to the letters, his scalp began to prickle, as if his intellectual curiosity had transformed itself into a physical reaction. "You've broken the code, haven't you," he said eagerly.

"Not entirely. I *have* found a key to those symbols. Be patient, and I shall explain." Seward cleared his throat. "The author is familiar with Gematria, handed down to us from the Jews through the Spanish scholars of the Cabbala, though it is definitely of still older extraction. The Greeks knew of it, and of course it was much used by adepts of the Hermetic school. When we were in Prague, you might recall, we met the last of these great scholars, friends to Dee and Fludd who have since died or gone into obscurity. You may not have heard, Fludd himself has been dead these five years –"

"Enough about Fludd," Laurence interrupted, pacing about. "Tell me about the code."

"I repeat," Seward said crustily, "I did not complete the transcription."

"Why not?"

Seward pursed his lips, an oddly secretive look on his face. "There wasn't the time. I did, however, uncover the makings of an astrological chart. The date of birth is the nineteenth of November, 1600."

Laurence ceased pacing and frowned at him. "Whose is it?"

"That of His Majesty King Charles."

"Good Christ." They were silent for a moment, then Laurence asked, "What does it predict?"

"Let's find out." Seward had already copied down on fresh paper a series of figures from the original documents, with their decoded equivalents beside them. On another clean sheet, he drew a perfect square, measuring the sides carefully with a ruler, and scored two lines across it diagonally from corner to corner. Then he marked the midpoint of each of the square's sides and linked these points to form a second square, resembling a diamond shape, within the first. The diamond now contained four smaller diamonds, with eight smaller triangles around it that touched the corners of the outer square. "Twelve spaces in all, for the cabal of twelve houses," he informed Laurence. "And in the spaces, I shall fill in the figures." Laurence observed, chewing on his lip, as each was entered and Seward pored meticulously over the whole.

"I don't like to trust another man's calculations," he muttered at last, "but if the mathematic and the reading of the stars are correct, His Majesty has only a short time to live. Two years or a little more. And he will die through violence." He dropped his quill, sending a small splash of ink across the chart, and gazed up at Laurence.

"You're thinking the same as I am, aren't you," Laurence said, his throat suddenly constricted. "Whoever made these calculations is plotting to kill him."

"That is a wild assumption."

"Why else would someone cast his horoscope?"

"There might be many reasons. Queen Elizabeth had hers cast regularly by Dee."

"I'm sure Dee wouldn't put it in a code that no one could read."

"Calm down, Beaumont! His Majesty might have requested that it be done, for his own protection. Why, have you any grounds for what you suspect?"

Laurence paused. He hated to give credence to any kind of divination, yet if he were right, the potential consequences horrified him. He was being irrational, he told himself next. "No," he said. "I have no grounds."

"Well, we shall see once the transcription is finished. As for the code, I shall show you how it is designed. There is a key of repeated symbols. Are you paying attention, or must I take a rod to your backside?"

It took Laurence some time to understand how the key functioned, but eventually Seward brushed the sheets into a pile and handed them over to him. "It's up to you, now. You've plenty of work ahead of you, so go to it."

"But why can't we do it together this morning?"

The same odd look passed over Seward's face. "I am too busy with my own studies," he said, in a waspish tone. "Pray remember that I am not your tutor any more, Beaumont."

Laurence had a question on the tip of his tongue; it came out as a statement. "You *have* seen the code before, haven't you."

"Why do you say that?"

"Because what you did would be close to impossible otherwise. It's too dense, too difficult. I tried for months and got nowhere."

"Pray give me credit where credit is due. I am no humble initiate at such things."

"Neither am I."

"You have precious little knowledge of the Cabbala," Seward grunted, and Laurence knew he would get no more out of him on that score.

"What if the letters *do* concern regicide?"

"You will have to alert His Majesty! Such an expression on your face," Seward remarked, in a gentler voice. "As a boy, you were afraid of nothing and no one, much to your parents' consternation. Have some courage: Fortune dealt you the hand, and you will prove equal to it." He reached out and ruffled Laurence's hair. "I missed you. Few of my students had the ability to provoke me as you did."

"Thank God you're still here to provoke. Seward, I'll have to take the letters to my father's house. I'd rather not stay here in Oxford for the present."

"Why is that?"

"Some of the men I knew who fought abroad are pressing me to serve in their regiment," Laurence said quickly, as he tucked the papers inside his doublet. "I'll come back again once they've left to join the King, in the north."

Seward accompanied him to the door and unbolted it. "Don't let six years pass before we see each other again. I have every expectation of being dead by then."

"You can raise the dead, can't you?" Laurence winked at him. "Teach me how, and I'll revive you."

"Thank you, but I'd prefer the company of angels even to yours. One last thing: keep the letters secret until we have discussed how you should proceed. And when you visit me next, I should like you to bring the sword your gypsy stole. I might be able to glean something from it. Metal can be used to draw forth its owner, with certain magical operations. It can also speak, in its own fashion."

"How remarkable – a talking sword. It hasn't yet told me a thing."

"Your scepticism only betrays your ignorance. Now, be off with you, Beaumont," said Seward, pushing him out into the bright sunlight.

CHAPTER FOUR

I.

Laurence swore as he screwed up yet another wasted sheet of paper. He was almost sick with anxiety: after two weeks spent toiling over the letters, he still could not produce a full transcription, but he now knew that he had indeed uncovered a plot to kill the King. Yet he could put no names to the conspirators, nor could he establish where or precisely when they were planning to commit their crime.

With Seward's key he had unlocked one layer of the code, only to discover a further puzzle beneath. It was a mathematical cipher which, though challenging, he had unscrambled to identify words, and then parts of sentences. Nevertheless, huge gaps remained, sequences of numbers that must be in a different code altogether for which he had not the key. Even if he took the information to His Majesty, it was incomplete in the most vital aspects.

Folding away the papers, he left his chamber for the library, where he concealed them carefully inside one of Lord Beaumont's dustiest volumes. He replaced it high up on a shelf, tucking it for good measure behind several other tomes. Then he went downstairs as quietly as he could.

Lord Beaumont's valet, Geoffrey, stopped him at the front doors. "Her ladyship has asked for you, sir. She is expecting a guest today whom she particularly wishes you to meet. Might I ask where you are off to, sir?" Geoffrey added.

"To the river."

"Not to bathe? Oh sir, what if you catch a chill? Or drown, more like. Only witches and dead men float."

"Then I must be a witch."

"It's no joke, sir. There was a woman ducked at Moreton-in-the-Marsh just last year. She'd put a hex on her neighbour's cattle."

"Did she float?"

"No, she was sinking till they dragged her out. She died in gaol later, though – of a chill."

"Don't you worry – that won't happen to me," Laurence assured him, and hurried off.

Outside not a breath of wind stirred the humid air, and the sky was almost white, the sun invisible behind a film of cloud; there would be rain before nightfall, Laurence thought. He passed through the court-yard to open meadow, where the heat became more intense, and when he arrived at the riverbank he sat for a while, gazing at the water and the apparently aimless passage of dragonflies over its shining surface, before removing his clothes. As he waded in and dived under, the frigid temperature shocked his skin. He stayed below as long as he could, feeling the sucking sensation of mud beneath his toes as he reached bottom, and the soft reeds that stroked his skin. He closed his eyes, imagining fronds and fish moving at the same calm pace about him.

Resurfacing, gasping from the cold, he looked across the gleaming expanse of river to the far bank. It was not his father's property, and he had enjoyed trespassing there as a boy. Once he had scared some shepherds by springing out of the water stark naked, apart from the riverweed clinging to him. They had crossed themselves at first, think-ing him some sprite. Later they grew accustomed to him, and would explain in their thick Gloucestershire accents where to find the biggest fish or how to get an orphan lamb to take milk from a bottle, and why he should not touch a toad for fear of poison, or kill certain birds whose death brought bad luck. Where were they now, he wondered; some probably dead, some with sons whose lives might soon be interrupted or ended altogether by a war they cared nothing about.

A shout from the near bank caught Laurence's attention, and he turned to see a man dressed in black waving at him. He disappeared underwater again, hoping to be left in peace, but the second time he poked his head up the man was still there.

"You're alive!" he yelled at Laurence. "Wait, wait – I shall find a stick, or a branch you can cling onto!"

"I'm not drowning," Laurence called back.

"Sir, you must get out! The currents could pull you under."

"What currents?" Laurence asked, amused. He swam closer, until the water reached to his waist as he stood up in it. "It's all right. I know this river."

"You live nearby?" the man inquired, staring at the scar on Laurence's side.

"Yes."

"The land belongs to Lord Beaumont, does it not?"

"It does."

"Are you – are you acquainted with his lordship?"

"Yes."

"As it happens, I have just come from his house." The man's eyes had a sharp glint to them; in his sombre garments, with his beaky nose, he looked like an oversized crow hunting for worms. "I wanted to see his lordship's son, Laurence Beaumont, and a servant directed me to the river," he said.

"Who are you?"

"My name is Joshua Poole, sir. Are *you* Mr. Beaumont?" Laurence nodded. "I must speak with you about a . . . a confidential issue, and I should be most obliged, sir, if you might come out so that I have no need to raise my voice. I would prefer not to be overheard."

Somewhat uneasy, Laurence plunged through a tangle of reeds and lilies towards the bank. Poole modestly glanced away as he climbed out. He returned the courtesy by pulling on his breeches, and his shirt, to cover the scar. "So, Mr. Poole," he said, sitting down on the grass and wringing the water from his hair, "how can I help you?"

Poole sat down also, more gingerly. "I have come to make you an offer for some letters in your possession."

Laurence felt as though he had been punched in the stomach. "Letters?" he queried, when he found his voice.

"Yes. Some months back, they fell into your hands through an unfortunate circumstance. A robbery. Their owner desires their speedy return."

Laurence feigned polite confusion. "I don't know anything about them – you must have mistaken me for someone else," he said smoothly; he had used the line so often in the past.

"Allow me, sir, to refresh your memory. The theft of which I spoke occurred at a tavern in The Hague, one night towards the end of last winter. The thief was a young woman. I believe you would remember her."

"To be honest, Mr. Poole, whenever I was in The Hague there were always plenty of women, but none of them gave me anything to remember her by, for which I've since been truly grateful."

Poole did not crack a smile. "She was a gypsy. You left with her that same night and travelled together into France."

Laurence pretended to think back; always better to tell a version of the truth, rather than a total lie. "Oh – *her*. She gave me a song and dance about not being able to protect herself on the road, and I was stupid enough to swallow it."

"Was it not because of her theft that you quitted the Low Countries with such dispatch?"

"God, no! Someone was out to kill me over a game of cards."

"You went a long way with her, to the Spanish border, in fact. In all that time, she never spoke of the theft?"

"No. In fact I'd never heard of it until today. Though it doesn't surprise me," Laurence went on, affecting scorn. "Those gypsies have thieving in their blood."

"But she must have confided in you. She was your mistress."

"Please," he objected, with a laugh, "I wasn't *that* desperate."

"Did she have money with her?"

"Not that I saw. The only money she spent was mine."

"Are you sure she was not carrying any gold?"

"If she was, she hid it from me."

"One hundred pounds," Poole said, with renewed determination. "He will pay you one hundred pounds for the letters."

Laurence began tugging on his boots. "Really! What are they, *billets doux*?" Poole appeared not to understand. "Love letters?" Poole winced, as if insulted by the idea. "Whoever this man is, you should tell him to save his money and accept that they're lost. Knowing that girl, she probably used them to wipe her arse," Laurence concluded, rising.

"Mr. Beaumont," Poole said, speaking rapidly, "you are fortunate, born to noble estate, loved and esteemed by your family and friends. If you refuse to comply with his request, you might endanger them all."

"Are you deaf? I haven't got his letters."

"Sir, I must warn you that if you decline the offer, the matter will be out of my control entirely," cried Poole, struggling to his feet. "Please, sir, give them to me and take the money, and let this be the end of it."

"I'll say it one last time: I don't have them. And I don't appreciate your threats. Now please leave this property at once." Laurence strode towards the meadow; he could hear Poole behind him, panting to keep up.

"I shan't trouble you any more today, sir. You can find me in Aylesbury at an inn called the Black Bull. I'll give you a couple of days to reconsider." Laurence continued to ignore him. "You will not be left alone, sir, until you bring me the letters," gasped Poole. "Don't delay, or he will strike you where it hurts most!"

The sunlight dimmed abruptly, so that Laurence peered upwards. Storm clouds, heavy with rain, were massing in the sky; a fitting change in the weather, he thought, as he quickened his pace again.

"The Black Bull, sir!" Poole shouted after him.

Laurence made no response and indeed hardly noticed which direction he took, for his mind was careening from one disastrous possibility to another. He or someone close to him must know the conspirators. How else could Poole have found out so much about him? Or could that evil-eyed servant somehow have picked up his trail again, after all these months? It seemed inconceivable.

He ran back into the courtyard, determined to grab the letters, fetch his horse, and leave for Oxford immediately. Heavy raindrops had begun to fall and a flash of lightening split the sky as he darted indoors, only to be cornered again by Geoffrey, who appeared almost as agitated as he. "Sir, her ladyship's guest arrived over an hour ago. They have been waiting for you."

"Not now, not now," Laurence muttered, brushing past him to go upstairs.

Then his mother's voice rang out from the hall. "Laurence, come here, if you please."

With a grimace at Geoffrey, he entered to find his parents and sisters in the company of a woman he did not recognise. She was fanning herself against the heat.

"Laurence," said his mother stiffly, a pained look on her face as she examined his damp, rumpled clothes, "may I present to you Lady Morecombe."

Lady Morecombe rose and curtseyed, as he bowed. "Well, sir," she said, "if you are to be betrothed to my daughter Alice, should we not become acquainted? Do please sit." She indicated the chair beside hers with her ivory-handled fan. He did as she asked, his knees weak. What had he brought upon his family? And here they were, in perfect ignorance, merrily arranging his future. "You are nearly twice Alice's age," Lady Morecombe was saying, "although I would not guess it. You have decided rather late to marry, given your position in society. Were you too set in your bachelor habits?"

"To which habits do you refer?" he asked, inspecting her; her gown was low cut, and ill advisedly so, from what he could see.

"What I mean, sir, is this," she said, reddening under his gaze. "Her ladyship has addressed the matter, yet I should like to hear from your own mouth why you have not chosen to marry before."

"I haven't cared to," he said.

"Most men are delighted to relinquish their freedom, once they discover the advantages of a loving and obedient wife." Since he made no response to this, she was forced eventually to turn to Lord and Lady Beaumont. "It would be most distressing to me were there to be any delay in the wedding plans as a consequence of our political troubles."

"Few armies campaign over Christmastide," Lady Beaumont said. "Elizabeth and Mr. Ormiston are to be married then. If necessary, we can hold the weddings together."

"But it permits him such a short time to know his bride, or for her to know him," Lord Beaumont interjected.

"There is time enough," she told him firmly.

"Oh yes," agreed Lady Morecombe, scanning the hall as though estimating its worth. "A single meeting between them may suffice. Alice will make him a perfect helpmeet. I have taught her the arts of household management. She is expert in the preparation of sweets and light repasts. She has a fine hand at needlework. Her health has never failed her. She is even-tempered and devout, very devout. What more could a man ask?" she said, to Laurence.

"I can't possibly imagine," he replied, resisting an impulse to drag her from her chair and boot her out.

"My dear Lady Morecombe," said Lord Beaumont, as a clap of thunder rattled the windowpanes, "you should stay until the storm abates."

"She is to pass the night here," his wife informed him.

"Ah. In that case, might I steal Laurence away for an hour or so? He has promised to assist me with a translation."

"Of course," Laurence said, and jumped up.

"A most obedient son," Lady Morecombe remarked to Lady Beaumont, who coughed discreetly into her hand.

"Oh dear, oh dear!" exclaimed Lord Beaumont, as he and Laurence mounted the stairs. "I knew we had sprung this on you too fast. I did say as much to your mother, but I had not expected your reaction – such shock and dismay! Is the idea so awful to you?"

"I beg your pardon?"

"The idea of marrying Alice Morecombe! Laurence, you haven't heard a word I said. There must be something else troubling you."

"No, no."

"Then you would be prepared to meet the girl?"

"Why not," Laurence said, to put an end to the subject.

His father beamed at him. "Your mother will be so gratified, as am I. The Morecombes are old Gloucestershire stock, as you might remember. Her ladyship's late husband was active in Parliament, though poor health forced him to resign his duties some years ago." Once in the library he regarded Laurence again with consternation. "Why so hagridden, my boy? What is on your mind?"

"I have to go back to Oxford." Laurence attempted a more cheerful demeanour. "I promised to meet up with some friends of mine from the other war."

"When will you leave?"

He hesitated, incapable of producing any decent excuse to rush off to Oxford in the middle of a blinding storm. "In the morning, I hope."

"Good. You can take with you my response to Earle's letter. You promised to help me write it in a new cipher. We may as well go to it now."

"Can't we wait until I return?" Laurence asked hopefully; at present he felt that he could not have designed a cipher if his life depended on it.

"Now don't disappoint me, sir. I have chosen to transcribe a passage from Aristotle on kingship, rather fitting for the tutor of a prince. And I want to challenge Earle, so you must make me an ingenious device."

The passage from Aristotle unsettled Laurence in its irony, given how the King had been so much on his mind. Most of the words he encoded with a cipher that he had used before, but in his state even this process was arduous, and he had to keep putting down his quill to wipe the sweat from his hand.

"I'm not quite satisfied," Lord Beaumont said critically, at the end. "Add a hook to it. Something truly brilliant that will outfox Earle."

Laurence thought again, and an idea came to him. For one crucial line he would use the conspirators' cipher, which he had memorised, removing its more obscure mathematical digressions. But as the missive was sealed with the family crest, he pondered if he had tempted fate in borrowing from those other, deadly letters; and he also wondered who might be lying in wait for him on the road to Oxford tomorrow. He decided, as a precaution, not to take the originals with him. He would make copies that he could easily destroy if he were followed.

II.

The day after he and Juana had set out from The Hague, he asked her, "Who is it that's tracking us?"

"I haven't seen anyone."

"You lie worse than you sit a horse. He's the lone rider I pointed out to you this afternoon."

"It must be Saint-Etienne."

"He wouldn't be fool enough to come without friends, and he would have confronted us by now. He's had ample opportunity."

"Then how should I know who it is?" she said, shivering.

They travelled on south, past abandoned cottages, ransacked churches, barren fields, and remains of the dead quarrelled over by carrion birds. They were continuously soaked to the skin by rain or sleet, and their supply of food dwindled, for there was nothing to purchase or steal: with the countryside pillaged by one army after another, the local people were reduced to eating roots and vermin. Meanwhile they had to hide themselves and their horses from roaming bands of marauders, a rabble of beggars and cutthroats. And although he did not mention it to Juana, Laurence also feared that he might come across some party of soldiers who would recognise him and drag him back to face a hanging.

Throughout, Juana stayed true to her word: tireless, resourceful, quick to sense danger, she did not slow him down, and though she must have been aching from saddle sores, she never complained. He felt a growing admiration for her, tempered by a desire to be free of her as soon as he could.

Just north of the border with France, they stopped one evening to camp as darkness fell. With her usual resourcefulness, Juana coaxed a smoky fire from a handful of twigs and dried grass, and they sat warming their numbed hands, their stomachs growling.

"You are very quiet, Monsieur," she remarked to him. "What is it that you are thinking about?"

"That I'm hungry," he answered, tersely.

"No. You are worrying that you may be captured, by the army. Cecilia told me once, after she'd had too much wine, that you were a deserter." Laurence kept silent. "Why did you desert, Monsieur?"

"I was sick of fighting."

"You'd been a soldier for years. What made you stop, just like that? Was it something that you did?"

Laurence sighed and looked up at her. "Yes. And something I failed to prevent."

"You might feel better, for talking of it," she suggested.

She might be right, he thought. "Well," he began, "there was a town we'd laid siege to, I can't even remember the name of it. We'd taken our share of dead and wounded, so we were ready to celebrate when it fell. We sacked a warehouse and I found some barrels hidden away. We got drunk. Later, when we had to move on, I was ordered to round up a few of the men who were missing." He paused, and pulled his cloak more tightly about his shoulders.

"Go on, Monsieur."

"I found them with a woman."

"Nothing new to them, or to you," Juana murmured.

"Oh, but it wasn't my kind of entertainment. She was hugely pregnant – she must have been very near to giving birth – and they were raping her one at a time, as her children watched."

"Hmm. And what did you do?"

"I told them to leave her alone. They didn't approve. The last man, as he was finished, took his sword and stuck it right up her. Such a lot of blood – I'd never seen so much come out so fast. I was carrying two pistols. I shot him dead. The others bolted."

"You should have shot them all. They were animals!"

"Were they? I knew them as my companions, my comrades in battle who'd risk their lives to come to each other's aid – and to mine, for that matter. But after some privation and suffering, followed by victory and liquor, that's what became of them."

"They deserved to die. They killed a woman and her unborn infant."

"They didn't kill her." Laurence took a breath. "She was still screaming in agony. So I . . . I shot her in the head, as you might some horse that's no good any more. I shot her in front of her children. You should have seen their faces. It made me wish I'd fired that second ball into my own skull."

Juana frowned at him. "She would not have survived, and anyway, why should you carry this with you, as if you blame yourself? You surprise me, Monsieur. I have witnessed far worse cruelties, and learnt to put them from my mind."

"I've tried, but I can't seem to do that," he said, at which she smiled, as if to herself, and fed the last twigs to the flames.

III.

During his journey to Oxford on the morning after the storm, Laurence drew his horse off the road every so often into the shelter of trees, anticipating that a figure might be shadowing him, yet there was never anyone suspicious in sight. The hot weather had broken: torrential rain overnight had petered off into a steady drizzle, the wind blew cold, and the roads became bogged with treacherous puddles, in several of which carts had become hopelessly stuck. Even his own progress was slowed.

He arrived at Merton around six in the evening, tired and chilled. Leaving his horse at the College stable, he hurried over to Seward's rooms with the sword tucked under his cloak.

There he found Seward in fine spirits, sharing sack posset with a companion. "Take off that wet cloak, Beaumont, and sit down," he said. "I don't believe you've met Dr. Isaac Clarke."

Clarke more than filled his chair: his posterior and thighs spilled over the edges of it. The contours of his face resembled those of a well-nourished baby, and his old-fashioned scholar's robe was so strained over his belly that Laurence could glimpse the spotless linen shirt beneath it. "Ah, yes, you are Thomas' older brother," he declared, in a fruity baritone. "You left College before my time, but I took him in rhetoric. Is heredity not a mysterious thing," he added to Seward. "How one child of the same parents may be as different from another as a changeling."

"Beaumont resembles his mother, though he must be tired of hearing it remarked upon," said Seward, as he resumed his chair and draped the striped cat over his knees. "Clarke and I have been discussing Merton politics," he informed Laurence.

"We suspect that our Warden, Nathaniel Brent, is about to abscond to the rebels in Parliament," elaborated Clarke. "We should have predicted it earlier. He's full of venom for bishops, and quarrelled with Archbishop Laud on the issue of religious reforms at the College."

"He'll have to escape to his house in London when Oxford declares for His Majesty," Seward said, offering the silver posset cup to Laurence, who refused; from childhood he had detested the sweet, custardy drink. "Still, support for the King is not as strong here as we might hope. The merchants care only about their purses, and the students are unruly and without proper direction, liable to be swayed by any street demagogue."

"If Brent does run off," Clarke said, shaking his head, his jowls wobbling back and forth, "I fear he may take with him most of the College plate!"

Laurence sighed and glared at Seward, willing him to send Clarke away.

"Beaumont," said Seward, "you've something preying on you. You may speak freely in Clarke's presence."

"No, no." Clarke heaved himself up. "I shall be going. But, Seward, please listen to my advice about Illingsworth. He is liable to take advantage of you and could prove very dangerous indeed."

"No need to tell me," Seward said huffily, brushing the cat off his lap and reaching for his pipe. "I am already tiring of him."

"Don't lend him any more money and you'll be rid of the pest, that's what I say. Good night to you, Mr. Beaumont."

"Who's this Illingsworth?" Laurence asked Seward, when they were alone.

"A student of mine."

"I heard you'd given up teaching."

"I made an exception in his case. He's a very gifted boy whose parents can barely afford to keep him here."

"How very generous of you. Or has he found another way to pay you for his lessons?"

"Never mind him, you impudent fellow. Did you finish the transcription?"

"As much of it as I could. Enough to know that it *is* about regicide."

"Heavens," murmured Seward, and his hands shook as Laurence passed him the papers. "But these are all in your illegible scrawl!"

"I'll explain why I only brought you copies." In a rush, Laurence told of his encounter with Poole. "I don't understand how the conspirators found me. But there are so many people that might have known me in The Hague, a number of whom are here in England again. And they talk too much."

"Yet how could they have known about the letters when you didn't learn of their existence yourself until you reached France? No – it is my guess that the conspirators used magic to locate you," Seward stated sombrely. "If one of them is an adept of the Hermetic school, he might have employed a scrying bowl or a crystal to divine your whereabouts."

Laurence gave a derisive snort and sat forward. "Seward, in case something happens to me, I've left the letters in a hole in the wall near the gatehouse to my father's property." He described where Seward could find them, and then, reminded of his father, he took out the script for Dr. Earle and put it on Seward's desk. He was now so nervous about having used the conspirators' cipher that he felt inclined to burn it straight away, but Seward's grate was cold.

Seward was reading over his transcription. "This is unfinished. You did not apply yourself."

"Yes, I did, for days and nights, which is why I took so long in coming back here. The code concealed a mathematical cipher, which I managed to break parts of. But you see these numbers, in series? I think they represent names, of people and places crucial to the conspiracy. I couldn't make any sense of them, except where they refer to the King and his son Prince Charles. Those names I could assume from the context. But that's all."

"Your writing is too much of a dog's breakfast for my feeble eyes, and in this poor light. Tell me what you've found out."

"Remember you said that one of the authors had a bold hand? I have the impression that he's the master of the conspiracy," Laurence said. "The other letter I'm sure was written *to* him some time later, judging from its contents, and of course it's in the same hand as the astrological calculations." He stopped, to catch his breath. "I suspect that the second author invented the code, or introduced it to his master. If you compare the letters, the master has an assertive hand but he's blotted some of his words by hesitating over them. The second author's script flows perfectly, and the horoscope is in his writing. If he's familiar with astrology he could also be knowledgeable about the Cabbala. Just as you are." Seward furrowed his brow, as if he did not appreciate the compliment. "Anyhow," Laurence went on, "the money Juana stole was for arms, to be bought in The Hague, presumably."

"Wait – you think the master's letter is dated earlier. Start with that."

"He writes that he anticipates a war and must know the propitious time to act in order to save the country from ruin. He's convinced that the King himself poses the greatest obstacle to peace."

"And does he say how he reached that conclusion?"

"No, but he sounds as if he's a courtier well acquainted with His

Majesty. And he mentions others, both at Court and in Parliament, who might be persuaded to his side."

"Their names are still a mystery?" Laurence nodded. "And how will the deed be done?"

"The King will be spirited away to some place, also a mystery, and a hired assassin will take care of him. The master doesn't say how, but his own hands will look clean. Then he'll see to it that when Prince Charles takes the throne, he'll be appointed as protector until the boy comes of age. So I assume that the Prince, too, is well known to him and would trust him."

"And Her Majesty?"

"I couldn't find any reference to her. At any rate, that's the essence of the first letter."

"And the second, that you believe was written by his accomplice, our astrological adept?"

"It's all about business: how much the arms will cost, and when the purchase will take place, how they'll be shipped over and who'll receive them, though that was another name I couldn't transcribe."

"Dear God! Our master conspirator must be powerful indeed, to cherish such ambitions."

"But he has a problem," Laurence said, picking up the sheet of paper covered in bold writing. "He insists here several times that all correspondence must be destroyed immediately on receipt. His accomplice obviously disobeyed him and kept this very damning letter, I think to betray the conspiracy if need be, or to have a hold over him."

"No surprise, then, that the accomplice tried so hard to get all his letters back."

"And is still trying."

There was a pause; then Seward asked, "Did you bring the sword?" Laurence unwrapped it from the cloak and passed it to him. "I see initials inscribed on the blade," he said, after squinting at it, "but the script is so ornate I can't read them."

"I know. Neither could I."

"And a decorative pattern – of flowers."

"Look, Seward," Laurence burst out, "you must get away from here at once. I can't blame myself for showing you the letters since I didn't know what they were about, but I'll definitely blame myself for what might befall you next. These men may know I came to see you. They could be a threat to you, too."

"My life has been imperilled before," Seward said calmly. "I shall go, when I judge fit, to a house Clarke owns in the country."

"You should go tonight."

"No, no. In the morning, when my head is not fogged by sack posset, I shall study the transcription. That man Poole said he would give you a few days to consider his offer, after all. If I am successful, you must fetch the original letters and ride to His Majesty, wherever he may be. And I shall arrange an absence from the College, and pack my books, and so on."

"I'm staying with you until I see you out of here."

"The King's life is more important than mine."

"Not to me."

"If you insist, my dear fellow," Seward sighed, relenting. "Clarke will keep contact between us. I shall send you a message through him – he has my absolute trust. It will all turn out for the best, you'll see. As I told you before, when Fortune challenges, you must act boldly if you are to seize the advantage. She is a woman as well as a goddess, after all, and you've always had a way with the female sex."

Laurence smiled sourly. "I almost forgot to mention, my parents have found a wife for me. The daughter of some family in the neighbourhood."

"Are you to have your wings clipped at last?" Seward let out a wheezy chuckle. "It's about time."

IV.

While the musicians were tuning their instruments for a dance after the wedding feast, Radcliff drew Kate into the garden. "Open it," he said, pressing a small velvet pouch into her hand. As he watched her pull at the woven cord that fastened it, he suppressed anger. One necklace was all he could save of what Pembroke had given him for her. The other jewels he had sold off with some difficulty: there was only a buyer's market for such luxuries, with the country on the verge of war. Although he had been able to raise nearly a hundred pounds, he knew that was less than they were worth. And if Beaumont had indeed told Joshua Poole the truth, the sacrifice might be in vain. "If it doesn't please –" Radcliff began, but she interrupted him.

"It is beautiful."

"Rubies set with pearls," he told her, unnecessarily. "Allow me." She let him put it on, and it looked so splendid about her white throat that he dismissed all anxiety, imagining her as she would be in a few hours, in bed with him. "You must wear this tonight. Kate, now that we're married, we shall learn to know each other, and love each other more."

"You will be away, though, with your troop," she remarked, in her dispassionate way.

"I promise, I won't neglect you," he whispered, touching her skin beneath the necklace.

"We are neglecting our guests," she said, and turned back towards the house.

"Yes," he agreed, "and I must thank your brother properly. What a banquet he laid out for us."

"Richard's happy to be free of me."

"That's not true."

"But it is," she insisted.

As they returned to the brightness of the hall, he could not help asking, "Are *you* happy, Kate?"

"Very," she said, then she escaped him just as Ingram came over with his aunt, Frances Musgrave.

"Here's to the groom!" Madam Musgrave raised her glass; one of several, Radcliff guessed from the woman's flushed cheeks. "Will you spare me a gavotte, dear sir?" she continued amiably, as she took his arm in a powerful grip. "I was considered an excellent dancer in my youth, though I can't fathom any of the newfangled steps they practise at Court these days. Too slow for my liking. Not enough *brio*, eh, nephew?"

"My aunt is full of *brio* tonight," Ingram said, smiling at her.

"As I observe," said Radcliff. He knew that he ought to feel indebted to her, since she would be housing his bride for the next months, but he found her tactless and coarse.

Ingram's smile faltered as he surveyed the pillaged table, the knot of sweating musicians, and the lavish decorations. "Richard's outdone himself."

"Cheer up," said Madam Musgrave. "I've seen to it that you all won't be left destitute as a result of these festivities. Kate's our only girl and her parents would turn in their graves if we didn't send her off in style. She's a little spoiled, Sir Bernard," she went on, "and she knows nothing of men, apart from her brothers. She needs to be treated gently but firmly."

"I hope I'll give no cause for complaint," Radcliff said, bridling a little.

"Tonight shall be your first trial! Kate may be an inexperienced judge but don't press your case with too much dispatch. We women so appreciate an eloquent tongue before and after the due process of love."

"Aunt," Ingram said quickly, "I must speak with Sir Bernard about the troop. Just dull military stuff – would you excuse us, please?"

"With pleasure. My glass is empty. I'd better hurry to quench my thirst before the dancing starts. I shall let you go you for now, Sir

Bernard, but you still owe me a gavotte!" And she sailed away towards the refreshments.

"A spirited lady," Radcliff commented.

"There are few such ladies nowadays," laughed Ingram. "Her kind went out of style with old King James' passing. She was considered a beauty then." Radcliff examined her with more interest, trying to distinguish her natural attributes beneath the white lead make-up, heavily painted lips, and stiff, old-fashioned gown. "After her husband's death she had a string of suitors," Ingram told him, "but she refused to remarry. She's wealthier than all of us Ingrams put together and she's very astute where money's concerned. But she's also got a heart, Radcliff. She's been almost like a mother to us, most of all to Kate, who was so young when we lost our parents."

"I'm sure she is devoted to you. I only wish that Kate and I could settle down together in my own house, and have no more need to depend on Madam Musgrave's charity."

"Kate will be much happier at our aunt's. She and Richard are like chalk and cheese."

"I know. Though I can't help worrying . . . which is why I must ride for Longstanton tomorrow. I have to organize for payment of the new taxes the rebels are imposing, or else I could lose –"

"Radcliff, this is your wedding night!" Ingram clapped him on the back. "Let the future keep until tomorrow. But don't be away too long. Now that His Majesty has dismissed Parliament's latest offer, he must declare war very soon, even if he's been advised against it by his own Secretary of State."

"Yes – many people say that if my Lord Falkland weren't pledged to the King out of honour, he might have favoured Parliament's cause," Radcliff said, echoing what Pembroke had written to him in their last correspondence.

"That may be, but a man's honour is the greatest pledge he can give," said Ingram earnestly.

"It is, and Falkland is nothing if not honourable. That reminds me, whatever happened to your friend Beaumont?" Radcliff inquired, trying to sound casual. "Has he entered Falkland's service?"

"I don't know. We haven't talked since that afternoon at the Lamb."

"You should have invited him tonight."

"I told you, he and Richard aren't on the most cordial terms."

"I wonder if he's joined up with Henry Wilmot? I mean, he can't be undecided as to where he'll stand in this war."

"The truth is, I don't think he wants any part of it. But he might be persuaded otherwise. He told me he was going to consult Dr. Seward, who was our old tutor at Merton. Seward's sure to give him some wise advice."

Radcliff felt the blood rush from his face. "Did you say *Seward?*"

"Yes. Do you know him?"

"Er, no. But I might have heard *of* him somewhere," Radcliff added, with a brave shrug.

"I wouldn't be surprised; he's quite renowned in academic circles. Oh, look out, Radcliff," Ingram said distractedly, as a round of applause broke out amongst the guests. "The gavotte has been announced. You'd better ask Kate to take the floor, before my aunt catches hold of you."

In a daze, Radcliff sought out his wife and danced with her, his thoughts now far from joyful, that dread name ringing in his ears. Then he became aware that the music had ended; and the guests were hushed by a roll of drums.

"We must bed our married couple!" Richard exclaimed. "Ladies, to work!"

"Until soon, my love," Radcliff whispered to Kate, who avoided his eyes.

She was taken away by the women, to the cheers and hoots of the male guests, as Radcliff tried to compose his features and act as though nothing were wrong. Even without such dire news to oppress him, he would have had to fake enthusiasm as the gentlemen accompanied him upstairs shortly afterwards; he hated the vulgarity of the ceremony. In an antechamber to the bedroom, he undressed, and Richard held out a fresh linen nightshirt and robe for him to put on. Healths were drunk to his virility and to the fruitfulness of his bride. Entering the bedroom he felt temporarily nauseated, his nostrils filled with the scent of rosemary. For remembrance, he thought to himself, and used as much at funerals as at weddings. The curtains around the bed had been drawn back. A cluster of giggling women threw dried flowers and more herbs upon the counterpane beneath which Kate lay, her face strained and pale.

"Now may God bless you, my brother," cried Richard, "and may He bless your union tonight."

Radcliff allowed him to remove the robe and slipped into bed. "I *am* blessed," he said, "to have celebrated the greatest day of my life with my new family and dear friends. I thank you from my heart."

"Well, let them get to it," Richard declared, shepherding the crowd to the door.

Radcliff listened as their guests retreated down the stairs, and when all was quiet, he turned to her. He had envisaged this scene over and over again, yet all the pleasure he might have taken in it was now spoilt by his discovery of another shocking connection between Beaumont and himself. As he looked at Kate, he felt as if he were cursed with some evil enchantment; he did not even know if he would be able to perform. "Close your eyes, my darling," he said, and slowly he rolled on top of her. He kissed her lips, pulling up her nightdress under the covers. Her legs were icy, the muscles tensed, offering him no encouragement. He could not hope to enter her as he was. "Let me show you what to do," he whispered, and taking her cold fingers he guided them below his nightshirt. Her eyes opened, her expression a mixture of defiance and distaste. Immediately he released her hand, moving away so that they lay beside each other, looking up at the embroidered canopy of their bed.

"Kate, would you prefer to sleep?" he asked. "I won't take offence. I'm very tired myself, after the long evening."

"Please," she said.

He kissed her again, on the forehead, and with a short breath extinguished the taper by their bed. "Good night, my love, and sweet dreams."

He had requested of Ingram that they not be disturbed by carousers later on, as was the old custom, and at length, exhausted by feverish cogitations, he slept.

He dreamt that he and William Seward were in a dark place with wood-panelled walls, lit only by a single candlestick. Before them, on a table, was a bowl full of opaque liquid, and they were both concentrating upon the still surface, waiting for a vision to appear. For hours, it seemed, none came; and he knew that if he did not produce some result, Seward would cast him out as a failure, so he began to invent images of the most fantastic sort, conscious that he lied atrociously. Seward berated him, calling him a scoundrel and a counterfeit. Increasingly stung by the invective, he grabbed the old man by the throat. In the same moment he glanced over at the bowl and saw the reflection of Madam Musgrave's face laughing at him; and when finally he managed to draw his gaze away from her, he noticed that his fingers were closing around Ingram's throat, not Seward's. He tried to release his hold but it only locked more tightly. He witnessed Ingram's horror, and in the next second he woke.

Kate was asleep, her back to him. As he regained a measure of calm, a fury rose up inside him that fate should put such obstacles in his way, overshadowing everything, including his own wedding night. One curse had been lifted, however, for beneath the bedclothes he was hard and bursting with desire. At least in this most intimate part of his life, he would not be frustrated.

Intending to rouse her, he sat up in bed. "Kate," he hissed in her ear.

As though irritated, she shifted away from him. Flipping her onto her belly, ignoring her gasp of surprise, he dragged up her gown, baring her to the waist. He pressed his hands between her legs and buttocks, splaying her on the mattress, and penetrated her. When she moaned, his excitement increased, though he forced himself to pause, for he did not want to end too swiftly. But when he looked down and saw the root of his penis stained with her blood, a brute sense of triumph overwhelmed him. In one deep thrust he spent himself.

Instantly he felt ashamed: this was her first taste of their marital union, and he had possessed her as selfishly and artlessly as some yokel might tumble his wench beneath a haystack. "I'm sorry, Kate," he murmured. "That was not how I wanted it to happen. Next time it will be different, I promise."

She did not respond, and so he covered her with the bedclothes and went out to the antechamber to wash away the signs of their brief contact. As he was dressing, he heard her stir, and rushed in again. She was lying on her back, her eyes wide though oddly expressionless, gazing up at him.

"Kate, I have to leave," he said.

"So early?"

"Yes. You remember, dearest, I'm expected at Longstanton."

"When will you return?"

"As soon as I can." He bent to kiss her. "I love you, Kate."

As he straightened, he saw a flash of ruby beneath her golden hair. Reminded once more of his troubles, he wanted to tear the necklace off and rip it apart, but instead he left the room, shutting the door gently after him.

V.

Perched on the edge of Seward's desk, Laurence was examining the latest set of transcriptions. "Three days and you've got no further with these letters than I did."

"You're right." Seward pushed back his chair wearily. "All the names and places are in another code, and we're lost without the key. They could be using a slew of variations."

Laurence jerked his head in the direction of Clarke, busy packing books into a chest in preparation for Seward's journey. "Why did you tell him so much?" he asked, in a low voice. "I thought we were to keep all this between us."

"You must learn to trust him. I shall be seeking refuge at his house, don't forget."

"So, what now?"

"You should still take the letters north to His Majesty."

"But we don't even know who the conspirators are."

"The horoscope is sufficient evidence of a plot, together with those parts of the code that we have broken so far."

"What if he thinks the plot is connected to me in some way?"

"Why in heaven would he suspect you of any such thing?"

Laurence frowned at Clarke, who must have registered Seward's exclamation and had come nearer. "Before I left the German army, I was in just this sort of work," Laurence said, gesturing at the letters.

"Deciphering codes?" Clarke interjected. "Where's the offence in that? His Majesty will have men similarly employed in his own service."

When Laurence did not speak, Seward told Clarke, "I believe -Beaumont means that he was a spy for the Germans."

Laurence saw repugnance in Clarke's eyes. Always the same, he thought to himself. "Please don't ask me what I did there," he said. "All

I can tell you is that some of my past activities might prejudice the King's opinion of me."

"Could you not get a recommendation from your father?" Seward suggested, after a long silence.

"I nearly did, though I declined it." Laurence told him about Lord Beaumont's request.

"But that is perfect, Beaumont! Rather than approach His Majesty directly, you would do better to address my Lord Falkland. As your father's friend, he will trust you, and he has the authority to investigate what you have learnt thus far."

"I suppose," Laurence said, grudgingly.

Seward leant forward, his face very stern. "I must ask you to promise, however, that you will not mention my name to him."

"Why? You broke the hardest part of the code."

"We both have a past, Beaumont. As you know, my more esoteric interests often got me into difficulties that I haven't the strength to live through again. I shall do whatever is in my power to help you, but I do not wish to be associated publicly with this business."

Neither do I, Laurence almost added, for he could see where it would all lead, as though he were being sucked down inexorably into some evil swamp.

"Well," Seward recommenced, "let us make haste, you to Chipping Campden for the letters, and I into the depths of Oxfordshire."

"Seward, we have a supper at High Table tonight," Clarke put in, his frigid gaze still resting upon Laurence. "If you don't attend, people will wonder."

"I know. I'll sleep in your rooms tonight, Clarke, and be off at first light. You don't need to stay on guard, Beaumont," Seward added. "In fact, you would be making a mistake – you must not delay your mission on my account."

"What difference would it make, in any case, if he were to stay?" Clarke waved at Seward's possessions, piled up in the centre of the room. "The damage is done."

"For me, this is merely a temporary retreat." Seward smiled and patted Laurence's knee. "Stop looking so gloomy. The country air will do me good! I shall go mushroom picking, and Pusskins will become a champion mouser. And it is small trouble, if we can save His Majesty from these perfidious men."

"I would advise you, Mr. Beaumont, to make some alteration in your appearance before you visit the Secretary of State," Clarke said. "A shave and a change of clothes are in order at the very least."

Laurence opened his mouth to respond but Seward cut him off. "Make yourself useful and take down that box from the shelf, will you, my boy. Clarke, I think it will fit in the chest over in my bedchamber." Clarke glowered once more at Laurence before stomping away. "And now, Beaumont, we must bid each other goodbye." Seward gathered up the papers on which he had been working and passed them to Laurence. "The sooner you reach the Secretary of State, the sooner we all shall sleep secure."

"I don't give a fuck what he says," Laurence whispered, indicating the bedchamber. "I'm staying here tonight."

"I forbid it! And stop worrying about me."

As Seward hurried him out to the quadrangle, he asked, "When shall I see you again?"

"Talk to Clarke about that. No one else will know where I am. Now may God speed you on your journey."

Laurence nodded obediently, though he had already decided to come back to Merton after suppertime.

While he was saddling his horse in the College stables, he had the distinct sensation of being watched, and he turned to see a fair-haired youth, evidently a student, looking over at him from beyond the open doors. The boy then strolled off. Mere curiosity about a stranger, Laurence told himself, and he rode away knowing that on his return he would face Seward's displeasure.

VI.

"Where is my Pusskins?" Seward complained.

"He must not appreciate journeys," Clarke said. "We shall find him before morning. He is certain to manifest himself at the supper hour."

"True enough, Clarke. He is almost as much of an epicure as you are."

They watched the carter hoist Seward's belongings onto his vehicle and tuck a blanket over them. "This man will go as far as Witney," explained Clarke, "and there he'll be met by my housekeeper, who has a second cart to pick up your goods and bear them to their destination. If he's stopped on the road, there's not much information anyone could extract from him."

Once the cart had gone, they repaired to Clarke's chamber and enjoyed a sip of Malmsey against the damp, until the university bells chimed eight times and they had to set off for the feast. But they had not sat long in the hall when something soft and warm brushed Seward's leg underneath the trestle table. He looked down to see Pusskins, tail held high, fur standing on end, gums bared, hissing. When he tried to tempt the animal by flinging it a piece of meat, it backed a few paces away towards the doors and emitted a yowl so uncanny that the other scholars ceased talking and gazed at it in astonishment. Then it crept under the table again, and Seward felt sharp teeth on his shin.

"I cannot believe it," he remarked to Clarke. "He bit me!"

"Cats are not celebrated for their gratitude," someone said.

"My dear man," responded Seward, "God has endowed these creatures with keener moral understanding than he has most of us. Any cat could tell you that virtue must be its own reward, or else it is nothing but the vice of self-love disguised, and doubly vicious because it wishes to go unobserved."

"Well put," cried another. "Let's drink to that."

Seward was still eyeing Pusskins, now backed off to the door, swishing its tail. When Seward moved his chair, the cat made as if to run. When he sat back, it yowled at him. Since he had not once known Pusskins to do anything without a reason, he guessed that his cat wanted him to follow it.

"Gentlemen, forgive me," he said, rising. "In my old age I am forgetful – I left a taper burning in my rooms! I must make sure that I have not set fire to them. Clarke," he added, very deliberately, "would you please come with me?"

Clarke glanced regretfully at his heaped platter but acquiesced. "You know very well that was a lie," he grumbled to Seward, as they crossed the new quadrangle. "Why on earth must we go hunting for your cat when we could be enjoying ourselves at the feast? I had barely touched the first course –"

"Quiet," Seward interrupted.

Pusskins had now vanished. The dusk outside seemed more like deepest night after the brilliance of the hall, and they had only a small lantern to illuminate their path. Seward began uttering the chirrups that normally attracted his cat's attention at mealtime. "Oh, of course, Clarke," he said, "he will have gone to my rooms. We must stop there and catch him."

"Damn the beast," Clarke swore, and they headed off.

As they drew nearer, Seward handed the lantern to Clarke, to fumble for his key in the pocket of his gown. Then Clarke said, "I thought you locked everything up. But your door is ajar."

"Good God, so it is! Clarke, beware – some kind of mischief has been done." They both started as Pusskins scampered out of his chambers, across their feet, and in again. "It's safe," whispered Seward. "We can enter."

The lock had been smashed apart. He applied a fingertip to the door, and it swung wider to reveal shredded paper scattered everywhere, and furniture overturned. In the bedchamber, his mattress lay on the floor sliced through and eviscerated. His pillows had been torn apart, leaving drifts of feathers all about. Even his chamber pot had been cracked in two.

"A mercy you were not here," Clarke said, gazing about.

"And that there was nothing worth the taking." Seward stooped, picked up his cat, which had grown calm, and held it close to his chest. "My Pusskins," he said, "how nobly you acquitted yourself. Oh Clarke, I should have listened to Beaumont."

"Pah! He's to blame for all this," Clarke muttered, righting the only chair left, so that he could sit down.

"Don't make yourself too comfortable, my friend," Seward told him. "Whoever did this violence got no satisfaction out of it and may come back tonight. We haven't a moment to lose. We must ride out at once – and we shall take Pusskins with us."

VII.

Laurence had repaired to a tavern for some supper. Finding himself in a quiet corner, he took out the papers to inspect them again, and as his attention was drawn towards a particular arrangement of symbols, he suddenly remembered Dr. Earle's letter. He had not told Seward what it contained. On no account must it fall into the wrong hands.

At almost ten o'clock, he estimated that Seward would probably still be at High Table, but he could not bear to wait any longer and headed back to Merton. The College porter informed him that he had just missed Seward, who had left with Dr. Clarke half an hour before for an unknown destination. The change of plan surprised Laurence, and so he asked the porter to admit him, and rushed over to Seward's rooms.

He had not expected to see light in the windows, but neither had he anticipated that the lock would be removed, leaving a gaping hole in the wood. He opened the door, entering cautiously. All was silent. Inside, as he stumbled about in darkness, he was puzzled to encounter no furniture, not even the heavy old desk. In the bedchamber, he bumped into Seward's four-poster bed. Too big to move, he thought, but the mattress was gone. Seward had obviously chosen to leave early and was safely away, he reassured himself. Since he had nowhere else to sleep that night, he settled down on the uncomfortable frame of the bed, cradling his pistols across his chest for security, and closed his eyes.

CHAPTER FIVE

I.

The toll of bells woke Laurence in the morning, and immediately he sat up in shock as he saw Seward's wrecked mattress slumped like some dead beast in one corner of the bedchamber. In the next moment, he was unnerved to hear feet shuffling in the other room. Quietly he cocked his pistols, but when he rose from the bed, it gave him away with a loud creak.

"Tyler, is that you?" called a soft, youthful voice.

Laurence walked out. Before him stood the blond student he had noticed the day before; the boy's face would make an angel jealous. The expression in his cornflower-blue eyes betrayed both recognition and terror, as he stared at Laurence and the raised pistols.

"Who are you?" Laurence asked, lowering them.

"I – I am Harry Illingsworth. And you?"

"A friend of Seward's."

"You startled me, sir. Do you know where he is?"

Laurence shook his head, gazing about. Save for a lone chair, all the furniture had gone and the floor was strewn with debris and feathers, as if gusted there by a whirlwind. "When did this happen?"

"I have no idea. I just came for my lessons in Greek, as I always do."

"Not much chance of any lessons today, so you might as well leave," said Laurence.

A different look, flirtatious and crafty, now crossed Illingsworth's face. "Oh, but Dr. Seward never misses our morning hour together. Why don't we wait for him? I should enjoy getting acquainted with any friend of his." And he smiled seductively at Laurence.

Laurence hesitated. He had acted in such scenes before, and was not especially bothered to play out of character as long as matters did not progress too far. He was also curious as to who might appear on stage next. "All right," he said, smiling back. "But there's nowhere to sit. Let's go into the bedchamber."

The boy agreed at once, and they seated themselves on the frame of the bed, Laurence purposely close to him. "Dr. Seward and I have a special friendship," Illingsworth declared, with all the subtlety of a novice whore, his fingertips brushing Laurence's arm. "He finds me beautiful. Would you say the same, Mr. – ?"

"I certainly would," Laurence replied. He set down the pistols on his other side, and began to stroke the boy's neck. "What sort of things do you like to do with him, apart from your lessons in Greek?"

"We kiss sometimes," Illingsworth whispered, leaning forward with half-shut eyes, allowing Laurence a chance to reach inside his doublet for his knife. "Would you like to kiss me?" the boy added. Laurence moved even closer, so that their lips touched. "What else can I do for you, sir?" Illingsworth inquired after a while, his fingers straying in the direction of Laurence's groin.

"You can tell me who Tyler is."

The boy pulled back. "Tyler?"

"Yes. You called out his name, remember?"

"He's a . . . a friend."

"Another friend of Seward's?"

"Of mine. Dr. Seward hasn't been introduced to him yet," Illingsworth went on, more confidently.

"Then why would you expect to find him here?" The boy looked discomfited again and did not answer. "What's he like, this man Tyler?" asked Laurence, caressing the boy's cheek.

"He's a giant and has huge muscles. And he's got a walleye. He can't keep a straight gaze."

The Englishman's servant, thought Laurence grimly. He brought his knife to Illingsworth's throat. The boy tried to jerk away, gasping, but Laurence had him by the collar. "You came looking for *him*, not Seward. You knew Seward was already gone."

"That's not true!"

The boy flinched, as Laurence tightened his grip. "When did you first meet Tyler?"

"A – a few days ago. He said he'd heard I was in Dr. Seward's confidence, and he wanted to – to talk to Dr. Seward in private. He asked me to arrange it."

"What's his business with Seward?"

Illingsworth was wriggling about. "I swear to God, he didn't tell me!"

"I'd advise you to keep still. This blade is sharp and it could slip." Laurence remembered Clarke's comment about the boy. "Did Tyler pay you?"

"T-twenty guineas," Illingsworth admitted, as the point of the knife pressed against his white skin.

"I see. Is that why you're here?" The boy nodded fractionally. "And all he wanted was an introduction to Seward?"

"Yes!" Illingsworth whimpered. "When he arrives, he'll make you sorry for how you're treating me!"

"I doubt he'll have the time before I shoot him. And he'd be too late to save *you*."

The boy grew paler. "If you release me, I – I promise I won't say a word to him about you, nor about Dr. Seward. Please, sir, don't hurt me!"

Laurence hesitated again, the urge to violence burning in him like sexual desire. But he knew he could not shoot Tyler here in the College without risking arrest himself, and if they fought, he might lose, given the man's probable strength. And Tyler would have access to the papers he was carrying. The wisest course was for him to quit Merton as soon as possible.

He must have been eyeing Illingsworth as he contemplated murder, for the boy looked about to swoon. "Stay here, if you value your life," said Laurence, and put back the blade.

He gathered up his pistols and returned to the main room. Illingsworth had not budged an inch. The boy was not made for a game like this, Laurence reflected with disgust, and after a swift glance about the quadrangle, he walked out to fetch his horse.

II.

Lady Beaumont greeted Laurence at the doors with such uncharacteristic warmth that he was instantly suspicious. "To what do I owe such a welcome?" he inquired, raising his eyebrows at her.

"Thomas' wife, Mary, will be most relieved to see you," she said, helping him off with his cloak. "She is not at her best, mind you. None of us is."

She led him into the hall, where Lord Beaumont stood before the fireplace, his arm around the shoulders of a girl not much older than Elizabeth, pretty, although her face was red and swollen from crying. They both looked up, and Lord Beaumont declared, "Oh, thank heavens you are back in time!"

"In time for *what*?" Laurence asked, mystified.

"Thomas is very ill," explained Lady Beaumont. "His servant Adam arrived to tell us early this morning."

"The poor fellow is at Nottingham, where the King is gathering his armies," added Lord Beaumont. "He has the flux, which is widespread amongst the soldiers."

"That's no surprise," Laurence remarked, "with so many men crowded together."

"Call Adam," Lord Beaumont ordered his valet. "Laurence, you should hear it from him at first hand. He was in the saddle thirty hours straight – nearly killed his horse to get to us as soon as he could."

"He fears for Thomas' life, as do we," Lady Beaumont said shortly.

There fell an uncomfortable silence, punctuated by Mary's snuffling into her handkerchief, which Lord Beaumont broke with his customary tact.

"How was Dr. Seward, Laurence?"

"Very well, but he's gone into the country for a while," Laurence said, hoping that his father would not inquire about the letter to Earle.

"I trust he is not being harassed again by the College Warden? That dreadful man Nathaniel Brent should lose his post! Ah, here is Adam," Lord Beaumont exclaimed, as a stout young man with freckled cheeks entered the hall and bowed to them.

"Master Thomas got stricken while His Majesty's army was in Leicester," Adam began, on Lady Beaumont's request. "As we pushed towards Nottingham the fever became worse. When we arrived there I found him quarters away from the other sick, and a doctor to tend him. But his bowels are so disordered he can't keep a thing inside."

Laurence nodded, recalling his own past bouts of the same affliction. "How many days has he been feverish?"

"At least three."

"Is he vomiting?"

"Yes, sir."

"Could he hold down water?"

"A little."

"Is he throwing up any blood?"

"No, sir."

"Is there any in his shit?"

"I did not see," Adam replied, blushing.

"What would that mean?" Mary piped in.

"That it may be more . . ." Laurence hesitated. "Only that it might take him longer to recover."

"Laurence, we depend upon you," said Lord Beaumont, laying a hand on his shoulder. "We must send you to him, and God willing, once he is over the worst of it, you shall bring him home so that he can receive proper attention."

"As you wish," Laurence said. If His Majesty was in Nottingham, he thought suddenly, then so also must be Lord Falkland.

"Let me go too," begged Mary. "Should Thomas die, and I were not by his side, I could not forgive myself."

"No," said Lady Beaumont. "You would just be a nuisance."

"Don't worry," Laurence comforted Mary, "I promise I'll bring him home alive."

"You could write to him, my child," Lord Beaumont told her kindly. "That would lift his spirits."

"Do it at once," commanded Lady Beaumont, and the girl hurried off.

Adam had been shifting from one foot to the other, and now he blurted out, "I shall go to Nottingham, too, if my lord and lady will permit me. Master Thomas would wish it."

"If you want to come, I've no objection," said Laurence, "but I know what it's like to ride as far as you have without any sleep. If it hasn't caught up with you yet, it will later."

"I can keep pace with you, sir –"

"Leave us, Adam," interrupted Lady Beaumont. After he had obeyed, with a dour look, she cried to her husband, "Did you hear how rudely he spoke?"

"He's only anxious about Tom," Laurence said.

"That is no excuse. Laurence," she continued, "it is his lordship's dearest hope that you and Thomas be reconciled. You must seize this chance to mend the breach between you."

"Let us pray that it is not too late," Lord Beaumont murmured.

"Indeed." She tapped Laurence on the arm. "Come to the still room. Martha will have some remedies that may be useful to you."

"Of course," said Laurence, rather admiring her cool efficiency.

Along the way, she remarked, "I pray you have not given Mary false hope."

"She's unhappy that she can't be with him. I don't see the point of upsetting her even more."

"Goodness, since when did you acquire such delicacy of feeling?" she inquired sardonically.

"I don't know. I must have inherited it from you," he said, with a smile.

"Well, I am afraid I lose patience with that girl. She mopes about the house as if she felt life with us to be insufferable."

"Perhaps we *are* insufferable," Laurence suggested; and he could detect in his mother's face a hint of amusement.

As they entered the still room, Martha was assembling a list of medicines. "Agrimony, clove root, ginger, and wild carrot. Will you remember everything, sir?" she said to Laurence.

"You've known him since he was a child, Martha," said Lady Beaumont. "If nothing else, he has a good memory. What more do we need?"

"Opium," Laurence said.

"Martha, hand me the poppy tincture." Lady Beaumont wrapped the precious bottle in layers of cloth, and it was stored with the others in a leather bag. "Take this, Laurence, and find yourself some dry clothes. We cannot have *you* falling sick before you reach Nottingham. And if all goes right with Thomas," she went on, more agreeably, "we could be persuaded to delay your wedding until after Christmastide."

"Is that what you think of me?" Laurence demanded. "That I have to be bribed to take care of my own brother?"

"You misunderstand," she replied. "We know you will do your best, out of love for him."

Laurence looked her in the eye. "I'm glad that much is clear," he said.

Not an hour later, he rode out of the courtyard and across the park towards the gatehouse. A few yards away from it, he reined in by the wall surrounding his father's property and peered about, but saw no one. He dismounted, pulled out one of the stones and reached in to retrieve the conspirators' letters, which he had hidden wrapped in oil-cloth to protect them against moisture. Stuffing them inside his doublet, he climbed back into the saddle and headed through the gates, with a wave at the gatekeeper, who had come to open for him.

III.

"So you came that near to him," Radcliff said to Tyler.

"It galled me no end I couldn't catch him."

"I did not ask you to." Eager for a breath of fresh air, Radcliff got up to open the window, then remembered that the Black Bull's kitchen midden lay directly below it. Even the close atmosphere of his room was preferable to the stench of refuse. "How much did the boy give away, apart from your name?"

"Nothing else." Tyler sniggered. "He was so frightened of Beaumont, he'd pissed in his breeches. The little money-grubbing coward! If Beaumont *had* cut his throat, I wouldn't be a bit sorry."

"The boy may hear something soon. Someone is bound to gossip."

"I'm not so sure. He said that Seward's disappeared without a trace."

"Small wonder," said Radcliff, with heavy irony, "since he is, by reputation, a master of spells." He saw fear pass over Tyler's face and made a mental note: it was worth remembering what could scare a man like him. "So, what did you bring back?"

"Just some scraps of paper I found. Spells, maybe." Tyler hunted in his bag and produced them.

"Spells?" Radcliff stifled laughter. "These are copy lessons, for his students. In Greek, for the most part."

"That fits. He's got the Greek vice."

Radcliff rifled through them without interest until he came to a sealed letter. "Not much here. You must be starved after your ride." He held out some coins. "Poole is down in the taproom eating. Why don't you join him. And bid him come to me when he has finished."

"Aye, sir," muttered Tyler, and sloped out.

Radcliff's heart quickened as he opened the letter, directed to Dr. John Earle, in the care of Merton College. The seal bore a noble crest that he guessed must belong to the Beaumont family. As he scanned the contents, written in an elegant hand, he recognised the cipher and set to transcribing it. Half an hour's labour yielded most of the passage, which he remembered came from *The Politics* of Aristotle. "The inquiry we still have to attempt," it began, "is concerned with the King who does everything at his own discretion. An absolute kingship is a form of constitution in which a king governs at his own discretion and in all affairs. He who commands that law should rule may thus be regarded as commanding that God and reason alone should rule; he who commands that a man should rule adds the character of the beast."

On reaching the last line, however, Radcliff could scarcely believe his eyes, for it was in a different cipher, cunningly modified from the one he used himself in his correspondence with Pembroke.

"Appetite has that character," the line read, "and high spirit, too, perverts the holders of office, even when they are the best of men."

He grew dizzy, as he had upon meeting Beaumont for the first time. Beaumont and Seward had his letters. Why had they sent such a pointed message to Earle? They could not have cracked the last layer of the code, and found out any names of those involved, so how could they know that John Earle, Prince Charles' tutor, was meant to play an unwitting role in the scheme, keeping the boy safely distracted just as his royal father met with a fatal accident? Unless Seward had used his scrying bowl to fill in what blanks remained in the code. Radcliff shivered: it was perfectly possible.

He heard footsteps, and hastily locked the letter away amongst the other secret documents in his small travelling coffer. He tucked the key back inside his shirt, as there was a knock at the door. After wiping the sweat off his forehead, he said, "Enter, Mr. Poole."

"Tyler's gorging on a whole side of beef, or so it appears," Poole said scornfully.

"That gives us time to talk. I'm afraid Beaumont deceived you. He most certainly has my letters. Sit down, man," Radcliff told him next, for Poole's horror appeared almost as great as his own.

Poole crumpled into the chair that was offered him. "How did you learn of it?"

"Tyler brought me evidence from Seward's rooms that proves the code has been partially broken."

"After all my years in the courtroom, I could not detect a liar right in front of me!" groaned Poole.

"You should not blame yourself. Beaumont is practised at mendacity – he made his living off it."

"But what are we to do?"

Radcliff sighed; he had always appreciated Poole's faith in him, which was why he had kept from his devoted lawyer certain details of the conspiracy. All that Poole knew was that the Earl of Pembroke was seeking to secure a peace by setting up a private conference with His Majesty and certain other parties on both sides of the conflict, and that only in the last resort was the King to be detained by use of arms in order to expedite the settlement. "Listen to me," Radcliff said, "Tyler hasn't a clue as to the value of what he's given me, and I'd rather he not know. I shall send him back to Oxford to see if he can sniff out any more information. That boy at Merton College might be able to discover where Seward has gone. As for you, I want you to stay here in Aylesbury. There's a chance that Beaumont might decide to sell us the letters, now that he may think he's got all he can from them."

"After he has delayed so long? I doubt it! Sir Bernard, let me return to London. My wife will be fretting for me."

"I am sorry but wait you must," Radcliff insisted. "This is a convenient meeting place for us, and I cannot keep passing messages through your friend Robinson whenever I need you."

At once he regretted mentioning Robinson, for Poole became even more agitated. "I have not heard from him in over a week, sir. I pray he has not fallen into any danger, in his work for us."

"He'll come to no danger," Radcliff answered, with a confidence he did not at present feel. Like Poole, Robinson had not been trusted with full knowledge of what was to happen, but it would be a grave setback if he were to be caught and questioned. He was useful as a courier.

"And this business of your giving a false name to the innkeeper: what if he were to find out that you are not Mr. Rose?" Poole whispered.

"How would he ever find out? Hush," Radcliff added, hearing a heavy tread outside and then a louder knock. "Tyler, is that you?"

Tyler walked in, his breath stinking of meat and onions. "Well?" he said, his features alert, like those of a hunting dog ready to attack; if he had a tail, Radcliff imagined, it would be erect and quivering.

"You are to go back to Oxford and continue the search for Beaumont and Seward. Press the boy to ask everywhere after them."

"But I told you –"

"Use your ingenuity, Tyler! Poole shall remain here at the Black Bull. And as for myself," Radcliff concluded, wryly, "I must go to war."

IV.

From Adam's directions, Laurence found the old, ramshackle inn at which Tom was accommodated, now as busy as every other such establishment in Nottingham catering for the Royalist troops. He climbed up a winding, partly rotten staircase to the top floor, and as he reached the door, he smelled no longer the combined odours of ale and tobacco and rancid fat from the taproom below, but the sourness of a sick chamber. Before he could knock, a voice cried out, "Leave the food outside."

"I've come to see my brother," Laurence shouted back.

The door swung wide, revealing a room not much bigger than a cupboard, close and reeking. Apart from a bed, the curtains of which were drawn, the chamber was furnished with a table supporting vials, bottles and medical instruments, and a collection of soiled chamber pots.

"Your brother?" the speaker repeated sceptically. He was a short man with a single brown lock combed down over his pate to imitate the appearance of hair where none grew.

Laurence threw his bags on the floor and went to open the window. "Yes, I'm Laurence Beaumont, and I was sent here by our family. And who are you, his doctor?"

"I am, sir, and as such, I would recommend that you shut the window," the man ordered. "The draught will kill him."

Laurence paid no attention, tearing aside the bed curtains.

Tom's face was grey and wasted, his lips crusted with sores beneath his matted beard. He peered up dully. Then in his bloodshot eyes Laurence saw something register: either disappointment or despair, or a combination of both. His linen had probably gone unchanged since he had first occupied the bed, and his nightshirt clung to his chest like a second skin. "What are you doing here, Laurence?" he mumbled.

Laurence touched his forehead. "Oh, Tom, that's a high fever you have."

"Mr. Beaumont," the doctor intervened more politely, "may I introduce myself? I am Dr. Chapman, his physician, and let me assure you, sir, he is much improved since yesterday."

"Improved? What are you giving him?" Laurence selected one of the bottles on the table. Inside, wrinkled, blackened objects floated about in a viscous solution. "What's this? Pickled spiders? And this?" He indicated a curious instrument, a tubular metal construction attached to a plunger.

Chapman moved protectively towards the table. "The administration of clysters is of prime importance to the patient. He is taking a course of physics that will balance the humours in his body. I have been purging the effluvia with senna taken by mouth, and a pepper wash, by his nether parts. He has on waking each morning, and each night, a mixture of seethed egg yolks, peppercorns, and red wine. At midday, he takes a glass of ale containing a measure of grated dried stag's pizzle, mercury, and tincture of shepherd's purse."

"That would make anyone sick. And the spiders?"

"They restore the throat. With a drop or so of melted butter, they go down very easily."

"And come up as easily," Laurence commented, glancing at the chamber pots.

"Sir, the vomit is a sign of imminent recovery."

"He was vomiting when he came under your care. You're dismissed."

Chapman blinked at him. "Sir, I –"

"You may go."

"With all due respect, it was your brother who engaged me, and it is for him alone to dismiss me, should he so wish it." Chapman turned to Tom. "For the life of you, sir, do not allow him to interfere."

But Tom could not speak. He was waving feebly at the pile of chamber pots. Not a moment too soon, Laurence thrust one under his chin. He disgorged some frothing liquid and lay back with a moan. Laurence removed the pot and set it on the table; there was dark blood in the vomit.

"A person of your rank cannot be used to such unsavoury labours," Chapman observed. "You need me, sir, as much as he does." In response, Laurence picked up the bottle full of spiders and flung it through the window. "My remedies!" Chapman gasped, as more bottles disappeared. "My payment, at least, sir!"

From his pocket Laurence took a handful of coins and dropped them with a splash into the chamber pot. "Take it and get out now, unless you want me to kick you down the stairs."

Chapman grabbed the pot and made a rapid exit, not stopping to shut the door behind him.

"What's happening, Laurence?" Tom asked hoarsely.

Laurence did not reply, digging out from his bags a flask of spring water and a cup into which he mixed honey, a pinch of salt, powdered ginger, and some drops of Martha's poppy tincture. "Here," he said. "It should plug you up, and put you to sleep."

Tom had to be fed in spoonfuls, a process lengthened by his reluctance to ingest anything at all. He stirred fitfully for a bit, and then the drug worked its magic. Meanwhile, Laurence examined what remained of Chapman's alarming pharmacopoeia and wondered if he should have let Tom's body rid itself of the poisons naturally. Yet sleep was also curative, he thought. He would not have minded sleeping himself, for he was weary and saddle-sore.

He leant out of the window, and as he gazed down on the court-yard below, he thought of Mary and his facile assurances to her. He had seen men fitter and stronger than Tom waste away from this disease. He could not leave his brother until the fever passed, if in fact it did. His meeting with the Secretary of State would have to wait.

v.

Not a propitious day for declaring war, mused Falkland. It was more like November than late August: large clouds hung in the sky, gobs of rain spattered everyone's cloaks, and the King's speech, delivered with some garbling of words by a herald, was practically inaudible in the strong breeze that made the royal standard flap about like a nervous bird.

"How unfortunate that His Majesty changed his script at the last minute," Lord Digby remarked, shouting in Falkland's ear. "The other version was superior."

"Your work?" Falkland asked, one hand on his hat to keep it from blowing away.

"For the most part. Never mind, it would have been wasted on the wind. And what a poor showing," Digby went on, gesturing at the assembled troops. "I've heard Parliament has twice our number mustered in London. Any regrets, Lucius?"

"No man of conscience can be happy today," Falkland answered guardedly, "to see a monarch wage war against his subjects."

"Ah well, the die is cast."

"I think not. We can continue to negotiate. I have every faith in Culpeper's mission to London."

"But what is the chance that our terms for a settlement will be accepted by the radicals? All Culpeper will do is buy us some time – which, God knows, we need, to amass a decent fighting force."

"That smacks of duplicity. Parliament's Commissioners are men who just yesterday were our friends and colleagues. We must be honest and fair in our dealings with them. After all, they are some of them as eager for peace as we."

"Yet as the Gospel says, no man can serve two masters. Are you not content with the one you have chosen?"

"He is my King. I could not choose to side against him." Falkland looked over at His Majesty, who was mounted as usual on a very tall stallion. Beside him was his handsome young nephew, Prince Rupert of the Rhine, newly appointed Lieutenant-General of the Horse; and by Rupert was Boy, the white poodle that went with him everywhere.

"Young pup," muttered Digby, at which Falkland smiled. "And here comes your trusty spymaster Colonel Hoare, who worships the Prince as faithfully as does Boy," Digby added, as Hoare galloped up.

Hoare stopped briefly to salute them. He eyed Digby with undisguised loathing, then urged his horse over towards the Prince's.

"What a man," Digby exclaimed. "His face reminds me of a death's head. I really can't abide him."

"Nor can I. But thanks to you, I must tolerate him."

"Poor Lucius! Permit me to make amends by inviting you to a small collation after Council meets. Around ten o'clock. I have asked the Prince to attend but I don't expect he will."

"Have you two had a falling out?"

"Not as far as I am concerned," Digby replied with a hurt expression, smoothing down the feather in his hat. "But it is as if he has forgotten all about our months of friendship abroad, and now he treats me like some neophyte who has no business in a council of war. He doesn't seem to care how many people he offends with his brusque Teutonic manners. And he has offended a great many in such a small space of time."

"So what was your purpose in inviting him to sup with you?"

"To show the extent of my good will towards him, in spite of his less than gracious behaviour towards me." Digby stopped looking hurt and smiled at Falkland. "Please come, Lucius. Otherwise, if Rupert and his poodle fail me, I shall have to eat all alone, and that is so very dreary."

"I shall come," Falkland said; whatever Digby was machinating, he preferred to know as soon as he could.

Digby received him in quarters more comfortable than his own, explaining, "Unlike most of the townsfolk, my hosts are enthusiastic Royalists, and very partial to me – as they should be, since I have been made Governor of Nottingham."

"Oh yes," Falkland said. It was an honour recently bestowed and one that he had forgotten about.

"They have allowed me every indulgence," Digby effused, "including the use of their cook and this private dining chamber where I can entertain."

Falkland was unsurprised to find Prince Rupert absent from the table, at which three places had been laid, yet to his puzzlement he saw that Digby had another guest, a woman, who was seated by the fire at the far end of the room. When she rose to curtsey to him, he could not help staring at her, an impropriety most unlike him. But what on earth was Digby up to? They could not possibly discuss matters of state in her company.

"Isabella Savage, my Lord Falkland," said Digby, and to Falkland, "Isabella and I have known each other since we were children."

"You exaggerate, Digby," she told him, in a low, husky voice. "I was still a little girl when you first took your seat in Parliament. My lord," she said to Falkland, "I have often watched you there, from the galleries, but never had the privilege of a closer acquaintance. I am afraid I insisted on that privilege tonight."

"The privilege is mine," Falkland said, bowing.

"So, as of today you are both soldiers!"

"Lucius has some military experience already, with the Earl of Essex, in the Scottish campaign," Digby put in slyly.

How typical of him, Falkland thought, to disguise a little thrust as a compliment. "True, I served under Essex," Falkland said to Mistress Savage, "but we did not see much fighting, madam, and as you must know, His Majesty's attempt to pacify the Scots ended in defeat."

"And now Essex is your enemy. What a changed state of affairs."

"One I regret," he murmured, beginning to regret that he had come.

"Our simple repast is ready," Digby said, as the servant entered bearing a platter of stewed fowl and a large pie with a standing crust. "Isabella, you shall take the Prince's chair. Lucius, you shall sit opposite her. And I shall sit between you."

An obvious ploy, Falkland told himself, but it worked: throughout the meal, he had to look at her; and if he did not look, he felt an idiot that he should so studiously avoid her.

When she turned aside in conversation, he noted a classical cast to her profile and long, slender neck; face on, she enchanted him with her deep brown eyes, hooded by sleepy lids, and her lips, half smiling in repose; and as she moved her head, he glimpsed a flash of auburn in her dark hair. He admired the slim fit of her gown, a bronze silk that brought out the honeyed colour of her skin, and the emeralds dangling from her ears, and her gestures, rather lazy, as was her drawling speech; though he guessed, from what she said, that there was nothing lazy about her brain. She unnerved him, and not just because of her beauty: she talked with a most unfeminine confidence.

"Nottingham is the same as Coventry: hostile to us, one might argue," she remarked, tearing apart a wishbone. "My Lord Falkland, did you think it a good decision to raise the standard here? What do we have so far, a thousand men? If that?"

"His Majesty expects others, now that war has been formally declared," Falkland said.

"But he has just sent emissaries of peace to London. Why should the local gentry commit to him? And it's harvest time. How can you expect any farmer to desert his crops, when there's no absolute certainty of war and even less certainty of getting paid to fight, if war does break out?"

"Isabella, you are plaguing him while he is trying to eat," said Digby. "So quick she ought to have been in breeches," he giggled to Falkland.

"Are you insulting my sex?" she asked Digby, her eyes sparkling at him. "If so, I won't stand for it!"

"If I had my druthers, you would stand for Parliament! Lucius, don't you think that if women were given the same education as ourselves, they would prove as capable in the political sphere?"

"There are many examples to be found in history," Isabella said, before Falkland could answer.

"Our late Queen Elizabeth," Digby said.

"And my namesake, the Queen of Spain."

"These are princes, and may prove the exception rather than the rule," Falkland said at last. "And I would not think it proper for women to assume all of our duties."

"Which would you spare us, my lord?" she queried, with a devastating smile.

"The battlefield, madam, for one," he answered, hoping to silence her.

"Ah, but what of the Amazons?"

"My darling Isabella, are you prepared, as they were, to cut off a breast to go to war?" Digby said, giggling again.

"There would be no need. We are not still shooting bows and arrows, as they were," she responded.

"We may have to, if we continue to be so short of pistols and muskets."

"Then in the interests of self-preservation I shall certainly leave warfare to you gentlemen." She turned to Falkland, her expression more serious. "My lord, what do you believe might come of the negotiations?"

"Some compromise, before the violence becomes widespread," he replied.

"Would you go to London and plead for peace, if circumstances required?"

"Yes, I would, with all my heart," he said vehemently, "if it could put a stop to any bloodshed. And I may yet."

"His Highness Prince Rupert has been heard to say that we should not pander to rebels," she said. "What is your view, Digby?" Digby was nibbling on a quail leg; with his full cheeks, he reminded Falkland of a large, blond squirrel. "How you hate to commit yourself," she went on, with a hard little laugh.

"I follow the voice of reason, as does my friend Lucius."

"You follow a great number of voices, but chiefly your own."

"And what would *you* say, my dear?"

"That there is reason on both sides."

"Aha! It seems that neither of us wishes to divulge our true feelings about this war."

"Were you merely jesting, then, when you wrote from Holland to His Majesty urging him to take up arms against his people?" Falkland exclaimed, hearing his tone grow shrill with emotion.

Digby gave him a reproachful look. "Now, Lucius, you have hit below the belt."

"Do you deny that you encouraged him to it?"

There was a silence, during which Falkland caught Mistress Savage studying them both with great interest, as though expecting they might leap up and engage in physical combat.

"Must we argue?" Digby said, casting them one of his incandescent smiles. "I can never tolerate an argument while eating."

"Then let us attack a less controversial issue," Mistress Savage said hastily. "Tell me, gentlemen, has the Prince got himself a lover yet?

I wager there are more young hearts waiting to be broken by him than there are troops serving under His Majesty."

"Yours too?" Digby asked. "Or aren't you susceptible?"

"I fear I'm not. I think I prefer more experienced campaigners."

"You speak of *military* campaigning, I assume," he said, winking at her.

"Rupert has experience, even though he's only twenty-three," Falkland interjected, to steer their discourse into less ribald waters. "He served nearly ten years in his father's army."

"Don't mention it to our host – he is somewhat envious of Rupert's martial prowess," commented Mistress Savage. "Digby, I do believe you wish for war just so you may be proved as fine a general as you are a man of politics. Am I right?"

Digby for once appeared annoyed. "It is getting late, Isabella," he observed rather peevishly.

"Yes, I must go," she said, rising. Digby and Falkland got up also, Falkland with some relief. "Digby, would you have my maidservant called?"

"I shall fetch her myself," he said, and went out.

Another obvious ruse, Falkland thought, but what was the design behind it?

Mistress Savage came closer, and he saw that her eyes were not dark brown but hazel, shot with golden flecks. "My lord," she said quietly, "you know Charles Danvers, do you not?"

"As an acquaintance," said Falkland, frowning.

"He is estranged from his wife and has engaged in a love affair. His mistress, who is a friend of mine, told me that he is claiming you hired him as one of your agents. She does not lie to me. I think you would be wise to detach him from your service. He cannot even contain his own secrets, let alone those of anyone else."

"Madam, may I ask why are you offering me this advice?"

"Because of how you spoke out tonight," she replied, with apparent candour. "I would be sorry to see a man as noble as you come to grief. My lord, you are not like *us*." And she glanced towards the door. "We are – how can I put it – in the world, and you have not yet been polluted by its dealings."

She moved away from Falkland as their host returned with her maidservant, who held out her cloak for her to put on.

"Thank you for attending, Isabella," Digby said.

"And I thank you for the wonderful repast, and wish you both well with the recruits," she told them, in her former languid drawl. "And you with the peace negotiations, my lord."

"Thank you, madam," Falkland said.

"I hope we meet again, though it will not be for a while. I am soon to leave Nottingham."

Digby kissed her on the cheek. "I shall visit you tomorrow, my dear."

"Please do," she said.

After she had gone, they resumed their seats at the table, and Digby made a few humming noises in his throat. "I am sure you are speculating, Lucius," he said, at length. "Let me set matters straight. My wife and I are inseparable."

"There is no need to explain."

"But I would like to, in case you should have formed some mistaken opinion of Isabella. She is a sort of relative, to be precise. Her father is unknown to her. He is of noble blood. Her mother died when she was but four or five. Alas, the union from which she sprang had the sanction of neither Church nor state, and left her vulnerable, and that is why I took it upon myself to be her guardian. However, since she has attained an age at which she is able to lead her own life, I allow her perfect freedom. And, as you may judge, she makes full use of it."

"If she is your ward, is it not your responsibility to erase the stain of her parents' indiscretion by finding her a husband?" Falkland said abruptly, still rattled by what she had just told him.

"I shall, by and by. Someone very old and very rich who will die and leave her a grand estate."

"Yet she must still be subject to . . . to gossip."

"As are we all."

"With her bold talk, she does not make it any easier on herself."

Digby inspected him, simpering. "I so adore to watch each time my Helen of Troy makes her first impression on a man. Even you were not immune, Lucius."

"Oh for God's sake, Digby. I am as inseparable from my wife as you are from yours."

"But were you not horrified at the very idea that she should sacrifice one of those exquisite breasts to go to war? And they *are* exquisite, Lucius. I have seen them."

"Digby, please," said Falkland, blushing again.

"On one occasion only, when I had her painted by Van Dyke in ancient costume," Digby said, with an air of wounded innocence. Then he took a sip from his glass. "What were you and she speaking of, before I came in?"

"She made some inquiry about Charles Danvers," Falkland said, now wanting very much to leave.

"Danvers? Oh yes, I think he is paying court to a friend of hers. And who is Danvers to you?" Digby inquired, as if he were uninterested in the answer.

"Merely an acquaintance," Falkland repeated, berating himself for letting slip the man's name. "I should also retire, Digby. I have work to do still."

"Lucius, you must not let your duties overwhelm you," Digby said, sympathetically; but his eyes, like those of his ward, were calculating.

VI.

"Are you awake?" said Tom.

Laurence dragged himself up from the floor where he was resting, with his saddle for a pillow. "Yes."

"I think I'm hungry."

This was the first such comment that Tom had made in more than a week. For days he had hovered close to death, and although Laurence had moved him to a larger, airier room at the inn and had tended to him night and day, he was still vomiting, voiding, and delirious. Then at last there had been hope: he had slept soundly for some twenty odd hours and Laurence now knew on touching his forehead that the fever had passed.

"It was a near thing, Tom," he said.

"Were you here, all the time?"

"Yes."

"I suppose I should be grateful to you for looking after me."

"I don't want your gratitude – we're brothers." Tom said nothing. "We haven't always been at odds, have we, Tom?" Laurence went on.

Tom looked thoughtful. "Remember when we were boys, the day we jumped off the top of the barn?" he said eventually. "You thought I was a coward, didn't you. You thought I hadn't the guts to do it."

"I wasn't thinking at all. It was pure stupidity on my part. We could both have been killed."

"Then you went off to Merton, and when you next came home you were so pleased with yourself. You'd had your first fuck, and you couldn't stop carrying on about it."

Laurence smiled sheepishly. "How ridiculous of me. I'm sorry, Tom."

"Are you? You wouldn't even come near me, after six years, when I held out my arms to you. Even Ingram was embarrassed. And you had to make a joke of it, as you have of me ever since I was old enough to understand."

There was a silence during which Laurence wanted to ask Tom's forgiveness. But Tom had closed his eyes, as if he would sleep. "I have to go out tomorrow," Laurence told him. "I won't be more than a couple of hours."

"Do whatever you want," said Tom. "You always do, anyway."

VII.

There were soldiers posted outside the door to Lord Falkland's offices, burly men armed with pikes. Their disdainful attitude suggested to Laurence that although he had washed and shaved earlier, he should have heeded Dr. Clarke's advice to purchase some new clothes.

"Your name, sir?" demanded one of them. Laurence gave it, and he knocked and disappeared within. Laurence paced about, ignoring the other guards, until the man returned. "His lordship will see you," he announced, as if granting that favour himself, and Laurence was shown in.

It had been perhaps seven years since he had met Falkland at Chipping Campden, but Falkland seemed much older than that time would warrant. He sat before a trestle table piled with documents, a harried expression on his face.

"Laurence Beaumont," he said, smiling immediately. "Is his lordship your father well?"

"Yes, thank you, my lord."

"And your family?"

"All except for my brother. He fell seriously ill and is only just recovering. I've been looking after him for the past week."

"Here in Nottingham?" Laurence nodded. "Praise God he is feeling better." Falkland gestured for Laurence to take the chair opposite him. "As you must know, I was expecting you."

"You were?" said Laurence, with a frown.

"Yes. Your father wrote to me of your talents, and suggested that you might be interested to work for me as a cryptographer."

"Oh. But that's not why I came to see you, my lord." Laurence stopped, conscious that he had spoken too bluntly. "I came to bring you these," he began again. "My father knows nothing about them." He took a roll of papers out of his doublet, almost frightened to part with it, and laid it on the table.

"I have only a few days before I must go to London for the negotiations with Parliament." Falkland sighed, picking up the papers. "The truth is, I am rushed so from one thing to another that I do not have much time to spare. What are these documents?"

"They're letters in code, my lord, and my transcriptions of them. They concern a plot to assassinate the King."

Falkland dropped them hurriedly, as though they might scorch his hands. "How in heaven's name did you acquire them?" Laurence told the story as succinctly as he could, describing the difficulties he had experienced with the code. After he finished, there was a pause. "Let me see if I understand you," Falkland said, looking baffled. "We have evidence of a conspiracy, but we cannot discover the identity of the conspirators."

"Yes, my lord. That's the problem. But there might be some way to find out, with all the resources you have at your disposal." Laurence searched for words to convince him; of course, the whole affair must seem half-baked, even suspicious. "The conspirators are in England now, and they're breathing down my neck again," Laurence went on, and spoke of his meeting with Poole, though he kept to himself the wreckage of Seward's rooms at Merton, and his own subsequent chat with young Illingsworth.

"Are these men aware that you have broken part of their code?" Falkland asked.

"There's a chance they may be. My lord, I would urge you to investigate this as swiftly as you can."

"Let me first read the letters. Then we'll talk very soon, I promise. Where are you staying in town?" Laurence gave the address, which

Falkland noted on a corner of one of the documents. "Mr. Beaumont, you were some years in the Low Countries, were you not? Did you return to England because of this conspiracy, or because of the political unrest here?"

Laurence was saved from having to reply, for they heard a dog yapping outside and the door burst open. A tall, dark young man in an armoured breastplate strode in, followed by a white poodle. "My lord," he cried, a hint of German to his accent, "why won't you reconsider your mission to London? What is the point, after Parliament has rejected Culpeper's terms? It's as if the standard were never raised!"

Rising to bow to Prince Rupert, Laurence had to conceal a smile: it was common knowledge that the royal standard had been toppled over by heavy winds shortly after it had been erected.

Another man now entered, of middle age, who surveyed first the room and next Laurence. "My lord," he said, bowing to Falkland.

"We have not been introduced," the Prince said to Laurence.

"This is Laurence Beaumont, Your Highness," Falkland said. "He is the son of my friend and neighbour, Lord James Beaumont. He was lately serving in the war abroad." Laurence bowed again to the Prince. "And this is Colonel Hoare, Mr. Beaumont."

A professional soldier, Laurence guessed. Hoare was inspecting him as if he were some untrained recruit who should be whipped into obedience, and so he stared straight back, until Hoare looked away.

"How long were you in service, sir?" the Prince asked Laurence.

"About six years, Your Highness."

"Were you at Breda?"

"Yes, I was," Laurence said, hoping that there would be no more questions about his role in the siege, during which he had so belatedly discovered an enthusiasm for the Protestant cause.

"What a privilege, to take part in that glorious victory of ours," the Prince said, making an assumption that Laurence let pass. Out of tact, he also did not mention that he had more creditably fought at Vlotho in the same battle as had the Prince; it had been no glorious victory, but rather a crushing defeat for Rupert's older brother, Charles Louis, and Rupert himself had been taken hostage and held for three years in prison by the Hapsburg Emperor. "Whose regiment are you with?" the Prince inquired.

"I haven't enlisted as yet, Your Highness."

"I would welcome you in mine. We need every good man we can find."

"That would be an honour, Your Highness, and I'll certainly consider it."

"Mr. Beaumont," said Falkland, with an air of closing their audience, "I thank you for coming today."

"I thank you for hearing me out, my lord," Laurence responded, and after a last glance at the letters on Falkland's desk he excused himself, feeling uneasy, as though he had just played the wrong card in a game of high stakes.

VIII.

Falkland was waiting for some comment; and it came.

"Such a dark fellow – he reminds me of the Lascars I used to see hanging about the Harlemmer Port in Amsterdam," said the Prince.

"His mother is a Spaniard, Your Highness. That accounts for his looks."

"She's a papist, my lord?" inquired Hoare.

"No. For more than thirty years, as Protestant as you or I."

"And what was his business?"

"He merely came to bring me Lord Beaumont's greetings." Falkland turned to Prince Rupert. "I am saddened that you disapprove of our offer."

"By God I do." Rupert threw himself into the chair that Beaumont had recently vacated. "Why countenance the demands of rebels?"

Falkland thought of Mistress Savage, who had predicted the Prince's response so accurately. "Your Highness, we must at least try to reach a bloodless solution to our arguments," he said gravely.

"I wish you success, though I doubt you will have any." The Prince jumped up and stretched out his arms, yawning. "For a whole night's sleep I'd give a hundred of your offers to Parliament. Come, Boy, let's be off." And he left with his dog as swiftly as he had arrived.

"I must agree with His Highness, my lord," remarked Hoare. "You'll waste your breath in London."

"The Council is decided," said Falkland, "and I should remind you that I am not the only minister inclined to negotiate. I shall leave in five days' time, with Lord Spencer."

Hoare scowled disapprovingly. "Yes, my lord."

"Oh, and in my absence, and from henceforth, I do not wish you to assign Charles Danvers any confidential work," Falkland added, thinking again of Mistress Savage.

"I have assigned him none. It was you who asked that I employ him as an agent, my lord." Falkland was silent: he could not deny this. "He has his uses, nonetheless," Hoare acknowledged. "There is often an advantage to such indiscreet fellows. No one believes them when they tell the truth. And his love of drink puts him in the company of men similarly inclined, who are also apt to be blabber-mouths. But why your sudden request, my lord? Have you heard some news about him that has disturbed you?" Falkland hesitated, inadvertently laying a hand on the papers Beaumont had given him. "From Mr. Beaumont, perhaps?"

"No," said Falkland.

Hoare pointed at the documents. "What are these, my lord?"

Falkland passed them over with a certain reluctance. "I have not even read them yet. Mr. Beaumont brought them to me, along with such a muddled tale of codes and conspirators that I could scarcely follow it."

Hoare took time to examine them. "My lord," he said, afterwards, "there is treason written here! I must question this man at once!"

Falkland glared at Hoare, disliking his peremptory tone. "There is no need. I have promised to see him again myself."

"Then I strongly advise my presence at your next meeting." Hoare pulled out a sheet, which he thrust under Falkland's nose. "Look, my lord."

Falkland squinted at it and then at Hoare. "The Bible may forbid the casting of horoscopes, Colonel Hoare, yet it is scarcely a treasonable offence."

"Indeed it is," Hoare objected, a superior expression on his narrow, pallid face, "when it charts the life and death of our King."

Part Two

England, September–October 1642

CHAPTER SIX

I.

Four days after Laurence had met with the Secretary of State, he received a message summoning him to another audience at six o'clock the following morning. "Must be something to do with our father," he told Tom. "It's an ungodly hour for an appointment, but Falkland says he has to set out for London immediately afterwards."

"I want to go home," Tom announced, sitting up in bed. "I'm well enough to ride."

"We can leave once I've seen him," said Laurence, although he wondered whether this would be possible: Falkland might insist that he remain in Nottingham to discuss the letters. "I should make sure our horses are fit for the journey," he added, and hurried out before Tom could become too interested in his dealings with the Secretary of State.

He rode over to the fields outside the city where the cavalry was at drill, and for an hour or so he watched Prince Rupert's and Henry Wilmot's divisions at their manoeuvres. Prince Rupert's men were the more organized and clearly worshipped their leader; an advantage in battle, Laurence thought, even if they were not yet trained to discipline.

By sunset, the riders were sweating and the horses flecked with foam. As orders were sounded to break rank, Laurence hailed Wilmot, and they walked their mounts to the village around which the cavalry was billeted.

"Come to join up with me, have you," Wilmot said, stating a fact rather than asking.

"Or I might serve with Prince Rupert," Laurence said, to nettle him.

"I suppose you think I'm envious of that boy, but for the moment we're the best of comrades," Wilmot chuckled, though with a sarcastic edge. "He keeps reminding me how we fought together at the siege of Breda. As though I can ever forget it. The wound I got there still plagues me." He smiled at Laurence maliciously. "You were at Breda, weren't you."

"Er, yes."

"Is His Royal Highness aware that you were with the Spanish then?"

"I don't believe he is."

When they had settled at a table in a nearby tavern, Wilmot observed, "You know, Beaumont, there's a lot of rumour flying about concerning your time abroad. It can't surprise you, of course. With your looks, you stick out like a sore thumb. None of your shadowy past bothers me, however. To be frank, it interests me. You could do me a favour."

"What sort of favour?"

"I need a cipher for my correspondence. And I'm telling you, man, you'll be a lot better off with me than with Prince Rupert. If you served with him, you'd have to answer to Colonel Hoare, who's in his regiment and is also Lord Falkland's spymaster."

Laurence recalled the iron-jawed soldier in Falkland's chambers. "What kind of man is he?"

"Hoare's spent his whole life climbing up through the ranks, and he's a mean bastard," Wilmot said, filling their cups. "I knew him from the Scottish War, and I once saw him thrash a fellow almost to death just for stealing a loaf of bread. He's fiercely loyal to the Prince, far more so than to Falkland, I'd wager. He shares Rupert's view that the only way to teach the rebels a lesson is on the battlefield."

"He can't like it that Falkland is negotiating for a peace."

"He doesn't. And I'm sure he knows that Falkland would love to be rid of him. But he's too good at his work."

"To be honest, Wilmot," Laurence said casually, "it rather amazed me to learn that Falkland was made Secretary of State."

Wilmot seized on this. "You weren't here – you don't know how it happened. He never wanted the office, but Digby, amongst others, pushed him forward. Digby couldn't have it himself, because nobody trusts him. Like you, he has a dubious record in terms of his loyalties."

"How so?" Laurence asked, ignoring the barb.

"It's quite a tale. Over two years ago, he was caught duelling in the precincts of Whitehall and was imprisoned for it, much to his disgruntlement. Perhaps he thought the King would intervene on his behalf. Anyway, when he first entered the House of Commons, he took up with the radicals who were howling for the Earl of Strafford's blood. Then he declared in Parliament that he wouldn't support any such thing. But his speech had got out in print, and he had to issue an apology to the Commons, to excuse his shift of allegiance."

"How very embarrassing for him."

"Embarrassment is not a word in his vocabulary," Wilmot sniggered. "Why, he changed his tune again completely once he moved up to the House of Lords. This January he was urging the King to prosecute five of His Majesty's loudest opponents in Parliament. The Queen was won over to the idea, and I heard that she and Digby encouraged the King to go in person to the House of Commons to secure their arrest."

"A shocking breach of parliamentary privilege," remarked Laurence, laughing.

"And a slap in the face for the King. They'd been alerted ahead of time and escaped downriver by barge. But by then the whole city was in an uproar."

"What happened to Digby?"

"Oh, he tried to wiggle out, claiming the King had been ill advised and that he'd had nothing to do with it. He was summoned to the House of Lords to explain himself, whereupon he promptly sailed for Holland. That was when the King also fled, with his family, to Hampton Court." Wilmot grinned and licked his lips. "The best I've saved for last. Digby was fool enough to write to His Majesty from abroad advising him to take up arms against his opponents. Digby's correspondence was intercepted and read out in Parliament, and he was impeached, just as the Earl of Strafford had been – charged with treason for levying war against the nation. That's why he was arrested when he got back to England recently. Yet again, by some miracle of diplomacy, he managed to wiggle out. Ever since he's been busy ingratiating himself with the King."

"And what's his strategy with Falkland?" Laurence inquired, to return to the Secretary of State.

"Think about it! Digby has enemies not just in Parliament but within our camp, too. Falkland, on the other hand, is universally respected. Digby must have counted on improving his own image by championing someone so principled, while pulling Falkland's strings at the same time."

"To achieve what?"

"Parliament will ask Falkland for some major concessions if a peaceful settlement is to be reached. Digby's removal from the public stage will be one of them. The radicals might even demand that he be put on trial."

"You mean he's relying on Falkland to keep him safe from prosecution?"

"Yes, and no." Wilmot poured them more from the jug. "Call me cynical if you like, but I believe Digby urged Falkland into office precisely because he's an unsuitable candidate. Digby's setting him up to fail – and along with him, the peace negotiations."

"You *are* a cynic," Laurence said, laughing again, though Wilmot's theory intrigued him. "In your view, is there any chance of peace?"

"I think Falkland is pissing in the wind." Wilmot regarded Laurence through narrowed eyes. "So what do you say – will you enlist with me?"

Laurence sighed. His feelings had not changed about army service, yet it was becoming evident that he would not be able to avoid it indefinitely now that war had been officially declared. "You'd have to give me a certain amount of latitude," he said. "I've some business to sort out."

"You want to come and go as you please?"

"Only for a while."

"Hmm. Will I get my cipher?"

"Yes, I promise."

"Then we have an agreement. Look who's here," said Wilmot, in a louder voice. "Our mutual friend. Everything well in the camp?" he asked of Charles Danvers, who had sauntered up to their table.

"The opposite, I'm afraid," Danvers said, taking a seat. "The men are arguing with the quartermaster about their rations. They didn't have their full share of cheese today, and what they did get was mouldy."

"Oh, bugger it – I must deal with them." Wilmot rose and slapped Laurence on the shoulder. "Don't forget what we discussed."

"I won't," Laurence said, smiling up at him.

"Good old Wilmot, you can always depend on him to look after his troops," Danvers said, when Wilmot had gone. "You two were having a very deep conversation. What about?"

"Just politics," Laurence said.

"Did he by chance mention his own foray into the political arena?" Laurence shook his head; Danvers was clearly dying to explain. "He was chucked in the Tower of London last June and then expelled from Parliament, on a charge of plotting to bring the army into Parliament to intimidate the rebels."

"Was he, indeed."

Danvers winked at him slyly. "Wouldn't have been a bad thing if it had worked. Beaumont, what plan have you for tonight?" he asked, in a different tone. "There are some actors I could introduce you to. Actresses, to be precise, not boys in women's clothing. They're from France."

"A more enlightened country than ours," Laurence commented.

"I'd say – I don't know why people here are so averse to putting a woman on the stage. The ladies were invited to perform in London this spring as a novelty, but with Parliament ready to close down all the playhouses, they had to escape from the capital. They came to Nottingham to beg His Majesty's assistance with papers of safe conduct or some such thing. You speak French, don't you? Mine's atrocious. I'll take you to their lodgings in town."

"All right," said Laurence, with a shrug. He had to ride back into Nottingham in any case, and felt he deserved a few hours of female company after all the time he had spent at Tom's bedside.

The actresses turned out to be a disappointment. Even in the dimly lit room where they received their visitors, Laurence could see that two out of the five were well past their prime. Danvers had obviously established a special rapport with the only alluring one amongst them. Another was scarred from the smallpox, while the youngest, a plain girl of about sixteen, looked about to die of shyness when Laurence addressed her.

The women were pathetically grateful to be able to communicate with someone in their own tongue, and although hospitable, they must have been very low on funds, for the wine they served him was pungent and sour. Out of courtesy he choked down a glass, but when he saw that Danvers and the prettier actress had disappeared, he assumed to practise a language more universal than French, he decided to leave.

As he was saying good night, the young girl asked if he would mind translating an official paper that had been granted to them for their journey home. Reluctantly he agreed, and she led him to another chamber where she said they might find some writing instruments. Walking with her, he felt oddly heavy and clumsy: he had to concentrate on putting one foot before the other, and when she sat him down on a low couch, he could not resist closing his eyes for what seemed to him only a second. With an effort, he opened them again to find her on top of him, her expression more frightened than lustful.

"What are you doing?" he asked, hearing the slur in his words.

"Monsieur Danvers said you would like to make love," she told him.

"Well he was wrong."

He tried to get up but his limbs would not respond. Her face hung above him like a misshapen moon, and then, abruptly, the moon was eclipsed.

II.

Laurence woke with a pounding headache. He heaved himself off the couch and staggered over to look out of the window. The sun was high in a lucid expanse of blue. A beautiful day, he thought irrelevantly. He had long since missed the hour of his meeting with Falkland.

In the main room, he found one of the older women in her dressing gown taking breakfast. When she saw him, she stood and curtseyed. "Monsieur," she said, "thank you for sparing my daughter. Monsieur Danvers promised us an escort to the coast if we would provide you with an evening's amusement. Yet my girl would have paid too high a price. *Elle est pucelle.*"

"Where is he?" demanded Laurence, feeling an ominous queasiness in his guts.

"He left earlier this morning. I am sorry, sir – I see you are not well."

"I'm not. You must excuse me," he mumbled, and she showed him to the door.

A couple of armed men in buff coats were waiting outside. "He looks sick as a dog!" one of them jeered.

"Mr. Beaumont," the other said, "you're to come with us."

As they cuffed his wrists behind him, he was overwhelmed by an impotent rage: he should have guessed that he had been drugged as soon as he tasted the wine, which he could taste again now as it threatened to come back up. But why?

They led him to Falkland's rooms, where he was dismayed to find Colonel Hoare sitting at the desk, which had been tidied beyond recognition, parchment stacked in neat piles, quills in regimental alignment beside the inkwell. Hoare was equally tidy, his hair and beard impeccably groomed, his collar spotless.

"Free him and leave us," he said to the men, who removed Laurence's handcuffs and departed. "Mr. Beaumont, my Lord Falkland insisted that I convey his regrets to you, but he could not delay his journey on your account. Are you suffering from some sort of ague, sir?"

Laurence did not reply, his teeth clenched together to avoid the further humiliation of vomiting. So Danvers was in Hoare's pocket, and back in Oxford when he had dropped those heavy hints about his clandestine employment, he must have been fishing to recruit Laurence into the Colonel's service.

Hoare produced the conspirators' letters and tossed them onto the desk. "How did you come by these?"

"I have already explained that to Lord Falkland," Laurence answered, after swallowing hard.

"I confess, sir, that I am disinclined to trust the convoluted story you gave him. For I know about you," Hoare went on gloatingly. "You were a parasite in the foreign war, and you're home expecting to play the same old game. But here you've an advantage: you can use your father's connection with his lordship to inveigle your way into his good graces, and hoodwink him into believing that you came by these letters honestly. I can see it all: the prodigal son redeemed by uncovering a plot against the King's life! Oh, what glory would accrue to you! Well it won't be quite that easy. If his lordship cannot see through your machinations, I certainly can. Now tell me the truth. How did you get the letters?"

"It was just as I said to Lord Falkland."

"As if I'd buy that!" snorted Hoare. "Your noble father must rue the day he engendered you. Born so high, only to sink so low – a turncoat mercenary who spied for both sides in the conflict abroad."

"I worked only for the Germans," Laurence retorted. "How can you condemn me for that, when you're in the same business?"

Hoare sat forward, regarding Laurence in consternation. "You would compare us, when your record is so very black? You fought with Spanish troops, so why should you not have been a mole for them, too, when you have Spanish blood in your veins? Let me warn you, sir, the onus is upon *you* to prove that you are not a regicide as well. For I suspect you were involved in this conspiracy, and decided to sell it out once you got to England! How else could you have broken such an intricate code without anyone's assistance, as you claimed to his lordship?"

Laurence covered his mouth. "I'll show you," he said, "but not now."

"About to puke, are you?" Hoare laughed shortly. "I'll not have you fouling his lordship's quarters, so I suppose I must wait. Tomorrow morning, would that suit?" he inquired, with savage politesse. "We shall examine the code together, and you can demonstrate to me how you unveiled its mysteries, and why you could not unveil them *all*. Good day, Mr. Beaumont. And don't try to run – my guards will be onto you."

The guards marched Laurence back to his quarters at the inn; he could hardly walk for the cramp in his stomach, and his head was spinning, as much from Hoare's lecture as the after-effects of the drug.

Tom must have heard him clambering up the stairs, and opened the door with an angry gesture. "Where were you last night?" Laurence pushed past him, ran to the window, and spewed copiously. "Have you caught my flux?" Tom asked, with more concern.

"No," muttered Laurence, still spitting and wiping his nose and mouth.

"You got drunk! I should have known you'd do a thing like that. By Christ, will you never change! Lord Falkland must have been disgusted with you."

"I never saw him; my appointment was postponed until tomorrow," said Laurence with what dignity he could muster, as he crawled into a corner and wrapped himself in his cloak.

"Liar," Tom said. "You were too full of booze to wake up for it."

To this Laurence made no reply. Almost immediately sleep engulfed him, and he began to dream he was on the road again with Juana. As they passed through a dark landscape full of the horrors of war, there was not just a single rider but an entire army after them. And as he turned to look, he saw Colonel Hoare's face on every man.

III.

A wet snow was falling as Laurence and Juana arrived at Lille, not more than a hundred miles from Paris. After many vain inquiries he managed to secure them a damp cellar in a village inn, though the landlord was quick to identify Juana's origins. He exacted a high price and ordered her to stay hidden downstairs, out of respect for his customers, he said. When Laurence went to fetch her some food, he discovered that these were mostly soldiers, swilling drink and playing at dice or cards before the fire, where a haunch of mutton roasted on the spit, watched avidly by a couple of mongrel dogs.

Once Juana had eaten, she curled up in the straw and gave a satisfied belch. "Not ready for bed, Monsieur?" she asked.

"No," he said. "I might join a game of cards upstairs. Keep the pistols with you. You know how to use them, don't you?"

She assured him that she did.

He had not been apart from her for days, and was enjoying his temporary freedom in the warmth of a good fire, winning easy money. Then a fellow who had left the table briefly came back with a leer on his face.

"The landlord says you're riding with a wench," he remarked to Laurence. "Seems our friend paid a tidy sum to get her in," he informed the others. "And by God, he'd have to – she's a gypsy."

The men started to laugh contemptuously. "Eh well, a cunt's a cunt," one of them said. "I've had a few in my time that weren't too choice, and I'm not alone, am I, boys? Some will even fuck their own sheep, for want of a woman."

"I could think of worse," another added. "Why, when you've had your fun there's no nagging afterwards. And if there is, you can slice her up and eat her!"

They howled at this witticism. When Laurence did not, the first man stared directly at him. "Vermin, them gypsies are. Shouldn't be allowed to live. I wouldn't touch that whore of yours if she was the last woman on earth."

"That's lucky for you," said Laurence. "Because she wouldn't have you anyway."

The man had just launched out of his chair, fists curled, when a shot rang out, sending the taproom into confusion. Moments later, the landlord hurried over. "You come with me," he hissed in Laurence's ear.

Laurence hastily obeyed, cursing himself for leaving Juana on her own; she might be lying dead in her nest of straw. But there she was at the entrance to the cellar, very much alive and clad only in her thin shift, struggling to escape from a youth who was trying to pin her by the arms.

"She bit me, Father!" the youth complained.

"I was attacked!" she shouted to Laurence.

"By this little sod?" he asked, wrestling the youth off her.

"No! A big man came at me with a knife!"

"Her cock-and-bull tale," said the landlord. "Pierre, bring the lantern. Let's find out what mischief she was up to."

They all descended. At the far side of the cellar, a door was banging open and shut in the icy breeze. The shot had passed through it, leaving a small hole. Laurence could see no other signs of disturbance, except that Juana's clothing and some of the straw bedding lay scattered about, as did the contents of their saddlebags.

"A fine oak panel destroyed," said the landlord. "That'll cost you five gold pieces. And I shall hold your horses as security. Be gone early tomorrow and don't come back." He waited for his payment, and then he and his son departed with the lantern.

Laurence sat Juana down in what remained of the bedding. "What happened?" he asked.

"I – I was asleep, Monsieur," she stammered, "and the next thing I knew, there was a light in my eyes and a knife at my heart. The man spoke to me in some foreign language and made me open the saddlebags. Thank God he couldn't see the pistols or the sword – I'd tucked them deep in the straw. He hunted and hunted through everything. I was too scared to cry out. He forced me to undress, and went through all my clothes. I didn't know what he was looking for! He even made me lift up my shift." She moaned, covering her face. "*Qué deshonra*, Monsieur! No man has seen me like that since my husband."

"Go on," Laurence whispered.

"When he had finished groping me, he went to search our things again. So I felt underneath me in the straw for one of the pistols and I pointed it at him. He came at me, but he kicked over the lantern and then the pistol went off. He ran out through that door."

"Was he the man we saw on the road?"

"I don't know! But he had the evil eye."

"What do you mean?"

"Just that," she replied impatiently. "He may come back, Monsieur! Let us leave!"

"And go where, in this weather? We'll rest until daylight. Now put some clothes on before you freeze to death."

She made no complaint as he assisted her to dress. Afterwards he gave her both of their cloaks, and chafed her hands to bring the blood back. She continued to shake, so he put his arms around her to keep her warm, and eventually they slept.

In the morning, he imagined himself back at Simeon's house and wondered lazily which of the girls was with him, her back flush against his chest and belly, and her rear tucked into his groin against the hard length of his morning erection. Then he remembered. This was as close to Juana as he had ever been. For a while, he let himself think of her as he had seen her last night, with her slender hips and small rounded breasts undisguised by layers of clothing. Obviously he was missing what had been a regular part of his life at the brothel, but he knew he could seek no satisfaction here.

Braving the frigid air that greeted him as he emerged from their cocoon, he unbolted the door. Beyond were fields of mud, suffused with dull light. A few stars continued to glow in between the clouds, and there was no one about. The cold made him forget his desire, and he went to the stable where he saddled his horses, threw a sack of feed over one of their backs and led them out, towards the cellar door.

Juana was sitting with their saddlebags neatly packed, Simeon's sword resting at her feet. She looked refreshed and happy, which made him suspicious.

"Have you told me everything you know about last night?" he said.

"Of course I have," she replied innocently. And he knew that she was lying.

IV.

"Mr. Beaumont," said Colonel Hoare, "take a seat. You look much improved since yesterday. Now let us see how much of an expert you really are. What do you make of this?" he added, passing over a sheet of paper.

"Suppressed vowels, and a sequence of numbers for the rest of the alphabet," Laurence said, after a pause.

"And the next?" Hoare inquired, passing him another.

"Cardano's cipher."

"Which works how?"

"If you select every third letter before a punctuation mark and put them together, you have your message."

"The next?"

"Trithemius' alphabets."

"I suppose you are acquainted with all fourteen of them, and the words corresponding to each letter," Hoare remarked sceptically.

"Yes."

"What does the letter A signify in the first alphabet?"

"A is Jesus, B is God, C is Saviour –"

"Give me O in the eighth."

"Peace."

"O in the thirteenth."

"Virtuously," said Laurence, wondering when this would stop.

"I never understood why the method was so popular. A waste of paper and ink, and tedious to memorise. Next page, if you please, Mr. Beaumont."

"It's a design cipher, based on a four-part grid."

"And the last?"

"Trithemius again. His cipher table."

"You are well versed in the essentials," Hoare admitted, with obvious disappointment. "But your code, as you are aware, bears no relation to the methods we have just discussed. How did you crack the first layer of it?"

"The cipher is based on a table –"

"I mean the code. Without the code, the cipher is impossible to read."

Laurence was dreading this line of interrogation; if only he had paid more heed when Seward had helped him transcribe the documents. "It's derived from the Cabbala," he began, and slowly he explained how each of the ten Sephiroth pertained to the figures before him, and how, with this key, one could obtain a numerical value for the figures themselves.

"And where did you get your learning?" Hoare asked. "Have you friends amongst the tribe of Israel?"

"I had the benefit of an education while I was at Oxford," Laurence said, not bothering to hide his sarcasm.

"Then why can you not break the last part of the code and supply me with the conspirators' identities?"

"Because I haven't got the key. It's like Trithemius' alphabets, but in this case it must consist of a series of numbers privately agreed upon by the correspondents. They can invent as many variations for their names as they want, to make sure that there are no repeated frequencies. It's impossible to crack. Anyone versed in ciphering will tell you the same thing."

Hoare must have known this already, for he did not pursue the issue. "My Lord Falkland said that you were visited by one of the conspirators, who asked you to sell him back the letters. Tell me about him." Laurence described the meeting, after which Hoare said thoughtfully, "So, this lawyer is waiting for you at the Black Bull in Aylesbury."

"He was, weeks ago. He'll have given up on me by now."

"If the regicides were patient enough to follow you all the way to England, there's a chance he might still be there. You shall go and sell the letters, as he bade you."

"And lose the only solid evidence we have?" exclaimed Laurence, aghast.

"You won't go alone. I'll send some of my guards with you. Once the transaction is completed, they shall bring him in to me. I'll have the letters, and with luck and some persuasion he will confess, and we can net the other conspirators."

"If he sees me with your guards, he may be frightened away."

"Then you'll be the lure, and they will come in to perform the arrest once you've done your work. If no meeting occurs, they will bring you back to me. And let me remind you what's at stake if you try any tricks. I still think you may be implicated in the plot. I can have you held as my prisoner whenever I desire, and use all the means at my disposal to wring the truth out of you – a process with which I believe you are very familiar." Laurence shut his eyes briefly; so Hoare knew of this, too. "Lord Falkland won't help you," Hoare continued. "He told me to deal with you as I saw fit. I am offering you a last opportunity to prove yourself loyal to us. You shall set off tomorrow."

"Fine," Laurence said, assuming a coolly polite tone, "but I can't go straight to Aylesbury. As his lordship may have told you, my brother has been ill, here in town, and I'm on strict orders from my father to take him home. It's on my way south. It won't cost me more than a day's delay."

"Are you attempting to escape me?"

"I wouldn't be so foolish. My life is in danger from these conspirators. I have every interest in helping you to catch them." *Although I have no faith in your tactics*, Laurence added to himself.

"We'll see about that. My guards shall go ahead with the letters. I won't let you near them until it is absolutely necessary. Do you know the village of Thame, between Oxford and Aylesbury?"

"Yes."

"I shall give you four days to get there," Hoare said, with a magnanimous air. "My guards will be waiting for you at an inn called the Rising Sun. Make sure you are not late. Good day, Mr. Beaumont."

"Good day, sir."

Laurence walked out past the guards and into the street, where to his fury he saw Charles Danvers loitering. Danvers advanced with a hesitant smile that vanished as he noticed Laurence's expression. Laurence seized him by the front of his doublet and smacked him across the face so hard that he stumbled back.

"By Jesus!" he shouted, touching a finger to his lip, which was bleeding. "What did you do that for?"

"Would you like some more?" Laurence took a pace towards him and boxed him on the ear.

"For God's sake," cried Danvers, "I never meant you any harm!"

A few men passing by had stopped to watch. "Get at 'im!" one of them yelled enthusiastically to Laurence, who shot out a last punch that sent Danvers to the ground, moaning and clutching his chest. Laurence considered leaving him there but in the end gave him a hand up.

"Look, man," he gasped, "the drug was Hoare's idea, not mine. He said he would like to recruit you for –"

"Please don't try to excuse yourself," Laurence said into his reddened ear. "And in future I suggest you stay away from me."

Danvers opened his mouth to protest. Then a grin lit up his face; he was looking past Laurence, who turned, as a coach rumbled towards them. From within a woman was calling out Danvers' name.

"Another actress?" Laurence queried icily, when the vehicle had drawn to a halt.

"No, it's Mrs. Sterne," Danvers replied, apparently surprised.

"Charlie," she said, craning out of the window, "I've come all the way from Oxford for you!"

"Sweetheart, I'm unutterably flattered! You were right," Danvers murmured to Laurence. "She *must* be in love with me."

"Then she must be short of a brain," Laurence said, without lowering his voice.

A second woman now leant forward and gave Danvers her hand. "Charles, who is your friend?" she asked, her voice remarkably husky, as though she were recovering from a bad cold.

"Laurence Beaumont," he said, and to Laurence, "Mistress Isabella Savage."

She smiled at Laurence so dazzlingly that he almost smiled back. What a face she had: like some Botticelli nymph's, though she was dark rather than blonde. And her skin, exposed by the low neck of her russet silk gown, was glowing, without the pasty whiteness of most English gentlewomen. "Sir," she said, "how is it that we have not met?"

"He was abroad until lately," Danvers explained. "We knew each other from the foreign war."

"Are you also serving with Henry Wilmot?" she inquired of Laurence.

"I may be," he said, though after his talk with Colonel Hoare he doubted he could.

"Gentlemen, I am having some company at my quarters tonight. It is by way of a farewell, since I'm leaving Nottingham tomorrow. Would you join us?"

"Charlie, you will, won't you?" Mrs. Sterne said.

"I shall indeed!" Danvers said.

Mistress Savage fixed Laurence with her languorous eyes, in which he saw little flashes of gold. "And you, Mr. Beaumont?"

"Thank you, but no," he said. "I must leave tomorrow as well, early."

"Where are you going?" He told her about returning Tom to Chipping Campden. "Then we shall be on the same road," she exclaimed. "I am headed back to Oxford. We could travel together. If your brother is sick, he will be far more comfortable in this coach than in a saddle." She was right, he thought; Tom was still very weak. "Please," she insisted, and he could not refuse, although instinct warned him that he might be making things more complicated for himself than they already were. "I'll come for you at seven in the morning," she added, with another bewitching smile.

Mrs. Sterne blew Danvers a kiss. "Until later, Charlie!"

Mistress Savage gave a signal to the driver and the coach moved on.

"I think Isabella fancies you," observed Danvers.

"I'm unutterably flattered," Laurence told him, imitating his servile manner towards Mrs. Sterne.

"Well let me tell you, Beaumont," said Danvers, with an offended air, "she has connections in high places and she reports everything to her friend Lord Digby. So you should keep a guard on your tongue around her."

"And you should have yours cut out," Laurence spat back, which left Danvers appropriately speechless.

V.

"You hired a coach?" Tom asked, as it drew up.

"Not exactly," Laurence said. "Someone has offered you a ride in hers."

Mistress Savage swung open the door. In contrast to the day before, she was dressed sombrely in plain grey with a broad lace collar covering her neck up to her chin, none of which diminished her beauty. When Laurence introduced her to his brother, she inquired, "How are you faring, sir? Better, I hope?"

"Yes, thank you, madam," Tom said. *Who is she?* he mouthed silently to Laurence, but he got no answer.

"We must avoid Leicester, gentlemen," she told them, as Tom climbed into the seat opposite her. "This coach belongs to the Earl of

Bristol and was lent to me through the courtesy of his son, Lord Digby. They are both disliked by Parliament these days. Leicester is rebel territory, and I should not want any stones thrown at our conveyance."

"Whatever you wish," Laurence said, not really listening, expecting Colonel Hoare's men to appear at any moment and seize him.

But on the road south out of Nottingham, no one stopped them. The Colonel must be keeping to his word, Laurence thought.

At midday, as they broke to take some refreshment and water the horses at an inn, Tom could not eat; he was a sickly shade.

"Are you all right, Tom?" Laurence asked.

"Of course I am," Tom said stoutly.

Late into the afternoon, however, the coach pulled up and Mistress Savage swung open the door. "Your brother requires the close stool," she informed Laurence. "Digby's father had the foresight to provide such a thing under the seat."

"Oh no, I'll tell him to get out," he said.

"Please don't. He's embarrassed enough at having to ask. And in fact I would prefer to ride." She jumped down, without waiting for assistance. "You can oblige me by lending me his horse."

"It hasn't had much exercise recently. Are you sure you can handle it?"

"Let us see."

She ordered the driver to put her saddle on it, and they started off. In spite of his worries, Laurence could not help admiring her grace, and the lines of her figure as she rode with perfect control, following the horse's every motion. "You are very taciturn, Mr. Beaumont," she observed, at length. "Is it a habit with you?"

"Forgive me, madam," Laurence said. "So, do you live in Oxford?"

"I have no fixed abode," she replied in her lazy drawl. "There are people in the city I must visit."

"Aren't you afraid to travel alone?"

"I can rely on Digby's driver in case of any misadventures, of which

I've had none. In fact I get bored, sitting in that coach all by myself. I am so delighted that you agreed to accompany me. How long have you been back in England, sir?"

"About a month and a half," he replied, privately amazed at how much had transpired since then.

"You returned to fight?"

"No."

Something in his tone must have silenced her. Darkness was falling when she next addressed him. "We'll turn off the road," she said, "along this track. We shall spend the night at a house nearby."

"My brother and I can't impose. We'll find some other accommodation."

"You'll find nothing else hereabouts, the countryside is very desolate. And you cannot prejudice your brother's health by depriving him of a good night's sleep."

Again, he acknowledged, she was right, and he thanked her.

The coach took a narrow path, scaring away flocks of birds that were picking at the shorn wheat stalks, and over the crest of a hill, Laurence saw the house. It was of motley design, part stone, part timber, and part wattle and daub, agglomerated over generations. Some dogs barking vociferously in the yard must have alerted its owner, for as the coach drew up an elderly man emerged from the doorway holding a lantern in one hand. "Dear Isabella," he cried, "I was wondering when you might arrive."

"My faithful friend!" she said, dismounting easily and running to hug him. "We have two more to our party. This is Mr. Laurence Beaumont." Laurence dismounted also, and bowed to him. "Mr. Beaumont's brother, Thomas, is in the coach and may need to be taken to bed, I fear. He's still weak after a bout of the flux. As for us, we are thirsty!"

The man laughed at this, and introduced himself to Laurence. "John Cottrell, Mr. Beaumont. My servant will tend to your brother while we're at table. I'll have some hot broth prepared for him."

It was only the three of them at supper. The night was mild, and the casements were open all about, letting in sweet country air and the noise of crickets. While they ate, Cottrell talked of the weather and the harvest, and the gleaning rites celebrated by his labourers; but eventually he began to yawn. "We simple folk aren't used to staying up after dark unless there's a moon and work can be done," he explained.

"There is a moon tonight," said Mistress Savage.

"But she's a virgin still, a mere slip of a girl. Well, I'm to bed. Stay and drink as long as you wish, and pay no heed to me."

"Thank you," Laurence said, "but I should see to my brother."

"I'll show you to your chamber. Isabella, we shall put you in the one next to it, facing south."

"I know," she told him, nodding. "I shall be up soon."

As Laurence and Cottrell ascended, Cottrell asked, "I hope it won't inconvenience you to share your brother's bed?"

He insisted that it would not, and they said good night.

The doorway to the bedchamber was so low that he had to duck his head to enter. Woodruff and lavender were strewn upon the floor in the old fashion, and Tom lay fast asleep on one side of the bed, snoring lightly. Not feeling tired himself, Laurence went over to the window and looked out at the ripening moon yellow in the sky, in a feathering of bright stars, and at the fields spread out, dotted with neatly rolled bales of hay. He could hear pigeons, from a nearby cote, and, as before, the rasp of crickets. Perhaps in some other country house Seward was looking out at the same moon, he reflected.

He sat down on his side of the bed and dragged off his boots, then started to unbutton his doublet. His throat was tight and his eyes stung, as though the herbs were affecting him; their scent overpowered the small chamber. But it was not that, he knew. Cottrell had reminded him of a quiet life tied to the change of seasons rather than the tumult of unnatural events, the life led by most people that was now closed to him. In a little over a month he had succeeded in threatening the future of his family and ruining Seward's tranquility, and if the duties and obligations of his rank had always weighed upon him, he would now have to fight in a war that he did not care about, for a side itself poisonously divided. The coded letters and his own past had made him a slave to Colonel Hoare, and he was being chased by a bunch of regicides. Fate had spared him so many times from death abroad, only to bring him home and play on him this awful joke.

His brooding was disturbed by a scream, short and sharp, then a moment later Mistress Savage called out his name. He opened the door, and at the sight of her felt considerably less gloomy: she wore a nightgown of the finest muslin, and her dark hair hung in loose, heavy curls about her shoulders.

"A bat," she whispered. "A bat has got into the hangings of my bed. You must remove it for me."

"I'm at your service," he said, and followed her into her chamber.

She shut her door and motioned to a tiny black shape clinging to the curtains around the bed. "You will think me a coward. In general, I'm not, but I have a particular loathing for these creatures."

"Why don't you blow out the candle," he suggested.

She did so, retreating as he shook the curtain, and the animal flew off obediently through the open window. "Thank you, Mr. Beaumont!" she said, as though he had just rescued her from some fire-snorting monster, and the triviality of her fear as compared to his own dismal plight struck him as so absurd that he began to laugh. "You are laughing at me!" she exclaimed, giving him a push, which he allowed to send him onto the bed.

"Oh no," he said. "We all have our fears." Her gown, with the faint moonlight behind it, was quite diaphanous. He was most intrigued as to what she would do next.

She reclined beside him, and he could see the curves of her breasts, and the faint shadow of her nipples beneath the gauzy fabric. "It is nice to see that you can laugh. Your expression earlier today was positively forbidding. I hardly dared open my mouth lest I say something to provoke your further displeasure." She paused. "Mr. Beaumont – may I call you Beaumont?"

He nodded, trying not to appraise her too obviously. "What should I call you?"

"Isabella. I cannot have you call me Savage. Not on such short acquaintance, at any rate! But I am sure we are going to be friends." A promising start, he thought, and waited for her to continue. "Beaumont, I have some idea why you are in such a foul mood. So I am offering to help you."

"Why?" he asked, wondering just what had been said at her little party the previous night.

"Don't frown at me like that. I suppose you are suspicious of me because you have heard that I am Digby's mistress. It is untrue, and a gross slander to both Digby and me."

"Why would I care whose mistress you are," he said, at which she looked piqued. "I mean – it's none of my business. I'm very grateful for your generosity towards my brother, and your friend Mr. Cottrell has been –"

"I am aware that you have been put in a most difficult position," she interrupted. "And I have an idea as to how you can get out of it."

He gazed into her eyes a moment longer. "Perhaps you should shut the window," he said, rising from her bed. "Another bat might fly in. Good night, Isabella."

She leapt up and grabbed him by the arms. "Beaumont, listen to me. Trust me to help you."

About to remove her hands, he gave in to temptation and kissed her instead. She offered no immediate resistance, and he was beginning to contemplate leading her back towards the bed when she stamped on his foot. "How dare you take such liberties," she said, although she sounded more challenging than angry. "If I want you, I shall tell you so."

"Won't I have any choice in the matter?"

"I believe part of you has chosen already," she murmured, and touched him lightly there, making him shiver.

"Who's taking liberties now," he said, hopeful that she might take more.

Then he heard Tom's voice, from the corridor outside. "Excuse me for disturbing you, Mistress Savage, but have you seen my brother?"

"What do you want, Tom?" Laurence snapped.

"I – I'm not well."

Laurence swore mutely.

Isabella was smiling. "You had better attend to him. We shall talk again tomorrow. Good night, Beaumont."

"Good night," he said.

Laurence caught a faint snigger from Tom on entering their room. "How far did you get with her?" Tom asked him. He did not respond, still coping with the physical discomfort of unsatisfied desire. "So sorry I spoilt your fun," Tom laughed quietly. "You lecherous old goat. Is that how you repay her kindness, by trying your best to fuck her?"

Laurence took a deep breath to master his temper. "You said you were unwell, Tom, so why don't you go to sleep. You'll need your strength for tomorrow."

The following morning at breakfast, Isabella seemed in excellent spirits and announced that she would take Tom's horse again. As they resumed their journey, she asked Laurence, "Did you like Mr. Cottrell?"

"Very much," he said.

"He and his wife nursed me through a difficult illness once, long ago, and I have not forgotten his kindness to me, nor his wife's. She is dead now, bless her soul. Let us ride towards Northampton," she went on more briskly. "There is an old road that should be serviceable in this weather." After they had gone some miles, she urged her horse nearer to his. "Beaumont, may we talk again?"

"Why not."

"I shall be direct, if you don't mind. I know that Colonel Hoare has pressed you into his service. Such work is not altogether new to you, I hear." Laurence said nothing. "If you aren't aware yet, Hoare despises Falkland's peace overtures to the rebels, and is eager to have his lordship replaced by a Secretary of State less pacifically inclined. In fact, I have cause to believe he is now working towards that end. If he is not stopped, he could seriously damage Falkland's reputation – which surely you would not wish," she added, when Laurence remained silent. "Your father is a good friend of his lordship's, is he not?"

Laurence heaved a sigh. "Isabella, why are you telling me all this?"

Her eyes lingered on him in such a way that he was reminded of his frustration the night before. "Because I've taken a fancy to you," she said, as if reading his thoughts.

"So quickly?"

"Yes. And I am worried for *you*, as well as for Falkland. Hoare is an odious upstart who abuses his agents terribly if he has the faintest suspicion that they might cross him. He expects them to come to heel like obedient dogs. And you are not that kind of man, if I am any judge of character. Beaumont," she persisted, "you will be close to him. You might be able to catch him out, in his scheming."

Laurence started to laugh. "Now I understand! You're not Digby's mistress, you're his errand boy. He must want to get rid of Hoare for his own reasons." She glared at him. "It's the truth, isn't it?"

"No, it's not. And in time you will regret not listening to me."

He laughed again and shook his head. "What I do regret is my brother's interruption last night. *That* was most ill-timed."

"By God, you are presumptuous."

"I'm being *direct*. And with respect, I don't need any more of your help, thank you very much." He wheeled his horse about and cantered back to the coach, which had been trundling along behind them. "Stop," he said to the driver.

Tom stuck his head out of the coach window. "What's the matter, Laurence?"

"Get out, Tom. You said you were fit to ride, and we'll make better speed on horseback."

As Tom hesitated, Isabella approached them. "He can continue with me as far as Banbury," she said, in a clipped tone, "even if you prefer not to."

"Oh no," said Laurence. "We wouldn't dare take any further liberties with you."

She scowled, and jumped down from her horse. "Then put my saddle back in the coach." He did so, replacing it with Tom's. Once Tom had vacated the coach, she entered and slammed shut the door. And on her command, the coach took off.

Tom was chuckling as he mounted his horse. "Too bad for you, Laurence," he remarked. "And she was such a beauty!"

Too bad indeed, Laurence thought, but after the trouble that Juana had brought upon him, he did not intend to make the same mistake twice.

VI.

He and Juana had arrived at Paris without further incident. Either they had lost their pursuer or he had been satisfied by his search at Lille, for they saw no more of him, and as they rode along the banks of the Seine, Laurence felt a new optimism. Here at last was life untouched by war: there were boats unloading plentiful cargo of wines and cloth, and hawkers peddling hotcakes and birds in cages and ribbons and strange fruits to the milling crowds of people. Entering the heart of the city, he was surprised how well he could remember its geography from the last occasion that he had visited, on his foreign tour with William Seward.

Once they had stabled the horses, he took Juana to market to buy a change of clothing, and then, much against her will, to a bath-house. Afterwards they repaired to a tavern, where he ordered a lavish meal.

"It's the last we'll have together, so it might as well be the best," he said.

"Let me stay with you tonight, Monsieur," she begged. "I swear I will be gone tomorrow."

Feeling relaxed and indulgent, he agreed. It was dusk, and rainy, and he did not like to think of her sheltering in some damp alleyway, so he bought them two private chambers in a hostel.

When he came to say goodbye to her the next morning, she clung to him, pressing her face against his chest. "You are the only *gadjo* who has ever treated me with any respect," she moaned. "Let me stay."

"Come on, Juana," he said, laughing. "This city is as rich as The Hague. You'll do just as well here picking pockets." Without another word, she pushed him away as though insulted, seized her belongings, and rushed out. "Goodbye to you, too," he muttered after her.

He lazed about contentedly in bed until suppertime, then went to the same tavern as before, and ate and drank with some officers from the young King Louis' court who later invited him to a social gathering. Here he fell into the company of two women, and he spent the night with them, in a tangle of limbs, only to return wonderfully sated to his own hostel in the early afternoon.

Juana was sitting on the floor, her baggage beside her, at the door to his chamber. In her lap was a purse of expensive calfskin, and she wore a new, gaudy yellow dress. Her hair was curled and pinned up to imitate the French fashion, though crudely, as if she had done it herself. Her lips bore traces of paint. All these additions to her toilette had the effect of making her look younger, more vulnerable, and cheap at the same time.

"What are you doing here?" he asked, puzzled by her transformed appearance.

She gave a sorrowful sniff. "I can tell where *you've* been. You reek of perfume."

When he unlocked the door, she entered without being asked and planted herself on the bed, holding the purse to her chest.

"Juana, what more do you want," he said. "I did as I promised, didn't I?"

"Yes, Monsieur. And that is why I came back. I owe you a confession. The man who attacked me at Lille is the one we saw on the road."

"Ah, so you finally admit it."

"He tracked us all the way from Simeon's house." She unfastened the purse and emptied out a heap of gold coins. "I took this from the Englishman that Marie had in bed with her the evening we left. The one who chased us is the Englishman's servant." Laurence stared at the coins and then at her. "You can't be upset with me, Monsieur," she went on, in a defensive tone. "I needed money for the journey, and it was a clean theft, as clean as any of your card tricks. I took his sword, too, the one I told you that Simeon gave to us. He did not see me, because Marie had already drawn the bed curtains. Not even the servant saw me then. But we rode out in such a hurry, remember? That's how they knew to come after us."

"Why didn't you tell me before?"

"You would have abandoned me!"

"No I wouldn't have, though by God you'd have deserved it. This is English gold, newly minted," he remarked, sitting down beside her to examine one of the coins, on which was stamped the profile of King Charles. "Hundreds of pounds."

"It's ours now," Juana said.

"It's *yours*. You're a rich woman, you won't have to steal again."
More gently he added, "You've made your confession. Now you can
leave. Goodbye, Juana, and good luck spending your fortune."

He lay back and closed his eyes, hoping she would make some
move to depart with her wealth. Then to his amazement he felt her
hands inexpertly caressing his thighs. "Well, well," he said, sitting up
again, and grabbed her by the wrists. "Have you reconsidered our terms
on setting out? Is that why you got yourself all dressed up? It's not in
the best of taste, but you show your intentions clearly enough."

She pulled her hands away, and whispered, "The servant is here in
Paris, Monsieur. Yesterday, I saw him following me. I . . . I thought I
had lost him, but he may be waiting to catch me outside." Neither of
them spoke for some time; Laurence was too angry. "Monsieur," she
continued, "he knows your name. That night in the cellar, he kept
talking at me and shaking me, and I couldn't understand any of what
he said, except for your name: Beaumont. He must have asked about us
at Simeon's. No one inside the house would have betrayed you, but the
grooms hated you because you had your freedom with the women.
They hated us both."

"I should hate you, too," Laurence said quietly. "You put my life in
as much danger as yours, and only when you think you need me again
do I find out about it."

"But, Monsieur, you must help me! The servant will kill me
whether or not I give back the money."

"I wouldn't blame him in the least."

She burst into tears, which seemed genuine, and he felt a kind of
pity for her, that she should have guarded her virtue so zealously for
years, only to offer it to him as a last resort and find herself humiliated.

He started to gather up the coins and replace them in the purse
but stopped on noticing an odd lump beneath its silk lining. Ripping
apart the fabric, he drew out some folded sheets of paper, durable but

so thin as to be almost transparent, covered in lines of writing. "This is a code, or a cipher," he said, inspecting them. "Why didn't his servant find the purse when he attacked you?"

"Because of the dark," she said miserably. "And I had buried it deep in the straw, along with his sword."

"Then he wasn't looking for the money when he told you to strip off your clothes. He was after these papers. That's why he searched you as he did. Christ!" Laurence exclaimed, studying them with new interest. "They must be worth as much to his master as the gold. Perhaps more."

"How could paper be worth more than gold?"

"I don't know. And I don't understand why he didn't ambush us long ago, to get what he wanted."

"You would have fought him off," she declared, with childlike confidence. "You would have killed him."

"If I didn't then, I may have to now."

"Bless you, Monsieur –"

"I'm not doing it for you, I'm doing it for myself. And if I hear another lie from your mouth, or if you give me any more nonsense, I'm finished with you." She nodded resignedly, which amused him, even though he was still angry. "And one last thing." He detached the pins holding up her coiffure and tossed them aside. "Don't wear your hair like that again. It doesn't suit you at all."

VII.

At Stratford-upon-Avon, only about twenty miles from Chipping Campden, Tom suffered a relapse. Laurence fed him the remains of the opium, and they pressed on, stopping just a couple of times for Tom to ease the gripe in his belly. Late in the night, they reached the gatehouse to Lord Beaumont's estate. Laurence ordered the gatekeeper's son to run ahead with news of their arrival, and then arranged for a litter to carry Tom the rest of the way, while he followed, leading their tired horses.

Lord and Lady Beaumont were waiting with Mary at the entrance to the hall, and as he walked in, they bombarded him with anxious inquiries about the invalid. When they were assured that Tom's life was in no danger, and once he had been put safely to bed, accompanied by his wife, Lord Beaumont observed to Laurence, "You look worn out, sir. It seems we shall have to nurse you both back to health!"

Laurence could not even smile; he had spent too much time on the road with Tom, and he now feared that the Colonel's men might arrive at the house to arrest him before he could get to the meeting place near Aylesbury. "I can't stay," he said. "I have to set out again at first light tomorrow."

"On what business?" his mother asked.

"It's a private matter."

Lord Beaumont frowned at him. "Did you perchance pay a call on Lord Falkland in Nottingham?"

"Yes, I did."

"Has it any connection with your need to ride out so early?" When Laurence hesitated, his father said to Lady Beaumont, "I should have informed you, my dear. I suggested that Laurence inquire whether he could be of assistance to Falkland. He is so clever with figures and languages and ciphers, I thought there might be a place for him in Falkland's service. And I must confess," he added to Laurence, "I wrote to him on that subject."

"So he told me," Laurence said.

"I hope he also told you that I did impress upon him your concerns, and that I wished him to treat you well."

Laurence groaned inwardly.

"Well treated?" cried Lady Beaumont. "My lord, have you taken leave of your senses?" She turned on Laurence. "What have you agreed to do for him? Has he employed you in some kind of . . . underhanded occupation? For if you made any such commitment, I will not allow it!"

"Oh my dear," murmured Lord Beaumont. "Falkland would never bring dishonour upon our son."

"Tell me, Laurence," she insisted.

How astute she was, he thought, and how unworldly was his father. "I've made no commitment to Falkland," he answered, with absolute truth. "In fact, when I was in Nottingham, I enlisted in Wilmot's Horse."

They appeared astonished. "I must congratulate you," his father said, at last. "We were aware how hard it would be for you to take up arms again."

"But why not serve with Thomas' troop?" objected Lady Beaumont.

Was nothing ever good enough for her, mused Laurence. "Wilmot's an old friend of mine, and I owe him a favour," he replied. "You'll have to be satisfied with that."

CHAPTER SEVEN

I.

On the way to London with Lord Spencer, Falkland pondered yet again why Mr. Beaumont had failed to keep their appointment. He still refused to accept the explanation Colonel Hoare had offered that morning, as they waited a whole hour for the man to appear.

"Beaumont's a complete and utter scoundrel," he had told Falkland, after describing what he had learnt from his investigations amongst the veterans of the foreign war. "I reckon he was lying to you about how he acquired those letters. He may know more about the regicides than he was willing to admit, and after he saw you, he probably lacked the nerve to defend his concocted story. As I said, my lord, you must let me question him."

"That I forbid," Falkland had insisted, appalled by Hoare's imputations, as by his eagerness to interrogate Mr. Beaumont, given what the process would entail. "And I don't believe you. He was begging me to act on the intelligence."

"Then will you alert the King as to a plot that threatens his life?" Hoare had inquired, coldly.

"I must know more about it first, from Mr. Beaumont. I shall speak with him myself upon my return. And afterwards of course I shall address His Majesty."

Colonel Hoare tended to place too much faith in the veracity of rumour, Falkland thought, and whatever were Beaumont's sins abroad, his father had written him a high recommendation. He deserved another hearing.

On arrival in the city, Falkland found it as noisy, crowded, and smelly as always; he could not understand how anyone would choose it over the peace and cleanliness of the countryside. But many things had changed: playhouses were closed, the taverns were half-empty, and the apprentices had left work to train with their own bands to defend the capital. Even women were employed digging earthworks, skirts kilted up, singing psalms as they wielded their shovels. Apparently all the churches had been stripped of the art that they had housed for centuries, and while Falkland did not share his mother's Catholicism nor her love of Episcopal trappings, he was sad to imagine statues defaced, and frescoes and panels whitewashed over.

It saddened him further to realise, as he began negotiations with Parliament at Whitehall, that he had embarked upon a bootless mission. From the outset, he had predicted that the King had not gone far enough in agreeing only to put a formal end to hostilities if both sides withdrew the accusations of treason each had brought against the other. And so, in a private conversation with the leaders of Parliament, Falkland extended His Majesty's terms, saying that the King was ready to consent to a thorough reformation of religion, and to anything else that they could reasonably desire. He knew that he might be compromising himself, for His Majesty had just once, and very vaguely, intimated such broad concessions, but in the end Parliament voted to reject even these. Falkland sent a messenger post-haste to Nottingham with the news, then sat in his coach alone and wept.

On his last night in the capital, he and Spencer were invited to attend a feast in the Banqueting House, to signal a close to their visit.

He wondered if the location had been selected to heap upon them a final insult. For the House, constructed and decorated richly in honour of His Majesty's father, King James, whose resplendent form had recently been depicted on its ceiling by Rubens, had formerly been the scene of many royal ceremonies and pageants. How ironic, Falkland reflected, that he must now sup with men who might blow out his guts if he met them on the battlefield. Nonetheless, social decorum had to be observed, and so he and Spencer, in full regalia as members of the House of Lords, would go to break bread with the enemy.

He returned to dress at the house where he was staying, that of his friend Edmund Waller, who had been one of a minority in Parliament that voted to accept His Majesty's peace terms. As he walked in, he was surprised to hear music: Waller must have come home early from the Commons and was now in his parlour playing an air on the bass viol, with another man at the virginals. Falkland listened, unwilling to disturb them, the minor key suiting his mood. But they had heard his footsteps and broke off.

"Falkland," cried Waller, coming out to him, "you tried your best."

"Parliament has given me what amounts to an unequivocal declaration of war," said Falkland. "How could the King possibly commit to withdrawing his protection from his advisors and, yet more outrageous, have them pay the costs of this war as traitors to the realm?"

"Pym and his allies would love to see Lord Digby's head stuck over Traitor's Gate," Waller remarked, with a smile.

"Mine too, perhaps."

"No, my dear friend. You have their respect, and always will. And be comforted. London is far from lost to the King. He has only to march as far as Reading, and he'll see that his capital has not deserted him. I'll write to you, and keep you apprised of the climate here."

"I pray you, be careful," Falkland warned. "Letters can be intercepted. For you, especially, as a Member of Parliament, it would be unwise to risk anything of the sort. And now," he added, with a sigh, "I must prepare myself for the banquet."

Yet it was not as much of an ordeal as he expected. He had been seated beside the Earl of Pembroke, who behaved very graciously towards him, and expressed deep regret that an impasse had been reached.

"My lord," Falkland said, as the last platters of a meat and fish course were cleared away, "I am pleased to discover that you have not hardened yourself against His Majesty, after your last encounter at Newmarket when he rejected your own peace petition." The King must have incurred Pembroke's wrath long before, Falkland thought, when he dismissed him from the position of Lord Chamberlain. It was amazing that Pembroke should seem to bear no grudge. Falkland had always known him to be a choleric sort, sensitive to the slightest breach of his dignity.

"He is our anointed King, may God preserve him," said Pembroke. "At any rate, if a campaign this autumn can't be avoided, which I fear it can't, Englishmen will at least be taught what it is to spill each other's blood on home soil. When the armies break for the winter months we will have more of a chance to negotiate a peace."

"Unless one side emerges triumphant," Falkland pointed out.

"But that would leave the other desirous of revenge and restitution. My lord," Pembroke went on more urgently, "I think we have much to discuss. Would you permit me to take you in my coach wherever you are staying tonight? We could then talk a while undisturbed."

"Very well. I am at Edmund Waller's house."

"The poet?"

"Yes, and my good friend, although I had lost touch with him lately because of our country's woes."

"We have all lost touch with friends – another reason we must speak."

After the company rose for a final health, Falkland said his goodbyes, gave instructions to his servant Stephens to follow him, and accompanied Pembroke outside.

"The Banqueting House always brings me back to the old days of King James' reign," Pembroke observed, as they settled themselves in his coach. "I was quite a favourite with him, until George Villiers displaced me in his affections, and got created Duke of Buckingham for it."

"At least you did not meet your death at the hand of an assassin, as did the late Duke," Falkland reminded him.

"Too true that being a favourite of kings has its dangers," Pembroke said, with a hint of bitterness. As the horses picked up speed, he began again, "I should like to lay before you a proposal. I ask you to mention it to nobody as yet, not even your closest allies. Have I your word?"

"My lord," said Falkland, "I cannot be party to anything that might harm His Majesty's interests, nor will I betray the confidence of anyone who has chosen to serve him."

"Be assured," Pembroke said earnestly, "I would never seek to impugn your position as Secretary of State."

"My position is not at issue here. My concern is to do what is right. Whether it is perceived as such, I do not care. I must satisfy my conscience."

"That is exactly why I would discuss this matter with you! Because you are a man of honour and principle who loves his country and abhors bloodshed. As do I, my lord, as do I!"

Falkland took a moment to respond, surprised by the heat in Pembroke's voice. "What is it that you propose?"

"We need to form an alliance of moderates on both sides: like-thinking men, such as ourselves. Before the end of the autumn campaign there is little to be gained by open discussion, so we have almost three months to prepare the ground."

"And if there *is* a clear victor?"

Pembroke shook his head vehemently, his fierce, aquiline profile exaggerated by the flame of the single lantern within the coach. "My lord, a civil war does not end in clear victory. The defeated tend to rise again, perhaps in five or ten years, perhaps in the next generation. And most of us do not want to shed the blood of a brother or a cousin or a friend. So how can war be stopped, after today's vote, you may ask."

"I do indeed," said Falkland.

"By a strong and decided group of us who can present King and Parliament with a *fait accompli*, a well-knit agreement amongst principal ministers to govern our kingdom according to new laws. Our immediate task is to approach those whom we think might favour such a scheme, and canvass their views, without being explicit as to our plan."

"Behind His Majesty's back? We won't succeed."

"He will be ruined if we do not!" Pembroke shut his eyes tight for a moment, as if imagining this calamity. "His nephew Rupert may win him every battle in the field," he continued in a more forceful tone, "but too many of his subjects have made it evident that they will not accept his governance as before, and he will have to find an accommodation, whatever the outcome of an armed conflict! With the sword you may hack off a branch. But if the root remains, what have you achieved, other than to strengthen its growth?"

Falkland could not deny this. "And who are you considering, on the King's side?"

"After you, Culpeper, Lord Spencer, and Edward Hyde, the lawyer. And Lord Digby, possibly."

"Digby? You can't think of *him* as a potential ally!"

"He is now generally detested here, I grant you. But two years ago he moved in Parliament for a select committee to remonstrate with His Majesty on *the deplorable state of the kingdom*, if I recall his exact words. He was not always inimical to our aims, and he could be swayed."

"Swayed too easily," Falkland said, picturing Digby's round, angelic face and duplicitous blue eyes. "He shifts like the wind."

"Then start with those you can trust. I shall do the same. There are many here who actively disagree with the radicals. Your friend Waller proved as much in voting for your terms of peace." Falkland nodded, guardedly. "We must correspond with each other within the month," Pembroke said, "in a secure code known only to the two of us."

To Falkland's relief, the coach had arrived at Waller's house and was slowing to a stop. "Within a month?" he queried. "That is too soon."

"But are you agreed, my lord?" Pembroke seized Falkland by the arm, as though he might fly out of the coach to avoid committing himself. "Is this not the sole means of preventing our country from disaster? The King toys with one policy and another, and in the meanwhile, we could negotiate a thousand times and go nowhere. Will you join me?"

"Let me consider it. I cannot be rushed into deciding. Indeed, as I often say, when it is not necessary to make a decision, it is necessary *not* to make a decision."

"You may be certain, my lord, that some decision is very necessary at this juncture!" Pembroke fell silent as his driver came and swung open the door, drawing out an ingenious little set of stairs for Falkland to descend onto the street. As Falkland was about to make use of them, Pembroke held him back again. "You know Dr. John Earle, do you not?"

"Yes," Falkland replied. "He is very dear to me and my wife."

"He was once my chaplain. He left my service when our politics did not agree." Pembroke sighed heavily. "It is my fondest wish to heal the breach between us, and beg his pardon. Earle was also, you see, my spiritual counsellor, and I am much in need of his guidance these days. Would you be so kind as to take him a letter from me?"

"I should be glad to," Falkland said, trying to conceal more amazement; he had not imagined Pembroke capable of such humility.

Pembroke reached into a side panel in the cushioned wall of the coach and withdrew a slim, sealed document. "I shall remember this, my lord," he said, handing it to Falkland. "And I look forward to our further communication."

II.

At Thame, Colonel Hoare's guards greeted Laurence with evident mistrust, and they also had worrying news: some of the Earl of Essex's troops were on their way to occupy Aylesbury for Parliament.

"If we all descend on the Black Bull together, we may scare our man off," Laurence told them, though he thought the chances of finding Poole there were worse than slim. "And we should scout the place, before trying to arrest him. He may not be alone."

The guards, on orders not to lose him, disliked receiving his instructions. After much argument, Laurence rode the nine miles or so into Aylesbury accompanied only by their chief, Corporal Wilson. They stabled their horses at the Black Bull, and walked into the taproom, where Laurence made inquiries of a maidservant.

"What d'you want with Mr. Poole?" she demanded.

"I'm an old friend of his," he said. "Haven't seen him in a long time."

"He's been staying for weeks now," she said more amiably. "But he's not in. He went out just this morning and hasn't returned yet. He's got our cheapest rooms, sir, at the back."

"More than one room? He must have company, then."

"Not at present, sir, though there are a couple of men who come and go."

"I might know them," Laurence said to Wilson, who was listening keenly. "What are their names?" he asked the woman.

"I've heard Mr. Poole address one of them as Tyler." Laurence shrugged, as if he had never heard of any Tyler. "I've no idea about the other."

"Can you describe him?"

"He's a gentleman, sir, always polite and well dressed, with light brown hair and a touch of grey in his beard."

"Hmm. Could be any number of my acquaintances."

"When do you expect Mr. Poole?" Wilson interjected.

"I can't say, sir."

"Would you please pass on a message?" Laurence asked. "Tell him Mr. Beaumont will await him here, around eleven o'clock tomorrow. And thanks for your trouble," he added, slipping her a few coins.

Outside they looked about, checking the number of entrances to the inn and calculating where the guards should be stationed so as to be inconspicuous, if Poole appeared at the meeting. Then they took a stroll around the back of the inn. The conspirators had chosen their accommodations well, Laurence thought: their windows gave directly onto a kitchen midden, the reek of which would dissuade anyone from loitering. But there was a thick vine clinging to the wall just below Poole's window that appeared sufficiently sturdy to support the weight of a man, and might allow the possibility of breaking in.

As he and the guards ate supper in Thame that evening, Laurence suggested how they should proceed. "Wilson and I will ride in together, but I'll enter the taproom by myself," he said. "The rest of you should get to Aylesbury in good time. There are enough of you to post a single man at each exit of the inn, with about five to spare who should hold off on an arrest until Wilson gives the signal."

"Who's issuing orders here?" objected Wilson, though in the end he accepted the plan.

Hoare had instilled in his men a fair sense of discipline, but over supper, at Laurence's subtle prompting, they indulged rather too freely in ale and mutton stew, and he gained some unexpected advantages: first, he discovered that Hoare had told them very little about their mission, other than that they must capture Poole, and second, by midnight they were all fast asleep in the large communal chamber. Even the man told to keep watch on Laurence was snoring away, his pistol on his lap.

Laurence rose stealthily and crept out, and down to the stables, then saddled his horse and headed again for Aylesbury. Silence had fallen over the town, and he met no one on the street, not even a night watchman. At the Black Bull, all was just as peaceful. He tethered his horse and passed into the back courtyard, disturbing only a family of rats as it tunnelled through the kitchen refuse. He saw light at a window of Poole's rooms. Breathing through his mouth to avoid the stench, he sought a foothold at the base of the vine and tested its strength before levering himself up until he hung almost parallel to the window. As he was wondering how long he could hold on, the casement flew open.

"Why didn't you tell me what was in those papers I brought you?" came an angry voice that he guessed must belong to Tyler. Someone replied, too quietly for Laurence to catch any words, though he felt a ripple of excitement: Poole did indeed have company. "I knew Beaumont would make something of your code," the first voice said, "him and that old warlock Seward." Laurence cursed under his breath: Tyler must have found the letter to Earle while he was ransacking Seward's chambers. "Don't think I can be played for a simpleton just because I'm not schooled as you are," Tyler carried on, sneeringly. "I'd say the more you learn, the less you see things for what they are. I can fix Beaumont tomorrow, as he arrives."

"As you fixed that poor boy in the College?" Laurence recognised Poole's voice, full of revulsion. "And what if he doesn't have the letters on him?"

"He will." A head emerged from the window, and Laurence squeezed himself back against the wall, out of sight. Someone spat into the yard, then the head disappeared, and an arc of liquid surged from within, finally dwindling to a patter of drops. "I pissed on a rat," Tyler laughed. "Nearly drowned it."

"Would you shut that casement," came a third voice, extremely faint, and the window closed.

Laurence slid down from his perch and ran back to his horse, inhaling deeply to rid his lungs of the foul air. The third voice seemed somehow familiar, although he could not place it.

On his return to Thame, he roused the guards. As he was explaining how Poole was not alone, they glowered at him as if they trusted him even less than before. "We could make the arrest tonight," he urged. "These other men must be Poole's accomplices. We'll have all three of them."

"No, we'll stick to the plan," Wilson declared. "And from now on, Mr. Beaumont, no more tricks."

Laurence lay down to rest until morning, sleepless, bemoaning this lost opportunity. After breakfast, he and Corporal Wilson galloped off for Aylesbury in tense silence. Wilson would only pass him the letters once they had arrived at the entrance to the Black Bull's taproom, but at least he did not insist on their going in together.

As he walked through the door, Laurence half expected Tyler to be hidden in some corner, waiting to ambush him. Instead, however, he found the serving woman he had spoken with the day before.

"You asked me about that gentleman, sir," she said. "His name is Mr. Rose, according to the innkeeper. He and Tyler got here yesterday evening, not long after your friend Poole." She pointed across the room to a table where a hunched, black-clad figure was sitting. "There he is, sir."

Poole looked much as he had on the last occasion, worn and fretful. "You've kept me waiting, Mr. Beaumont," he said, standing to bow as Laurence approached. "I almost gave up on you."

"Better late than never," said Laurence, taking a seat opposite his.

"Do you have what I asked for?"

"Do you have my money?"

Poole placed a cloth bag on the table and opened it so that Laurence could see inside. Laurence, in turn, produced the letters, and laid them in front of Poole, who frowned at them in such a way that Laurence suspected he had not seen them before. How strange, and a pity to find out too late: he could have been given copies, rather than the real documents.

"This is all of them?" Poole inquired, confirming Laurence's suspicion.

"Yes. What else did you expect?" he said.

"Why did you deny you had them, back in August?"

"I thought I might be able to make more off them than you'd offered me. Unfortunately, I couldn't. I must thank you, Mr. Poole," Laurence went on. "This money will buy me passage out of the country. I'll be leaving as soon as I can, and this time I won't return. I don't like what's happening here."

"Who does," said Poole glumly.

"By the way," Laurence asked, on a whim, "why did you say the owner of these letters had been robbed at a tavern?" Poole frowned again. "It wasn't a tavern, it was a bawdy house. The best in The Hague, as a matter of fact. I should know. I used to live there." Poole gaped at him. "So you were lied to about that. You've got some nasty bedfellows, Mr. Poole. That servant of your master's, for one. He must be straining at the leash, eager to finish me off. Tell your master it's not worth the trouble."

"You could still talk, if you broke the code," Poole ventured.

"You must be well aware that I couldn't break all of it. Besides, what would I say?" Laurence leant closer, to whisper in his ear. "That there's a plot to spirit away the King and murder him, but we don't know who the assassins are, nor how nor when nor where they intend to do the deed? It's an absurd tale with an even clumsier plot, of which I now have not a shred of evidence. Goodbye, Mr. Poole." He grabbed the bag and rose, but on seeing Poole's face he sat back down again, quickly. "My God! Weren't you told how it would end?"

Poole was rigid with shock; he had not even touched the letters. "I – I don't know what you mean," he quavered.

"It's not my business how much this man has lied to you, but you should make it yours if you want to get any older. To be frank, I'm glad to be rid of them," Laurence said, indicating the letters. "They were becoming a burden to me. Now the burden is yours."

"I thank you, Mr. Beaumont," Poole said, as though he meant the opposite.

"Oh no, I thank *you*."

Laurence turned once on his way out, and saw that Poole had not moved. He was equally dumbfounded at this turn of events, and sorry for Poole, who might be tortured and hanged for a crime of which he was innocent. There was no way to save him. Laurence had to save himself, and execute the most difficult stage of his plan.

He found Corporal Wilson alone. "My men haven't come," Wilson said urgently. "I don't know what's kept them."

Laurence swore and rushed back into the taproom, with Wilson behind him. Poole had now vanished, no doubt upstairs to deliver the letters to Mr. Rose. "Let's try the back entrance," Laurence told Wilson, who cocked his pistol. "We can get in through the kitchen door and go up to his rooms."

Just as they were crossing that other, foul-smelling courtyard, a shot blasted past them. Tyler, Laurence thought. They ducked, but a second ball caught Wilson on the arm. He cried out, dropping his pistol. And all of a sudden they heard a new sound: the combined thunder of hooves and clink of steel, far too loud for the ten or so riders they had been anticipating.

"Parliament's troopers," gasped Wilson, as the courtyard became a flurry of activity, people racing hither and thither.

"Let's move," Laurence said, and they pushed through the confusion to find their horses.

Mounting hastily, they charged onto the street. A party of some hundred cavalrymen were approaching in their direction. Laurence veered off towards the fields, Wilson a short distance behind, and they spurred their horses to a gallop, leaping over the hedgerows, until they were some miles to the west of town.

"Slow down!" Wilson cried.

Laurence reined in and saw that Wilson's sleeve was dripping blood. "Oh Christ," he said. "Let me see the wound." He tore open the cloth and examined it. "I'm sorry – that ball was meant for me." With his knife he cut a strip from his own cloak and bound Wilson's arm tightly, after which they let their winded animals move at a trot.

"I can't jump no more hedges, sir," Wilson panted.

"I'm *sir* to you now, am I? All right, we'll go back to the road."

Parliament's troops must have passed by not long before on their way to Aylesbury, for the road was strewn with moist piles of horse dung. "Essex may have occupied Thame by now," Laurence said. "I think it would be safer for us to head straight for Oxford."

"How far is that?"

"About sixteen miles."

Wilson clenched his jaw and nodded.

They skirted Thame and continued on the main road again towards Wheatley, their pace slackening. At this rate it would be some time before they reached the city, and Wilson was still losing blood. Then, up ahead, Laurence saw horsemen. About to pull Wilson into a thicket of trees to hide, he stopped. "Your comrades," he remarked dryly.

Some of their horses were bleeding from shot, and a guard was dead, lying crosswise over his saddle. Another fellow had a gash to his thigh.

"What happened?" Laurence demanded of them.

"We skirmished with a few rebel stragglers on the road to Aylesbury – thought we'd show 'em what we were made of," one boasted.

"Took down more than we lost," the wounded fellow put in.

"You stupid arses!" Laurence yelled. "And what the fuck are you doing here?"

They looked more sheepishly at each other. "They gave us chase," the first man admitted. "We had to retreat. Wasn't no point in going back to Thame or we'd run into more of them."

"Now, then, Mr. Beaumont," said Wilson in a stern voice, as though regretting his earlier lapse of authority, "Colonel Hoare will want a word with you."

"I look forward to that," Laurence told him, in the same tone.

III.

A fortuitous escape, Radcliff congratulated himself, as he raced out of Aylesbury at breakneck speed. He wished he could have seen Beaumont dead, but Tyler had been chafing for a kill and would not fail him this time; and inside his coffer were all his precious letters, reunited like a happy family. He could not keep the coffer with him, since he was obliged to rejoin his troop, so he headed first towards Madam Musgrave's house at Faringdon, where he thought he might find a secure place to hide it. He also very much wanted to pay a visit on his wife.

The journey took him much longer than it should have, since he had to dodge military patrols all the way, and when at last he arrived, he guessed at past ten o'clock, the house was in darkness. He knocked loudly at the door and waited impatiently until Madam Musgrave's old butler answered to him. Then she descended wearing what appeared to be a relic of her days at Court, a padded dressing gown studded with pearls; her coarse, dyed hair was concealed by a huge nightcap, and she was blinking away sleep.

"Sir Bernard, why did you not warn us that you were coming?" she cried, embracing him. "You see that we keep country hours here, but I would have been better prepared, and Kate, too. I shall have her called."

"No, please," said Radcliff. "I am only too ready for bed myself."

"Naturally you are," Madam Musgrave said, with a salacious smile.

"I mean, madam, that I am tired from my journey."

"Well since you have been so inconsiderate as to disturb *my* slumber, pray share a drop of sack with me before you go up."

They went to the hall, and the butler brought them each a large cup of the sweet wine, and a platter of marchpane biscuits that Madam Musgrave instantly attacked. "I am always peckish at night," she said, in between mouthfuls, spilling crumbs amongst the pearls on her gown. "So, where have you been?"

"At my estate in Cambridgeshire," Radcliff lied. "I am doing my best to prepare the house, in case the enemy –"

"Have you hidden your plate?" she interrupted. "And your livestock, can you disperse them in any way? As for me, I will not let the rebels slaughter so much as a single one of my sheep if I can help it." She took a swig of wine, and crunched on another biscuit. "A pity you could not bring your valuables here. I have a priest's hole upstairs that the papists made good use of in Elizabeth's reign. I shall not hesitate to conceal whatever I can in there."

"Is that so," said Radcliff, suddenly very interested. "I might prevail upon you to store a small coffer of mine that I carried with me. It contains a few items, family heirlooms that I should not want to fall into the hands of Parliament if Longstanton is invaded. I also put in there a gift for Kate's next birthday," he added, thinking quickly. "I want it to be a surprise, so if you please, say nothing to her about my coffer."

"As you wish, sir. But what is the world coming to, that we must resort to such measures to protect our own goods!" Madam Musgrave exclaimed. "And how can those men who presently sit in London think themselves more fit to rule than their rightful King!"

"Is Kate well?" Radcliff asked, to cut short her pontificating.

"Yes, though she spends too much time reading and musing by herself. She does not enjoy sporting pursuits, as I did at her age. She is lonely for you, I think, Sir Bernard." Radcliff forced a smile, though he felt irritated, as before, that Madam Musgrave should lecture him about his wife. "For how long can you stay?" she inquired.

"No more than a night, I am sorry to say. I left my troop under the command of some sound fellows who served with me in the campaign abroad, but since we may be engaging with Lord Essex's army, I must rejoin them as soon as I can. Madam," he concluded, "might you show me the priest's hole, before I retire?"

When they had finished their wine, he took his coffer and she led him up to the third floor of her house, through a passageway into a disused, wood-panelled bedchamber. There she guided him to the carved stone mantelpiece over the fireplace. "Watch," she said, and pressed firmly at a panel on the wall nearby. It flipped open to reveal a small lever that she turned, before moving back to the mantel. Placing both hands on one of its stone curlicues, she shifted it away and pointed out to him another lever. "Turn it clockwise," she ordered, and as he did, he was amazed to see a far larger panel in the wall slide away, leaving a gap just big enough for a man to squeeze through. She grabbed a candle and went in, as he followed, descending along a narrow staircase to a door on their left-hand side. She pushed it wide, and they entered a little room festooned with cobwebs, various objects packed against its walls.

"Does Kate know of this place?" he asked, peering about.

"Yes, but she doesn't know how to get into it, and she never visits the third floor," Madam Musgrave replied, with a chuckle. "Don't worry, sir. Your surprise won't be found out."

He stored away the coffer, they ascended, and she slid back the panel to close the hole. "I thank you, Aunt," he said, delighted; he could not have invented a more secret location. "Now you will excuse me."

"Go to your beloved, sir. You newlyweds have much to catch up on."

Tiptoeing into Kate's chamber, he could hear the sound of her breathing, regular in sleep. But after he had undressed, and as he was climbing into bed, she started and cried out.

"Shhh, Kate, it's me," he said.

"When did you arrive?"

"But an hour ago. How I've waited to be in your arms again." He kissed her, parting her lips with his tongue and caressing her face and hair. When he unfastened the front of her nightgown and touched her breasts, she did not resist, so he took her as she lay, on her back, entering her as gently as he could. He kissed her with more passion, and in contrast to their last time together he held back his own climax until he heard her breath quicken, although whether from excitement or from the vigour of his thrusts he could not tell. "Are you close?" he whispered. "My darling, are you close?" Perhaps she did not understand, for she said nothing, and he could restrain himself no longer.

He stayed in her afterwards, enjoying the warmth of her body. Then he realised that she must be uncomfortable under his weight, and he rolled to one side, cradling her head on his shoulder. He felt cleansed, as though the moment of orgasm had washed away all anxiety. His error in The Hague could not come back to haunt him. And now, at almost forty, he had only two and a half years to wait for the fulfilment of his and Pembroke's hopes, if his calculations on that all-important horoscope were correct.

IV.

Radcliff had first met Philip Herbert at the Pembrokes' family seat, Wilton House, in the autumn of 1629. Then twenty-six and hungry for advancement, Radcliff had settled on Herbert as a possible means to this end, detecting in the man an even stronger hunger for power than his own, which encouraged rather than chastened him. Named after an uncle, the distinguished soldier and courtier Sir Philip Sidney, Herbert had not yet inherited the earldom from his older brother, William, but had nevertheless secured prominence under the new king Charles. His Majesty was a familiar guest at Wilton, where the

Herberts could show off their collection of paintings and sculpture, stables rumoured to be the best in the country, and grounds teeming with game. The King had appointed Philip Herbert his Lord Chamberlain, as a tribute to the favour in which the former monarch James had held him. Yet William stood between Philip and the title, and this, Radcliff quickly ascertained, was the fly in his ointment.

When a friend of Radcliff's fell sick and could not attend a hunt arranged on the Wilton estate, Radcliff had gladly accepted to go in his stead, and made sure to stay near Philip Herbert's side as they galloped after their prey. At the end of the chase, sweaty and breathless, they had exchanged courtesies, and Radcliff conceived of a scheme to attract his interest.

It took months of cultivating common acquaintances, running small errands, and sending the occasional gift to Herbert, simple but well chosen, until eventually Radcliff was invited to Wilton to attend a masque. Herbert seated him close by his side and seemed to be study-ing him as he watched the spectacle, the theme of which was the triumph of true religion over the corrupt and scheming Roman church. Afterwards, Herbert beckoned him out into the gardens to talk.

"I do fear for the Protestant cause abroad," Herbert began, as they strolled about, inhaling the mild spring evening air. "His Majesty could be keener in his support for it. And ever since the Duke of Buckingham's tragic murder last year, he appears to be listening more and more to the Queen's advice." Radcliff kept silent, aware that he was being tested in some way. "Understand me," Herbert continued, "I am utterly devoted to His Majesty. But I worry that the Queen and her priests will try to bring us back under the yoke of papism. Look what misery our country endured less than a hundred years ago under Queen Mary! Must we see more Protestant martyrs burnt at the stake?"

"All those of our faith must be as worried," murmured Radcliff.

"You seem a judicious person. Have you no desire to stand for the Commons?"

Radcliff smiled and shook his head. "I have my views, but I am not a good speaker. I leave public life to others more suited for the role."

"You prefer to remain offstage, is that it? Yet you don't strike me as a man who likes obscurity. You've plenty of time to reconsider, at your age. Where is your estate?"

"In Cambridgeshire. It's modest, but it gives me a healthy income," Radcliff added, untruthfully: he could not be seen asking for any favours, money least of all.

"Are you married yet?"

"No, my lord."

"Enjoy your freedom while you have no provincial wife to embarrass you," Herbert advised, with a harsh laugh. "Now, what can I do for you? I assume you have some preferment in mind, or you would not be so assiduously courting me."

"If I may speak plainly, my lord," said Radcliff, his answer well rehearsed, "I believe you stand in need of my skills."

"Your skills?"

"Every man wants to know what the future might bring him. A great man especially."

"What do you mean by that? Tell me *plainly*, if that is how you would speak."

"I am trained in the casting of horoscopes. I was told by a master of the art that I had a natural talent for it."

"Ha! What else can you do, raise spirits? Find the philosopher's stone?"

Radcliff assumed a hurt expression. "Let it be forgotten, what I said. Forgive me. I should never have presumed upon your patience."

Herbert stopped walking and turned to him. "Presume upon it again and tell me how you gained your training."

Radcliff smelt victory, in spite of Herbert's disdainful tone. "The adept who instructed me is an Oxford scholar, a student of the great John Dee and Robert Fludd. He recognised my abilities and was able to hone them as no one else could."

"There are countless rogues who lay claim to such learning," Herbert said, "although Dee *was* an exceptional man." Radcliff's heart quickened at this: he had mentioned the name on purpose, knowing that Dee had been well received in former times by Herbert's uncle and aunt, Philip Sidney and his learned sister Mary. "I would need proof," Herbert went on.

"And I would be neither so rash nor so conceited as to make a vain boast."

"Of what benefit could your horoscopes be to me?"

"I repeat, every man wishes to know what the future may bring him."

Herbert said nothing for a while. "You can foretell events?" he asked, at length.

"I have had success at it more often than not."

"A necromancer, are you?"

"No, my lord."

Herbert walked on, and Radcliff followed, anticipating what he would be asked next. "Could you foretell the time of a death, for example?"

"It is possible."

"The matter must go no further than the two of us." Herbert stopped once more to face him, looking straight into his eyes. "I'll do worse than ruin you, if you blab about it."

"I swear by Jesus Christ that your confidence is safe with me."

"Then I'll give you a chance to prove yourself. My brother is most concerned about his health. He has had fits – he is of an apoplectic nature – and they have worsened of late. He wishes to know how much longer he has to . . . to prepare himself for the end." Herbert heaved a funereal sigh, and Radcliff rejoiced inwardly.

"If you will supply the necessary information as to his exact place and hour of birth, I shall do my best to assist him," he said.

In the event, his calculations were astoundingly accurate, even by his standards. The third Earl was struck down by a severe fit on the tenth of April 1630, just a day earlier than predicted. Philip Herbert, at last Earl of Pembroke, declared that he and Radcliff would both benefit from a closer association. And so Radcliff pledged himself to the man's service, feeling like an explorer setting out to discover immeasurable wealth and glory, but guided by an uncertain map, and driven to depend upon fellow travellers who might fail him in the last resort.

v.

Seward placed his silver bowl upon the table, filled it with water, and sat down to gaze into it. Practice had taught him how to banish from his mind the distractions of the physical world in order to seek out knowledge inaccessible to most people. But tonight he was worrying about Isaac Clarke, who had ridden back to Oxford earlier in the day because of rumours that Parliament was about to occupy the city. Poor Clarke was afraid that his collection of rare books might be taken out and burnt by some philistine rebel soldiers.

With an effort, Seward tried to focus on the object of his scrying, and as he turned his thoughts to Beaumont, he seemed to wander backward rather than forward in time, as if to wrestle the future from the past.

They had been introduced in Lord Beaumont's library, just before Beaumont was to come up to Merton. Seward could still recall that first impression. The boy owed nothing to his father but his height: the clear golden skin, the inky hair, the fine bones, and the alien set of his green eyes came unmistakably from his mother, although his mouth was different, softer and more mobile. He was all arms and legs, and ill-groomed. And when he smiled at Seward like some teasing elf, Seward had been instantly smitten.

"You will be studying with a veritable jewel in Merton's crown," Lord Beaumont had told the youth proudly. "As his former student, I can attest to his excellence. It is not often that a scholar of his age and seniority is prepared to take on the duties of tutorship, so you must be on your best behaviour, Laurence."

The boy had not been at College for more than a week when he was late for a lesson. "What kept you, Beaumont?" Seward said. "I am obliged to punish your tardiness unless you've a good excuse."

"I fell asleep in prayers again." Without the least shame, Beaumont unhooked his breeches from behind, pulled up his shirt and displayed his hard little backside. He had been beaten so violently that blood had been drawn. "Dr. Middleton's work," he said, as he restored his clothing, adding with a wink, "He very much enjoyed it, too. I bet he's pulling away at his yard as we speak."

From then on Seward took care to avoid any unnecessary physical contact with the boy, suspecting that his charge had given him a subtle warning, and when Beaumont deserved punishment, as he often did for his laziness and general disregard for rules, Seward had it meted out by one of the other tutors.

The following April, Seward and he were summoned to Chipping Campden by a terse note from Lady Beaumont. They were escorted to her chamber, where she received them alone.

"Dr. Seward, my son has committed a serious offence," she announced. "A maidservant in our employ is four months gone with his child, I assume begotten during his Christmas holiday here. She has been dismissed, of course, but the blame rests on him." Beaumont flushed, which Seward had never seen him do before. "Will you admit to your wanton act?" her ladyship demanded of him.

"Yes," he said, bowing his head and shuffling his feet.

"And how will you make amends?"

"I – I don't know."

She turned to Seward. "What sort of an education is he receiving!"

"My lady, he has not been allowed to consort with any females while under my authority," Seward affirmed, knowing that Beaumont had been notably absent on some nights. He would sneak in later smelling of cheap perfume and a slightly fishy scent that Seward guessed must be the odour of a woman's intimate parts. He himself had never been with a woman in all his life, and the very thought of it repulsed him.

"Laurence, you may go," she ordered. Afterwards she said to Seward, "We have decided to send him away for a period of continental travel, to separate him from any influences which might encourage him to further debauchery. At my husband's recommendation, he will be in your trust. Lord Beaumont will arrange matters with the College. But, Dr. Seward, how has Laurence picked up such unchaste habits? From the other boys?"

"I cannot say," Seward replied; she was making a fuss of nothing, in his view. "He deserves your reproach, my lady, but the passion of youth does lead to temptation. I do not seek to mitigate his offence, yet many of us have fallen into similar errors, in our early years."

As he finished his banal speech, he was perplexed to see that she had lost her air of command and looked almost frightened. "What are you implying, Doctor?" she said, in a tight voice.

"My lady, only that he should be pardoned. He has an impulsive, giving nature, and –"

"In this case he has given too much of himself," she said, regaining her composure. "You must instil in him greater moral sense or we shall have to find someone more vigilant to supervise him."

Their interview ended, and Seward was shown into the library, where Lord Beaumont greeted him kindly, asking if he would mind an absence from the College.

"I shall be more than happy to forego my duties there for a while," Seward answered.

"Then it is settled. We are grateful, Dr. Seward. I know that Laurence is very fond of you."

"As I am of him."

"Between us two," Lord Beaumont said, almost apologetically, "I am not in the least concerned if he sows a few wild oats. I just wish he would venture outside the confines of his own household so that his mother would not have to know. Though I'd prefer that he have a good clean country girl, rather than lie with town prostitutes," he added, smiling. Seward cleared his throat; Beaumont had evidently done both. "And now, Dr. Seward, permit me to introduce you to my younger son, Thomas. In five years he shall follow Laurence to Merton College, God willing."

A child was playing at the far end of the room, swinging a toy sword about in combat with some invisible assailant. On Lord Beaumont's request he came to them obediently. He was blond and fair-skinned, his blue eyes round and widely set, his nose and plump cheeks spattered with freckles, and he bowed solemnly to Seward. Like a miniature gentleman twice his age, Seward thought, and the picture of Lord Beaumont. Then, as though the secret had been whispered in Seward's ear, he understood why he had awoken such fear in the irreproachable Lady Beaumont.

The call of a nightjar brought him back to the present, and he wondered, as he had so many times, who Beaumont's true father could have been. A Spaniard, most likely. Beaumont had no clue to this day, and he so loved the man he considered as his father that Seward would never disabuse him.

About to give up and empty the silver bowl, Seward caught an image reflected in the water. It was the face of a man he had once known. His gut contracted painfully, and he stumbled back in shock. This was a sign: he must tell Beaumont the truth about the coded letters. He should not have kept silent so long, deceiving a dear friend, but he had been afraid for himself. Rumours had dogged him for years. He had endured the whisperings of jealous academics, suffered the confiscation of his books and alchemical equipment, and faced accusations of sorcery. He had even feared for his life. In his waning years, all that he desired was peace and obscurity in which to pursue his journey towards spiritual enlightenment. His past had surfaced, however, to threaten not just his life but that of the King. He had been cowardly, he realised, as only the old can be.

Now another image came to him unbidden, not in the bowl but in his head, of the pattern on the Toledo sword that he had left with Isaac Clarke for safekeeping. "Oh, what have I wrought?" he exclaimed to himself, and inked his quill to compose a note to Beaumont. Then, as swiftly, he reconsidered. He could not trust such information to paper. He would have to tell Beaumont in person.

VI.

Diana was sitting with Margaret in the parlour, both of them trying not to laugh while her eldest boy recited lessons from his hornbook to the nurse; the poor woman, being illiterate, could detect none of his mistakes. On Diana's lap, her younger child babbled away happily, playing with a coral-and-silver rattle.

"Sir Robert is home early today, madam," said Margaret, as they heard the sound of hooves in the courtyard.

Diana thought of that other day when her husband had arrived back early, nearly a month ago. Out of tact, or perhaps a reluctance to know more, Robert had not once mentioned Beaumont again. She was grateful for this and had been especially solicitous towards him ever since.

Quickly she handed the child to the nurse and rose to look out of the open window; Robert was dismounting from his horse, and as he marched towards the house, she saw his face. "Something is the matter," she murmured, and hurried to greet him.

She reached the foot of the stairs just as Robert walked in. "Oxford has surrendered to Parliament," he said, tearing off his cloak with unwonted violence.

"Oh my God!" she cried. "But Sir John Byron had command of our defences –"

"He left a few days ago. The King is short of men, and I assume Byron's regiment could not be spared, so the rebels had an easy time of it. The common townsfolk have always favoured them, and you should have seen them lording it about the streets, burning books and aiming shots at every statue of the Virgin that they could find. What's worse, we merchants must now do business with this occupying force at prices it has set to its own advantage, or else have our goods confiscated. We have been given until the end of the week to decide."

"Surely *you* will not treat with the enemy."

"As if I had a choice! How much would you have us lose?"

"Oh, forgive me, sir," she whispered, embracing him.

"I should send you and the boys away," he said, more gently.

"You may send them. I won't leave you."

He kissed the top of her head. "Bless you. Oh, I almost forgot. You will be receiving a visitor shortly. I met Mistress Savage in the High Street."

"Isabella Savage? Goodness, it has been years since I last saw her," Diana said, amazed. "What can she be doing in Oxford?"

"You will have to ask her yourself. I was sorry for her today – her splendid coach was trapped in an alley, and some drunken soldiers were pelting it with dung. I sent one of my men after them with a whip, and they staggered off. I cannot believe she would risk travelling with only her driver for protection. Very foolish, but then I never had a high opinion of her. I told her to come to my house immediately, before she could be set upon again."

"You acted most courteously," Diana said, knowing Robert's antipathy for Isabella.

"My love," he said, smoothing her hair with his fingers, "let's be brave and pretend that everything is as it should be. And now I'll read over my accounts for a while. It is not as though I can conduct any other business under the present circumstances."

Diana attempted a smile, and returned to the parlour. "Take the children to play in the kitchen yard," she ordered the nurse. "I don't want them disturbing Sir Robert." To Margaret she confided, "Oxford is lost to the rebel army. Not a word to the servants."

"Oh my lady!" gasped Margaret, "what will become of us?"

"I wish I knew. And I have a guest arriving, Mistress Savage. We must make up the spare chamber for her. Come, it's best that we keep ourselves busy."

Not long after they were finished, a coach drew into the courtyard pulled by four sweating chestnut horses. Diana ran to meet it, watching eagerly as the door swung open and Isabella emerged without the assistance of her driver, who was unloading her baggage. She wore the plainest dress and her hair was dishevelled, yet for all that she had not changed, Diana thought, with a touch of envy.

"What an ill-mannered bunch those troopers are," she said, hugging Diana. "Thank heaven Sir Robert chanced by."

"I dread to imagine what might have become of you otherwise. You must stay with us, no question of it. We have already prepared your chamber. But do you not have even a maidservant with you?"

"My last one I let go, she was stealing from me," Isabella replied. "I did not have time to hire another."

"Dear me," said Diana, scandalised as Robert had been that her friend should travel alone. "You must want to refresh yourself."

"Later. Let us talk first. Do you have children now?" Isabella inquired, with an odd, melancholy sweetness to her expression.

"Two boys, four years old, and eighteen months."

"You are lucky." After a little pause, Isabella smiled in the languid way that Diana remembered well. "And you are as pretty as ever. So many women lose their looks after childbirth."

In the parlour, Diana called for Margaret to bring them fruit cordial, while Isabella pinned back her hair.

"It's been almost a week since I set out from Nottingham," she told Diana. "One of the axles broke on the coach, and I had to spent a couple of nights waiting for it to be repaired. I was sleeping in a veritable outhouse, for there were no inns about. I have flea bites over every inch of me."

"You came from Nottingham?" Diana asked, sitting forward. "Then do you know if the King is marching south?"

"His army will have left yesterday."

"To liberate Oxford?"

"Alas, no. We encountered a scout outside Banbury who said that His Majesty is bound for the west to swell his ranks before engaging with the enemy."

"You are better informed than any of us in town."

"If this first battle is to decide the war, I dislike our chances. Essex's army is far superior in size."

Diana chose to switch to a lighter subject. "Whose coat of arms is that on your coach, your husband's?"

Margaret had entered with a flagon and glasses; she was examining Isabella from the corner of her eye.

"No, no," Isabella replied, laughing. "I am still unwed. It is that of Digby's father, the Earl of Bristol."

"So your noble patron is still looking after you," Diana remarked, feeling envious again.

"Yes, though in the end I wish I had travelled less ostentatiously. Those drunks would not have pestered me if I had been on horseback."

"How *could* you journey by yourself at a time like this?"

"As a matter of fact, two gentlemen accompanied me when I started out. Then there was an altercation, and I continued on my own."

"Had they been true gentlemen," Diana observed, as she filled their glasses, "you would not have been left unescorted."

"How right you are, my dear. I shall chastise Mr. Beaumont at the next opportunity."

"Did you say *Beaumont*?" exclaimed Diana, almost dropping the flagon.

"Yes. They were brothers. Laurence and Thomas Beaumont."

"Why – they are – they are kinsmen to Sir Robert. Distant cousins."

"Ah!" Isabella paused again, as if to absorb the information. "Do you see much of them?"

"Oh no, very little." Diana took a sip from her glass, now wishing Isabella would speak of something else.

"They are both wed, I assume."

"Only the younger brother, Thomas. The eldest was to be married some years ago. Then he . . . he went abroad, to fight."

"Is that so! They are both remarkably good-looking, are they not, though in such a different manner. Which do you find the most handsome?" Diana hesitated, uncomfortable at the idea of Beaumont and her friend together. "I am certain that you have devoted some thought to the issue, or it would not provoke such colour in your cheeks," Isabella teased. "Let me see if I can guess." Yet she got no further, for Margaret suddenly jumped up and ran to the window.

"Soldiers, my lady!" she cried.

Diana hurried over. Horsemen were trotting into the courtyard; they had the orange sashes of Parliament about their waists, with cockades of the same colour in their hats. They dismounted, and an officer wearing a polished steel breastplate approached the house while the others stood at ease, inspecting their surroundings.

"Margaret, fetch Sir Robert," she said. "We should go down."

"No," said Isabella, who had remained seated. "Let them come to us."

They waited, hearing the clink of spurs below, until a servant arrived with the officer, whom he announced as Colonel Goodwin. "My Lady Stratton," said the Colonel, as he removed his hat and bowed, "please forgive me for intruding. I come on the authority of Lord Say, Lord Lieutenant of the county of Oxford."

Robert now burst in upon them. "Colonel Goodwin," he said, "if you wish to know my decision as to the terms you offered –"

"No, no, sir. We promised you time to consider how you would dispose of your merchandise, and the word of Parliament may be relied upon. I am here for another reason altogether. I received news of an incident in town this afternoon. A woman was importuned in her coach by some of our troops, who have since been detained and shall be strictly disciplined for their misconduct." Goodwin eyed Isabella with polite mistrust. "It appears that the coach in which she was travelling bore the Earl of Bristol's coat of arms. It is, I believe, the same vehicle that I saw just now in your courtyard. Madam, might I ask your name?" he inquired of her.

"Mistress Isabella Savage, sir," she said, regarding him demurely.

"I should like to know whether Lord George Digby accompanied you on your journey and might at present be in this house."

"He is not," Robert said. The Colonel seemed dissatisfied with his response, looking from him to Isabella, who did not speak, to Diana, who was baffled by the whole exchange. "You may inspect every corner," Robert told him, "if you wish to confirm the fact for yourself."

"Madam, do you make a habit of roaming the country alone?" Goodwin asked Isabella.

"I am used to making journeys by myself when I must," she said in her low drawl. "I had not anticipated that Parliament's troops would treat me with anything but respect. Yet I have seen my error, and I shall be sure to correct it in future."

"From whence were you travelling?"

"Nottingham, sir."

"I must search whatever baggage you brought with you."

"Whose orders are these?" Robert demanded, "and to what end?"

Goodwin ignored him. "Mistress Savage, are you a courier for Lord Digby?" When she did not reply, he addressed Robert. "Surely you know that Lord Digby stands accused of treachery against the realm. Now, Mistress Savage, would you please answer me?"

Diana expected her friend to quake with fear, yet Isabella seemed unconcerned. "I am no one's courier," she said, "but by all means search my things. I would ask, however, that your men do no damage to the Earl of Bristol's property."

"We must impound the coach and horses," said Goodwin, less politely. "Have your belongings brought in here. And I must trouble you with further questions, while the search is conducted."

"I shall complain to Lord Say," shouted Robert.

"It is upon his order that I act." Goodwin produced a sealed roll of parchment and offered it to Robert, who did not open it.

"Sir Robert," said Isabella, "I thank you for defending me, but we must let the Colonel do his duty."

Once her belongings had been carried in by his soldiers, Goodwin motioned for Diana and Robert to leave, and closed the door.

"If they find what they are looking for, we shall be undone," Robert said, drawing Diana into the garden. "Goodwin could impound not just the coach and horses but everything we own!"

They paced up and down in terrified silence. Then at last a soldier arrived to summon them back to the courtyard. Goodwin had completed his search.

"Please see that Mistress Savage does not leave the house," he said to them. "We shall post a guard around it, just in case. And tell her to send out no messages."

"Have you any evidence to support the accusations you levied against her?" Robert asked.

"No, but I may well find it hidden somewhere in Lord Digby's coach. And if so, I shall have to take her into my custody. Good day to you both."

The soldiers mounted and followed the coach as it rolled away; and only when all was quiet did Robert and Diana go back indoors. In the parlour, they found Isabella examining the floor, which was strewn with her garments. A jewellery box also lay there, without its lid, its silk lining ripped to shreds, disgorging a tangle of necklaces and earrings.

"Such boors," she commented disdainfully.

"Is it true?" Robert exploded. "Are you Lord Digby's courier?"

Diana saw her friend's face alter, as though she had been asked to indulge some immodest query. "Since when has it been a crime to offer assistance to one of His Majesty's most favoured counsellors? But as I am in your debt, Sir Robert, and have brought this grief upon you, I shall tell you: Colonel Goodwin will find nothing to compromise you when he searches that coach."

"Will you swear on your honour?" he said, with open sarcasm.

"On my honour," Isabella said, her tone frigid.

CHAPTER EIGHT

I.

Slipping on the wet flagstones and splashing through puddles, Laurence hurried across the dark quadrangle and banged on Dr. Clarke's door.

"Mr. Beaumont," Clarke said, opening for him, "you look like a drowned rat. Were you questioned by the soldiers at the gatehouse?"

"No. I waited for them to go off duty."

"Why are they here at all?" groaned Clarke. "As if a bunch of old men and boys would pose any threat to Parliament! Those who wanted to fight have already enlisted. Enter, sir, and pray dry yourself by the fire."

"Thank you," Laurence said, stripping off his cloak, and then his soaked boots and doublet. Clarke was surveying him with evident distaste as he left pools of water on the floor.

"Might I borrow a cover of some sort?" he asked courteously, determined not to quarrel with the man this time.

After his reluctant host disappeared into the bedchamber, he looked around. The main room, unlike Seward's, was free of academic clutter. Rich tapestries hung on the walls, chairs were sociably positioned about the blazing fireplace, and on a table napped by a Turkey rug stood a chessboard with pieces disarranged. "I interrupted you in the middle of a game," he remarked, as Clarke came out and tossed him a blanket.

"Against myself. For the most part I have no trouble winning, with one side or the other. Tonight I arrived at a stalemate. Do you play?"

"I do, yes." Laurence peeled off his shirt and wrapped himself in the blanket; Clarke was still inspecting him as though he had just made some shameless display of himself. "Dr. Clarke, I have to see Seward. You must tell me where your house is."

"Near Witney, in a village called Asthall, about thirteen or fourteen miles' ride from Oxford," Clarke said, grudgingly.

"How is he?"

"Well enough. I was there with him, until my servant arrived to say that the enemy had taken Oxford. I rushed back as fast as I could. Thank God the rebels had not tampered with my rooms." Clarke paused, his fat face very grave. "I learnt, however, of a dreadful event that happened here last week. A boy named Illingsworth was murdered. His corpse was found in a corner of the stables. His throat had been severed to the bone. His breeches were about his ankles, and a broom-handle had been stuck up his nether parts."

Laurence sighed and sat down by the fire. The boy was a little sneak, but he did not deserve that. It must be Tyler's work, as bestial as the man had sounded in conversation with Poole and Mr. Rose.

"There is more," Clarke added. "In his fist was a ring with Seward's initials on it. Seward must have given it to him at some point, though I never saw him wearing it. Perhaps the killer found it in his pocket."

"Seward is under suspicion, even though he was away at the time?"

"Yes. The College Warden, Nathaniel Brent, has always hated him. Brent is encouraging the boy's parents in the idea that Seward enjoyed unnatural relations with their son, who may have threatened to expose him and was therefore dispatched on his order."

"Is there any proof against him, apart from the ring?"

"None but idle rumour, yet the Warden is demanding that he attend the inquest. Brent has sided with Parliament, which reigns here currently in all matters. The inquest is bound to find against Seward, and if he stands trial, the charge of sodomy alone might be sufficient to ensure his execution. My servant went to Asthall to warn him."

"What a disaster. I hope to God he stays hidden."

"You are also implicated." Clarke fixed Laurence with a glare. "Someone has bruited it about College that Seward received several visits from you recently. There might even be suspicion that you were his accomplice in the murder."

Laurence was tempted to laugh: how much worse could things get? He rose and wandered to the table. Selecting a black knight, he slid it across the board. "Your king will have to move."

Clarke came to see. "Where to?"

Laurence picked up the white king and set him in a sheltered square. "You can't abide me, can you," he said.

"If you want the truth, I can't. By the look of you I would hazard a guess that you were much the same to Seward as was young Illingsworth – what would it be – fifteen years ago."

"Which do you find the most distasteful, that I might share Seward's inclinations or that I involved him in something that threatens his life?"

"*That* you most certainly have!" snorted Clarke. "And both are connected. I always thought desire led him astray."

"It's led me astray, too, but I wasn't his boy. I like women."

Clarke lowered his eyes for a moment, then raised them again, accusingly. "You already knew about the murder, didn't you. You seemed not a bit surprised when I told you."

Laurence hesitated, unwilling to trust someone who so obviously loathed him. "Yes," he admitted, and he told Clarke about his visit to the Black Bull, in Aylesbury, and the conversation he had overheard.

"Dear me, Mr. Beaumont," said Clarke, when he had finished. "Such a pity the regicides escaped you. What did Colonel Hoare have to say to you afterwards?"

"He wasn't pleased. Nor can he be happy that I gave him the slip, on the march towards Stafford."

"Was that altogether wise? If he has the Secretary of State's authority to treat you as he wishes –"

"It was a necessary risk." A thought occurred to Laurence, and he shivered beneath the blanket. "I'm almost certain that Tyler's still in Oxford. He killed the boy not just to incriminate Seward but to flush me out, too. I can't go to your house now, or I might lead Tyler straight there."

Clarke nodded warily. "What will you do, then?"

"Find him, of course. He spent months trying to catch me abroad. It's about time for *me* to catch *him*."

Clarke disappeared again into his bedchamber and emerged carrying the Toledo sword, gingerly, as if it might spring up and attack him. "You may want this," he said, handing it to Laurence. "Seward left it with me, but I haven't much use for it in my profession. Are your clothes dry yet, sir?"

"Dr. Clarke," Laurence said, with another sigh, "I regret having to trespass on your hospitality, but I've got work to do and I need a place to stay until it's done. Someone must have seen Tyler at the College. It may not be safe for me to ask, but *you* could. He's easily spotted," Laurence went on, and gave Clarke a brief description of him.

"I shall make inquiries," Clarke agreed. "And now, sir, before I retire, why don't we finish this game." He plodded over to the table and motioned for Laurence to join him. "Black or white? I think black has the advantage."

"White, thank you," Laurence said, yawning. "I'd rather lose quickly and get some rest."

II.

The next day, Clarke departed for breakfast to glean what he could from the other scholars while Laurence investigated the site of the murder. He knew one of the grooms at the stable, who showed him where Illingsworth's body had been dumped behind a tall bale of hay. "Butchered, he was," the groom said, with morbid fascination. "We couldn't scrub out all the bloodstains." He pointed to some brownish traces splattered across the stone wall.

"Was it you who found him?" Laurence asked.

"Thank God no, sir. It was my friend Laythrop. He was so shaken by it that he quitted the College the same day. He said he won't come back until they catch the murderer."

"Have you ever seen a big, tall fellow around here, with a cast in his eye?"

The groom shook his head. "You might ask at the porter's lodge, sir."

Laurence took his advice, and discovered from the porter on duty that a man resembling Tyler had visited Merton but a month ago, exactly when Seward's rooms had been invaded. Unfortunately, that was the last time any of the porters had seen him, yet Laurence knew from experience that there were ways of breaking in and out through the ground-floor windows.

"You be careful, sir," the porter said ominously. "There's a lot of gossip circulating about you and Dr. Seward. If I were you I wouldn't tarry here. The authorities are eager for an arrest."

Clarke returned to his rooms some hours later, his expression grim. "No one that I spoke to has glimpsed hide nor hair of Tyler," he told Laurence. "But one thing is certain: you are far from safe at the College, Mr. Beaumont. I suggest you take lodgings in town, if you wish to continue your hunt. I am already sheltering a wanted man at my country house. I cannot shelter you as well.

It is bad enough in Brent's eyes that I am Seward's closest friend."

"I understand," Laurence said, and he fastened on the sword, collected his pistols, and bade Clarke goodbye.

When he went to fetch his horse at the stable, he found the same groom talking with another College employee, probably a cook, to judge by his grease-stained apron. "Soldiers, eh?" the cook was muttering. "What'd they do for their sins?"

"Thieved from the garrison's coffers, or so I heard," the groom replied. "They'll draw a crowd tomorrow. Everyone likes a hanging, whether they'll admit it or not."

Laurence listened as he saddled his horse. A hanging, he thought to himself; precisely the sort of event that Tyler might enjoy.

III.

In the crisp light of dawn, Tyler made his way to the Castle wall where a stage had been erected and a throng of spectators were gathering. Nobody in the crowd seemed to know what the condemned men had done to suffer such a fate; not that Tyler cared. He was only disappointed that one of them went off too easily on a nice clean drop. The other gave more sport, kicking and squirming in the noose to speed his end. When it was over, the hangman cut them down and started selling pieces of the rope to those who believed such trophies might bring them luck.

Tyler bought himself some breakfast at a stall where a woman had set out oatcakes. He was munching away, entertained by the hubbub around him, when he noticed a dark head above the crowd. "Can't be," he whispered, a warm, triumphant sensation creeping over him. "But it is!"

Wrapped in a long black cloak, Beaumont was leaning against the wall viewing the scaffold with a bored expression on his face. An instant later, as if magically, his gaze shifted towards Tyler's own. Their eyes met, and Tyler smiled, predicting panic in return. Beaumont also smiled, which so confused Tyler that he hesitated, and then found his way barred by a knot of housewives armed with capacious baskets. By the time he pushed the women aside, Beaumont had vanished.

Tyler rushed to where he had been and espied him strolling along a side lane by the wall. Panting with anticipation, Tyler drew out his sword as he left the crowd behind. Rounding a corner, he had to slacken his speed: some cavalry soldiers were galloping towards him. He hid the sword beneath his cloak until they were well past, at which point Beaumont was nowhere to be seen.

Swearing, he turned one way, then the other. His hunter's instinct led him to a small alley littered with refuse that ran between two dilapidated buildings on the opposite side of the Castle. Moving warily to the entrance, sword ready, he plunged in. It was like night after the bright sun, and his boots slipped in the slime underfoot, the smell as foul and ripe as that of the Black Bull's midden. He would do more than piss on this rat, he told himself. Then he felt his hat fly off, as though a breeze had lifted it, and an even greater darkness descended: cloth, tight over his face and round his neck. A sharp blow behind his knees made them buckle. He dropped his sword as he tried to stop himself from falling, but he went face down in the muck, blind as a newborn kitten. Someone jumped on top of him, and a cord was put around his neck over the cloth, and tightened more securely. And on his right temple came the hard pressure of a pistol's muzzle.

"Don't move or you're dead," said his attacker.

"There – are troops – around the corner!" Tyler gasped, as the noose cut into his flesh.

"I don't give a fuck." Tyler became still as he registered the hatred in Beaumont's voice. How strange, he thought, that they should now be locked together like mating animals, after all the months he had spent following him. "Who are you working for?" Beaumont asked, loosening the cord a little.

"None of your business."

"Spit it out while you still can."

"Kiss my arse. I'm not telling you a thing."

"Come on, Tyler," Beaumont said, tightening the noose suddenly, nearly choking him, "who is he?"

Tyler felt the noose slacken again marginally, and he gulped for air. "Some grand nobleman in London. I'm not privy to his name."

"What about Mr. Rose, where is he now?"

"I don't know." Beaumont hit him with the butt of the pistol, grazing his cheek; he had to make a bid for time, while he searched for a means to escape. "He's gone north," he blurted out.

"Is he with the King's forces?"

"Aye."

"Which regiment?" Beaumont hit him more violently. "Answer me."

The noose tightened, then slackened once more. "Pr-Prince Rupert's," Tyler stuttered. The tension on his neck was agonizing, but he estimated that Beaumont did not weigh much, for all of his height.

"Is he an officer?"

"Aye."

"What rank?"

"I don't know."

"How many others are in with you?"

"One more, maybe," Tyler admitted, thinking of Poole's friend, Robinson.

"You liked watching those boys hang, didn't you," Beaumont whispered, and the noose sliced deeper again. "Do you want to die as they did, shitting in your breeches?"

"No!"

"Then you'd better talk. Who else is in on your game?"

Tyler prepared himself to act. With his right hand he reached out and grabbed for Beaumont's left, thrusting up with the whole of his body. He tossed Beaumont off, but could not know where the pistol might have gone. He lashed out with his fists. Beaumont moaned, and Tyler felt him pull away, perhaps to retrieve the pistol, or to aim it. Akin to Samson, sightless and desperate, Tyler clenched his teeth, seized Beaumont's clothing and rammed his forehead into what he hoped was Beaumont's nose. He heard a louder moan. Beaumont must have lost the pistol, or he would have fired it by now, Tyler reckoned. Dragging himself to his feet, he ripped at the cloth before his eyes. It gave way only partly, yet enough to let him distinguish Beaumont's figure on the ground. He rammed the toe of his boot in Beaumont's groin. Beaumont let out a yelp and curled up protectively. In the next second came a crack and a flash of light, and Tyler felt burning in his right shoulder.

"God damn you," he roared, and lurched out of the alley. Another ball whizzed past his ear, scalding it; he was in sunlight again, able to see more, careering down the lane. Hearing voices and the returning thud of horses' hooves, he shouted for help. Beaumont had now emerged, doubled over, and was stumbling in the opposite direction.

"Get him, get him!" Tyler yelled, as the Parliamentary soldiers pounded down the lane. "He went that way! He's a Royalist spy – get after him!"

They clattered off, leaving him shaken that he should have revealed to Beaumont what little he had. Then he heard a volley of shots. Praying that the troopers had a deadlier aim than Beaumont, he staggered back to his lodgings.

IV.

Only sheer force of will drove Laurence from the alley: his genitals felt mashed to a pulp, he was retching from pain, and his nose streamed blood. He heard horsemen approaching and headed for the river, scrambling on all fours through brambles and stinging nettles. As shots were fired overhead, he stuffed his pistols inside his doublet and slid into the cold water, where he submerged himself, lungs bursting for air. At length, it seemed the troopers had given him up for dead and ridden away. He clambered out, panting, and lay on the muddy bank, shielded by tall reeds, nursing his groin.

He should have strangled Tyler there and then, he thought bitterly, rather than try to extract information from a man twice his size and as strong as an ox. Now all he could hope was that he had wounded Tyler mortally, or at least bought himself a chance to reach Asthall without being pursued.

Although numbed to the core, he waited a while for any sign that the troopers might return. Then, fearing arrest at every step, he threaded his way through back streets and yards to the inn where he had left his horse.

About an hour later he arrived, tired but relieved, at Asthall. He could feel swelling around his eyes, and he was starting to sneeze, his nose leaving bloody streaks on his sleeve as he wiped it. Never mind, he thought; Seward would look after him.

A woman answered the door. She was as round as Clarke, her large red hands covered in flour. "You must be Mr. Beaumont, Dr. Seward's friend! That's a terrible bruise on your face. What happened to you, sir?"

"I was in a fight," he said.

She invited him into the front room, which was as cosily appointed as Clarke's lodgings at College, the air fragrant with the odour of baking. Seward's striped cat was stretched out, basking on the flagstones before the fire. All that the scene lacked was Seward.

"Where is he?" asked Laurence.

"He's not here, sir. He went to Oxford just yesterday."

"Oh no!" Laurence almost keeled over, and she had to steady him. "Why?" he demanded.

"He didn't say, but he left you a letter in case you visited in his absence." She bustled over to the chimneypiece and then returned with a slim, folded piece of paper. "I must get those pasties out of the oven before they burn. You sit down here, sir."

She guided him to a chair and left him slumped in it, ready to weep like a child. What madness or naïveté had drawn Seward out of this haven into the clutches of his enemies? He would surely die, if not by Tyler's hand, then by that of the law as Parliament saw fit to execute it.

Laurence ripped open Seward's letter; it was in a code they had invented together years ago. "Please," he said, when the woman reappeared, "I need a quill, and some ink."

She gave him what he requested, and he began to transcribe the few lines. "The boy's spirit has been haunting me these past nights," Seward had written. "I must give it rest, or I shall find none myself. I have looked into my scrying bowl. All will be well, so have no fear. I know the author of the horoscope, but I cannot trust his name to paper, as I shall explain when I next see you. Go to His Majesty and alert him of the danger. Confide in no one else. Then come to join me in Oxford." At the end was a postscript: "The Cabbalistic code was my invention."

A surge of anger rose up in Laurence. Seward must have recognised the code as his own when he first set eyes on the letters. Why had he not said so?

V.

Army life did not suit Ingram, from what he had seen of it. Corporals Blunt and Fuller treated him like a schoolboy, and he was heartily tired of listening to yet another anecdote about their glorious campaigns abroad. Although physically tested by the endless drills, he had not yet slept a single night through, and he was unaccustomed to such a complete lack of privacy in everything he did. He could not even move his bowels in peace and quiet.

Radcliff had returned a week earlier, apologetic for his long absence. "Some business at my estate," he had explained to Ingram.

"Has it been pillaged, as you feared?"

"No, though my steward told me that some of my neighbours have been less fortunate. Oh, and I stopped by Faringdon. Your sister is in fine health, praise God, and your aunt, as ever. They send their best wishes. You should write to Kate," Radcliff had added. "She is worried about you."

Ingram was worried too, which was why he had not written. The thought of combat horrified him, and the endless delay before they would see any action only increased his dread.

On the evening of the twenty-second of September, Radcliff called his officers to attention. "Sir John Byron has occupied Worcester. He can't hold it alone against Essex's forces, so Prince Rupert must now go to his aid with eight troops of horse and ten companies of dragoons. We leave at first light."

Blunt and Fuller let out a cheer.

"Excellent news," Ingram said, belatedly, and noticed his brother-in-law look at him as though recognising a weakness for which Radcliff had no pity.

The camp was restless that night as the word spread. For hours Ingram tossed and turned on the hard ground; and when the men roused themselves to a cold breakfast, he could taste almost nothing of it.

Once on the road, however, he became infected by the general excitement. Peasants in the fields stopped their work to stare as the cavalry passed by, in advance of the dragoons, singing songs both bawdy and patriotic. The cornet of each troop of about sixty or so men held aloft its colours, whipped about by a pleasant breeze, and their progress was marked by the beat of drums and the jingle of spurs. Prince Rupert galloped up and down their ranks on his white horse, making inquiries, checking a poorly maintained weapon, or sparing a few words of encouragement. Also with them, Ingram heard, were Rupert's younger brother, Prince Maurice, and Lord Digby, as well as the King's Commissioner of Horse, Henry Wilmot.

They journeyed with only short breaks until dusk, and had covered nearly forty miles when they camped down on the banks of the River Severn, before the last push to Worcester. Everyone was talking confidently about a victory, some even predicting that if they smashed Essex's army here and now, it might be just a few weeks before the King could march triumphantly back into London.

As Ingram was eating supper with Radcliff, Tom Beaumont walked over, a broad smile on his face. "So, Ingram," he exclaimed, "you're to be blooded tomorrow."

"As are you," Ingram reminded him. "You've lost weight, Tom."

"I was ill with the flux," Tom said, as if he did not want to talk about it.

Ingram introduced him to Radcliff, who appeared surprised and interested. "Brother to Laurence? With which regiment are you, sir?"

"Wilmot's Horse," Tom replied.

"Where *is* your brother these days?" asked Ingram.

"I don't know. He claimed he was also to serve with Wilmot, but I haven't yet seen him in the ranks. Are all these your men, Sir Bernard?"

"They are, sir," Radcliff answered.

Tom surveyed them with the air of a veteran, which greatly tickled Ingram, imagining what Beaumont would say if he were there. "Well, must be off," Tom announced. "Good night to you, Sir Bernard," he said, bowing to Radcliff. "Good night, Ingram."

Radcliff gazed after him as he left. "Such a contrast," he murmured to Ingram. "How far apart in age are they?"

"Five years."

"And you are the same age as Beaumont, are you not?"

"Give or take a few months – he turned thirty this past June. My birthday is in mid October."

"You are a true Libra, balanced, and ready to see both sides of an argument," Radcliff said warmly. "And which day was he born?"

"The sixth of June. Why do you ask?"

"Our stars at birth exert a crucial influence on character in later life, don't you agree?"

"Perhaps, but Beaumont wouldn't. He's a sceptic about such things."

"Ah, well, I'd have liked to know him better, for your sake," Radcliff said next, in a tone that puzzled Ingram.

"You talk as if he's dead!"

Radcliff cleared his throat. "Dear me, I pray not – I want us to be friends."

"You shall be, in time," Ingram said, wondering what had become of Beaumont, and whether he had enlisted after all.

They reached Worcester the next day. Many years of peace had left its defences in a sorry state, and the Prince declared that he had no intention of wasting valuable troops in attempting to secure it for His Majesty, so they would retreat again. They had received intelligence that the main body of Essex's army was closing in, but that his artillery had lagged behind, slowed by the thick clay soil of the local roads. To cover the rest of the Royalist troops as they removed themselves from Worcester, Rupert took his cavalry a couple of miles out towards the little town of Powick. There they dismounted and positioned themselves in a small depression just north of the River Teme, preparing to harass the enemy as it crossed over at Powick Bridge. Dragoons were sent to line the tall hedgerows that grew along the narrow lane leading to the bridge, as the troops of horse waited in the field into which the lane opened.

It was a dry, windy afternoon. The horses were drinking at the Teme, and the men were at ease, their breastplates removed for comfort when, from far off, they heard the thunder of hooves. At once the alert was given: Prince Rupert was ordering a charge on the enemy as soon as it came into view. They had not even time to buckle on their armour before mounting. Their dragoons fired first on Parliament's cavalry-men, who were moving only four abreast down the lane. The Prince had laid a clever trap: the cavalry had no opportunity to draw up in formation while under attack. Ingram got a view of these fellows, no different from himself; and his stomach cramped with fear at the thought that he must shoot to kill.

He raised his pistol with one hand, struggling to control his excited horse with the other. Over yells from both sides and the neighing of beasts, he caught Radcliff shouting, "Hold your fire until the last minute! They're breaking! They're breaking already!"

It seemed impossible to aim over the thick ranks of their own side. Ingram realised that the enemy was attempting to back up and re-form, but to no avail. A small party had escaped, forcing its way through the Royalist ranks, but the remaining riders, unable to follow, panicked and fled along the far edge of the field. Some were taken down by Royalist shots and thrown into the hedgerows, their mounts plunging off with empty saddles into a nearby copse of hazel trees. Rupert and the other officers rushed forward on the hapless bunch that had been caught at the mouth of the lane. Soon the air was full of acrid gunpowder that brought tears to Ingram's eyes, and his ears rang with the terrible cacophony of screaming and clashing steel and exploding shot. An enemy soldier, pressed from behind, was coming straight at him. He fired, but his hand was trembling and he missed his target. Someone else must have shot at the same time, however, for the man cried out and clutched his arm as his horse reared. He slipped out of the saddle, and Ingram saw him no more.

Squinting through the smoke and dust, Ingram was swept along in the rout, as the King's troops pursued the enemy towards the river.

Parliament's officers were bellowing for their men to stand their ground, though the troopers would have none of it and rushed on, in pathetic disorder.

In little more than an hour the action was over. As the air cleared, Ingram saw the bodies of men and horses littered about, awkwardly splayed in death. He felt a strange distance between himself and the surrounding scene, as though he had been an actor in some well-crafted drama that would soon end, everyone rising, smiling and unhurt, to brush off their costumes. He watched the enemy prisoners, crestfallen wretches, being disarmed and herded together on foot, their mounts roped up in a separate part of the field. One stout, red-faced officer wept over another man whose cheek was cut open and covered in blood, a large, darker stain flowering over his belly. Not far from the front hooves of Ingram's horse, a severed arm lay on the muddy turf, its hand still gloved. He had a moment of faintness, and could not breathe.

"Easy, now," said Radcliff, reining in beside him.

"Thank the Lord you're safe," Ingram said.

"And you?"

"Not a scratch."

"All I have is a small cut to my thigh. I should have worn a longer coat and his blade would not have pierced me. But I gave him worse, poor soul." Ingram looked down at the cut and swallowed hard. "Ingram," Radcliff said, "you did well today, as did we all. Can't you hear our troops rejoicing?"

As they fell into rank for the journey back to Worcester, a sensation much like drunkenness seeped into Ingram's veins. No longer faint, he was cheering with the rest of them, feeling part of one greater brotherhood. Even Blunt and Fuller offered him congratulations.

They left the wounded prisoners in the city; then, with those captives fit enough to travel, they moved about twenty miles northwest to Tenbury to set up camp and tend to their own injured. Ingram was exhausted with the deep, almost drug-like fatigue that Radcliff had told him always came over men after a battle. That night he slept soundly for the first time since he had joined the army.

VI.

From Oxford, Laurence rode over a hundred miles northwest to reach the King's camp at Chester. His immersion in the river had left him with a hacking cough and he could stop just briefly to rest his horse, since he was passing through territory even more hostile to the Royalist cause than Nottingham had been. When he arrived, he was too late to secure an audience with His Majesty, so he spent the night in a field, coughing and spluttering so much that he could hardly sleep, despite his exhaustion.

In the morning he went to the royal quarters only to encounter Lord Falkland leaving them, accompanied by his manservant.

"Mr. Beaumont, what are you doing here?" Falkland asked sternly. "And why did you disappear from Colonel Hoare's service without his permission?"

"I've come to see His Majesty," Laurence replied, ignoring the second question.

Falkland waved away his servant. "About the regicides?" he whispered to Laurence.

"Yes, my lord."

"So you would take the matter into your own hands! The King has enough to concern him, at present, without your addressing him on an issue that he would in any case delegate to me."

"Have you informed him that someone is plotting to assassinate him?"

"Sir, he hears daily of a thousand conspiracies –"

"I wonder about that," Laurence shot back. "Forgive me, my lord," he added hastily, "but it's vital that I see him."

"Alas, Mr. Beaumont, he may not be inclined to receive you."

Laurence sighed; he could guess why. "I know what Colonel Hoare thinks of me," he said, "but I brought you those letters in good faith. And I would have come to meet you again before you left for London if he hadn't prevented me."

Falkland nodded, his expression softening. "It was Hoare who suggested employing you, under my auspices, to hunt out these assassins."

"To prove I'm not mixed up with them, as he seems to suspect. We would have caught them in Aylesbury if his guards hadn't fallen into a most unnecessary skirmish with Essex's men. *And* we lost the letters. We're just lucky that I made copies of them."

"True. Yet according to him, we have three of the conspirators' names."

"But no material evidence."

"Well if you are here to see the King, I presume you've learnt something new."

"Yes, I have." Laurence decided to rearrange the facts a little. "When I listened in on the conspirators' conversation at Aylesbury, I overheard one of them, Tyler, say that he might head for Oxford. The reason I didn't mention this to Hoare when I reported to him was that I wanted to go to Oxford alone, without his men tagging after me. In the end, I managed to find Tyler and got some information out of him. But we fought, and he escaped me – he's an enormous man, much stronger than I am."

"What is the substance of this information?" Falkland inquired keenly.

"He said that Mr. Rose is an officer serving with Prince Rupert. And the chief conspirator is some important nobleman in London. Tyler claimed not to know his name."

Falkland looked disappointed. "That is all?"

"It's a start," Laurence said, barely controlling his annoyance. "My lord, please let me work on my own and report straight to you. Hoare and his men will only slow me down."

"I cannot do that, sir. You must go and apprise Hoare immediately of these developments. He is in Shrewsbury, where we will be marching in a couple of days once we pick up as many levies as we can."

"On that subject, I've enlisted with Henry Wilmot."

"Have you? Your father suggested to me that you did not care for active duty." Laurence had to smile; so Falkland thought him a coward, as well as a reprobate. "Mr. Beaumont, I am sorry that your relations with Hoare are less cordial than you might wish, but you must obey me. Don't try to circumvent my authority again – or his, for that matter. Prince Rupert's regiment is also at Shrewsbury. Perhaps you will find Mr. Rose within his ranks." Seized by a fit of coughing, Laurence could merely nod in response. "I shall impress upon His Majesty the danger he may be in," Falkland added, as though to placate Laurence further. "The more we know about the conspirators, however, the easier it will be for me to convince him."

"Yes, my lord," said Laurence, his throat thick with phlegm.

"And I shall attempt to ensure that Colonel Hoare will treat you more respectfully in future. Good day, sir."

Laurence bowed, and waited until Falkland had gone before spitting on the ground.

VII.

Throughout supper Mistress Savage had been peculiarly quiet, Margaret observed, as though she were turning something over in her mind. After Sir Robert and Lady Diana had retired to bed, she asked Margaret to come with her to her chamber. Margaret obeyed, though uneasily: what could the woman want of her?

"I must leave Wytham," Mistress Savage said, closing the door behind them, "but I cannot afford to endanger your master and mistress by involving them in my departure. Today there were not as many soldiers posted outside, and tonight there may be fewer still."

"You cannot be so reckless!" Margaret chided. "If they catch you, Sir Robert will be blamed!"

Mistress Savage smiled cunningly. "The rebels should not have shut down London's playhouses – they might have learnt a thing or two about disguise. I shall dress myself as a boy."

"Your face as much as your figure will betray you!"

"No, no – I've done it before, with some success. All I ask of you is that you find me clothes and a hat. I shall pay you handsomely."

"I wouldn't take your money," Margaret said, scowling at her. "What if Sir Robert wakes up?"

"His bedchamber is too distant for him to hear me."

"How will you carry all your belongings?"

"I need very little. The lighter I travel the better."

"Where do you intend to go?"

"That is not your affair. Please, Margaret," she said testily, "just find me some boys' clothing and I shall take care of the rest."

Margaret crept downstairs to the servants' quarters, her legs wobbly with fear. The potboy was about the same height as Mistress Savage, and he had an old pair of breeches and a doublet that would suit; it would serve her right if they were crawling with lice. After Margaret had begged them off him, she unearthed a battered hat of Sir Robert's and a short, moth-eaten cloak left behind by some visitor.

She returned to find Mistress Savage stripped to her shift.

"Dear me, I shall not impress the ladies in this costume," Mistress Savage commented, laughing, when Margaret showed her the garments.

She did not dress immediately, but gathered a bowlful of ash from the fireplace, mixed it with water and dirtied her face, neck, and arms. Around her mouth she painted a hint of darker shadow. She next removed the shift and with a knife cut two broad strips from the lower part of it. These she tied together and wrapped several times about her breasts. When she pulled on what remained of the shift, it now hung straight down over her flattened bosom. Margaret was watching jealously throughout, wondering how many men had enjoyed the privilege of that body; Sir Robert had once said to his wife that Mistress Savage must have won Lord Digby's patronage on her back.

"Tell me, Margaret, is your mistress in love with Laurence Beaumont?" she inquired, as she fastened the breeches to the points on her doublet. Margaret said nothing, stunned by Mistress Savage's perspicacity. "If I have caused her difficulties, *he* could ruin her. I scarcely need to remind you that she is a wife and a mother, and enjoys a decent position in life. He, as far as I can judge, is something of an adventurer, and probably a breaker of hearts."

"All that was years ago, and it is quite over now," Margaret retorted. "So you see, she has no need of your advice."

Mistress Savage was stuffing some coins into a pair of kid boots that she had also blackened with ash. "Ah, then they *were* once lovers," she remarked, to Margaret's dismay, as she put on the boots. "Poor Diana – she is not made for adulterous affairs."

"Perhaps you have more experience in that domain than she."

"Undoubtedly," agreed Mistress Savage, laughing again. She wound her hair into a tight knot, grabbed the hat and stuck it on her head. "So, how do I appear?"

"Better than I had expected," Margaret admitted.

Mistress Savage reached into her trunk and pulled out her jewellery box. "Here," she said, holding it out, "choose something for your pains. They won't bite! Hurry and choose." But Margaret refused. With a short sigh, Mistress Savage dumped the contents into a cloth, wrapped it up and tucked it down the front of her breeches. "I shall send for everything else later," she told Margaret, throwing the cloak about her shoulders and seizing a small pack that she had ready. "Thank you, and goodbye."

And good riddance, Margaret added silently, as Mistress Savage let herself out.

VIII.

"After the victory at Powick, all of Shrewsbury rejoiced," Colonel Hoare told Laurence, his voice cracked with emotion, as they marched along the street with his escort of guards. "You should have seen Rupert's entrance into town. It was a magnificent day. What a rout!" Hoare continued, almost dreamily. "One of their colonels died swearing he'd made a mistake in taking up arms against His Majesty. The rest of them ran whimpering to Essex afterwards and must still be licking their wounds. We shall move on London as soon as the King returns. One more battle could finish Essex. The sooner the better for us – the merchants hereabouts have raised money to supply the infantry, but not our horse. We've had to squeeze what we can out of the local landowners."

"Then you must be very popular in the neighbourhood," Laurence commented, wary of Hoare's newly amicable attitude towards him; the man had not even berated him for his absence.

"Quite so," said Hoare. "Have you heard what they're calling Rupert? Prince Robber. He's an impatient lad, naturally, used to doing as is done abroad, demanding tribute in short order. But the English can't understand that sort of warfare." Hoare now hesitated, regarding Laurence more thoughtfully. "Your brother fought at Powick. I hear he distinguished himself by his zeal."

"I'm sure he did," Laurence said, though he disliked the idea of Hoare knowing Tom. "May I ask where we're going?"

They had turned down a small street with warehouses on either side. He began to feel choked by the sickly smell in the air, of dye used on the woollen fabric produced in that part of the country.

"Our men will have new coats and breeches for their next engagement," Hoare carried on, as if he had not heard. "Blue for Prince Rupert's Lifeguard, red for the King's, and so on. It's as well or else we cannot tell ourselves apart from our enemies."

"Unless they choose the same colours."

"Ah, yes, there is that possibility," Hoare agreed with a laugh.

They went inside one of the buildings where the stench was even stronger. The Colonel had made himself a rudimentary office there, with a table and chairs, and several chests set around them. Another, interior door was heavily barred. Laurence could detect some muffled voices on the other side, as of men arguing, and then, more distinctly, a cry.

"Wait in the lane," Hoare ordered the guards, who withdrew. "I learnt today that there may indeed be a Mr. Rose in the Prince's regiment," he said to Laurence. "You shall bring him in for me. But first, however, you shall undergo a small test." He removed the bar on the interior door, and opened it. "This way, Mr. Beaumont."

In the adjoining room, above the reek of dye, another smell more powerful and familiar greeted Laurence's nostrils: of sweat and blood and excrement combined. A naked man hung suspended from a beam in the ceiling, his feet dangling inches from the floor. Rope bound his wrists behind his back so that the full weight of his body tugged at his shoulders, slowly dislocating them. His buttocks were smeared with his own filth and crisscrossed with markings from a lash. On his chest and back the same pattern was repeated.

The room was windowless, lit by a brazier and a couple of torches thrust into holders on the wall. Three soldiers attended the prisoner: a scribe seated on a bench before a small table, his quill and paper at the ready, and two men standing, who bowed to Hoare and Laurence with jovial complicity.

"We've been teasing him since last night," said one, "but he's a tough nut to crack." He picked up a leather strap caked in gore and struck at the man's thighs. As though to contradict him, the man let out a scream.

"You *have* been teasing him," Hoare said. He seized the strap from the soldier and sent it curling across the man's face, where it left a broad red line. The scribe quickly turned aside.

"Our prisoner says his name is Peter Robinson," Hoare told Laurence. "We believe he is a mole for Parliament. He was caught asking questions about the location of Prince Rupert's troops, and he had a message on him that he stuffed in his mouth and swallowed as we arrested him. You must make him cough it up."

"Why me?" Laurence asked. "He's *your* prisoner."

"You should know by now that you are in no position to pick and choose your assignments," Hoare said, his amiable manner vanishing. "Take this as a warning, sir. I'll string you up just like him if you play about on me again." And he raised the strap, poised to lash at the man's groin.

"You should stop," Laurence said, keeping his voice purposely cool. "Or he'll be dead before he talks."

"Ah yes, you would know about that," Hoare observed, with heavy irony. "Come, sir, share your technique with us. Or would you prefer to work alone, as you did in Oxford? I'll give you a chance. Not more than half an hour, mind, and if you have nothing from him, I shall take my disappointment out on you. Do I make myself clear?"

"It's hopeless," Laurence protested. "He's about to faint."

"So work quickly. Search Mr. Beaumont and make sure he's not armed," Hoare said to the soldiers, and they took Laurence's knife from him. "Now, sir, do your bit, or when I get back I shall have you pulling out his nails and crushing his fingers one by one. Come along, boys."

The soldiers and scribe left, and Hoare followed, with a backward grin at Laurence, who felt desperate: the hardest task of all, he knew, was to obtain any sensible intelligence from the mangled wreckage left behind by other interrogators. As for that final threat of slow torture, he had watched it inflicted before and did not care to witness it again. He grabbed the scribe's bench and set it near the beam, then climbed up to untie the rope. It was difficult to support Robinson while lowering him, and the man moaned as he was laid on the ground. Laurence struggled next to loosen the knots about his wrists but the rope had sunk too deep into his flesh.

"What are you doing to me?" he gasped.

"I'm trying to help you," Laurence said.

He jumped up and looked frantically around the room, a cold sweat breaking over him. On the scribe's table he spied a blade for sharpening quills; he snatched it up and used it to saw at the rope but its edge was blunt. After some minutes of hacking away and tearing at the rope's frayed ends, he finally released Robinson's arms, and turned him over. He fetched a cupful of water from a barrel standing nearby, then shifted the man into a sitting position and brought the cup to his lips. Most of the water trickled out again, mingling with the blood on his face.

"Robinson," hissed Laurence, "you're very brave to hold on, but what they'll do to you next will be even worse than what you've already suffered. If you talk to me, I'll make them stop."

The man shook his head. "Whether I talk or not, I am as good as dead. If you truly want to help me, finish me now! Put me out of my pain!"

Laurence wiped his own perspiring brow. "You have to give me something first. What was in that message?"

"Please just cut my throat," Robinson implored him.

"I can't," he said, shuddering, imagining the agony that dull blade would cause.

"Then find another way! Oh, hurry!"

"I will. Just answer me, and I will."

"I did no wrong!" the man burst out.

"Then what was in the message? Tell me, and I'll do as you ask."

The man hesitated, before whispering, "Do you swear?"

"I swear. These men who tortured you are no friends of mine," Laurence added. "Whatever you say to me, I'll keep to myself. I promise you, on my soul."

Robinson grimaced. "Why should I trust you?" Laurence said nothing; he could think of no reason. But his silence seemed to have an effect on Robinson, who shifted one bloody hand to place it on his, and mouthed, "Water." Laurence gave the cup to him again, and afterwards Robinson breathed, "It was a letter to further the peace – there was no evil intent behind it."

"Then why the secrecy?"

"There are some in P-parliament who would consider its author disloyal for seeking a reconciliation with the King." Robinson rested his head back against Laurence's chest, evidently exhausted from the effort of speaking.

"Who wrote the letter?" Laurence helped him to more water. "You must tell me. We haven't much time."

Robinson nodded, then panted in short bursts: "P-Pembroke. The Earl of Pembroke."

Laurence frowned: this made no sense. Pembroke was engaged in open peace negotiations with His Majesty's delegates, Falkland included. "And who was to receive it? Someone here, amongst the King's troops?"

"I cannot risk *his* life."

"You won't, if his intentions are as honourable as yours," Laurence urged, shaking him gently by the shoulders. Robinson howled, and Laurence immediately stopped, realising that the man's shoulders were already out of joint. "Please, Robinson, please – tell me who was to receive that letter," he begged, "and I'll take away your pain."

"It was – Sir – Sir Bernard Radcliff," stammered the man.

"*Radcliff*?" exclaimed Laurence, completely astonished: how could Ingram's brother-in-law be involved in this?

"Now do it!" Robinson told him, too spent to catch his reaction. "Do it, for the love of Jesus."

Laurence could use neither knife nor rope, or Hoare would see exactly what he had done. With one hand he pinched the man's nostrils together, and with the other sealed his mouth, trying not to look into his eyes as they bulged wide. Then he knelt on top of his chest, knowing that Robinson would struggle instinctively for air no matter how much he yearned to die. Laurence's grip kept slipping in the blood drawn by Hoare's lash, and the flesh, soft and pulpy to the touch like rotten fruit, oozed through his fingers. He had to exert all of his strength. At last he felt Robinson's body grow limp. He checked that the man had ceased breathing, waited a moment to catch his own breath, rose and walked over to the door. He was shaking as he opened it.

Hoare lunged into the room, followed by the soldiers. "What in hell is this?" he snarled at Laurence. "Why did you untie him?"

"His heart must have given out. He was dead when I cut him down." Laurence shoved aside the soldiers and gained the other room before anyone could grab him. But the outer door, as he might have expected, was locked.

"Did he talk?" demanded Hoare.

Laurence paused to compose himself, then turned about. "He said he was trying to deliver a letter to the King, concerning the peace negotiations."

"A letter from whom?"

"He had no opportunity to explain. I told you, you'd pushed him too far."

"And I have not yet pushed you far enough! Was that all?"

Laurence merely stared at Hoare, possessed by a brutal desire to smash his teeth in and pound at his face until it was beyond recognition.

Perhaps Hoare sensed this, for he took a step back. "Very well, Mr. Beaumont," he said, unlocking the door.

"May I have my knife, please?"

Hoare smiled down at Laurence's outstretched hand, which was bloodstained, with raw flesh packed beneath the fingernails. "How is it, to be back in the saddle again?"

"An unmitigated pleasure, sir," Laurence replied.

Hoare stopped smiling and passed him the knife. "Bring me that third man – Mr. Rose. And don't be too long about it, or I'll be in danger of losing my patience with you."

CHAPTER NINE

I.

Most of Prince Rupert's cavalry was scattered wide across the countryside around Shrewsbury, requisitioning supplies or simply pillaging, in preparation for the long march on London, and new levies were flooding in from Wales and the northwest, overcrowding the camps. When Laurence asked amongst the men for Mr. Rose, some did not know the names of their commanding officers, and even when they did, he could hardly understand their impenetrable accents. Then at last he learnt from one of Rupert's troopers that there was a Mr. Rose in their ranks who had just gone out with a foraging party.

"Not an officer, sir," the fellow told him. "Can't be over eighteen, that lad, still wet behind the ears."

All the while, Laurence had been turning over in his mind two pieces of information: what the tortured man had confessed about Radcliff and the Earl of Pembroke, and the description of Mr. Rose that the serving woman in Aylesbury had provided. This last fitted Radcliff curiously well, he thought.

"Keep looking," Hoare said, when Laurence reported back to him. "And I shall keep an eye on *you*."

Wilmot must have had the same idea, for Laurence received an order to meet him in his quarters at the house of an alderman in town.

"Where have you been, Beaumont?" he demanded. "Your private business has taken too long. I need the cipher you promised me for my correspondence. Until I get it, you're not going anywhere."

"Then you'll have to talk to Colonel Hoare," Laurence said. "He found out about my work abroad for the Germans, and he wants me to serve him in the same capacity."

"I'll gladly tell him to go and fuck himself," Wilmot responded, laughing. "He can't pull rank over the King's Commissioner of Horse. As for you, Beaumont, Mr. Fulford, my generous host, will find you a spare chamber here, so you can scribble away undisturbed."

As soon as he was settled in his room, Laurence wrote to Clarke for news of Seward. Couriers were both difficult and expensive to hire, and over a week passed before he received Clarke's disheartening reply. Seward was being held in Oxford Castle, in the custody of the Parliamentary governor, pending a criminal inquest for which no date had yet been set.

"Nor have formal charges been laid," Clarke went on, "which is an outrageous violation of habeas corpus. He is not the only one to suffer likewise, for the rebels are hard pressed to keep order in the city, and whomsoever they accuse of wrongdoing is sent straight to the Castle, to rot at their discretion. As a result, that place is horribly overcrowded and full of disease. I visit him daily, but he has wasted despite my efforts and any small illness could carry him off. The College has failed to rally to his aid. Even those who were his friends have turned cowards, too frightened of the Warden to speak out against this injustice."

Laurence could only hope for a victory over the Parliamentary army massing under the Earl of Essex: if the King triumphed, Oxford would be liberated. Yet it might be too late for Seward, he realised despondently.

"There's a fellow called Thomas Beaumont in my regiment," Wilmot said to him one evening. "He raised his own troop. Any relation?"

"He's my brother."

"Hmm! I saw him in action, at Powick. He's got guts."

"I'm sure he has."

"Do I detect a little fraternal discord?"

"No, merely a difference of character."

"How's my cipher coming along?"

"It's almost finished."

"About time. We'll be leaving Shrewsbury in under a week. Then you'll have to fulfil the other part of our agreement. I told you, I'm going to put you in my Lifeguard."

"To be honest," Laurence said, "I'd rather just be a humble soldier."

"Humble, my arse," Wilmot growled back.

Laurence sighed; he appreciated Wilmot's offer, but he still had to locate Mr. Rose. He also wanted to talk with Ingram, who might know something about Radcliff's connection to Pembroke. Strange, though, that he had not mentioned it to Laurence when he first spoke of his new brother-in-law.

The next day Laurence completed the cipher. As he and Wilmot were poring over it together in Mr. Fulford's parlour, a blond, smartly dressed gentleman walked in.

"My Lord Digby," exclaimed Wilmot, bowing.

"You're very comfortable here, Wilmot, more so than where I am," Digby remarked. "And who, pray, is your friend?"

"Laurence Beaumont, my lord."

Digby surveyed Laurence, his blue eyes curious. "Ah yes," he murmured ambiguously. "Wilmot, might the house have accommodation for another person?"

"Don't raise your hopes. There's not room enough for you and all of your retinue, my lord."

"Oh, it's not for myself that I ask, but for a lady who cannot tolerate my inferior lodgings, which are perishing draughty. She has been unwell, you see. She came to Shrewsbury after a misadventure in Oxford, and a journey that was even more insufferable. She lost my father's coach to Parliament and nearly lost her life getting away from the rebels." Isabella Savage, thought Laurence, with a flicker of interest. "In fact," Digby said, "she is waiting outside."

Wilmot began to laugh. "So you didn't plan on being refused."

"I try not to be, as a rule. I shall summon her."

As Digby was about to go, Mrs. Fulford entered and dropped them a curtsey. "My Lord Digby," she said, "what an honour! Is that your wife you have with you?"

"No, madam. My dearest Anne has not followed me on our campaign. She is at home with our children. The lady you saw is my ward, Mistress Savage," he continued, his eyes again on Laurence, who pretended not to notice. "She is indisposed, and I was about to beg you the favour of sheltering her under your roof for a few days until she recovers her health."

"It would be my privilege," said Mrs. Fulford. "I shall help her in."

When the women arrived, Laurence caught Wilmot appraising Isabella with a lasciviousness that vexed him, even if he might have predicted it. Mrs. Fulford was supporting her, one arm about her waist, as though she were unable to walk unaided. Her face had a sallow hue, and she was dressed not in her plain travelling costume but in an ill-fitting dress that hung loosely on her frame.

"Isabella Savage, this is Henry Wilmot, gallant Commissioner General of His Majesty's Horse," Digby said. "I think you and my ward are already acquainted, Mr. Beaumont."

"Yes, we are," said Laurence blandly, and he and Isabella exchanged the appropriate courtesies.

"Where are your things, madam?" Mrs. Fulford asked.

"Such baggage as I had was left behind, in Oxford," Isabella replied.

"You shall want for nothing in my house. My lord, gentlemen, I must put her straight to bed," said Mrs. Fulford, and the women disappeared.

"Straight to bed is where *I'd* like to put her," Wilmot told Laurence, under his breath.

"I do thank you, Wilmot," Digby was saying. "And now I shall leave you, for I have much to accomplish tonight." His eyes strayed to the papers on a table between Laurence and Wilmot, and he wandered forward to inspect them. "What's this – an exercise in algebra?"

"Yes, my lord," Laurence said, silently daring him to ask more.

"Are you receiving some instruction from Mr. Beaumont?" Digby asked Wilmot. "He's a clever fellow, or so I've heard."

"I'll walk out with you, my lord," Wilmot said, glancing at Laurence as he ferried Digby off.

Laurence snatched up the papers to convey them to the safety of his chamber, but at the foot of the stairs he was stopped by Mrs. Fulford. "Mistress Savage wishes to speak with you, sir," she said. "You will find her in the front room. How lovely she is!"

"Er . . . I suppose," Laurence said.

"Mr. Beaumont, are you immune to *all* women?" whispered Mrs. Fulford, taking a step closer to him. "I think of you sometimes, at night, as I lie in my bed. Perhaps you have thought of me?"

"Every night, madam, before I go to sleep," he told her, with the utmost gravity. "I think of you and your husband's kindness, and I pray that God will reward you both for it." And he squeezed by her, running upstairs in a few bounds.

He found Isabella settled in a big four-poster, tucked beneath a thick counterpane. She now wore a modest, high-necked nightgown that he guessed must belong to their hostess, and her hair, loose upon her shoulders, had been combed to a glossy sheen. "How are you, Beaumont?" she said in a friendly manner, as if they had not parted on bad terms.

"More to the point, how are you?"

"I am mending slowly. It's a quartain fever that afflicts me at regular intervals, like an unwelcome but familiar visitor. Although it goes away, it always leaves me very weak." She motioned for him to sit down beside her, which he did, at a respectable distance. "While in Oxford I stayed with Diana Stratton, a friend of mine, and more than that to you, as I discovered." He must have shown his surprise, for Isabella went on, "Don't worry, she did not betray any past secrets, but it was quite clear to me that she is still in love with you, even though you are evidently finished with her."

"What was this misadventure you had in Oxford?" Laurence asked.

She frowned at his evasion. "Parliament's troops made me a virtual captive at Sir Robert Stratton's house because of the coach I was travelling in. They accused me of carrying intelligence for Digby, though they found none at all. Then I felt I had overstayed my visit – Sir Robert and I have never rubbed along. So I escaped by means of an old subterfuge."

"Which was?"

"I disguised myself as a youth."

"You're joking! You mustn't do it again."

"I do as I please. And *you* have no right to reprove me. You abandoned me on the road with only a coachman to protect my honour."

"Very true," he admitted. "I'm sorry for that, Isabella."

"Beaumont," she recommended, after a pause, "you know what I said about Colonel Hoare seeking to have Falkland removed from office? I have discovered someone who can bear witness to the fact, a man named Captain Milne who used to be one of his guards until they quarrelled a short time ago. He has seen Hoare intercepting his lordship's private correspondence, opening it and then resealing it in such a way that Falkland would have no idea that it had been tampered with. Hoare is also keeping a record of anything that interests him."

"Really," said Laurence. "Captain Milne should inform Falkland at once."

"Milne is in Prince Rupert's regiment, as is Hoare. He's afraid that

Hoare might find out if he goes anywhere near the Secretary of State. But *you* could warn Falkland, so that he is at least aware of what Hoare is doing."

"Why not warn him yourself?"

"How can I, when I am tied to my sickbed?" He cast her a sceptical look. "You still mistrust me," she said crossly. "What was it you called me last time – Digby's errand boy. I have never been so insulted."

"Well you do seem to enjoy male disguise," he observed.

"Try just for one day being a woman in a world ruled by men!" She heaved a short sigh. "Beaumont, will you talk to Falkland? Can't you see the trouble that unscrupulous spymaster of his could bring upon him?"

Laurence stood up. "You must be very tired. I should let you rest."

She opened her mouth, perhaps to insist again, then clearly changed her mind. "Yes, I am," she said, smiling at him. "But will you come and see me later, to entertain me?"

"I could send Wilmot to keep you company," he suggested, as he went to the door.

"Please don't. I haven't the strength to fend him off. Though I gather that I am quite safe with *you*, Beaumont," she said, her eyes now sparkling at him. "Mrs. Fulford tells me that you are the consummate gentleman."

"I certainly am, as far as *she* is concerned," Laurence said, and he heard Isabella laughing as he closed the door behind him.

II.

The following day, after much internal debate, Laurence called on Lord Falkland, who had returned from Chester with the King and was lodged near the quarters occupied by the royal household.

"His lordship is busy," the Secretary of State's manservant declared, when Laurence had given his name.

"I'll wait. Please inform him that I come on urgent business."

With a supercilious stare, the manservant guided him through a passage into a large herb garden.

As Laurence was waiting, walking up and down the paths, a tall, dark-haired boy arrived carrying a book under his arm, accompanied by two attendants in royal livery. "Go away, I want to read," the boy said, and shooed them off.

He had not noticed Laurence yet. He sat on a bench and opened his book where a marker had been inserted between the pages. He had a swarthy, pleasant face, although not handsome, the cheeks a little pouchy, the lips full, and the eyes a molten brown. Looking at him, Laurence felt a sudden wave of hatred for the conspirators who sought to kill this innocent boy's father. It must be stopped, he thought.

Then Prince Charles saw him and said, "Hello," as if glad to be distracted. "Who are you?"

"Laurence Beaumont, Your Highness."

"Are you here to see Lord Falkland?"

"Yes."

"He's talking with my tutor, Dr. Earle. Dr. Earle sent me out because my yawning disturbed their conversation," the Prince explained. "Sit down next to me, Mr. Beaumont. Are you a foreigner?"

"No, but my mother is," Laurence said, obeying his instruction.

"Mine too. She is abroad," the boy added in a mournful tone, "and I'm not sure when she will come home."

"What are you reading?" asked Laurence quickly.

"Thucydides, on the Peloponnesian War. My other tutor, Dr. Hobbes, suggested it. I'm at the fifth book."

"The Melian debate."

"Yes! The Melians were brave, weren't they, to resist such a superior power."

"Things ended rather badly for them."

"That's true," Prince Charles acknowledged. "But if they had sub-mitted to Athens they would have been made slaves. I should prefer to die nobly than to be enslaved, wouldn't you?"

"I don't know. Death might be a worse fate."

The boy examined him pensively. "Whose regiment are you with?"

"Wilmot's."

"Wilmot's a good fellow, isn't he! Were you a soldier before, as he was, in the Low Countries?"

"Yes."

"I might have guessed! You have that look about you."

"That look?" Laurence queried, smiling.

"As if you know far more about death than I do," the Prince said, with impressive sagacity. He reached forward, to touch Laurence's wrist. "How did you get that scar?" Laurence hesitated. "Come, answer me," the boy said, in a voice of impatient command.

"Someone didn't appreciate my luck at cards."

"And you've another scar on your mouth. What was that from?"

"That? I can't remember."

"I'll bet you can, but you don't think it a fit story for my young ears," Prince Charles said, as though he had heard that phrase too often for his own liking.

"You're absolutely right," Laurence agreed. "And it most definitely isn't."

The boy guffawed. "The things everyone tries to hide from me! Since I'm to be King some day, I should learn as much as I can about my people, wouldn't you say?" Again, Laurence had to agree with him. "So now you must tell me your story."

"Well," Laurence began, "I once became friends with a woman who was married to a very jealous man."

"You mean she was your mistress," Prince Charles interrupted, his brown eyes gleaming.

"I've never liked that term – it has implications of ownership. At any rate, her husband –"

"Oh, what a nuisance," cried the Prince, squinting over Laurence's shoulder. "Here are Dr. Earle and Lord Falkland. We shall have to stop talking about mistresses. They wouldn't approve. This is Mr. Beaumont," he announced to them, as they approached.

"Lord Beaumont's eldest son, Laurence?" Dr. Earle said. "I met you a long time past when you were a boy not much older than our Prince. You were to come up to my College, Merton, as did your father, to study with William Seward."

"Yes. He was my tutor for about five years."

"You took your *Magister Artium*?" Laurence nodded. "Then Mr. Beaumont is something of a scholar," Earle told Prince Charles. "Not many young noblemen stay to finish one degree, let alone two."

"I know he is," the Prince said. "We were discussing the Melian debate."

"You were? Scarcely a topic for hilarity, yet I could swear that I heard you laughing. Now, Your Highness, we must not take up any more of my Lord Falkland's precious time. Please give my greetings to your father, Mr. Beaumont. Does he still keep up his splendid library?"

"He does," said Laurence, thinking of the stormy afternoon he had spent amongst those books, at work on a cipher that Earle never received.

"And his collection of Titian and Rubens and so many other continental masters rivalled most that I have seen, those at Wilton House included." Earle turned to Falkland. "By the bye, I have not yet answered the letter you brought me from my Lord Pembroke."

Laurence started at the name, then recalled what his father had told him: Earle was once chaplain at Wilton House.

"I have not exactly answered him yet myself," Falkland murmured back. "But we shall speak of him another day."

"And Mr. Beaumont, we must finish our discussion of Thucydides when we have a chance," the Prince said, grinning and stroking his lower lip with a finger.

"It would be my pleasure, Your Highness," Laurence said, and bowed.

"Good day, my lord," the Prince said to Falkland, who also bowed; and the Prince and Earle departed.

"Although Prince Charles is only twelve," Falkland remarked to Laurence, taking a seat on the bench, "he is wise beyond his years."

"That he is."

"Pray sit, Mr. Beaumont." Falkland cleared his throat. "I understand that you have been frustrated in your efforts to catch Mr. Rose, but that you assisted Colonel Hoare in interrogating a spy he had arrested."

"My assistance wasn't needed; the man was pretty much dead by the time I arrived," Laurence said flatly.

"But he was alive long enough to reveal to you that he had some message for His Majesty about the peace negotiations." Falkland stopped, regarding Laurence intently. "Colonel Hoare thinks that you did not tell him everything you got out of his prisoner."

"I didn't."

"Why not?"

"I'll explain, my lord, though I must ask, for your safety and mine, that you keep what I say in complete confidence."

"You ask much of me, when I have been given fair cause not to trust you."

"In your position, my lord, it might be best to trust no one." Laurence got up and scanned the open windows overlooking the herb garden. "May I request that we move?"

"Are you afraid that someone might be listening?"

"I'd prefer not to risk it." He drew Falkland to the other end of the garden, where, after looking around once more, he said, "Hoare's prisoner confessed to me that he was on a mission for the Earl of Pembroke."

"Pembroke?" exclaimed Falkland, so sharply that an inchoate idea surfaced in Laurence's mind, like a first, faint whiff of scent caught by hounds before the chase.

"Yes. It seems Pembroke was concerned that he might be accused of disloyalty to his own side, so he wanted to communicate in secret. The message was not for the King, but for someone else in His Majesty's service – I presume an agent of Pembroke's – Sir Bernard Radcliff."

Falkland tugged at his moustache. "I don't know of him."

"By coincidence, I do. He's married to the sister of a friend of mine. And he's serving with Prince Rupert."

"Was that why you lied to Colonel Hoare, to spare Radcliff from arrest?"

"Of course! The interrogation I had to take part in was botched thanks to Hoare's excessive violence. If that man had been treated differently, we might have had far more out of him." He noticed Falkland shiver, despite the warmth of the autumn sun. "Hoare is not just inept, my lord," he went on. "He's also strongly opposed to your desire for peace, as you must be aware. And I've heard a rumour that he may be opening and reading your private correspondence."

Falkland gaped at him. "He could not be so treacherous!"

"He wouldn't consider himself treacherous, my lord. He's the sort of man who sees things in black and white. He'll do whatever he believes is best for His Majesty's cause, which in his view does *not* include a peaceful settlement. If this rumour has any truth to it, he may be hoping to undermine your efforts in that direction."

"They may be undermined anyhow." Falkland plucked a twig from a nearby bush, of fragrant lavender, and began to tear off the leaves methodically, one by one. "Yesterday the Earl of Essex sent an emissary to us, asking His Majesty to listen to another petition from Parliament. It contained the same old terms: that he return to Westminster, abandoning to their merited punishment all those counsellors who had misled him into declaring war. His Majesty refused to listen to it on the grounds that he would receive nothing from a proclaimed traitor." He shook his head, adding, "After our victory at Powick, Essex should have recognised that his petition hadn't a chance."

"Is peace still possible?"

"I must have faith that it is," Falkland replied, though gloomily, as he tossed aside the naked twig. "And you?"

"I'm not altogether sanguine. But then I've been told I have a jaundiced view of human nature," said Laurence, with a smile.

"You have seen at first hand what war can do."

"Yes, well, as far as peace is concerned, the Earl of Pembroke evidently shares your faith," Laurence remarked, in an offhand way. "It would be interesting to know if he confided any of this to Dr. Earle."

Falkland jerked up his chin and narrowed his eyes. "Allow me to clarify, sir. I sat beside his lordship at a banquet in London last month. Afterwards he gave me a letter. He merely said that he desired to renew his former friendship with Earle." Laurence nodded, as if accepting the explanation. "And all his lordship said to *me* was that he regretted our present discord, and wished it had not come to bloodshed."

"Then what did you mean when you told Earle that you hadn't exactly answered him?" Laurence could not help asking. He was aware that his question verged on impertinence, yet the scent that he had picked up earlier was growing more distinct.

"Mr. Beaumont, I am not obliged to answer you," Falkland retorted.

"Forgive me, my lord," Laurence said, pretending apology. "However, you might learn something of Pembroke's intentions from Sir Bernard Radcliff."

"Are you suggesting that *I* arrest him?"

"You could call him in for an audience – *without* alerting Colonel Hoare. And in future, my lord, I would urge you to be extremely vigilant not to say or write a word that Hoare could use against you."

"What about the plot to regicide? He will expect you to work for him –"

"I must *appear* to be working for him. Please, my lord, don't let him hinder me in my own investigations. I promise to tell you everything I find out, just as I've been frank with you today."

"This rumour about my letters being opened – can you obtain some proof of it?"

"I could try," Laurence said, reluctantly.

"I do admire your skill in negotiating these dark corners, Mr. Beaumont," Falkland commented, in a rueful tone. "If only I had spent less time in my library, and more out in the world."

"You're out in the world now, my lord."

"So I am," said Falkland. "And what a world it is."

III.

Ingram was currying his horse after another day of drill exercises when he saw Beaumont gallop up on his graceful black stallion. "Here you are at last!" Ingram cried, as his friend dismounted.

"I meant to find you earlier but you know how things are," Beaumont said, shrugging. "You look tired, Ingram."

"I am. We've had new men come in who have no training yet, and some of our poor beasts contracted the founder and we had to shoot them. Radcliff went off this morning to buy more, though good mounts are scarce these days."

"So you're not quite prepared for a victorious march all the way to London?"

"I think we'll have a fight with Essex before we get there. I heard from Tom that you've enlisted with Wilmot."

"I'm in his Lifeguard," Beaumont admitted, as if embarrassed.

"It pays to have such friends!" teased Ingram. "And I'm proud of you," he added more seriously. "I know you weren't keen to join up."

"In the end I hadn't much choice. How was your sister's wedding?" Beaumont asked, to Ingram's surprise, for he did not generally show an interest in such events.

"It passed off well, though I felt sorry for Kate that she had no honeymoon. Radcliff left the following day to visit his estate in Cambridgeshire. I didn't see him again myself until the middle of September."

"He was away from his troop for a whole month?"

"I know, it was a long time, but he's desperate to keep his property from being confiscated by the rebels. They've imposed the most outrageous taxes on anyone in his neighbourhood who doesn't support them."

Beaumont hesitated, toying with the reins of his horse. "Ingram, did he ever express any doubts about where he'd stand in this war? After all, most of his county has gone the other way."

How odd, Ingram thought, before answering: Radcliff had asked him much the same question about Beaumont. "That would make no difference to him! He came home ready to fight for his King, as he did bravely at Powick."

"I thought he came home to get married," Beaumont said, with a playful smile.

"That, too," Ingram agreed, smiling also.

"How was Powick? For you, I mean."

"I can't say I enjoyed it. And ever since – you may think me foolish, but I've had a premonition that either Radcliff or I won't come out of the war alive. I dream about it now and again."

"That's natural."

"But – if it *were* to happen, would you go to Kate and tell her, so she doesn't have to hear by some vile official letter? Promise, Beaumont," Ingram insisted. "It's important to me. She's such a peculiar girl – not easy to like, in some ways. But we're very close. And of course Radcliff is devoted to her."

"I promise, but promise me in return that you won't dwell on this. Sometimes the more a man fears dying in battle, the more it tends to happen. Not that I suggest you act the hero. I never did myself, and I wouldn't recommend it to anyone I cared about."

Ingram felt a deep pang of affection for his old friend. "I wish you were riding with us," he said.

Beaumont squinted at him mischievously. "You've got Radcliff, haven't you?"

"He doesn't make me laugh, as you do." Ingram nearly mentioned Radcliff's persistent curiosity in Beaumont but held off. Beaumont would not appreciate it, he knew, and he so wanted the two men to be friends. "That's a handsome pair of flintlocks you have there," he remarked instead, pointing at the pistols in the holsters of Beaumont's saddle. "I didn't get a proper look at them on the night of our drunken foray. May I?" Beaumont pulled them out for him, and he weighed them in his palms, impressed by their lightness compared to his English wheellocks. They were indeed beautiful, of highly polished wood inlaid with a decorative silver pattern. "Where did you find them?"

"In Bremen, I think it was, though they're French-made. I won them in a game of dice."

"By luck or trickery?"

"Probably a bit of both."

"You won't see many of them around here." As Ingram replaced them in the holsters, he noticed a sword tied to the saddle. "And how about this?" he said, fingering the ornate hilt. "Another game of dice?" Beaumont did not answer, but took it down for him. "A far cry from our broadswords, damned clumsy things," Ingram said, as he unsheathed it admiringly. "Radcliff would be envious. When he was in the Low Countries this past spring, he lost a sword that must have been as fine as yours. He had it crafted to his design, even had his initials embossed on it." Ingram made a few passes in the air with

Beaumont's, sensing how comfortably the grip embraced his hand. "No, now I remember. It wasn't lost. Some thief sneaked off with it while he was eating at a tavern."

"At a tavern?" Beaumont repeated. "What bad luck. Was anything else stolen from him?"

"Yes, money, I believe, though it was the sword that upset him most. But then he wasn't expecting a woman to rob him."

"The thief was a woman?"

"That's what he said."

Beaumont's gaze was riveted on his own sword, and as Ingram returned it to him, he inspected the pattern on the hilt as if seeing it for the first time. "It just occurred to me," he said, looking up blithely. "I didn't give Radcliff a wedding present. Please deliver this to him with my compliments." He handed Ingram the sword, in its green scabbard. "And tell him I hope it makes up for the one he lost."

"Beaumont, you can't! You'll need it soon, if we engage with Essex."

"I'll borrow another from Wilmot," Beaumont muttered, as though to close the subject.

"Why don't you wait, and give it to Radcliff yourself?"

Beaumont appeared to consider, then shook his head. Typical, Ingram thought, his friend had always hated being thanked. "But do me a favour," Beaumont said. "I want to know the look on his face when he first sees it."

"I can predict that," Ingram told him. "He'll be dumbstruck."

IV.

On the evening before the King's army moved out of Shrewsbury, Laurence called on Isabella again. When he entered her chamber she was lying dressed on the counterpane, propped up by cushions, her head bent over a thick volume. She smiled on seeing him and patted a spot on the bed beside her.

"In our difficult times," she said, closing the volume with a dull thud, "I find it appropriate to study the Bible. But I am still mired in the earlier Books."

"Violent stuff," he commented, sitting down.

"Yes – I have reached the part where everyone has just been circumcised. All those males, I should say, who were not wandering about in the wilderness. I wonder why the custom is not still respected to this day amongst Christian people."

"If you were a man, you might be relieved that it isn't."

"Ah!" Her eyes widened. "Have you personal knowledge of the subject?"

"No, though a couple of times I've seen evidence of it. Not all my friends have been Christian."

"Then you have a broader acquaintance than I. Beaumont," she went on more gravely, "I think you've been avoiding me. You haven't come here all week."

"Wilmot's kept me busy at drill," he said, which was true; he had not even found an opportunity to ask Ingram about the sword.

"You might have visited me in the evenings, instead of tippling with him downstairs."

"You seem better," he observed, to deflect the issue.

"I am. Mrs. Fulford has lavished me with attention. She is most distressed, by the way, that you gentlemen are leaving tomorrow. But I, too, shall be joining the dreary procession of camp followers. Digby says there are even more whores amongst them than wives, and of the wives, many will be turned into whores by the end of this campaign," she concluded, with a hard little laugh.

"Why did he bring you to this house, Isabella?" Laurence inquired, moving nearer to her on the bed.

"To recover from my illness. Why else?"

He let the question pass. "Thank you for telling me about Captain Milne. I think I'll go and speak to him after we camp down tomorrow night."

"No! You cannot go near him!" Isabella burst out, confirming to Laurence that he should be wary of her offer. "Don't you see? If he has heard that you may be working for Hoare, you'll scare him into silence. *I* must address him first – he will require persuasion to come forward."

"What sort of persuasion did you have in mind?"

"You are annoying," she snapped, heaving the Bible at him with both hands.

"Ow," he cried, as it smacked him on the kneecap; and he picked it up and held it away from her.

"Give it back!" she ordered, though she had started to laugh, not as she had before, but in a spontaneous, unaffected manner. "Beaumont, I'm sick of us arguing," she said, once she had composed herself. "Can we be friends again?" She extended her hand to clasp his, as would a man. "Now, will you let me address Captain Milne? And then you can bring him to Falkland." Laurence shrugged, and nodded. "Did you speak to his lordship about this?"

"Er . . . not yet."

"You should." She released his hand and glanced away. "I pray you are not all slain in battle, before we can arrange the meeting."

"At least it would be the end of our tribulations," Laurence joked.

She did not seem amused. "You mustn't be too valorous, Beaumont, when you are in the field."

"You've no need to worry about that."

They regarded each other in silence, and he had the impression that she was lonely in a way that he understood. He would have liked simply to hold her. But he rose to leave.

"Good night, Isabella," he said.

"Good night, Beaumont," she said, with a sweet, triste smile.

Back in his chamber, he stared out of the window into darkness, twisting Khadija's bracelet round and round his wrist. He should get rid of the damned thing, he thought; it was blackened from wear. Shutting his eyes, he tried to picture Juana's face, and was disturbed to find that he could recapture only the sketchiest memory of it, though he could easily recall so many other faces from his past. Perhaps, in the words of Khadija, the poison had left his system. But to acknowledge this was no consolation.

v.

"You have stopped going out these past nights, Monsieur," Juana remarked one evening in Paris, as they ate supper together.

He paused to reflect. Though he was not sure why, more and more he had tended to stay at home with her in their lodgings not far from the fashionable Marais, wasting his time over the indecipherable letters. A month had slipped by without any sign of the Englishman's servant, and Laurence would have suspected that she had lied about seeing the man in Paris, if not for the fact that he could rarely persuade her to leave the house, and only with him.

"It is nearly May," she continued, deliberately. "The roads should be dry by now." He made no reply. "Monsieur, I should like to set out for Spain."

"Why not," he said.

"So you will come with me!"

"Oh, Juana, don't start that again."

"Have you never been to your mother's homeland?" He shook his head. "Are you not curious to travel there?"

"Not for the moment," he replied, thinking that he was not taking advantage of the city's pleasures as he should. He had become too lethargic, too habituated to her company; they were behaving like some old married couple.

That same evening, he went out prowling in search of amusement. At a drinking house nearby he struck up conversation with a party of men and women who were celebrating someone's birthday. They were young, attractive and lively, and flirtatious in the French style, teasing each other about their latest conquests, and boasting as to how ingeniously they had managed to deceive their spouses. He found himself enjoying their urbane cynicism, and as the night wore on, he could predict how it would end. A coquettish creature named Angelique suggested that he and she take a room; and afterwards she insisted on another assignation, and then another.

Over the next week, however, he wearied of her moods, her obsessive attention to matters of dress and social etiquette, and her interminable stories about an overzealous husband of whom she clearly hoped he would be envious. Just the sound of her voice began to irk him, particularly since she refused to shut up even during the act of love. One day he rose, dressed, kissed her goodbye, and left without telling her that it was finished between them.

Juana had not once asked him where he had been, and he thought no more of the affair until, on a sunny morning as he was lazing in his chamber, three men burst in and hauled him from his bed. In the bluntest terms, they introduced themselves as Angelique's husband, brother, and father. Unarmed and outnumbered, Laurence could not win the fight that ensued, and eventually the aggrieved husband sliced open his lower lip with a stiletto while the other two held him down. They were about to tear off his breeches and inflict worse damage when he was rescued by the arrival of Juana, brandishing the Englishman's sword. Her ear-splitting shrieks alerted some lodgers from next door, and the intruders were chased away, though they swore to return.

"What knaves, to come at you three against one," Juana said, hunting out a clean cloth to staunch the blood dripping from his mouth. "Who were they?"

"Never seen them before in my life," Laurence mumbled, shaken.

Very gently, she attended to the wound; and as he looked up at her face, he considered it more beautiful, without a hint of artifice, than Angelique's could ever be, even with all the skilful tricks she employed to improve upon nature.

"Now we both have enemies here," said Juana. "Let us leave Paris, Monsieur."

He agreed, pondering nonetheless how conveniently the incident had worked in her favour. "As thanks for saving my manhood, I'll take you to the Spanish border," he said. "That's my limit."

By afternoon they were packed and had set out, walking their horses over the busy Pont Neuf, through crowds of people buying and selling from shops that lined the bridge. Juana seemed a little nervous, as she always was in public, glancing about surreptitiously and staying very close by his side. Then suddenly he felt her grip his hand. "Look behind you," she hissed.

He turned, expecting to see Angelique's vengeful kin coming after him. But instead, at a distance, he espied a more familiar figure, tall and bulky, wearing a hat pulled low over his face.

VI.

"Not gone ten bloody miles," Wilmot grumbled, as the Royalist army made camp after their first day on the march; there were fourteen thousand men settling down for the night across a swath of countryside. "At this rate, we'll reach London by Christmas."

"Essex must be moving no faster." Laurence held out a leather flask. "Here – from Mrs. Fulford."

"Bless her heart." Wilmot sampled the contents. "How could you reject a woman of such singular forethought, you ingrate? I suppose you had your sights set on the luscious Mistress Savage. Tell me, did you get up her nightgown before we left Shrewsbury?"

"No. Did you?"

"She said she would have liked it," Wilmot said complacently, "but she was worried that I might catch her illness."

"How considerate of her," said Laurence, feeling buoyed by this news. "Wilmot, I'll see you later. I have to talk to a friend of mine."

He had ascertained earlier where the main body of Prince Rupert's Horse was encamped. After an hour of riding about and making inquiries, he found Radcliff's troop and was fortunate to spot Ingram leaving the fire around which his companions were huddled. Moving off towards a clump of bushes, Ingram stopped to unlace. Laurence waited for him to finish before addressing him.

"Good to see you, man. Where are you camped?" Ingram asked, as he refastened the front of his breeches.

"About three miles north."

"Not very clement for the middle of October, is it. I wish I'd brought a thicker pair of stockings. You know, Beaumont, I've been wanting to speak to you." He led Laurence a little further away from the camp before speaking again, in a lower voice. "You remember what you asked me, about Radcliff and the sword?"

"Ah yes," Laurence said.

"You wouldn't believe – that day I gave it to him, I'd never seen him act so strangely."

"Why, what did he do?"

"Well," Ingram began, "as I may have told you, he'd gone off to buy some horses, but he couldn't find any for love or money, and he returned very disappointed. I thought it would cheer him tremendously to receive your gift. But as soon as I mentioned to him that you'd come by, he turned pale as a ghost."

Laurence caught his breath. "That *is* strange."

"He turned even paler when I showed him the sword. And when I said it was a wedding present from you, he became almost angry! He said he didn't understand why you would part with your sword when we were about to engage in battle."

"And what did you say to that?"

"I told him it was just like you – how when we were at Merton together, I'd have to bite my tongue on many occasions because if I let slip that I admired something of yours, you'd wear me down with all the arts of persuasion if I refused to take it." Laurence smiled, touched by the warmth in Ingram's tone. "He made some comment to the effect that generosity comes easily to those born into wealth," Ingram continued. "I found that snide. I said – and I know you'll forgive me, Beaumont – that you were always in funds, but not because of your birthright. I suppose I wanted to provoke him, so I told him that you looked after yourself by gaming, which ensured your freedom from the family purse, if not from their judgement. I even told him you paid for my first woman."

"I *did*?" Laurence murmured, his mind on Radcliff.

"Don't you remember? You insisted that I couldn't pass my seventeenth birthday without losing my virginity at an Oxford brothel. And that night the deed was done, though too fast for me to be proud of it. You kindly assured me that I would improve with practice."

"I'm sure we've both improved since then," Laurence said, laughing. "Did Radcliff share any similar confidences in return?"

"No! He told me such pursuits were unworthy of me, and he hoped I'd given them up. That made *me* angry, and I said if he thought the sword was unworthy of *him*, he should give it back to you. He apologised profusely then. I think I'd struck on a sensitive issue. I've observed before that he has a sore spot when it comes to social rank, and he may resent you for what you are, and for your

ability to be generous. But he *was* grateful, in the end." Ingram hesitated. "Why did you ask me that question – about how he would
receive the gift?"

"Oh, just to know what sort of person he is," Laurence replied.

"You gave him a priceless sword to test his character?" Ingram
shook his head. "I think you did it for me, because I esteem him. And
that's the sort of person *you* are. The sort of friend, I should say."
Laurence said nothing, but wished guiltily that this were true.
"Beaumont, why not join us by the fire? I'm sure he'll be glad of a
chance to thank you. If it doesn't matter to you, it does to me."

"Then I shall," Laurence said.

As they came nearer, he saw Radcliff rise and break into a smile
that was impossible to read in the poor light. "Mr. Beaumont, I can't
express how overwhelmed I was by your present," he said smoothly,
indicating the sword hanging at his side. "There are few craftsmen
more skilled than the Toledo swordsmiths. Did you obtain it when you
were in Spain?"

"No, in The Hague." Laurence moved closer, to observe him.

Radcliff returned his gaze with perfect sang-froid. "It must have
cost you a fortune."

"On the contrary, it cost me almost nothing."

"Indeed. Well I'm still honoured, although I pray you do not regret
your largesse."

"Why should I?"

"You may not find another sword as well made before we go into
battle. As we both know, those inferior blades often snap in the midst
of a fight."

"I'll have to watch out, then."

"That you will," Radcliff agreed, his voice now distinctly tense.

"Good night, Sir Bernard," Laurence said, bowing courteously.

Radcliff blinked several times but made no response.

Ingram took Laurence by the elbow and steered him away, back towards the bushes. "For God's sake, man," he chided, when they were out of earshot, "Radcliff did thank you for the sword. Why insult him by telling him how little you paid for it?"

"I was only being honest."

"What *is* there between the two of you? It's as though –"

"My dear friend," Laurence interrupted, "I'm sorry if I annoyed him, but you know me, I can't help myself in these situations. And he should loosen up a bit. He's got no sense of humour."

"Well, *you* should know by now that not everyone appreciates *yours*. I shall have to calm his ruffled feathers."

"I hope I haven't ruffled yours," Laurence said, as he mounted his horse.

"No, no," Ingram said, starting to smile. "Experience has inured me to your provocations. Good night, Beaumont."

"Good night."

With a sigh of relief, Laurence nudged his horse's sides and trotted away. Perhaps he had been unwise to bait Radcliff in front of Ingram, yet it had been worth the risk. There was still no tangible evidence to confirm that Radcliff and Mr. Rose were the same person, and Radcliff might well have had his pride wounded upon receiving an extravagant present so casually tossed off by someone of higher rank. But his voice had the timbre of Mr. Rose's in Aylesbury, and after years of studying the most insignificant tics and gestures and flickers of the eye, Laurence felt certain that he had his man. If Radcliff was involved both with the conspiracy and the Earl of Pembroke, then what might be the true aim of Pembroke's secret negotiations? Intriguing, Laurence thought. He should suggest that Falkland be cautious in any dealings with Pembroke, just in case. And he must also be careful. Any accident might happen in the midst of combat, and it would be most ironic if he were to end up skewered by a Toledo blade.

VII.

"Those idiots are going to be a disaster in the field – they won't listen to what they're told," Laurence remarked to Wilmot, who was riding just beside him, as the Royalist army snailed through the countryside; some of the younger nobles were bolting impetuously in and out of rank on their fine mounts, as if the rules of military discipline did not apply to them.

"Weren't you the same at their age?"

"No. I came into war at the bottom, with the foot soldiers. If we didn't listen, we'd get starved or whipped into obedience."

"Ah yes, the Spanish foot. Must have been rather a surprise for you, given your cosseted upbringing."

"It was. Have you ever carried a pike for ten miles?"

"God, why would I! I've only served in cavalry," Wilmot responded, with such disdain that Laurence burst out laughing.

The march from Shrewsbury had been slowed by bad weather, lack of organization, and a shortage of supplies; and as the regiments halted late on an unseasonably bitter afternoon in the fourth week of October, it was discovered that only the King and his immediate circle could be accommodated at the nearest village, Edgecote. Prince Rupert's men had to seek billets at another village, Wormleighton, while the greater part of the army, including Wilmot's men, camped spread out for miles over the surrounding fields. No tents were available for cover, firewood was scarce, and as darkness fell they were all cold, worn out, and hungry. Wilmot left to attend a meeting of the Council of War, as they sat shivering over a meagre fire.

Half listening to Wilmot's officers speculate about how soon the armies would meet, Laurence pondered whether he should urge Falkland to arrest Radcliff straight away. It was hardly a good time, when they were about to engage in battle. And should he not wait, until he had incontrovertible proof?

He had come to no decision when Wilmot reappeared some hours later. All the officers crowded around, anxious to hear what action had been agreed upon. "Byron's regiment is to march on Banbury and surprise the rebel garrison," Wilmot announced. "The rest of us will stay behind. Intelligence came in that Essex is still on his way from Worcester, so there's no prospect of a fight just yet."

This settled the question for Laurence: while the men were voicing their collective disappointment, he slipped off to find Falkland. It was cloudy overhead, and pitch black once he rode away from the fires. After twenty minutes or so, he calculated that he must soon encounter another Royalist encampment, or hopefully someone who could direct him to Edgecote. He had perhaps gone too far, he realised. Then he spotted a cluster of lights ahead, probably from more campfires.

"Who goes there?" shouted a voice, out of the night.

Startled, he reined in. A pikeman was standing just a few feet from him. He heard the sharp sound of flint being struck, and a match flared up, illuminating the man's face.

"You with the cavalry?" asked the pikeman.

"Yes."

"Then what are you doing out here?"

Laurence hesitated; the man had a strong London accent. "I was sent to find some of my men who went looking for firewood," he replied, assuming an aristocratic tone. "I think I've lost my way back."

"You've missed your camp by a long mile, sir – head north, past Kineton Church," the man said more respectfully, indicating the route.

"Thanks," said Laurence, and he started off again feeling less than reassured. To his knowledge, there were no Royalist cavalry billets at Kineton.

"Your password, sir," the man yelled after him. "You didn't say the password."

Laurence gave a laugh and swung his horse about. "I'm sorry," he said, returning to the man. "I seem to have forgotten it." From the pommel of his saddle, he took down his flask, since refilled with wine less tasty than Mrs. Fulford had provided. "Small comfort," he said, passing it over, "but you must be freezing."

The man took a swig. "Very generous of you, sir. It *is* a bleeding cold night."

He returned the flask to Laurence, who fortified himself similarly. "You're a Londoner, aren't you," Laurence said. "So am I. Whereabouts do you live?"

"Why, I was born and bred in Southwark myself, sir. Do you know it at all?"

"Very well, though I've been away for some time – six years, in fact – fighting abroad. Tell me, have there been any changes in the neighbourhood?" Laurence inquired, passing over the flask again.

The man stopped to consider. "One of the bear-baiting rings was torn down, and the poor Cathedral's in some disrepair. The old Tabard Inn is still standing, however, you'll be glad to hear. I've got soused more often than I can remember at that place," he added, chuckling, before taking another swig.

"What about Mistress Edwards' house in Blackman Street?"

"Fancy establishment – too fancy for the likes of me, sir, though perhaps not you, as I can tell you're a gentleman. But Parliament's been closing all of them brothels, so like as not it's gone. I wish I were back in the city, sir," the man confided next. "I could have joined the Trained Bands and slept safe in my own bed, instead of marching over hill and dale till my boots wore out. And this wilderness don't agree with me. I've never been out of London all my life till now." He emitted a belch. "Still, old Robin Essex won't let us down, will he? Did you see him this morning, smoking his pipe as though nought were amiss."

"Yet he must be worried."

"He must, at that. How come the ordnance got stuck behind us? Short of draught horses, they say. I say there's some at the top who are short of brains – no offence, sir, if you're one of them – but poor Essex must make up the slack, and he'll be blamed if the King steals past him and threatens London."

"So he will." As the man handed him the flask, Laurence noted with regret that it was almost empty. "I'll have worries of my own if I don't get back to my men. Good night to you."

"What's your name, sir, if you don't mind me asking, in case we meet again?"

"Harry Illingsworth," said Laurence. "And yours?"

"Peter Ascroft, sir." Laurence held out his hand, which Ascroft grasped as if it were a privilege. "Now you follow a straight path, sir," he said, blowing out his match, "and if I might be so bold, sir, the password tonight is 'Praise Jesus.'"

"Thanks for reminding me."

Laurence waved goodbye and headed off in the direction of Parliament's army, to take a look at the enemy camp. As he rode through the fields, the password was useful in fooling two other sentries, enabling him, with the aid of his last few drops of liquor, to glean more information. Then he decided not to press his luck any further and retreated as fast as he could, hoping to rejoin his own side.

After a couple of miles, he dimly heard some riders ahead. "Hold your fire," he shouted, as they closed in on them, pistols at the ready. They were Rupert's men, so he gave the Royalist password this time, reining in, and they followed suit, their beasts snorting and stamping. "I'm with Wilmot's Lifeguard," he explained.

"At ease, boys," called out one of them, moving forward. "Lieutenant Clement Martin, sir," he said, with a brief salute.

"Laurence Beaumont. Do you know that Essex has reached Kineton?" Laurence asked him next.

"No, but we suspected as much. As we got to Wormleighton we ran into some of his quartermasters hunting out billets in the village. We arrested the bunch of them and His Royal Highness has since ordered us out on reconnaissance. Were you in Kineton?"

"Very near. We still have the advantage. Essex is more ignorant of our movements than we are of his, and he has no artillery for the moment." Laurence recounted what he had found out from Ascroft and the other sentries, and what he had seen of the enemy camp.

"You must inform His Highness the Prince," said Martin. "Carter, go with him," he added, to a member of his troop. "We'll follow once we've confirmed your report. Make speed, Mr. Beaumont."

Laurence did not speak and neither did his escort as they raced back to Wormleighton. Carter took him to a farmhouse where another part of Rupert's regiment had made camp. Much to Laurence's irritation, he saw Corporal Wilson standing at the door, and then Colonel Hoare emerged.

"What brings you here?" he asked Laurence, with frigid politeness.

"I'm to report to the Prince, on Lieutenant Martin's command," Laurence said, as politely.

"Don't you try to get around me," Hoare said, abandoning all pretence of civility.

Laurence ignored him and dismounted, about to enter the house, but Prince Rupert himself suddenly came striding out, his cloak flapping behind him, Boy at his heels. "Mr. Beaumont, is it not?" he asked. No wonder his men loved him, Laurence thought, with such a memory for names. "Have you news?" And he paced about, listening keenly, until Laurence had finished. "When Martin returns, we shall call another meeting of Council," he said to Hoare. "If all this proves correct, the attack on Banbury must be countermanded. Instead we should strike at Essex before he knows of our position." He turned back to Laurence. "Where was it, again, that we last met, sir?"

"In Nottingham, Your Highness."

"Mr. Beaumont is an agent of mine," Hoare intervened, in a proprietary tone.

"I thank you, sir – you've done His Majesty a vital service tonight," the Prince told Laurence, and hurried away, followed by Boy.

Laurence suppressed a laugh: a complete blunder on his part had turned out to his benefit, and he was thoroughly enjoying the rancorous scowl on Hoare's face.

He was about to climb back into the saddle when Hoare seized the reins of his horse. "Whatever you did tonight, Beaumont, you're sleeping on your other mission. If you make it through until tomorrow in one piece, you're mine. I won't let you wander off any more, no matter how many of your high-flown friends try to prevent me."

"Good night to you, then, sir," said Laurence, bowing.

After such unexpected good fortune, he decided not to risk another foray into the dark countryside, but rather mounted and galloped back to Wilmot's camp. If his luck held, he would speak with Falkland after the battle.

CHAPTER TEN

I.

"Ingram," whispered Radcliff, shaking his arm to wake him.

"What hour is it?"

"Six o'clock. We have orders to fall into rank on Edgehill."

Ingram sat up, his face still flushed and his eyes puffy from sleep, like a child's. "I don't understand. I thought we weren't going to fight."

"Prince Rupert's scouts found out that Essex arrived at Kineton last night. The Prince wanted to move straight away and catch him unawares, but that plan was overruled. We'll give him battle today, instead."

"This could decide the course of the war," Ingram said soberly.

"Yes, it might," said Radcliff, although he had foreseen in His Majesty's horoscope that the conflict would not be over, whether King or Parliament triumphed on this momentous day. He felt choked, as though he were about to cry; if he had less self-control, he would have embraced his brother-in-law, who was now looking at him with a candid trust that pierced his heart. "You remember what I bade you do?" he asked.

"Take Kate your letter."

"On condition that you are absolutely certain of my death," Radcliff reiterated.

But death in battle was not what he most feared for himself; what concerned him was the plan he must execute. He had to let himself be captured by the Parliamentary forces. As an officer he expected to be given quarter if he surrendered his arms, and there was a safe conduct from the Earl of Pembroke sewn inside his doublet that would allow him to enter London. Nevertheless, what he was attempting could easily go awry if His Majesty's forces proved victorious.

Dawn had already broken as they assembled on the crest of the hill, in the right wing, along with the rest of Prince Rupert's Horse. The infantry was apparently still some miles away, and so the cavalry dismounted to wait. They could see their own breath and that of their horses in the misty air and, beyond the mist, the sparse shapes of trees.

Radcliff squinted over to the left, where Wilmot's men were assembling. Beaumont must be with them, he thought, and he offered up a brief prayer that some Parliamentary soldier would do him the favour of slaughtering the man. After that gift of the sword, he knew that Beaumont had fingered him. They were playing a waiting game, in the middle of the greater game of war, but at least he had his letters safely hidden away, he reminded himself.

"Colder than a witch's teat on this hill," Ingram commented, as he fiddled with his pipe and a damp match.

"And we'll be here a good few hours before we see any fighting," said Radcliff.

At midday, as a pale sun climbed the sky amidst grey clouds, Ingram pointed to their left flank. "The infantry is arriving. That looks like Colonel Gerard's regiment over on the other side of Prince Maurice's."

They watched the long columns move into position, many of the infantry armed only with clubs and cudgels. To the right, the King's Lifeguard had been given pride of place, on their own request, covered by a regiment of dragoons whose inferior mounts would be used only to ferry them from one part of the field to another. Then the order came for everyone to shift from the top of Edgehill to the plain below. The probable aim, Radcliff explained to Ingram, was to provoke an attack by Essex, since the Royalist troops were short of rations and should fight as soon as possible before they lost what energy they had.

Once the move was accomplished, a cheer surged up from the assembled men at the sight of His Majesty riding up and down, the young Princes Charles and James behind him. The King wore a dark breastplate, a cloak lined with ermine, and a fine plumed hat; his sons were as richly attired, and waving vigorously. He halted to deliver a speech that could barely be heard over the brisk wind that rippled and tore at their standards. Prince Rupert also took his turn to give each troop some words of counsel, reminding them yet again to go in with the sword and hold fire until the enemy scattered, so as not to waste valuable shot. Next, the chaplains began praying, and the men bared their heads in response.

"I wish it were over," Ingram sighed.

"Soon enough," Radcliff said, wishing the same.

Over the sloping field lay the enemy horse into which they would be charging. Finally they heard drums, and then the boom of guns on both sides. Their own heaviest cannon were firing from a position almost directly to their rear, and the noise was terrible, although the enemy shot whistled harmlessly past them. Their horses were neighing and jumpy, unaccustomed to such clamour. When the smoke cleared a little, their infantry raised a shout as news filtered through the ranks that the centre of Parliament's line, mainly composed of foot soldiers, had suddenly deserted the field before it could be charged. And while they were still absorbing this information, Rupert gave the signal to advance.

Ingram's face was very white. "God keep you," he muttered to Radcliff.

"You too, brother," Radcliff said.

They were off, starting at a trot in good order, cantering, and then galloping up the crest of the hill, all of them bellowing their battle cry,

"For God and the King!" The enemy was firing carbines at them before they were in range, the shots landing somewhere in the mile of field between. To Radcliff's astonishment, a whole troop of Parliamentary soldiers appeared to turn coat and join the King's ranks; and the enemy horse, faced with Rupert's inexorable advance, abruptly fled. Just as at Powick, the Royalists were drawn into a chase, having scarcely fired a shot. Radcliff saw Ingram almost topple from his saddle and then right himself as they pounded across the turf. The village of Kineton rose out of the hills as they sped on, with loud cries of triumph; and rapidly they arrived, catching and firing on some of the enemy cavalry in the narrow streets. They took out their swords when they reached Parliament's baggage trains, and the plunder began.

A horde of soldiers descended with delight upon a richly liveried coach: that of the Earl of Essex. Others were busily stealing from the supply wagons, meeting with almost no resistance. Radcliff reined in his mount, as he heard his corporals yelling in a vain effort to reassemble his troop, though he knew from experience that few men would listen when there was booty to be had, even if work remained to be done upon the battlefield. In the chaos, he sought a chance to escape, but was foiled by his corporals, who kept reporting back to him dutifully, just as he had trained them to do.

The beat of drums and the shrilling of a trumpet alerted them to a new danger: some of Parliament's cavalry must have arrived too late to join battle and were now converging on Kineton, fresh, and ready to attack the marauders. Prince Rupert, on his great white horse, was struggling to wheel the Royalist forces about. Several of Radcliff's men were felled by pistol shots. At last the Royalists turned to head back to the field. Time to seize the opportunity, Radcliff decided. As he was swerving away from the main body of retreating troops, Ingram appeared at his side.

"I'll go back and gather the rest of our men," Radcliff shouted.

"No!" Ingram cried. "You'll get yourself killed! They'll find their own route."

A shot rang out and Ingram's horse screamed. Plunging to the ground, it trapped him underneath. Radcliff thought that it was dead, until it kicked violently, rolled to its feet and galloped off towards the battlefield, following the other Royalists. For one shameful second he was tempted to leave Ingram and flee.

"Ingram!" he yelled. "Speak to me, brother!" He leapt down and tugged Ingram's body aside so that they would not be trampled. He heard a bullet fly past, and felt a stinging sensation in his arm as he helped Ingram to stand. Ingram's left leg must have been crushed by the horse's fall and could bear no weight, and he seemed dazed; although his lips were moving he made no sound. "Take my horse," urged Radcliff, and managed to lift him into the saddle. When he thrust the boot of Ingram's damaged leg into the stirrup, Ingram shrieked and doubled over the pommel. Radcliff beat the horse's rump with the flat of his sword, and the animal sprang forward carrying its unwieldy burden. At once he lost view of them in the smoky air; and as a knot of Parliamentary cavalry thundered up, he had only a moment to throw aside his weapons and go down on his knees in the thick mud. "Quarter!" he begged. "Give me quarter! I am an officer! I am unarmed! In God's name, give me quarter, I pray you!"

II.

"We must rally the men for another charge," Falkland cried to Wilmot, over the din.

"Most of our horses are too blown," Wilmot yelled back.

After more than four hours of battle, they had been unable to claim victory. In the fading light, between clouds of floating smoke, they could see that Parliament still held rank on the field.

As had Prince Rupert's Horse on the right flank of His Majesty's line of battle, Wilmot's on the far left had routed the enemy at the outset, chasing Lord Feilding's cavalry northwest. Digby's regiment, following behind, had wheeled about to attack the rear of the Parliamentary line. Feilding's men had scattered, but Wilmot's were tired and winded by the pursuit. As they straggled back to the field from Kineton, after some looting and the capture of many Parliamentary colours, Wilmot received news from one of his scouts that events were not turning completely in their favour. His Majesty's personal Lifeguard, brave and determined to be more than a show troop in their elaborate uniforms, were suffering heavy losses along with most of the infantry. Meanwhile, with Rupert's regiment missing from the field, Parliamentary cavalry had poured through the gap on the right flank towards the King's gun battery and disabled many of the cannon. The remaining Royalist troops could not be made to regroup and attack in proper military order.

"Oh, for a regiment of hardened Swedish mercenaries," Wilmot complained, as he and Falkland gazed upon the disorder before them: men moving as if weighted down as they tried to raise their swords, their horses' mouths flecked with foam. On the blood-soaked turf lay wounded, dying, and dead, some heaped together indiscriminately, some alone.

"Can we not finish this once and for all with a last charge?" Falkland pleaded, his voice rising with desperation.

"We've as good as won the day, my lord," Wilmot said. "Why not live to enjoy it. Our men are exhausted. They won't be much use until they've had some rest."

Falkland was so disappointed that he could not speak. He had hoped for a swift end to the war with this one action, followed by some honourable agreement between Essex and the King. It was not to be. The core of Essex's army would continue to hold its ground, as would the King's disorganized forces.

They heard the Royalist foot firing at the enemy until night fell. Then came an awful stillness, though not a silence, as Wilmot bade his drummers beat an order for his cavalry to join the rest of the army a couple of hundred yards to the side of Edgehill, where they would make camp.

"Cheer up," Wilmot told Falkland, as they retreated. "We've raided enough of Essex's supplies that he'll be short of his supper, as well as his coach."

"I am so sorry," Falkland began, tearfully.

"What for?"

"Look about you. How many lost, Englishmen all of them."

"Not all. There's a bunch of hapless Welsh levies amongst them who deserved to be cut down, they made such a poor showing." Wilmot peered this way and that, twisting in his saddle. "Hoy! Danvers!" he said, as Charles Danvers breezed past them on his horse.

Danvers was grinning and brandishing a huge flagpole in one hand. "I bring you Colonel Feilding's colours." Wilmot guffawed and punched his arm, making him nearly drop the pole. "Beaumont's hauled back a cask of wine," he added, "but it's going fast, so you'd better hurry if you want to partake."

"Trust Beaumont to think of such a thing," Wilmot said. "How practical he is. Come, my Lord Falkland, let's raise a cup in honour of the day."

"No, thank you," Falkland told him, offended by their levity; they were behaving as if they had just returned from a successful hunting expedition.

After they rode off, he tried to pray out loud, but his throat was thick with the acrid gun smoke and the dense fog that had settled over the battlefield. He felt cold, much colder than the chill air warranted, every limb trembling, his jaw locked; and yet sweat was pouring from him, down the back of his neck and face, stinging his eyes. As he was removing his gloves to wipe his damp palms he felt his signet ring, engraved with the family crest, slip off. Uttering a rare curse, he dismounted to hunt for it. He could see nothing in the gloom, and after a while he knew that he must give it up as lost.

III.

Laurence was in a farmer's barn with Wilmot, Danvers, and some others, quaffing wine and inspecting the goods pillaged from Essex's train. He had done his share of the violence with weary distaste, for Parliament's cavalry were still mostly raw and hesitated too long to draw blood, though they would grow used to it in time. All he wanted now was to get very drunk.

"Hey, Beaumont, isn't that your brother over there?" Wilmot pointed towards the door.

Begrimed with gun smoke like the rest of them, Tom wore an anxious expression as he bowed to Wilmot. Laurence poured him a cup of wine that he gulped back in one swallow. Then he announced breathlessly, "Ingram's been hurt. His horse fell and crushed his leg. The surgeon might have to cut it off."

"Oh God, I hope not," Laurence murmured, horrified, knowing too well the likely consequences of such an operation in the field. "Can you take me to him?"

"That's why I came to find you."

"Where was your troop today, sir?" Wilmot demanded of Tom.

"We were transferred this morning to His Royal Highness Prince Rupert's regiment, sir."

"Why's Rupert poaching my men? Who ordered it?"

"I – I got the order from Colonel Hoare, sir."

"Beaumont, did you know about this?"

"No," said Laurence, with a questioning look at his brother.

"And what was His Royal Highness thinking, to let you run riot all the way to Kineton?" Wilmot said to Tom. "We could have made short work of Essex if he'd kept his right wing in the field."

"Our wing did exactly the same thing," Laurence reminded Wilmot, who gave a little snort and turned back to Danvers.

Laurence followed Tom out and they walked side by side through the camp, their boots squelching in the thick mud. "Thanks for coming," Laurence said.

Tom nodded shortly. "I must admit, I didn't expect you'd fight. When you weren't with us at Powick, I assumed . . . oh, well, what does it matter now."

They pressed on in silence through the crowds of men, some sitting or lying on the cold, muddy ground, some groaning from their wounds, and others talking quietly together and ministering to the needs of those worse off than they. The air stank of blood and powder, and from the distance came an agonized chorus: hundreds of horses were dying, strewn about the surrounding fields.

"How do you like war so far?" Laurence asked with a grimace. "Isn't it splendid?"

"It *was* splendid," Tom said, in a hushed voice, "when we were charging at the enemy. I've never known such a thrill in all my life. And to ride with the Prince was an honour."

At the mention of Rupert, Laurence stopped and took his brother's arm. "Tom, you must be on your guard with Colonel Hoare. Don't trust him."

"Why do you say that?"

"Because . . ." Laurence hesitated; he could not tell Tom the truth. "Because of what I've heard."

"From what *I've* heard, he's amongst our finest soldiers and he's trusted by Prince Rupert, which is recommendation enough for me. You've been listening to your friend Wilmot, haven't you," Tom exclaimed, pulling away. "Everyone knows that Wilmot's deadly jealous of the Prince. No wonder he'd try to slander Colonel Hoare."

Tom strode on again and Laurence had to run after him. "This has nothing to do with Wilmot. I mean it, Tom – watch out if Hoare begins to pay attention to you."

Tom laughed sourly, his old hostile expression returning. "Now I understand. *You're* jealous – of *me*! My troop was specially selected by Hoare to fight under His Majesty's most talented officer, and you could have been with us sharing the glory but for your prevarications."

"Don't be so stupid," Laurence said. "I couldn't give a shit about any of that. I'm warning you off Hoare for your own good."

"Out of brotherly love?" Tom sneered, and he walked away.

Laurence swore at himself. His vague, condescending advice about Hoare would probably make Tom respect the man even more. But why, he wondered, had Hoare brought Tom's troop into the Prince's regiment? At present, however, his chief concern was Ingram, who might already be suffering unspeakable pain at the hands of some ill-trained surgeon.

He eventually found Ingram laid out in the open with many other wounded men, his legs covered by a blanket. "Beaumont," he said, his face contorting as he sat up. "Tom must have sent you. Did he tell you I broke my leg?"

"Yes. Has anyone seen to you yet?"

"No. I was told that I'm not an urgent case." Ingram attempted to smile; then he gasped as Laurence pulled out his knife and drew aside the blanket.

"I'm going to cut your boot off, not your leg. Don't move." Laurence prised the leather from Ingram's flesh, sliced downwards and peeled it away. "Thank God the bone hasn't pierced your skin. We'll bind up your leg to keep it from moving, and then you should have it set as soon as possible, before the swelling gets worse." He thought quickly. "I'll take you to my father's house. It's not more than a couple of hours' ride, and you can be well looked after."

"I should stay with my troop."

"What for? By the time a surgeon gets round to you, we could already be at the house."

"But surely Wilmot needs you."

"Not as much as you need your leg. I can catch up with him tomorrow morning."

Ingram sniffed and muttered, "What friends I have – first Radcliff, and now you. Radcliff saved my life today, Beaumont." Laurence did not respond; he was busy tearing the blanket into strips. "If he hadn't dragged me out of harm's way after I fell, the enemy cavalry would have ridden right over me. And he gave me his horse. Because of that he's either dead himself or a prisoner at Kineton. Beaumont," he said urgently, wincing as Laurence started to bandage him up, "I must know. Could you go and ask if any prisoners have been exchanged?"

"If you're to make this journey we should start at once."

"Please, I beg you!"

"Oh, all right. I'll give it an hour, no more. Don't let anyone near you, Ingram. If a surgeon does come by, tell him your leg's been set."

Ingram nodded weakly. "Thanks, Beaumont. I won't forget this."

At first, all that Laurence could discover was that a number of distinguished officers, particularly amongst the King's Lifeguard, had been slain, and others taken hostage by Essex. As yet no exchanges had occurred. A list of casualties was apparently being compiled in another part of the camp, but once he arrived there, no one seemed to know who had been set this thankless task.

He ventured onto the plain of Edgehill, where he could still hear the moaning of stricken men and beasts, and where the scavengers, military and civilian, had begun the gruesome work of stripping those unable to defend themselves. It was perhaps as unsafe to wander around now as during the heat of battle, he thought, and he was about to return to Ingram when Lieutenant Martin galloped up to him with a party of soldiers.

"Mr. Beaumont," he said, "did Wilmot send you on another errand?"

"No, I'm looking for someone from Prince Rupert's Horse: Sir Bernard Radcliff."

"Radcliff? I saw him at Kineton, as we were hurrying out. He was on the ground," Martin added, more sombrely.

"The rebels weren't ready to show much mercy after we'd sacked their wagons," one of his companions put in. "I'd say he must be dead."

"But no one actually saw him killed?" Laurence asked.

"Not I," said Martin. "Still, I wouldn't hold out hope if I were you. It was there that we suffered most of our losses. At any rate, we should head back to camp and get some rest. His Majesty may decide to press through the remains of Essex's forces tomorrow and march straight for London."

So Oxford might not be liberated after all, Laurence realised, feeling heartsick; this was bad news for Seward.

He hurried to fetch his horse and borrow another for Ingram, then returned to where his friend was lying, obviously in even greater pain than before. "Beaumont," Ingram said in a faint voice, "what did you find out?" Laurence sighed and told him. "I see." Tears were welling in his eyes. "I hate to ask one more favour of you, but do you remember what you once promised, about Kate? She's at my Aunt Musgrave's house in Faringdon. Would you take her a letter from me?"

"Faringdon's close to Oxford. It must still be held by Parliament."

"Please, man. I don't want her to hear from anyone else."

"First let's take care of *you*," said Laurence, helping him to rise.

IV.

Madam Musgrave reminded Laurence of an amiable Flemish brothel madam he had once known; she would have been attractive some twenty years ago, and still possessed an overblown charm. "Why did I not meet you at Kate's wedding, Mr. Beaumont?" she inquired, once they were settled before the fire, drinking wine.

"I wasn't invited. Richard's not very fond of me."

"He's not altogether fond of me, either," she said, laughing, "but he couldn't afford to please himself on that score. Kate has been staying here since her betrothal, and if things continue as they are, I expect to have her for a while. Walter's my favourite, however, and I'll make no secret of it. He has the sweetest nature." She took a sip from her cup, and her expression grew more serious. "I cannot thank you enough for what you did for him. And to come all this way –"

"It's not necessary," Laurence interrupted. "I love Ingram like a brother."

They were silent for a while. Then she asked, "And Sir Bernard?" He explained what he had heard from Lieutenant Martin. "Dear me," she said. "The uncertainty will be almost worse for Kate than knowing. Though she won't reveal her true feelings to me. She's such a cold fish, that girl. I don't understand her, and to be frank I believe her husband may be at the same loss."

"He looks a bit of a cold fish himself."

"I won't argue with you, sir. But he has a title and land, and Richard is in awe of him and was anxious to find a match that Kate wouldn't refuse. She had refused enough of them already. Where *is* she?" Madam Musgrave called out to a maidservant. "Tell her again that she has a visitor." She turned to Laurence. "The girl spends hours in her chamber, sir, and she must be bored and miserable, yet when I try to entertain her with a game of cards, or ask her to sing for me, it is as bad as pulling teeth. Do you sing, by any chance?"

"Never," Laurence said. "It's against my religion. But I do like a game of cards."

"Thank God for that. We shall have a hand after supper. I insist that you stay and eat with us, sir. Ah, at last," she declared, as Kate entered.

Kate must have been no more than sixteen when Laurence last met her, and since then she had fulfilled the promise of her youth. She resembled some northern goddess, her carriage very erect, blonde and blue-eyed, and perfect in her features. She inspected him coolly, as though he were a worshipping devotee, so he appraised her in return with rather less hauteur and saw her lips twitch disapprovingly.

"Mr. Beaumont has ridden from Chipping Campden, at great peril to himself, just for your sake. There was a great battle yesterday that he has news of," said Madam Musgrave, pouring more wine for them all. "Here, have a cup, my dear."

"No, thank you, Aunt," Kate replied, sitting down.

"I think you might need it, before you hear what he has to say."

Kate accepted the cup, without drinking from it.

"I'm a friend of your brother's, Lady Radcliff, though you won't remember me," Laurence said.

"Yes I do, sir. I hope he is well," she went on, her reserve faltering slightly.

"Not altogether. His horse fell on him during the action. But he was lucky – he only broke his leg. I took him to my father's house, and he had it set this morning by a good surgeon, so you mustn't worry about him."

"We are in your debt, sir," she said.

"No, no. It was your husband who saved his life." From his saddle-bag Laurence withdrew the letter that Ingram had written to her after the operation. It was a surprisingly thick missive, he now noticed, although he could not remember his friend taking long to compose it. "Perhaps you should read this," he said, passing it over.

She took it, and as she broke open the seal, another sealed letter fell out and tumbled to the floor. He bent to retrieve it for her and then hesitated.

"Is this your husband's writing?" he asked, of the few lines on the cover.

"Yes. What of it, sir?"

He paused again, to control his excitement; the hand exactly resembled that on His Majesty's horoscope. "Nothing," he said.

Kate was perusing her brother's note. "I am not to read Sir Bernard's letter unless I know for certain he is dead. Sir Bernard wrote the same instructions," she said, eyeing his. "'To be opened by my wife, Katherine Radcliff, upon my certain decease and no sooner.' What should I do, Aunt?" she inquired.

Laurence gritted his teeth, willing her to open the second letter.

"In your place, I would read it, Kate," said Madam Musgrave. "Since it may concern what is now your property, you have every right."

Kate looked from her to Laurence. "Mr. Beaumont, is it possible that he is still alive?"

He hesitated yet again; he could not lie to her about so grave an issue. "He might be," he said, at length. "We must hope so."

"Then I shall wait, until I find out for certain," she said, lowering her eyes.

Damn her obedience, thought Laurence. And her reaction amazed him: either she was exerting magnificent self-control, or she did not care much for her husband.

After supper they sat at cards. Madam Musgrave suggested that he stay the night, and he agreed, for a private motive: he was burning to get his hands on Radcliff's letter. While she dealt the first round, he considered the possibility of stealing into Kate's chamber late in the night. But if she were to catch him, he would have a hard time explaining himself, and she might cause a highly unpleasant scene.

"You have an enviable proficiency at the game, sir," Madam Musgrave told him, as he shuffled the deck for another round. "You could make a living off it, were you born to less happy circumstances."

He merely smiled.

"I think, Aunt, that I may retire soon," said Kate, her frown expressing undisguised contempt for such a trivial pastime.

"Oh, come now! Mr. Beaumont, you must know some tricks that might entertain her."

He looked at Kate, thinking that no sleight of hand could possibly achieve that end. Ingram was right: she was not easy to like.

"Here, allow me, sir." Madam Musgrave took the deck from him. "Kate, you have only to pick a card."

With the air of an adult humouring a difficult child, Kate selected the knave of spades. *More appropriate than you know*, Laurence could not help remarking to himself.

"'How absolute the knave is!'" Madam Musgrave quoted. "'We must speak by the card, or equivocation will undo us.'"

"I beg pardon?" said Kate, blinking at her.

"From a play – a tragedy, about a Danish prince, who could not make up his mind."

"Whether he should kill the man who had murdered his father and married his mother," Laurence added. "Don't you know it, Lady Radcliff?"

"I have never been to a playhouse, sir."

"I used to go quite often with your brother," he said, remembering how disconsolate Ingram had been after the death of his wife a year or so into their marriage. Laurence had taken him about Southwark and shown him some of its many attractions, some more licit than others.

"Walter did not tell me," she said, as though in reproach not of Ingram, but of Laurence for leading her brother astray.

Madam Musgrave winked at Laurence. "He must have had his

THE BEST OF MEN 333

reasons! So, Kate, are you ready? Put the card back." As he watched her thick, capable, none too clean hands deal out the cards, Laurence tried to imagine what Ingram would say, were he to learn that Sir Bernard Radcliff, the excellent soldier, the dear relative trusted with a precious sister, was plotting against the King's life. Then Madam Musgrave nudged his elbow. "Mr. Beaumont, you are far away."

"I'm sorry, madam. I'm just a little tired, and I must leave early tomorrow."

"I am also tired," said Kate, getting up with alacrity. "Thank you for bringing my letter, sir. Good night, and I wish you a safe journey. Good night, Aunt."

When she had gone, Madam Musgrave set aside the cards. "I shall not keep you long from your bed, sir, but help me see that all is locked up. The servants are sometimes neglectful."

"Of course," he said, and he accompanied her about the house as she went from window to window, and to the doors, checking that each was shut fast.

They were at the stair, and she had given him a candle to light his way, when she held him back and whispered, "What disturbed you so about Sir Bernard's letter?"

"It wasn't the letter," he replied hastily. "It was Lady Radcliff who disturbed me – it's as if she doesn't love him at all."

"Walter assures me that she does. And Sir Bernard is deeply in love with *her*. If he is still in this world, that is."

"I wish my inquiries on that count had been more successful," Laurence said, with genuine regret.

"What might he have written to her, for him to place such a condition on her opening it? It *must* concern his property, which he has gone to great pains to secure from Parliament. He was so worried about his house being ransacked that he stored a coffer of his here – he said he feared to leave behind certain family valuables at Longstanton."

Madam Musgrave heaved a sigh. "If we were to receive confirmation of his death, Kate must see what is inside it."

She might not like what she found, thought Laurence, his own curiosity instantly aroused. He should have been more pessimistic as to Radcliff's chances of survival. Kate had come so close to breaking that seal.

Madam Musgrave surprised him by leaning forward to plant her lips on his cheek. "I do declare, sir, I haven't seen such skill at gaming since my days at King James' Court. And if I were as young as I was then, I would not permit a handsome fellow like you to escape with only a chaste kiss. Now off to bed, and I shall wake you at dawn, though if you have need of anything before you go to sleep, my chamber is to the right hand of the stairs, and I shall be up soon. You may take the one on the left."

"Thank you," he said, wishing he could ask which was Kate's. "Good night, Madam Musgrave."

Once in his room he removed his boots and blew out the candle. Keeping his door an inch or so ajar, he peered out. A few minutes later he saw his hostess stomping upstairs, followed by her maid-servant. They entered her chamber, and for a while he heard voices in conversation. Eventually there came a loud thump, as of someone settling heavily into bed, and silence. He waited, until reassured by the snores emanating from her chamber. Slipping past it in the narrow corridor, scarcely daring to breathe, he very cautiously tried each of the other doors on that floor. Only one was fastened shut, and he discerned from his investigations that it must be Kate's. Frustrated, he returned to his room, and paced about. Then he stopped short. How on earth could he have forgotten the message that Seward had left him at Clarke's house? Seward knew the author of the horoscope, and therefore Seward knew Radcliff.

V.

Dressed in the robes of Lord Chamberlain, Pembroke was sitting beside His Majesty in the Banqueting House, with young Prince Charles nearby. The King fastened on Pembroke his expressive Stuart eyes with their drooping lids, so like his father's, and asked, "Are you my f-f-riend, Herbert, or my enemy?" Pembroke declared his undying allegiance in the warmest terms, yet even as he was speaking, the boy Charles rose and cried, "Take him from here, and when he is hanged, drawn, and quartered, put his head on a stave at Traitor's Gate for all to see his disgrace." Pembroke turned in horror to the King; and a yet more terrible thing happened. His Majesty's head seemed to flop from one side to another loosely, and next toppled altogether from his shoulders and into Pembroke's lap. Pembroke tried to rid himself of the object, but it stayed as if glued to his robe, and he began to scream.

In a sweat he awoke, clutching his throat. The recurrent dream became more vivid each time, although it always stopped short at the same point, flinging him back to consciousness, heart pounding in his breast.

He must not let it agitate him so, he told himself sternly, as he had on countless past nights. His conscience should be clear: he was working to save his country from the stranglehold of popery and cut short the bloodshed that had already broken out in the land. He had recognised what must be accomplished and had chosen to act alone. And Charles Stuart's destiny was written in the stars, sanctioned by a Divine Hand. Pembroke himself was merely God's instrument, executing His will. The death of one would preserve the lives of many, bringing peace and prosperity to the realm, so that England would stand out again as a beacon of true faith to the whole of Christendom. With God's grace and the secret powers that Pembroke hoped soon to acquire, he would start a cleansing tide that would in time purge out the whore of Rome, her priests and her armies too.

He deserved some revenge, he thought next. He had served the former King James dutifully, allowing the old sodomite to caress him and lean upon him and slobber over him when he was a pretty young man. All the while he had courted Prince Henry, heir to the throne and noble defender of the Protestant cause at home and abroad. But Henry had died in the flower of his youth, of fever or perhaps of poison, and his brother, that unworthy, stuttering dwarf Charles, had become king in his stead.

Lying back, Pembroke could recall as if it were yesterday the fateful incident in the summer of 1641 that had cost him the office of Lord Chamberlain. Lord Maltravers, the Earl of Arundel's impudent son, had set out to provoke him during a meeting at the House of Lords, and he had lost his temper, a mistake to which he was prone. He had slapped the boy's face. When they were both sent to the Tower, he thought that would be the end of it. Yet King Charles had been waiting for just such an excuse to remove him from office and appoint the Earl of Essex in his place, in a belated attempt to appease Parliament and to please the little buck-toothed Queen, who Pembroke knew harboured an intense hatred for him.

"You and your papist wife," Pembroke said quietly, into the darkness. "You should not have humiliated me."

He was about to shut his eyes when rapid steps approached his door, and his servant's voice called, "My lord, please forgive the disturbance, but Mr. Rose is come to see you."

"Have him wait in my antechamber," he called back, tossing aside the bedclothes. He got up, removed his nightcap, put on his dressing gown and padded slippers, combed his thinning hair, and went out to receive his guest.

Radcliff's face was shockingly grey, his eyes circled with shadow. His buff coat was stained with dried blood, and his right arm was in a sling.

"Bring him refreshment," Pembroke ordered the servant, "and then leave us in privacy until I ask for you again." He and Radcliff waited to talk, exchanging agonized glances; like lovers too long separated, Pembroke thought wryly. At length his servant brought wine and a platter of fruit, bread, and cheese, then withdrew.

"So our plan succeeded," Pembroke observed.

Radcliff nodded. "Upon capture at Edgehill I feared for my life, but your document of safe conduct was respected, and here I am."

Pembroke now noticed the green leather scabbard at Radcliff's side. "How the devil did you recover your sword?" he cried. "You told me it was stolen on the same night as my money!"

Radcliff laid a hand on it, as if to comfort himself that it was still there. "It came back to me by a coincidence that can only have been fated, my lord. A friend of my brother-in-law Ingram gifted it to me as a wedding present. Since it was originally *your* gift to me, its return can only augur well for us."

"*What?* You mean it travelled across the sea to you, as though drawn by magnetic force? I would more easily believe that it was never stolen than swallow a tale like that!"

"It is the truth, my lord, which is often more unlikely than a lie. The man who gave it to me also fought abroad. He happened to purchase the sword in the very same place that I was robbed – The Hague."

"A pity he could not have found my gold, as well!" Pembroke sneered. Had Radcliff pocketed the money himself? Though if so, why arrive with the sword in evidence, and such an unlikely explanation? "I am disappointed," he went on in the same caustic tone, "that with all your astrological skills you could not foretell this extraordinary event."

"My lord," said Radcliff, speaking in a tense whisper, "I am not some mountebank that cozens old women for a penny to find their missing thimbles. What I practise is both art and science, and it has not failed you in the past, as far as I can remember."

"I spoke in jest, man," Pembroke said, uneasily; he still needed Radcliff's skills, even if the business of the sword left a nagging doubt in his mind. "What happened to your arm?"

"Grazed by a ball. The wound has festered a little with the strain of riding."

"Why did I not hear from you after Robinson delivered my message to you at Shrewsbury?"

Radcliff stared at him in obvious consternation. "I received no message!"

"By Jesu's blood! I sent him over a month ago, to inform you of what passed between Falkland and myself when we met. He did not return to report to me, which I found perturbing; he is usually so reliable. The message was in our code, and contained nothing that could damage us, but if he were seized and put to torture, he might reveal our names."

"He knows only that we are striving towards a peace."

"Yes, thank God, no more than that," Pembroke agreed. "And we are amongst many these days. Here in Parliament, the radicals are falling from favour. You may depend upon it, peace talks will begin again soon." He eyed Radcliff warily. "I now see fit to tell you: since late summer I have been corresponding in secret with His Majesty. I have offered my services unreservedly to his cause and pledged never to take up arms against him."

"Did you have to go quite that far, my lord?"

"Why not? The more he trusts me, the better." Pembroke gulped back his glass of wine, a thrill passing through his veins. "As I said in that message to you, Falkland has effectively promised to re-establish communication between myself and Dr. Earle. When Falkland was in London I gave him a letter for Earle, begging Earle's forgiveness if I had ever offended him. Neither man will resist my advances, I know," he concluded, smiling to himself. There was a silence, during which

Radcliff gazed blearily at the floor. "What's the matter?" Pembroke said.

"Excuse me, my lord, it is my wound that ails me."

"Oh, I meant to ask – did your bride like the jewels I gave you for her?"

Radcliff seemed to wince. "Yes, thank you, my lord. When I last saw her, she was wearing one of the necklaces."

"The diamond?"

"No. She was most taken with the ruby and pearl collar."

"She has modest tastes! That was a mere trinket, compared to the others. And were her favours worth the wait?" Pembroke added. "Anticipation can be more exciting than the act itself, especially with an untrained girl."

"My wife delights me in every respect," Radcliff answered stiffly.

"Then you must have been sad to leave her bed! God willing, in another month or so we shall all spend Christmas with our families. How I miss Wilton! I had no chance to hunt this autumn and my estate must be overrun with fine buck." Pembroke broke off; Radcliff looked as if he were about to faint. "We must attend to your wound," Pembroke said, and rang a bell to summon his servant. "Mr. Rose shall stay for what remains of the night," he told the man. "See to his comfort, and fetch the surgeon. He has a bad arm that requires care. Mr. Rose, we shall talk again tomorrow."

VI.

After a tortuous ride from Faringdon to Oxford evading enemy patrols, Laurence headed straight for the Castle to reconnoitre the area. He considered risking a visit but was not sure that Seward would still be imprisoned there. As dusk began to fall, more and more soldiers came riding back in through the main gate, and he knew he could not linger without attracting their suspicion. He had no choice but to go again to Dr. Clarke.

At Merton, he found that gentleman on his way out of the door. "What in God's name are you doing here, Mr. Beaumont?" Clarke exclaimed, his face flushing with anger.

"Let me in," Laurence said, and Clarke reluctantly opened for him. "Is Seward still in gaol?" he demanded, pulling off his cloak.

"Yes, he is. As you may be, if you don't get out of Oxford at once."

"How is he?"

Clarke sighed and waved Laurence to a chair. "I am trying everything in my power to move his case forward, sir, to no result thus far. But I did succeed in having him transferred to a new cell, away from the common pound, and his health has greatly improved. Indeed, I have been permitted to visit him almost every day and bring him nourishing food, and books, to relieve the tedium of his confinement. He is as well as can be expected. And he would *not* wish you to venture any mad escapade on his behalf. Tell me, sir," Clarke went on, in a different tone, "have you news of the battle between His Majesty and Essex's army a few days ago? It's all we can talk about here."

"I was in it," Laurence said.

Clarke questioned him eagerly about it, remarking when he had finished, "So His Majesty could be marching on the capital as we speak. Well, as for me, I should get my supper. Don't stir from my rooms, sir, until I return."

Once alone, Laurence sat forward and rested his head in his hands. *How to free Seward?* he asked himself. An hour passed, and another, and he grew increasingly restless. Then at last Clarke burst in, very excited.

"I have glad tidings! The Warden is packing to leave for London! And why must he flee? Because the King is on his way to reclaim Oxford! Lord Say has called the townsfolk to prepare for an attack within the next day or so!"

"That *is* good news," Laurence admitted.

"We must be patient. If the city is liberated, our friend will be too."

"But he's facing a charge of murder. He may yet go to trial."

"With Brent out of the way, the charges will not stick! There's nothing you can do for him, sir," Clarke added. "You may sleep here tonight and rejoin your regiment on the morrow."

Laurence acquiesced, settling down as before on the floor of Clarke's main chamber. But he could not sleep. It occurred to him, as he tossed and turned, that the conspirators had been counting on Parliament to hang Seward. Tyler was on the loose, and perhaps Radcliff as well. They must know that their hopes could be foiled by the arrival of Royalist forces.

When he heard the university bells chiming out four o'clock, Laurence rose and lit a candle. Hunting out a sheet of Clarke's paper, he scribbled a couple of lines on it, signed it with a flourish that he considered suitably illegible, sealed it up, and stuffed it in his doublet. Then he charged his pistols, removed his spurs, grabbed his cloak, and exited quietly. In the stable, he saddled his horse and walked it out through the gatehouse, managing not to rouse the porter on duty.

There was only a thin moon to light his path, but he knew the territory well, apart from the recent city fortifications. He mounted and rode south, passing Corpus Christi and Christ Church Colleges, and then west, without encountering a soul. The city seemed deep in slumber, as on any other chill early morning before dawn.

Troopers were mustering at the Castle walls, no doubt headed for the northern boundaries of the city to anticipate the invading Royalists. Laurence heard the jingle of harness and hooves pounding on the cobbled street, though it was too dark for him to see how many soldiers had stayed to guard the prison. He brought his horse up against the wall and stood in the stirrups to get a higher grip on its rough stones, then dragged himself over, jumping down on the other side. Torches burned at the gate, which he avoided, looking instead for a window that might offer him entrance, but there was none within his reach.

A sentry stood not far away, shuffling his feet to keep warm, and humming to himself. Laurence could not get past unnoticed. Slowly, step by step, he crept up on the man, who fortuitously took off his hat to scratch his head just a second before Laurence's pistol butt crashed down on it. Two more blows felled him, and he got a fourth on the ground. Seized by a sudden inspiration, Laurence stooped to strip off the man's orange sash, which he tied about his own waist. It was a poor disguise, he knew, and as liable to fail him as the rest of his plan.

Retrieving his pistols, he ran towards the main gate and across the courtyard, through a set of open doors, into a large chamber with a vaulted ceiling. Here he looked around, concealed by one of the thick supporting columns, their shadows starkly defined by the light of torches that blazed upon the wall. Prisoners were crowded in iron cages on either side of an aisle, some sleeping, some clinging to the bars in a dejected manner. The floor, strewn ineffectually with hay, was a wash of sewage. At the far end, a couple of guards sat on a low stone ledge, muskets propped beside them. They were eating, apparently undeterred by the odour.

Laurence screwed up his courage and strode out, along the aisle between the cages. "Stand to attention," he yelled, in his most imposing military manner. The guards jumped, nearly dropping their breakfast of bread and cheese. "I come with an order from Lord Say, to release a prisoner by the name of William Seward into my custody," he continued, before they could speak. "Take me to his cell." The men frowned at each other and then at him. "What are you waiting for?" he snarled.

"Order?" queried the oldest of the pair, putting his food down carefully on the ledge. "I wasn't told about no order."

"You should watch your tongue. Who is in command here?"

They glanced at each other again. "Captain Flynn, sir, but he went last night to drill the troops out by Gloucester Green," the younger man said.

"How the hell could he leave the Castle so poorly defended?"

"Those was his orders, sir," said the other man. "I am in charge, in his absence."

"And who are you?" snapped Laurence, willing them not to ask the same question.

"Ensign Crawley, sir."

Laurence glared at him until he looked down at his boots. "Well, I suppose I must deal with you." He took the parchment from his doublet and proffered it to the ensign, who broke the seal with grubby fingers and inspected it officiously. Laurence tried not to laugh: the untidiness of his own writing had frequently earned him criticism, but in this case its legibility was not helped by the fact that Crawley had the letter upside down.

Crawley gave him back the parchment and nodded to his companion to pass him a bunch of keys. "This way, sir," he said to Laurence. They went through an archway into another chamber, less stinking than the last, where the cells were divided by walls rather than bars, each with a wooden door into which a small peephole had been cut for the benefit of the guards. "What does Lord Say want with him, sir?" Crawley asked Laurence, his tone now deferential.

"He's not just a murderer but an enemy spy. He will be interrogated and then hanged."

"That ancient fellow? I'd never have thought it."

"He's a known witch, too," Laurence added, for good measure.

"That I can believe," Crawley said.

"Has he had any visitors?"

"Yes, sir. Someone else from the university, a Dr. Clarke, has come every day, to bring him food and books. And not a moment ago, I let in his nephew."

"His *nephew*? At this hour?"

"Yes, sir. He came with a basket of provisions. I ain't seen him before, sir."

As Crawley fitted a key into one of the doors, Laurence stayed his hand and peered through the peephole. Inside, Seward was lying on a pallet, half obscured by a huge, familiar figure standing over him. "Open the door quietly and go back to your post," Laurence whispered to Crawley.

Moving away so that he would not be seen as it swung wide, he cocked his pistols. As he stepped into the doorway, pistols raised, Seward saw him and let out a cry. Tyler turned and with amazing speed hoisted Seward up as if he weighed less than a child, holding him in front of his own body like a human breastplate.

"Good evening, Mr. Beaumont," he said softly, his face registering no surprise.

"Good evening, Mr. Tyler," said Laurence. "Sorry to have missed you on the last occasion."

"More narrowly than I missed you at Aylesbury. I spent a few weeks in bed nursing my shoulder after that. And you clipped off my earlobe." Laurence risked a glance at Seward, whose eyes were now shut tight. "So," Tyler continued, in the same calm voice, "I can be more use to you alive than dead. In fact, I might tell you some things that you'd like to know." He paused, and then went on less patiently, "Put down your weapons, and let's agree to be out of here."

He moved just a fraction, perhaps to gauge Laurence's response, and exposed his face. It was the best that Laurence could hope for, and he fired with the pistol in his left hand, praying that his aim was true.

At such short range the impact of the shot sent Tyler flying against the wall. His face was blown open, one eyeball hanging loose from its socket on a strand of flesh, the other socket a well of blood. Seward had collapsed on the floor. "I thought you'd never do it," he murmured to Laurence, as the guards ran in.

"Don't give me any trouble," Laurence ordered him, for their benefit, "or I'll shoot you, too. He was another Royalist agent," he said to them, nodding at Tyler. "No doubt passing messages to this fellow. We'll find out soon enough, even if you take a little persuading," he said nastily, to Seward.

"Did you have to kill him, sir? We could have arrested him for you," said Ensign Crawley, examining what remained of Tyler's visage.

"You couldn't arrest your own mother. Search the body."

Crawley's efforts yielded no more than a knife and a few coins, while the basket that Tyler had brought for Seward contained only a loaf of bread and a slice of meat pie.

"Put the prisoner in irons," Laurence said next.

"Sir, we've got none to spare."

"Then tie his hands behind his back and take him to the main gate. Carry him if you must. And don't you try me," Laurence spat at Seward, afraid of any error that might give them away. He marched ahead of them through the gaol and past the astonished prisoners. Out in the courtyard, he could see the sky paling with dawn. More soldiers came to gawk, although they maintained a respectful distance.

Crawley was hovering about nervously, like a schoolboy waiting for his master to leave. "What shall we do with the dead spy, sir?"

"You can fuck him up the arse for all I care," Laurence replied. "I'm going to remember you, Ensign Crawley. Next time you slack off, I'll have you stripped of your rank and flogged senseless. Good day to you."

"Good day, sir," said Crawley, saluting shakily.

With a brutality that was not lost on the soldiers, Laurence seized the rope around Seward's wrists and hauled him out through the gate and into the street beyond. To Laurence's relief, his horse was where he had left it. He lifted Seward into the saddle, mounted behind him, and kicked the beast into a gallop. Neither of them spoke until they neared Merton College, when he slowed it to a trot.

"That was a fine performance, Beaumont," Seward told him, in a remarkably strong voice.

"It was pure luck," said Laurence. He knew what they were both thinking: had he come on stage a minute later, Seward would have been dead.

VII.

"There was method to his madness, I grant you, but he could have got you both killed," observed Clarke, as he arranged a pillow for Seward to sit up in bed.

"I should not want Beaumont for my superior officer," Seward jested gaily, rubbing at his wrists where the rope had chafed them. "He nearly bit that poor ensign's head off. Didn't you, my boy!" Beaumont said nothing. He was watching them both, eyes narrowed and glittering like those of a cat about to fight. "What's the matter with you?" Seward asked. "You should be in high spirits after your marvellous feat of daring!"

"Was it Sir Bernard Radcliff's name that you held back from me?" Beaumont exploded furiously.

Seward stared at him. "Yes, it was."

"And it was you who gave him the code. Why didn't you say it was yours when I first showed it to you?" Beaumont tore the orange sash from his waist and hurled to the floor. "You lied to me – or you concealed the truth, which is just as bad!"

"I planned to tell you but fate intervened."

"That's no excuse."

"I know," Seward conceded, his joy deflating; he felt suddenly frail and helpless. "How did you find him out?"

"Your story first," Beaumont said, grabbing a chair for himself.

"Very well," Seward sighed. "My acquaintance with Radcliff began six or seven years before your time, Beaumont. He'd studied at Cambridge for his bachelor's degree, and he was interested in the great Hermetic teachers, in cryptology, and astrology, of course, which was why he'd sought me out. We often discussed codes, both ancient and new, and the code he used in those letters was one we had worked on together."

"My God," exclaimed Beaumont. "Go on."

"He had such a quick mind," Seward said, remembering. "And I took such pleasure from instructing him that I grew almost giddy with it. I saw in Radcliff someone to whom I could pass on the learning of my great masters, Dee and Fludd. Indeed, I thought then that I would never find a better student. But over time I became uneasy, as he showed signs of worldly ambition. He had a mind to preferment in the foreign embassies, because the estate he would inherit in Cambridgeshire was on such poor land that it could barely keep a gentleman's household." Beaumont frowned as if this meant something to him, though he did not interrupt. "And then we had a disagreement. He wanted me to teach him the art of scrying. I felt he was not ready for it and would use the knowledge for venal purposes. So I refused. That was why he broke with me. I never saw him again."

"He already had most of what he wanted from you."

"Far more than I realised. I not only taught him to cast horoscopes, for which he had a genuine aptitude, but I revealed to him part of what I knew about a Hermetic order, the Knights of the Rosy Cross."

"And who are *they*?" Beaumont asked brusquely.

"A Protestant Brotherhood dedicated to the enlightenment of Europe, to freedom from the yoke of Rome, and to the revival of learning in politics, the arts, and the sciences based upon the mathematical and alchemical synchronicities between microcosm and macrocosm." Seward hesitated, catching Beaumont's annoyance with his long-winded answer. "They seek a revolution, my boy, as well as a revival: to cast off centuries of misguided, superstitious scholarship that has accumulated ever since Aristotle's teachings were bastardised by the Roman Church. Dee was almost certainly connected with them, and I know Fludd was, though he always denied it. Radcliff had heard that I had been Fludd's student and must have thought I was a member of the order."

"Well, *are* you?"

"If I were, I would not tell even you."

"What could Radcliff expect to get out of this Brotherhood?"

"Secret knowledge brings many kinds of power," Seward murmured.

Beaumont let out a harsh breath. "Can you be more precise?"

"Please, Beaumont, I am too weary to discuss such deep and complicated things just now, but to give one obvious example, the power to control others and bend them to your will. A power most useful in politics."

"He failed with you."

"Ultimately, yes, and he would be unable to gain admittance to the Brotherhood for the same reason that I would not teach him how to scry. There – now you know everything," finished Seward, dropping his head back upon the pillow.

"Not quite," Beaumont said, in a low voice. "Why did you hold back on me?"

"Out of selfish fear," Seward replied sadly. "I have had so many troubles in the past, and so many false charges brought against me. I did not want my association with Radcliff to come out into the open. I am ashamed of myself, Beaumont. Can you forgive me?"

Beaumont gazed at him for a moment, then smiled. "Of course."

"Now I have told you my story. It is time for yours."

Beaumont rattled his off, ending with his glimpse of Radcliff's writing on the letter. "And here's what I've been thinking," he said, "though I can't prove any of it. Radcliff is working for the Earl of Pembroke, who is negotiating in secret for a peace. But what if these negotiations are a cover for some less noble scheme? Why should he be courting the Secretary of State *and* Dr. Earle?"

"Earle was his chaplain," Clarke put in.

"Earle is also Prince Charles' tutor. And my father says Pembroke had a grudge against the King. Wasn't he dismissed from office as Lord Chamberlain for some offence?"

"Hardly sufficient to turn him into a regicide!"

"That's where my theory falls down," Beaumont acknowledged.

They were quiet for a while; then Seward said, "Do you remember, Beaumont, the design on that sword? Of roses. And the form of the sword is like a cross."

"And Mr. Rose is the name that Radcliff's been using. So what does all that mean?"

"Radcliff and his master are employing the Brotherhood's symbols for more than their correspondence, which may hint at a yet broader aspiration on their part."

"Good Christ! Isn't ruling a kingdom by proxy enough for them?"

"Maybe not. Their whole purpose in committing regicide might be to adopt a course from which our present monarch has thus far refrained, to the disappointment of many an Englishman. If the master of the conspiracy could establish himself as the young prince's protector and restore peace to the kingdom, he would then be free to enter the foreign war in full force in order to crush the Hapsburg Empire, and perhaps Rome itself."

Beaumont made a little whistling noise through his teeth. "I can't imagine anything worse than to drag England into that quagmire."

"If he succeeded, however, he would be seen as the saviour of the Protestant faith and the champion of a new empire. And I suspect he wishes to invoke the Brotherhood's blessing for his actions," concluded Seward, shuddering at the idea.

"What would be wrong with that? You just said the Brotherhood aims to free us from the yoke of Rome."

"On the contrary, Beaumont, it would be a disaster! The Knights of the Rosy Cross seek spiritual and intellectual enlightenment, whereas he is seeking worldly power for its own sake! They would never sanction the murder of a Protestant king, nor of any king at all! This usurper would spit upon their symbols: the cross, an image of Christ's suffering and the suffering that we must all endure to reach wisdom, and the rose, the symbol of love." Seward paused; Beaumont was frowning in concentration, the same look he used to wear as a student when puzzling over some difficult lesson. How much he had risked at the Castle to rescue an old man, Seward thought, wanting to hug him. "Eros' crown was made of roses, my boy," Seward continued, "but the rose is also a symbol of secrecy – Eros gave a rose to the god of silence. The Brotherhood does not wish to be known – its alchemical secrets can be too easily abused. Had I not been so foolishly deceived by Radcliff, I would never have trusted him with such knowledge."

"Eros is two-faced, both creative and destructive," said Clarke.

"And can make a man blind, as I was. Radcliff may also have blinded his master, tempting him with more prophecies, such as the one he made about the King's death."

"Do you believe in prophecies?" Beaumont asked abruptly.

"Yes, but, as they say, we must beware of false prophets."

"How can you tell the false from the true?" he persisted, with an interest that surprised Seward.

"The true have nothing to gain by their predictions and take no reward for them. Beaumont," Seward went on, "after Radcliff left Oxford, I heard that he had become secretary to a member of the House of Lords. I did not inquire who."

"It might have been Pembroke. I should ask Ingram about that."

"We'd still lack evidence of Pembroke's guilt. It is a terrible charge to bring against a noble so well-reputed and honoured, and a perilous thing for us, should we levy it wrongly."

"If he did not fall at Edgehill, Radcliff must be arrested and interrogated," Clarke declared.

"I suggested something of the sort to Falkland even before I was certain of Radcliff's guilt," said Beaumont. "I wish I still had those letters. It's thanks to Hoare that we lost them. All he's got left are my transcriptions, and all *we* have are my copies."

"Not any more," Seward confessed. "I thought it best to destroy them before I fled from Merton."

"Christ, what a pity!" Beaumont gave a short, despondent laugh. "Oh and I forgot to tell you, I've learnt that Hoare could be a threat to Falkland. He can't tolerate the endless peace negotiations, and he may be reading Falkland's private correspondence, trying to catch him out in some indiscretion with Parliament. I warned Falkland, and he asked me to bring him some proof of it."

"Let us hope this matter does not interfere with his pursuit of the regicides," said Seward anxiously.

Beaumont nodded. "Just the same, though, I'd like to see Hoare dismissed as soon as possible."

"Gentlemen, we have had a great adventure this morning," intervened Clarke, as if to terminate the conversation. "We may yet have more, when the King's army arrives."

"And then pray heaven I can clear my name, and Pusskins and I can move back into my rooms," Seward added. "And what about you, Beaumont?"

"You already gave me my orders," he said, with a sardonic smile. "I have to find Radcliff."

Part Three

England, November 1642–April 1643

CHAPTER ELEVEN

I.

After a victorious sweep into Oxford, the King's forces had pushed southeast to menace the capital. Parliament was renewing its peace overtures, even as it hurried to strengthen fortifications around London in case of an attack. From a position of strategic advantage at Reading, His Majesty declined to receive one of its chief Commissioners. At the same time, Prince Rupert was making quite clear his disdain for a settlement by pillaging the local countryside and skirmishing with any Parliamentary troops he found there.

Meanwhile, Laurence had searched vainly for Radcliff's name on the list of casualties from Edgehill and was now convinced that he must still be alive.

"If he's a person of any quality he may have been taken hostage to London," said Wilmot, when Laurence consulted him one evening. "The rebels will wring some money out of him and then swap him for a prisoner of ours. Why, what's your interest in him?"

"He's the brother-in-law of a very good friend of mine, Walter Ingram." Laurence pretended to think for a moment. "Wilmot, have you ever considered how valuable it might be to have some better intelligence about London's fortifications?"

"Are you suggesting you could sneak into London and not get caught?"

"I know I can. With Rupert chasing down all the Parliamentary forces between here and the city, there won't be enough troops to stop every man travelling alone, especially at night."

As Laurence had anticipated, any praise for the Prince instantly raised Wilmot's hackles. "All right, Beaumont," he said. "But I want you to swear that you won't share your information with anyone else before I see it." Laurence swore obediently. "When do you propose to leave?"

"Tonight, if I have your permission."

"Tonight, eh?" Wilmot burst into laughter. "I'm well aware that you've your own reasons for making this journey, but if they keep you away too long, all friendship aside, I'll see that you pay. And if you do get caught, don't expect any help from me."

"That's understood," said Laurence.

He gained the city outskirts just as the sun began to rise. At the Chelsea turnpike, he stabled his mount at an ostler's yard and waited until dusk in the quiet meadows nearby, before walking down towards the river. Eluding some sentries near Tothill Fields, he stole passage on one of the barges carrying goods downstream and hid, crouched amongst sacks, his legs horribly cramped. When it pulled into dock just short of the Bridge to unload, he jumped off, into familiar territory not far from Blackman Street, where he hoped to seek shelter.

Mistress Edwards' brothel had once been as busy and well reputed in London as Simeon's house in The Hague, yet when Laurence arrived all was silent in her street, and the place itself was boarded up with a sign pasted on the door: Closed by Order of Parliament. As he stood reading it, the contents of a chamber pot were tossed from a window above, narrowly missing his head.

"For Christ's sake, watch what you're doing," he shouted up.

"Lord bless us!" cried a female voice that he recognised, and Mistress

Edwards' maid peered out of the window. "If it isn't Mr. Beaumont!"

"Sarah," he said, "may I come in?"

The window slammed shut. Soon the front door opened. "Gracious, sir, I can't believe it – haven't seen you in years," Sarah whispered, closing the door behind him.

He clasped her hands in greeting and asked eagerly, "How are you all? Well, I hope?"

"Oh no! What hardship we've fallen upon, sir! Mistress Edwards has been thrown in the Fleet Prison with some of the ladies, and we who are left have barely a penny between us. We've been asked to pay so much tax on everything you can think of, and we're nigh on starving."

"You've had no custom?"

"A little here and there," she replied, "but the ladies must be ever so sly about it. And the men who come here know how miserable we are. If the ladies don't agree to their price, they say they'll call in the authorities."

The main room where Mistress Edwards used to receive her guests was completely blocked off, the entrance roughly plastered over. Sarah showed Laurence upstairs, into a bedchamber stripped of its former luxurious hangings. There he found three women wrapped in blankets sitting round a fireplace in which a lump of coal smouldered; two of them he knew, the fancifully named Cordelia and Perdita, while the other must have arrived after his time. They all looked to him thin and pale, though appealing nonetheless, for Mistress Edwards, like Simeon, had taste.

"Welcome back, sir!" cried Cordelia, jumping up to embrace him. "This is Mr. Beaumont, Jane," she added, to their companion. "One of our favourites, he was!"

Jane rose and curtseyed. "Pleased to meet you, sir."

"We thought you didn't like us any more," Perdita reproached him. "Where've you been all these years?"

"I was abroad, or else of course I would have come to see you." He shivered; he could see his breath in the air. "It's freezing in here."

"We've no more coal," said Cordelia.

"Any wine, then?"

"Not a drop," Sarah apologised.

"Can you buy some?"

"I could buy whatever you want, sir, if I only had the money."

He gave her a few pounds for provisions, and after she hurried off, he sat talking with the others, who told him what a sad decline they had witnessed since Parliament ruled the city.

"No playhouses, no bear-baiting, no music except for hymns – no fun," Cordelia lamented.

"You ain't with the rebels, are you?" Jane asked.

He shook his head. If the Royalists were to lose this war, he thought now, life would be unbearable: it seemed as if Parliament were bent on suppressing every pleasure available to Londoners. "I'm here looking for information that may help His Majesty's cause," he said. "And as a matter of fact, you might be able to help *me*, because I won't be able to go about the city openly."

After Sarah returned, and they were all invigorated by food, drink, and a blazing hearth, he began to describe what he would like them to do, then stopped, on hearing a heavy tread on the stair beyond.

"That's just the old Dutchman, Meyboom, what sleeps in the garret," Sarah said. "Calls himself an artist, but he can't get his paintings sold any more, so all he does is signs." She gestured to a corner of the bedchamber. "There's a whole stack of his canvases. Bowls of fruit and flowers and dead birds, most of them."

Laurence got up to inspect them; they were not unskilfully executed. "Do you think he's hungry?" he asked the women, who glanced at each other and began to laugh uproariously, as if this were a foolish question. "Take him up what's left of the meal, and tell him I want to speak with him in the morning."

"And may we send poor Mistress Edwards a hot dish tomorrow?" Sarah asked.

"Yes indeed." He found himself yawning. "So . . . where might I sleep?" he inquired, with a smile.

Cordelia giggled and nudged Perdita, who said, "You can have your choice of beds, sir."

That night he chose Cordelia's, for he had known her longest, and he had not forgotten some of her more ingenious talents.

The next day, as they lay together, she observed, "If we were starving for a decent meal, I think you were hungry for something else."

"You're right, I was, and thank you for it," he said, kissing her affectionately.

He was feeling hungry again when there came a knock at the door.

"Mr. Meyboom to see you, sir," Sarah called out.

"Well, isn't that a nuisance," Cordelia teased, pinching Laurence on the rear as he launched out of bed. "And just look at the state of you!"

"Most inconvenient," he agreed, taking his time to dress before opening to the Dutchman.

Meyboom was grey in hair and beard, and hollow in the chest, his face pale from the same inadequate diet as that of the women. His shabby garments were dust-coloured with wear save for a few bright splatters of paint on the front of his doublet. "Mr. Beaumont, I thank you for the sustenance last night," he said, in ponderous English. "What may I do for you?"

Laurence addressed him in his own language. "I would like to commission a painting. Not a still life – a mythical subject. A scene with two Greek gods, Eros and Harpocrates."

"Ah – I have read my classical authors," Meyboom answered proudly. "Eros gave a rose to Harpocrates, the god of silence, to keep him from revealing the weaknesses of the other deities."

"That's exactly what I wish you to portray. There'll be some text, as well, but it can come later. When could you start?"

"As soon as you supply me with a small advance to purchase the necessary materials, sir."

Laurence obliged with a large advance, and Meyboom left contented.

"What a tongue, Dutch – sounds more like spitting than speaking," Cordelia said. "Now then, Mr. Beaumont, what about those new gowns you promised us?"

The four women were disappointed, however, when they heard what Laurence had in mind. "Must they be so plain?" Perdita asked, wrinkling her nose.

"Very plain," he said. "Collars up to your chins, and caps over your ears. And no paint on your faces. Mr. Meyboom can use all the paint he likes, but not you."

"Oh, I get your meaning – we're sinners disguised as saints!" Jane said.

It was Jane, suitably apparelled, whom he sent out towards Whitehall to inquire as to the whereabouts of the Earl of Pembroke's house. On the pretext of selling eggs she called there and, after a day or two, became friendly with the kitchen boy. In exchange for a cuddle, she learnt that a Mr. Rose had been staying a while back to heal from a wound. He had since gone, the boy knew not where.

When she reported this to Laurence, he was so delighted that he gave her an enormous hug, picking her up off her feet. "Jane," he exclaimed, "I can't thank you enough."

"It was easy, sir," she said, as he set her back down again. "We are all actresses, we whores. If only they'd let a girl on the stage."

"If only there was a playhouse still open," Cordelia grumbled. "Our turn now, Mr. Beaumont. What are the rest of us to do?"

"I'll tell you," said Laurence.

Over the following days, as Mr. Meyboom painted away upstairs, the women toured London using their various wiles to extract intelligence from unsuspecting citizens and Parliamentary guards alike. Gradually two images began to take shape: one a map of the city's defences in Laurence's blotted scrawl, and the other, on canvas, a depiction of the two gods. Meyboom claimed to be a quick worker and estimated that the painting would be finished and dry in a fortnight's time. Laurence was perfectly happy to wait, even if he could not leave the house for fear of the city militias. He slept late, and when all was quiet during the afternoon he worked on his map. Each evening the women brought him fresh details, which they would discuss over supper, and then he would retire to his choice of bed.

"Well, sir, how does it strike you?" Meyboom inquired at last, as they examined his creation.

Against a background of rustic scenery, the semi-clad Eros held out a red flower to Harpocrates, who stood in his traditional pose, a finger to his lips. Between them was a tomb, on which lay a sword in a green scabbard.

"It's excellent," Laurence said. "And now there's one more thing I want you to include." He gave Meyboom a small piece of paper, which the artist had to put on his spectacles to read. "If you please, copy what I've written, right here on the canvas."

Just past the middle of November, Laurence called the women together and revealed to them his map. At the far eastern extremity of the city was a bulwark at Gravel Lane, the beginnings of another in Whitechapel Road, a redoubt near Brick Lane, the same at

Hackney and two at Shoreditch in the northeast, batteries at Mountmill and St. John's Street End, a large fort at the new River Upper Pond, and so on round to the northwest. The western approaches, which might prove most interesting of all to the King's strategists, were being covered by further batteries, forts, redoubts, and breastworks, and finally, on the south side of the Thames, a fort at St. George's Fields; another close to the brothel, at the end of Blackman Street; and one more in the Deptford Road.

"Your hard work," Laurence told them gratefully.

"We've the blisters on our feet to prove it," Sarah said, laughing.

She then went up to summon Meyboom, who descended promptly with his canvas and sketches. "Thanks to your commission, sir," he said, "I shall not have to paint any more signs until the New Year."

The women had been recompensed as copiously as Meyboom, and Laurence had also given them money for Mistress Edwards to hire a lawyer and pay the fine to free herself and the other ladies from gaol.

Laurence burnt all Meyboom's sketches, along with his own notes, in the fireplace; then Cordelia rolled the canvas up, wrapped it in layers of cloth, and fastened the whole with string. Jane had instructions for its delivery, through a series of bearers who could not be traced to Blackman Street, once Laurence was out of the city. That evening, they indulged in a final celebratory feast.

"Dear Mr. Beaumont, why d'you have to leave us?" Perdita cried, resting her head on his shoulder; she was tipsy from too much Canary wine. "We was having such fun."

"I'll come back again soon, and I trust by then that Mistress Edwards will be out of the Fleet," he said, feeling sorry for them: Parliament, in its endeavour to root out vice, had only changed their lives for the worse.

II.

Tom had come to adore Prince Rupert. Daring and resolute, Rupert endured hardship with his men, inspiring them equally by his personal example and his brilliance as a military tactician. The King had not pledged to lay down arms during the peace negotiations, so when it was reported that London's Trained Bands were marching out of London ready to defend the city, Rupert had considered this sufficient cause to continue hostilities. On the twelfth of November, early on a misty Saturday morning, his men had attacked the enemy garrison in Brentford.

Some of Parliament's forces scattered immediately. Others held their ground, and the two sides fought, much to the horror of the civilian population, laying waste to houses, gardens, and orchards. It was Tom's first experience of street fighting, and he felt temporarily alarmed to be shot at from upper storeys and around corners, yet the Prince's reputation drove fear into the enemy, and soon Parliament's troops were in retreat, herded like cattle into the nearby river or into roped-off compounds, where they were held as prisoners of war. Once all opposition had been crushed, Rupert's men broke into the houses of Parliamentary sympathisers and looted whatever seemed of value, from linens and plate to casks of wine and ale. They threw mattresses out of windows, sending a cloud of feathers into the street, tore sides of meat from larders, and chased the women, harassing the prettier ones and insulting the rest. Tom and his troop stormed into a chophouse and ransacked it, tumbling jars from the shelves and helping themselves to a tray of freshly baked pies. They were already drunk, and pissed in unison against the counter before they left.

The next day, Parliament had sent barges loaded with ammunition downriver to aid what was left of its army near Brentford, but Rupert's sharpshooters exploded one and sank a few others. Only when Essex drew up the Trained Bands at Turnham Green was the onslaught halted, for he had twice the Royalists' number and easier territory to defend. The King's infantry fell back, with Rupert's cavalry protecting its retreat. At Reading, His Majesty resumed negotiations with Parliament, which was still furious about the sack of Brentford, and his army took a well-deserved break.

Colonel Hoare had been extremely cordial towards Tom during the recent action, complimenting him on his troop and taking pains to find him a decent billet at Reading. On his return from a foraging expedition one evening, Tom was intrigued to find a message requesting him to meet with Hoare alone, at a crossroads on the outskirts of town.

Hoare was waiting there when Tom arrived. "All's well with you, Mr. Beaumont?" he greeted Tom briskly.

"Yes, sir, thank you," said Tom.

"And your men?"

"On fine form."

"Good. Let's walk our horses, shall we?" They dismounted and led their beasts by the rein some way, until Hoare stopped and turned to him. "Tell me, have you seen your brother of late?"

"No, sir," Tom replied, guardedly, "not since Edgehill. He must be with Wilmot's Horse, as he was on that day."

"What is your view of the King's campaign thus far?" Hoare asked next, rather unexpectedly.

"I regret that we're no nearer to London, sir," Tom said. "And I'm tired of Parliamentary Commissioners. If His Highness the Prince had his way, there'd be no more talk of peace and we'd have chased Essex to Westminster by now. The rebels should be punished, not coddled with concessions," he went on with more assurance, sensing Hoare's approval. "The war could be won before Christmas if we marched on London straight away. At the first hint of Prince Rupert's advance, those tailors and dyers would throw down their arms."

"His Majesty is too patient," sighed Hoare, patting his mount's glossy neck. "And there are some around him, some of his most trusted advisors, who have an interest in weakening his resolve to fight."

"Then they play into the hands of his enemies."

"They are well intentioned but misguided. For example, I am sorry to say that my Lord Falkland, due to his conciliatory disposition, may be ill-suited for the office of Secretary of State at a time such as ours." Tom said nothing, although he agreed. From his own acquaintance with Falkland at Chipping Campden, he had always considered him a scholar uninterested in politics and utterly averse to war, much like Lord Beaumont. "If we could persuade His Majesty of this," Hoare said, "we would do him and our country an immense service. Not by casting aspersions on Falkland's loyalty, of which there can be no doubt, but by demonstrating that he and his allies will only hamper the successful prosecution of the war." Tom nodded vigorously but still did not interrupt. "Has your brother ever mentioned to you his involvement in espionage while abroad? Or that he is presently an agent of Lord Falkland?" Hoare inquired, his tone more confidential.

"No, sir!" said Tom, shaking his head in amazement; this cast a new light on his brother's comings and goings from army duty.

"It was I who employed him," Hoare said, "hoping that his impressive skills would be useful to his lordship." Tom frowned: in that case, why had Laurence warned him to beware of the Colonel? "Yet I have a grave situation on my hands. There is reason to suspect that his lordship, in his earnest desire for peace, may be putting those skills to his own end, in order to communicate secretly with Parliament."

"Beg pardon, sir!" Tom gasped. "Are you suggesting that my Lord Falkland is behaving treacherously? And that Laurence is abetting him?"

"Certainly not," Hoare answered, so emphatically that both horses started, whinnying. "In truth, I am sad for Falkland. He cannot see how his enemies will abuse his trusting nature. And your brother, I am sure, is acting out of respect for his lordship. Your father and Falkland are close friends, are they not?"

"They are, sir."

"It would be most . . . *tragic* if any of this were to come out. Both Falkland and your brother would be seriously compromised."

"Of course, sir," Tom murmured; what a stain it would be upon his family's honour, he thought.

"And that is why I require your help. I should like you to relay to me, in person, whatever you might find out about your brother's dealings with Falkland."

"Yes, sir," Tom said, knowing that he must obey, but discomforted nevertheless at being asked to spy on his own kin.

"By the bye, he is not with Wilmot," Hoare added. "He has not been seen in the regiment for over two weeks. I hear from my sources that he went to London, apparently with Wilmot's blessing." Tom remained quiet, his amazement transformed into understanding: naturally Hoare was dangerous to Laurence, because he could ferret out Laurence's clandestine doings for the Secretary of State. "I am counting on you, sir," Hoare said, "and I am sure that you will not disappoint me. I think you have much promise as a soldier, Thomas Beaumont, and I should know – I have been in service since I was a boy of twelve. A man could not choose a better education."

"Thank you, sir," Tom said, blushing.

"May I look forward to hearing from you?"

"Yes, sir." Tom bowed smartly. "I am proud to do whatever I can to further His Majesty's cause." But he did not feel entirely proud as they mounted and galloped back to town together. Instead, he felt a deep mortification that the Beaumont name might be prejudiced by his brother's conduct, and also a solemn responsibility: it was up to him to protect his family, as much as to serve the King.

III.

"Who could have brought this here?" Pembroke demanded of his servant.

"We have no idea, my lord. It must have been left at the gates over night."

"Were you *all* sleeping?" Pembroke took a paperknife and slit the cord around the package, then unravelled several yards of cloth to find a rolled-up canvas. It was not the first time that a painting had been sent to him unsolicited: his interest in art was well known, and many people had tried to curry favour with him by offering some item from their private collections. Usually the gift would arrive accompanied by an obsequious missive, but in this case there was none.

He brought the canvas to the window, the better to appraise its elegant lines and subtle use of colour. The Northern school, he opined, for it lacked the dramatic intensity of an Italian or Spanish master. As the artist must have intended, Pembroke was struck by a detail: the red rose proffered by one figure to another. It led his eye towards the marble tomb between them; and his gaze drifted downwards, to the sword upon it. Further down still, he noticed the inscription on the side of the tomb: a short line, in the code given to him by Sir Bernard Radcliff.

"What the devil is he playing at, to send me such a message," he muttered, and ordered away his servant. Returning to his writing table, he inked a quill and copied down the line on a sheet of paper, and then searched in a hidden drawer for his book of transcriptions and set to work. "It cannot be," he groaned. "It cannot be." His heart was thudding, as after one of his nightmares. He looked hard at the canvas, and again at the script to ensure that he had made no mistake, but he was correct: *The rose has betrayed your secret.*

IV.

"Just a few days?" bawled Wilmot, as Laurence walked into his quarters. "You and your bloody impertinence!" Laurence handed him a roll of parchment and waited patiently as he unfurled it with a violent gesture. "What is this – some sort of joke?"

"It's a map. You'll have to excuse my lack of skill as a draughtsman –"

"I'm in no mood to excuse you of anything," Wilmot retorted, but his eyes gleamed as they darted across the paper. "Read it for me, Beaumont," he said, at length. "Make sense of it." Once Laurence had finished, Wilmot started to smile. "God's balls, you must have been to every corner of the city! How did you avoid arrest? By making yourself invisible?"

"I considered that," Laurence said gravely. "But even so, I couldn't have done the work alone – it would have taken me too long. I had to summon up my familiars and send them out in whatever form would attract the least notice." Wilmot stared at him, half credulous, until Laurence could not keep a straight face. "Never mind how I got the information, Wilmot," he said, laughing. "Do you like my map any better now?"

"I do, yet you still make me very curious. Have you shown this to anyone else?"

"No, just as I promised you."

"Then I shall take full credit for your discoveries when I present them to His Majesty." Wilmot gloated a minute more over the map, before rolling it back up. "So, did you find that fellow Radcliff?"

"I'm afraid not."

"Remarkable that your imps couldn't sniff him out. Well it happens I've a letter for you from your friend Ingram that might provide you with some clue. Oh, and there's another from our friend Mistress Savage, and a third, which I couldn't decipher." Wilmot rose to fish about in a chest full of papers. To Laurence's annoyance, the seals on his letters had been broken. "I have to know what you're getting up to behind my back," said Wilmot, shrugging as he passed them over.

Laurence began with Ingram's, though he would have opened Isabella's first had Wilmot not been watching him so closely.

The leg was mending, Ingram wrote, and he could walk without pain if he did not put weight on it; one of Lord Beaumont's grooms had made him a pair of crutches to help him regain his mobility. Laurence skipped over the next paragraph, in which Ingram thanked him and the Beaumont household for all their kindness over the past month. Then Ingram continued,

> I had word yesterday from Kate that set my mind at ease. Sir Bernard Radcliff was amongst those prisoners of Essex who were marched off to London. He bought his freedom after much negotiation and the payment of a heavy ransom, poor man, and all the while he was suffering from a wound to the arm that he had sustained at Edgehill. Without the loving care that I was fortunate to receive, he developed an infection, which kept him some time longer in the city, waiting for it to cure. He must now be on his way to rejoin the troop, if he has not already done so. I am infinitely grateful to you for delivering our letters to Kate after the battle. In the end, she was wise not to open Sir Bernard's.

Ingram concluded with a sincere prayer that he and Laurence would see each other soon.

In contrast to his warm effusions, Isabella's note was a couple of lines, and started with a curt apology for troubling Laurence about such a trivial issue. "I regret to inform you," she went on, "that my milliner has demanded a higher price for those Italian gloves I promised you as a gift for your mistress. Until then, I beg you to wait. I am close to striking a bargain with him."

"Who's the lucky lady, Beaumont?" Wilmot inquired suspiciously. "And what's so special about the Italian gloves?"

"With all respect," Laurence said, "it's none of your business."

The last letter was from Seward, encoded as always, and even shorter than Isabella's. He was back at Merton. Apparently his old enemy the Warden had paid off several witnesses and threatened others to suppress evidence in his favour, but at last he had been officially cleared of all charges.

v.

Falkland thought that Mr. Beaumont looked extremely healthy and cheerful as Stephens ushered him in. He sat down uninvited, crossed his legs in a most ungentlemanly fashion, and cast Falkland a dazzling smile.

"It is nearly the end of November," Falkland told him irritably, after dismissing Stephens. "Almost two months since we last spoke."

"You must be pleased, my lord, that His Majesty has agreed to withdraw his forces from Reading," Beaumont commented, ignoring Falkland's veiled reproach.

"I am, yes. It demonstrates his goodwill in treating with Parliament, and once we are quartered in Oxford for the winter, I believe we shall be able to resume talks on a less hostile note."

Beaumont raised his eyebrows, as if he thought there was small chance of that. "Have you seen any signs that your correspondence has been tampered with, my lord?"

"Not thus far. And what progress have *you* made, Mr. Beaumont?" Falkland caught him hesitating, and added, "Fear not, sir – we can't be overheard."

"One of the conspirators, Tyler, is dead. I'll explain the circumstances later. But the other, Mr. Rose, was using a false name. He is most definitely Sir Bernard Radcliff, the man who married my friend's sister. I've seen his handwriting on a document in her possession. It's the same as on one of the letters I brought you. So I have to wonder, what does this tell us about the Earl of Pembroke?" finished Beaumont, resting his light eyes significantly on Falkland.

Falkland cleared his throat; the information impressed him, yet as always he felt that Beaumont was keeping something back. "We have no grounds to accuse the Earl of Pembroke of complicity in the plot," he objected.

Beaumont smiled again, sceptically. "My lord, what did you and Pembroke discuss last September?"

"I told you before. He said that he wanted to strengthen relations amongst us moderates."

"Oh? No, as a matter of fact, you neglected to mention that," Beaumont remarked, at which Falkland's face grew hot. "What else, my lord?"

"That's all," said Falkland, reluctant to admit that Pembroke had written to him since, urging him again to cooperate on a private alliance.

"Is it?" When Falkland was silent, Beaumont said, "According to the horoscope, His Majesty is to die in June, less than two years from now. Has Pembroke ever said anything to you about that particular date?"

"Indeed he has not! Mr. Beaumont," Falkland hurried on, "you were to bring me proof of Colonel Hoare's duplicity."

"I think I can, but you may have to wait a bit longer."

"I shall be attending your sister's wedding in December, to which your father generously invited me. Might you have something for me by then?"

"I hope so. My lord, what about Radcliff? We know *he*'s guilty –"

"Do you have the letter with his writing on it?"

"No, but I could find a way to get another sample of his script, through my friend, perhaps. You might take him into custody. At least we wouldn't lose him again. Or better yet, have him shadowed."

"I can do neither without Colonel Hoare learning of it. I am sorry, sir. We must settle one issue before the other."

"Are you afraid to discover the truth about Pembroke?" Beaumont inquired, as if it were a casual question.

Falkland stifled an urge to curse. Were his thoughts so transparent? "It could affect the negotiations," he replied.

"An understatement, if ever I heard one," murmured Beaumont, giving Falkland a keen look, as though contemplating whether to say more on the issue. Then he seemed to shake himself, and added only, "We may appear to have plenty of time to catch these regicides, and of course you're still hoping for some happy outcome from your talks with Parliament, but I suggest you be very guarded in your dealings with *one* of the Commissioners." Stephens entered again, interrupting them, rather to Falkland's relief. "Oh well, don't be discouraged, my lord," Beaumont went on, more amiably. "Just watch out for the wolves in sheep's clothing. They're quite common these days."

"Please excuse me now, Mr. Beaumont," Falkland said. "I am due to sup with Lord Digby."

Beaumont got up, a mischievous expression on his face. "Speak of the devil. Or of the wolf, I should say." And he bowed to Falkland and departed, with a friendly nod at Stephens on his way out.

"A peculiar person, my lord," Stephens observed, as he helped Falkland on with his cloak.

"He is. Would you be inclined to trust him?"

"No, my lord. He resembles an Italian," Stephens elaborated.

"Thank you, Stephens, I shall bear your view in mind," Falkland said, and went out to his coach.

Over their meal, Falkland found Digby unusually quiet, but at last, as they were served a course of braised game, he announced, "You will be happy to hear that Prince Charles has conquered his measles. The King's physician thinks him well enough to travel."

"Then he will leave Reading tomorrow in procession with the King."

Falkland was silent for a while, watching Digby eat, which he did in small bites, possibly to counter his tendency to plumpness. "Be honest, my lord," said Falkland, "you think me like Sisyphus with his rock, trying again and again to reach a peaceful settlement."

"No, I admire your determination. But do you truly think that His Majesty shares it?"

"I must pray he does."

"Or else the radicals in Parliament would be vindicated in their opinion that he is not being quite open with them," Digby said, with a little smile. "Still, there is another way to end the war. With enough foreign troops –"

"If His Majesty imports troops from Ireland, he will destroy any chance of reconciliation with Parliament."

"Who said anything about the Irish?"

"Irish or French, what does it matter. You know what every Englishman fears. A Catholic invasion to re-establish the supremacy of Rome in this country."

"Every *Protestant* Englishman, I think is what you mean. Did your mother not convert to the Roman faith, along with your younger brother?"

"We both have Catholics in our families."

"We do, yes. I argued long and hard with my cousin Kenelm, trying to bring him to see reason. Alas, he remains adamant in his beliefs."

"Belief and reason are old enemies. A pity there is not more tolerance. We are all children of Christ."

"If every Englishman agreed with you, the kingdom might not be in this sorry state." They were silent for a while, chewing their food. "I cannot wait to return to Oxford," Digby began again. "I had such a wonderful time as a student at Magdalen College. And you will be nearer to home."

"Not twenty miles away," Falkland said, thinking longingly of his wife and boys.

"You must miss your intellectual gatherings at Great Tew – Tom Hobbes, John Earle, William Chillingworth – superb scholars, all of them."

"It seems much like an idyll to me now, to sit about at leisure with good friends discussing everything under the sun."

Digby took a sip of wine and mopped his lips. "Do you by any chance know a Lord Beaumont, who has a house not far from yours?"

"He was often my guest, as I was his."

"He has a son who is serving with Wilmot, Laurence Beaumont. You must know him, too," said Digby, in the probing tone that Falkland detested. "I met him when I was – yes?" Digby inquired of his servant, who had hurried in unexpectedly.

"My lord, Mistress Savage is here to see you."

He looked flustered. "What can this be about? I apologise, Lucius."

Mistress Savage entered a moment later, her cheeks tinged pink from the cold. "My lords, forgive me for disturbing you," she said, as they rose to bow.

"What is it, my dear?" asked Digby, coming to put an arm about her shoulders. She frowned at him and then at Falkland. "Go on, go on," Digby urged.

"I have news from London. The day before yesterday, Parliament intercepted a message that was to be smuggled upriver to one of the King's secretaries. It was from some person in the Queen's suite, and describes the assistance that he may expect from abroad. The Queen has promises of aid from Denmark, France, and the Low Countries. She is about to send over a hundred and twenty thousand pounds, and will land in England herself very soon. If the King can take Kent, London will be blockaded. If the city refuses to surrender, the King of France will lend three regiments of Englishmen in his service for an invasion."

Falkland blinked at her, speechless with shock and dismay.

"How did you hear this?" said Digby.

"From the wife of a certain Member of Parliament. A most trust-worthy source."

Falkland felt sick. All along the King had been negotiating in bad faith, and Parliament now had the evidence to prove it. "We have been made fools of," he exclaimed, "with our talk of peace."

"It cannot be such a surprise to you," Digby told him soothingly. "Her Majesty was publicly seeking help from the Danish king, who is after all His Majesty's uncle, and we ourselves received his envoy here. What will be difficult to explain is the inopportune time."

"Inopportune?" repeated Falkland, his voice rising. "By Jesus, it is worse than that! Parliament will think us a bunch of liars!"

As if the heat of Falkland's reaction embarrassed him, Digby turned to Isabella. "Has His Majesty been alerted yet?"

"No."

"Then Lucius and I must beg an audience with him at once."

How can I even look him in the eye, Falkland thought, but he nodded.

Digby gestured at his kidskin shoes adorned with satin rosettes. "Excuse me for a moment, I must put on my boots to go out in this nasty weather," he said, and bustled off.

Falkland sat back down, trembling, and drained his glass of wine. Mistress Savage slipped into Digby's seat and laid a hand on his arm. "I have news for you, also, my lord."

"You do?" he asked apprehensively.

"If you have not heard this already, Colonel Hoare has been inspecting your private correspondence. There is an informant, Captain Milne, who has seen him opening it and taking notes afterwards, I presume about whatever content he might use against you. Milne is in Prince Rupert's Horse. He cannot come to you until the armies retire for the winter or Hoare may find out. But when the time comes, he will bear witness."

"I ask you again," said Falkland, wary of her connection to his host, "why are you extending yourself for me?"

"Out of respect for you, my lord. And for another man, who has an enemy in Hoare."

"Who is that?"

"Mr. Beaumont. He will help me to arrange your meeting with Milne, which of course must take place in absolute secrecy. You may rely upon Beaumont."

"May I, Mistress Savage?"

"More than you can rely on the King," she said, very softly.

VI.

"We move out early tomorrow," Wilmot told his officers. "Just a day's ride, we'll camp for the night and then attack the rebels at Marlborough the next morning. It will be good sport. More to the point, in one swoop we'll block enemy access to the wool trade and complete our line of defence to the southwest."

"How unfair of you, Wilmot, to leave Prince Rupert none of the glory," Laurence reproved him, as the officers dispersed.

"It's our last action before we hole up for Christmastide and I want my name on it," Wilmot retorted, grinning.

They set out at dawn: Wilmot and Lords Digby and Grandison had amongst them four troops of horse and six hundred dragoons. Artillery completed the train. Wilmot had selected smaller guns, demi-culverins and sakers, to make better speed on the road, and before they left, he had sent his scouts ahead to report on the town's defences. They journeyed towards Wantage, then turned west past the enormous White Horse, carved into the chalky soil in some bygone age. The mid-December wind blew bitterly cold across the Downs as they camped, waiting for the artillery to catch up.

The sky was still dark when they re-formed to approach on

Marlborough, and in the small hours of morning on the fifth of December the guns began to roar, followed shortly by a cavalry attack.

The townsfolk were at a strategic disadvantage: along the broad High Street stood a number of well-proportioned inns with wide stable-buildings that were easily penetrated by one wing of the Royalist cavalry, while the other wing filled the street. They were shot at ineffectually by snipers posted at upper windows and barricades, but faced no serious opposition, and the fight was soon over. Then, as at Brentford, the looting began. Dwellings, stables, barns, and warehouses were stormed and prisoners seized, along with bales of cloth, huge cheeses, barrels of wine, and hogsheads of oil. Wilmot's men discovered a stack of Bibles and used them to fuel a bonfire that blazed away as the citizens were rounded up and forced to crack open their coffers.

Laurence was watching these proceedings with resigned disgust when Digby called him over. "A wealthy merchant lives here," he said, pointing to the house opposite. "Let's see what we may have off him."

The man was alone in his parlour when they strode in with some of Digby's officers; the servants were fleeing upstairs, where the rest of the family had presumably taken shelter.

"Five hundred pounds, sir," Digby declared. "That is the price of your liberty, to be paid within four days at the latest. I hazard a guess you spent more than twice that amount on your splendid furnishings and would not care to see them destroyed."

The man fell to his knees and burst into tears. "You blackguard soldiers have plundered me so, I can give you no more than a hundred!"

"How very unfortunate for you. Mr. Beaumont, pray hold your pistol to his skull and see if he hasn't five hundred pounds."

The man shrank from Laurence, who had raised his pistol reluctantly. "Spare my life! I've eighteen children to maintain and will have nothing left to keep them!"

"Eighteen children?" Digby exclaimed. "Did you hear that, Mr. Beaumont? Does it not seem to you an excessive number?"

"It certainly does," said Laurence, amused by Digby's air of outrage.

"God damn me," Digby continued to the man, who winced at the blasphemy, "if you will be so short of money, why not tie the creatures up two by two together and drown them, as we do kittens?"

Laurence began to laugh, at which the man railed at him, "You are an impious creature, to find humour in the tormenting of a Christian gentleman!"

"And you, sir, are incontinent," Digby said. "You might as well claim half of Marlborough as your progeny. If you will not drown them, I'll gladly undertake the duty for you. Where are they hidden?"

At length, after Digby had suggested stringing him up at his own door, the man promised to surrender his five hundred pounds, and they left him.

"I must congratulate you, Mr. Beaumont," said Digby, scanning the chaos around them. "That old miser was more appalled by your sinister face than my threats. No doubt he'll enjoy retelling the story to his horde of grandchildren."

"Or to the enemy pamphleteers," said Laurence.

"Hmm. Pamphleteers, eh? You give me a thought. When we are back in Oxford, I believe I might engage your services, if Wilmot will allow me."

Laurence made no reply.

Once stripped of valuables, Marlborough had to be garrisoned for the King, but by the time the Royalist army rode out, shopkeepers were reopening their businesses and the town had been restored to relative calm. It was a slow journey back to Oxford with prisoners, horses, and cattle in tow, and piles of booty stuffed into every available vehicle, but as Wilmot had anticipated, they were greeted as conquering heroes upon their arrival. The Court was in residence, Christmas festivities had started, and news of the victory at Marlborough only heightened the atmosphere of optimism, as well as the boasts of the pro-war party. At Christ Church College, where he was quartered, His Majesty threw a banquet to congratulate the Cavaliers, as they had come to be known.

Laurence had been seated between Wilmot and Charles Danvers, with whom he had no desire to exchange a single word. They were all drinking heavily, surrounded by an adoring female audience. Then Digby sailed up and made himself a place at the table. He looked exceptionally sober, and smug.

"Why in God's name aren't you as cut as the rest of us, my lord?" Wilmot demanded.

"Later, later. Mr. Beaumont," Digby said, beaming at Laurence, "I've a proposition for you. Where are you staying?"

Wilmot answered for him. "Alas, Beaumont is *not* staying. His sister is to be married in a few days, and he tells me he cannot miss the event. Are you trying to steal him away from me, my lord?"

"I was not aware you owned him. What do you have to say to that, Mr. Beaumont?"

"I don't have any owner that I know of, my lord," Laurence said politely.

"Really! I was told that Colonel Hoare thinks he owns you. As he owns our friend Danvers here."

Danvers flushed and tossed back his wine.

"If you're trying to provoke an argument, my lord," Wilmot said, "we are in far too good a humour to rise to the occasion. For an argument, I mean." He drew the nearest woman onto his knees and put a hand on her breast, which she did not discourage from dipping below the front of her dress. "We are perfectly capable of rising in other ways."

Digby giggled. "I'm sure you are, sir! Ladies, don't you find Mr. Beaumont an exotic morsel? If I did not know him for an Englishman, I might suspect he has a lick of the tar brush in him. Hot climes breed hot blood, or so it's said. If I were you, my dears, I'd be tempted to discover the truth of it."

"Now *there's* a recommendation," observed one of the young ladies; the prettiest, Laurence noted. Slight and dark-haired, she wore a dress of pale silk that glowed and shimmered in the candlelight, and she was examining him with eyes rather like Isabella's, though wider set, in a heart-shaped face.

"Leave him be, my lord," Wilmot growled at Digby. "And drink up."

Shortly after, Laurence excused himself; since the campaign had drawn to a close, he was at last free to visit Seward, and he had much to recount.

"Off to smell the flowers, are you?" Danvers said. "Me too."

Out in the open quadrangle, breathing chill winter air, Laurence realised that he was drunker than he thought. Danvers had stopped to urinate against a wall. "Beaumont," he said, over his shoulder, "I told you, it's not true about Hoare. You can't believe Digby – he's just trying to make trouble."

"I couldn't give a toss, either way," Laurence said, walking off. "Good night."

A few seconds later, he heard the rapid click of heels on the cobblestones, and a hand tugged at his cloak. He turned abruptly, expecting Danvers, but it was the woman from the banquet. "Mr. Beaumont," she said, "I had thought to leave also. My chamber is not far, in Corpus Christi. Would you accompany me there?"

"Yes, madam," he replied, after a brief hesitation; she had slipped her arm in his. "Have you no cloak?"

"I'm not cold," she said, but he took his off anyway and wrapped it over her shoulders.

She was a lady of rank, he thought, judging by the tasteful, expensive style of her clothes. She should have a servant with her. "Are you alone?" he asked, feeling suspicious.

"I am now," she sighed. "My gentlewoman was drinking to excess and is quite incapacitated." When they reached the College, she returned his cloak. "Would you see me to my chamber? I had difficulty with the key." He hesitated again; he was unarmed, about to enter some unlit corridor, and there could be any number of surprises awaiting him behind her door. Yet she beseeched him again so sweetly that he agreed.

As she had said, it took him some time before the key would turn in the lock. He opened the door, removed the key, and was about to place it in her palm when she murmured, "Aren't you going to give me a good-night kiss?" He looked down at her, and the aphrodisiac effect of liquor crept over him. Her lips were soft and her mouth tasted of something sugary. "I would so like to know you better," she whispered afterwards, pressing her breasts against him.

She manoeuvred him into the chamber, which was large and elegant, suggesting that she must indeed be someone of importance, and after a quick glance about he shut the door with his foot. He unfastened her gown, slipped it from her shoulders, and began to kiss her again. Then he stopped. "Are you sure you wish to know me this well?"

"Yes. Lock the door."

In the darkness, after certain other preliminaries, he raised her petticoats and happened to run his hand over her belly, only to discover that she was some months pregnant. "Is your husband here in Oxford with you?" he inquired warily, recalling his past experience with an irate spouse.

She shook her head and pulled him closer. "He died of his wounds after Edgehill. We were married four years, and loved each other very much. Please, sir," she said, her voice hoarse with desire, "make me forget him for the night."

She was certainly in need, raking his back with her nails and biting his neck. She panted so loudly that he had to muffle her mouth with his, although the squeaking of the bed frame would have been sufficient to give them away to anyone passing. After a while he shifted her about, to avoid the distracting swell of her stomach. "What have you touched inside me?" she cried ecstatically; and he thought, not for the first time, what a shame it was that so few women seemed familiar with this sensitive spot within their own bodies. The ceiling of heaven, he had once heard it called.

They continued on until he felt himself on the brink; and when it ended, her panting quietened. She gave him a last kiss, lay back in bed closing her eyes, and mumbled, "You may let yourself out," before apparently succumbing to sleep.

Easing away from her, he laced up his breeches, and was ready to exit from her chamber when he heard noises outside, of slow, dragging footsteps. He unlocked the door, and looked out. In the corridor another woman was tottering towards him. Even from a distance, he could smell the alcohol on her breath. Her eyes flickered as he emerged. "Who are you?" she demanded. "Where is my Lady d'Aubigny?"

Laurence felt a slight alarm, hoping that the episode would not become public knowledge: Lady d'Aubigny's late husband had been a cousin of His Majesty. Oh well, he thought next, at least he could not be accused of impregnating her.

"Where is my Lady d'Aubigny?" repeated the gentlewoman drunkenly.

"In her chamber," he said. "Allow me," he added, as she grabbed his arm for support. He took her in, laying her down on the bed beside her mistress, then left them and closed the door.

When he reached the street outside, he had the taste of sugar on his tongue and Lady d'Aubigny's floral perfume lingering in his nostrils. After his enjoyable hour with her, he felt full of energy. He walked the short distance to Merton, where a yawning porter admitted him.

Seward, as usual, had not yet gone to bed, and greeted him with a hug as he entered. "Look at me, home at last – as is Pusskins, too!" The cat was padding in circles around Laurence's feet, emitting loud purrs. "He is thanking you," Seward explained, "for your gallant conduct in Oxford Castle. Sit down, Beaumont, and give me an account of your exploits since then."

"Well," he began with a smile, throwing himself into a chair, "I can now confirm without a doubt that Pembroke is our chief conspirator."

Seward listened avidly as he described his sojourn at Blackman Street and the gift he had arranged to be delivered to the earl's house. "Eros and Harpocrates!" Seward crowed with glee. "Not only will he be in a frenzy of suspicion against Radcliff, but he may think that the entire Brotherhood of the Rosy Cross is after him, bent on revenge for the misuse of their symbols. Have you told Falkland about the painting?"

"No, though I nearly did. He wants me to sort out his problems with Colonel Hoare before we make any move on the regicides. I urged him to arrest Radcliff and hinted as broadly as I could that Pembroke was involved, but he insisted that we wait. He's afraid of prejudicing the next round of negotiations with Parliament."

"I think you made a mistake in not disclosing all that you knew! Surely if he were aware that Radcliff had been staying with Pembroke, he would be convinced they were both guilty as sin."

"Perhaps. But I agree with him that it would be best to have Hoare out of the way before we question Radcliff. Radcliff will keep silent for as long as he can, just like Harpocrates, and I don't want Hoare butchering him before we can make him talk." Laurence paused, then added, "When I was at the house of Ingram's aunt, just before I came to Oxford last time, she happened to mention that Radcliff had stored a small coffer with her. His correspondence might be in there."

"Can you invent some excuse to go back and conduct a search?"

"If you can think of a good one, I'll use it – once I've fulfilled a prior commitment. My sister Elizabeth is getting married the day after tomorrow, and if I don't attend, my mother will disown me."

"It amazes me that she did not do so years ago," Seward said, laughing.

VII.

Ingram was playing backgammon with Elizabeth and Anne in the parlour, a fire warming his back, his leg propped up on cushions, a glass of sack and a plate of cracknels beside him on the table. He felt at the same time happy and a little sad, because it was his last day with them, although that might be for the best: he had grown too fond of Anne during his convalescence. He would also miss Elizabeth's teasing, so like her oldest brother's, and the charming, learned conversation of Lord Beaumont.

Chipping Campden seemed to Ingram a world of its own. He was still surprised to wake up every morning in such a magnificent bed, his clothes freshly laid out for him, and to descend to a breakfast of gargantuan proportions, given the numbers at table. For excluding the legions of servants, butlers, maids, grooms, and so forth, the Beaumont household was curiously empty, and his lordship received few visitors. Apart from Tom's wife, Mary, there were no other relatives living there, and no gentlewomen attending her ladyship, of whom everyone clearly stood in awe, including her husband. The two daughters led a remarkably untrammelled existence, reading whatever they wanted from their father's library and discoursing with self-assertion on topics that Ingram considered more suitable for an Oxford scholar than a pair of young, nobly born females. They also spoiled him with an affection that he had never enjoyed at home. Towards Mary they were less affectionate and occasionally even mean, though Ingram understood their impatience with her: she lacked their wit and spontaneity, and her habit of weeping at the least excuse had become more pronounced of late, now that she was with child. Today morning sickness had kept her in bed, and neither he nor the girls felt her absence.

"Laurence once said that there are thirty-six different throws possible with two dice," Elizabeth observed, as she waited for her turn at the board. "If you know every combination, you can tell where to leave a blot with the least chance of being hit."

"Good Lord," Ingram exclaimed. "Who could remember them all?"

"*He* can, which is why we don't like playing with him any more," Anne said.

At this moment, there came the clink of spurs outside and Beaumont himself walked in. Both girls rose immediately to greet him.

"We were speaking of you – and here you are!" Elizabeth remarked delightedly.

"How's the leg, Ingram?" he inquired, once they had all sat down again.

"The surgeon thinks it will heal a bit shorter than before," Ingram said, "but that's a small price to pay." He smiled at his friend. "You look very well. I gather you survived the first campaign of the war unscathed?"

"Yes, by some miracle," Beaumont replied, lounging back in his chair.

"Laurence, you must persuade Ingram to stay for my wedding," begged Elizabeth. "He claims he has to leave for Newbury tomorrow, for Christmastide."

Beaumont stole a sip from Elizabeth's glass, earning a slap on his wrist. "You can't go when I've only just arrived," he said to Ingram. "I'll take it as a personal affront."

"I'm sorry, truly I am, but Richard is expecting me." Beaumont rolled his eyes. "And Kate and Aunt Musgrave have come from Faringdon. Radcliff is joining us, too, once he's paid off the troop."

"You mean to say their company is more stimulating than ours?"

"You will miss a wonderful feast," Elizabeth put in. "All the local gentry are to attend, including the Secretary of State!"

"Yet Kate must be longing to see you and her husband again," Anne said. "You never told us, Mr. Ingram, was it you who first introduced them?"

"It was, yes," he said, recollecting. "I brought him to Richard's house some time ago. He was so struck with Kate that he wanted to press his suit immediately, but he'd accepted a commission to fight abroad. In the end he was away for three years. He couldn't free himself from the Dutch service until early last spring."

"And when did *you* first meet him?" Beaumont asked, toying with one of the dice, flipping it over and over deftly between his fingers.

"After you left England, in thirty-seven. I was in a bad way, at the time." Ingram became suddenly conscious of Anne beside him. "I'd wanted to marry again," he went on, "but as I delayed my proposal, afraid of being rejected, someone else made a better offer. I was crushed, and drowning my woes – and that's when it happened."

"How, exactly?" Anne said.

He paused, to choose his words. "I was taking a walk about Southwark very late one night, when I heard shouts and the sound of blows coming from an alley. So I went to see what the trouble was. A poor costermonger had been set upon by thieves – he might have been murdered, had Radcliff not appeared and chased them away."

"Thieves are as plentiful as rats in that neighbourhood," Beaumont said, a little smile curling the edges of his mouth. "I wonder what Radcliff was doing there, at such an hour."

"He was on business."

"A most important business – as was yours, I'd guess," Beaumont added, winking at Ingram, who glared back.

"He was delivering a contract, a deed of sale that his lawyer had drawn up. He told me afterwards that he would never visit Southwark again if he could help it. He wasn't often in London and barely knew the city."

"So he didn't sit for Parliament?"

"No. He hasn't much interest in affairs of state."

"No friends in high places?"

"He hasn't told me of any," Ingram said, bemused. "Why do you ask?"

Beaumont shrugged, still fiddling with the dice. "What about his estate, is it a good piece of property?"

"I've only been there once, before he had a chance to begin his improvements. It wasn't much then," Ingram admitted. "But he said he's bought more land and drained the parts that were swampy. And he refurbished the whole of his house."

"That must have cost him a lot," Beaumont said, now looking surreptitiously at his friend through his eyelashes, in a way that Ingram recognised from years ago. He was trawling for information. But why? Had he not found out enough about Radcliff when he gave him the sword?

"Laurence," interrupted Elizabeth, "you are to be presented to Alice Morecombe at my wedding." She squinted at her brother naughtily. "We might have another betrothal in the family."

"I'm not marrying her," said Beaumont, and threw an arm round his friend's shoulder. "I'd rather marry Ingram."

"No thank you," said Ingram, shoving him off and pretending to laugh along with the rest of them, though he was a bit cross with Beaumont, and embarrassed at himself.

Of course, it was Beaumont who had introduced him to the house in Blackman Street, otherwise he would not have dreamt of setting foot in such an expensive place. Beaumont was friendly with Mistress Edwards and with the whores, and would call on them solely to talk or play at cards; there were always plenty of women who needed no financial inducement to share his bed. Yet how utterly wrong Beaumont was to assume that Radcliff might also have patronized the brothels of Southwark! When the two of them were better acquainted, Ingram thought, Beaumont would understand his mistake.

VIII.

After the family had all bade Walter Ingram a fond goodbye, Lord Beaumont stole off to his library to avoid the manic scenes taking place everywhere else, as the household prepared for Elizabeth's wedding. When he descended some hours later, he was surprised to find her all alone by the fire, roasting chestnuts.

"I hope you have spared a few of those for me," he said, settling in his armchair and stretching out his feet towards the hearth.

"There aren't many left," Elizabeth told him. "I sent for more but all the servants are so busy they have forgotten us. Laurence went to the kitchen, instead."

"Ah, Laurence!" Lord Beaumont repeated contentedly. "He seems in higher spirits than he was this past summer. Military service must suit him, although I would not have imagined it from what he told us."

"It is so wonderful to have him home again," said Elizabeth. "Our family was not the same without him. I have been thinking," she went on, "as I am about to become part of another family, that I know almost nothing at all about my own mother's. Ormiston finds this most peculiar."

"I suppose it is," Lord Beaumont agreed. "But my parents bore such ill will towards us when she first arrived in England, that she must have chosen to break completely with her past in order to appease them – not that they ever accepted her," he finished sadly.

"Did her sisters resemble her?"

Lord Beaumont tried to recall. "They were fairer in complexion, though they were younger than she and might have grown to look more similar in later life. But there was one member of her family who was her spitting image: her cousin Antonio."

"What was he like?"

"Proud as a peacock – a common Spanish failing!" Lord Beaumont chuckled. "And he was excessively vain of his handsome looks and fashionable attire. Your mother and her sisters all adored him, as girls are wont to be impressed by swaggering young fellows. Though I trust that I managed to eclipse him, in the end," he added, smiling, "for she has not once mentioned him over the course of our married years."

"He sounds like a proper fool," Elizabeth declared, with the certainty of youth.

"Nevertheless, he acted kindly towards me when there were others in her family who opposed our union. I was considered a heretic, you see."

"Because you were a Protestant?" she exclaimed, her eyes now wide with interest.

"Oh yes. They were scandalised that she should consign herself to the fires of hell by converting from the true faith. Although your mother's line was not entirely free of scandal in the past. It seems that an ancestor of hers was suspected of having Moorish blood, which was at the time, and still is, a terrible slur upon the honour of a noble Castilian household."

"It must have been far worse for someone in her family to marry an infidel than a heretic."

"There would have been no *marriage* as such," Lord Beaumont confided, lowering his voice. "I believe it was the result of some slip on the distaff side. Quite a pleasing fancy, in my opinion. I do admire the Moors! They excel both as scholars and soldiers, and their architecture in Spain awed me with its magnificence."

"How I should like to travel there," Elizabeth sighed, as she peeled a chestnut for him. "Sometimes I wish I were a man, so that I could go wherever I chose. Why could I not have had a tour of the continent, as Laurence did?"

Lord Beaumont was phrasing a reply to this but had no chance to deliver it, for Thomas marched in, his cloak dusted with snow, followed by Adam. As they were exchanging greetings, Laurence returned carrying a basket of chestnuts; and Lord Beaumont was sorry to notice his sons nod at each other with evident reserve.

"Adam, tell the butler to bring us all a cup of my finest claret," he commanded hastily. "We shall drink a health, in thanks that we are reunited at last."

Yet to his dismay, as soon as they were served Thomas launched into a passionate tirade. "I must say, I fail to understand why His Majesty is still receiving Parliament's Commissioners! What a waste of time."

"War is a great evil – an utter waste of *life*, Thomas, as he is aware," Lord Beaumont admonished. "Members of his own family fell at Edgehill. I count myself lucky that you are both with me now, when other families are mourning their lost ones."

"But the war's nearly won."

"Not quite," Laurence said, "or he wouldn't be so desperate for foreign aid."

"Are you referring to the Queen's message about help from abroad?" asked Lord Beaumont.

"Yes, I am. It did seem somewhat ill-advised that His Majesty should be trying to secure military assistance during the negotiations," Laurence replied, with marked irony.

"Why should he not?" Thomas shot back.

"Because he could completely undermine them, of course. If you were on Parliament's side, would you trust him in the same circumstances?"

"Why should he trust *them*, when they've taken up arms against him! They're traitors."

"You can't brand them all as traitors, Tom. Many of them fought with the greatest reluctance. Many of us, too, for that matter."

"So you support Lord Falkland's party?"

"I doubt he'll achieve his aim, but he has a lot of courage to keep trying."

"For a peace at any cost?"

"I'm sure he has his limits. He chose to side with the King."

Tom seemed pensive; then he said, "How far would you go to placate the enemy?"

"If I were Falkland?"

"No. I'm asking you."

Laurence shrugged. "I think neither side can be placated, especially after His Majesty's flirtations abroad."

"And there is too much inflexibility on those issues that brought us to war in the first place," said Lord Beaumont. "Come," he went on, "let's drink to a cessation of hostilities, however temporary, and the beginning of the festive season."

Thomas raised his glass, a strange light in his eyes, as though he had reached a conclusion to some internal debate; and he was very quiet until the other women joined them and they were called to supper.

IX.

The next morning, Laurence hoped to speak with Tom alone, to warn him in more convincing terms about Colonel Hoare. He was even prepared to tell Tom part of the truth regarding Hoare's scheming against Falkland. But he missed his opportunity: some of Tom's friends from the troop, John Ormiston amongst them, had ridden over early, and all day they were engrossed in boisterous discussion of the recent campaign.

Everywhere Laurence went in the house there was confusion: his sisters in frantic chatter over their gowns; his mother snipping at the servants; and more guests pouring in, the courtyard choked with coaches, and the stables teeming with grooms currying and feeding travel-weary horses. As he skulked back to his chamber, he pondered what he would tell Falkland the next day. He now wished that he had tried to find Isabella Savage in Oxford to see what progress she was making with Captain Milne.

Before the supper to fete the arrival of the wedding party, Laurence submitted to a series of tedious introductions while being steered about by his father, all under his mother's scrutiny. Eventually Lord Beaumont presented Robert Stratton to him. "Our cousin's wife is not in attendance," Lord Beaumont explained, "though for a happy reason. She is expecting a third child." Laurence bowed to Stratton, who was regarding him balefully. "I shall leave you two to become reacquainted," Lord Beaumont said, oblivious to Stratton's hostile attitude, and wandered off to hail some other guests.

Stratton looked about, then faced Laurence squarely and hissed at him, "What happened between you and my wife when you visited my house this past summer?"

Laurence was lost for an answer. How much had Diana told her husband? And why would she confess to an affair now, when it was a thing of the past?

He must have taken too long to respond, for Stratton's face was turning purple. "I see my worst fears have been confirmed! Mr. Beaumont, it is my belief that you importuned her that day. To preserve her dignity, I have not asked her to speak of it, but if I catch you near her again, I'll have more than words for you. You are a menace to all decent women!"

"You flatter me, Sir Robert," said Laurence, unable to conceal a smile.

"I did not intend a compliment," said Stratton, through his teeth, and he turned on his heel and strode away.

At table, Laurence was relieved to find Elizabeth and Ormiston seated on either side of him. "You must get to know each other," his sister said. "I shall insist upon it."

"I've promised Elizabeth to corner you after we've eaten," Ormiston added.

She leant towards Laurence, to whisper in his other ear. "Don't tell him about our little talk."

Laurence shook his head; some months ago Elizabeth had besieged him with questions as to what she might expect on her first night with Ormiston, and he thought he had given her a fair idea.

Much later, after most of the older guests, his parents, and his sisters had retired, he and Ormiston went into the small parlour. Tom's group had occupied the warmest spot by the fire, but Ormiston said that he preferred not to join them.

"I'm worried about Elizabeth," he confessed to Laurence. "This is a palace compared to our house in Hereford, and it's not what she's used to. I'm afraid she'll be homesick. She'll have my sisters for company, but they're not her age, and they're spinsters who hate the slightest change in their daily existence."

"Why didn't they marry?"

"They had offers and turned them down. Then the offers ceased to come."

Laurence remembered Ingram's sister, who had apparently spurned a few suitors before accepting Radcliff. "Women shouldn't have to wait to be asked," he said.

"If they didn't, they'd turn the world upside down."

"What would be wrong with that?"

Ormiston began to laugh. "Elizabeth warned me that you have some rather dangerous opinions. At any rate, it all turned out well for us. She and I are in love. I pray you're as lucky; she told me that you'll be meeting a prospective bride tomorrow."

"Yes, but I'm not –" Laurence broke off on seeing Tom approach, a drunken grin on his face and his gait unsteady.

"What are you doing all by yourselves?" he exclaimed. "Come over here with the rest of us!"

Ormiston glanced at Laurence. "Shall we?"

Laurence agreed, against his better judgement.

Tom surprised him by draping an arm about his waist as they went. "Gentlemen," Tom cried, "meet my older brother." He could not hold his glass without spilling what was in it, and his friends were in much the same condition. "He's a veteran of the Low Countries," Tom continued, slurring his words, "but you'd never know it, because he's so tight-lipped about his service there. Laurence, won't you share some of your adventures with us?"

"Not now, Tom," Laurence said, gently detaching his arm.

"But I've heard you had more than a few of them. In fact, I've heard the most curious things about you." Tom belched into his free hand. "Which is why I wonder what you're doing *here*. You see, boys," he added to his friends, "my brother seems to dance in and out of this war as he pleases. And he's an admirer of our Secretary of State. They both think that we should kiss and make up with the rebels, instead of teaching them a lesson. Isn't that so, Laurence?" Laurence merely sighed in reply. "All this talk about peace is worth less than a fart. If you're not with us, you're against us. That's what I say. What do you say, brother?"

"Whatever you like." Laurence caught Ormiston looking discomfited, as did even Tom's friends. "Let's go for a walk outside, Tom – you need fresh air," he suggested, leading him towards the parlour door.

"Now I understand why you wanted to set me against Colonel Hoare." Tom was swaying perilously on his feet. "Because he knows the truth about you and your secret duties for Lord Falkland. He told me himself."

"Please, Tom, let's discuss this tomorrow when you're sober," Laurence said, eager just to shut him up; what else would he blurt out, in his stupefied state?

Tom clutched at a wall to recover his balance. "S'not right. S'not right what you're doing. You might as well betray us to the enemy. If you haven't yet." With the grandiose theatricality of the very drunk, he held a finger to his lips. "Won't say a thing, though. Mustn't disgrace the family." Then he hurled his glass to the floor, glowering all the while at Laurence as if he would have liked to dash it in his face, and staggered out.

CHAPTER TWELVE

I.

Laurence was shivering with cold, even though the church was full
and braziers had been brought in to heat the tall box pews. It was
a Sunday, and throngs of local people stood behind the Beaumonts, the
Ormistons, and their assembled wedding guests: gentry, merchants,
farmers, and labourers, along with their big-bellied wives and excited
children, were craning to get a view of the spectacle.

He had not visited the church for years. It seemed smaller to him,
and more oppressively crowded with family monuments. To his left
side lay the tomb of the first Laurent de Beaumont, depicted in effigy
with full chain mail and armour, his broad sword in hand and his
feet resting on a faithful hound. Wall tablets hung above a sealed crypt
that accommodated the bones of more ancestors, various Laurences
amongst them; there were yet more under the stone flags; and in a
chapel to the left of the family pew Lord Beaumont's father, another
Laurence, was entombed with his wife, their alabaster figures resting on
an enormous canopied marble bed. Nearby a small memorial housed
the remains of Lord and Lady Beaumont's sons James and Charles,
who had died in their infancy. Laurence could scarcely remember them;
they were both gone by his fourth year. He raised his eyes to a large
painted board before him where the Ten Commandments in all of their

terrifying glory were inscribed. He had liked to read them as a boy and imagine breaking each one without exactly knowing what crimes some of them entailed, and now it occurred to him that he had succeeded beyond all childhood expectations.

As he reached up to pull at his collar, which chafed uncomfortably where Lady d'Aubigny had bitten him, he caught his mother's eye. She wore the same puzzling expression, vaguely haunted, with which she had greeted him earlier in the morning when he had come downstairs in the dark, olive-green suit of clothes that she had ordered for him. He looked away, at Tom, who was staring ahead resolutely, perhaps struggling to control a queasy stomach from last night's debauch. They had not exchanged a single word today.

II.

"Like the aftermath of a battle," Falkland commented to his wife, Lettice.

"Such extravagance," she said soberly. "What is left could feed a village."

It had been an epicurean feast. For the first course, brought out in strict array, were salads, simple fricassees, boiled and roasted meats, some served hot and others cold, and rich stews. For the second course appeared lesser and then greater fowl and finally more hot and cold baked meats in standing pies and tarts. Both courses also included dishes of fish and crustaceans for guests of delicate appetite. All were arranged in a strategic display according to colour and texture around a pasteboard replica of Lord Beaumont's house, complete in every detail. Venetian glasses and silver plates were changed with each course, along with the cutlery. Falkland had detected bafflement on the part of some guests, who were clearly used just to eating with knives, as they saw the ivory-handled forks set at each place. Butlers and other servers who must have been brought in from the town for this special event scurried to fill vessels with Lord Beaumont's best wines, Elsertune from the Rhine and fine Gascons from Bordeaux. Meanwhile the musicians played on bravely, over the babble of voices and the clinking of glasses.

Amongst the many conversations that Falkland could discern, war was the main topic. Some talked of brothers, cousins, or nephews who had gone over to Parliament. Others lamented those who had fallen early in the King's campaign. For the younger generation, it was an opportunity for much boasting and posing: His Majesty's enemies were dogs and traitors, and there was lively competition over who had been exposed to the greatest peril in the field, or survived the worst wounds.

Beaumont was seated beside a rather colourless girl, or so she appeared in contrast to him. Whatever he was saying to her had made her giggle, so that the glass in her hand tipped, spilling wine on the damask tablecloth.

"She may be betrothed to him, Lady Beaumont told me," Lettice said. "Her name is Alice Morecombe."

"He's never mentioned it," said Falkland. "I know the Morecombes," he added; Lady Morecombe was something of a dragon, as he remembered her.

After hours of feasting, the third and final course arrived. There were marchpanes decorated with Lord Beaumont's coat of arms in gold leaf and sugar icing; preserved fruits and pastes, comfits and choice fresh fruits, so rare in the winter season; almond fools and sweet cream-cheeses; and lastly, delicate wafer cakes. No two dishes of a single kind stood together. The servers presented little bowls of scented water for the guests to rinse their fingers, and a cunning display of fireworks shot up from the pasteboard house, alarming a few of the ladies present. Then, with the pouring of sweet Malmsey wines and Xeres sack, the speeches began: from Lord Beaumont welcoming everyone; from John Ormiston to proclaim his happiness upon marrying Elizabeth; and from Ormiston's uncle, regretting that John's father had died too soon to witness this day. As the wine flowed, the guests grew rowdier and less inclined to keep their seats, some disappearing to relieve themselves or stroll about to counter the effects of the banquet. Lord Beaumont's replica house was in ruins amidst half-eaten pastries and wine stains.

When the long trestle tables were finally being folded and put aside to make room for dancing, Falkland caught Beaumont's attention and waved him over.

"He has his mother's eyes," Lettice whispered. "I don't like them. I feel as if they could see through you."

"Sir," Falkland said, as Beaumont walked up, "that was a splendid repast."

"All too much for me," he muttered, smiling, as he bowed to Lettice.

"My dear, might I have a moment with –" Falkland began, and as always Lettice understood at once, and excused herself. "Is there a more private place where we might talk?" he asked, once she had gone.

"This way," Beaumont said, and guided him out of the hall towards a parlour that opened off it.

There they found Tom and some other fellows smoking by the fire. Beaumont seemed to hesitate on seeing them.

Tom got up at once to greet Falkland. He was not so tall as his brother and of heavier build, bearded rather than clean-shaven, with strong, fair, Norman features. A true English nobleman, Falkland thought, and he sounded it, too, with his well-enunciated speech. "Share a pipe with us, won't you, my lord?"

"Thank you but I don't take tobacco," Falkland said. "I'm afraid the smoke makes me cough."

Tom was examining Falkland and his brother searchingly.

"Let's go outside," Beaumont told Falkland. He requested their cloaks from a servant, and they went through the main doors into the courtyard.

As they walked towards the stables, he loosened his collar and started to rub the side of his neck. "I have to confess – I haven't been able to get the proof you asked me for, regarding Colonel Hoare."

"I also have a confession to make," Falkland admitted. "I was not forthcoming, as regards my communications with Pembroke. You must realise how hard it is for me to know on whom I can rely," he concluded, realising as he spoke that he had used Mistress Savage's very words.

Beaumont nodded, as if he sympathised. "What is he suggesting?"

"An alliance of moderates, as I told you, to negotiate a limit to the powers of both His Majesty and Parliament, and an agreement on the religious question. In London, I had said to Pembroke that I would do nothing underhand. But since the King himself was less than truthful with Parliament's Commissioners, I might have been tempted."

"Has Pembroke written to you again?" Beaumont asked, as they passed through the doors of one of the stable buildings.

Falkland heaved a sigh: he might as well tell all. "Yes, Mr. Beaumont, he has. He says my friend Edmund Waller has agreed to join him, and the Earls of Holland and Northumberland, in the Lords. On the King's side, he is most interested in myself, Edward Hyde, Culpeper, Secretary Nicholas, and Dr. Earle. A peculiar choice, that last."

"Earle is tutor to the Prince. Don't you think he'd be essential in what Pembroke wants to achieve?"

"I am still not convinced of –"

"Shh," said Beaumont, and Falkland heard crunching footsteps in the snow. They waited, listening, until the noise faded. Beaumont looked around before resuming in a hushed voice, "Do you have his letter with you?"

"No, it's at my house. It is not in the same hand as the coded letter that you showed me."

"He may have dictated it. How did you answer him?"

"I said that I must learn more before I could commit myself. Mr. Beaumont, after you and I last saw each other, I was issued a warning about my correspondence by someone else: Mistress Savage, Digby's friend. She also said that there is a Captain Milne in Prince Rupert's Horse who has actually seen Hoare interfering with my letters. She has offered to arrange for me to meet him."

"You have nothing to lose by it."

"And she told me to trust you." Falkland paused. "She seems attached to you."

"What makes you think that?" Beaumont sounded amused, but Falkland could not quite read his expression in the dim light.

"I believe she –"

"God damn it," exclaimed Beaumont, as they were disturbed now by louder footsteps.

A drunken guest blundered into the stable, arms outstretched to prevent himself from falling. "Who's there?" he mumbled. "Gentlemen, could you help me get back to the house?"

"Yes, of course, sir," Beaumont said, with an edge of impatience.

"This is not a good time for us to speak," Falkland told Beaumont quietly. "Come and see me tomorrow morning at Great Tew."

"I shall."

They assisted the fellow out, and back to the main doors of the house. As they entered, the same manservant came to take their cloaks and whispered something to Beaumont. He whispered back, and the servant went off.

Beaumont turned to Falkland, his eyes bright. "She's here. Isabella Savage, I mean."

"Was she invited to the wedding?" Falkland inquired, surprised.

"No, but she may have news for us about Captain Milne. I've asked for her to be directed to my chamber. Why don't you come up with me and we can all talk together?"

Falkland thought it best to decline. Lettice would be searching for him and he did not wish to be seen with the uninvited and very alluring Mistress Savage, knowing how people enjoyed their gossip. "I would prefer not," he said. "My wife is tired, and we shall be going home shortly. Make the arrangements with Mistress Savage, and call on me as we planned."

"As you wish. Until tomorrow, my lord," Beaumont said.

As Falkland looked about for Lettice, he noticed Thomas Beaumont watching, his expression unsmiling and intense, like a hunter marking his prey, as his brother bounded up the stairs. Then Falkland was distracted, as Lord Beaumont touched his shoulder. "My dear friend! I believe the young couple are about to be bedded with full ceremony, a fearful process that I did not have to endure in my time. Nor you, I gather."

"No – my marriage was a rushed affair," Falkland agreed, smiling. "Everyone was so against it. My father never forgave me for choosing Lettice, in the three years he lived afterwards. You were one of the few to see her qualities and to show us support."

"I, too, had disobeyed my parents in my choice of wife. And in both cases our affections have held strong."

"I hear that your eldest son is to take a bride," Falkland remarked, espying Lettice coming towards him through the merrymakers.

"Yes, young Alice Morecombe. His mother and I are very happy for it; he has kept us waiting too long."

"Might I be attending another nuptial feast in the near future?"

"God willing, my friend, God willing," said Lord Beaumont cheerfully.

III.

As Laurence opened the door to his chamber and found Isabella standing before the fire in a long hooded cloak, he felt a little ripple of excitement. She removed it with a dramatic gesture to reveal her dark, low-cut gown, and he could smell her perfume, delicate yet haunting.

Her hair was drawn back with a few stray curls at her forehead, and from her ears hung tear-shaped pearls.

"Such a mansion your father has," she declared. "And look at you, all dressed up." She examined him with a critical air. "I am not sure how I like you best, as a ruffian or as a nobleman."

"Well I know how I'm most comfortable," he said, unbuttoning his doublet and pulling off his collar.

"I saw Robert Stratton downstairs, though thank God he did not see me. Is Diana with him?"

"No. She stayed at home."

"Is she ill?"

"She's pregnant."

"Ah," Isabella said, her husky voice casual, as she picked up a book by his bedside and leafed through it.

"Have you spoken with Captain Milne?"

"A few days ago," she replied, putting down the book to turn to him. "He has agreed to meet Falkland in Oxford, on Christmas Eve."

Laurence sat down on the bed and leant back against one of its carved oaken posts. "That's less than a week away," he said thoughtfully. "Will he bring some sort of proof to show Falkland?"

"He stole a page from Hoare's records that apparently contains information to which Hoare could not have been privy other than through devious means. Falkland will recognise it, Milne claims. However, we have a slight problem. Milne won't go near Falkland's quarters – he's too petrified of Hoare – so we shall have to arrange the meeting somewhere else. My lodgings, possibly," she added, taking a step closer to Laurence, who caught another waft of her seductive perfume. "I have a chamber at the Blue Boar. Are you acquainted with it?"

"Yes. But I'm not sure Falkland would like that. I asked him to come up here with me to see you and he refused."

Isabella gave her hard little laugh. "He thinks I'm not respectable. Fair enough, we'll find some neutral territory that suits everyone concerned."

"I can discuss the details with him tomorrow. Then I'll come straight to you in Oxford."

She clapped her hands together. "At last! The end of Colonel Hoare!"

"Digby will be pleased," Laurence said, to see if it would provoke her.

"We shall all be pleased," she rejoined evenly, settling herself on the bed. Then she kicked off her shoes and smiled at him. "What a very good thing it is that Falkland did not accompany you. Because he's right about me. At the moment, I do not feel in the least respectable."

"Is that so."

"Come here, Beaumont." She grabbed him by the front of his shirt and they both fell back against the coverlet. He was almost on top of her. Their mouths met, and their tongues. She seemed in no hurry, which excited him even more. "Now," she told him, in a low whisper, "take all the liberties you want with me."

"On your command," he said.

He moved away to lift her skirts, hoisted her legs over his shoulders, and bent his head between her thighs. She tasted clean, like a courtesan; he had always found that it was the upright woman who avoided soap and water, as if virtue were a sufficient guarantee of hygiene. "Yes," she hissed, as he licked the rise of her flesh, and down, and around, until it became silken with moisture. When he applied his tongue more firmly, she tangled her fingers in his hair, and spread wider for him; and she shuddered against him. "How sweet," she murmured. "I want more." He was about to comply when suddenly her legs became rigid on either side of him. "Stop!" she ordered him.

He extracted his head from the warm tent of her skirts, brushing his hair out of his eyes only to see Lady Morecombe in the open doorway.

"Mr. Beaumont," she said, in a sepulchral tone, "what *are* you doing?"

"Madam," he responded, after a brief pause, "if you truly have no idea, I believe your husband's been neglecting you."

"My husband has been cold in the grave these past seven years!"

"Oh," said Laurence. "I'm sorry for that."

She remained motionless, staring. "I was told that you had to speak with me."

"It seems you've been misinformed."

"I shall call off the betrothal! Your father shall hear of this, and your mother! The entire neighbourhood!"

"The whole world, if you choose. Now would you please leave us alone?"

Lady Morecombe snorted angrily, and shut the door on them with a bang.

"Dear me," said Isabella. "Were you meant to marry that woman's daughter?"

"I don't think I'll have to any more."

She burst into peals of laughter so spontaneous and genuine that he joined in; and for a while they both lay helplessly convulsed on the bed.

"Beaumont, how you amuse me," she gasped, "but perhaps it would be wise for me to disappear."

"No." He jumped up and went to bolt the door. "We won't be interrupted again – though I'd like to know who sent her up here," he added, throwing himself back on the bed.

Isabella began to unlace his breeches. "Well, well," she said, lifting his shirt to caress his sex with practised fingers, "let's find out what you can do with this." And she drew him inside her.

How superior was experience to innocence, he thought, as she moved her hips in harmony with his own, alternately squeezing and releasing him; and occasionally she would pull away to tease the tip of him before plunging him deeper again. Then her body arched towards his, and he looked into her gold-flecked eyes. "Now!" she exclaimed, and obligingly he timed his release with hers.

"I wish we could be naked, skin to skin," she said afterwards. "These clothes are a nuisance."

"They are," he agreed. "What did you tell Lord Falkland about me?" he said next, on impulse.

"That he should trust you."

"Nothing else?"

"No."

He loosened her dress and lowered it beneath her breasts, so that if he would not see her naked tonight, he might at least explore as much of her as possible; and there was nothing to disappoint beneath her clothing, no inadequacies cunningly concealed by a talented seamstress. Ready for her again, he felt as if he might make love to her for hours, watching her expression to see what pleased her. But when she gripped him fiercely, her breathing harsh in his ear, and with a finger artfully placed, drove an intense thrill through his body, he could not contain himself.

"How fine that was," she sighed. "A pity I can't stay here all night."

He withdrew from her, regretfully, and when she sat up, he fastened her dress. Her hair had come loose of its pins, so he knelt behind her and restored it neatly, as the women at Simeon's house had taught him. "Such unexpected skills," she remarked. "I should hire you for a chambermaid."

They heard a babble of voices growing louder, and then the thunder of feet up the stairs and past his door. "Sounds like a herd of cattle," he said.

"Yet another bedding."

She stepped into her shoes as they listened to masculine cheers and the shrieking of female voices. Gradually the noise became more distant.

"It should be safe for you to slip out," he told her.

She pulled on her cloak as he opened the door and checked in both directions. "Fear not, Beaumont," she said, giving him a light kiss, "I shall have everything arranged, you may depend upon it." She ran a finger along the side of his neck. "And you must explain these teeth marks, at some future date. I am almost certain that *I* did not put them there." Before he could speak, she was gone.

In a buoyant mood, he changed into his old clothes, loaded his pistols and bundled them in his cloak, then ran downstairs, where he found Geoffrey sweeping a floor littered with broken glass.

"These people," Geoffrey complained, "they can't hold their liquor, and we must clean up after them in all corners of the house. And Lady Morecombe just took her daughter and left with her suddenly, we don't know why. Who'd want to go out so late, and in this foul weather?"

Some men now came roaring down the stairs. Tom was amongst them, red-faced but not as drunk as the night before. "Laurence," he cried. "How was she? Boys," he called to his friends, who gathered around him, "he just had a woman in his chamber. I'll bet she's a juicy piece and wouldn't object to another tumble. Is anyone game?"

"Be quiet," said Laurence, realising who had inspired Lady Morecombe's unsolicited visit.

Tom seized him and twisted him about, sending his pistols clattering to the floor. "You've dishonoured our family!"

"Enough, Tom."

Tom paid no attention. Unsheathing his sword, he pointed it at Laurence's chest. "Arm him," he snapped to one of his friends, who pulled out a rapier and thrust it at Laurence. "Take it, or I'll run you through," Tom shouted, pressing in his own blade, piercing the fabric of Laurence's doublet.

"Go on, then, if that's what you want." Laurence laid a hand on the blade, as if to push it further in.

Tom's expression changed from fury to incredulity. In that second, Laurence yanked the blade from him, threw it away, and punched him twice. Tom's head jerked back and he collapsed.

"No more entertainment for tonight, gentlemen," Laurence said to Tom's friends, who shambled off.

He and Geoffrey lifted Tom into a seated position and propped him against the wall. He was dazed, with a bloody nose and another trickle issuing from the side of his mouth.

"What cowards," Geoffrey muttered. "Not one man dared stop him."

"You'd better fetch some cloths and hot water," Laurence suggested.

"You'll need more attention than Master Thomas, sir."

Laurence looked to see the palm and fingers of his right hand bleeding freely. Making a fist, he crouched down beside Tom. "What possessed you to do that? If you have an argument with me, settle it privately, for God's sake, and not in our father's house."

"What about you, bringing that whore under his roof?" Tom demanded scornfully. "You're worse than a whore yourself."

They were silent until Geoffrey brought what was needed. As Geoffrey mopped the blood from Tom's face, Laurence wrapped up his own hand, then picked up his cloak and pistols, bade a quick good night to Geoffrey, and made his way to the stables. His cuts were bleeding through the bandage once he had finished saddling his horse, and he rode off dreading what might await him upon his return. His mother would have words for him, he knew, but he was more concerned about how the fight would upset his father.

At Great Tew, after waking the servants, he was received by Falkland's wife in her dressing gown. "Mr. Beaumont, what brings you out at such an hour?" she asked, her face taut with anxiety. "It's past three in the morning."

"I beg pardon for disturbing you, Lady Falkland, but I have to see your husband."

"He is not here. He left as soon as we came back from Chipping Campden. A messenger had arrived with an urgent summons to fetch him to Oxford."

"What was it about?" Laurence asked, her alarm infecting him.

"He did not tell me. Oh, sir," she exclaimed, as she saw his hand, "you are hurt."

"I'll have to find him," Laurence said, thinking that if Falkland had come upstairs with him to meet Isabella Savage, there would have been no scandal and no fight. At the same time, however, he could not entirely regret how events had transpired.

"Let me change your bandage," Lady Falkland insisted. "Come into the parlour, sir." He waited there, his hand aching more sharply, while she sent for a basin of water and clean linen. "You should not ride such a distance," she said, as she unwound the soaked cloth. "It will only aggravate the bleeding."

"I've no choice. Do you have anything for the pain?"

She exchanged a word with her servant, who went away and came back with a cup and a small, corked bottle. She pulled out the cork and poured a few drops into the cup for Laurence; it was not poppy, but some other, sour-tasting stuff. "Mr. Beaumont," she said after he had drunk it down, "my husband does not often confide in me about matters of state, but ever since he came home he has been so agitated. What could be troubling him?"

"You must ask him yourself." While she dressed his hand, the cuts began to throb. "If you don't mind, I'll take some more of that," he said, reaching for the bottle.

"Sir, it's very strong," she protested, but he swigged down a mouthful.

"May I keep it with me?" he asked.

"Yes, sir, though be careful – what you have had is quite sufficient."

He stuffed the bottle inside his doublet, and she accompanied him out to his horse. As he mounted, he noticed that she was holding back tears, and he extended his good hand to grasp hers. "Now don't worry too much about your husband," he consoled her.

"I cannot help but worry! He must have told you about our two young sons – I only pray he will see them grow to manhood." She sniffed and added, "Oh, dear, sir, you would not understand; you have no children."

"Well, in fact, I'm not altogether sure about that," he said, with a smile.

She also smiled, weakly, and released his hand. "Thank you for your concern. And give him my love when you find him."

IV.

In the shimmering waves of heat on the horizon appeared a massive coach and four, with armed soldiers riding postillion at either side. At first Laurence took it for some chimera of his imagination, since the glare of the sun was making black spots dance before his eyes. He blinked, but saw it again, moving closer. As the coach slowed in front of him, he reached for Juana, who had been standing by his side. He touched thin air. She had vanished, and the soldiers were raising their pistols to train them at his chest. He wanted to move or cry out, but his limbs were frozen and he could make no sound. Then a dark, malevolent face appeared through the coach window: Khadija's.

"*Ayúdame!* Help me, help!" a voice screamed, and he realised that Juana was also in the coach, struggling to escape as Khadija held her fast by the wrists. Still he was paralysed, unable to come to her aid. She howled and shrieked, crashing her body against the walls of the coach so violently that it rocked to and fro, but Khadija seemed possessed of infinite strength and would not let go.

As suddenly, Juana fell silent. The coach ceased to lurch about, and Khadija smiled, with unmistakeable triumph. "This witch will trouble you no more," she told him, fixing him with her penetrating gaze. And the coach sped off.

Her words must have released Laurence from the enchantment, for now his limbs had the power to move. He tore after the coach, and at last he caught up and grabbed on to the window frame. The driver's whip lashed out at his hand; and in the same moment he saw inside the coach. It was empty. He felt shock, and a sharp sting as the whip sliced again into his flesh; then he knew that the pain was real.

He opened his eyes and looked about, completely disoriented until he recognised the hangings on Seward's bed, upon which he was lying fully clothed.

"Finally you are awake," said Seward, coming in. "You've slept for over ten hours."

"How did I get here?"

"Habit must have guided you, for you were almost insensible when you arrived."

Laurence squinted at him. "When was that?"

"You stumbled in about midday and fell on my floor. I spoke to you, but you were incoherent, and then unconscious. What on earth was the cause of it?" Laurence felt for the bottle in his doublet with his left hand, and passed it to Seward, who sniffed at the contents. "Belladonna may be one of the ingredients – dangerous in any quantity. Let me see your other hand." Seward unwrapped the bandage; it was dark with dried blood and glued to the cuts, which began to burn and bleed as they were exposed. "How did you acquire these injuries?"

"My brother challenged me to a duel last night, after our sister's wedding. I had to take his sword away from him."

"Why did you quarrel?"

"I don't want to discuss it."

"The deeper cut will require stitching. Let us go into the other room, where the light is better." Laurence obeyed, and Seward sat him down in a chair. Though still mildly stupefied, he had to swallow back nausea as the needle dug into his skin, and after a while he stopped watching.

"Seward," he said, "in a few days' time Falkland will talk to the man who saw Hoare opening his correspondence. A friend of mine, Isabella Savage, is helping to arrange the meeting." He described his earlier conversation with Falkland in the stables, and his hurried ride to Great Tew. "Falkland's wife was in such a panic over this urgent summons that I became nervous about it myself. So I came here and managed to find his quarters, but his servant said he was in conference with the King. That was when the drug started to overwhelm me. My heart was racing, and yet I couldn't put one foot in front of the other. I don't remember any more."

Seward was studying Laurence's face, in between stitches. "I could not but notice, as you entered, that you were wearing a most captivating scent – attar of roses, orrisroot, musk, and a touch of frankincense, if I'm not mistaken."

"I didn't know you had such a keen sense of smell," Laurence remarked.

"Who is this woman Isabella Savage, and why should she volunteer to assist Falkland?"

"Lord Digby is her guardian. Digby hates Colonel Hoare."

"Ah, I see: it will be as convenient for them as for you, if Hoare falls from grace. But that does not explain the perfume. Was it because of her that you and your brother came to violence?"

"In part."

"My dear boy!" Seward tied a neat knot with the thread and snipped off the excess with a pair of scissors. "And on your sister's wedding night! I hope you were discreet."

Laurence thought of Lady Morecombe and began to laugh. "I'm afraid we weren't, though it wasn't exactly our fault."

Seward rose and went to his cupboard, from which he selected various jars and a pestle and mortar. "You need a poultice, to stop the wound from suppurating," he said, and they were quiet for a while as he prepared it. "Just watch out where desire leads you," he advised, on his return.

"You speak from experience," Laurence observed, smiling.

"Indeed I do. Now, I have some news for you, on the subject of our regicides. Since my return to College, I had a most fruitful chat with John Earle. Pembroke sent him a letter through Lord Falkland."

"Yes, yes, I knew about that. What did Pembroke want?"

"To reconcile with Earle, despite the political differences that had caused them to argue. Earle said he's in Pembroke's debt. He had been Pembroke's chaplain at Court in the early thirties, and was bestowed the rectory of Bishopston, in Wiltshire, for his service. A very generous living."

"What did you say to Earle?"

"That he should investigate Pembroke's motives before making any decision. I think it was enough to put him on guard."

"He *should* be on guard," Laurence said vehemently.

"Beaumont, it's high time you told Falkland about your trip to London."

"I know. And now I also know where Radcliff is: at his brother-in-law's in Newbury."

"It will be a rude interruption, if you seize him there."

"I'll have to draw him out. But I'd rather wait until next week, by which time Falkland should have Hoare safely under arrest."

"Yes, that's not a bad idea." Seward applied the poultice to his hand and bound clean linen over it. "You called out a name when you were dreaming: Juana. Was she your thief?" Laurence nodded. "So you have not yet forgotten her."

"I have, and I haven't," Laurence answered honestly. "It makes me ashamed, that I should be capable of forgetting."

V.

They had outpaced the Englishman's servant as they started to cross the Pyrenees, and Laurence felt confident that it would be impossible for him to track them through the dense pine forest. Even they themselves had trouble keeping their bearings.

After some hours they came across a clearing where the ferny undergrowth had been cut to cover a humble shelter built of sticks. Juana jumped down from her horse to poke about inside and emerged flourishing a child's toy crudely carved out of wood. "The people left their belongings here, Monsieur! Maybe they were chased out."

They set off once more, and had not gone far when they heard the rushing of a stream ahead, and encountered a path that they followed for about a mile until the sound became clearer. "Look, Monsieur, a *patrin*!" she cried, and dismounted again to pick something from a bush. It was a small bunch of reeds tied together with a cunning knot. "I'm sure they were *Roma* who made that hut. They left the *patrin* as their mark, for other travellers to find."

They rode on, Laurence ahead. As they were approaching the banks of the stream, his horse whinnied and reared, almost throwing him off. On the ground before him lay what had startled it: the body of a child, swollen and pulsing with maggots. He turned about quickly, to prevent Juana from following. "Some dead animal," he said, for he did not want to upset her with the truth. "Let's avoid it, for the sake of the horses."

They left the path to break through the undergrowth, and reached a point at which the stream broadened into a deep pool, reflecting back the pure blue of the sky. They were both thirsty, and she rushed to kneel and scoop up mouthfuls of water. He was about to drink also when a cloud momentarily obscured the sun, and he could see down into the pool. There were two shapes below, a man and a woman tied together and swaying in the slight current, their bodies trapped by underwater reeds. The woman's long hair swirled about her head like a plume of seaweed, the sole thing about either of them that had not become hideous in death.

Juana was about to return her hand for more water when he snatched her away. "That water's not clean." And he pointed to the bloated, decomposing bodies. "You should make yourself sick," he urged. "Stick your finger down your throat."

But she continued to stare downwards, as if she had not heard him. "They were the people from the camp," she whispered. "They were murdered by the *gadje*, as was my own family."

They moved on at once, but after a short interval, as Laurence glanced behind him, he noticed that she was riding so slowly that he had to rein in for her to catch up. The sun gradually began to dip in the sky, and as twilight came, he had no idea where they were. When he looked back for Juana again, she was crumpled over her horse's neck, her head sagging on her chest as though someone had shot her, both arms about her waist. She allowed him to help her from the saddle and pry them away. Her dress strained where it usually hung loose, her stomach distended as if she were pregnant. Shaken by a dreadful convulsion, she clapped a hand over her mouth, and vomit streamed through her fingers. Choking it up, she fell on the ground, but when he tried to assist her she fought him off, crawling to the side of a tree to drag up her skirts and squat. He retreated and turned aside. Modest as she was about her bodily functions, she would hate him to witness this indignity.

When he came back later, she was lying motionless on the ground. As he picked her up she did not respond, eyes closed, her mouth encrusted with earth and vomit, her breathing laboured. He carried her over to their belongings, made her a bed with what covers they had and wiped the mess from her face. Then she stirred and spoke to him deliriously in her own language; and in Spanish, she muttered, "Don't mark my grave. It is bad luck. Promise you won't mark my grave."

"I promise you won't die," he said, though he knew how near she was, and the thought of burying her in the forest appalled him, as he imagined her body dug up and torn apart by wild creatures.

Listening to her ragged panting and the sounds of the forest, he tried to stay awake for her, to be companion to her last moments, if need be. Yet he must have drowsed, for when he woke the sun was high above the treetops. Juana lay still in his arms, her eyes shut. He cursed out loud, sick with guilt; then his despair lifted as he felt the air from her nostrils, and the cooler temperature of her skin. She was asleep.

After some hours, her eyes opened and she gazed up at him. "You are crying, Monsieur," she whispered, in a ghost of her normal voice.

It was then that he realised he had come to care for her far too much. She had manipulated him and lied to him; and she had only offered herself to him once, in shame, and out of sheer desperation. If they stayed together, she would just use him again. They must part as soon as she was strong enough to travel on her own.

The next day she seemed much better, but she was in a filthy state. He took her to the riverbank and against her protests washed her thoroughly. She wept and hid her face from him as his hand slipped between her legs, where the worst of the dirt clung; and he was embarrassed also, because in touching her, he had been aroused.

The journey out of the forest exhausted her. On the following day near evening, as they reached the town of Pamplona, he discovered that no amount of money would persuade an innkeeper to admit her. Plague had been spoken of in the countryside, he was informed, and everyone knew that gypsies spread the disease. One sole hope remained: the Sisters of Mercy at the convent might be persuaded to shelter her in their hospice.

When she understood that he was about to leave her there, Juana grabbed on to him with all her strength, shrieking as though possessed. He had to surrender her baggage to the Mother Superior hoping that it would not be inspected, for he had tucked the purse full of gold inside. "How like animals they are, these gypsies," the Mother Superior commented. "No dignity. Yet God made us all, did He not, and His purpose is mysterious to the sinful minds of men." Juana was wrestled off him by a couple of stout nuns and dragged away, screaming his name. And so, he reflected, it was done.

He should have left Pamplona, but he ended up wandering about town until he came to a large hostelry where he took a room and slept late, waking thick in the head as though he had been drunk the night before. At a nearby stewhouse he bought a bath and sat in the steaming water, trying to convince himself that it was all for the best, for Juana as for him; and while he was dressing, a woman proposed to him the usual service. He thought this might afford him some relief, though when they were finished, he felt even gloomier. At a tavern, he tried to get drunk.

Back in his chamber in the early hours of morning, as he lay sprawled on the bed, he was disturbed by a knock at the door. "Monsieur, how could you abandon me to those bitches?" Juana cried, sweeping in. She was clad in a voluminous nun's robe, and from beneath it, like a conjuror, she produced the purse. "The Mother Superior had hidden it in her cupboard, but I broke the lock and took it out when she was at prayers!"

She tossed it on the bed, bent down to grasp the hem of the habit and stripped it off. More slowly she unfastened the dress below it, and removed that also. In her thin shift, she approached him, took his hands and placed them on her breasts, then ran them over her belly to her groin.

"Juana, what do you want?" he said, as wary of her advances as he had been in Paris. But this time she was bolder, and he was in no mood to resist.

She said nothing, kissing him, her teeth bruising his lips. Then she ripped apart the front of his breeches. He was achingly hard, and when he drew her to him and entered her, she was moist and open.

"Why did you do it?" he asked later, as they lay side by side on the bed.

"You were waiting for me," she replied evasively. "And I knew you would choose the nicest inn. You still had plenty of money, although I had the gold." She grabbed a handful of coins from the purse and set them in a neat line from her throat to the rise of her pubic bone. "Am I not handsome, dressed so?" And seizing his hand, she buried it between her legs, at which he gave in to her again, like a man tumbling wilfully over a precipice.

In the weeks that ensued, there was no question of them separating: he did not suggest it, nor did she, and she seemed as eager for him as he was for her. The more he had her, the hungrier for her he became, though she was neither skilled nor adventurous as a lover. He was so intoxicated with her that he scarcely noticed her asking after her tribe in every village they passed. She must have learnt something, for she insisted that they travel yet further southwards, to Granada.

Crossing the river Ebro at Logroño, they headed over the mountains into Castille towards Guadalajara, and then down to the barren plains of La Mancha, where the temperature soared and they gladly shed much of their worn clothing. The heat was a balm to him, and soon they started to resemble each other, burnt to the same dark colour in their faded rags. He had the impression that they were disappearing into the landscape, the hours passing seamlessly from day to night, and day again. He lost track of the month, unable to remember if it was late in May or early June. Then the cold returned, as they made the hard trip over the Sienna Morena, after which, with much relief, they descended into warmer climes, where the sun became powerful once more.

One day, while watering their horses at the banks of the Guadalquivir, they spied a great coach in the distance thundering towards them surrounded by clouds of dust. The only other human presence they had witnessed for some time had been the occasional peasant and his donkey, so this seemed to them a remarkable sight. The vehicle was drawn by four white Andalusians with shining manes, and the soldiers riding postillion were armed.

"They must be wealthy people," Juana commented. "The brigands in these parts will be after them."

"I hope they don't shoot us first," Laurence said apprehensively.

The coach slowed before them and a man peered out. His complexion was jaundiced and he was sweating beneath his plumed hat. To some passenger within he muttered, "Gypsies, my dear!"

A woman's face now appeared at the coach window, her hair in ornate curls about her temples, her cheeks flushed, rich jewels dangling from her ears. "*Mira*, Don Fernando," she said, "they are half-naked, like beasts of the field!" At this, Laurence saw Juana tugging up the front of her dress and folding her arms over her chest, to hide the mild curve of her breasts. He himself was without a shirt and felt unpleasantly exposed.

"Ask them," Don Fernando said to one of his soldiers, who growled sharply, "Which way to Jaén?"

The woman, meanwhile, continued her inspection of Laurence and Juana. "How unfair, that such precious white teeth should be gifted them!"

"If your skin were as black as theirs, your teeth would shine as bright. You," Don Fernando said, beckoning to them, "open your mouths wider for the lady. Show us these pearls that nature has wasted on swine."

Laurence nudged Juana's elbow; she was bristling visibly at the taunt. "Keep calm," he whispered.

"Open your mouth, girl!" the soldier yelled at her, jumping down and brandishing a whip.

She gave him a haughty glare, her mouth clammed shut. Predicting trouble, Laurence stepped in front of her and addressed the occupants of the coach in his most correct Castilian. "Excuse me, but if you desire the road to Jaén, you missed it some way back, at the crossroads. You should take the right-hand path."

"*Madre de Díos!* Where did you learn to speak like that?" the woman demanded. "Were you a servant in Madrid?"

"That's a musket wound on his side," Don Fernando said, pointing. "He's too tall for a gypsy, and his eyes are too strange a hue. What are you, you scoundrel, a half-breed Moor? A deserter from the army?"

"No, sir," Laurence said, impressed by the accuracy of his last guess.

"Does the girl tell fortunes?" the woman inquired.

"I'm afraid not," Laurence replied.

"Then open her mouth for us, boy," said Don Fernando. "Show us her teeth." When Laurence did not move, he said to the soldier, "Give her a lick of the whip."

They were silent save for the snorting and stomping of the horses in harness, then the soldier swung his arm back. Laurence anticipated the whip's trajectory, and caught the leather tongue as it cracked down.

"By the devil's arse, let go, you son of a bitch!" cried the soldier, attempting to free the whip, to which Laurence hung on, though it stung his palm and fingers.

"They are worse than beasts," announced Don Fernando. "And I don't like the look of this rogue. It could be a trap, and he may have friends ahead." He waved at the driver. "Let's be off!" Laurence released the whip and the soldier went back to his horse, uttering more curses. And the coach wheeled about and rattled off.

Juana flopped down on the ground as though her legs could no longer support her. "Monsieur," she said, "why did you put yourself at risk for me again?"

"Because I would do anything for you," he blurted out.

"Then never desert me!"

He fell on his knees in the dirt beside her, unable to credit what he had just heard. "When you find your people, you won't need me any more," he said, willing her to contradict him.

"I shall always need you. This I swear by God, by the Virgin, by my very soul." Taking his hand, she kissed his palm, where the whip had left a vivid welt. "No one can part us, as long as I have life in my body."

He should have laughed off her declaration, or said nothing and remained sceptical. But instead, like an idiot, he let himself believe her.

VI.

Lord Falkland's manservant greeted Laurence as always, with a brief inclination of his head. Tickled by his pomposity, Laurence asked, "What's your name?"

"Stephens, sir," he said, raising his eyebrows, as if it were an impertinent question. "His lordship is not in his chambers. He is taking some air." Through the window he indicated a courtyard bordered with rose bushes where a short figure was pacing about.

"Thank you, Stephens," Laurence said. "Do you ever smile?"

"I have not had cause for it lately, sir."

"Hmm. And how is his lordship?"

"With all due respect, sir, you would do better to ask him yourself."

"I shall," Laurence told him, and went to join the Secretary of State.

"Mr. Beaumont," Falkland said rather curtly, as he approached, "I thank you for your message yesterday, and I am sorry that I was too occupied to see you then." Since he offered no explanation, Laurence let this pass. "How much did you reveal to my wife?"

"As little as I could. She was worried about you and what took you to Oxford."

"Yes, yes, I can understand why," Falkland murmured, running a hand over his face; he was grey with fatigue and his hand trembled.

"If I were you, I'd be honest with her, but that's just my opinion. What do I know about wives." Laurence frowned at him. "Are you well, my lord?"

"I am merely tired. I have not slept since I left Great Tew. What . . . what news do you have for me?" Falkland said next, under his breath.

"I'll bring Captain Milne to you on Christmas Eve."

"Where?" Falkland's eyes now darted about, as though Milne might spring out from around some corner to surprise them.

"In Christ Church, at eleven o'clock. It should be busy at that time with the midnight service. You must go alone to the Lady Chapel and kneel down as though praying. If you don't see me within the half hour, leave. If there should be any change of plan, I'll let you know before then, or Is – Mistress Savage will."

"Can we depend upon her?"

"At this point, we haven't much choice," Laurence said, more irritably than he had intended.

"As I've said to you before, I'm not used to intrigue. Far more your province than mine."

"Oh, one more thing, my lord," Laurence added, in a low voice. "I meant to tell you when we spoke at the wedding, but if you recall, our conversation was somewhat abruptly curtailed. I went to London in November to look for Radcliff, who was missing from his regiment after Edgehill. I suspected that he'd been taken there as a hostage. I was wrong. He was at Pembroke's house all the while."

Falkland blinked at him. "My God! So you've known since November that Pembroke is master of the conspiracy."

"Yes. And I don't care about your negotiations. I want to bring in Radcliff next week. We can interrogate him together."

Falkland nodded; he appeared dazed. "As you think fit, Mr. Beaumont," he said.

VII.

Tom looked down at Mary as she lay pale and weak in their bed, and then at his mother. He wanted to rage out loud at the injustice of it: his child was lost.

"You have not yet begun to endure what is a woman's lot," Lady

Beaumont was telling Mary. "Now bid your husband goodbye, and no more tears."

"You won't be away too long?" Mary begged of him.

"Promise I won't," he said, and touched her cheek with his lips.

"Thomas," said Lady Beaumont, as they descended the stairs, "admit that you think the sight of your face after the fight provoked her to miscarry."

Tom fingered his bruises, less swollen for three days of remedies from the still room. "Why else would it happen?" he responded bitterly.

"She told me she had the pains earlier and was bleeding before she went to bed that night."

Tom said nothing. He still held Laurence responsible.

When they entered the hall, they found Lord Beaumont with Elizabeth, Ormiston, and Sir Robert Stratton, who had prolonged his stay on the excuse of a bad cold.

"Thomas, you must not be too discouraged," Lord Beaumont said. "Stratton was just telling me that his wife Diana slipped her first child, and yet they have now a pair of fine sons and another babe on the way. It is well known that Nature deals so with imperfections. Aristotle, if my memory serves me correctly, once wrote –"

"On the subject of imperfections," Lady Beaumont cut in, "I received word today from Lady Morecombe that she has decided to overlook Laurence's misconduct. Alice is prepared to do so as well. It does not much surprise me, given how those Morecombes stand to benefit from the marriage."

Tom gaped at her. "So there'll be no more consequences for him than if he'd broken wind and neglected to apologise? He *arranged* for Lady Morecombe to witness that disgusting scene! He did it all on purpose, can't you see?"

There was an awkward pause.

"Thomas says he must leave for Oxford," announced Lady Beaumont.

"Should you not be with your wife, given her circumstances?" Lord Beaumont objected.

"I wish I could stay, but there's an issue of supplies for my troop that I must attend to," Tom said, struggling to subdue his anger.

"I shall ride back with you, if I may," Stratton said. "My lord, my lady, you have been too hospitable, and I thank you both."

As Stratton went to ready himself for the journey, Ormiston took Tom aside. "What's the true reason for your going, Tom? It's Christmastide: we'll have no action for a month, at least. Are you intending to find your brother?" Tom glowered at the floor. "You must forget your quarrel. What he did with that woman was in poor taste, but if he had fought with you afterwards, God knows what greater damage might have been done."

"I've no need of your advice," Tom spat back, livid. "And if you want to keep the peace between *us*, you won't interfere again."

On the way to Oxford, Stratton suggested that he and Tom break their journey at Woodstock, now stuffed to the seams with Royalist billets, and get a meal in an alehouse. This they did, and while they sat thawing their feet before the fire, drinking from their mugs, Stratton remarked, "It must have been a very low sort of trollop who came to your brother's chamber that night."

"I know who it was: her name's Isabella Savage," Tom said. "She's one of those women at Court who live upon their looks and their cunning. And, of course, their easy virtue."

"Dear Christ! It is my misfortune to know her too!"

By the time their meat had arrived, served on hearty slices of bread in the old style, they were assembling a fuller list of her crimes.

"Digby's courier, is she," Tom muttered; so she might have visited his brother for more than carnal purposes that night. "And she escaped from your house dressed as a boy? Hard to believe she'd fool anyone in that guise."

"Because of her, my entire household was confined at Wytham and I lost some lucrative contracts," Stratton complained. "If I see her again, I shall be tempted to wring her neck. As for your brother –"

"I should wring *his* neck."

"I have more cause. I strongly suspect that he once had the gall to make advances to my wife."

Tom feigned appropriate surprise and dismay. "When?"

"This summer, on his return from the other war."

"She must have been horribly affronted."

Stratton picked up his mug and toyed with it. "She will never again receive him alone, nor do I ever want him in my house. Out of discretion, I've not mentioned it to your parents, nor shall I tell my wife the details of this latest unsavoury episode. She still has a misguided affection for that Savage creature, and as it is she cannot bear to hear so much as your brother's name, after his outrageous behaviour towards her." Poor Stratton, mused Tom; either he had too much pride to admit that he had been cuckolded years ago, or he was unaware of the fact. Stratton took a quick gulp of ale, straightening his shoulders. "I'd call him out myself if he came anywhere near my door, but he'd probably refuse to settle with me as a gentleman should, just as he refused you."

"We can only pray that he'll get his comeuppance one day," Tom said, setting down his mug and rising. "Well, sir, let's cover those last miles, since we've eaten our fill."

"I trust our conversation shall remain private, sir?" Stratton asked anxiously.

"I give you my word," Tom assured him.

CHAPTER THIRTEEN

I.

At half past nine o'clock on Christmas Eve, Laurence left Merton College for the Blue Boar. He had arranged to call on Isabella shortly before he met Captain Milne, who was to be waiting for him in the cloisters of St. Mary's Church; he would then take Milne to Christ Church. But his conversation with Falkland had made him somewhat uneasy about Isabella's role in their plans, so he had decided to set out early; he half anticipated surprising Digby in her chamber, or possibly even Milne.

In the streets, he encountered only bunches of revellers on their way to or from some Christmas celebration. The Blue Boar's horn windows were bright with candlelight, and he could hear exuberant voices carousing within. As he entered, he inhaled the smell of tobacco smoke and the mixed odours of roasting meat and spiced ale. Festooned with branches of holly, yew, and mistletoe, the small taproom was crowded with people laughing, and singing and raising cups.

He pushed through them, then quietly mounted the stairs to Isabella's chamber and listened outside her door for a moment. Hearing no voices, he knocked.

"Who's there?" she called out.

"Me," he replied.

She admitted him, shut the door behind him and bolted it; there was no one else in the room. "I did not expect you for at least another hour," she said curtly.

"I beg your pardon, should I go and come back later?" he inquired, with mock politesse.

"Of course not."

He removed his cloak and tossed his pistols on the bed. "Is anything wrong?"

"No."

"Then why are you trembling?"

He reached for her, but she pushed him away. "Beaumont, this is not the time."

"We have plenty of time."

"Oh, I see, now I know the reason for your excessive punctuality."

Irritated, he shot back, "Have you seen our friend Digby recently?"

"Yes." She turned on him a bright smile. "And in fact we spoke of you. He hoped you might help him: he is about to publish a broadsheet, to assist the King in spreading news of his victories and discrediting the nonsense going about London these days as to his Cavaliers' awful atrocities," she carried on, as though delivering some speech that she had memorised. "Women raped and children skewered on muskets! Prince Rupert's dog is even being portrayed as a satanic familiar. It is hilarious what people are willing to believe. But since many Londoners are now pleading for an end to war, Digby thinks they deserve better information to sway their allegiances."

"Better information, or better lies?"

"Why so cynical? If you agree to help, Digby might get you exempted from military service this spring. He needs reliable intelligence from all parts of the country to be reported quickly to Oxford, so that the broadsheet can be printed weekly and then distributed in London. He might have it reprinted there, if we cannot import sufficient copies. I shall organize for it to be smuggled into the capital, under the best cover in the world: women's skirts."

"How ingenious," he said, laughing. "Your idea?" She nodded. "What's he going to call his broadsheet?"

"*Mercurius Aulicus.*" She hesitated, surveying Laurence, then resumed in a brittle, careless tone, "Do you know you have an admirer at Court? That poor young widow Lady d'Aubigny is besotted with you, or so rumour has it."

"You shouldn't listen to rumour," he said dismissively.

"Well, beware. She's a flighty girl and has deluded herself that she has a gift for politics. And she is practically the King's cousin."

"Isabella, have you anything to drink?"

"No."

"I can go down for it."

"Would you?" Suddenly her expression changed and she became herself again. "Beaumont, I am so dreadfully on edge. I hope Captain Milne doesn't disappoint us tonight."

"And *I* hope Falkland doesn't." He smiled, to reassure her, and took a step towards her. "I forgot to tell you how much I like your perfume. Let me guess: attar of roses, orrisroot, musk . . . and . . ." He bowed his head to her neck and sniffed. "Perhaps a touch of frankincense. Am I right?"

"Why, yes!" she said, visibly impressed. He was about to venture yet closer when they heard the toll of church bells. "That's ten o'clock," she reminded him. "You should fetch the wine."

Down in the taproom, Laurence had to elbow his way through the crush. Someone tried to grab his arm, but he paid no attention until, over the din of voices, he heard a man cry, "I've got him!" He recognised a couple of Hoare's guards peering out of the crowd at him, and another nearby, who had attempted to seize him. He kicked that man in the shins, shoved his way back towards the stairs, raced up to Isabella's chamber, hurried in, and slammed and bolted the door. "Hoare's men are downstairs," he whispered urgently.

"What shall we do?" she gasped.

He flung wide the window. There were more guards below, Corporal Wilson amongst them; they had surrounded the tavern entrance.

"You can't – it's too far down," Isabella protested, as he hoisted himself over the sill. "Beaumont, you'll break your neck!"

Men were now hammering at the door. It gave on its hinges as Laurence was squeezing his shoulders through the window frame. "Throw the pistols down after me," he called up to her.

But she disappeared as though she had been snatched away, and Corporal Wilson's face loomed over him instead, grinning. "Mr. Beaumont, we meet again!" Laurence released his hold and fell, then scrambled on hands and knees down a narrow alley beside the tavern. There was no exit, he quickly realised. "He's down there!" Wilson yelled to his companions below. They rushed after Laurence, dragged him out into the street, and began to assail him with blows and kicks, until he was writhing about on the wet ground.

A pair of shiny boots approached and stopped in front of his face. "Mr. Beaumont," said Colonel Hoare, "a happy Christmas to you."

"And a happy one to you too," Laurence managed to reply, just as two guards marched Isabella out of the tavern.

"What right have you to treat him so?" she demanded of Hoare, attempting to tear herself free from them.

"I need to get some answers from him," Hoare said calmly. "I shall also detain you for a while."

"You are a brute, sir!" she shouted. "Lord Digby shall hear of it!"

"He may hear of it, madam, but he has no power to prevent it." As if to emphasise his point, Hoare sank one smartly booted toe into the pit of Laurence's stomach.

"Let her go," panted Laurence.

Hoare delivered another kick, lower than the first; Laurence retched and nearly fainted. "As I think you should recognise by now, Mr. Beaumont, you're in no position to order me about. Take her to my quarters," Hoare told the guards, who led her off. "And as for you," he added to Laurence, "I have a special place."

II.

A horde of young carol singers had arrived at Richard Ingram's door hoping for cakes and ale in return for their performance. Radcliff accompanied Richard, his wife, Dorothy, and Madam Musgrave to hear them, for Kate and Ingram had gone off together to talk; and as the children trilled and warbled, he assumed a genial smile that belied his own roiling thoughts.

He felt everything slipping out of his control, and for reasons that he could not fathom. First had come the news about Tyler. Having heard nothing from him since they had parted at Aylesbury, Radcliff had bidden Poole to go looking for him. In the last week of November, when Radcliff was with his troop, he received a letter from Poole informing him that Tyler had been shot dead in Oxford around the time that the city fell to the King. Poole had made inquiries at the gaol in Oxford Castle, and the description of Tyler's killer matched Beaumont precisely. Meanwhile, Seward was back at Merton and it seemed the charges against him had been dropped.

After reading the letter, Radcliff bore such a hatred for Beaumont that he wished he could do away with the man at once. But it was too risky, for the moment. Their waiting game would continue.

And then there was Kate. From the day Radcliff arrived at Newbury for the holiday, she seemed continually to avoid him, or else she would eye him piercingly when she imagined he was not looking. They rarely made love, and when they did, he sensed that she dreaded his caresses. Madam Musgrave tried his nerves with her gross comments; and she too gave him odd glances occasionally, as though she knew some secret about him that was not to his credit. Although Ingram remained the same as always, even-tempered and affectionate, this was small solace.

At length the carollers were shepherded into the kitchen by Madam Musgrave, and Radcliff went to join Kate and Ingram. As he might have predicted, Kate immediately left on the excuse of seeing to their refreshments.

"What's been bothering you these days?" Ingram asked, his innocent concern like a scourge to Radcliff's troubled soul. "You don't appear to be enjoying yourself here as you should."

Radcliff selected the only matter that he could discuss with his brother-in-law. "It's Kate. She is so aloof with me lately."

"Oh, now, she's always like that," Ingram protested, but not strongly enough.

"She is not aloof with you."

"No, but women are strange creatures." Ingram paused, at the sound of footsteps.

Kate returned with wine, poured out three glasses, and sat down with an air of trying hard to be agreeable.

"Did those young rascals get their fruitcakes?" Ingram asked her.

"They did. Aunt Musgrave has eaten almost as many. I wonder that she'll have any appetite for supper. To Richard's disapproval she was calling for a game of cards before we eat."

"My aunt fancies herself a cardsharp, Radcliff," Ingram said. "But we haven't played thus far because my brother holds such pursuits in low regard."

Unsurprisingly, Radcliff thought. Richard had succeeded in losing most of his property without resorting to games of chance. "There can be no harm in the cards themselves, as long as one doesn't bet money on them," he observed.

"You should have seen her with your friend Mr. Beaumont," Kate murmured to Ingram, in what was clearly intended as a private aside. "She'd have played cards with *him* all night."

Radcliff started at the name. "What did *you* make of Mr. Beaumont, Kate?" he asked, assuming an offhand tone.

"I am obliged to him for bringing me the letters, after Edgehill," Kate replied, very properly.

"Yes, indeed, as am I. My dear," he went on, an unpleasant idea occurring to him, "I know that you did not open mine, as I had requested, but I had written some instructions to that effect on the letter itself. Did he happen to read them?"

That same piercing look crept into her eyes. "How could he have?"

"Your letter was enclosed in mine," Ingram said to Radcliff. "He wouldn't even have seen it. And why would it matter if he had?"

"Those instructions were for Kate, in confidence. One cannot always trust people to be discreet."

"Indiscretion is not amongst Beaumont's faults," Ingram said, rather crossly.

"Forgive me, Ingram, but you forget that I don't know him as well as you do," Radcliff said, with a conciliatory smile.

Ingram grunted in assent, as he lit his pipe. "It's true though, Kate – he certainly must have charmed Aunt Musgrave," he began again. "She called him a delectable young devil."

"He is not attractive to *me*," Kate said. "It is as if he is of . . . of some other *breed* than the rest of us. And there is something impolite about his gaze."

"There you go, Radcliff," Ingram said, smiling. "At least he won't steal Kate from you."

Radcliff hesitated, to swallow his outrage at the suggestion. "Why, is he in the habit of luring married women away from their husbands?"

THE BEST OF MEN   4 3 3

"He has at least once or twice in the past, and I don't believe he owes his success entirely to his looks."

"Oh, naturally, with his wealth and noble blood –"

"That's not what I –" Ingram checked himself, casting a glance at Kate.

"If *he* were wed, I am sure *he* would not appreciate such behaviour from others," she commented, wrinkling her nose as at some disagreeable smell.

"He may be married soon, to the daughter of one of Lord Beaumont's neighbours."

"Then all the husbands in England will be the safer for it," Radcliff said, with an artificial laugh that tailed off as Richard Ingram entered, with Joshua Poole.

"Those impudent boys will not leave the kitchen," Richard was complaining. "They intend to eat us out of house and home, by all the evidence. Sir Bernard, you have a visitor."

Steeling himself to betray no hint of his surprise, Radcliff introduced Poole to Ingram and Kate. "Mr. Poole is my lawyer. What brings you here, sir?" he asked Poole.

"Some documents regarding Longstanton that require your signature, Sir Bernard," Poole said, humbly. "I must apologise for bothering you with them, given the season."

"No, no," said Radcliff. "I must have overlooked them on my last visit."

"You may go to my counting office," Richard said. "You'll find pen and ink where I keep my books."

Radcliff hurried Poole from the room. Once they reached the office, he demanded harshly, under his breath, "Why did you show your face here?"

"It was not my choice, sir." Poole appeared more bedraggled than normal, his thin features bitten by cold. "My Lord Pembroke called me to his house last week and asked what tidings I had of your affairs. I thought it best to tell him that Tyler had been stabbed to death in some taproom brawl, and that it was nothing to do with us."

"What did his lordship make of it all?"

"He made no comment about it. But he sent me to tell you at once not to correspond with him for the present," Poole went on. "And he stressed most categorically that you must cease using the code that you gave him."

"Why?" Radcliff asked, a cold sweat passing over him. "Does he think it unsafe?"

"He did not explain."

"How did he seem to you, Poole? Was he angry?"

"No, sir. The opposite, in fact. He said he was much encouraged by the political climate in London. The war is growing unpopular there, and its staunchest advocate, John Pym, is ill and frequently absent from Parliament. Even he might not carry the Commons in a vote to continue hostilities, and the Lords are inclining to reach a settlement this spring. His lordship even remarked that we may have no need to detain the King by use of arms, as you had planned in the last resort, in order to negotiate a peace."

"If I am not to communicate with his lordship, what then would he have me do?" Radcliff said, in a faint voice.

"Lie low until he comes to Oxford early in February as a Commissioner for Parliament. When he arrives, he will leave you directions at the Lamb Inn." Poole blinked at Radcliff like some sad old blackbird. "Sir Bernard, in the case of a swift resolution to our country's woes, I may choose to retire from your service. I've been plagued by heart trouble, and a quiet life would suit me better."

"Yes, yes," Radcliff said, hardly listening.

"I fear my friend Robinson is no more," Poole whispered next.

Radcliff could not contradict this; he felt a sudden sympathy for

Poole, caught up in a business he knew so little about. "Are you suffering from a cold, sir?" Radcliff said, more kindly. "I can ask Madam Musgrave to spare you a bowl of soup."

"Thank you, Sir Bernard," Poole said, as he blew his nose into his handkerchief, "but I would prefer to leave for London straight away."

III.

"What's wrong between you and Radcliff, Kate?" Ingram burst out finally. They had both been silent, ever since Radcliff had left with his lawyer. "Are you concerned that man might have brought him bad news about his estate? Or is it something else?"

She bowed her head, then looked up again and said quietly, "Walter, I know for a fact that he has not set foot in Longstanton for months."

"Don't be absurd! He went there on and off throughout the campaign – too often, for his troop."

"Away, yes, but not there." She took a breath. "I wanted so much to confide in you, yet I was . . . afraid."

"No need to fear," he encouraged her.

"Before Aunt Musgrave and I came here, Sir Bernard's steward stopped by her house. He was on his way to Hungerford, to spend the Christmas season with his wife's family, but he wanted to pay his respects to me for Sir Bernard's sake. He said that all was well at Longstanton. Parliament has made absolutely no move to sequestrate it, even though Sir Bernard has been unable to afford the taxes that are being levied on all the neighbouring Royalist estates."

"Are you sure he was Radcliff's steward?"

"He showed me proof, in Sir Bernard's writing; he'd thought to bring it, as we had never met before. And he asked me why the master had been absent since the summer." Ingram muttered an exclamation. "I did not know what to say," she continued, "except that my husband was busy at war and would visit when he could. Where can he be, when he claims he is at his estate?" she demanded agitatedly. "And why has it remained untouched by Parliament? Walter, my husband and your own friend is lying to both of us. He told the same barefaced untruth in front of his lawyer! Is that man party to his secret?"

Ingram shrugged, mystified. "Have you spoken of this to Aunt Musgrave?"

"No. But do you recall Sir Bernard's fuss about his letter, which I now curse myself for not opening? The moment he arrived, he made me return it to him. It must contain some answers!"

"You should ask him outright, instead of letting your imagination run riot."

"And your friend Mr. Beaumont is hiding something, too," she rushed on. "When he caught sight of the letter –"

"So he *did* see it?"

Kate blushed. "Yes, he did. It fell on the floor as I opened yours, and he picked it up for me. He looked stunned for a second, and inquired whether it was my husband's writing on the letter. I said yes, and then he pretended there was nothing to it."

"That is odd," admitted Ingram. He would have dismissed the whole tale, yet now he recalled how very interested Radcliff always was in Beaumont, and how Beaumont had questioned him about Radcliff that last time they saw each other.

"Walter, you must talk to Mr. Beaumont and find out what he knows."

"Yes – but no matter what, Kate, your husband is devoted to you."

"I pray he is not lying about that, too!" she moaned, wringing her hands together. "Until we can learn more, don't tell him anything. Swear you won't."

"I swear."

"And you will talk to Mr. Beaumont?"

"I'll ride to Chipping Campden before December's out. But stop fretting, Kate," Ingram reassured her. "There must be some simple explanation for all this."

IV.

On the night of his arrest, Laurence had been manacled and conveyed at gunpoint to Oxford Castle. Hoare's guards had marched him past the common pound, now full of Parliamentary prisoners, and up several flights of stone steps to a solitary doorway. There they removed his manacles, stripped him of his knife and spurs, and of what money he had on him. They pushed him inside, where by the light of their torches he could tell he was in one of the Castle's garderobes. Before the door clanged shut, he saw a dry space that he could occupy, barely four foot in length, and less in width. Everywhere else the floor was covered in slippery mould. Close to his little patch, a stone seat with a hole in it projected over a shaft, above and below which towered walls stained with centuries of human waste. He could not stand up fully, so low was the ceiling, the atmosphere was so putrid that his gorge rose whenever he took a breath, and he was shivering with cold, since he had left his cloak at Isabella's chamber. From time to time he had to huddle back to avoid being splashed as buckets were emptied down the shaft into the conduit of sewage beneath the Castle, sending a fresh reek to combine with the staler odours of his cell.

He attempted to sleep, but the freezing draughts and the sheer stench of the place deprived him of rest. Counting the hours, marked by the striking of church bells, he wondered how Hoare had known where to find him. And how much could Hoare know about the meeting that was to have occurred later that night?

Shortly after midday came the tramp of feet and the grinding of bolts, and the door opened to reveal the Colonel himself. "Mr. Beaumont, do you like your quarters?" Hoare inquired, standing some distance from the threshold.

"Oh yes, so thoughtful of you to supply the jakes," replied Laurence. "Few cells can be as well appointed. What am I charged with?"

"I've a great many questions to ask you, sir," said Hoare, brushing off the one Laurence had put to him, "but I'm in no immediate hurry, since it is the festive season. You may continue to enjoy your solitude for a while, and then we'll speak again."

"Is Mistress Savage still in your custody?"

"You care about her, do you? She's a pretty bitch, I'll grant you." With this, Hoare stalked away, and his guard shut the door again.

Over hours that turned into days and nights, Laurence recognised that through all the hardships of war he had at least faced injury and death in the company of other men. Isolation in a veritable sewer began to wear far more insidiously upon his nerves, and after a while he could think of nothing but being warm again, and of breathing clean air that did not catch in his throat and nostrils.

On what he thought was his fourth evening, a new guard came to deliver his scant ration of bread and water. He was now so desperate that as the door was about be shut on him again, he stuck his hand in the way, risking crushed fingers.

"Fetch Colonel Hoare," he begged. "I have to talk to him."

"You get back in," the guard muttered, giving him a shove, and bolted the door.

Another slow hour went by, then Laurence heard approaching footsteps. To his surprise, the visitor was not Hoare but Charles Danvers, dressed in a suit of crimson velvet trimmed with lace beneath a cloak of the same shade, with an ornamental rapier at his side, and a pair of fine calfskin boots dyed to match his clothing.

Laurence jumped up and slithered to the doorway, from which Danvers had since retreated, pressing a hand to his nose and mouth. "Beaumont!" he said, his speech muffled. "What an atrocious hole!"

"What's the charge against me?"

"I'm not sure."

"Does Falkland know where I am?"

"I've no idea. You look terrible!"

Laurence was seized by a fit of coughing, after which he spat over his shoulder. "Hoare must want me to die of gaol fever. Another night in this place and I may."

"I'm sorry, man. You'll have to wait to see him; he's left Oxford for a bit. As soon as he returns, you'll be able to set things to rights."

"Set *what* to rights? I don't even know why he's arrested me. Tell Falkland that he must come and get me out."

"He's at Great Tew, with his family. It's Christmastide, remember."

"Would you go there for me? Please, Danvers."

"I'll do what I can." Danvers turned to the guard. "Private Wright, is Mr. Beaumont not permitted some decent food and a blanket?"

"Colonel Hoare said he wasn't to receive nothing from outside," Wright said, with the confidence of one performing his duty.

"What money do you have on you?" Laurence asked Danvers. "You still owe me from the last time we played cards."

"What you going to buy with it, where you are?" Wright growled, as Danvers hunted in his pockets.

"That's an excellent question," Laurence said; and he fancied he could hear Wright thinking.

"A man should pay his debts," Wright said, at length.

Danvers surrendered some coins, which Laurence stuffed in his pocket. "Beaumont, Isabella Savage came to see me yesterday. She's free, you'll be glad to hear. Digby made sure of that. She said you took a nasty beating when they arrested you. She seemed most upset on speaking of it. She wanted to come here, but Hoare's forbidden you any visitors."

"What are *you* doing here, then?"

"He must have made an exception in my case," Danvers said, with a childlike assurance that failed to deceive Laurence.

"I'm glad to see you, anyway," he said quickly; in his straits he needed even this false friend.

Danvers readjusted his cloak. "It's late, Beaumont. I'd better go."

"You must talk to Falkland," Laurence implored him. "Will you do that?"

"I'll try," he said, and sped off.

As Laurence could have predicted, Wright did not immediately shut the cell door. He strolled about, fingering his matchlock pistol, apparently in deep cogitation, then stopped to regard Laurence, who was still at the doorway. "It does occur to me," he said, "that I've disobeyed orders letting you take that money."

Laurence counted it out and piled it a few inches away. "Go on, it's yours."

Wright started to move towards it but reconsidered, to Laurence's immense frustration; he had been ready to spring up and make a grab for the pistol. "You won't catch me with that trick," Wright said. "Toss over the coins." And he scooped them up lovingly. "Well, Mr. Beaumont, you *are* a fool, easily parted from his money."

"That may be, but from Danvers you have only five pounds out of the fifty I lent him."

"And so?"

"And so there's more money in it for you, if you treat me well."

"Colonel Hoare don't have it in mind to treat you well."

"Think about it. My friends aren't poor. If you let them in to see me, you could make an easy profit. You're not Hoare's slave. He doesn't need to know everything, does he?"

Wright merely snorted in response and left, bolting the door. Not long afterwards, however, in the spirit of Christmas charity, he said, he brought Laurence a blanket, threadbare and stiff with grime, and a hunk of mouldering cheese, both of which he threw on the floor as he might a bone to a dog.

V.

Falkland was so deep in thought that he jumped up a little tardily after his guests to applaud Lettice's performance at the virginals.

"A glass of Malmsey?" she suggested to everyone, and they drew their chairs in by the fire while Stephens came round with the sweet wine. After some healths were drunk, Falkland's neighbour, Sir Henry Paget, complimented Lettice on the jam tartlets that she had made; and they became quiet, munching and sipping.

"Poor Lord Beaumont – what a scene at his daughter's wedding," Sir Henry remarked eventually. "His eldest son was always incorrigible, but he surpassed himself on that occasion. He was caught with a woman in his bedchamber!"

Mistress Savage, Falkland thought, a twinge of alarm passing through him. "He might have wished to speak to her more privately," he said. "The wedding was such a loud affair, one could not hear oneself think."

"According to Lady Morecombe, who by accident witnessed them together, he was speaking to her very privately indeed – and not to her mouth," Sir Henry added, with unmistakable emphasis, although a couple of the ladies exchanged querying frowns.

"But is he not betrothed to Lady Morecombe's daughter?" Lettice asked.

"Yes, and I hear that Lady Morecombe graciously permitted the arrangement to continue despite everything. I would be less inclined to forgiveness. I should not let any child of mine near him."

"I found him perfectly respectful, even kind, when he came here that same night to see my husband," Lettice said, at which Falkland felt immediately uneasy.

Old gossipmonger that he was, Sir Henry pounced on this. "I did not know you had dealings with him, my lord. Lady Beaumont told me at the feast that he was serving with Wilmot's Horse."

"He is," Falkland said. "And my wife is right, as ever. He is not such a bad fellow as one might suppose, and I am sure we would all agree that what an unmarried man does in his own bedchamber is his business and no one else's."

Sir Henry flushed at the rebuke.

"Sir Henry, you have such a fine singing voice," interjected Lettice hastily. "Would you care to grace us with an air? I shall accompany you." And the rest of the evening passed without further mention of Beaumont's name.

After the guests departed and Falkland came at last to bed, Lettice was still sitting up by candlelight. "My lord," she said, "I have been patient, as a woman should, yet you owe me some explanation. You barely eat, you sit pondering in the dark, and tonight you were as distraught as ever I have seen you. That was not lost on our company. Sir Henry wanted to know if you were suffering from some malady, he considered you so unlike your usual self. Lucius," she went on, reaching for his hand; she rarely used his Christian name, and he felt pain on hearing it. "I have shared many hardships with you. You cannot shut me out. You know whatever passes between us will never be repeated by me to anyone. Tell me your worries."

He sank onto the bed and put his head in his hands. "Oh my love, all that I believed in has been turned upside down." She was silent, caressing his back. "In Council, His Majesty talks of peace, which you know I have worked towards honestly throughout the years, even before I took the office of State. But from abroad the Queen encourages him to pursue hostilities while misleading Parliament's Commissioners about his intentions. More openly, Prince Rupert and Digby are urging him not to treat with rebels. They want this abominable slaughter to continue! And I must be his mouthpiece, when the Commissioners come to Oxford. He will use my reputation to cozen them into thinking that he is ready to compromise." He laughed sourly. "Naive, dithering Falkland! I am well aware of his opinion of me."

"Lucius, it cannot be so!"

"I tell you, there is more honour in the Earl of Essex's heart, in John Pym's, and John Hampden's, and in many of the other so-called rebels, than I can find in that of my King." He sighed, and went on, "If only his duplicity were my sole concern. Lettice, my own spymaster, Colonel Hoare, may be working to have me forced out of office. He, too, is of the war party, and I suspect him of hunting for proof that I am in secret contact with Parliament, offering concessions of which His Majesty would disapprove."

"What a perfidious man! You must dismiss him at once. After all, you are quite innocent of such a thing!"

"Of course I am," he told her, although he was thinking of that conversation back in September, in Pembroke's coach; as he had said to Beaumont, he might so easily have agreed to an alliance with the King's would-be murderer. "But some people believe otherwise. As you know, I talked with Mr. Beaumont at the wedding feast. His brother Thomas must have overheard some of what we said and misconstrued it, thinking that Beaumont is assisting me in these communications with Parliament. Thomas reported to Hoare, who went straight to the King and asked permission to detain Beaumont for questioning. And the King agreed," Falkland murmured, closing his eyes.

"But can it not be explained to His Majesty that Thomas made a simple mistake?"

Falkland sighed again and turned to her. "Alas, what he overheard could prejudice me, although Beaumont and I were talking of something else altogether." He hesitated; should he tell her about the conspiracy? In the end, nervous to mention Pembroke's name, he gave her a modified version of it.

She stared at him, aghast. "Was this why Mr. Beaumont came here to find you after the wedding?"

"No. He was also helping me to obtain proof of Hoare's treacherous behaviour towards me. We were to meet on Christmas Eve, when he would bring me a witness to it, but he did not appear. The next day I learnt of his detention from an ally in Council. Naturally, Hoare will interrogate Beaumont about the conspiracy. He is convinced that Beaumont has not been honest with him about all the details. And he's right: Beaumont mistrusted him and was bringing information straight to me." Falkland paused; such an irony that he had trusted Hoare over Beaumont. "If I know Hoare," he began again, "he will want all the credit of unveiling the regicides for himself."

"Why not pursue these men without him?"

"I cannot do that. All my agents are too loyal to him." Except Beaumont, Falkland reflected, whom Hoare could not control.

"Then you must put pressure on His Majesty to secure Beaumont's release," Lettice insisted sensibly.

"My dear, I spoke to the King as soon as I found out, and told him that Hoare's allegations were groundless. But I am afraid he did not entirely believe me. Hoare has assured him that Beaumont will not be kept for long; he said Beaumont was one of his best agents. And now I can only pray he sticks to his word."

VI.

"Both of us are too old for such a venture," Seward grumbled, as he and Clarke made their way early in the morning to the Blue Boar tavern.

"It was you who conceived of it," Clarke pointed out.

Over a week had passed since Beaumont had set out for the same location, and Seward had spent many sleepless nights worrying why he had not resurfaced after his meeting with Lord Falkland. Had the planned encounter with Captain Milne ever happened? If not, where was Beaumont? Although Seward generally avoided female company, he had decided that he must talk to Mistress Savage, and he brought along Clarke for moral support.

In the taproom of the Blue Boar, the tavern keeper directed them to an upstairs chamber, saying that Mistress Savage kept late hours and might not yet be awake. Undeterred, they ascended, Clarke puffing at the exertion, and Seward knocked at the door.

"Who is there?" asked someone from within. The voice was unlike that of a woman; to Seward it had more the quality of a youth's, newly broken.

"Dr. Clarke and Dr. Seward of Merton College," Clarke announced in his authoritative baritone.

The door opened a margin, and the muzzle of a pistol poked out at them. Clarke clutched Seward's arm. "Beaumont's," Seward said to Clarke, indicating the pistol, and to her, "Mistress Savage, we are friends of his."

She lowered it. "Then be welcome."

To Seward, she resembled one of those lascivious spirits whom the Church Fathers claimed were sent to torment the dreams of honest men. Her heavy-lidded eyes might have graced the portrait of some Italian Madonna, yet in her mouth he read the promise of vice rather than virtue, as in her tumbled hair and the contours of her body, ill-concealed beneath a flimsy nightgown and a satin wrap. She did not apologise for her déshabille but waved for them to take a seat on the unmade bed, at which Clarke lowered his bulk gratefully. Seward remained standing.

"What is your relation to Mr. Beaumont?" she asked.

"I have known him for fifteen years," replied Seward. "I was his tutor when he was a lad up at university." She turned to Clarke, who said nothing, and so Seward added, "Beaumont left my rooms on Christmas Eve to call on you. I haven't heard from him since and hoped you might be able to shed some light on the matter."

She considered them a while. "Let us be straight with each other. Did you know he was to meet with my Lord Falkland that night, after he came here?"

"Yes, madam," said Seward, reluctantly.

"Someone – I cannot guess who – must have informed Falkland's spymaster, Colonel Hoare, of this. Hoare's guards surrounded the tavern, seized Beaumont, and took him to the Castle, where he is presently being held."

Seward and Clarke exclaimed aloud. "Who else knew that he was to come to your chamber?" Clarke asked sternly.

"Only he and I . . . or so I thought until now," she said, eyeing them both. "I was taken into Hoare's custody also, and questioned. I told Hoare that Beaumont had visited me for the reason many men will visit a woman at night. He could lay no charge against me other than that of having loose morals, and he could not stop Lord Digby from securing my freedom the next day."

"You were to provide the informant on Hoare," said Seward.

"Ah, so you were privy to it all! Yes, he was waiting to speak to Falkland. Now he will not come forward, fearing arrest himself. I shall do what I can to make him reconsider, but in the meantime Beaumont is at Hoare's mercy."

"What is the charge against him?"

"Hoare would not tell me, nor can I find out. Hoping for some information, I went to see a mutual *friend*," she continued, speaking the last word as if she disliked the taste of it. "Charles Danvers has been into his cell and says that he is being kept in the most disgusting conditions, and has fallen sick."

"Who is this Danvers, and why is he permitted access?" Seward demanded.

"Danvers is a sorry wretch without a mind of his own. He knew Beaumont abroad, and he is an agent of Hoare's, who wants him to encourage Beaumont to talk, in lieu of sterner measures, probably to wring out some false confession about Falkland's doings with Parliament."

"Men such as Danvers are often unknowing agents of evil," Seward said bitterly, "and the first to get trodden upon."

"As he deserves, by the sounds of it," Clarke expostulated.

"Yes," she said, "though he did confide in me that the fellow guarding Beaumont's cell might be bribed to let a visitor in, as long as Hoare doesn't find out about it. For obvious reasons I cannot go to the Castle again, but you gentlemen might have better luck."

Clarke frowned at Seward. "I don't advise it."

"While I have a particular detestation of that place," Seward said, remembering his own confinement within its walls, "I must concur with Mistress Savage. We are sufficiently harmless in appearance, and if we come bearing gifts –"

"There I can help you," said Mistress Savage, rising from the bed. She went to a trunk in the corner of her room from which she selected two fine necklaces and a pair of earrings. "Take these to the pawn shop in Catte Street. They'll fetch their price at this time of the year, when all the gallants in town are bent on showering their mistresses with baubles. If they contribute to liberating our friend, I shall be happier than I could ever be in wearing them."

"Madam," said Seward, "you must have strong feelings for Beaumont, to make such a sacrifice for his welfare."

"I must look to my own welfare as much as his," she responded indifferently. "Hoare is no friend of mine."

"We thank you. Well, sir," he said to Clarke, "we should get us to Catte Street. Oh – and madam, might I take Beaumont's pistols with me, in the hope that I may return them to him once he is out of gaol?"

"Yes, and his cloak which he also left here." She had it folded neatly, and held it a moment, stroking the cloth gently with her fingertips, before surrendering it.

"We thank you again, and good day, madam," he told her.

Clarke only nodded at her as they departed, laden with their spoils. "She is no better than a strumpet, despite her fancy trappings," he opined to Seward, once they were out of earshot. "Never trust a woman, that's what I've always said. And plain is bad, but pretty is worse."

"She is more beautiful than pretty," Seward corrected him, "and beautiful women are by far the most dangerous. Though they hold no appeal for me."

"Nor me," Clarke agreed.

"Just as well, for you are no Adonis, with that monstrous belly of yours."

"And nor are you, you rack of old bones."

They quitted the Blue Boar for the shop in Catte Street, where all went as Mistress Savage had anticipated. Having disposed of the jewels, they walked back to Merton to discuss how to approach Beaumont's guard at the Castle. As they gained the new quadrangle, Seward espied a man waiting outside the entrance to his chambers.

"Dr. Seward," said Walter Ingram, "do you remember me?"

Seward felt suddenly alert; Beaumont had told him of Ingram's relationship to Radcliff. "I do indeed, sir," he answered.

When they had made their greetings, Ingram requested a private talk, and so Clarke went off to his own rooms.

"I don't flatter myself that it is my company you seek, after all these years," Seward said to Ingram, showing him indoors. "Are you looking for Beaumont?"

"Yes. I went expecting to find him at Chipping Campden, but he vanished a fortnight ago, on the night of his sister's wedding, and hasn't been heard from since. His parents are both very angry with him. Do you know where he is?"

"In detention at Oxford Castle."

"Why? What trouble is he in?"

"I wish I could tell you," replied Seward, with partial truth.

VII.

Laurence was roused from a febrile sleep by the squeaking of a bolt.

Danvers peered into the cell, holding his nose. "Beaumont, I'm getting you out."

"Did you see Falkland?" Laurence asked, hearing his voice tremble.

"Not yet, but what matters is, you'll soon be free. You poor fellow, you've been almost two weeks in that shit hole. My God, how you smell!"

Laurence was so shaky from lack of nourishment and exercise that he allowed Danvers to help him down the stairs. They passed through various passageways into a far more habitable part of the Castle; then Danvers stopped and said, "In here." They entered a chamber where a fire blazed in the hearth. There was a table set with food and drink, and a servant in attendance. On a sideboard nearby stood a bowl, a jug of steaming water, and shaving implements.

"Sit down, man. You'll feel better with some of this inside you," said Danvers, pouring him a cup of wine.

Laurence sat and accepted it, his hand quivering; what trick was being played on him, he wondered, as he downed the contents. The alcohol caught in his throat and he started to cough. "Now I want to leave," he said, when he had recovered.

"You will, but Colonel Hoare has to speak with you." Laurence glared at Danvers. "You should eat something, Beaumont, to get your strength back."

"I hope he paid you well for this," Laurence murmured.

After tasting a small amount of stew and drinking more wine, he let the servant help him to wash and shave. Almost as soon as he was finished, Hoare strode in.

"Mr. Beaumont, you are refreshed, I trust," said Hoare, inspecting the room as if he were measuring it for new furniture. He stopped beside Laurence's chair and laid a hand on his shoulder. "We did work together quite well, sir, and I should like us to do so again. I have no interest in keeping you cooped up when we've business to finish." Hoare glanced at Danvers. "Off you go." Danvers disappeared obediently, with an anxious backward frown at Laurence. "Now, sir," Hoare began again, "we both know that Falkland has been in talks with certain Parliament men, and that you are abetting him. It's not a serious issue, in all likelihood, but we must have it out in the open. Supply me with the details, and I shall set you free."

"Why am I even here?" demanded Laurence. He was well aware that ten or so days in solitary confinement were nothing compared to Hoare's usual methods; either the arrest had not been authorized or else Hoare was on orders not to mistreat him.

"I am sorry to confess," said Hoare, "that your brother Thomas described to me a conversation that you had with Falkland at your sister's wedding." Laurence sighed; so the footfalls in the snow that night had been Tom's. "He also warned me Mistress Savage might be party to your work for Falkland," Hoare continued, his face smug. "That is how we found you. My men had been watching the Blue Boar for some days. Out of duty, I told the King, and he is permitting me to investigate."

"Is Falkland also in gaol?"

"No, no," laughed Hoare. "He is with His Majesty and the rest of Council, preparing for the next round of negotiations with Parliament. As you may imagine, the King wished to sort out this little indiscretion before the Commissioners arrive at the end of January. It is as well that he should be able to trust his Secretary of State not to agree to any overgenerous terms with the rebels, don't you think?"

"He *can* trust Falkland," Laurence said, "and whatever my brother heard, I can explain."

Hoare's face became animated. "You and Falkland mentioned names: the Earl of Pembroke, Edmund Waller, Hyde, Culpeper, and John Earle. The first two are on Parliament's side and the others purport to be on His Majesty's. Be honest, sir: are they not in secret league together?"

"Not at all," Laurence exclaimed, though he cursed his mistake in giving Hoare such an entrée.

"Then in what context were you talking of these men?"

"I can't remember exactly. We may have been discussing the peace negotiations."

"That's not good enough, I'm afraid. Mr. Beaumont, Pembroke has been in correspondence with Falkland, and Waller is Falkland's close friend. Tell me what they are scheming at, and we can protect him from any repercussions."

"*Scheming at?*" repeated Laurence. "Sir, I'm sure if you address Lord Falkland, he'll be happy to show you whatever Pembroke wrote to him and answer any questions you might have, and you'll find nothing to support your ludicrous theory."

Hoare let out a frustrated breath; he must not have any damaging evidence against Falkland yet, Laurence realised, with some relief, and he had not asked at all about what had been supposed to happen on the night of Laurence's arrest. "Let us move on to another issue: the conspiracy to regicide," Hoare said next. "I am driven to conclude that you found out these traitors already, but decided to subvert me by reporting your intelligence directly to Falkland." Laurence made no reaction; he had expected this. "Let me state clearly, sir, that I no longer report to him myself but to the King, *on the King's own order*! I want the names of the conspirators. I want to know everything, indeed, that you have withheld from me."

"I don't know any more than you do. Why don't you let me go after them, instead of holding me back? You're wasting my time and Falkland's – *and* His Majesty's," Laurence concluded scornfully.

Hoare flared up at once. "You think because of your father's title that you are nearer to the King's confidence than I am? Well, you are not! And my opinion of you hasn't changed. To me you are still a parasite, used to sailing through life on the strength of a name, while those of us less fortunately born must prove our worth through diligence and hard work!"

"You're quite the democrat, sir," Laurence remarked. "Given your views, perhaps you should be fighting on the other side in this war."

"May I remind you," Hoare said, colouring, "that my loyalties are not in doubt, but yours most definitely are. I have been patient with you. I could have strung you up the same night I brought you in, and beaten you within an inch of your life."

"Then why didn't you? Because you've no right to, that's why. And you had no right to detain me in the first place."

He caught the truth of his assumption in Hoare's eyes, but only for a moment. "His Majesty has granted me the power to do whatever I can to persuade you to talk," Hoare snapped at him. "And believe me, I shall."

"Take me before the King," Laurence retorted. "I'll answer any question he may put to me, to the best of my ability. But I won't answer to you."

Hoare went to the door and called for his guards, to whom he muttered a few quiet words. Two of them picked Laurence out of his chair and held him up while the others pummelled him in the ribs several times, then in the small of his back, and in the belly. He crumpled, choking. When he raised his head again, Hoare punched him hard on the cheek, leaving the familiar taste of blood in his mouth. His eyes watered, but he forced himself not to cry out. Instead, he spat a thick thread of red-flecked saliva across the polished toes of Colonel Hoare's boots.

"You'll be sorry you did that," Hoare said, "just as you will regret your childish instinct to defy me. All right, boys."

As the guards hauled Laurence back to his cell, he felt reassured on one score, even if his own circumstances remained uncertain: Hoare could not have learnt of the planned meeting on Christmas Eve, or else he would have wanted information about it. The double arrest had merely been a stroke of luck for him. And now that Isabella was at liberty, she might yet prove resourceful enough to set up another rendezvous between Falkland and Captain Milne.

VIII.

Kneeling alone before the altar in Magdalen College chapel, Digby found his mind veering more to the profane than the sacred, so excited was he about the imminent release of the first issue of *Mercurius Aulicus*. At length, unable to concentrate on his prayers, he got up from the pew, brushing dust from his breeches; he should consider leaving a bequest in his will for the better maintenance of his old college, he mused. On his way out, he paused at a monument in the antechapel to view the inscription, and as he was reading about the unfortunate brothers, John and Thomas Lyttleton, both drowned seven years ago while one was trying to rescue the other, he heard Isabella call his name.

"Your servant told me you were at prayers here," she said, walking along the aisle towards him. He thought she looked tired and downcast, though beautifully dressed as always. "Digby, I shall come to the point. You were such a saviour, in rescuing me from Colonel Hoare. Could you not at least –"

"My dear friend," he interrupted, with a shade of exasperation, "how often must I repeat myself? It is not the same for Mr. Beaumont. His Majesty has allowed Hoare to question him, and though he may grow a hermit's beard and waste away a bit on his prison diet, Hoare can't do any more to him than that. His rank will protect him."

"It has not so far." She seemed about to continue in this vein, then said abruptly, "I thought we both wanted Hoare destroyed."

"Nothing would delight me as much. We have been hampered, however, by the Secretary of State's ill-conceived chit-chat with Parliament."

"How can you believe Hoare has any evidence of that! You have probed Falkland endlessly, trying to make him admit something of the sort, and he has proved himself loyal to the King."

"Yes, but I think he has his moments of doubt." Digby began to imitate Falkland's high-pitched, squeaky voice. "'We must put an end to the violence! This country is being torn apart, the earth soaked in English blood!' How many times have I had to listen to him vent his moral indignation – and how it bores me," he concluded, in a tone that would usually make her laugh.

"Falkland is an honest man," she said, almost angrily. "That is why you must stand up for him – and get rid of his enemy."

"My dear, you are so staunch in his defence, and yet I have an idea that it is not *his* fate that most concerns you," Digby said, watching her face. "Are you by any chance smitten with Mr. Beaumont? Was I wise to leave you alone together in Wilmot's quarters last October?"

"How trivial you can be! If Falkland goes, you and Prince Rupert will be open rivals in Council with no one to keep the peace between you, and after the Prince's glittering record in this past campaign, you will lose out. Moreover, Hoare will only gain in status, as one of the Prince's most devoted and experienced officers."

"Not necessarily; his fate will depend on who might succeed Falkland as Secretary."

"If Rupert has the King's ear, that would certainly not be you."

Digby conceded with a nod. "Well, what of Mr. Beaumont? *Have* you fallen for him?"

"Are you jealous, Digby?" she inquired, her eyes flashing at him. "You are never jealous."

"I have always been content for you to take whomsoever you desire to your bed," he replied, with complete honesty, although for the first time he felt a trifle insecure in his influence over her. He knew what passion could inspire in a woman's heart, as in a man's. "You are not about to marry him, for God's sake," he went on, rather vindictively. "Lord and Lady Beaumont would take a fit, in their Palladian mansion! I can just imagine them." He started to giggle but stopped on seeing her expression, which had grown closed and cold.

"Who *shall* I marry?" she said. "I am twenty-six years of age, far from virgin, and in all likelihood barren. My face and body have been my fortune, but they cannot last forever."

"I'll find you someone, as soon as you wish to surrender the title of Mistress and call yourself a wife. Though, of course, you can be both wife, and mistress to whom you choose, if we find an agreeable husband." Digby saw her mouth tighten and was instantly full of remorse. "Please forgive me, Isabella," he said. "You know how much I love you. I shall always look after you as I would my own sister."

"Yes, I do know that." Isabella gave him a kiss on the cheek and turned to leave.

"Where are you going now, my dear?" he asked.

"Oh, nowhere you should follow," she told him, and let herself out of the chapel before he realised that she had not answered his question about Beaumont.

CHAPTER FOURTEEN

I.

For three days after Laurence's preliminary interrogation, Danvers visited the cell regularly, squatting outside with a handkerchief pressed to his mouth. He claimed that he had gone to Falkland begging him to intercede, and that Falkland had said he could do nothing for Laurence. This seemed hard to believe, but if it were true, Laurence did not like the consequences for himself. He was utterly furious still to be in captivity.

On the fourth day, Danvers condescended to move closer to him, braving the stench. "What's the point of you rotting away here, Beaumont?" he exclaimed. "Don't you see how futile it is? Think of what Hoare might inflict on you if you keep being so pigheaded."

"I won't let him take Falkland down," Laurence said. "And he'd be a fool to try and extort a confession from me. I don't even think he has the authority to hold me here."

"Then why hasn't Falkland come to your aid by now?" Laurence had no reply to this. "Besides, Falkland won't come to any grief if he's demoted," Danvers went on. "He hates his office, as I'm sure he must have told you. Everyone says he's not suited to it –"

"What are you, Hoare's parrot?" Laurence interrupted coldly.

Danvers flushed. "You have to change your mind, Beaumont, before it's too late. Don't you remember, in the other war, that fellow who got his prick shot off in battle? We both agreed we'd rather be dead than be unable to fuck any more, and to have to make water through a straw. You'll suffer if you don't talk. Hoare could hurt you badly – perhaps beyond repair."

Just as he finished speaking, Private Wright leant in through the cell door and beckoned to him. They muttered together in subdued tones, then he returned with a panicked look on his face. "Beaumont, I have to go. We must say goodbye." He put out his right hand but Laurence would not take it.

Soon after his departure, the clump of boots echoed up the stairwell. The bolt was shot, and the door swung wide. "Mr. Beaumont," called out Hoare, "my patience with you has not been rewarded as I'd hoped. It is now time for me to change tactics."

The guards wrestled Laurence downstairs and through a low corridor, dark except for a few guttering torches, into a chamber as evil-smelling as his cell. Inside, neatly arranged, were a vertical rack, a barrel full of water, and a selection of whips and stout wooden sticks. They tied Laurence to the rack with his arms in front, and hoisted him aloft. The wrenching on his shoulders and the bonds cutting into his wrists made him gasp with pain.

"You have no right to do this to me!" he yelled at Hoare.

"I can do as I please," Hoare said, smiling. "For you are now like one of those poor souls wandering in limbo: everyone has washed their hands of you. Even my Lord Falkland is staying away, anxious not to compromise himself. I shall give you one more chance, sir." He ordered the rack to be lowered, so that he and Laurence were face to face. "I want the truth about your exchange with Falkland that night, and I want the names of the regicides. That is all. I am not attempting to unseat his lordship. In fact, I am protecting him. If you also desire to protect him, you will answer me."

"I've told you the truth."

"Not about the regicides." Laurence stared him in the eye, as he had on their very first meeting, and again Hoare looked away. "Go ahead, lads," he ordered the guards, and Laurence was hoisted up once more.

He took a deep breath, knowing that he must feign yet greater distress than he felt. After a series of blows to the chest, stomach, and groin, however, he was no longer pretending. One of his ribs cracked, and he cried out so loudly that Hoare called off the guards, drew a cup of water from the barrel and approached to hold it to Laurence's lips, but Laurence would not drink.

"Who are the conspirators?" Hoare demanded.

"I've told you all I know," Laurence repeated, between gritted teeth.

"Stubborn, aren't you," Hoare said. "We'll see how long you can last."

He signalled to the guards, and as the beating started again, Laurence felt the crack of a second rib, and burning in his chest. He forced himself to relax in the bonds, although they were eating into his skin, and let his head flop down and his eyes close. The tension on his wrists and shoulders lessened suddenly as he was lowered from the rack; then the guards dunked him head-first, up to the waist, in the barrel, sending liquid coursing up his nose and down his throat. Plunged into this aqueous hell, he seemed to see red, as if his brain had become suffused with blood. At length, he was pulled out and thrown to the floor. He did not move or make a sound, though he was dying to rid his lungs of water. Then came a pressure on his stomach and chest that made the fluid surge up out of him; and he tried not to choke or open his eyes, for if he did, the torture would continue.

"Not a touch of the whip," he heard Hoare say, "and he's fainted like a girl with the green sickness. That's it for now, boys. Put him back in the cell."

Laurence bit his tongue to keep himself from groaning as they lifted him up, and he must indeed have fainted then, for he knew no more.

II.

Diana had reached her fifth month of pregnancy without incident, which delighted Sir Robert, and he was in even greater transports of joy when he received an invitation, for the sixteenth of January, to pledge his services in person to His Majesty at a banquet at Christ Church College for all the most important Oxfordshire gentry.

"You shall accompany me, my dear," he told Diana, "for you are not so big with child as to appear ugly yet."

As she and Robert queued to perform their obeisance before the High Table, where the royal party was seated, he distracted her with an exclamation. At one end of the long board was Isabella Savage, conversing with the man to her left. "My Lord Digby," Robert whispered in Diana's ear. "And that is my Lord Falkland on her right. Yet what is *she* doing here?" he added, as though Isabella were some cheap dross masquerading as gold.

"You know very well that she is Digby's friend," Diana said, trying to catch Isabella's eye; and finally Isabella noticed her and smiled, but with a peculiar lack of assurance.

When the feast drew to an end, the dancing began. His Majesty's partner was a lovely young brunette as pregnant as Diana. "My Lady d'Aubigny," Robert informed her. "She was married to His Majesty's late cousin who was killed at Edgehill."

"How very sad that he will never see his baby." Diana was looking elsewhere: Isabella had just left the hall. "Pray excuse me, sir. I must go and find the privy offices."

"Why now? They are playing the pavane, which we may join in without harm to your health, if Lady d'Aubigny is any example."

"I cannot wait," she insisted.

"Oh, go, then, and hurry back. We might catch the last of it."

Threading her way through the crowd, Diana felt a pang of nostalgia as she remembered slipping away from another state occasion on that hot summer evening when she and Beaumont had first made love. Then her child stirred a little within her, as though issuing a mute reproof, and she forced herself to dismiss the memory.

At the doors, Isabella was talking with a blond man, tall and slim, of martial bearing. They were obviously in some argument, yet drew apart when Diana approached. Isabella looked pale and harassed. "Lady Stratton, may I present Captain Milne," she said. "She is a friend from Court, whom I have not seen in an age," she told Milne, who bowed, then inspected Diana with rather too bold an interest. His face, although otherwise comely, was marred from the smallpox.

"Captain," Diana said, "would you be so obliging as to permit us ladies a moment together?"

"Only if I may claim Mistress Savage for a *dance* later this evening," he replied, as though the word had some special significance, his gaze on Isabella. "I believe you said you owed that to me, madam, for my services."

"Yes, sir," Isabella said, in a strained tone. "I always keep a promise."

"I'll look forward to it," Milne said, and after giving Diana a last swift appraisal, he walked away.

"Of what services was he speaking?" Diana asked.

"He is being of assistance in a . . . ah, well, a political matter."

"Isabella, how *could* you disappear like that from Wytham?" Diana reproached her. "It caused us such trouble!"

"Robert must think very badly of me, even more so than before."

"I'm afraid he does, though it has not changed *my* opinion of you."

Diana hesitated. "Have you by chance heard the news about Mr. Beaumont?" she asked next, without exactly knowing why. "Laurence Beaumont, that is."

A veiled expression came into Isabella's eyes. "What news?"

"He is to be married. Sir Robert learnt of it while he was at Chipping Campden last month."

Isabella frowned, as if digesting this information, then smiled gently at Diana. "You were in love with Beaumont, weren't you."

"Who told you –"

"No one had to. I guessed from you, who are as open as a book."

"It was no more than a . . . a youthful flirtation," Diana murmured, caught out.

"I see. My dear, you are blessed with so much, in your husband and your children. Never forget that," concluded Isabella; and she glanced towards Captain Milne, who was watching them from the doors.

"Is he importuning you?" Diana asked, disliking the man's predatory air.

"He is one of many nuisances that I must contend with. But nothing in life is perfect. Now you should go back to Sir Robert, or he will be worried." With the same gentle smile, Isabella gave her a kiss on the cheek and they said goodbye.

In the hall, the pavane had ended, and the musicians had struck up a more vigorous tune. "What kept you?" Robert complained, as Diana returned to her seat.

Annoyed by his tone, she answered frankly. "I encountered Isabella Savage on my way. I could not be so rude as to ignore her."

At once he reddened and seized Diana by the wrist. "As your husband and master, I forbid you absolutely to associate with that – that *whore* ever again!"

"Sir Robert, please! You may detest her, but you have no justification to insult her so."

"My wife," Robert retorted, "I should perhaps have mentioned to you before – it was *she* who Mr. Beaumont had in his chamber, on the night of his sister's wedding."

Diana could not look at her husband. Suddenly she recalled Isabella's questioning her about Beaumont at Wytham, asking whether she found him handsome, and then the tender counsel of a few moments ago. How long had Isabella and he been lovers, she wondered to herself, agonized, inadvertently brushing her cheek as though to wipe away Isabella's kiss.

III.

Laurence felt too muddled to calculate how many days had gone by since his return to the cell, where he no longer noticed the stink. He leant his head against the slimy wall, taking shallow breaths through his nose to stop himself from coughing, which was excruciating to his broken ribs. As waves of fever passed through him, he shivered, wrapped in his inadequate blanket, teeth chattering. Dreadfully thirsty, he reached for the bowl of brackish water that Wright delivered to his door each morning, but it was dry.

Then he heard the familiar tromp of boots outside, and shrank back in his corner as the door opened. Hoare stood in the entrance flanked by his guards; with the light behind him, his face remained in shadow. "How are you faring, Mr. Beaumont?" he inquired, his tone courteous.

"How do you think," Laurence whispered back.

"Not too well, I'd imagine. I have a surgeon waiting to attend to you, and then I shall release you – if you will only answer my questions." Laurence shook his head. "Dear me," Hoare said quietly, "and I considered you an intelligent man."

He motioned to the guards. Laurence could not suppress a cry as they bore him once again down the stairs.

This time he was stripped of everything but his breeches and strung up by the ankles. His chest burned so much that he could hardly draw breath. The soles of his feet were subjected to Hoare's whip while the guards beat him about the body. With the blood rushing to his head and stinging his eyes, he was entering what seemed to him a new dimension of consciousness: very little mattered except where the next blow would land and how he could endure it. Hoare's repeated questions were drowned out by his own yells. Then the beating stopped and he saw Hoare's face upside down, pushed up against his.

"Look at you now, Mr. Beaumont," Hoare said. "Drenched in your own sweat and blood and piss. I doubt Mistress Savage will fancy your sorry arse by the time *I'm* finished with you. That's good for today," he told the guards; and Laurence felt the rope slacken.

IV.

Lord Beaumont strode into his wife's office, a letter in his hand. "I must go at once to Oxford," he announced.

She looked up from her account book with a startled frown. "Why, my lord?" He gave her Dr. Seward's letter, which she scanned in dismay. "What mischief has Laurence done this time," she murmured as she read on. "But there is no explanation here as to why he is under arrest!"

"Seward will tell me when I arrive, as he says. I doubt he would alarm me unnecessarily, my dear. Our son is in trouble, and my presence is requested. That should be sufficient reason for me to go."

She set aside the letter, still frowning. "Why not write first to Dr. Seward and ask what offence Laurence has committed before you involve yourself? My lord," she continued, "you know how wayward he has always been, keeping low company and drinking, and brawling – and God knows what else that we did not hear about. On his last visit, he showed us that he has not altered one whit over the years. Such a shameful scandal he caused! In that instance he did not pay as he should have, and yet again he has disappeared without so much as a word of apology to us. Now he may be receiving his just deserts for some other misdeed, the nature of which Seward is probably too ashamed to disclose on paper. But may I remind you that our son is a grown man, not a child to be rescued by his father! He must learn to take responsibility for his actions."

"I see your point," Lord Beaumont admitted, though he was not fully convinced. "Very well, my dear, I shall write. It will mean only a day or two's delay, in any case, if he truly needs my help."

"I thank you." Then she went on, as though she could not stop herself, "I have never liked that Dr. Seward. If Laurence had been more strictly governed during his years at College, he would not have turned out as he did."

"Madam," said Lord Beaumont, "pray remember that Seward was my tutor, also, and Thomas' for a while. I believe that disproves your argument."

She studied him, her expression less severe. "I know how much you love Laurence, and please do not think me uncaring towards him. Yet he still has no respect for the privileges and duties that life has granted him. I was hoping that service abroad might have changed his character. Clearly it has not. So tread with caution in this matter, my lord. We cannot afford any further disgrace to our family name, nor can we allow the arrangements for his marriage to be prejudiced again."

"Quite so," Lord Beaumont agreed; and he went off to his library, to pen a letter to Seward. But deep in his heart, he feared that he was making a mistake.

v.

Laurence stirred dizzily, aware of some unaccustomed warmth against his bare skin. As he opened his eyes he saw Danvers beside him, crammed into the small space.

"Beaumont," Danvers said, "I've been arrested by Hoare."

"No you haven't," Laurence told him, in a croaking whisper. "He just put you in here for the same reason he let you visit me."

"I wish that were so, but it's not. He's received some news that set him on edge. I couldn't find out what it was, but he's in a hurry now to make you talk. And I've got something to tell you that may persuade you to change your mind," Danvers babbled on frantically. "Just before Hoare took me in, I heard from a fellow at Court that His Majesty has secret plans to support a revolt of the Royalists in London this spring. And Falkland will be in charge of it."

Laurence tried to make sense of this, his wits slowed by pain and fever. Danvers must be lying, he thought; Falkland would never take part in any plan that would compromise his negotiations with Parliament, if not doom them altogether.

"So you see," Danvers began again, "Falkland's the same as everyone else, pursuing His Majesty's interests, whether openly or covertly. I don't understand myself why he'd be communicating with Parliament at the same time, as Hoare maintains. Maybe to disguise the plans for the revolt, which would be clever, wouldn't it?" Laurence said nothing, still following with difficulty. "Yet the fact remains, he's not what you believed him to be, so you might as well do as Hoare asks, and he says he'll free us straight away. If not, he says he'll beat us both! And you can't take much more."

"No, I can't," Laurence murmured.

Danvers did not speak for a long while, during which Laurence closed his eyes, trying to sleep. "After the things we've done, Beaumont, where would we go if we were to die?" Danvers asked next. "I mean, to heaven or . . . or to hell?"

Laurence dragged open his eyes and squinted at him through the gloom. "This is much like hell, wouldn't you say?"

"Don't you believe in a life after this one?"

"No."

"I pray you're wrong." Danvers' mouth contorted into a wobbly grin; he looked about to cry. "I had a letter yesterday from my wife. We'd been living apart, even after I ended with Mrs. Sterne. She – she wrote to me to say she wished to – to make up." He dashed a tear from his cheek. "If I get out of this place, I – I swear, I'll change. A man can change, can't he, Beaumont?"

"I suppose."

"Oh God, oh God," Danvers sobbed. "Why am I here? What have I done to deserve this? All I've ever tried to do is please people! Where's the sin in that, I'd like to know?" When he got no answer to his rhetorical questions, he began banging on the cell door, shrieking for Private Wright. "I can't bear it! Let me out! Let me out!"

Laurence stuck his head in his arms to dim the noise, as Danvers cursed and implored, and continued to proclaim his innocence in the face of injustice. When at last he quietened, keening to himself, Laurence was able to drowse off to the sound, as if to a lullaby.

Then Laurence felt hands seize him roughly by the shoulders, to carry him out. Danvers followed, a guard behind him. In the downstairs chamber, Hoare was waiting. He drew Danvers aside and asked him something that Laurence could not hear, to which Danvers replied in the negative.

"More's the pity for you," Hoare muttered, and he had both Danvers and Laurence bound by the wrists and hoisted aloft, not a foot apart from each other. "Mr. Beaumont," he said, "do you know that old rhyme about the telltale? Allow me to remind you. 'Telltale tit, your tongue shall be split, and all the dogs in town shall have a little bit.' Your brother was a telltale, wasn't he, and Danvers here has told a few tales in his time. Now it's your turn. I've just discovered that you are conspiring against me, and that you have an informant who's been talking to Lord Falkland – yes, and even to the King – trying to paint me as a traitor to his lordship. Who is he?" He unfurled the whip and lashed it across Laurence's jaw and cheekbone. Laurence yelped, blinking away the water that sprang to his eyes. Hoare turned to Danvers. "Can't you give him a little encouragement?" And he sent the leather strap flying again, grazing Danvers' face, which provoked an immediate result.

"I did, sir, I did!" Danvers cried. "I told him Falkland wasn't worth protecting! And I've news for you – if you'll –"

"Be quiet! I want to hear from Mr. Beaumont."

"But sir, I beg of you, take me down and I'll give you valuable information!"

"Let him go," Laurence pleaded, mistakenly, for Hoare's expression changed, as if he had indeed received news, and he tossed aside the whip. From his belt he pulled out a knife with a curved blade, which he started to whet on a leather strap. "Mr. Beaumont, I am going to slit his tongue and make you eat a piece of it if you will not reveal who this informant is," he said, approaching with the knife; Danvers was now wailing incoherently. "Boys, make sure he watches." The guards grabbed Laurence's head and pried his eyes open, so he had no choice. "Well, sir? Who has been spreading tales about me?"

Laurence saw the knife come closer. "I'll tell you! Let him down and I'll tell you."

"You'd better tell me all – *all* that you've been keeping from me! Will you, sir?"

At this, Laurence balked. Hoare stepped forward, and with the help of another guard prised apart Danvers' jaws and seized his tongue. In vain Danvers tried to pull away as Hoare sliced into it vertically. Danvers screeched and jerked, his mouth dripping red, his blood spattering Laurence's face. Then he went limp, his body tugging on the ropes.

Hoare persisted until he had bifurcated the tongue, so that it resembled that of some exotic snake. "It won't kill him," he remarked of Danvers, laughing, as he made another quick cut to the tongue.

"Boys, Mr. Beaumont has seen enough. You may let go." They obeyed, and Laurence could shut his eyes. "Now, however, you shall sing, unless you're hungry," Hoare declared. "Come, let's hear you." But Laurence found himself incapable of speech, as if his tongue had frozen in empathy with that of Danvers. "Open his mouth," Hoare told the guards, and stuffed in a wet, slippery thing, like a slice of raw liver. A hand sealed Laurence's lips forcibly, and he felt his head being tilted back. His stomach heaved and acid rose up his throat, which they were stroking, so that he had to swallow, though he gagged and retched immediately as they released his head. Afterwards they began to beat him again, and he vomited once more when hit in the groin. His vision grew murky. He could hear Hoare ranting at him, as from far off, and he felt a strange peace: he was near death, and glad of it.

VI.

Falkland ordered his troopers to rein in their horses. Mistress Savage stood at the Castle gates clad in a long, hooded cloak. "I am coming in with you," she said.

"Madam, a gaol is no place for a lady," he told her.

"Perhaps not, my lord, yet I must insist." Falkland was about to object when she asked coldly, "How do you think you got the evidence for what you are about to do?"

"From Captain Milne."

"Yes, but *how*?"

Falkland examined her; and he understood. "As you wish," he said, dismounting. "I pray Hoare has kept Mr. Beaumont in reasonable conditions all this time," he added as they walked through the gates, his men behind them.

"Small chance of that." Her voice was now unsteady, and he hoped she would not swoon when confronted by the sights and smells of a prison.

They were directed to Hoare's quarters, where they found him sitting at a desk, paring his fingernails with a little knife. He rose, clearly surprised that Falkland should appear unannounced, and more surprised still to see Mistress Savage. "My lord," he began, but Falkland cut him off.

"Colonel Hoare, you are henceforth relieved of your duties, to be detained here at His Majesty's pleasure." He motioned to his soldiers, who surrounded Hoare, cocking their pistols and aiming them at his breast.

"My lord, what is this?" Hoare said, glancing from the pistols to Falkland.

"I have a warrant for your arrest on a charge of treachery. Mr. Beaumont must be released. Have him brought here at once." Hoare did not move. "I am His Majesty's Secretary of State, or have you forgotten?" Falkland shouted at him. "Bring him to me!"

"Think, my lord," Hoare said with a hint of menace, "else you regret your haste. If you levy this charge of treachery against me, how many other treacheries might be revealed, which I know of?"

"You may reveal whatever you wish. We shall be most interested to hear you speak in your defence."

Hoare turned sharply and marched out, Falkland and Mistress Savage after him. His guards were in the corridor, outnumbered by Falkland's men. "Show his lordship up to Mr. Beaumont's cell," Hoare said. "I would advise the lady to remain here."

"You know where you can put your advice," she spat at him.

"Stay," Falkland ordered his soldiers, "and cuff his wrists."

As he and Mistress Savage ascended the stairs, the air became close and fetid. They penetrated a dark corner, and the guard ahead of them signalled for them to stop; he unbolted a door, then stood back as it swung open. The reek of sewage was now mixed with some sweeter, rotten, cloying odour. Falkland pinched his nostrils together and took a gasp through his mouth, while Mistress Savage pressed the edge of her hood to her lips. The guard handed him a torch, and he peered inside. Two men were collapsed upon each other in a clumsy embrace.

"Take them out," he said, his throat full of saliva; and they were hauled forth and laid side by side, like a pair of carcasses at the slaughterhouse. "Sweet Jesu," he exclaimed, gazing down at them.

Their faces, illuminated by the torch, were covered in blood. Danvers' eyes were open, staring into nothing. Beaumont's were shut. Save for his breeches, he was naked and filthy, and his rib cage, contused and so discoloured that it might have been painted in shades of black and purple and red, stuck out unnaturally above his hollow belly. Danvers was dressed in a suit of which he had been particularly proud. How sorry he would be to see it now, Falkland thought. Then he felt ashamed, in the presence of such horror, that his mind should seek refuge in the trivial. As much to restore some shred of dignity to Beaumont's corpse as from his own inability to look at it any more, he removed his cloak and draped it over the body.

"How long have they been dead?" he asked of the guard, not wanting to know the answer.

"I can't exactly say, my lord," he replied. "This one was but a day and a night in the cell." He prodded Danvers with the toe of his boot. "At least they are in peace, after their sufferings."

"How shall I tell Lord Beaumont," Falkland whispered to himself.

All of a sudden, as if she had been pushed, Mistress Savage fell to her knees and slumped forward; and the guard made a similar observation as had Falkland, about this being no place for a woman. But then she sat up and gently drew back Falkland's cloak to bare Beaumont to the waist.

"Give me your hand," she said to Falkland.

He bent towards her and extended it, with a slight, guilty repugnance; and as she placed it upon Beaumont's chest, he felt beneath his fingers an undeniable heat and movement.

THE BEST OF MEN 471

VII.

"My boy," said Seward, gruff with relief, as Beaumont's lids fluttered open. "You are in good care," he added hastily, observing his friend's dazed look. "My Lord Falkland removed you from your cell two days ago, though you are still in the Castle, and too frail to leave for the nonce. Hoare is under arrest. He must have given you up for dead, a fate that I sincerely pray awaits him after he stands trial."

Beaumont tried to move his head, and winced. "D-Danvers?" he breathed.

"He did not survive. He may have expired from the shock of what was done to him, for he had not been touched otherwise. As for you, you will heal in time. Drink this." Seward helped him to a measure of opium tincture; he grimaced with pain as he swallowed it. "Now rest," Seward said. He touched Beaumont's forehead, checking its temperature, then left the room, shutting the door quietly.

Ingram was waiting outside. "So?"

"He has regained his senses."

"Oh thank heaven!" Ingram paused for a moment, obviously holding back tears. "Could he speak?"

"He could, but I would not let him. I gave him a sleeping draught."

They went into the adjoining chamber, where Falkland and Mistress Savage were talking in low tones, although they stopped on seeing Seward.

"He is conscious at last," he said.

"Praise God!" Falkland exclaimed. "Mistress Savage, we were not too late." She said nothing, regarding him with an indecipherable expression.

"Nonetheless, he is in a wretched state," Seward reminded them. "It will take careful nursing for him to recover, and even then there may be some lingering effects from the torture."

Falkland shook his head in consternation. "Hoare must have completely lost his mind! I knew he was a brutal fellow, but to go so far – what possible purpose could he think it would serve? If I'd known he would use such disgusting cruelty, I would have overstepped even His Majesty's authority to stop him." Seward said nothing to this, and he caught Mistress Savage narrowing her worldly eyes at Falkland. "At any rate, we shall have no trouble securing a conviction," Falkland went on, after an uncomfortable silence. "Beaumont can testify to my lawyers when he is sufficiently recovered, and then I suggest that he be conveyed to his family home. Might I ask you to arrange this, Doctor?"

"I would prefer that you do," Seward replied, "since it will be up to you what you wish to reveal to his family about his work for you. I could not write of that to Lord Beaumont, which is probably why his lordship demurred when I asked him to come to Oxford."

"I shall have to prepare him, in advance of his son's arrival. Will you go with Beaumont?"

Seward hesitated, thinking of Lord Beaumont's wife. "Again, my lord, I would prefer not."

"Allow me to take him to Chipping Campden," Ingram said to them quickly, "if your lordship can obtain me a short leave from service when the time is right. I owe it to him, Seward," he added, his voice catching a little.

"Then it is decided." Seward glanced at Mistress Savage. "What think you of our plan, madam?"

"It appears very sound," she murmured, with a hard smile.

"Allow me to accompany you to your quarters," Falkland said to her. "Dr. Seward, I shall visit again tomorrow."

"That will not be necessary, my lord. I shall send to you when Beaumont is ready to provide the deposition. But before you leave, I did have one query. How was it that His Majesty was suddenly persuaded to sign the warrant for Hoare's arrest, after permitting Beaumont to languish in gaol for almost a month?"

"Mistress Savage's informant, Captain Milne, finally bore witness to His Majesty that Hoare was spying on me. And another person interceded most powerfully on Beaumont's behalf: my Lady d'Aubigny, widow to the King's cousin. I am not sure how she learnt about what had happened to him," Falkland concluded, looking significantly at Mistress Savage, "but we owe her our thanks."

"I did not know Beaumont had such a friend," Seward remarked, his gaze straying in the same direction as Falkland's.

"Nor did I. Well, shall we be on our way, Mistress Savage?"

"Yes, my lord," she said, accepting his arm. "Dr. Seward, please remember me to Mr. Beaumont, when you next speak with him. Good day, Mr. Ingram." And she sailed out of the room as though she were leaving some inconsequential social event.

VIII.

As Parliament's Commissioners entered the lofty hall at Christ Church, Pembroke saw the King rest his eyes upon each one in turn, as though chastising them for their disloyalty. Pembroke himself received a warmer reception, which he attributed to the secret pledge of faith he had made to His Majesty. When he bowed, he was acknowledged with a regal nod that would have gratified him were he not now so worried about the future.

Representatives from the House of Commons filed in after the Lords, Edmund Waller at the tail of the procession. Waller broke into a smile, and went so far as to go up and kiss His Majesty's hand. Pembroke was amazed to hear the King say, without taking pains to lower his voice, "Though you are the last, Waller, yet you are not the worst, nor the least in my favour." Some of the delegates on both sides began to mutter amongst themselves but Waller seemed unabashed, as did His Majesty; they might have been alone in the room together. What a sycophantic display, Pembroke thought, jealous of Waller nonetheless.

As the Earl of Northumberland read out the Treaty propositions, the King interrupted constantly. He demanded refinements and explanations, and he sighed from time to time, as if to suggest the extremity of his tolerance in even listening to the articles. Falkland was obviously trying to maintain a composed demeanour, yet he must have been ashamed that the Commissioners were received with such open disrespect. It was lucky for him, Pembroke thought, that two of the greatest warmongers on the King's side, Prince Rupert and Lord Digby, were already on campaign in Gloucestershire, unwilling to await the outcome of these negotiations.

When Northumberland, red in the face, had completed the reading, His Majesty allowed an awkward silence to ensue before addressing the Commissioners. He expressed his strong dissatisfaction with the propositions, and finished crushingly, "Those who principally contrived and penned them had no thoughts of peace in their hearts, but to make things worse and worse. Yet I shall do my part, and take as much honey out of the gall as I can." With that, he rose. "I thank you, Lords and gentlemen," he said, and with a cool smile, this time directed at no one in particular, he left them.

After his exit, debate on the propositions was impossible. Falkland made a brief speech welcoming the Commissioners and invited them to sup at Christ Church that evening, and the assembly broke up.

Pembroke managed to catch Falkland on his way out of the hall, and drew him into a corner of the quadrangle. "Not a felicitous start, my lord," Pembroke remarked, "except for our friend Waller, towards whom His Majesty appears to show a marked fondness. Surely you must now see the wisdom of my idea," he continued, under his breath. "With the Queen expected to set sail any day now for the English shore and Prince Rupert threatening to seize the Cotswolds wool trade, why should His Majesty cede on the issues we have put before him, when he senses himself ahead in the game? Our only chance for peace is to talk apart from him. May we, tonight after the feast? I can bring Waller and Northumberland to your quarters."

Falkland shook his head curtly. "It is too much of a risk. There will be spies about, and if it were discovered that we were holding secret meetings, we might all be compromised."

"But, my lord, we are missing a great opportunity! Have you heard from John Earle?" Pembroke inquired, fear rising in him. "He has responded to me only in the vaguest terms – as have you, for that matter."

"I have been too occupied of late to speak with him. He may share my instinct for caution."

"All I asked was for us to renew our friendship," Pembroke objected. "What is so compromising in that?"

"I would not know." Falkland bowed, doffing his hat. "Now, please excuse me, my lord."

"Silly little man, what you call caution is merely your own cowardice," Pembroke muttered to himself, watching Falkland cross the quadrangle, head bowed, his cloak flapping in the early February breeze.

Pembroke turned back towards the hall, still smarting from Falkland's almost hostile prevarications, when it struck him: what if they were based on reliable intelligence? Could Radcliff have betrayed him to the Secretary of State?

IX.

It was midnight when Radcliff arrived at the meeting place, near an abandoned windmill some miles northwest of Oxford. Pembroke's coach was waiting for him, light flickering in its windows. He must not show his trepidation, he reminded himself, as he dismounted and looped his horse's bridle over the branch of a nearby tree.

"Please, sir, get in," he heard Pembroke say, and he obeyed, immediately reassured by his lordship's smile and the timbre of his voice. "How is that arm of yours? Fully healed?"

"Yes, my lord," Radcliff said, relief washing over him. Just as Poole had informed him, Pembroke was not angry at all. "What news of the negotiations?"

"I fear that His Majesty is, as ever, intransigent, if not contemptuous of our proposals. And I had no opportunity for a private audience with him, as I had hoped, before we laid them before him. Sometimes I tire of striving, the future of this kingdom weighs so heavily upon my shoulders," Pembroke sighed. "Had I not been forced to assume such a burden, I would have stayed quietly at Wilton, completing the additions to my house and garden, and enriching my collection of art." Radcliff did not interrupt, enjoying the warmth of the coach and Pembroke's air of confiding in him, as in old times; Poole's visit to Newbury had alarmed him for nothing. "Have *you* any interest in art, Sir Bernard?" Pembroke asked, in the same friendly manner.

"Interest, yes, but I'm not the expert you are, my lord," Radcliff said, adding ruminatively, "I'd like to have a portrait done of my wife some day."

"Yes, you should, before age and childbirth take their toll. Do you know of any talented artist who might execute it?"

"For that, I would defer to your lordship's recommendation," Radcliff answered, settling back on the padded seat; he had not found Pembroke so amicable since his departure for The Hague with the ill-fated purse full of gold.

Pembroke regarded him more closely. "There are many new masters emerging from the Dutch school. Their services can be bought quite cheap, or so I gather." Radcliff nodded, hearing a change in Pembroke's speech: it had become deliberate, even expectant. "Are you acquainted with any of them?"

"No, my lord. I should be grateful for an introduction – though of course you must have far more pressing concerns at the moment."

Pembroke continued to survey Radcliff, in the dancing flame of the lamp that hung from the ceiling of his coach. "In truth I do," he said finally. "Sir Bernard, I have spoken with John Earle, and I swear, it is as if he has been warned off me. I had asked him if he would again act as my spiritual counsellor, as he once was, but he claimed that his duties as tutor to the Prince of Wales made it impossible for him to do as I asked." How sensible of him, thought Radcliff; who could rescue a soul as proud and greedy as Pembroke's? "It was evident that he considers his friendship with me over," Pembroke went on. "We have thus lost a vital thread in our scheme: without Earle's confidence, it will be far more difficult for me to win that of the young Prince."

"And my Lord Falkland?"

"He is yet more off-putting. I did wonder why. But then I got wind of a rumour that he may have been in clandestine talks with some members of Parliament, against the King's wishes. Perhaps that is the cause of his wariness towards me: he may fear for his reputation," he concluded, boring into Radcliff with his small, greyish eyes.

"Perhaps," Radcliff agreed uneasily, wishing that Pembroke would spit out what was on his mind.

"Has any detail of our plans for His Majesty *ever* leaked out to *anyone*?" Pembroke barked, startling him.

"Certainly not, that I am aware of!"

"What about our code? Apart from you and I, does anyone else have knowledge of it?"

"No, my lord. For that reason I was most puzzled when Poole told me that I should desist from using it for our correspondence."

"I shall tell you the reason. In November past, a message was delivered to my London house, *in our code*, though the author is still a mystery to me."

Radcliff allowed himself to look as aghast as he felt. This had to be Beaumont's doing, but how in heaven's name had he learnt that Pembroke was involved in the conspiracy? Had Seward used his occult skills to divine the truth? "That is – incredible," Radcliff stammered. "What was the substance of it?"

Pembroke hesitated once more, his thin lips working. "That there is a traitor in our midst," he said, at length.

"Do you think – oh, no, my lord!"

"Then who? Joshua Poole? Tyler?"

"Neither was privy to the code! And Tyler could barely read or write!"

"So we come full circle, back to you," said Pembroke, with deadly logic. "If you cannot find out where the leak occurred and how far it has spread, and demonstrate to me that it is *stopped permanently*, I shall have no choice but to end our association." He took a quick, furious breath. "Have you forgotten what you owe me? I have supplied you with money, protected your estate, given you jewels for your wife! But thanks to your blunder in The Hague, I have no store of arms for my own security. And that ham-fisted bully you hired got himself killed in a drunken squabble, Poole told me. Now your precious, unbreakable code has somehow been cracked. Christ's blood! What will go amiss next? All that you seem to do well is to cast horoscopes!"

"My lord," Radcliff protested, "I am fully conscious of my debt to you. I have put complete faith in you, and I assure you, I am staking my all on your success. If you fail, I am undone. You must know that."

"Then you had better move fast on my instructions, or else I shall find myself another stargazer," Pembroke retorted acidly. "And with Tyler dead, we must secure a new man to dispatch our prey."

"I promise I shall do as you ask," Radcliff assured him. "I shall replace Tyler."

"No. Leave that to me. And no more promises. I want results."

"How should we communicate, from here on?"

"Use the lawyer, if you must. Good night," said Pembroke, pushing open the coach door with a violent jerk of his foot.

"Good night, my lord."

Radcliff descended from the coach and managed to bow before Pembroke slammed the door and yelled at the driver to whip up the horses. At this instant, he hated Pembroke; and he thought of the letters secreted away in Madam Musgrave's house, most of them in Pembroke's characteristic, forceful script.

X.

"It was a fine fight in and about Cirencester, and when the town fell we took twelve hundred prisoners," Tom wrote to his father, in the dim glow of a tallow candle. "They are now being marched back to Oxford, and I regret that I shall not see the Commissioners' long faces as they arrive. My troop did me credit, no one killed and only a couple lightly wounded. If Gloucester had also fallen to the Prince, we would have had the whole county secured. Yet His Majesty can now safely communicate with his forces in the southwest, and halt the supply of wool to London. Prince Rupert has two thousand head of horse. He has been promised four thousand pounds a month, and a regiment of foot to keep Gloucestershire for the King."

"Master Thomas," Adam called, from outside Tom's tent. "There's a messenger come to take you to His Highness Prince Rupert."

"Just a moment," Tom shouted back, excited, as he dashed off: "I send this by Adam, praying to God you are all in good health, my dear wife especially." Before leaving with the messenger, he gave Adam instructions to take his letter and ride the short distance to Chipping Campden that same night.

The Royalist regiments were camped mostly in the open Gloucestershire fields, still scattered with patches of snow. Tom shivered as he walked the half mile to Prince Rupert's accommodations, and when he entered, his damp cloak began to steam immediately in the welcome heat. Surrounded by their chief officers, the Prince,

Wilmot, and Digby were all at supper together, and Tom's mouth watered as he smelt the roast wildfowl and freshly baked bread on the table before them.

"Mr. Beaumont," the Prince said, in his direct fashion, setting down his knife, "your men fought well today. You must visit my quartermaster, on your way out, and he will issue a barrel of ale and extra rations for your troop. It's a cold night out there, and hunger makes a man even colder."

"I thank you, Your Highness, on their behalf," Tom said, very pleased, and a little sorry that he had been unable to include the Prince's words in his letter.

The Prince motioned to one of his officers, who filled a tankard of ale and handed it to Tom. As he drank, he could see both Wilmot and Digby eyeing him.

"Have you heard lately from your brother, sir?" Wilmot asked him, when he had finished.

"No, sir. I last saw him at Christmastide, at my father's house. I thought he was in your service."

"He must not have been allowed pen and paper, in his gaol cell," Lord Digby remarked to Wilmot.

Confused, Tom looked from them to the Prince, who said to him, "Did you not know of his arrest?"

"No, Your Highness!"

"My dear fellow," Digby said, "how peculiar, and how appalling, that you should have been kept in ignorance."

"Your brother was detained in Oxford Castle at the end of December, on suspicion of colluding with the rebels," the Prince explained.

Dumbfounded, Tom could not respond at once. "Oh – but that is – is impossible, Your Highness! There must be some mistake," he added, thinking of his private report to Colonel Hoare; he had not suggested anything so grave as this.

"An *egregious* mistake," stressed Digby.

"But you may comfort yourself that he has recently been freed," said the Prince. "One of my captains has evidence that he was falsely accused."

"I – that is, my family and I are most obliged that Your Royal Highness should condescend to pay attention to my – my brother's case," stuttered Tom.

"It is not just his case. Are you acquainted with Colonel Hoare?"

"I am, Your Highness."

"It was he who took your brother into custody and treated him with unwarranted violence, beating him almost to death and killing another man imprisoned there. I have yet to find out why he did them such a wrong. Thus far Colonel Hoare's reputation has always been unimpeachable."

"Ah, well, we can all be impeached," Digby observed languidly. "I have been impeached by Parliament, though I confess I tend to consider it as more of a compliment than an injury to *my* reputation."

He and Wilmot started to laugh but were silenced by the Prince's frown.

"Mr. Beaumont," Wilmot said in his sneering way, "was it not Colonel Hoare who ordered your troop to be transferred from my regiment to that of His Royal Highness just before we gave battle at Edgehill? I think you told me so yourself."

"Yes, sir, though I did not ask him for the transfer."

"Yet you must know him as more than an acquaintance."

"Not much more, sir," Tom said, shrinking inside.

"What difference does it make whose regiment he fights in, as long as the war is won," Prince Rupert put in brusquely. "Good night, Mr. Beaumont, and for your men's sakes don't forget to stop with my quartermaster."

Tom bowed again and tried to make a dignified exit, although he felt as if his heart were stuck in his throat.

CHAPTER FIFTEEN

I.

Laurence was still slipping in and out of consciousness. Even under the influence of opium, it hurt simply to breathe, and whenever he coughed, he felt as if his rib cage were about to burst apart. Most worrying of all, he had suffered internal injuries; for days, there was blood in his urine. When not drugged, he wished he were dead. Sometimes when drugged, he did not really care if he lived. Once his fever abated, he found himself repulsed by the wreck that his body had become, and humiliated that he needed help with the most basic functions. Unable to bear the thought of his father seeing him as he was, he forbade Seward to write to Lord Beaumont about what he had suffered. Instead, he dictated a message explaining that his arrest had been an error and that he was now out of gaol, but was presently recovering from an illness he had caught there.

When he told Seward about the planned uprising in London, his old tutor dismissed the possibility that Falkland might have a hand in it. "I want to know the truth," Laurence insisted, though Seward declared him still too unwell for a meeting with Falkland, or for any other visitors.

After lying in bed for five interminable weeks, however, he lost patience. Defying Seward's orders he got up to hobble around, which aggravated his cough, cracking open a rib again. "*Festina lente*," warned Seward, "or you could suffer a serious relapse. But I shall send word to Falkland that you are ready to give your deposition."

On the last day of February, as he brought Laurence's nightly dose of opium tincture, he announced that Falkland would arrive in the morning with his lawyers. "If you think yourself so much better, you must stop taking opium soon, my boy," he remarked. "It is very addictive."

"Oh, for God's sake, you know I can't cope without it," Laurence said, determined not to lose his only relief from pain. "Seward, why hasn't Isabella Savage come to see me?"

"Do you expect *me* to understand the vagaries of women? Now sleep, Beaumont. You will need all your energies for tomorrow."

Laurence shut his eyes, waiting for the blissful moment when the drug would begin to seep into his bloodstream and he could enjoy its transient oblivion. He felt stifled, as though some invisible creature were pressing the air from his lungs and constricting his throat, and with each inhalation he fancied that he could smell the reek of the jakes on his skin. Yet he must have slept, for he dreamt.

The guards were stringing him up. The cords ate at his wrists, his shoulders throbbed, and he was tired of resisting. That was not the worst of it. Tom hung beside him; and not Tom as he was, but as a boy of ten years old, scared and whimpering. Hoare seized the boy's tongue and was about to slice into it with his knife, asking, "What will you do to save him, Mr. Beaumont? Though why save him? He's a telltale, isn't he, of the most reprehensible sort!" As the blade neared Tom's mouth, a cascade of blood stung Laurence in the face. He was unable to wipe it away, because his hands were tied. It filled his mouth until he had to swallow it; and he jerked awake.

Seward was standing by his bedside. "A terrible racket you were making."

Laurence's sheets were soaked in sweat, as was his nightshirt. The bandage on his left wrist had come unravelled during the night from his tossing and turning, and as he watched Seward tying it back up, he realised that Khadija's bracelet was gone. "Seward," he asked, "when you first tended to me here, did you take something off my wrist, a strip of leather?"

"My dear fellow, that day there was nothing to take off you but your breeches," Seward replied, pouring water into a basin for Laurence to wash. "What was it, anyway?"

"Nothing," said Laurence quickly. "Nothing at all."

By the time that Falkland entered with Stephens and two lawyers, Laurence was feeling no pain, having cadged a double dose of opium from Seward for the occasion. He could detect a change in Falkland, who looked much thinner, and pale.

Falkland examined him tentatively in return, and addressed him as though he were the victim of some disfiguring accident. "Mr. Beaumont, I must thank you for offering to provide your testimony when you are still in convalescence. I trust you have the strength for this?"

"Let's find out," Laurence said.

The lawyers asked question after question, while Falkland listened, sighing now and again. They often interrupted Laurence, seeking clarification. But when he described Hoare's single act of brutality against Charles Danvers and what had happened immediately afterwards, they did not ask him to repeat himself. At length it was done. The document was read back to him, and he signed it.

Falkland then sent out his servant and the lawyers, motioning for Seward to stay behind. "Sir," he said, sitting down in a chair close by Laurence's bed, "there is no way in which I can express my gratitude to you. Before you leave the Castle for Chipping Campden, I shall write to your father about the circumstances of your imprisonment."

"Please don't, my lord," said Laurence. "Allow me to tell him in my own time."

"If you so wish. But in all conscience, I cannot cause you further distress given what you have endured, which is why I have decided to release you from my service. I shall pursue the regicides without you. I did meet with Pembroke while he was here in Oxford," Falkland rushed on, as Laurence opened his mouth to interrupt, "and I declined to engage in any private conferences with him, though not so abruptly as to suggest that I knew anything. Earle saw him too and more definitely refused further communication with him, on Dr. Seward's advice. My next step will be to arrest Sir Bernard Radcliff and have him interrogated."

"At last! But by whom? Or do you propose to do it yourself?" Falkland coloured at this. "No, my lord, you must wait until I'm well enough to assist you."

"I am surprised, sir, that you would want to witness another interrogation, let alone participate in it."

Laurence sat forward in the bed. "I've come this far with you – don't cut me out now. These men are a threat to me, my family, and to Seward."

"My lord," Seward intervened, "you have no spymaster at present. You would indeed be wise to wait."

Falkland sighed again. "Then I shall. Once more I am indebted to you, Mr. Beaumont."

"Let's not talk about debts," said Laurence, relaxing back against the pillows. "I have an interest in finishing this business, that's all."

"My Lady d'Aubigny sent her good wishes to you, for your recovery," Falkland went on, in a lighter tone. "When you are better, you might find the opportunity to thank her. She used her influence with His Majesty to expedite your release."

Laurence was surprised: no one had told him of Lady d'Aubigny's efforts on his behalf. His hour of pleasure with her had paid off more handsomely than he could ever have expected. "And have you seen

Mistress Savage?" he asked. "Seward said she was with you when you got me out of the cell."

"I have," Falkland said, a little awkwardly. "She too sends you her greetings."

"When does Hoare go to trial?"

"As soon as I can spare time to attend the proceedings. I am still busy with Council at present, and he can afford to sit in gaol and ponder his fate."

"Will my brother be called as a witness?"

"Undoubtedly. Hoare will require him to state that there were solid grounds for him to interrogate you, and for the aspersions cast upon me."

"I hope our father doesn't hear about all this," Laurence said, starting to cough.

"At any rate, I shall write to you at Chipping Campden and give you a full report of the trial. And I did write to Danvers' wife, to tell her the tragic news."

"He spoke of her just before he died. He said he loved her and he was sorry he had wronged her."

"I shall make sure she knows."

"My lord, he said something else: that there's to be a Royalist revolt –" Between more coughs, Laurence went on. "In London. He said you were party to it, but I didn't believe him."

"Did he talk of it to Hoare?" Falkland asked, in a near whisper.

"He would have, if they hadn't slit his tongue first." Laurence coughed again, hugging his ribs. The opium was beginning to wear off and he felt a sinking in the pit of his stomach: Danvers had not lied to him. "It's true, isn't it. Why?" Falkland gazed at him uncertainly as he sobbed for breath. "Why would you risk prejudicing the negotiations, and the esteem of Parliament?"

"Beaumont, hush, and take some of this," Seward advised, bringing a cup of water to his lips. "We should leave him, my lord," he said to Falkland.

"Not until you tell me why," Laurence demanded, pushing aside Seward's hand. "My lord, you owe it to me."

"He is the King I elected to serve," Falkland said, with a melancholy smile, "and it is, after all, his right to issue a Commission of Array in his own capital. I had no choice but to swallow the indignity of participating in a venture that goes against my principles."

"Politics is a choice of evils, Beaumont, as you are aware," Seward observed.

"True enough," said Laurence wryly. He pitied Falkland: what a heart-wrenching compromise for one so morally upright. "My lord," he added, "about the conspiracy – before we interrogate Radcliff, I want to find those letters I sold back to him. Otherwise he may be very hard to break. We need that evidence."

Falkland glanced at Seward, who said, "He's right again."

"Radcliff can't afford to carry the letters on him or to leave them to be discovered at his estate," Laurence went on, "but I think I know where they might be." And he told Falkland about the coffer that Radcliff had hidden at Madam Musgrave's house.

"I can authorize a search of the house immediately," Falkland said.

Laurence shook his head, stifling another cough. "Please don't. She's part of my friend Ingram's family. If it's at all possible, I want them protected from any association with Radcliff's guilt. Let me look for the letters on my own. If I have no success *then* you can order a search."

"How are you going to accomplish that, Beaumont?" Seward queried. "You can't even walk yet."

"I have an idea," Laurence replied. "Just give me some time."

Falkland rose from his chair and touched Laurence's shoulder. "Mr. Beaumont, I know you share my desire to deal with this conspiracy quickly. How long will it take until he is well enough to venture out?" he asked Seward.

"A good two weeks if not more," Seward answered firmly.

"I shall give you two more after that to find the letters, Mr. Beaumont. If you've had no luck by then, I shall issue a search warrant. Thank you, again, sir, and I pray you enjoy a speedy recovery. Good day, Dr. Seward."

"What is this idea of yours?" Seward asked Laurence afterwards.

"What if, instead of going home, I went to stay with Ingram's aunt?"

They regarded each other in silence. Then Seward began to smile. "First you must be fit to travel."

"Make me so," Laurence said.

This was not as easy as he had hoped. Without opium he was plagued by nausea, cold sweats, and a constant, maddening itch all over his skin. Seward treated him to various foul-tasting herbal decoctions to counter the withdrawal pangs, permitted him wine to dull the aches of his body, and forced him to eat and take gentle exercise. At last his bruises faded to a lighter shade of purple, and his ribs knit together more firmly. But he could not walk ten paces without pausing to catch his breath.

Seward proved a relentless taskmaster. "You're worse than Hoare," Laurence complained, sweating and shaking, during one of their perambulations about the Castle courtyard.

"On your request, Beaumont."

"I know." Laurence peered up at the high walls surrounding them. "And I can't stomach this place any more."

"Are you ready to leave it?"

He nodded, and smiled. "You old bastard, I think you've been enjoying yourself all the while. You've never had such an obedient slave in me."

"Not in fifteen years," Seward agreed, tugging his ear affectionately.

II.

Although Beaumont had been packed into the coach cushioned all round with bedclothes, Ingram noticed him gasping and wincing at each jolt. It was their hard luck that the route north from Oxford into the Cotswold hills had flooded in the spring rains, and that they had had to take a westerly detour towards the market town of Witney. After two hours of slogging through mud and potholes full of water, with regular breaks to free its wheels, the coach had covered less than eight miles.

Beaumont was continually coughing and spitting out of the coach window. "I can't let my family see me like this, Ingram," he said at last. "I'll go anywhere else, but not there. Please, man, don't take me there."

He seemed so distraught that Ingram knocked on the roof for the coachman to pull up. "Where on earth can I take you, then?"

"There must be somewhere else. What about your aunt's house at Faringdon?"

Ingram paused to calculate. They would not reach Chipping Campden that day, while Aunt Musgrave's estate lay roughly fourteen miles south. They could stay overnight and push on in the morning, when Beaumont might be more reconciled to the idea of going home. "All right," he said, at which Beaumont managed a faint smile.

"Ingram, I'm in a lot of pain. I think Seward gave you a sleeping draught for me. Can I have some now?"

"I must confess," said Ingram, as he searched for it, "I'm surprised that Dr. Seward allowed you out of bed, in your condition."

Once he had taken the medicine, Beaumont murmured, "Thank you." Then his eyes shut, and he ceased to make any noise.

At about six in the evening, the coach finally drew up in Aunt Musgrave's courtyard. Ingram eased himself out and limped towards the house, his bad leg stiff from the damp and sitting still. He heard the dogs barking, and was much reassured to see her ancient butler come out of the front door bearing a lantern. When she emerged, she gave him a motherly hug.

"Dear Aunt," he mumbled, into the prickly fabric of her ruff. "Sorry to arrive without any warning."

"No apologies are required for my favourite nephew. But where did you get such a splendid coach? Were you knighted by His Majesty?"

"No, no – I've my friend Beaumont with me. He's been extremely ill and we were on our way to his family seat at Chipping Campden, but I was afraid the journey would be too long for him, without stopping for the night. Where are the grooms?" he asked of her butler.

"You will have to tend to the horses yourself, Walter," she said. "My fellows are gone to join the army, their heads filled with talk of Prince Rupert and his Cavaliers. I've been left with a couple of beardless boys and dotards such as my old retainer. The cowmen and shepherds had more sense and stayed behind. But my best mounts have been seized by Prince Rupert's troops. Sweeping the commons, they call it. Robbery, is what I say. His Majesty will make few friends amongst us country folk if Rupert continues to pillage our goods."

"It's a necessity of war, Aunt, both sides have been driven to it," Ingram reminded her.

"Necessity be buggered. He should pay for what he takes."

Ingram called for the coachman and they manoeuvred Beaumont out of the vehicle.

"Mr. Beaumont," Aunt Musgrave said, in a shocked voice, as they carried him into the better light of the hall, "what are those marks on your face? Did someone give you a whipping?" Beaumont nodded, squinting at her. She directed them upstairs to a chamber, and when he had been lowered onto the bed, she herded Ingram and the others out. "Off to the stable, this is women's work," she told them.

Ingram obeyed at first, though foreseeing her even greater shock as she discovered more about Beaumont's injuries, he had the coachman finish the remaining chores and rushed back into the house.

Kate was at the foot of the staircase and grabbed his arm as he tried to ascend. "What is wrong with Mr. Beaumont?"

"He's been very ill, Kate. Let me go to him."

"Walter, did you ever ask him about . . . about my husband?"

"Do you ever think of anyone but yourself?" Ingram reproached her, pushing past.

In the bedchamber, Aunt Musgrave and one of her maids were removing Beaumont's doublet. "What are all these bruises from?" she exclaimed, as she took off his shirt.

"Lord Jesus!" the maid cried, flinching.

Aunt Musgrave ordered her out, shut the door, and faced Ingram gravely. "What happened to him, nephew?"

"He was detained and horribly mistreated by Lord Falkland's spymaster," Ingram replied. "It's a complicated matter that I can't fully explain now, but we'll be gone tomorrow," he hurried on. "I only have a few days' leave to travel with him and then I must return to my troop."

"Tomorrow? He is far too weak to go anywhere." Ingram agreed privately, as they took off the rest of Beaumont's garments. "He shall stay here with me until he is able to complete his journey," she declared, pulling the bedclothes over her patient and rearranging the pillow beneath his head. "Walter," she resumed, more quietly, "Why has Sir Bernard not once written to his wife since she last saw him? I consider it remiss, for a newlywed husband. She wrote several times, but this month she held back – to know for certain whether she was with child. Which she is."

"How wonderful!" Ingram hugged his aunt again. "He'll be overjoyed, as am I."

"Tell him that he should convey his joy to Kate, or else she may become so jittery as to miscarry. I can't answer for her moods and she has been stranger than ever, since the holiday at Newbury." Ingram tensed, recalling his conversation with Kate about the steward's visit. "By the bye," Aunt Musgrave said, breaking in on his thoughts, "is our Mr. Beaumont aware that you are in love with his sister?" Ingram gaped at her. "Oh Walter, any idiot could tell. At Christmas you mentioned Anne Beaumont's name so many times that I was getting bored with the sound of it."

"Might *she* have guessed?"

"If she has a woman's instinct. Will you make her an offer?"

"How can I? I've no fortune. And the Beaumonts are such a grand family. They can trace their line back to the Normans."

"Pah," she said, "that's nothing. Ours goes back to Adam and Eve. Faint heart never won fair maid. What have you to lose by asking, save a little pride?"

III.

When Madam Musgrave woke Laurence the next day, he felt an initial confusion on seeing her; his arrival the night before had been quite a blur to him thanks to Seward's medicinal skills.

"Good morning to you," she said. "Walter looked in on you earlier. He didn't want to rouse you to say goodbye. He's gone back to Oxford. You're to rest here, Mr. Beaumont, and only when you are better should you attempt the journey home."

"Thank you," he said, genuinely grateful.

She reached below the bed and held out a chamber pot. "A man should not go so many hours without answering the call of nature." He took it, hesitantly, much to her amusement. "Bashful, are you? You've not much left to be shy about with me, sir – I undressed you last night. What a beating that wretch must have given you," she added, shaking her head.

"Ingram told you, then," Laurence remarked, wondering what precisely his friend had said.

"A very little of it. Now, you need some peace and quiet. It will be my privilege to have you as a guest after all you did for Walter and his broken leg. Besides, Kate will be glad of some younger company."

"Lady Radcliff is still at the house?"

"She is. We came back together after spending Christmastide at Newbury." Madam Musgrave threw up her hands. "She is with child, and utterly miserable at not hearing from her husband in so long."

What had happened to him, Laurence wondered; had Pembroke decided to make an end of him after receiving that painting?

"Can you manage on your own?" said Madam Musgrave, indicating the pot. "I could send my butler to assist you."

"Oh no," Laurence answered, smiling, "that won't be necessary."

IV.

With Clarke and Earle, Seward arrived promptly at the university hall that had been assigned as a courtroom, but they had to sit waiting until well past the appointed hour for the trial to begin. Spectators were still filing into the galleries and the lawyers were busy in consultation. Seward saw Mistress Savage take her seat beside a blond young man he guessed to be Captain Milne. Near Milne were several of the soldiers from the Castle, all witnesses for the prosecution, Seward assumed. On one side of the room were Falkland, his lawyers, and the officers of the court, on the other side the jury, and between them the judge on his dais. The gallery above was packed with courtiers, mostly ladies dressed as if for an entertainment.

The noise of the crowd fell to murmuring as Hoare was marched into the dock, accompanied by an armed guard. Seward felt a surge of anger, then an unsettling puzzlement: Hoare showed no fear, but defiance, more like a commanding officer than a prisoner awaiting trial on hanging charges; and as these were read out by the clerk, he looked over calmly at Falkland.

Hoare stood accused of murdering Charles Danvers, causing severe bodily harm to Laurence Beaumont, and malignant tampering with Lord Falkland's correspondence in order to defame him and subvert his authority. Hoare submitted a plea of not guilty. The prosecutor next embarked on an elaborate speech to the jury, detailing dates and times, the witnesses who would be brought to testify, and depositions to be presented. The prisoner would speak in his own defence, and call those witnesses of his own who might disprove the case against him. Laurence and Thomas Beaumont were both on his list.

By two o'clock, however, the prosecutor had yet to finish his speech, no witnesses had been sworn in, and the jury was becoming restless. The judge announced that the court would adjourn and reassemble in an hour. As the galleries emptied, Seward glimpsed Mistress Savage coming through the crowd towards him. He signalled that he would follow her, and made his excuses to Clarke and Earle before joining her outside.

"How is Mr. Beaumont?" she inquired, with no perceptible emotion.

"He has been recovering at his family home," Seward replied, continuing more honestly, "He still has no idea of all that you did to help him."

"Let us keep it that way. Falkland must wish that he were here, more than ever."

"Why so?"

As she bent her head towards him, Seward scented again the expensive perfume that he had once noticed on Beaumont's clothes. "Doctor, this too should be a secret between us, with one exception: Mr. Beaumont needs to know of it. Digby informed me that His Majesty is sending a Commission of Array to London, authorizing all citizens opposed to Parliament to take up arms for the royal cause. The plan was hatched last year, but the time did not seem opportune to execute it. Now His Majesty believes that the Queen's recent arrival in England will stimulate an upsurge of enthusiasm in the capital, and win over those who are still hesitant to join him. In Parliament, Edmund Waller has undertaken to act as an intermediary between the citizens and any members of the Lords or Commons who would declare for the King. And Falkland has accepted to organize the correspondence between Oxford and London." She stopped, regarding Seward with her intense hazel eyes. "Perhaps His Majesty was inclined to test him, by assigning him such a vital role in the uprising. It is likely to come to fruition in May."

"A perilous endeavour," observed Seward.

"And what occurred to me is this: to whom may Falkland turn, to manage these secret communications?" Beaumont, Seward thought; and how difficult it would be for him to refuse this other duty, since he had shown himself so keen to assist Falkland with the conspiracy. "Yes, *him*," she said, in a whisper. "He has proved that he can be trusted, under the greatest duress. If only he were not so useful." Abruptly she put on a smile, which Seward guessed was for the benefit of Digby, who was strolling up to them.

"What sublime weather!" Digby cried. "More like July than the middle of March. Who is your distinguished companion, Isabella?"

"Digby, may I present Dr. William Seward of Merton College."

Digby examined Seward with interest. "I have heard of you, sir. Are you not renowned for your knowledge of astrology?"

"It is one of my pastimes, my lord. I cannot claim any expertise."

"Oh no? In any case, it seems a tricky business. Her Majesty the Queen consulted astrologers before setting sail for the English coast, and they warned her against making the journey because of some unfavourable conjunction of the planets. But she prayed to our Lady of Liesse, *et voilà*, she was safely delivered to our shores."

"A happy miscalculation on the part of her astrologers."

"Or else divine intervention. Isabella, should I ask Dr. Seward to see into your stars?"

"Please don't," she said, with a bright laugh. "I prefer to be surprised by fate."

"As do I," Digby concurred. "Is Dr. Seward preparing you to take a place at Merton? With her brains," he said to Seward, "she could outwit any of our undergraduates."

"The day has not come when women are allowed such a privilege," she murmured.

Nor will it ever, thought Seward, if there is a God in heaven.

"If it does, I worry for us men," laughed Digby. "Doctor, have you had a chance to read a copy of my new broadsheet, *Mercurius Aulicus*?"

"I have not."

"Its concerns are more mundane than the rotations of the planets, but it is informative nonetheless. I shall have the latest issue delivered to Merton, if you like."

"I thank you, my lord."

"So what's your opinion, will Colonel Hoare be spared a traitor's death?"

"I hope not."

"I wonder why Mr. Beaumont is not in attendance," Digby said to Mistress Savage. "I thought he'd have liked to see his foe brought down."

"Digby," she said, taking his arm, "listening to all these speeches has given me a terrible thirst. Let us find some refreshment before we return to the courtroom."

"Certainly, my dear. We shall see you in there, Doctor," Digby called back to Seward, who bowed and watched them go, chatting merrily as if they had not a care in the world.

V.

On his third morning at Faringdon, Laurence could play the invalid no longer; he had only ten more days to find Radcliff's letters. When Madam Musgrave poked her head into his room late in the afternoon to ask how he was, he announced that he wished to dress and come downstairs. She looked surprised, but later expressed her great pleasure as he descended on trembling legs, disappointed at how much weaker his muscles were after being bedridden again.

She invited him to the fireside, advancing his chair nearer to the blaze.

"Has Lady Radcliff had any word from her husband yet?" he inquired, with an air of polite concern.

"She has not, poor girl," said Madam Musgrave, "though Walter must have told him her news by now. I urged her not to worry too much, sir. Nothing can be amiss with him or else Walter would have informed us, even if Sir Bernard has not the grace to write himself."

There was a pause, during which Laurence searched for a way to steer the conversation towards his desired object. "You have a very beautiful house," he remarked. "Has it been in your family long?"

"No, sir. My husband's father, Marmaduke Musgrave, bought it upon its confiscation from a Catholic nobleman, back in the reign of Queen Bess. The fellow had apparently been plotting some mischief against her."

"What happened to him?" Laurence asked, thinking of certain other conspirators.

"He and his wife fled to France. Others in their household were not so lucky. You see, Mr. Beaumont, the house was used as a refuge for priests sent from the Spanish Netherlands to convert us all back to popery. They had a priest's hole built into the walls, and mass was held every Sunday in a bedchamber on the third floor, near the secret entrance. After they left, one of the priests was discovered, still hidden. A servant had betrayed him, and he was hanged, drawn, and quartered at Tyburn," she concluded, with grim relish. "My servants believe that he haunts that chamber. They've heard knocking and the sound of footsteps."

"Have *you* ever heard him?" Laurence said, smiling; he could not picture Madam Musgrave frightened by anyone, living or dead.

"No, but I rarely go up there; all those stairs are too much for my old knees. The last time was months ago, when I placed some valuables in the hole so that no soldiers from either army could come stealing from me."

"Very wise. Soldiers are a greedy lot."

They stopped talking as Kate entered the hall, and Laurence rose to bow. She appeared to him as haunted as any spectre, with dark circles about her eyes and a blotched, unhealthy complexion.

"Mr. Beaumont," she said, in a rather accusatory tone, "you must be much better."

"I am, thank you, Lady Radcliff," he said, faking a wince as he sat down again.

"Such a change we've wrought in him since he arrived," Madam Musgrave observed, beaming at him. "We were just speaking of the priest's ghost, Kate. Have you been witness to his knockings and bangings?"

"I have not, Aunt, and I hope I never am," Kate answered, her face grave.

"We must ask Sir Bernard, the next time he calls on us, if he saw any strange apparition when he put his coffer in there," said Madam Musgrave, winking at Laurence, who could hardly believe his ears. Then her expression changed and she flushed a bright pink.

"What coffer?" Kate asked, frowning at her.

"Oh my dear," she exclaimed, "I was not supposed to tell you!" Laurence glanced from Kate to her, tantalized, waiting for her to continue. "He left it with me last September. He said it contained some family relics from Longstanton, and a present that he wished to give you on your next birthday. He wanted to surprise you with it. How indiscreet I've been! Promise you won't say a word to him about this?"

"Certainly, Aunt," Kate said, after a hesitation.

"You know, Kate," Madam Musgrave went on more softly, "when

we were in fear of his life after Edgehill, I was tempted to fetch it for you anyway, in case he might have stored a copy of his will there, which he would have been sensible to do."

Kate nodded; her eyes were now on Laurence.

"Do you believe in ghosts?" he asked her, as though to resume a lighter conversation.

"I do, sir," she replied. "The Bible tells us there are such things, that can be raised by witchcraft."

"Hmm. Well God knows, I've seen enough dead people, but not one has come back to haunt me."

"You should spend a night in the hole, sir," suggested Madam Musgrave, in her former bantering tone, "and try to catch the spirit at his pranks!"

"I should," Laurence agreed, thrilled at the ease with which he might achieve his goal. "You must take me there some time."

Over supper, he framed his request more directly, but Madam Musgrave must have taken it as a joke. "If I can spare a moment to indulge your whim, sir," she said, laughing. "I'm short of labourers at one of the busiest seasons, what with the new crops coming in and the sheep starting to lamb." She then embarked on an agricultural discourse, encouraged by some courteous questions on Laurence's part.

Meanwhile Kate was pushing her food about on her plate, just pretending to eat. Something was bothering her, Laurence felt sure.

There were no cards after the meal. Madam Musgrave hurried them off to bed, saying that she must rise at dawn to oversee her fields. Laurence retired with her well-thumbed copy of *The English Husbandman* under his arm. "Any landowner should be familiar with it, and you did express an interest in the subject," she had said, pressing the volume on him as he went upstairs.

In his chamber he flicked through the pages, listening until the house was quiet, and restraining himself for another hour, as an extra precaution. Then he took off his boots, lit a fresh candle, and slipped out of his room and down the passage, remembering the last time he had prowled about hoping to steal Radcliff's letter from Kate. But on this occasion he climbed the narrow, winding flight of stairs up to the third floor, where he had never yet been. He could distinguish several closed doors along a similar passageway, and next, to his amazement, a quivering ray of light at the very end; the priest would need no illumination to conduct his nocturnal rounds. Blowing out his own light, Laurence advanced to the last door, which was wide open.

Within he saw a huge bed frame, bereft of its canopy and hangings. All four walls were wood-panelled in a linen-fold pattern. On a carved mantel above the fireplace stood a single lit taper. Kate hovered there, clad in a long white nightgown, her back to him, running her hands methodically over and over the mantel's decorative knobs and curlicues. Her repeated attempts yielded no result and she uttered a short, frustrated sigh; her taper was guttering, casting sinister shadows across the room. She would soon have to stop searching, he estimated, or else be left in darkness.

He retraced his steps, tried the latch on one of the other doors along the corridor, and entered. Although the door closed quietly, inside he tripped on what he guessed to be a pile of broken furniture, stubbing his toes. He was too late to muffle a yelp of pain: so much for concealment. Then, inspired, he grabbed a heavy piece of wood and let it drop with a satisfying thud to the floor. He picked it up again and struck it at the rest of the pile, producing a clattering sound, after which he groaned mournfully several times. This was enough: he heard a gasp and the patter of bare feet along the corridor and down the stairs. He waited, lest Kate summon up the courage to return, but after a while, hearing nothing more, he emerged.

Without the advantage of his candle's light, he had to extend both arms just to negotiate the corridor. Once in the other chamber, he felt along the panelling to the fireplace, and repeated the same motions as Kate. He had no more success than she, and he started to tire from the unwonted exertion. *Reculer pour mieux sauter*, he told himself. Tomorrow he would ask Madam Musgrave again, and if she would not oblige him in his inquiries, at least Kate had supplied him with a vital clue.

The next day he was up before the maidservant could arrive with his breakfast, though too late to corner his hostess; she had long since set off for the fields. He found Kate at table, and judging by her haggard face, she had probably not slept at all. Immediately he was ashamed of the cheap trick he had played on her.

"You look tired, Lady Radcliff," he said, sitting down beside her.

"I passed a wakeful night, sir," she admitted, locking and unlocking her slender fingers, and twisting her wedding ring about.

"Here," he said, and poured her some ale, of which she took a tiny drink. "Is something troubling you?"

He waited for her to speak of the ghost. But what she said next was most unexpected. "How well are you acquainted with my husband?"

"I've only met him on two or three occasions, with Ingram," he said, shrugging.

"Do you recall when you came last October to bring me Sir Bernard's letter, how it fell and you picked it up for me?" He nodded. "You gazed at it as if it meant something to you."

"It meant nothing to me at all."

"I believe it did. At Christmastide, Sir Bernard asked me whether you had read what was written on the cover. When he asked me, I evaded his question, because I remembered yours as you clapped eyes on the script. You asked me pointedly if the writing was my husband's."

"It wasn't a pointed question, just an idle one."

"I am not sure I believe you. At any rate, I now wish I had opened that letter. Because I think it would have explained why *he* is lying to me," she finished, with a catch in her voice.

Laurence blinked at her in astonishment. "Lying about what?"

"He claimed he was absent at Longstanton – oh, so many times, to me and to Walter," she replied, and told Laurence how his steward had informed her otherwise. "I should have confronted him straight out, this Christmastide. I was too cowardly. Instead I implored my brother to ask you what you knew. But he has not asked, has he?" Laurence shook his head. "A Mr. Poole, who is Sir Bernard's lawyer, called while we were at Richard's house, apparently to get his signature on some papers to do with the estate. Again he lied before Walter and me, saying he had been there. And he was not the same after Mr. Poole left, as though he had received bad tidings."

"About the estate?"

"That is one possibility," she said, darkly. "When Walter brought you to the house a few days ago, I made him promise to demand an answer from Sir Bernard. I have heard from neither him nor my husband since." She broke off, wringing her hands. "I am in such distress! I would rather my babe be stillborn, if –"

"*If?*"

"If he is hiding from me the truth – that he is in secret league with Parliament!"

Laurence started. "Good God. Why would you jump to such a conclusion?"

"Longstanton has been untouched by the rebel armies, when all the neighbouring households loyal to the King have suffered. Don't you find that peculiar?"

"Not necessarily –"

"And why was I only to read his letter when I could be certain of his death, if it did not hold some shocking revelation? Oh, if I still had it! But he asked for it back."

"Why didn't you read it after you spoke with his steward?"

"It was sealed. Sir Bernard would have found out." She was tugging at her wedding ring so violently that it flew off across the table, and Laurence had to retrieve it for her. "Mr. Beaumont, I have a strong feeling that what is in the coffer holds some clue to this mystery. And *that* is why he did not tell me about it! You must help me find it in the priest's hole, and open it for me."

"But you don't need my help," he said, though what he was about to suggest alarmed him. "Have your aunt fetch it for you."

"She is so interfering! She will want to know why I asked for it, against my husband's expressed wish. And what if my fears are confirmed?"

"Lady Radcliff, I don't even know where this priest's hole is —"

"Within a bedchamber on the third floor! There's a device some-where on the fireplace that you must press to spring the door."

"Can't you enter it by yourself?"

Her gaze faltered. "Please," she begged tremulously, "come. I – I *cannot* do it alone."

What to say, he thought. Should he refuse to assist her, she might yet screw up her courage and succeed where they had both failed. "Let me consider it," he told her; he must not sound too eager, since she was already suspicious of him. "I'm a guest in this house, and it does seem a bit dishonourable that I should invade your aunt's property without her permission. It's different for you."

She looked about to protest when, most fortuitously, he heard Madam Musgrave's loud voice calling his name, and the approaching clump of boots.

"Sir," his hostess cried, marching into the hall, "I require your help!" She was wearing a skirt of motley red and brown hue and a rough jerkin. The colours on her skirt were stains, of blood and dirt, and her face was streaked with sweat and more dirt. "My birthing skirt," she said, indicating the garment. "It brings me luck every year. Yet now my finest dairy cow is in calf, poor creature, too early in the spring for my liking. You must lend a hand – or an arm, to be precise."

"I'm so sorry," he said, "but I don't know anything about cows."

"After reading my *English Husbandman*? But that's of no import. Oh, do make haste, sir," Madam Musgrave said impatiently, and he had to obey, catching a stricken frown from Kate.

Madam Musgrave hurried him from the house, through the courtyard and into a barn by the dairy, where her cowman and a stable boy stood beside an enormous, supine cow, her belly swollen and heaving. "Nat, Sam, how is she?" she asked them.

"It's either her or the calf, ma'am – or even both, is what I fear," the cowman replied.

"We must have the calf out dead or alive. Don't you fret, Sam," she added kindly, to the boy, "Mr. Beaumont will reach it. See how long his arms are."

The cowman murmured approval. "I couldn't myself, sir." And he showed Laurence his own short, muscular arm, slimed up to the pit.

Laurence took a step back. He felt dizzy and nauseous, though he did not know why: he had seen far worse sights than a cow in labour.

"I'll not lose such a valuable beast on account of your squeamishness," Madam Musgrave told him. "Strip to the waist, or your clothes will be dirtied." Unbuttoning his doublet, he cast it away and drew off his shirt; he was swallowing, in a determined effort not to be sick. She pushed him down on his knees by the animal's nether parts, and ordered her cowman to lie on the front legs while she and Sam secured the rear ones. "Now, Mr. Beaumont, search for the hooves. Grab them and pull." He gazed at the cow's buttocks, filthy with excrement, and its opening, impossibly distended and raw. "Go on!" said Madam Musgrave. "Think of her as you would any woman about to bear a child. It's only nature, for Christ's sake." He shut his eyes and an image flashed before him, of Danvers' bloody mouth. "Do as I say, sir, or I shall kick your arse to kingdom come!" she yelled.

He curled the fingers of his left hand into a fist and plunged in. Further and further he reached, trying to keep his face from the ordure and to follow Madam Musgrave's instructions over the agonized lowing of the animal. Then he touched something small and hard, and another, and found a grip on them. He was afraid to pull too vigorously and eased his fingers higher to catch the legs.

"Go to it!" Madam Musgrave bellowed in his ear. "Pull, pull for all you're worth."

He pulled. Like a plug stuck in the neck of a bottle, the calf would not budge. He tugged again, his free hand on the cow's flank to provide resistance. The channel that encased his arm contracted, and he almost lost his slippery hold. There came more contractions and then, as though the plug had finally loosened, a surging motion towards him. Again, he pulled and pulled, and opened his eyes to see his upper arm emerge from the hole, sticky and red, and then his forearm, and his hand clutching a pair of spindly legs; and the calf came out in a massive gush of fluid, the fetal sac broken and glued to its body.

Aunt Musgrave slapped him on the back. "Well done, sir, well done!"

"But it's dead," said Laurence, overwhelmed by disappointment.

"Nay," the cowman said. He gathered the calf up and placed it before its mother, who began to lick it, and it stirred and made a noise. "Strong wee thing, naught wrong with her," he announced, as Madam Musgrave bent to admire it.

Laurence staggered up and went outside, shaken, and loath to inspect the mess on his arm. Yet when he did, he was not revolted, but foolishly pleased with himself.

"Mr. Beaumont," said Madam Musgrave, joining him a second later, "I've a mind to name that she-calf after you. What is your Christian name? I seem to have forgotten." Once he told her, she complained, "Can't make a girl's name of that. Beaumont's no better."

"Then why don't you call her Kate, after Lady Radcliff?" he suggested.

They began to laugh so much that Madam Musgrave had to wipe her eyes with her birthing skirt, leaving more streaks on her face. "With your aptitude for husbandry, sir, I think I shall put you to work in the fields," she said. "It will add meat to your bones and colour to your cheeks – and I need all the hands I can find." She must have seen him hesitate, for she added, with a playful smile, "Although if you think such labour beneath your dignity as a nobleman, I could always pack you off home."

"Of course it's not," Laurence said hastily. "I'll be glad to assist you however I can."

VI.

Radcliff's troop was preparing to ride out of Oxford as part of a contingent of about twelve thousand horse and dragoons, seven hundred foot, and carts loaded with six cannon, all under the command of Prince Rupert and Digby. They were to launch an attack on the small, ardently Parliamentarian town of Birmingham, some eighty odd miles away, which had generously provided fifteen thousand sword blades for the rebel army and supposedly still held a cache of plate stolen from His Majesty's baggage after Edgehill.

As dusk fell, Radcliff walked amongst his men, checking weapons and rounds of shot, noting the condition of their horses, and seeing to any arguments that arose in the distribution of supper. He was feeling oppressed from the sheer burden of what Pembroke had assigned him: to stop the leak, as Pembroke had so bluntly said. It was far too late for that, and Radcliff hoped Pembroke would understand that he was now on campaign, and could make no immediate progress. Meanwhile, Ingram had taken a short leave the week before; to solve a private issue, was all that he had told Radcliff. Since his return he had been oddly uncommunicative, apart from bringing news of Kate's pregnancy, which made Radcliff yet more nervous about his own future.

As he sat down by the campfire to eat the rations that Corporal Blunt had saved for him, Ingram was there filling a pipe. "Brother," Radcliff said, in his friendliest tone, "I cannot cease thinking about our Kate. I wonder if it will be a boy or a girl," he added, though he was fairly sure from her horoscope that their first child would be a son.

Ingram only grunted, puffing out a cloud of smoke.

"So tell me, what was this private issue that you disappeared to attend to?" Radcliff asked.

Ingram straightened and took the pipe from his mouth. "What about all the times *you* were away, Radcliff? Even the men have been talking. And you always give the same excuse."

"Because it's the truth."

"I know it's not. Before Christmas, while Kate was at Aunt Musgrave's, your steward called on her, to pay his respects –"

"My steward?" Radcliff interrupted, a shiver running along his spine. "Ah yes, he has family in the area. Why did she not mention this to me?"

"I'll get to that. He was very polite, she said, and most informative, as well." Ingram paused, scanning Radcliff's face. "He said you had not been to Longstanton in months. She couldn't understand your lying, and she was too fearful to ask you the reason for it."

"By Jesus!" Radcliff muttered. "When did she tell *you*?"

"At Richard's. The night your lawyer came by."

Radcliff's belly knotted. "Why have you waited so long to reveal this?"

"I hoped you would explain, of your own accord. But for her sake, I could wait no longer and nor can she. She'll make herself ill with worry, Radcliff."

Radcliff breathed a sigh. What evil fortune had cursed him for over a year; and now he could possibly lose the trust and love of his wife and

brother-in-law. He must give Ingram the same story that he had told
his lawyer, but if Beaumont had ever dropped any hints to Ingram
about his covert activities, the story might fail to convince.

"Ingram," he said, "would you respect a man for trying to do what
he believes is right, even if it places him in danger, or even disrepute?"

"I would."

"And you do respect me, don't you?"

"I always have. Are you that man?"

"Yes. And I shall explain, as far as I can, why I was forced to lie to
those I hold most dear." Radcliff sighed again, and began. "Many years
ago, after my university studies, I became secretary to a nobleman of great
prestige." Ingram frowned at this, though he did not speak. "I left his
employ because I believed all Englishmen should uphold the Protestant
cause abroad," Radcliff continued. "But when the schism widened
between King and Parliament, he wrote to me. He said he was attempting to find some means of reconciling them, in order to avert bloodshed.
He had sided with Parliament and could not work openly towards this
aim, so I agreed to assist him. After all I'd seen in the foreign war, I
thought he was justified, even if others might see his actions differently."

"As less than honest."

"Yes. Though in politics, honesty is not necessarily a virtue. There
you have it. I am his messenger, his emissary, if you like, to those
Royalists who might favour his plan. It was he who I had to meet,
whenever I went away."

From Ingram's expression, Radcliff knew that he was struggling,
both to understand and to accept what he had heard, although such
things went against his nature; and Radcliff loved him, in that moment,
more than ever before. How sad, Radcliff thought; it was like deceiving a child. "Who is he?" Ingram asked.

"That I cannot reveal. I took an oath of secrecy. As it is, I've told
you too much."

"Is he protecting Longstanton from Parliament?"

"Yes. So you see, I have much at stake, as have Kate and our babe." Radcliff took from his doublet the sealed letter to her and showed it to Ingram. "What I've said to you is written here. I had wanted to tell her the truth but only when it could not hurt her."

"If you can trust me, you can trust her. Send her the letter."

"It could be intercepted. My life may be forfeit, and my honour and my estate, if anyone else learns of what I am doing."

"Your life?" exclaimed Ingram, looking shocked.

"The best of intentions can appear treasonous at a time such as ours, and I am just small fry. My master would consider me worth sacrificing, if he believed that might save our country from destruction. And I cannot argue with him." *Pembroke is even ready to sacrifice Charles Stuart, King of England*, Radcliff added to himself; but the King's death was anyway fated. "Have I still your respect, brother?" he said, reaching for Ingram's hand.

Ingram squeezed his in return. "You do, but I wish you could break free of him, so that you had no need to lie to anyone. And I wish you would take Kate that letter as soon as you can."

"Then I shall go tomorrow after drill," Radcliff told him, "and be back before we set off for Birmingham the next morning."

Part Four

England, April–October 1643

CHAPTER SIXTEEN

"Mr. Beaumont, time to get up – we've work to do!" Madam Musgrave shouted, outside Laurence's door.

He struggled out of bed yawning, having scarcely slept. Kate had begged again for his help to get into the priest's hole, and after prevaricating a little he had agreed. Late into the night they had tried in vain to find the hidden mechanism. Although Kate never mentioned the ghost, she was quaking with fear, gasping and clutching his sleeve at the smallest noise. Weary of these histrionics and eager to get her out of the way in case he actually succeeded, he had told her to retire and let him continue alone. But he had enjoyed no better luck.

Downstairs, as he was taking a quick breakfast, Sam ran in flourishing a letter. "The carrier just brought it for you, sir, from Oxford," the boy told him importantly.

"Thank you, Sam," Laurence said, recognising Seward's neat, old-fashioned handwriting on the cover.

Sam was peeking at it. "Is that how your name looks, sir?"

"Yes. Can you read?" Sam blushed and shook his head. "Nothing to be ashamed of." Surreptitiously Laurence had fished a coin out of his pocket, and now he began to stare at Sam's rather prominent left ear. "What have you got there?" he inquired.

"Where, sir?" said Sam. Laurence touched his ear gently, produced the coin as if from thin air, and tossed it to him. Sam gazed at it, awestruck; then Laurence started to laugh and he followed suit. "How did you do that, sir?" he wanted to know.

"Magic," replied Laurence, with a shrug.

Sam looked anxious. "It won't vanish, sir, will it?"

"Not if you keep a close eye on it."

"Thank you, sir! Thank you!" said Sam, and he scampered off, while Laurence ripped open Seward's letter, which for once was not in their code.

Seward wrote that the trial of Colonel Hoare had opened five days earlier but was taking far longer than anyone had predicted, due to his dragging out rules of procedure and harassing witnesses so doggedly that he had been able to twist their testimony in his favour. He must be a more skilful lawyer than he was an interrogator, Laurence thought, surprised. Hoare had managed to cast a bad light on Captain Milne, offering evidence that the man had a grudge against him and was a habitual drunkard and a swindler. And Laurence's deposition had been ruled inadmissible, since Falkland had taken it without the presence of a neutral party. Hoare therefore demanded the right to question Laurence about his association with the Secretary of State and the demise of Charles Danvers. Hoare was also asking for all his own private documents, seized by Falkland upon his arrest. And now the trial had ground to a halt until Laurence Beaumont could testify in person. "You must come to Oxford at once," Seward concluded.

Just as Laurence finished reading, Madam Musgrave rushed in with an alarmed expression on her face. "Nat's arrived back from town to tell me that there are soldiers coming! They may be rebel troops! You must take one of my horses, sir, and flee."

"No – they might catch me on the road." He hesitated. "Why don't I hide in the priest's hole?"

"I suppose you could," she said dubiously.

"Please," he insisted. "And tell no one in your household where I am."

"Very well, sir. Gather whatever property you brought with you and meet me on the third floor."

He was already waiting for her at the head of the stairs as she plodded up carrying a flask, a wrapped bundle, and, with typical practicality, a chamber pot. In the bedchamber, she went over to the fire-place, but rather than operating some mechanism on the mantel, as he had expected, she pressed first at a panel on the nearby wall. It opened, to reveal a small lever. Kate had not known about this, he thought. Madam Musgrave turned it, and only then approached the mantel. She moved aside part of the carved stone, beneath which was a second lever. He held his breath in anticipation as she wound it clockwise. A large panel on that same wall suddenly slid back with miraculous ease.

"There's a staircase within," she said. "Count the steps as you go down. There are twelve, for the apostles of Jesus Christ, as I was told as a child." Brushing aside cobwebs, he lowered himself into the space, and descended the stairs. "Are you at the bottom, sir? Then feel to the left of you for a metal latch and push hard." He did, and a door creaked wide.

The priest's hole fitted between two walls. The ceiling was so low that he could not stand up straight, and the close, mouldy atmosphere reminded him unpleasantly of his cell in Oxford Castle. Without light he could not see a thing, though there was a draught from above; the place must somehow have been vented.

"It is not commodious, sir," Madam Musgrave yelled down. "The priests cannot have been as tall as you. Are you sure you wouldn't prefer to escape by horse?"

"No, this will be much safer," he called back.

"Come and I shall lower you these supplies." He stumbled up to the entrance, and she passed them to him. "I'll open up the panel and knock loudly when the danger has passed. Good luck to you, sir – and perhaps your wish shall be granted, and you'll have a spirit for company," she said, patting him on the shoulder. Then she gave him a lighted candle, to see his way down again.

Shut up in the hole, he appreciated her forethought: the flask was full of wine, and the bundle contained a loaf of bread and a hunk of cheese, and more candles. He sat on the floor and assessed his surroundings. Against all four walls were stacks of belongings. He began to rifle about. There were chests, none locked, that contained clothing layered with dried herbs to keep out moth, an ancient shield emblazoned with a faded coat of arms, and a broken spinning wheel. There was even some evidence left of the priest, for a wooden crucifix still hung on one wall with a silver Christ upon it, now blackened and almost indistinguishable, and amidst a pile of books Laurence found a Catholic missal, its pages glued with mildew.

Finally, in a corner behind a roll of bedclothes, he discovered a small, padlocked chest. He felt within his doublet for his knife to attack the lock, but realised that in the rush to hide he had left it behind in his chamber. He could not blow the lock open with his pistol; a shot would make too much noise. His candle guttered, and he lit another, gazing hungrily at the little coffer. Then he reached up and loosened the crucifix from the nail that held it to the wall. The thing was made not of silver but of some baser substance. He pried the Christ figure off easily, for the wood was partly rotten, and with his pistol butt bashed one of the outstretched hands into a more pointed form, to insert in the keyhole. It would not turn.

He stopped and took some wine. He was sweating, the room suddenly hot and oppressive. He removed his doublet and sat for a while, frustrated. Of course, he thought next, the *nail* would fit. He plucked it from the wall, ran it back and forth into the hunk of cheese to grease it thoroughly, then tried it in the lock. He had to light another candle, and after much fiddling and dropping the nail, and cursing as he hunted for it on the floor, he pushed it in again and found a slight purchase. He twisted it gently and heard a click, and the lock fell open.

He paused a moment to calm himself. The chest might only contain some of Madam Musgrave's treasures. But to his joy there were letters. The top few he recognised as those he had sold back to Joshua Poole. Beneath was a bundle of new correspondence, in the same code, in Pembroke's hand, which was all he could distinguish in such dim light. Digging deeper in the chest, he brought out a quill, some blank sheets of paper made of the same distinctive parchment as the letters, a bottle of ink and a seal without initials, and in a small velvet pouch, a pair of gold earrings. He took part of the blank sheaf of paper, calculating that it might come in useful, and tucked it away in his doublet with the correspondence, then put back the other items and shut the chest. Slipping the padlock back into place he checked to be sure it had locked and returned the chest to its former position.

Though giddy already, he drank off almost the whole flask. The conspiracy was foiled at last, he reflected, and his life could change after more than a year of being hounded and nearly murdered, and of endangering friends and family.

As the flame of his candle dwindled to a mere speck and flickered out, and as the wine began to work its way into his system, a lassitude born of sheer relief flooded over him. Closing his eyes, he curled up, his head on the roll of bedclothes, and dozed off.

He dreamt that he was walking with Khadija in the Alhambra Palace, her indigo robes rustling as she moved, and she was telling him a story about the end of Moorish rule in Granada. "One of its last kings fell in love with a Spanish slave girl," she was saying, "and she converted to his faith. She became his second wife. His first grew jealous and angry, thinking that her own son might not succeed to the throne."

"And the wives fought?" he asked.

"No. The King did, with his eldest son, who defeated him. Years later, the son was defeated by the Christians and forced to sign away his kingdom." Khadija turned to him, her face glowing. "The slave girl took a Muslim name when she married – Zoraya, the morning star. But her Christian name had been that of a queen."

Khadija now grasped him by the hand and led him in silence through the labyrinthine palace, past ornate columns and arches, their multicoloured tiles festooned with Arabic inscriptions, and then through endless, enormous rooms that grew more and more obscured by shadow; and he was afraid.

II.

He and Juana reached Granada in the blazing heat of early June with only one horse: he had had no choice but to shoot hers after it had broken a back leg. The animal's death unnerved him, as though it were an evil portent, for Juana was now questioning other travellers, many of them gypsies, as to the whereabouts of her family. He assumed from her disappointment that she had not yet gleaned any information.

In this southern city she was received with less prejudice, however, and they were able to buy a room at the largest inn, with a view of the Alhambra Palace in the distance. Looking out upon it, he could not help thinking sadly of his father, who had often talked to him of its colourful history when he was a boy.

In bed that night, he was visited by an insatiable lust, as if by filling Juana with himself he could bind her to him more tightly. At dawn, he opened his eyes to see her standing naked by the window, her interest attracted by some scene in the street below. She had put on weight: her ribs were hardly visible, her stomach curved where it had been hollow, and her breasts were fuller. She pressed both hands over her belly, smiling with such an air of private mystery that he felt excluded, and more terrified of losing her. As she turned about, he pretended sleep.

He heard her rummaging on the floor for her clothes, and dressing, and tiptoeing to the door. The latch squeaked open and shut, and he imagined her running down the stairs, out into the blinding sunshine. He waited, sweating beneath the thin sheets. Would she ever return, and what held him back from following her? But not long afterwards she burst back into the room, a jubilant smile on her face.

"My people are camped not far from Cadiz," she announced. "It will be some days' ride, so we must set out straight away if we wish to catch up with them. We must buy another horse – no, two good horses, to make faster progress." Jumping on the bed, she threw her arms about him. "Are you not glad for me?"

He did not answer.

During their journey, they had no intimate contact. She claimed that she was sore after their night in Granada, and he guessed that she was punishing him for it, as they travelled over the Sierra de Almijara, past Ronda, to Medina Sidonia, and further west still. Secretly he hoped that she had been given false directions, or that her people had moved on elsewhere. Then one evening, as dusk began to fall, they espied on the horizon a column of wagons and horses moving along the crest of a hill, lit by the red glare of sunset. Before he could stop her, she galloped across the plain to meet it. When she came abreast of the column's leader, they leapt from their mounts, and the fellow picked her up off her feet and spun her about so that her skirts danced in the breeze. Jealousy surged through Laurence: in all the time he had known her, he had been the only man that she had allowed to touch her. He spat his bile out on the sand, and stayed where he was.

At last Juana and her companion remounted and rode in his direction, the ragged column following them more slowly. Juana drew up, the fellow a pace behind her on a fine black stallion; he was holding it on a short rein, clearly unused to a horse of such mettle.

"Who is he?" Laurence asked her.

"My cousin, Pedro, also known as el Guerrero, for he fought in the wars like you," she replied.

He and Pedro inspected each other with mutual animosity until the rest of the column arrived: there were more men on horseback, women and children and bawling infants in carts drawn by emaciated donkeys, and a half dozen ill-assorted dogs, their coats full of mange. Even after his own experience of a vagabond's lot, Laurence found them a pitiful sight.

"And all these are my people," Juana declared proudly.

III.

A banging noise startled Laurence awake; he was in a state of acute sexual arousal, for the first time since his beatings. Comforted by this, despite the inconvenience, he scrambled over to open the door. Madam Musgrave's face was looking down at him through the small exit at the top of the stairs. "Sir! You can come out now!"

Willing his tumescence to subside, he stuck the bread, cheese, and flask into the empty chamber pot and handed them up to her. Then he went back for his own things and emerged, his doublet held strategically in front of him.

"Can you believe," she said, as she slid the panel back into place, "the troops went right past my house without stopping, and then who should arrive but Sir Bernard Radcliff!"

"Radcliff?" he repeated, his arousal quickly dissipating.

"Yes! He wanted to get in here straight away, to fetch his precious coffer! I managed to put him off for a bit so that he wouldn't find *you* instead. Goodness, you look pale, sir, though no wonder – you haven't had any fresh air for hours."

"Where is he?"

"With Kate, but I shall be calling them for supper shortly. Now go and wash off all that dust – there's hot water in your chamber."

Laurence thanked her and descended to his room, his heart beating wildly. He had just closed the door behind him when he heard a knock and Radcliff's voice. "Mr. Beaumont? May I enter?"

"In a moment, if you please," he responded, as he pulled out the letters and stuffed them under his mattress. Ripping off his doublet, which was covered in dust and cobwebs, he turned it inside out and threw it on the bed, took off his shirt and used it to clean his breeches. Then he went over to a side table, where a jug and basin stood waiting for him, and poured out some hot water. "Come in," he said, a little out of breath, starting to wash.

Radcliff entered, smiling affably. "How are you, sir? Aunt Musgrave told me you are here recovering from a dreadful ordeal at the hands of Lord Falkland's spymaster." When Laurence said nothing to this, he went on, "I trust you are feeling better?"

"I am, thanks," Laurence replied, busily soaping.

Radcliff indicated the bed. "May I sit?"

"If you like," said Laurence ungraciously, though he was tempted to smile as Radcliff settled himself there.

"It is a shame that I must set out again after supper," Radcliff said next. "My men are readying for a march tomorrow; Prince Rupert is to attack Birmingham. When did *you* arrive at the house?" he demanded, more bluntly.

"About a week ago. Why do you ask?"

Radcliff appeared to be making some mental calculation. "You must have been in very poor shape," he commented. Abruptly he rose and approached Laurence, studying him up and down, as though appraising his physique.

"If you don't mind, Radcliff," Laurence said, wishing he had kept on his shirt, "could we have this conversation after I finish my ablutions?"

"But we might not have another opportunity to speak together in private." Radcliff looked away, as if pensive. "Remember that summer day in Oxford when we first met? From all that Ingram had told me about you, I judged you to be the sort of fellow who cared only for wine and women. I have since revised my opinion. I now see your qualities, sir. You are admirably free of any hunger for power, or for the respect of others, which often amounts to the same thing. You are that rare creature, an *honest* man." They were both silent for a while, Laurence marvelling at Radcliff's effusive praise. "However," Radcliff resumed, in a less friendly tone, "I know you are not here for the reason you gave Madam Musgrave. I also know what you are up to, and what you suspect about *me*. But I should warn you that things may not be as they seem." He stopped once more, clearly waiting for Laurence to speak.

Laurence picked up the jug and tipped it over himself, splattering Radcliff's clothes, at which Radcliff had to jump back. "You should listen to me," he hissed angrily, flicking off the droplets. "I am not what you think I am."

"Really?" said Laurence, drying himself on a towel. "Then what *are* you? Another honest man?"

Radcliff looked about to answer when they were interrupted by Kate. "Sir Bernard, Aunt Musgrave is asking for you!" she called, from the door. Radcliff had left it ajar, and now it opened an inch or two, as though she might enter.

"Wait there for me, Kate – Mr. Beaumont is not decent," he said.

Nor are you, Laurence wanted to add.

"We *must* speak before I leave," Radcliff murmured to him, and walked out.

Laurence dressed and hastily brushed away more cobwebs and dust with the towel, then whipped open the door to see if Radcliff might be lingering outside. He had gone, but Kate was still there. "He has my letter," she whispered. "I saw it in his doublet pocket, while he was changing his shirt. And the seal is still intact!"

"What do you want me to do about that?" Laurence inquired

impatiently; he was hoping somehow to steal away from the house before supper.

"I must read it! Please help me get it from him!"

Laurence considered; he did not want Radcliff chasing him on the road to Oxford, and besides, the contents of her letter interested him. "We'll dose his wine at supper," he said. "I have a drug that will put him to sleep. Now go down at once and stay close to him. Don't let him out of your sight."

She nodded and ran off, without a word of thanks.

He retrieved the other letters, rolled them up tightly and concealed them in his doublet, then grabbed the vial of Seward's medicine from his bedside before descending to the kitchen. There he procured from the cook a thin-bladed knife of the kind used for filleting fish, and some thread, after which he joined Madam Musgrave's party at the fireside. She was exclaiming over the household's lucky escape from the soldiers on patrol. No one referred to his absence or where he had spent it, and he had to hope that Radcliff would not find out.

At table, he sat on Radcliff's right side. Opposite him, Kate picked at her food in the usual way, while Radcliff shovelled his down, obviously in a hurry. Laurence ate as slowly as Kate, longing for an opportunity to slip him the drug.

Madam Musgrave was in an ebullient mood. "Let's drink a health: to your coming child, Sir Bernard, and to the safety of my property," she said, motioning for her butler to serve them wine.

Laurence waited until the old man came between him and Radcliff to fill Radcliff's glass, then deliberately shot out an elbow, sending a cascade of wine across Radcliff's lap. "Oh, how clumsy of me!" he said, as Radcliff leapt up, glaring at him. "I'm terribly sorry," he added, and as the women fussed over Radcliff's sodden breeches, he dumped the contents of the vial into Radcliff's glass.

Radcliff was too distracted to notice, though Kate did; Laurence caught her fixing on the glass as she resumed her seat. He nudged her knee under the table, and she looked away.

"Drink up, everyone," Madam Musgrave encouraged them all, and Radcliff emptied his glass reluctantly, grimacing at the taste. Another round was poured, and she chattered on and on, as Laurence prayed that the drug would take effect before the end of the meal. "Mr. Beaumont," she said eventually, turning to him, "you did not tell me, where did you hone your skills at the gaming table?"

He shrugged and smiled. "Oh, here and abroad."

"Yes, Ingram informed me that you are a consummate cardsharp," said Radcliff, with leaden emphasis.

"Such fast fingers," Madam Musgrave said, through a mouthful of stew. "I told him he could make a living off it!"

"Perhaps he has," Radcliff murmured, rubbing his eyes.

"I did for a while," Laurence admitted.

"When was that, sir?" Kate asked, giving Laurence a kick under the table with the toe of her slipper; Radcliff had leant back in his chair and was stifling a yawn.

Laurence kicked her back somewhat harder. "In between campaigns, when I was abroad."

"How curious that both you and Sir Bernard fought over there and yet you never once encountered each other," Madam Musgrave said to him, waving to the butler for a third round.

"I believe Sir Bernard was in the Dutch service," Laurence said, as the butler refilled their glasses. "I fought mainly with the Germans. Though it *is* strange that we didn't cross paths." He gave Radcliff a sidelong glance. "Especially in The Hague, which was where most of us went during the winter months."

Radcliff appeared not to be listening; his eyelids drooped promisingly.

"Sir Bernard, were you much in The Hague?" she asked.

"What, madam?" he said, shaking his head as if to clear it; he was beginning to struggle, Laurence knew.

"In The Hague, sir," she shouted, as though to a deaf person.

Radcliff blinked, and half rose. "Please excuse me . . . I must go up and prepare for my journey."

"You have plenty of time to get back to Oxford before dawn. Stay a while before you ride out."

"Madam, I cannot," he told her, one hand on the table to steady himself. Then he almost fell, clawing at the back of his chair.

"Sir Bernard, what is the matter?" she inquired. "Do you feel unwell?"

"I . . . I must have taken too much wine."

"I think you should rest for a while, sir," she advised, as he staggered to his feet. "It would be dangerous to ride in your condition."

"Yes, sir," Kate joined in solicitously. "Just sleep for an hour or two and you will feel much improved." Radcliff said nothing; he was tottering about like a drunk. She rushed to her husband's side. "Mr. Beaumont, he needs support! Can you take his other side?" Laurence obliged, and together they steered him towards the stairs and up to her chamber.

"I might be sick," Radcliff muttered, slumping back on the bed. "Give me the pot."

Kate fetched it, but his eyes had already closed.

"Help me lift him so we can take off his doublet," Laurence told her. When this was done, he shook Radcliff by the arms. "Wake up," he urged, "wake up." Kate had retreated into a dark corner, clutching the doublet. Laurence shook him more roughly, to no response.

Kate returned to the bedside, indicating to Laurence that she had the letter, and they hurried out. "Your drug must be very strong," she whispered anxiously. "Are you sure you didn't give him too much?"

"He'll be fine, though he may sleep for longer than a couple of hours," Laurence replied, in fact not at all sure whether the dose was safe. It would be quite a setback if Radcliff were poisoned before Falkland could arrest him.

"What now?"

"I have to break this seal. Go down and tell your aunt that you're staying with him because he feels sick. Then check on him again before you knock on my door."

Back in his own chamber, Laurence heated the knife's thin blade in the flame of a candle and then ran it under one edge of the seal until the wax began to soften, at which point he inserted the thread beneath it. Alternating between knife and thread, he peeled the wax off in one piece. It left a roundish stain.

He opened the letter. First were the expected details about Radcliff's property at Longstanton, and the arrangements to be made for his funeral and burial in the village church should the circumstances of his death permit. Kate was to send for his lawyer, Mr. Joshua Poole, who had offices off Fleet Street in London, and whom she could trust to attend her in her widowhood. Radcliff wrote next that he had been forced into the service of a nobleman who had once employed him, and who was trying to bring the King to agree to a secret settlement that would end the war. Radcliff had hidden this from her and her family, and if the whole affair were prematurely exposed, he added, some might even see him as a traitor. But whatever she might hear of him, he had died so that other Englishmen could live, and his marriage to her had been the greatest joy of his life. He commended her, and any issue that might have come of their union, to her brothers' care. And in a last paragraph, he mentioned a coffer that Madam Musgrave was keeping for him in the priest's hole. Upon his death, Kate must open it and burn whatever papers she found there.

A pity that Radcliff had not been explicit about Pembroke's identity, Laurence thought, but in any case the letter was no use as evidence, for here was the same expurgated version of the plot that must have been told to Joshua Poole.

He heard Kate knocking and bade her enter.

"He's dead to the world," she said, looking pleased; but when Laurence handed her the open letter, she frowned. "Did you read it?"

"Lady Radcliff, I have *some* honour," Laurence retorted. She read it herself and afterwards seemed bewildered. "Well?" he asked.

"He is not what I feared," she said, in a guarded tone.

"Then give it to me and I'll put back the seal." He warmed the knife again and with it replaced the fragile circle of wax, as she watched closely.

"It's absolutely perfect," she exclaimed when he had finished. "How did you learn to do that?" He said nothing. "You have gone to such pains for me. Why?" She was beginning to smile; and he knew what was on her mind. As did most beautiful women, she assumed that he would be drawn to her as a fly to jam. She did not want him, but she wanted to be secure in her powers of attraction.

"To allay your worries," he said blandly. "Now go and put that letter away where you found it. And you should stay with your husband, in case he *does* get sick – he might choke on his own vomit."

She hesitated, as if unsure whether to thank him or to take umbrage at his advice. In the end she did neither and simply left the room. He waited only a short time before snatching up his cloak and few possessions and letting himself out quietly.

Downstairs Madam Musgrave was still sitting at the table. "Such a disappointing conclusion to our party!" she said. "Sir Bernard has no head for liquor."

"It happens to us all occasionally," he remarked.

"At least I can count on you to keep me –" She broke off, seeing the cloak over his arm. "Do you have to go out somewhere, sir?"

"Yes. To Oxford, on urgent business."

"Ah. Has it to do with the letter you received this morning?" He nodded. "I shall ask no more questions, sir." She got up from her chair, then drew closer to him and whispered, "But – you may not know – Sir Bernard is full of questions about *you*. It may be that he was just a trifle anxious for his wife's virtue, while you were here. I happen to remember my nephew saying that you never had much respect for marriage vows, if a woman took your fancy."

"How indiscreet of him to mention that," Laurence said, laughing, and nearly added that, with respect to Kate, Sir Bernard had absolutely no need for concern. "Madam, might I borrow a horse from your stable? I'll see it's brought back to you soon."

"Of course, though I'm afraid you won't like your choice of mounts, sir; our Robber Prince stole the best of them."

"Thank you." He took her hand and kissed it. "And thank you for everything you've done for me. If ever there's anything I can do for you in return . . ."

"You owe me another visit, sir." She enveloped him in a bear-like embrace and kissed him on both cheeks. "I have grown most fond of you, and I pray that we shall soon be related by marriage!"

"By marriage?" Laurence echoed, wondering exactly how fond of him she had become.

"Yes! Walter confessed to me that he is head over heels for your sister Anne."

Laurence burst out laughing again. "Why didn't he tell me?"

"He's afraid your family would not have him. Now, I ask you to keep this to yourself for the present, but I intend to leave him my estate, so that he can marry as he wishes and won't have to go begging crumbs from Richard's table. So if your sister is agreed, but your family poses an objection, you may explain to them what I have in mind."

"She'd better agree, or I'll be very disappointed in her," Laurence said warmly, as Madam Musgrave saw him to the door.

IV.

Radcliff stirred awake, a sour taste in his mouth. He was lying alone on the bed fully dressed, though his boots had been removed. Only vaguely could he recall Beaumont and Kate carrying him upstairs the night before. How had he become so intoxicated by a few cups of wine?

Clambering off the bed, he went to the window, which looked out over Madam Musgrave's kitchen garden, and saw her bent double, rump in the air, planting some seedlings in the ground. The day was bright, with soft white clouds scudding across the sky. Opening the casement, he called down, "Aunt Musgrave, what hour is it?"

She straightened, massaging her back. "It must be about eleven of the clock, Sir Bernard. No headache, I trust?"

"No, madam. Pardon me for yesterday evening," he added, hoping that she might enlighten him as to whether he had disgraced himself.

"It must have been fatigue," she said generously.

"Whatever it was, it has passed, thank God. I have to leave soon. I shall come down shortly, to say goodbye."

He sat back on the edge of his bed, about to put on his boots. Then he noticed the stains on his breeches, and recalled Beaumont spilling the wine, and the odd taste of his own first glass. Panic gripped him. He threw aside the boots, grabbed a candle, and raced upstairs to the third floor, along the corridor, and into the last chamber. His hand shook as he manoeuvred the levers that opened the priest's hole. Lighting the candle, he stepped inside, then hastened down the stairs and through the door to the hiding place. It took him only a moment to find his coffer, where he had left it last autumn, and he felt somewhat less alarmed until he tried his key in the lock, which did not turn with its normal facility. When eventually it clicked open, he reached within, and his fingers met the crisp texture of parchment. Too crisp for his much handled letters, he realised, swinging back the lid. And as he looked inside, he saw that Beaumont had taken all of them.

He tore out of the hole, not bothering to close it, and ran down the three flights of stairs, nearly slipping in his haste, to the kitchen. Pushing past the cook and the potboy, he rushed into the garden beyond.

"Madam Musgrave!" he shouted.

"She's not there, sir, she's in the courtyard," the cook said, giving him a perturbed look.

He hurried back into the house and through the front door, his breath burning in his chest, to find Madam Musgrave talking with the stable boy, Sam, who was in tears.

"Now you stop that, little fellow," she was saying. "I'm sure he would have liked to say goodbye to you, but you were abed long before he rode out."

Radcliff inhaled deeply, to control his voice. "Madam Musgrave," he said, "has Mr. Beaumont left this house?"

She turned to him, her eyes widening as she surveyed his face and stockinged feet. "Why, yes, Sir Bernard, last night. He had some business in Oxford. My dear sir, you must be coming down with an ague!" she cried next. "What on earth –"

"Where is my wife?" Radcliff snapped. When she did not answer at once, he marched into the house and started yelling Kate's name.

Kate emerged from the hall. "Sir Bernard, you are awake! Are you –"

He did not give her time to finish, seizing her by the wrist and dragging her upstairs, and into their chamber, slamming the door after them. She was cowering, as though afraid he might do her violence. "Sit down, Kate," he ordered, trying to sound gentler. "I have a great deal to tell you, so please do not interrupt. I shall start from the beginning. Your brother told me about my steward's visit here. I did lie to you, as you know. Now I shall tell you the truth, but you must promise me that you will keep it secret, for the sake of your life, mine, and that of our child." After she had pledged her word, he launched into the story that he had recounted to Ingram. "My love," he said, at the end, "you remember my letter, that you did not open?" She nodded, trembling, as he took it from his doublet. "I want you to read it." She broke the seal, and obeyed, glancing up at him from time to time with the same frightened air. "You will note my directions about the papers: where I had stored them, and what to do with them in case of my death," he went on, as she raised her eyes to him again. "These documents are missing. They could utterly ruin me if they were made public."

"Who could have taken them?"

"Mr. Beaumont did – last night, after he put me into a drugged stupor."

"Mr. Beaumont?" She shook her head from side to side. "But – but what would he want with them?"

"He is an agent of the Secretary of State."

"No, it cannot be! Oh," she exclaimed more hotly, "he is despicable! Beyond despicable!" She gasped. "So that was why! Soon after he arrived, he got up and came downstairs, though I had been given to understand he was so very ill. And that first evening, he asked Aunt Musgrave about the priest's hole! She must have showed him how to get into it without telling me! Sir Bernard, what will you do?" she concluded, in a despairing voice.

"Go after him and get my letters back," Radcliff said, though he knew this would be impossible; by now, Beaumont must have delivered them to Falkland.

V.

"Let me have a look at one of those blank sheets," Seward said, as he and Laurence sat at his desk poring over their transcriptions of the letters.

"Is this like scrying?" Laurence asked, as Seward examined the paper with avid concentration. "Can you see something that I can't?"

"We should have caught such a simple device." Seward held the page over the flame of his candle and a pattern blossomed slowly upon it. "Look, roses adorned with drops of dew, or of blood, aligned in the shape of a cross just as on the sword. The symbol Radcliff and Pembroke stole from the Knights of the Rosy Cross. More secure than a signature, which they need never put to any of the letters. And they would always be sure of their correspondent. If the paper did not have the mark, they could tell it for a forgery."

"Ah," said Laurence. "Thank you so much for explaining."

Seward swatted at him with the page, then sat back to fill a pipe. "Let us review what we now know from the first set of letters we transcribed and the new ones you found in the chest. You may start."

"Pembroke has three safe houses, one near Reading, one in Oxford, and one close to his estate at Wilton. His plan is to take the King on a hunting expedition. The King is accidentally killed. The Queen is given a choice: exile or acceptance of the new regime, under the rule of her son."

"A neat operation, to remove the head and leave the body intact."

"Oh, come, Seward," Laurence protested, "who'd believe the King's death was an accident? Certainly not the Queen. It's well known that she hates Pembroke."

"There will be witnesses, Beaumont, reliable ones who saw it happen. And the assassin won't be left to tell tales. Think of the shock and sorrow it will cause. All Englishmen will temporarily forget their quarrels and unite to mourn His Majesty. Pembroke will emerge as the architect of a new harmony between Parliament and young King Charles II. England will be restored to its full, Protestant glory and Pembroke can shift his ambitions to the continent." Seward drew on his pipe before continuing. "As to the other conspirators, apart from Radcliff there's reference to a courier, who must have been Robinson, and to a lawyer, who must be Poole, and to Radcliff's servant, Tyler.

THE BEST OF MEN 5 3 3

There may be more working for Pembroke, though I would say very few."

"There *must* be more. He'd need a private army to seize power."

"He cannot depend solely on force. I would guess that he is doing precisely what he told Falkland: building an alliance of supporters in Parliament and in Oxford. Falkland would be especially useful in gaining their confidence. If a sufficient number are won over, then Pembroke can choose the moment, propitiously, with Radcliff's astrological guidance, to lay his peace proposals before His Majesty. He may even have entered into some secret pact with the King, to facilitate the deception."

"But it's *all* deception."

"Not entirely. It lays the ground for what Pembroke hopes will follow. Suppose there is a truce, and he invites the King to hunt at Wilton. Or the war carries on, and he takes the King out somewhere near his safe house in Oxford. Naturally Earle is vital here to draw Prince Charles into the net, to separate him temporarily from his father so that the murder can be done."

"I'm not convinced," Laurence said, shaking his head. "It all seems so . . . fallible. And why would he put all his trust in Radcliff, when the man could so easily betray him, and indeed may have been planning to, all along?"

"Radcliff can be persuasive. He won me over, for a time."

"Well *I* never liked him."

"You wouldn't," Seward said dryly. "He is not your sort – too proper a gentleman by far."

"And I bet Pembroke doesn't trust him any more."

"Pembroke may have accused Radcliff of treachery as soon as he saw the painting. He may also feel threatened on another front. While you were in Faringdon he came here to Oxford again, with the other delegates from Parliament. He met with both Earle and Falkland, who have since told me that he urged them more forcefully to join his secret alliance. Earle refused outright, as I had advised him. Falkland was less adamant, yet unenthusiastic."

"We should keep Pembroke guessing. If he knows we're on his scent, he could sail for the continent and take refuge there for as long as he had to, and if Parliament were to win this war, he'd return with no damage done to his reputation."

"Yes, I quite agree with you. Beaumont," Seward went on, in a speculative tone, "what if Radcliff is really about to turn him in?"

"That's what Radcliff is bound to claim, once he's arrested. It's his only way out of a traitor's death – if I haven't already killed him with that drug of yours."

"No, no. It may give him a bellyache, but no more."

Laurence sighed and yawned, stretching. "God, I'm tired. So what's happening here in Oxford? I want to be prepared before I see Falkland tomorrow."

"Hoare's still being a menace in the courtroom," replied Seward. "He is arguing that Danvers died of shock and that the murder charge is utterly spurious. And your brother has yet to testify. Hoare may be pinning on him the hope of impugning Falkland's good name *and* yours, needless to add."

"Has Hoare mentioned the conspiracy yet?"

"Oh yes. In his opening speech he claimed it as part of his justification for interrogating you. He said he would introduce as evidence the transcriptions you made of those first coded letters, and a record he kept of your meetings."

"We have to make sure Hoare can't use any of this in court. Pembroke may be watching the trial – from a distance, of course. We don't want him getting too interested."

They both mused over this, then Seward said softly, "I am delighted to see you on form again, my boy."

"I am for the most part, though I haven't got my full strength back."

"It will come, God willing." Seward cleared his throat. "I should alert you as to some other news. Mistress Savage knows about the uprising, from Digby. She told me that –"

"When did you last see her?" Laurence interjected.

"At Hoare's trial. She says the revolt will happen in May. A Commission of Array will be smuggled into London, to set it off. Waller is involved, and Falkland will take charge of all correspondence between Oxford and London. She believes Falkland may ask you to assist him in these communications."

Laurence groaned. "I suppose I'll have to."

"You virtually begged to fill Hoare's shoes when you gave his lordship your deposition."

"Yes, but first he *must* deal with the regicides." Laurence hesitated, fingering the blank sheet of paper. "Did she tell you where she's lodged?"

"I presume you refer to Mistress Savage. She is still at the Blue Boar."

"Once I've delivered the letters to Falkland, I'll go and see her."

"Can you not wait until the end of the trial?"

"Why should I?"

Seward did not answer immediately, puffing away on his pipe. "From what I know of her, she could be a dangerous woman," he said at last, through a cloud of smoke. "I hope you're not cherishing any amorous feelings for her. Or lustful ones, either," he concluded, beetling his brows at Laurence.

VI.

"You did it, sir!" Falkland exclaimed, as he scanned the letters. "I'm completely amazed!"

"I had some luck," Beaumont said, with one of his charming smiles. "So," he went on briskly, "Radcliff has probably rejoined his troop and is moving north towards Birmingham. If you give me a small company of men, we could bring him back to Oxford within the next couple of days."

Falkland sighed, inspecting him. Though slightly gaunt and sallow in complexion, he seemed untouched by his ordeal in Oxford Castle, apart from the scars on his face. Yet Falkland remembered him lying outside that noisome cell, bloodied and barely alive. How resilient he was, Falkland thought, a little enviously. "I know you are eager for an arrest, sir," he said, "but circumstances have altered since your return, and although we are not having much joy of our current negotiations with Parliament, we might prejudice them if we were to make any startling announcements – or arrests."

Beaumont screwed up his eyes as if he could not credit what he had just heard. "What are you saying?"

"Just that. We have to wait."

"But you wanted Radcliff detained last year and I asked you to hold off until I could find evidence of his guilt! Now we have it – there's nothing to stop you. He can give you all the answers, which you'll certainly require before you take in Pembroke."

"I would act, sir, but it is His Majesty's request that we delay."

Beaumont's expression changed to one of combined outrage and disgust. "It's *his* life that's at stake here! How much more urgent can this matter be?"

"Nevertheless, it is complicated. He refuses to believe the man is a regicide."

"Show him the letters! They're in Pembroke's hand!"

"There is no signature on them. They might be forgeries."

"Pembroke's mark is on the paper."

"You have no proof that it *is* his mark."

"Oh for God's sake! We'll get a confession from Radcliff!"

"How could we be sure it was the truth? He might be lying to save his life."

Beaumont laughed scornfully. "How many men have been con-demned in half an hour on less evidence than we have before us?"

"I have to agree with you on that," Falkland said. "Which brings me to the main reason for the King's delay. The memory of the Earl of Strafford's fate still haunts him. In signing the earl's death warrant, he sent to the block a faithful servant. Pembroke is yet more to him: a close friend, beloved by his father, who has sworn never to take up arms against him."

"And we know why," Beaumont said, in a furious whisper. "To dupe the King into trusting him!"

"Yes, but His Majesty will not be moved. As long as the supposed conspirators are under watch, he says he is not afraid of them. And in any case, my hands are tied until the middle of May."

"When the Commission of Array will be proclaimed in London." Beaumont swore rather inventively under his breath. "If London were truly so strong for the King," he said next, "don't you think it would have risen last year after Edgehill, when his army got as far as Reading?"

"As I told you, much has changed of late. There is discontent in many quarters. The citizens are rebelling against the exorbitant taxes they must pay to support the army, and are openly accusing the radi-cals in Parliament of feathering their own nests with the proceeds. And then they are complaining about the destruction wrought by Puritan vandals to so many buildings in the capital –"

"Every time His Majesty has been caught trying to pull the wool over Parliament's eyes, the citizens of London have rallied behind their leaders," Beaumont interrupted. "The date he's chosen is well over a month away, too long to keep a secret, which is not that secret as it is. Parliament has an efficient web of spies." Falkland nodded resignedly. "And wouldn't it strengthen his chances of success in London, if he could show that one of the chief negotiators in Parliament had designs on his life?"

"Without more proof he will not consider that an option. Please, sir, may we close this topic and turn to another?"

"Yes, my lord," Beaumont said, with an exasperated sigh.

"Tomorrow Hoare will call you as a witness. How do you propose to handle the questioning?"

Beaumont smiled, deviously this time. "You have all his private documents, don't you, and my transcription of the first letters." From the confusion on his desk, Falkland pulled out a leather book and a roll of dog-eared papers in Beaumont's scrawling hand. Beaumont flicked quickly through the book. "Pembroke knows that someone's on his tail, but he mustn't find out who, or how close we are – he could easily escape us. Naturally he'll be interested in this trial, since Hoare has talked about a conspiracy to regicide. So I intend to deny that the plot ever existed."

"But that would mean lying under oath!"

"That's right. And we must stop him getting his hands on any of this evidence. With nothing to support his claim, he'll be sunk," said Beaumont, slapping the book down on the table with a loud thump.

Falkland almost laughed at the bold-faced daring of his strategy. "How can we do that?"

"These are state secrets, my lord. The King must understand that we can't have the conspiracy broadcasted about while Pembroke and Radcliff are still free. Deny Hoare's records to the court on His Majesty's authority. And I think, before tomorrow, that you should pay a visit on Hoare."

"To what end?"

"To tell him he has no case. Let him sweat with fear until the morning."

"But his guards will bear witness that he questioned you about the conspiracy!"

"If you remember, I told him nothing."

"They went to Aylesbury with you, to arrest Poole!"

"Yes, but they knew no more than that he was a criminal of some sort and that we were ordered to bring him in. And anyway, they're slavishly loyal to Hoare; they're bound to tell his version of the story. Without evidence, their testimony won't stand up against mine. They're only commoners, my lord," Beaumont added, facetiously. "Well, do we have a plan?"

Falkland nodded, his stomach churning at the risks involved. "I shall have to speak to the King. If he is agreed, I could go to the gaol this evening."

"You might take the judge with you, so you can't be accused of subverting the course of justice," Beaumont said, with the same devious smile.

"I shall." Falkland began to smile also. "Mr. Beaumont, I hate to nag you about such a trivial thing, but could you please make sure that you are dressed appropriately for your appearance in court?"

"Don't worry, my lord – I've already enlisted the services of a tailor."

"Then tell him to send me the bill," Falkland said.

VII.

After his audience with Falkland, Laurence went immediately to the Blue Boar, and bounded upstairs to Isabella's chamber. The door stood wide open, revealing a servant on her knees scrubbing the floor. "Mistress Savage has moved to rooms downstairs," she said, on his inquiry, and told him where to find them.

He thanked her. About to go, he walked over to the window and looked down to the alleyway. In daylight, he could see the drop. Isabella had been right: he might easily have broken his neck before Hoare captured him.

He followed the servant's instructions to a door off the main taproom, and with slight disappointment heard a male voice within;

Isabella was not alone. He knocked, and after a while a man opened. He was a little shorter than Laurence and blond, his moustache and beard reddish in colour. His face, good-looking in the way of northern Englishmen with Viking blood, was lightly pitted. Had Laurence been introduced to him abroad, he would have taken him for a Swede. "You must be Mr. Beaumont!" the man said, smiling. "I'm Captain Milne. We were to meet, on Christmas Eve."

"Ah yes," Laurence said. "Pleased to make your acquaintance."

Milne waved him into the room, which was a small parlour with another door off it. In the room was a table covered in jugs and bottles, and Laurence guessed from Milne's speech and relaxed deportment that he must have been imbibing. Isabella, who had been seated at the table, rose to curtsey. Her cheeks had an unnatural colour to them, of rouge; and in her eyes, dark and shining like wet glass, Laurence read no welcome, but a strange, dispirited expression, as if she were not happy at all to see him.

"Mr. Beaumont," she said, in her husky drawl, "how good it is that you are so recovered."

"Yes, I heard the Colonel gave you some pretty hard knocks!" guffawed Milne.

"And how are you?" Laurence asked her.

"Oh, the same as ever," she replied, with a smile so manifestly fake that it wounded him.

Milne came over to her and patted her on the rear. "My sweet lady and I were having a little drink. Won't you join us, sir?" Laurence did not respond, busy stifling his rage, though he knew it was unfair. Milne seemed oblivious, pulling out a chair for him and searching amongst the jugs. "Damn it, my love, we've finished every drop! Wait here with her, Mr. Beaumont, and I shall fetch some more from that cheapskate tavern keeper." And he departed whistling, a jug in either hand.

"What are you doing with him?" Laurence demanded at once, as equably as he could.

"That should be obvious, to a man of your experience," she said, sitting down again.

He hesitated, examining her. "I . . . I came here to thank you. I know you went to the Castle with Falkland, that day I was freed."

"Yes I did – just to see the look on Colonel Hoare's face when Falkland arrested him," she said, with her hard laugh. "It was well worth my trouble!"

He nodded, and there was another silence between them. "Isabella, you don't have to stay with Milne," he blurted out. "You . . . you can't *like* his company."

"You mean that I should prefer yours?"

He felt himself flush. "I wouldn't be so presumptuous."

"You have been in the past." She sighed, fiddling with one of her earrings. "Well, Mr. Beaumont, I accept your thanks. Is there anything else you have to say, before you leave?"

He gazed at her, wishing she would show some emotion towards him other than indifference, but she was behaving as if he were not there at all. "No," he told her, at length. "Good day, Isabella." And he bowed to her, and walked out.

In the taproom, he bumped into Milne returning with the wine. "Going so soon?" Milne said cheerily.

"I forgot I had an appointment," said Laurence, trying to pass him by.

"But I'd like a quick word with you first, about the trial. Come, over here." Milne steered him to a nearby table and they sat down. "I suppose you're aware that Hoare's done all he can to discredit me," Milne began. "I'm glad you can bear witness to his evil deeds. You must be itching for revenge, as am I."

"What's your quarrel with him?" Laurence asked, although he was not especially interested to hear.

"He made a fool of me, in front of the rest of his guard. I nearly challenged him to a duel, there and then," Milne declared, with a proud toss of his head.

"Why didn't you?"

"He would have had me shot for insubordination. And now he's defamed my good name in court. Still, he's the prisoner, and we shall get to spit on him after he hangs." He leant back, squinting at Laurence. "Are you a close friend of Isabella's?"

"No."

"Hmm. I had wondered if you were her lover, in the past." Laurence did not grace this with an answer. "Well let me tell you," Milne confided, "she's got a wonderful talent for grasping things as they stand."

"What things?" Laurence said, wanting to slap him.

"The *affairs* of men," he sniggered; then he modified his tone. "When this trial is over, we must all celebrate together – you and me and Isabella, and Digby and Falkland, of course. She'll take me far, I can already see," he said, grinning up at the taproom's smoke-stained ceiling. "Not that I don't deserve it; I've paid my dues, believe me. You wouldn't understand, being so highly born, how life is for the rest of us. That's the whim of Fortune for you. But since Fortune's a woman, as they say, a man can always have the advantage of her. It's what I aim to do, upon my soul."

"I wish you the very best of luck." Laurence got up from the table, for if he had to listen to any more about Milne's future prospects, he would have felt inclined to curtail them altogether. "Now you must excuse me."

As he strode off, he heard Milne shout after him, "See you in court, sir, and mind you give the bastard his just deserts!"

CHAPTER SEVENTEEN

I.

Seward arrived in court anticipating a tense session, although Beaumont had insisted that all would go well. He was looking astonishingly smart in a new suit of black clothes, which Seward had admired earlier.

"Paid for by the Secretary of State – but I chose the colour," Beaumont had informed him, with a smile.

The judge ordered the prisoner to be brought forth, amidst much whispering and some jeers from the public benches. Hoare's linen was soiled and his beard needed trimming, yet he wore the same proud, impassive expression that he had maintained throughout. Beaumont was then summoned and sworn in; while respectful, he wore an air of aristocratic hauteur quite unlike his customary demeanour.

"Mr. Beaumont," commenced the lawyer for the prosecution, "according to your deposition, you were too ill to attend the trial until today as a consequence of the severe tortures inflicted upon you by the accused. Is that so?"

"It is," Beaumont said calmly.

"The accused has stated that you were employed by him, with the full knowledge and agreement of my Lord Falkland, to assist them both in gathering covert information. Is this true?"

"No. But I have on occasion offered some advice, to the Secretary of State alone."

"The accused has averred that, in September of last year, you gave my Lord Falkland some documents obtained by you abroad containing evidence of a conspiracy against the life of His Majesty, and that his lordship employed you to find the conspirators. Is this so?"

"Colonel Hoare is very attached to conspiracies, most of them imaginary," Beaumont replied, with unconcealed contempt. "In this case, he has constructed one against the Secretary of State. He would fabricate any lie to have Lord Falkland removed from office."

"A slanderous accusation!" Hoare interrupted, but the judge silenced him.

"Why should he desire the removal of my Lord Falkland?" the lawyer asked.

"Because he detests it that his lordship wishes to save the lives of our countrymen by bringing a negotiated settlement to the war – as His Majesty also wishes," Beaumont added.

"Now pray answer me directly, sir. Is Colonel Hoare's claim false?"

"As false as he is himself."

"It is *he* who is false!" yelled Hoare, glaring incredulously at Beaumont.

"He has claimed further that you were helping his lordship in private negotiations with some members of Parliament," the prosecutor continued. "Is there any truth to *this*?"

"None whatsoever."

"Even under torture, you did not admit to involvement in any such thing?"

"No I did not, as the accused can attest."

"Yet he says that he has evidence not only of the conspiracy but also of these other private dealings."

"Then I should very much like to see it."

"Do you hold the accused guilty of the murder of Charles Danvers?"

"Yes," said Beaumont, looking at Hoare for the first time.

"Sir, has my Lord Falkland tried in any way to influence your testimony?"

"In no way."

"You are not seeking to protect him, because of the friendship he has with your father, Lord Beaumont?"

"He does not need my protection. He is completely innocent of any wrongdoing," Beaumont answered flatly.

"I thank you, Mr. Beaumont," the lawyer said.

So far, so good, thought Seward. From the rumblings of the spectators, he could tell that they were on Beaumont's side.

It was now the prisoner's turn to question the witness. "Mr. Beaumont," said Hoare, "may I remind you that you are under oath. Do you honestly deny that I employed you to investigate the conspiracy to which you alerted myself and my Lord Falkland?"

"I do," Beaumont said, with the merest impatience, "because there *was* no conspiracy."

"I shall provide the court with ample proof that you are lying, and that I most certainly employed you as one of my agents. Did you not urge Lord Falkland to mistrust me?"

"Yes, I did."

"Why?"

"I think I have explained to the court why he had every reason to beware of you."

"So you were working to undermine my authority, and my position, as his servant."

"Oh no," said Beaumont. "I believe you were doing that work all by yourself."

Careful, boy, don't get too cocky, Seward warned him mutely, hearing muffled laughter from the galleries.

Hoare blinked and shuffled his notes. "During your years abroad," he recommenced, "did you not fight first with the Spanish army, and then turn coat to fight with the Dutch, and then with the Germans, from whom you also gained employment as a spy?"

"Yes, I did."

"Not a great example of your probity, is it," Hoare observed.

"I have not hidden my past from anyone."

"Are you not ashamed of it, sir?"

"Of which part should I be ashamed?" Beaumont inquired, raising his eyebrows.

"Of turning coat, sir!"

Beaumont cast him a bemused look. "Since you have in your regiment a number of men who fought with the Spanish, *that* can hardly be accounted a crime. Later I made a moral decision to shift my allegiance, once persuaded that the Protestant cause deserved it more. And unless you would condemn yourself as well as me, I see no shame in collecting intelligence for an army in the field."

"A *moral* decision?" Hoare repeated. "You would speak to me of morals, when you have none?"

"Colonel Hoare," said the judge, "who is under question here, you or this witness?"

"My lord, I am simply attempting to suggest that his testimony is not to be relied upon. Mr. Beaumont," Hoare went on, "after *deserting* from the German service, did you not return to England intending to continue in the same profession, that of a spy?"

"I did not."

"What a waste of your expertise. For you are, are you not, expert at writing ciphers and codes?"

"I have some skill at it but I've given it up, as one gives up a vice," Beaumont said lightly.

"It would be the only vice that you have ever given up. And you had not yet renounced it when I interviewed you on the subject of those treasonous letters you had produced. Indeed, you demonstrated your genius by breaking large parts of the code in which they were written."

Beaumont gave a short laugh, as if in consternation. "Sir, the genius is entirely yours, for inventing them in the first place."

"Do you deny that I sent you, with a party of my own guards, to arrest the conspirators in Aylesbury last September?"

"I do."

"My guards have testified otherwise, and truthfully so, as God is my witness!" Hoare glowered at him. "Mr. Beaumont, would you not perjure yourself a thousand times if you thought it to your advantage?"

"Must I answer that?" Beaumont said, to the judge.

"Colonel Hoare, what do you seek to gain by harrying Mr. Beaumont?" the judge said. "Keep in mind, we are here to discover your guilt or innocence, not his."

"My lord, if I may obtain access to my own records as I requested from the outset of this trial, I can prove that I hired him, that he brought Lord Falkland this treasonous correspondence, and that he conspired to turn his lordship against me. I had full justification to interrogate him in Oxford Castle! He is one of the biggest liars in the kingdom!"

"Sir, pray keep your accusations to yourself, or you shall stand in contempt of this court." The judge turned to Falkland. "My lord, may the court have access to these documents?"

"I am afraid not, on the express wish of His Majesty," said Falkland gravely. "They contain confidential information regarding matters of state. I have here a letter from him, to that effect." And he handed it on, through his lawyers.

The judge scanned it, then addressed Colonel Hoare, who was shaking with anger. "Sir, I regret that the court cannot overrule His Majesty's decision. Your case will have to proceed without these records."

"My lord, this is a perversion of justice!" cried Hoare.

"Once more, sir, I warn you to contain yourself. Mr. Beaumont, you may stand down," the judge said.

Beaumont bowed his head, acknowledging judge and jury, and walked past the prisoner's dock without a single look at Hoare. As he passed beneath one of the galleries, a woman rose and tossed her fan down to him. He paid no attention but Seward craned to catch a glimpse of the owner. She was young and dark-haired, her pretty heart-shaped face very animated.

II.

"Thomas Beaumont," said Hoare, in a strained voice, "will you admit that you came to me in December last, with news that your brother Laurence Beaumont was assisting my Lord Falkland to negotiate terms in private, with the enemy?"

"Yes, but I – I was in error," Tom said, attempting to keep his own tone even.

"Did you not expect me to investigate the truth of your assertion?"

"I did not expect you to use violence against my brother."

"Yet surely I would not be fulfilling my duty to His Majesty to let such information go without discovering the truth of it?" Tom was silent. "Have you not suggested, sir, to myself and to others, that your brother led a reprehensible life as a mercenary abroad?"

"Whatever he may have done there, since his return he has been fighting with Wilmot's Horse, and did good service at Edgehill," Tom replied more confidently.

After some murmuring between Falkland and the prosecutors, another paper was handed up to the judge, who read it before delivering it to the clerk of the court. "Let it be entered into record," he said, "that His Highness Prince Rupert and Henry Wilmot, Commissioner General of His Majesty's Horse, made particular mention of Laurence Beaumont's bravery at Edgehill in scouting for enemy troops and thereby securing intelligence that proved of immense value to His Majesty's armies on the eve of the battle."

Hoare tried to probe Tom on Laurence's association with Falkland, but the court was now muttering its displeasure with the prisoner's aggressive tactics. The judge had to intervene yet again as Hoare started to rant against both Beaumonts. "If you have no more reasonable questions," the judge said to Hoare, "I must request you to hold your peace."

At last Hoare complied, and a lawyer for the prosecution rose to cross-examine Tom. "Mr. Beaumont," he said, "did you have any quarrel with your brother, at the time that you overheard his conversation with my Lord Falkland?"

"My brother and I have had our differences now and again, but they are unconnected with matters of state," Tom said.

"Then why in heaven's name did you not ask him outright about that conversation, before reporting it to the accused?"

"I would have, but he left the house shortly after he and his lordship talked. I have not seen him since, until today."

"Why did you choose to report to Colonel Hoare, and not, for example, to His Highness the Prince, in whose regiment you served?"

"I was . . . I was not so sure of what I had heard, to warrant troubling His Highness," Tom said, feeling the blood rise to his cheeks.

"And yet this flimsy suspicion of yours could have cost your brother his life," the lawyer said, "and my Lord Falkland his office."

Tom took a deep breath. "I acted thoughtlessly. But I now understand that Colonel Hoare entrapped me, bending my words to his purpose, to take the liberty of abusing my brother and defaming our Secretary of State."

"These brothers are both perjurers," declared Hoare, and he refused to re-examine the witness.

Tom left the courtroom trembling, to find Laurence waiting outside. "Thank you, Tom," he said.

"*Was* there a conspiracy?" Tom whispered.

He noticed a familiar, evasive expression cross Laurence's face. "I can't talk about that."

"And Lord Falkland? Is there any truth in what Hoare said of him?"

"No, none at all," Laurence replied, now gazing straight at Tom.

They were quiet, examining each other. "You don't look so badly," Tom ventured, "for what was done to you." Laurence gave a little shrug. "Did you hear that my wife lost our child?"

"When?" asked Laurence, moving closer.

Tom retreated a step. "The day after Elizabeth's wedding."

"I'm so sorry," Laurence said, with such concern that Tom had to turn from him and swiftly walk away.

III.

"I assume you have good news," Laurence said, as Seward flung open the door to his chambers.

"I do! Hoare was found guilty on all counts. In his final address to the jury, he made a spectacle of himself, lashing out against you, your brother, Captain Milne, and my Lord Falkland for sending an innocent man to his death. He even remarked upon your absence, claiming that you must be too ashamed to show your face, after lying so baldly to the court."

"He wasn't altogether wrong on *that* score," admitted Laurence, with a rueful smile.

"Then let us pray he may be treated more mercifully on the Day of Judgement."

"What hypocritical nonsense! Don't pretend you give a shit if he burns in hell. Was Isabella there?" Laurence could not resist adding, for he had not seen her in court when he gave his testimony.

"No. Milne came alone."

"Ah. Seward, I got a letter today from my father. He said it was urgent that I come home at once."

"You should inform Falkland. He is on his way here as we speak."

Soon afterwards, Falkland entered unaccompanied and greeted them more brusquely than was his habit. "Your advice was sound, Mr. Beaumont," he said, "though I wish I'd had no need to follow it. By nature I'm not fond of taking wild risks, nor am I practised at tampering with the due process of law."

"Ah well, fortunately for you, my lord, I have no such scruples," Laurence said, annoyed to be damned with faint praise.

"I did not mean that as it came out," Falkland apologised. "I have you to thank for the successful conclusion of this trial. Should we not question Hoare, before his sentence is carried out, to determine whether he recruited any others in my service to work against me?"

"If I were you, my lord, I'd let him die with what dignity he has left. You'd spend your time more profitably in building a new network of agents who share your political views and can be depended on."

"I must have your help there."

"You will, but not immediately. My father wants me to come home first."

Falkland looked distinctly embarrassed. "I am afraid I contradicted your wishes and wrote to Lord Beaumont, in strict confidence, about what you did for me. He might have heard anyway about the trial and I wanted to give him a true account."

Laurence sighed shortly; so that was what had prompted his father's letter to him. "Afterwards, my lord, I should like to return to my regiment," he said.

"I shall ask Wilmot to release you, sir. My need of you is greater than his."

"No, my lord. If you want me back, you know what you must do. Arrest Radcliff."

"I, too, am chafing at His Majesty's delay as concerns the regicides. Yet as I've told you, I cannot force him into action."

"Then please don't force me. I'll be at Chipping Campden for only a few days, and after that, you can summon me from Wilmot's service should circumstances require."

"Very well." Falkland bowed to them. "Good day to you both, gentlemen."

"What a transformation in him," Seward remarked to Laurence, when he had gone. "I imagine that he has learnt from you the value of acting expediently."

"Are you suggesting that I've corrupted him?"

"Well, you may perhaps have loosened his ethical moorings," Seward said, with a dry chuckle.

IV.

As Pembroke reviewed his servant's written account of the trial of Colonel Hoare, his curiosity turned gradually to cold fear. The condemned spymaster had sworn to the existence of a conspiracy to regicide, even though the man who had supposedly uncovered it testified that the whole affair was a fiction invented by Hoare himself to disgrace Lord Falkland. This witness, Laurence Beaumont, must be the son of someone Pembroke knew, Lord James Beaumont of Chipping Campden, and was clearly very loyal to the Secretary of State. It also emerged at the trial that he was an expert in ciphers. Far too close to home, Pembroke thought, horrified.

He had visited Lord Beaumont's house many years before; the son would have been a boy then, and he had no memory of him. But he had not forgotten Lord Beaumont's wife. Her exotic face had so entranced him that he had envied her husband in having such a jungle cat for his bed, despite her haughty mien; there had been an awkward moment at table when Pembroke had spat out a bone onto the floor, and Lady Beaumont had frozen him with her unearthly emerald gaze as if he had just lowered his breeches to defecate. From his servant's description, her son had inherited her looks.

V.

On the way to Chipping Campden, Laurence pondered whether he should have called again on Isabella. But he still winced at the memory of her cold reception last time; worse yet was the thought of her in bed with Milne.

He arrived to find Lady Beaumont, Anne, and Tom's wife at their embroidery in the hall. To his surprise, Alice Morecombe was there as well, stitching at a frame, and he saw her redden the moment she set eyes on him.

Lady Beaumont rose to greet him, her expression a mixture of anxiety and relief. "Laurence, your father has passed many a sleepless night worrying about you. You do remember Alice," she added.

"Yes. Good day to you," he said, bowing to the girl. "I heard from Tom about your child," he told Mary. "I'm very sorry."

"It was God's will, sir," she replied, her face solemn.

"Now," said Lady Beaumont, "to the library." She took Laurence's arm and guided him in that direction, remarking as they climbed the stairs, "You are fortunate; as you may guess, Lady Morecombe has granted you a second chance."

"How *ever* did you persuade her?"

"With much diplomacy, but it is done. Since then Alice has remained at the house, the better to become acquainted with us. We must have your word on the betrothal, Laurence. You cannot shame your father twice." At the library doors she stopped and whispered, "You do not know what a blow it was for him, to hear of all that happened to you."

"I asked Falkland not to write. I wanted to explain myself."

"Too late," she said crisply, and knocked.

"Pray enter," Lord Beaumont called from within.

Laurence was shocked on seeing the alteration that less than four months' time had wrought in him. His hair and beard were more white than grey, he appeared shrunken in height and thicker about the middle, and his face had a high, purplish colour. At fifty-seven or thereabouts, he had attained an age that many would consider old, but whereas before he had not shown his years, now they seemed to weigh him down. Even Seward, at close to seventy, possessed a more sprightly air.

He embraced Laurence for a while without speaking, and afterwards inspected him, murmuring, "My beloved son, to think of such pain inflicted upon my own flesh and blood! And how I blame myself for not coming to your aid!"

"Please, you mustn't," Laurence insisted, feeling equally at a loss for words. "It's all in the past, now, and you should forget about it."

Lord Beaumont brightened a little. "We have Alice Morecombe with us. What a sweet child she is! I am sure that you will come to like her as we do."

"She *is* still a child," Laurence said.

"Not so," Lady Beaumont objected. "She has been having her monthly courses for a year now."

Laurence almost laughed, then caught his mother's frown and restrained himself. "Thank you," he told her, "for that interesting information."

VI.

"Mr. Meyboom," said Pembroke, as a thin, plainly dressed man appeared and bowed before him, "I have been some time in finding you. Would you please cast your eyes on this." And he unveiled the tableau of Eros and Harpocrates, which he had had framed elaborately in gilt. Meyboom surveyed it without any change in expression; typical phlegmatic Netherlander, Pembroke thought. "Is it your work?"

"Yes, my lord."

"Who commissioned it?" Pembroke demanded, his heart thudding in his breast.

"The gentleman did not give his name."

"Describe him to me." Meyboom hesitated. "Come on, come on! What did he look like?"

"He was young, perhaps between twenty-five and thirty, and tall."

Pembroke let out a derisive snort. "You are an *artist*, sir. Can you not supply me with more detail than that?"

"His hair was black, and he was dark-complexioned. If he had not spoken English without a trace of an accent, I would have judged him to be of Spanish or Italian origin. He also spoke my language fluently."

"What else, what else?"

"He had green eyes, my lord," Meyboom said slowly. "A striking shade of pale green."

VII.

Laurence stood staring at the marbles on either side of the doors into the hall. He could envisage the naked youth with a serpent and the nymph with her cluster of grapes hacked to pieces by the soldiers of Parliament, who had destroyed so many other statues judged idolatrous about the country. The youth, as he viewed him now, seemed hardly a match for the reptile coiled threateningly about his right leg.

Over the past week, Laurence had felt in a similar situation himself. His father had besieged him with questions about his duties for the Secretary of State, his relations with Hoare, and his incarceration. "And what was Thomas doing in all this affair?" Lord Beaumont had wanted to know. "I must find out from him."

"There's no need, he did nothing wrong," Laurence had assured his father, and after that, upset by Lord Beaumont's decline, he had averted any further discussion of the subject.

Meanwhile, his mother thrust him into the company of Alice Morecombe at every opportunity. She was, he supposed, no worse than other girls of her rank and age, but he had little to say to her. Although she was not shrewish in temperament, like the last girl his parents had selected for him to marry, she had neither wit nor charm nor intellectual curiosity. How to escape this betrothal, he wondered.

"Laurence?" He turned to see Anne smiling at him. "Such a glum face you had on! Would a game of backgammon cheer you? Elizabeth and I haven't played since December, when Mr. Ingram was here."

As soon as she spoke the name, Laurence needed no more information as to her feelings. "He's in love with you, Anne. Would you accept if he asked for your hand?"

"But he won't," she said gently. "I can no more marry him than you can avoid marrying Alice."

Remembering Madam Musgrave's instructions, Laurence kept silent.

Tomorrow he would rejoin Wilmot, he decided, as he and his sisters shifted their black and white pieces across the board. Yet first he had to disabuse his parents and Alice Morecombe of their notions about his marriage.

Before supper that evening the weather cleared, and he asked Alice out to walk in the garden. "I've got a confession to make," he said eventually. "I believe in honesty, don't you?"

"Yes, sir," she said.

"I'm in love with someone else."

"Oh!" She covered her mouth with her hands, then dropped them and stammered, "Do you . . . do you wish to marry *her*, instead?"

"She's not a woman who could ever be my wife. It was she who your mother found with me, that night."

Alice's face puckered, as if she had tasted something rotten. "Mr. Beaumont, please take me back to the house."

"Not yet. I want you to know that after we're married I shan't give her up. You won't have to see or hear of her. I'll provide for her as I choose, and any children I might have by her will receive a settlement on my death, though no amount so large as to compromise the finances of the estate. And only yours will carry my name. It's an equitable solution, don't you think?"

"I think it is scandalous!" Alice exclaimed.

"Forgive me, but it's not unusual."

Alice gaped at him. "How could you expect me to accept those terms?"

"You'll have to. Both of our families are in agreement."

"Sir, I can tell you that when my mother hears of this, there will be no more talk of a betrothal!"

He laughed and shook his head. "If she wasn't deterred by what she saw when she had the misfortune to enter my chamber, she'll be amenable to what I propose. I don't intend to hurt you, Alice, but you must understand: I'm nearly twice your age, and you can't expect me to change my ways, let alone break with a woman I care for above any other." Alice started to cry. "I'm sorry. I thought you would appreciate the truth," Laurence said, reaching for her hand.

"You are not sorry," she expostulated, shaking him off. "And I would not marry you if you were the last and the richest man in all England."

She fled, leaving him alone amidst the neat ornamental flowerbeds. And so, he thought, what his mother's diplomacy had worked to achieve was now undone. He had never before treated anyone so manipulatively who deserved it so little. He was also rather disgusted with himself for using Isabella to get rid of her; yet how easily it had come to him, to say that he was in love.

Alice did not come down to supper on the excuse of a headache, and he made sure to retire early. The next morning, Geoffrey woke him with the news that Mistress Morecombe had left Chipping Campden before dawn in the family coach. "His lordship and her ladyship wish to speak to you," Geoffrey finished, with an ominous look. "They are waiting in the small parlour."

The moment he entered, his mother snapped at him, "Laurence, what did you tell Alice Morecombe yesterday?"

"It hardly matters," he said. "The fact is, the arrangement would suit neither of us. I *will* take a wife, but I've seen too much of the world for you to decide for me. You must let me choose my own bride. You chose for yourself, didn't you?" he asked his father.

"I did," Lord Beaumont acknowledged heavily. "Yet how long must we wait?"

"Until I find her," replied Laurence; and to his surprise, he met with no further objections.

VIII.

Wilmot's troops were busy trying to secure the area around Reading when Laurence rejoined them; the garrison was so undermanned that it was at risk of falling into enemy hands, and Wilmot feared he had not the strength to prevent this. Prince Rupert and Digby could offer him no aid; they were raising siege at Lichfield in order to forge a path north, so that the Queen could travel safely to Oxford. Since Rupert had insufficient cannon to blast a hole through Lichfield's walls, his foreign engineers were mining them. It was an innovative tactic never yet attempted on English soil, Wilmot admitted grudgingly to Laurence.

Their fears about the fortifications at Reading were soon confirmed: despite a valiant effort on the part of a combined Royalist force to come to the town's aid, it capitulated to Parliament on the twenty-sixth of April. Just two days later, Laurence received a message from Oxford requesting that he call on Lady d'Aubigny at Corpus Christi College.

"Better go," Wilmot said. "Can't turn your nose up at a nice piece of snatch."

Laurence laughed, but he felt uncomfortable, knowing very well who had thrown her fan from the galleries after he had testified at Hoare's trial. He had not wished to encourage her by retrieving it, but he should at least have had the courtesy to thank her for assisting in his release from gaol.

He got to Oxford late in the afternoon, left his horse stabled at Merton, and walked to her lodgings. Outside her door, as if dropped by magic from some sunnier clime, stood an African pageboy in Oriental dress. The boy bowed, doffed his turban, and said in a high, piping voice, "Mr. Beaumont?" Laurence nodded apprehensively, reminded of the cold December night when Lady d'Aubigny had some trouble with her lock.

As the boy ushered him in, he saw that she was alone, clad in a loose robe, lying on her bed; she was no longer pregnant. She did not rise but offered her hand for him to kiss. "Dear sir, how pleased I am to see you. You may leave us and shut the door, Ibrahim," she told the page, who obeyed. "Mr. Beaumont, did you attend the hanging today? Colonel Hoare finally went to the gallows this very morning."

Why had it taken so long, Laurence thought, though he was relieved that he had not had to witness the event. "My lady, please forgive me," he said. "I should have thanked you earlier for what you did for me when I was in prison."

"It is Mistress Isabella Savage you should thank. If she hadn't begged me on her knees to help, I would never have known you were in such difficulties." So, Laurence realised, Isabella had extended herself far more on his behalf than he had known. Yet she was still with Milne.

"Sit beside me, sir," commanded Lady d'Aubigny. She lifted his chin with her forefinger and examined his face. "I do believe that these marks of your captivity render you more attractive than ever. It is my wish that we may soon spend some time together, once I am fully restored to health after the birth of my dear little boy." She was now stroking his thigh. "You know I have dreamt of you and the pleasure you gave me. My late husband possessed neither your experience, nor such a superb –"

"Please, your ladyship," Laurence interrupted, edging away from her as her fingers trailed further upwards. "You must allow me to explain. On that night, I was overwhelmed by your loveliness, but my behaviour was not that of a gentleman."

"Sir, I did not mind in the least."

"No, no. I took advantage of you in your bereavement." He tried to coax some moisture into his eyes. "And my offence weighs more heavily on my conscience since then, because you saved my life. I was – I was too ashamed of myself to see you again."

"There is no need for you to be ashamed. In fact, I wish you would be entirely shameless, sir," she said, fluttering her eyelashes.

"Your ladyship, the more I stay, the harder it becomes –" He stopped, to correct himself. "I mean, the harder you make it for me to do what I know is right. I really must leave."

"Oh no," she said, as he stood up; she wore the same look of spoilt entitlement that he had seen in Kate. "Please wait, Mr. Beaumont," she added, abruptly dropping her flirtatious manner. "As I have helped you, I want you to help me. I am going to London next month, on a matter of extreme importance, and Lord Falkland agreed that I might borrow you for this mission."

"*Borrow* me?"

"You are his agent, are you not?" Laurence did not reply as a suspicion took shape in his mind. "And you do know about the plans for London."

"Your ladyship, I'm bound to secrecy in whatever he tells me," answered Laurence, his suspicion confirmed.

"No surprise he values you so. It was Mistress Savage who inspired me when she told me how she arranged for *Mercurius Aulicus* to be smuggled into the capital under women's skirts, which is how I can bring in the Commission of Array. That document itself, signed by His Majesty, will confirm how and when the uprising is to take place. We expect to deliver it by the middle of next month."

Laurence could not hide his dismay. "You're very brave, my lady, but I honestly believe it would be a mistake. You'll be spied upon from the moment you enter the city."

"Why should Parliament take any notice of me? After all, I own a house in London and have every reason to visit there. Pray consult with Falkland, who will make all the necessary arrangements. It will be such fun," she concluded gaily, "to travel with you!"

After bidding her goodbye, Laurence rushed straight to Falkland's chambers, so angry that the servant Stephens stepped back in alarm on opening the door to him. His lordship was out, Stephens said, eating with Lord Digby in a tavern close by.

Laurence hurried there and was shown into a dining room where they were alone together at table. His expression must have had a similar effect on them as it had on Stephens, for both men regarded him with a startled air.

"Good day," he said to them, with a curt bow, and to Falkland, "My lord, we must speak in private."

"We shall go outside." Falkland rose quickly. "Excuse us, Digby."

"By all means," Digby said, "but would you honour me by joining us afterwards, Mr. Beaumont? There is something *I* should like to discuss with you, as well."

Laurence merely nodded, and walked out ahead of Falkland.

"I've just seen Lady d'Aubigny," he began, as soon as they could not be overheard. "Did you suggest to her this trip to London?"

"No. She volunteered herself. His Majesty was delighted with the idea."

"What is he thinking! He might as well send Prince Rupert's dog with the Commission in its mouth. Why didn't you ask me yourself if I would go with her?"

"Because she insisted on speaking to you first. I told you last time that I might need you, and now I do. She will be travelling by coach, with her friend Lady Sophia Murray. Lady d'Aubigny's late husband had a seigneurie in France, and the pretext for her visit to London will be to discuss the issue of this property with the French Ambassador. Should anything go amiss with the uprising," Falkland continued in a lower voice, "the Ambassador will offer you sanctuary."

"I'm most comforted to hear that."

"For heaven's sake, enough of your sarcasm, sir!" Falkland burst out. "None of this was my choosing, yet I am duty bound to fix things as best I can. And because I am acutely aware of your desire to move on the regicides, I have managed to extract a concession from His Majesty."

"We can take in Radcliff?" Laurence asked, more hopefully.

"Not him, I am sorry to say, but the lawyer, Joshua Poole. You must bring him to me for questioning. And when you are in London, you will deliver some correspondence to Edmund Waller."

"Which is His Majesty's main purpose in sending me, of course. He's giving us the arrest just to keep us happy."

"Dear me, Mr. Beaumont, I shall never try to pull the wool over *your* eyes. Meet me tomorrow at my chambers and we shall determine how you should proceed. Does ten o'clock suit you?"

"Yes, my lord."

"I thank you," Falkland said, with a weary smile. "And now shall we return to Lord Digby?"

When they entered the room, Digby was still eating while a servant fussed about him, fluffing a pillow on a stool where he had propped his leg. "I have a wound in my thigh, incurred during the siege of Lichfield, Mr. Beaumont," he explained, as they sat down. "I had been working waist-deep in mud like a trooper with his Royal Highness the Prince – we were draining a moat and attempting to build a bridge across it, as the enemy took practice shots at us and dragged off what prisoners they could. I finally extracted myself from the morass, then a ball struck me. Shaved off an inch of flesh. As a result, I was too incapacitated to witness the first mine sprung on English soil."

"So he did it," Laurence said. "Quite a feat!"

Digby shrugged, pouting.

"It seems you had not just your leg wounded, but your pride also, my lord," Falkland observed. "He argued with the Prince, I am afraid," he told Laurence, "and ended up resigning his military command."

"So you're not a soldier any more, my lord?" Laurence queried.

"Not for the present, sir," Digby said, "though as consolation here in Oxford I was able to watch Colonel Hoare step off into infinity. But where were *you*? I did not see you at that august event."

"I was too late. I've been serving with Wilmot and only arrived this afternoon."

"Ah yes, so you were near Reading! Poor Wilmot! He must have been so tirelessly scouring the area for the finest claret to serve his officers, that he could not give assistance to the garrison." Laurence let this pass, amused in spite of himself. "Oh, then you cannot have heard," Digby continued, in a more serious voice. "Mistress Savage is sick. You might recall, when we met at Shrewsbury this past autumn and you were doing your interesting mathematics for Wilmot, that she had a quartain fever – it is the same illness again. And I fancy that Captain Milne's reappearance can be no aid to her recovery."

"I thought he was at Lichfield, too," said Falkland.

"He was, but he seized upon the excuse of a small head wound to return to Mistress Savage's bower. I am sure she was not happy about it. What would you say, Mr. Beaumont?" Digby asked, scanning Laurence with his round blue eyes.

"I can't speak for her," Laurence replied calmly.

"If Milne is bothering her, why do you not tell him to go to the devil?" Falkland exclaimed. "You are her legal guardian. You should protect her from such unsavoury characters."

Digby looked momentarily abashed. "I would, but she and I have had a dispute."

"You are arguing with everyone these days!"

"Yes, so it seems. Mr. Beaumont," Digby recommenced, "you would do me an inestimable favour if you would only pay a visit on her. I am most worried about her health and should like to have some report of it. Or, even better, to have banished from her bedside anything that might cause it to deteriorate."

Laurence frowned at him. "Are you asking me to get rid of Milne?"

"Why not? She was instrumental in getting *you* out of gaol. She even pawned most of her jewellery to bribe your guards, though she refused to tell me until I demanded to know where her best pieces were. Some of them I had given her myself! And I might argue that, if not for your sake, she could have avoided this unpleasant situation with the Captain."

"I think her loyalty to you also played a part in it."

"A minor role. Well, sir, will you oblige me?" Digby asked impatiently. "I happen to know that Captain Milne is sadly impecunious and all his creditors in town are hounding him. He might be lured away by the promise of a reward, which I would not expect you to put up yourself. I shall gladly provide you with a sum sufficiently tempting to a man in debt. You may call for it at my quarters in an hour or so."

Laurence eyed him a little longer, then said, "As you wish."

Laurence found Seward in his rooms at Merton in the midst of some alchemical operation, a steaming alembic on the hearth. "Beaumont," Seward said, "when did you get to town?"

"Sorry, Seward, I've no time to talk. A quartain fever – what do you have for a quartain fever?"

"Are you sick?"

"No, it's for Isabella."

Seward grumbled a bit, but at length he selected a remedy from his collection of vials and jars. "This is a tincture of Jesuit's bark. Expensive and most difficult to come by." He described how it should be administered, adding, "Don't waste a drop, and bring me back what you don't use."

Laurence grabbed the vial and bolted out in such haste that he forgot to take his pistols with him.

At the Blue Boar, Milne hailed him with the same joviality as on the last occasion. "Was it not a fine thing, to see Hoare kick off?" he cried.

"Oh yes," Laurence said, with an amicable smile. "How's your wound?" he asked, indicating the bandage about Milne's temples.

"I'll survive it," Milne said, grinning. "So what brings you here?"

"Digby sent me with a remedy for Mistress Savage."

"Ha! He hasn't the balls to come here himself, since he and Isabella quarrelled. Pray enter, and meet my friends." Milne took him into the room, where two other men were sitting at cards. "Ruskell, Pickett, this is Beaumont. Do you play primero, Mr. Beaumont?"

"I do."

"A favourite of good Queen Bess, they say. You can join us if you want, but it's a rich game, I should warn you."

"That's all right by me."

"Beforehand, we should give Isabella her medicine. She's in the bedchamber." Milne guided him to the inner door, which was partly open. "My sweet, Digby had Mr. Beaumont run along with something for your fever. Go in, go in," he added to Laurence. "I must return to the table, or those fellows will tamper with my cards."

The bedchamber was dark and stuffy, and beneath the scent of Isabella's perfume Laurence could detect the smell of sweat. The curtains were not drawn about her bed, where she lay propped up by pillows. She looked ghastly, far sicker than she had been at Shrewsbury, and as she saw him she turned her face away.

He took a moment to compose himself. "This is Jesuit's bark," he said, producing the vial. "Very effective, according to Seward. Will you have some?"

"I will sample poison at this stage. I cannot feel worse than I do." He poured a few drops into a glass by her bedside and gave it to her. She drank it off, and rested her head back again. "Has Digby told you my news?" she resumed with forced cheer, though she was shivering under the thick layers of bedclothes. "Captain Milne has offered to marry me." Digby neglected to mention that, Laurence thought, but he said nothing. "I explained to the Captain that he was unlikely to get any issue of me," she went on, "yet he said he would have me anyway, if he could be paid a dowry by his lordship in order to rebuild his finances, which are in as sorry a state as I am."

Laurence bit back an exclamation. "And what did Digby say to that?" he asked.

"He refused. He has other plans for me, and he thinks I shall acquiesce, as he always expects me to acquiesce to his every scheme. Hence our disagreement. He must have sent *you* just to rub a little salt into my wounds."

"What do you mean?" Laurence said, wishing she would look at him.

"Only that he can be vindictive, sometimes. But let us return to Captain Milne. Is he not noble? Most men want children of their wives."

"How – how do you know you can't have a child?"

"Why should you care?" When he did not answer, she continued bitterly, "When I was quite young, there was a married gentleman who had his way with me. He hated the prospect of supporting a bastard, and so he sent me to an old crone skilled in removing such obstacles. It was a hideous process, as you may imagine, and it must have damaged me, for since then I haven't had cause to repeat it. If not for my dear friends, the Cottrells, who nursed me back to health afterwards, I would have lost all will to live. I did not tell Digby until some years later; he would have killed the man, and in so doing ruined his own political career. And that would not have repaired what was done to *me*. Now, Mr. Beaumont, why so moved by my story?" she inquired, finally meeting his gaze. "It must be familiar to you, or have you never troubled to learn the consequences of *your* sport?"

"Yes – I –" He broke off, blinking, and swallowed. "So, what will you do?"

"I should at least consider Milne's proposal, but the fact is, I despise him. Perhaps he will die in battle. War has its uses, after all." She paused, as from the room beyond came the noise of raucous laughter and clinking glass. "I heard *you* are to be married soon."

"No, I'm not."

She studied him, frowning, then closed her eyes. "Oh, Beaumont," she exclaimed, in an altered voice, feeble and despairing, "when I am this sick I wish I were dead."

He reached out and took her clammy hand in his. "I'll look after you, Isabella. I won't let Milne near you again, if that's what you want."

Her mouth trembled, though she spoke clearly. "Don't make me any promises that you cannot afford to keep. Besides, you did not come here of your own accord, and don't pretend otherwise."

"I would have come to you, I swear, had I known how you felt about –" Laurence stopped and dropped her hand, for as if on cue, Milne had appeared at the door, framed by light from the room beyond.

"Have you had your medicine like a good girl, Isabella?" he asked.

"Yes," she replied. "And now I must sleep."

"Good night, then, my sweet." Milne shut the door after Laurence. "I hope you've enough money on you, sir. We're playing for high stakes."

"You certainly are," said Laurence, taking a seat at the table.

Milne poured everyone a round of wine; and as the game progressed, Laurence lost Digby's money effortlessly.

"Bravo, Mr. Beaumont," Milne commented, shovelling up the coins. "You accept your disappointments like a gentleman. But then I hear your father's not short of change."

Milne's friends balked as the wagers grew and the wine ran out. At length, Pickett threw in his cards. "Too steep for me," he said. "I'm leaving."

Ruskell lasted only one more hand, murmuring something about the hour.

"You'll stay, won't you?" Milne said to Laurence, who nodded, smiling. "I'll just get us another jug."

As Milne went to the taproom, Laurence slipped outside and into the alleyway, where he satisfied an urgent need, born as much from nerves as from the wine. He now had to win consistently if he was to clear out the Captain's pockets, and if he could not somehow effect Milne's departure through bribery, he would have to find some other means to leave with Isabella, who was so weak that he might well have to carry her. And Milne wore a sword, while he had neglected to bring his pistols with him.

He got back before Milne, who immediately asked to inspect the deck of cards. "It's not that I don't trust you, but you never know what can get into a man when he's been losing all night."

Laurence shrugged and asked him to deal. Milne lost the first round with apparent grace. At the second, he gave a murmur of discontent. By the third, he was cursing, and in less time than it took them to drain the jug, he was down to a couple of shillings.

"The tables have turned," he said, in an uncertain voice. "I'm afraid it must be an early night for us, too. I can't play any more, unless you'll permit me to owe you if I'm out of luck."

"I don't like debts," said Laurence. "I'll suggest a bargain, however."

"What's that?"

Laurence sat back and cleared his throat. "Mistress Savage told me you and she are to be married."

"So we are."

"I'm very happy for you both. And you're doing her an immense kindness, which she deserves after the life she's had to lead."

"It doesn't matter to me that she had her lovers," Milne declared generously. "Once she's my wife, we shall begin anew."

"You're an enlightened man, Captain. I agree with you, I've always thought virginity was overprized. I far prefer a woman who knows what she's doing." Laurence counted out his gains and pushed them to the centre of the table. "Over eighty pounds." Milne surveyed the coins with poorly disguised covetousness. "Now, I heard from Digby that you happen already to have a few other debts. At how much would you estimate them?"

"Three or four hundred. Why?"

"You can have what's in front of you, and four hundred more if you give me this one night alone with her."

Milne gasped and laid his hand on his sword. "Are you proposing to buy my wife?"

"She's not your wife yet. Come on, Milne. You'll have her to your-self for the rest of your days, and nights. It's a fair offer, and my last. You see, I'm getting married too, in a month. Some girl my mother picked out for me."

"I suppose that's how it must be, with your sort."

"After thirty years of freedom, I must do my duty."

"Look here, Beaumont, if you want a quick poke, there are plenty of willing ladies over in the taproom."

"But I want *her*. I'll be gone by dawn, then you can reclaim her."

Milne was calculating, his eyes on the table. "Just tonight?"

"Yes," Laurence said, disgusted. Milne had not once objected that she was in no condition to comply with the terms of their bargain, nor had he troubled even to consult her.

"How do I know you won't try to steal her from me?"

Laurence gave a deprecating laugh. "I'm about to take a wife! I don't need all the bother of a mistress."

"When can I get the four hundred?"

Reaching into Digby's purse, Laurence threw out some gold. "There's half. You can have another two hundred in the morning."

Milne still hesitated. "What's so special to you about Isabella, that you would pay such a sum for her?"

"You know what you said to me when we last met?" Milne frowned, obviously trying to remember. "You made me curious as to her skills. And as for the money, I've paid more in the past for a night's entertainment."

Milne shot him a resentful glance and began to sweep up the coins. "It's nearly midnight. Get to it, and be gone by sun-up. And I'll sleep out here."

"Oh no. I said *alone*. You can afford another bed."

"You're driving a hard bargain!"

"Then let's forget it." Laurence rose from the table, yawning. "Give me back my money, and I'll say good night."

"No, no, you win, Mr. Beaumont, but tell her I don't like it. If I weren't in such straitened circumstances –"

"I understand, and I'm sure she will too."

Milne stuffed the coins into his doublet, which sagged with the weight of them. "I won't oblige you again."

"I wouldn't ask it of you," Laurence said, and saw him out.

Isabella was lying in a sweat, her hair wet at the temples and her nightdress drenched as if she had exposed herself to a torrential shower; she must have been delirious, for she did not recognise him at first.

"Isabella," he said, seizing her face in his hands, "it's me."

"Beaumont," she mumbled. "Where is Milne?"

"He just left." He flung aside the bedclothes and helped her to sit up. "You must change, quickly. I'm taking you away from here."

"How did this happen?" she asked, holding her arms over her head, like a child, for him to peel off her nightdress. "Beaumont, what have you done? He is an excellent dueller, and if you have wronged him, he will kill you."

"He can go and fuck himself," muttered Laurence, hurrying her into dry clothes. "Now, is there anything else you need?" She pointed at some other garments and her jewellery box, all of which he bundled up, then he wrapped her in covers from the bed, and at the last minute remembered to snatch Seward's vial from her bedside.

"I'll be too heavy for you," she protested.

"No you won't," he said, picking her up and cradling her in his arms.

He stumbled to the door, through the other chamber, and into the taproom, which was almost empty save for a couple of men at the front entrance.

"Eh!" one of them shouted, "where do you think you're off to?"

"Captain Milne said he might try some underhand trick," the other added, moving towards him.

"Captain Milne should be warned," Laurence said, "and you should keep your distance. She has the plague. She has sores all over her. If you're not afraid to be infected –"

"Why aren't *you* afraid to catch it?" the first man questioned.

"I've had it already, so I'll take my chances. Tell Milne to burn everything in that room, and watch out. It could be only a short time before *he* falls ill."

Isabella groaned convincingly, at which they stepped back and allowed him to pass. "Beaumont, you are inventive," she whispered in his ear, as he staggered along the street.

In the end he put her over his shoulder, as he had carried wounded men from the field of battle, and since the Merton porter would hardly allow him entrance at such a late hour accompanied by a half-conscious woman, he went around to the back of the new quadrangle, by the meadows. There he let her down gently and propped her against the wall before rapping at Seward's windowpane.

"Seward!" he yelled. There was no answer, and no lights shone within. "Oh God, what now?" he exclaimed, more to himself than to Isabella.

"Hold me," she said, "and kiss me."

He was still kissing her when the window opened and Seward's head popped out. "Beaumont, is it necessary that I be dragged from my bed to witness such a display? I hope you did not forget my Jesuit's bark!"

"Of course I didn't," Laurence told him, and tossed him the vial.

CHAPTER EIGHTEEN

I.

From the front window of his house at Longstanton, Radcliff gazed out over the flat, sodden Cambridgeshire fields cloaked in a light mist of rain. "How did you guess that I was here?" he asked.

"I caught up with your troop after the siege of Lichfield, but you had just disappeared from their ranks," Poole replied, in an urgent voice. "In the vain hope that you would surface, I followed Prince Rupert's forces to Reading, then to Oxford. At last I spoke with your brother-in-law. He told me, much to my amazement, that you had written him some perfunctory note saying you had gone to London to see *me*!"

Radcliff turned to him and smiled. "It was all I could think of at the time."

"He was clearly discomfited to realise that you had made no such journey. I consulted your wife at Faringdon, but she had neither seen nor heard from you. When I brought news of my failure to his lordship, he flew into a rage. He has sent out his own men to find you. They may soon draw the same conclusion as I did and come knocking on your door," Poole finished, shaking his head despairingly.

Radcliff felt an unwarranted calm descend upon him, as before a storm. "How is my wife?"

"In fine health, sir, unlike myself." Radcliff now noticed the dry patches of irritated skin on Poole's cheeks, and the yellow tinge to the whites of his eyes. "I was delayed in seeking you out because his lordship ordered me to make inquiries in Oxford about a certain Laurence Beaumont, who had testified at the trial of Falkland's spymaster, Colonel Hoare. Hoare claimed Beaumont had brought him and Falkland intelligence about a conspiracy against the King's life, though Beaumont said in court that Hoare was lying."

Why had Beaumont covered up the conspiracy, Radcliff wondered, not that it much signified at this point. "What else?"

"Hoare went to the gallows last week. But my Lord Pembroke is determined to talk to Beaumont. Sir Bernard, do you see what peril you are in?"

"It is worse than you know," Radcliff said. "Somehow Beaumont found out where my letters were hidden at Faringdon. He probably got that old woman Musgrave drunk and weaselled it out of her. We may now assume with complete certitude that they are in Falkland's hands."

"Sweet Jesu!" After a moment, Poole asked, in a sepulchral whisper, "Are you and my Lord Pembroke plotting to assassinate the King? Beaumont told me so last September, when he gave me back the letters. Is that why I was never privy to your code? To prevent me from finding out the truth?"

Radcliff took a breath, dumbstruck. "Poole," he said, "you should have asked me about this when you came to Newbury at Christmastide – or even before – and I would have explained!"

"I was afraid of what might happen to me, if it *were* true," Poole responded, looking straight at him.

"But I longed to confide in you about the awful burden that I have been carrying!" Radcliff exhaled heavily. "In one of the letters Beaumont partially transcribed, Pembroke wrote that if the King became intransigent over terms for a peace, we might be driven to just such a dire solution. I was horrified. I realised that he would employ any means towards his aim, and that it was my bounden duty to thwart him."

"Why did you not inform His Majesty there and then?"

"How could I? I had to play along until I had incontrovertible evidence of Pembroke's designs, or else His Majesty would never credit my accusations against the word of an earl who was once his great friend. *I* would be the one to suffer. Yet that is what has brought grief upon me, Poole. It would have been safer for me to destroy that correspondence, exactly as Pembroke commanded me to do."

"You must go to the King at once and reveal everything! You are caught on both sides: by Pembroke, and by the Secretary of State, who can have you seized the instant you return to your troop."

"I cannot return," Radcliff said, with a wry laugh. "I have burned that particular bridge. We are in the last stages of a chess game, and few pieces are left on the board. Indeed, I am confounded that Falkland has not already arrested me."

"Surrender to him and make a full confession. He might prove merciful, in exchange."

"Or he might not, and I will suffer a more painful death than Colonel Hoare, to say nothing of the disgrace and impoverishment that will befall my wife and child. No, Poole, I have another option. To find Beaumont and convince him of my innocence."

"You are clutching at straws," said Poole, in such a scornful tone that Radcliff was roused to genuine fury.

"I am doing what I can to salvage my honour, and that of my kin!" he exclaimed. "In all my dealings with Pembroke, I was striving for a happier future for my family. You may call it ambition if you like, but if no one had ambition, we would still be dwelling in mud huts, as do the savages of Africa. I am not much better off than they." He gestured at the mouldy, water-damaged plaster buckling the walls. "Mark the deterioration in my house since the war took me away from it. A year and a half ago, Pembroke said he would give me money to drain my land. But as soon as he quarrelled with the King and hostilities broke out, he said he must abandon even his own building plans at Wilton House in order to work for a resolution to our country's woes. And so he sent his funds with me to The Hague, to buy arms – and the rest you know."

"No," said Poole, "I do not. When you were robbed, Sir Bernard, were you at a tavern, or at a bawdy house?"

Damn Beaumont to hell, Radcliff wanted to scream; the man had invaded and threatened to trample upon almost every part of his life. Suppressing his anger, he said, "Yes, Poole, I was at a brothel."

"You know very well that it is not the deed, it is the fact of your *lying* that troubles me!"

"You would have judged me badly for it, even though I was unmarried then. What would I have to do with any other woman, now that I have my wife? But can you imagine her here, Poole? She would be miserable, as I am, pinching pennies to make ends meet, struggling to give the appearance of prosperity where there is only a form of poverty more degrading, more crushing to the soul, than the life of a street-beggar! He is at least free of society's yoke and has no need to pretend that he is anything else. I am not afraid to die before my time, but what I will not tolerate is the obscure life of a country squire – not for myself, nor for my child."

"You misled your wife, too," observed Poole quietly. "She believes you to be wealthier than you are."

"I trusted that the wealth would come. And I still do," Radcliff added, swayed to optimism by his own performance. "We must not become discouraged; that is the weakness of inferior strategists, to give up when circumstances take a turn against them. Go to Pembroke and tell him that I'll attend him shortly. You shall hear from me soon. Now have I still your faith, Poole?"

Poole regarded him with gloomy resignation. "I have hitched my wagon to your star, Sir Bernard, and can only pray that it does not fall."

II.

Security measures around London had tightened noticeably since Laurence's last visit. Again he entered under cover of dark and sought refuge in Blackman Street. This time, however, Mistress Edwards' house wore a less dreary air. The sign alerting passersby to its closure had been removed and its façade whitewashed, and when he knocked at the door, a short, swarthy, unsmiling manservant whom he did not recognise opened it.

"Is Mistress Edwards at home?" he inquired.

"Your name, sir," the man asked, in a funereal voice, as he showed Laurence into the main parlour, which was now reopened but remarkably austere without its usual hangings, carpets, and bacchanalian paintings. The interior walls had also received a coat of whitewash, and the only objects of furniture were straight-backed chairs and a long table, on which were arranged, of all things, several prayer books. When the man had gone, Laurence entertained himself by leafing through them until Mistress Edwards arrived, walking as gracefully as someone half her age.

"Not out of business, Mr. Beaumont, though I came very close," she said, offering her gnarled hand for him to kiss. She was transformed, clad in a sober, dark blue dress with a plain, high-necked collar.

"But what business *are* you in?"

"The same as always, though I am obliged to disguise my establishment as a religious meeting house." He started to laugh. "It's no joke," she assured him. "Fifteen years I have spent in this street, a decent citizen making no trouble for anyone, and in a single blow these canting rascals in Parliament nigh on ruined me. The money I pay them in bribes, to keep a roof over my head!" She smiled, permitting him a glimpse of her large wooden false teeth. "Thank you, sir, for what you did for me last year. My girls wept with joy the day I got out of the Fleet. And they said you saved them from starvation, God bless you."

"Don't mention it. I should be thanking *them* – they were extremely helpful to me."

"Well, now, how many years has it been, sir? Six or more – and you're as kind on the eye as you ever was, no grey hair yet and no gentleman's paunch. Would you take a sip of wine and a bite of supper?"

"Yes, thanks. In fact, I was hoping I might stay here for a while."

"Of course you shall, sir, as an honoured guest."

"How are your ladies?"

"In fine fettle, the lazy creatures. They've gone early to bed, since it's a quiet night."

"And Mr. Meyboom, is he still in the garret upstairs?"

"No, he left just after my return. He'd come into some money, he said, and could afford to move away from the river. Said the damp air was bad for his chest. Try a spell in the Fleet, I told him – that could finish anyone off."

She sat down and shared some wine with Laurence at table, and as he ate, he thought of his conversation with Ingram about Blackman Street.

When he asked if she had ever received a client of Sir Bernard Radcliff's description, she replied in the affirmative. "Hasn't graced us for over a year, though."

"He got married."

"That don't stop most men from darkening my door. And have you a wife, sir?" Laurence shook his head, and pushed back his empty plate. "Not even a lover? You must have at least one! Might she be fond of jewellery, Mr. Beaumont? I've some trinkets for sale, if you . . ." Mistress Edwards hesitated, with the peculiar delicacy of a high-class bawd, and he understood at once. She was forced to sell off her own property, just to make ends meet.

THE BEST OF MEN 579

"I'd like to see them," he said.

Simeon had taught him about gems and their cut, and he found it easy to select Mistress Edwards' best necklace, for which he gave her more than her price.

That night he shared Cordelia's bed; she was already fast asleep and did not wake when he got in beside her. In the morning, even before opening his eyes, he was aware of a pleasant sensation passing through him; and as he drew back the covers and saw what she was doing, he let her continue. He had been full of frustrated passion for Isabella ever since bringing her to Merton, but after that one kiss she had not encouraged him, and he had refrained from anything more than a few friendly visits to her sickbed. Now he could not argue with the part of his body that Cordelia had coaxed to action. Nonetheless, the experience was like eating with a bad head cold: he did not enjoy it as much as usual.

Over breakfast, he told Mistress Edwards how the women had assisted the Royalist cause on his previous visit, and how they might help him again. Later that day, her maid Sarah dropped by Sir Edmund Waller's house with the gift of a dried-quince cake to be delivered directly to him alone. Falkland's correspondence had been baked inside. Sarah returned bearing a note from Waller asking for her to be sent again in two days' time, so that he could reciprocate with a special offering from his own cook. Meanwhile, Jane headed north across the Thames and westwards, to call upon the law offices of Joshua Poole in Fleet Street. Mr. Poole was away, his clerk told her, and had not said when he would be back. Claiming she was a distant relative of Mrs. Poole's just arrived from the country, Jane obtained an address off Holborn Hill where she went to look around, and in the evening, she was able to give Laurence a description of both Poole's offices and his house.

On the following day, Cordelia took a turn about Fleet Street and came home with news. "He's there. I had it from a girl who was sweeping the steps next door. And I saw him through his window – a sad little man with beady eyes."

All well and good, Laurence thought, but how to approach him? Poole's offices gave onto a busy public courtyard; no arrest could be made in broad daylight without attracting the attention of a Parliamentary patrol. His house seemed a more likely prospect: it stood at the end of a row of other dwellings and had only one door to the street; to the back of the house were gardens and then a field. The main obstacle was Poole's ferocious guard dog, which had menaced Jane at the garden gate.

"You ask my servant Barlow to go round instead, sir," Mistress Edwards suggested. "He was a great sneaksman in his youth – prides hisself on it, and still has his fingers in a bit of that trade, I suspect. But he's been with me four years and did time with me in the Fleet. You can depend on him for your life."

The lugubrious Barlow averred that he knew everything there was to know about housebreaking, and disappeared for an entire day to scout out the neighbourhood of Holborn Hill. Jane visited Waller and came back with a partridge that must have hung too long, for it reeked, as did what had been stuffed up it: a sealed document for Falkland. The next day Laurence gave Barlow funds to buy a couple of good horses, and at dusk, he primed his pistols and said goodbye to Mistress Edwards and her ladies.

No moon or stars were visible as he and Barlow walked the horses north through small streets and alleys, and over London Bridge. Barlow must have been acquainted with every nightwatchman's beat, for they were not stopped. When they reached Holborn Hill, they waited an hour or so, their horses tethered, in the fields behind Poole's house. Once every light inside was extinguished, Barlow crept to the front to keep watch, armed with a cudgel, while Laurence pushed through the garden fence and gained the back entrance.

Immediately he heard growling. He had come equipped with a hambone that he now tossed over the garden gate, and the animal fell upon it, gnawing greedily as Laurence stole past, up the path to the house. Following Barlow's precise directions, he jimmied open a window on the ground floor and squeezed inside, then moved towards the stairs beneath which the potboy apparently slept in a cupboard. "He won't wake, sir – the young 'uns never do," Barlow had said. "They're too worn out from their labours. It's the old who sleep lightly, I've found."

The potboy did not wake. Laurence had three more occupants with whom to contend: Poole, his wife, and the maidservant. "She's Poole's daughter's niece by marriage," Barlow had informed him. "That's why she has a chamber to herself, off his."

"What *don't* you know about them?" Laurence had exclaimed; the Secretary of State could use a man such as this.

At the top of the stairs Laurence found the door to Poole's chamber ajar. He entered quietly, wishing that Barlow could have told him on which side of the bed Poole slept. But the sound of masculine snoring was sufficient indication. He drew aside the bed curtains with the nose of his pistol, and stuck it against Poole's temple.

"Mr. Poole," he whispered. Poole stirred, then blinked at him in alarm. "Don't wake your wife," he hissed. "Get out of bed, find yourself some clothes, and come downstairs with me. I won't hurt you if you do as I say." Poole slid from his wife's side and fumbled for his garments and shoes. Then he and Laurence descended the stairs and went out into the garden.

"How did you get past my dog?" he asked, a stunned expression on his face, as he dressed.

"I gave it a bone. Poole, I have to take you to Oxford. The Secretary of State wants to talk to you. If you're frank with him, you'll be safe from any charges," Laurence said encouragingly, although Falkland had made no such promise.

"Please, sir, spare me from arrest," Poole begged. "My poor wife is not strong! She needs me!"

"I'm sorry, it's not my decision."

As Laurence guided him through the gate towards the horses, which were invisible in the darkness, he began talking in a rapid whisper. "Sir, I'll tell you whatever I can, if you will only let me be! I saw Sir Bernard Radcliff at Longstanton four days ago. He told me you have his letters. He also told me about the regicide. All along he intended to prevent it! He is now looking for you, to explain this. And the Earl of Pembroke is after you both. He heard about that trial and is bent on questioning you."

"Does Pembroke know what happened to his correspondence with Radcliff?"

"No. Indeed, he cannot even be aware that Sir Bernard kept any of –" Poole stopped, as a whistle pierced the air: Barlow's signal. From up ahead, as though in answer, came a soft whinny and a stamping of hooves.

"We have to move," Laurence said. "Take the near horse." But as he lowered his pistol to untether both mounts, Poole swung out most unexpectedly and struck him below the ribs, winding him. More impressive yet, Poole managed to clamber into the saddle and urge the horse on, knocking Laurence over as it bolted in the direction of the fields.

"Stop or I'll fire!" Laurence shouted after him, putting up his pistol again, though he could not see a thing.

Then he felt a tap on his shoulder. "Where's the lawyer?" Barlow asked, helping him up.

"He gave me the slip. He went that way, on one of the horses."

"No chance of catching him now. Make haste, sir, there are watchmen on the street."

Barlow seemed to possess a feline instinct in the night. He located the other horse's bridle easily, mounted, and had extended a hand to help Laurence swing up behind him when a series of sounds ahead of them made them freeze: first the loud neigh of a panicked beast, next a man's cry, and lastly a dull thud.

"He may have been thrown," Laurence said. "Let's go and find out."

They went forward into blackness, but the horse found them, looming out of the dark like some nightmare apparition. Barlow grabbed its bridle and nudged Laurence's elbow. "There's the lawyer – he's on the ground, sir."

Poole was slumped at the base of a tree. Laurence squatted down to touch what felt like a leg. "Poole, are you hurt?" He searched upwards and this time felt a warm stickiness on Poole's scalp. Then as he lifted him up, Poole's head tilted back at an unnaturally acute angle. "God damn it," Laurence swore, and to Barlow, "He's dead."

"In that case, let's you and I ride north and split up once we get close to the new fortifications. You can pass through a gap near Shoreditch."

They mounted and spurred the horses on, Laurence again tailing Barlow, as grateful for his cool efficiency as his astounding powers of vision.

At the appointed place, they reined in. "Barlow, you have to tell me," Laurence said, "how can you see so well in the dark?"

"Practice, sir. Just blindfold yourself and walk around for a bit. You'll soon have the hang of it. My father taught me. Since I was five years old, I been getting inside houses to open up the door for him. A darkman's budge, we call it."

"I wish I had your skills."

"Well, thank you, sir," Barlow said modestly, "but you ain't never had to be a thief."

"You're wrong there – and I hope we can work together again."

He gave Barlow a little extra for all the trouble and galloped away, disheartened; in one part of his mission, he had signally failed.

III.

"So did you nab the lawyer?" Seward inquired, after inviting Laurence into his rooms. "Is he with Falkland now?"

"No, I'm afraid he's somewhere else altogether," replied Laurence, taking off his cloak; and he described Poole's accident. "And as for the uprising, I think it's doomed from the outset. I brought Falkland a letter from Waller, written in the simplest of codes. What a fool, to put down every detail. I had to transcribe it for Falkland, and he pretended there was nothing to worry about."

"And what *is* the plan?" asked Seward, as Laurence sat down with a sigh.

"Waller estimates that a third of London will support the uprising, and four-fifths in the suburbs, though where he got his numbers from I've no idea. Then there are Royalists within London's Trained Bands. On the night they're assigned guard of Parliament's fortifications, they'll seize the magazine of arms and powder, and secure all major military positions. Certain prominent Members of Parliament will be taken hostage. His Majesty intends to dispatch a force of three thousand – horse and foot – to enter the city once the gates are thrown open. No one person knows the names of more than three associates involved. Waller says he has the support of Lord Conway and the Earl of Portland, in the House of Lords."

"That is the extent of it?"

"Not quite. Falkland told me I'll be travelling with a third companion, apart from my Lady d'Aubigny and Lady Sophia Murray, a Mr. Alexander Hampden."

"Any relation to the Parliamentary commander of the same name?"

"He's John Hampden's cousin."

Seward shook his head dismally. "And he can be trusted?"

"His Majesty trusts him, which has to be enough for *me*. Hampden is going to London to request an answer from Parliament to the King's demand of last April for the immediate surrender of his ships and forts." Laurence rose and grabbed his cloak. "I'm losing patience with Falkland. He should let me go after Radcliff and leave this venture to those who are already up to their necks in it."

"Instead he's thrusting you back into the lion's den. When must you depart?"

"The day after tomorrow," Laurence said, as he wandered over to Seward's bedchamber and took a glance around.

"If you are hunting for Mistress Savage," said Seward, "I sent her to Clarke's house at Asthall. I could not bend College rules indefinitely by keeping her here. She won't be out of town long. Lord Digby is finding her accommodation."

"Have they patched up their quarrel?"

"Yes, and a very judicious move of hers it was, too. No one else will look after her as he can."

"That scheming arsehole only looks after himself. I want to see her before I leave for London."

"No, Beaumont!" Seward exclaimed. "You cannot be distracted when you are about to undertake a vital assignment for the Secretary of State! My dear fellow, has your infatuation with Mistress Savage blinded you to reality?"

"Excuse me?" Laurence said, raising his eyebrows.

"You understand me perfectly well – as does she. In truth, for a woman, she is remarkably rational on the subject. Though she says she is indebted to you for your late exploit as her knight errant –"

"I must say, Seward, I do resent your discussing any of this with her when I'm not present to contribute to the conversation," Laurence interrupted acidly. "As for what I did, she did far more for me, intervening with Lady d'Aubigny and putting up with Milne, which could be why she quarrelled with Digby. He can't have liked her abasing herself with that pig. In fact, I wouldn't be surprised if she even helped with the testimonial from Prince Rupert and Wilmot." He stopped, on seeing Seward's face. "So you knew! Why in God's name didn't you say anything?"

"She insisted on my silence. How old are you, Beaumont, thirty or thirteen? If you continue with her, she will have no advantage of it. She is used goods, as she is well aware."

"How dare you speak of her like that!"

Seward moved forward and seized him by the sleeve. "Will you stop and listen to my advice?"

"Not about her," said Laurence, and he walked out, slamming the door behind him.

It was a clear afternoon, hot for mid-May, and his horse fairly flew over the distance between Oxford and Asthall. Along the way, he boiled with anger at Seward; at the same time, however, he could not be sure how Isabella would receive him. What if her embrace outside Seward's window had been merely an impulsive gesture of thanks for taking her away from Milne? She had been almost delirious at the time, and might not even remember that kiss.

When he rode up to Clarke's house, she emerged from the kitchen garden that bordered it as though he had conjured her up just by thinking of her. Her hair was loose, newly washed and still wet, draped over her shoulders, and she wore an apron and gloves stained with fresh mud.

As he dismounted, she dropped him a curtsey. "Mr. Beaumont, you have caught me again when I am at my most unkempt. I was planting vegetables, a novel experience for me."

Her tone and mode of address chilled him; the same as at the Blue Boar, he thought to himself. "Are you better?" he asked.

"Yes, thank you." She turned away, to the garden; the housekeeper was now approaching them, which gave him hope that propriety rather than indifference was inspiring her cool behaviour this time.

"Good day, madam," he said, to the housekeeper.

"Mr. Beaumont, we did not expect you," she said. "My Lord Digby was to send for Mistress Savage. His coach is due tomorrow." Isabella nodded in confirmation. "Let me wash my hands and I'll get you a draught of ale, sir," the woman added. "My boy can tend to your horse."

"No, thank you, I'll do it," Laurence insisted, darting a look at Isabella.

"As you wish, then. You may curry and water him in the barn, and put him out to graze in the far meadow. We're still safe from horse thieves in these parts. Mistress Savage, you will want to go up and dress your hair for the gentleman."

"I am not in the least concerned to impress Mr. Beaumont," Isabella said, removing her soiled gloves and handing them to the housekeeper. "But I should speak with him." She walked apart from Laurence to the barn, and as he unsaddled his horse she inquired, in the same formal tone, "How was your journey to London?"

"Not much of a success," he said, starting to brush down the animal's damp coat.

"Was it to do with the Commission of Array?"

"Partly."

She asked no more questions, pacing about until he finished his tasks. Then she accompanied him as he led the horse into the meadow and set it free. "I am most grateful to Dr. Seward for sheltering me at the College, and now here," she remarked, at length.

"Isabella –" he began, but she talked over him.

"Nonetheless, I shall be glad to return to Oxford. After sponsoring your game of cards with Captain Milne, Digby has paid him yet more money to desist from harrying me. And through considerable luck, Digby also found me a small house off the Woodstock Road, since I am not about to move back to my old lodgings. Do you know, it's over a month and that wound to his leg has still not healed. He has the most incompetent physician –"

"Isabella, I love you," Laurence told her suddenly; and as the words leapt out of his mouth, he knew that he loved her as he had never loved before.

She frowned at him severely. "That cannot be."

"Why not?" he asked, taken aback by her certainty.

"Think of who you are, and who I am. I have tried to keep a distance between us for your own good and mine, though I admit, my resolve did falter temporarily after you came so heroically to my rescue."

"Which was nothing, compared to what you did for me."

"Dr. Seward broke his promise."

"Digby told me, not Seward."

This seemed to perplex her, but she shrugged her shoulders. "Well, whatever the case, we behaved as friends should. Let's not spoil our friendship now."

"Don't you . . .?" He sighed: it was as he had feared. "I'm sorry. How stupid of me to think you might feel anything more than that."

She did not speak for a moment, her face softening. "Beaumont," she said, "I have always wanted to be your friend ever since I first saw you, but, to be honest, I did not believe you were capable of true friendship with a woman. I suspected that you did not have much of a heart – that you were just a better copy of Wilmot and the many others who have sought me out for the usual reason. Then, at Shrewsbury, I discovered that I was wrong. And I realised that I must on no account fall in love with you." There was a pause, which he dared not interrupt. "I armoured myself against temptation, and I was nearly invincible – until I saw the look in your eyes when I told you my sordid story. They say a woman's tears come cheap, and I have seen men cry before. I have even made them cry. Yet *you* – once more, you surprised me. And you were so sweet to me at Merton, candid as a boy in your affection. You had no need to declare it." She lowered her eyes and went on sorrowfully, "I do love you, though I shall recover from it in time, as I have from my quartain sickness. Go, Beaumont, and forget what you said to me today. It was a fancy of your imagination – a passing dream, from which you will soon awake clear-headed."

"No I won't," he murmured.

He stood gazing at her, and she at him; and she began to weep without making a sound, the water pouring down her cheeks. He could not bear to watch, for her grief was his own. Risking that she might push him away, he took her in his arms; and she clung to him tightly.

Unlike the night of the wedding, they had only grass for their bed, and they were quick with each other. Afterwards she appeared as dazed as he was himself. Then he remembered the necklace, and pulled it out of his doublet pocket. "This is for you. I heard you had to pawn your jewellery a while ago."

"So I did!" She gathered up her hair so that he could fasten it about her throat. "Thank you," she said, kissing him on the cheek. "I shall wear it with pride."

"Isabella," he told her, after they had restored their clothing, "I have to go to London tomorrow. You know why."

She nodded slowly. "Are you afraid of what will happen there?"

"I can tell you already. The uprising will fail."

"Will you be able to escape?"

"I can only hope so."

"I am afraid for you, Beaumont, more than ever. And if you do come back to me, which by the grace of God I trust you will, I shall still be afraid. Digby may not want us to be together. He likes his power over me, and he is a keen observer of human nature. We must be very careful."

"He should let you choose for yourself."

"Brave words, as brave as your profession of love," she said, kissing his cheek again. "You will have time to reflect, however, while you are away from me. And I would prefer you be honest if you change your mind. Will you promise me that? Don't spare me, if you have the smallest doubt."

"I promise. But you should stop doubting *me*."

"It is to protect myself," she reminded him, soberly.

The light was fading as they left the meadow, his horse trotting after them, and as they entered the house, Clarke's servant appraised them both, and the necklace, too, though she said nothing. She fed them a supper that they made an effort to eat, avoiding each other's eyes, and they retired, Isabella to her own chamber and Laurence to Clarke's. He slept soundly until late the next morning, when on his pillow he found a note in her flowing script. Digby's coach had come for her, she wrote, and she had not wanted to wake him to say goodbye. She would be praying for him, she added.

IV.

Pembroke strolled in the lush grounds of Wilton House, examining his garden with mixed discontent and self-congratulation. The work on it had begun more than ten years before, under the direction of Inigo Jones and the Frenchman de Caus, and was still only half done. Pembroke had planned a series of fountains and a bridge across the river, in Palladian style, but had managed to complete just the right-hand aspect of his design before he lost the King's favour and embarked on that other, grander plan that had since cost him both money and peace of mind. As he turned back towards the house, he was surprised to see Sir Bernard Radcliff walking with measured steps across the lawn towards him.

Radcliff removed his hat and bowed with his habitual dignity. "Forgive me, my lord, I am late in responding to your summons."

"More than a month," Pembroke said coldly, examining him; he looked as if he were afflicted with some wasting sickness.

"I was making progress on that issue we discussed, back in February. I now know who sent you the message in our code." Pembroke held his breath, waiting for Radcliff to continue. "Remember when we talked together in this same garden, in the autumn of twenty-nine, and I first mentioned the casting of horoscopes? I told you then that I had been instructed by a scholar, a Merton man. His name is William Seward. He sent you the message." Pembroke frowned: he had been expecting another name, that of Laurence Beaumont. "In truth," Radcliff said, "he is himself part author of the code."

"What? I thought *you* had designed it! You said so, when you gave it to me!"

"I did write much of it but the particular arrangement of cabbalistic figures was one that he shared with me when I studied with him at Oxford. I borrowed it for our purposes, certain that he would never find out. I thought he would be dead by now, for he was elderly even then. But he is very much alive and must have discovered everything about our scheme."

"How?" Pembroke asked, after a tense silence.

"I believe, through scrying – a means of divination. He may have used a crystal, or a mirror, or simply a bowl of any liquid substance, which, if I recall, was his favourite method."

Pembroke stared at him and then exploded into laughter. "By Jesus, how gullible do you think me?"

"William Seward is the sole man in England, to my knowledge, who is familiar with the cabbalistic figures as they appear in our code. As I said, he is its begetter. And his path crossed mine again last July, so he will have been reminded of me."

"Did you reveal any of our private affairs to him?" Pembroke demanded, now wondering if the mysterious Dr. Seward might be in league with Radcliff, against him.

"No, my lord. We did not even meet. While I was in Oxford raising my troop early in August, my brother-in-law, Ingram, introduced me to a friend from his university days. During the course of our conversation, the friend expressed a desire to call upon Seward at Merton College. Seward had been his tutor and Ingram's, though Ingram had never told me. It must have been this friend who mentioned me to Seward, quite accidentally, in passing. And Seward, probably curious as to what had become of me, must have gazed into his scrying bowl."

"What outrageous nonsense!" Pembroke cried.

"My lord, you said that your efforts to court the favour of Prince Charles' tutor, Dr. Earle, had been rebuffed. In your words, it was as if he had been warned away from you. He was. Earle is Seward's close friend." Pembroke laughed again, yet a small anxiety twigged within him: Earle was the Secretary of State's close friend, also. "And last week," added Radcliff, "Joshua Poole came by a very strange fate. His body was found in a field at the bottom of his garden. His neck had been broken and his skull caved in on one side."

"He must have been set upon by thieves."

"But he was not robbed. I spoke with his wife, who is in a terrible state. She said that the guard dog made not a single noise to alert the family of any intruder. Poole got up, dressed and left in the night, voluntarily it seems, without waking her. He may have been under the influence of some spell."

"This is all pure speculation!"

"I wish it were, yet I fear that I am next on Dr. Seward's list. He has visited me in my sleep every night this past month," Radcliff confessed, running a tremulous hand over his face. "He is overlooking me, I can feel it. And he will be overlooking you, my lord."

"Why has he not killed you, rather than Poole? Or me, for that matter?"

"I do not know. It may be that he is taking the smallest of us first."

If Seward wished to foil my scheme, Pembroke wanted to ask, *why would he reveal to me that it was betrayed?* Then he hit upon a better tactic. "Sir Bernard, I've something to show you," he said. "Come."

He marched Radcliff back to the house and up into the clock tower, the oldest part of the building. Here, in a room fusty for lack of use, he had stored the telltale canvas of Eros and Harpocrates. He unveiled it, watching for Radcliff's reaction.

Radcliff surveyed the work without a hint of shock or guilt; on the contrary, he appeared impressed. "How astute of Dr. Seward to throw suspicion on me. He wanted you to do away with me, and thereby destroy any link between him and the code, since it could implicate him in our plans if everything comes out. He has been accused of many dark dealings in the past."

"Did he teach *you* the art of scrying?" Pembroke asked curiously.

"Alas, no. I think he decided to keep that weapon to himself, once he had seen my gift for astrology."

Pembroke indicated the canvas. "A man by the name of Laurence Beaumont commissioned this. If we have been discovered as you suggest, he must be linked to William Seward. Get him for me, and bring him to my house in London. We shall then learn whether there is any truth to your absurd suppositions."

"But, my lord, how will I –"

"I shall give some particulars to aid you in your search for him. Fail me and I can assure you, without the benefit of astrological guidance, that you will have no future to speak of. I told you I needed another agent, and I have taken steps to remedy the problem. You are no longer indispensable to me, Sir Bernard. Do you hear?"

"Yes, my lord," Radcliff murmured.

"And bring me Seward, too. Once I have finished questioning him, you may be cured of your nightmares." *As I may be of my own,* Pembroke concluded, to himself.

V.

Had he been in a less pessimistic mood, Laurence might have viewed his next trip to London as a comedy of errors. From the start, Lady d'Aubigny and her friend Lady Sophia Murray maddened him with their indiscreet chatter and flirtatious giggling. Hampden he totally mistrusted. The only one of his fellow travellers who did not wear upon his nerves was the page, Ibrahim, an intelligent lad with a sense of humour as dark as his skin. Once they arrived at Lady d'Aubigny's mansion, Hampden went off to deliver His Majesty's letter to Parliament while Lady Sophia exited with Lady d'Aubigny, who had the Commission of Array tucked down the front of her dress. When they all returned in high spirits from their respective errands, they had a feast; and Laurence drank as much as he could, though it did not calm his nerves.

They waited for developments over two long days. Avoiding both Hampden and the ladies, Laurence whiled away the tense hours playing cards with Ibrahim. Then Hampden casually announced that he was going for a walk. This time he failed to come back, and Lady Sophia finally confessed to Laurence that he had been carrying a letter to the Earl of Dover's wife telling her to get out of London with her children as soon as she could, because a major political upheaval was about to occur. Laurence was horrified at Hampden's recklessness, compounding the danger to all of them. The next day, they learnt that the House of Commons had rejected the terms of His Majesty's letter, though a majority in the Lords had favoured renewing peace overtures. A member of the Commons suggested impeaching the Queen herself for taking up arms against the realm, and this proposal was passed and sent up to the Lords. And Hampden had been arrested.

Laurence would have quit London immediately but was under strict instructions from His Majesty not to leave the women unprotected. A week dragged by, punctuated by sullen arguments, during which he forbade anyone to leave the house. On the last day of May, they received more awful news: Sir Edmund Waller had been seized. Parliamentary soldiers had discovered the Commission of Array in his brother-in-law's cellar.

"I didn't give it to his brother-in-law, I gave it to a man called Chaloner," Lady d'Aubigny moaned, as Laurence hurried her and Lady Sophia off to the French Embassy.

Upon receiving them, the Ambassador curtly informed Laurence that he could offer sanctuary to the ladies and their servants only. Laurence raced off to hide at Blackman Street, while rumours flew about over the next few days and other arrests were made: Waller had incriminated many, including his own brother-in-law, who would surely hang. More disastrously for Laurence, Lady d'Aubigny and Lady Sophia Murray had been removed from the Embassy and taken as prisoners to the Tower of London.

"They won't suffer," Mistress Edwards told him. "They're pretty young women with handles to their names. Parliament will have mercy on them. But it's a good thing you weren't seized, or you'd be dancing the hornpipe at Tyburn along with the rest of those sorry buggers. And we won't have no more talk of peace from the rebels, mark my words."

A calamity for Falkland, Laurence thought. As for himself, even if he escaped arrest on his way out of the city, he would be in no strong position upon returning to Oxford, for he had disobeyed the King's orders.

VI.

After a gruelling ride back to Oxford, Laurence was summoned, with Falkland, to the royal chambers. They barely spoke as they walked over to Christ Church, both equally grim, anticipating a hostile reception from His Majesty.

"Mr. Beaumont, you were just a youth when last I stayed at your father's house on a progress through Gloucestershire," His Majesty observed, as Laurence bowed to him. "Those were less d-difficult times. Today I must demand some explanation of your conduct, sir. I b-believe you were asked to keep guard of my Lady d'Aubigny and Lady Murray during their mission. Why did you not remain with them?"

"I was declined sanctuary by the French Ambassador, Your Majesty," Laurence replied. "And had I insisted on staying, I could have done nothing to prevent Parliament from taking them into custody."

"He would have been arraigned and questioned also, Your Majesty," Falkland intervened, "under torture, no doubt."

And then hanged, Laurence added privately.

"You suffered torture before, did you not?" the King asked Laurence.

"Yes, Your Majesty."

"I can understand that you would not wish to undergo the same again. Nevertheless, it is hard for me to forgive your recent dereliction of duty, particularly as my own family is concerned." The King cast him a pained frown. "I remember how my Lady d'Aubigny made every attempt to help you when you were imprisoned."

"I am aware of that, Your Majesty, and am most beholden to her for her kindness," Laurence said, bowing his head.

"You repaid it very ill," the King said tersely. "Now, my Lord Falkland has alerted me to a plot that you brought to his attention – a potentially scurrilous affair, involving the Earl of Pembroke, whom I thought to be my friend."

"Your Majesty," Falkland interjected, "I most urgently require Mr. Beaumont's services to investigate it."

The King looked heavenwards, then at them. "It was to threaten my life when – a year hence?" he inquired of Falkland, with the suggestion of a smile.

"Yes, Your Majesty."

"And I was to enter into negotiations with his lordship, the earl, who would try to d-dispose of me in some cunning manner?"

"Yes, Your Majesty, as is clear from the letters you read."

"Well, then, forewarned is forearmed. I still see no need to act upon it, as yet."

"Your Majesty, there is every need," said Laurence, at which he felt Falkland's hand on his sleeve.

"Mr. Beaumont," the King said, "why hurry, when we are not in possession of all the facts. You could not have known this, but – unbeknownst to Parliament, also – his lordship pledged an oath of fealty to me last summer, and he has been true to his word. He has not taken up arms against me and has gone to considerable effort in rallying support for a peaceful settlement."

"That's part of his scheme. He hopes to gain your confidence."

"And you are eroding it, sir, through your impertinence." The King's smile faded. "My Lord Falkland, until I can hear from Lady d'Aubigny what occurred at the French Embassy, I should prefer that Mr. Beaumont not stray too far. Keep him in Oxford, my lord. Since he has a knowledge of ciphers, have him train your agents in that useful skill."

Laurence shook off Falkland's hand. "Your Majesty, you must be aware that Pembroke –"

"Mr. Beaumont, I am disappointed in you," snapped the King. "Do as I bid you, or else you shall find yourself under restraint. Good day, sir, and good day to your lordship."

"You ought to have been more diplomatic, Mr. Beaumont," Falkland scolded, as they walked back through the College grounds. "Other than Her Majesty the Queen, only Prince Rupert is allowed such freedom in addressing His Majesty, and even *he* may one day earn the King's displeasure for speaking his mind."

"Forgive me, my lord," said Laurence, unapologetically.

He expected another chastisement, but Falkland was staring mournfully ahead. "I am so aggrieved by my friend Waller's behaviour!

He betrayed and sent to the gallows a man virtually his brother! It is war that has corrupted him."

Laurence could not help thinking of Tom, though he merely commented, "You can't entirely blame him for trying to buy his own life, given the alternative."

"If His Majesty fails to reach terms with Parliament," Falkland said next, "I believe that I shall enlist soon as a regular in some regiment that has no connection to my political office. To serve as a simple soldier has more merit than this infernal game I am forced to play."

They had been walking side by side. Laurence now stepped in front of him so that Falkland had to stop. "You mustn't do that," Laurence said, feeling a rush of compassion for the man. "For your wife's sake, if nothing else, don't do it."

Falkland gave a little shrug. "Lettice would understand. She has always understood me better than anyone."

VII.

"It's very swollen today, my lord, and there is a discharge of pus," said the physician.

"You have no need to inform me," Digby said. "It hurts like the devil." A servant appeared and announced that Mr. Beaumont was here to see his lordship. "Excellent. Send him in," ordered Digby. He saw Beaumont hesitate at the door, evidently noticing his state of undress. "Mr. Beaumont, pray come and give me your view: why will my leg not heal?"

Beaumont advanced to look. "What have you been treating it with?"

"Everything conceivable."

"I would let it heal naturally, my lord."

Digby was examining him, as he inspected the wound. "If I were a woman, I would covet those luxuriant eyelashes of yours." Beaumont jerked his head up. "Don't you appreciate compliments?" Digby added.

"That would depend on who's giving them," Beaumont said, with a lazy smile.

Digby agreed, laughing; then he sighed. "How I hate to be an invalid, unable even to sit a horse comfortably. But you must know my frustration. Isabella tells me that when you were serving abroad you took a musket ball in the chest. Would you oblige me by showing me the scar?"

"Why, my lord?"

"To satisfy my interest in surgical operations."

Beaumont opened his doublet and pulled up his shirt, at which Digby emitted a low whistle. At that moment Isabella entered unannounced; she was wearing her bronze silk gown, and a necklace that Digby did not recognise.

"Gentlemen," she said, "have I interrupted you in some masculine pastime?"

"We are comparing our war wounds, Isabella," Digby said, "and Mr. Beaumont's far surpasses my little scratch." He saw her nod at Beaumont, who bowed to her, with no particular expression on his face. "Mr. Beaumont," Digby went on, "I have not yet thanked you for snatching Isabella from Captain Milne. I find especially delightful the fact that you won her from him at cards!"

"At your expense, my lord," Beaumont said, as he stuffed his shirt back into his breeches.

"There may be consequences, however," Digby said, wagging a finger at him. "I hope you are fast with a rapier, because he has sworn to call you out."

"So I hear. Might I ask why you sent for me, other than for a medical opinion?"

"I wanted to discuss my proposal about *Mercurius Aulicus*. You haven't forgotten? I need a man with a nose for information."

"Speaking of noses, Digby, you are offending mine," Isabella commented. "Your wound, or whatever you have put on it, stinks."

"You should clean off the poultice," Beaumont said.

"Would you undertake the task for me, sir?"

Beaumont looked directly at him. "You have a doctor here, my lord."

"But I should prefer that you do it."

Beaumont requested hot water and a sponge, and as he tended to the wound, Digby watched his long fingers at work and imagined them exploring Isabella's lovely skin. She was wandering around the room, fiddling with her necklace.

"What a stir in London," Digby began again. "I can just picture the beautiful but feckless Lady d'Aubigny caught by some prick-eared Puritan as she was smuggling His Majesty's Commission of Array in the bosom of her dress."

"She was not caught with it down her dress," Isabella objected. "You know very well that she had delivered it before her arrest."

"Allow me some artistic licence! I write plays, Mr. Beaumont, were you aware of that?" Beaumont shook his head. "Although you must admit, Isabella, even had I written it as a piece for the stage, it could not be more *épatant*. Edmund Waller spilling all to preserve his life, which will also cost him some ten thousand pounds in fines and banishment once he serves his sentence, and those others whom he inculpated cursing him with their last breath as they go to the gallows! No wonder Parliament declared the fifteenth of June a day of public thanksgiving, for delivering the city from evil. Yet, thank God, the ladies will be spared any punishment, other than a brief spell in gaol. There are still some honourable souls in both Houses." He waited for a response, either from Beaumont or Isabella, but they were silent, so he persisted, "What about you, Mr. Beaumont? You were in London at the time. What did you think of it?"

"Not much," Beaumont replied, in his laconic way. He dropped the sponge in the bowl of water, now tinged pink with Digby's blood, and wiped his hands on a dry cloth. "Don't let anyone interfere with the wound. Just put a clean bandage on it. And no more poultices, or you'll have gangrene."

"Worry not, sir, I shan't require you to amputate my limb."

"Some would pay money for that privilege," Isabella said.

"Yes, Prince Rupert certainly would, and probably Wilmot, too! That reminds me – is Falkland still keeping you from Wilmot's service, Mr. Beaumont?" Beaumont smiled at him again, rather challengingly this time. "How lucky for you. Though having seen that scar of yours, I can comprehend why you would choose to eschew the field of battle, to train his spies for him instead."

"Lest you did not get his meaning, Mr. Beaumont," said Isabella, "Digby is calling you a coward."

"Oh I don't mind," Beaumont said, with a laugh. "I've been called that by better men than him."

Isabella cleared her throat, as if suppressing her own amusement.

"Yet are you not a little in disgrace, sir, after the events in London?" Digby inquired, amused too, but simultaneously piqued by his retort. "I heard you had your wrist slapped by His Majesty for abandoning his young cousin's widow in her hour of need. Some might call that a cowardly act."

"None of us is beyond self-interest, my lord. But in this case, I would have been no use to her, or to His Majesty, had I let myself be arrested."

"Oh yes – once tortured, twice shy."

"Precisely. Good day to you, my lord."

"Please don't neglect me, Doctor Beaumont. You must come back and check on my progress."

"Of course. Good day, Mistress Savage."

"Good day to you, sir," she said, politely cool, though as soon as Beaumont had gone, she asked Digby crossly, "Why did you engineer this encounter between us?"

"I suppose it was unnecessary, since you are seeing quite enough of him these days, at your house," Digby said. "Or should I say, these nights. But I thought it would be entertaining to observe you two together. And I *was* entertained, mightily."

"Why did you ask him to clean your wound? To humiliate him?"

"No, to test the strength of his stomach. Now come here and let me see that necklace. It's new, isn't it. Whoever gave it to you has taste, as well as money."

"I might have bought it myself."

"When have you ever had to buy your own jewellery?" Gently Digby stroked her cheek with his fingertips. "How is he in bed, my dear? I confess to a certain curiosity. Does he live up to expectations? Such a tall fellow . . . he must be splendidly proportioned."

"Now you are being lewd, Digby. It doesn't suit you."

"And you are blushing, which suggests to me that I am right."

"You sound as if you would like to bed him yourself."

Digby threw back his head and chortled. "No, but I shall be pleased to work with him. In that respect, he and I are a match made in heaven."

"I cannot think of two more different people."

"Difference is healthy in a relationship. And we shall get along famously, for we harbour no illusions about each other. Somewhat like you and me, my dear. Besides, I have another motive."

"What could that be?"

"To eliminate any impediment to your happiness. He is a vast improvement on Captain Milne, so I intend you to be with your lover as often as you want."

"How gracious of you. I thought you wished to marry me off."

"In time, when you grow bored of him. You do have to wonder," Digby said, after a short pause, "what went on between him and those ladies, on the road to London." Isabella stopped touching her necklace and squinted at him. "Everyone knows of Lady d'Aubigny's lust for Mr. Beaumont," he continued, "and as for Lady Sophia, I have met cats in heat that are more modest. Do you think he could have done them both?"

"Why don't you ask him, when he next comes to visit you?" she said smoothly.

"I most definitely will!" Digby rejoined; her insouciance did not fool him for a second.

VIII.

Lord Beaumont picked up the letter that Adam had delivered from Thomas, and read it yet again: "There was a victory at Chalgrove Field. Ormiston fought bravely, but died of a wound to his stomach on the road back to Oxford. His last words were to send Elizabeth his love and that he regretted his time together with her was so short. He was not in any pain. We lost only twelve men, him amongst them. We buried him alongside the others, at Oxford, for we had no means to send back his body."

"To think that this war has made a widow of Elizabeth before her twentieth birthday," he remarked sadly to his wife.

"At least she is with us now," Lady Beaumont reminded him, for Ormiston's mother, stricken by the death of her only son, had taken to bed, and while his sisters fussed around her, Elizabeth had pleaded to return to Chipping Campden.

"A common grave," he lamented. "She will not even know where he lies. If it were one of our own sons!"

Supper that evening was a dismal affair. The small amount that Lord Beaumont could force down tasted worse than dust in his mouth, and the wine he drank aggravated a dizziness that had troubled him frequently of late. He retired, his head aching, and feigned sleep when his wife joined him, for he was too unhappy for conversation. But he did not doze until far into the night.

He dreamt that he was standing once again in the courtyard at Seville, young and shy and nervous, come to ask for the hand in marriage of Elena Capdavila y Fuentes. He stifled in the heat, moisture trickling off his brow and down the back of his neck. The sunshine blinded him, even as he sought shade beneath the almond trees, and he felt lulled into a stupor by the tinkling noise of the fountains. Then a figure emerged from one of the archways and beckoned to him. It was her cousin Antonio, dressed in dark olive-green velvet and a hat plumed with white feathers. Lord Beaumont approached and they bowed to each other.

"I must congratulate you," Antonio said, showing his perfect teeth in a wide smile. "Of all the girls, you picked my favourite – the eldest. Do you not notice in Elena a marked resemblance to myself?"

"You are very like," said Lord Beaumont. "But that is only natural, your mother and hers being sisters."

"Natural, is it?" exclaimed Antonio. And he guffawed with laughter, as if he had just heard the best of witticisms.

Lord Beaumont lurched to consciousness. Sun streamed through the bed curtains, and the birds were chirruping their morning chorus. He removed his nightcap, which was damp with perspiration. Why should such a dream have visited him, and why should it so disturb him? He had not thought of Antonio since last Christmas, when he had told Elizabeth the rumour about her mother's Moorish ancestry.

He remembered the one visit he had made to Antonio's home, a vast crumbling edifice some centuries old. His host had treated him cordially, pouring him excellent wines, though the food upset his stomach afterwards: too much oil and garlic, and meat kept too long in warm temperatures. Antonio had questioned him with great interest about his estate and his parents, and how they might accept his foreign bride; and Lord Beaumont answered frankly that he knew that it would not be easy, given the religious and political differences between England and Spain.

"Parents are a curse, are they not," Antonio declared, stretching out his elegant legs and putting his feet up on the table. "Though I can hardly complain. Both of mine are gone. My mother died bearing me." He paused, resting his pale eyes on Lord Beaumont. "Do you know, she had been wed six years without issue before I took root in her womb. Her husband was an elderly man reckoned by his doctors to be impotent."

"These apparent miracles do happen," Lord Beaumont remarked.

"He went to his grave a year after her, leaving me sole heir to a diminished fortune and this ancient pile of rubble. Which is why I had to become a soldier, and could not be, as you are, a man of leisure. We are all poor but noble," Antonio said, with a scornful laugh. "Look at Elena's sisters. Unless they are married off soon, how many of them will escape the convent?"

"If her father had not been taken by sickness in the Indies, he might have repaired their fortunes," Lord Beaumont pointed out.

Antonio removed his feet from the table and leant forward. "Let me tell you about him. It was said that he had infidel blood, from some misadventure on his grandmother's side. He courted *my* mother before Elena's – he was crazed with love for her and nearly killed himself when she was sold behind his back to a withered old prick. So he married her younger sister, to be near her as much as he could, without anyone raising an eyebrow. One he took through the front door of the Church, but the other –" Antonio winked at Lord Beaumont, who was struggling to follow his rapid Castilian. "As for me," Antonio continued, "before he set out for the Indies that last time, he forbade me to come to his house. Immoral, he called me! I came by it honestly."

As he listened, Lord Beaumont thought that Antonio must have few friends, to unburden himself so to a stranger. After that, they saw each other only once or twice and exchanged no more than courtesies. Lord Beaumont had been too preoccupied by his betrothed: when he departed with her from Seville, she was inconsolable at leaving her mother and sisters.

Sitting up in bed, he looked over at her while she slept, as desirable to him after more than thirty years as when they had first met. "My dear," he whispered, tapping her arm, "I have had the most extraordinary dream."

"What?" she murmured, and then her eyes opened. "Are you sick, my lord? Your colour is very high."

"It is the dream that has agitated me, though I am not sure why."

"Was it about Elizabeth?"

"No – about your cousin Antonio, of all people!"

As he described it to her, her expression changed from concern to appalled shock, and then to anger, as though he were deliberately insulting her. "If you love me, you will never speak of this again!" she cried, and launching from the bed, she swept out of the chamber.

Immediately Lord Beaumont felt heartsick: why, at a time of mourning and sorrow, had he been so thoughtless as to trouble her with memories of her past? He must beg her forgiveness. He threw off the covers and was getting to his feet when a mist dimmed his sight, and his legs grew numb. Then came a rush of heat within, as if his head were made of some explosive substance ready to ignite; and he clutched vainly for the bedpost, knowing himself about to fall.

CHAPTER NINETEEN

I.

A dam regarded Laurence sourly, then pointed towards a lone man hunched on the ground a little apart from the other soldiers in Prince Rupert's encampment. "Over there. *Sir*," he added, through his teeth.

As Laurence came closer, he saw that Tom was stripping and cleaning a pistol. The look of concentration on his face and the trim of his beard and moustache were so reminiscent of a younger, vigorous Lord Beaumont that Laurence hesitated painfully before speaking his name.

"What brings you here?" Tom inquired. "Have you at last come to offer your sympathies upon Ormiston's death?"

"Didn't you get my letter?" Laurence asked, though he felt guilty that he had not sought Tom out. Indeed, he had sought out no one lately save Isabella, often at the expense of his work for the Secretary of State.

"A few paltry lines of your scrawl!" Tom was clutching the pistol so tightly that his knuckles were white. "What if it had been Ingram? Do you think I would have let a day pass, if I could help it, without telling you how sorry I was?" He stopped, perhaps waiting for Laurence to speak, or to control his own emotion, before resuming more quietly, "You know how Ormiston died? In my arms, with his belly blown open and his guts hanging out. He spoke just a few words, and then he was gone. We only lost a couple of men, and he had to be one of them. Have you ever done that – held a man in your arms as he takes his final breath?"

"Yes, I have."

"Well, then." Tom started cleaning the pistol again with ferocious determination.

"Tom, there's more bad news – from home," Laurence said. "Our father has suffered an apoplectic fit."

"A fit?" Tom's eyes widened. "He's not – he's not dead?"

"No, but he's partly paralysed, and he can't talk. Our mother fears that he could have another seizure. She wants us both to come home. Falkland has granted me leave and will settle with the Prince for yours. We can ride out now."

"It's *you* he'll want to see – his heir."

"Oh for God's sake," Laurence exclaimed, "he might die. He may be dead before we even get there."

Tom was searching in his doublet. "Here, give this to Elizabeth." He held out a ring, which he dropped into Laurence's hand as though to avoid all contact with him. "Ormiston wished her to have it. You can make whatever excuse you choose for my absence."

"Please, as your brother, I'm begging you –"

"Ormiston was more of a brother to me than you've ever been, or ever will be," Tom cut in hoarsely.

"For the sake of our family, then. Please come."

Tom shook his head, and turned back to his pistol.

On the way north out of the city, Laurence called at Isabella's house. Her maidservant Lucy invited him in, smiling until she saw his expression, then motioned him quickly upstairs. At the bedchamber, he paused by the open door; Isabella was at her sponge bath. He watched, quite still, as if in disturbing her he might shatter everything between them.

She must have felt a presence, for with that endearing instinct of a woman caught unawares she crossed her arms over her breasts, to peer over her shoulder. "You!" she said; then like Lucy, she became instantly grave. "What is it, Beaumont?"

He picked her up, dripping wet as she was, set her on the bed and knelt down before her. "My father is sick. He may be dying. I have to go to him."

"Oh my love," she whispered. He rested his head on her lap and inhaled the fragrant perfume of her soap, wanting to stay, comforted by the simple warmth of her skin against his. But she drew him up, and looked very directly at him. "It was too good to last, wasn't it. We should accept what we knew all along. It must end."

"No," he insisted, trembling. "Whatever happens won't change my feelings for you."

"Beaumont, I told you once before," she said, "think of who you are and will be, and who *I* am. I cannot marry you, and I cannot give you children. All that I could ever be to you is a mistress, of whom you would eventually tire."

"Have some faith," he encouraged her, but she said nothing to this, and merely kissed him goodbye.

II.

"I trust I can rely on *you* not to dissolve into tears," Lady Beaumont told Laurence with unaccustomed gentleness, as he looked down at his father.

Lord Beaumont lay sleeping in bed, in his neat cap and gown, his mouth contorted on the right side. His skin was unnaturally pale. His hands, palms up on the coverlet, resembled inanimate objects that did not belong to him. If not for the rise and fall of his chest and the soft sound of his breathing, he might have been a corpse laid out for burial.

"We have hope – he is much better than he was," she went on, more briskly.

Laurence sniffed, before asking, "How so?"

"He can speak more clearly and has regained some movement in his frozen side. According to the physician, we may anticipate even greater improvement. Martha prescribed lily of the valley, in a tincture with wine, to regulate the heart. And walnuts ground to a powder – I do not understand the point of this last item, but it may be having some effect."

"She's following the doctrine of signatures. The walnut resembles the brain."

"Thank you for that interesting information," said Lady Beaumont, with a faint smile. "Have you seen Elizabeth?"

"Yes." He thought of his sister in her rose-pink gown, standing at the altar beside her husband. "I just gave her Ormiston's wedding ring – from Tom."

"Why is Thomas not here?" she demanded, her smile vanishing.

"He said he would follow me as soon as he could. Poor man, he's broken up – he loved Ormiston."

"More than his father?"

"Oh no, I'm sure not."

She sighed and lowered her eyes. "I was angry with his lordship, just before the fit came over him, and I cannot help thinking that I am partly to blame."

Surprised that she should confide in him, Laurence slipped an arm around her waist to comfort her, then realised that he had never done such a thing in his life. He could detect her equal amazement in the straightening of her spine.

"I must thank Lord Falkland, for permitting you to come," she remarked, moving away from him. "How is he, these days?"

"Not a happy man. Since the events in London, any hope of peace is finished. The war party is on the ascendant, on both sides."

"How long will he let you stay?"

"As long as I wish, unless some emergency arises," Laurence answered, knowing that Falkland's generosity was born of embarrassment, over His Majesty's stubborn indifference on the issue of the conspiracy.

III.

"Will you stop that?" Seward inquired of his cat. Tail high and back arched, it was winding in and out of his legs as he tried to solve a complex algebraic formula. "My dear Pusskins," he said, "it is four of the clock, the sole time of night when I can have peace and quiet, amidst all the chaos of Her Majesty's arrival on these premises. Pray let me concentrate! Clarke was wise, to seek refuge in the countryside," he muttered to himself.

Just then, the cat nipped sharply at his ankle, making him jump up. He was about to berate it again when a memory stirred within him. He looked through the window to the dark quadrangle beyond and saw no one. But a second later there came a knock at the door. He opened it a crack, to Sir Bernard Radcliff, and stepped back in fright.

"Dr. Seward," Radcliff said, "may I come in?" Seward admitted him, after which Radcliff inspected the room as though in a dream; he was hollow-cheeked, his eyes darting from one object to another. "Everything here is as I remembered it!" he exclaimed, as if he and Seward were still on the best of terms.

"No thanks to the depredations of your servant," said Seward, keeping close to the door in case he needed to make a quick escape; Radcliff was wearing his sword.

"Doctor, I am in need of your assistance," Radcliff confessed, in a humble tone.

"To cast a royal horoscope?" Seward said, with wary sarcasm.

"No, to finish the mischief just such a horoscope started. To stop a regicide."

"Go to His Majesty and make your confession."

"You know that if I do, I'll pay with my life and my family will be paupers."

"The price of treachery is ever steep."

"I predicted the King's death! I did not plan it."

"Liar! You would not be here at all, and nor would I, had you not been frustrated in your evil scheme! Why should I help you?"

Radcliff fell into Seward's chair and buried his face in his hands. "I want to save my wife and child from dishonour. No more than that." He looked up, beseeching. "You must have foreseen I would come to you."

"I thought you might address Beaumont first."

"I tried, when he was at Faringdon. Then he stole my letters and disappeared. Doctor, the Earl of Pembroke has shown me the painting of the god of silence. I assume you scried for Pembroke's name, for it was in none of the letters."

"My skills, in this instance, were unnecessary," Seward said, taking great delight in telling him. "Beaumont identified Pembroke long ago as the master of the conspiracy. And the painting was entirely his idea."

"By God!" whispered Radcliff. "Pembroke discovered that he sent it, however, and has asked me to bring him to his lordship's house in London."

"When was that?"

"Back in May, before the Royalist uprising was thwarted."

"Why did you not do it?"

"Of course I would not hand Beaumont over to him! My association with Pembroke is finished, and he must know it. He may already have sent someone out to kill me. Although he, too, is somewhat compromised in his activities these days," Radcliff added. "As one of the moderates in Parliament, he is under suspicion of involvement with the Commission of Array, and is being watched closely by Parliament's spies."

"Alas for him," said Seward, and pointed at Radcliff's sword. "Was it you who told him about the Knights of the Rosy Cross?"

"Yes, and at once he saw that their aim of establishing a wholly Protestant Europe fitted marvellously with his own ambitions."

Seward gave a dry laugh. "I hope he is not aspiring to enter the Brotherhood."

"He said he desired the privilege but had first to earn it."

"In that, he may be disappointed."

"In that, perhaps, but not in other respects," Radcliff said, his voice shaking. "I have cast his horoscope, on his bidding, and he is destined to live on for some years into a time of peace – well after the King's death. So there is reason for us to fear that he may still achieve his goal."

"Oh my God," murmured Seward. Radcliff had truly excelled at astrology and was unlikely to have made any mistake in Pembroke's chart, or indeed in the King's.

"Dr. Seward," Radcliff began again, more firmly, "I have been gathering information, to compile a list of Parliamentary spies operating in London and beyond. It could be of value to the royal cause."

"You would buy your neck with it?"

"No. All I can hope to buy is my family's good name, with that list and my testimony as to Pembroke's guilt. But now we have very little time."

"We?"

"Pembroke will not leave this business unfinished. He will want vengeance on both you and Beaumont. So you must realise, we have an interest in working together to bring charges against the Earl," Radcliff concluded, his steel-grey eyes fixed on Seward. "And if I were you, I would not hesitate to warn your friend."

IV.

Lord Beaumont was ensconced in a high-backed armchair in the library, his feet resting on a stool, while Laurence sat cross-legged on the Turkey carpet nearby, reading to him. He had requested a favourite work in Spanish, *Don Quixote*, and they had just reached the passage describing Dorothea's seduction, at which Lord Beaumont became visibly moved, occasionally dashing the water from his eyes with his handkerchief.

"'What is more,'" Laurence continued, "'Don Fernando's oaths, the witnesses he invoked, the tears he shed and, finally, his charm and good looks began to incline me forcibly to a course which proved my undoing –'"

"Oh, that a poor, innocent young maid should be so terribly wronged by that scoundrel!" interrupted his father, just as his mother burst through the open doors, a strange, panicked look on her face. Perhaps still absorbed in Dorothea's fate, Lord Beaumont did not catch her agitation. "My dear wife," he said, "is it not remarkable how well our son has kept his Spanish? He sounds as if he had never spoken anything else all his life."

"Put that book away," she snapped at Laurence, regarding it as she might some deadly weapon. "A letter has arrived for you. The messenger said it needed no reply."

Laurence rose and took the letter from her. "It's from Wilmot," he said, scanning it, hugely relieved that it was not a summons from Falkland. "Her Majesty has arrived in Oxford and has been installed at Merton College. And there's been a victory, at a place called Roundway Down, near Devizes. Wilmot and Byron crushed Sir William Waller's army – they killed or took prisoner about fourteen hundred men, and seized all of Waller's ammunition and his baggage. Her Majesty insisted that the King create Wilmot a baron, out of gratitude for his success. He's now Lord Wilmot of Adderbury."

"That has a fine ring to it!" said Lord Beaumont cheerfully.

Laurence started to laugh, as he folded up the letter. "It's going to make Wilmot unbearably smug."

Lady Beaumont's face relaxed into a small smile. "Now, Laurence, it is time for your father's nap. Pray go and call Geoffrey to assist him to bed."

When his father had been settled comfortably, Laurence excused himself, and as he often did when the weather obliged, he went down to the river to bathe.

Undressing at the bank, he waded through the shallows and plunged in, breaking the smooth surface. What could have inspired his mother's odd behaviour today, he mused, as he floated lazily on his back; she had been so much friendlier towards him since he had come home. Then he thought of Isabella. Over the three weeks or more since they said goodbye he had missed her like a part of his own flesh, yet he had written to her only once, to inform her of Lord Beaumont's recovery. Although he felt no less certain of his love for her, he knew that it had not been a particularly eloquent letter. In fact, he now worried that she might have found it inadequate. He should reiterate his feelings for her, but the words did not come easily to him.

Diving deep into a colder current of water, he surfaced gasping. Instantly his stomach contracted with fear: on the near bank, a man in black stood watching him.

He exhaled with relief on hearing Seward's voice. "Come out, Beaumont!"

Unlike Joshua Poole, Seward did not avert his gaze as Laurence emerged from the water, but examined him instead with more than academic interest. Eventually he said, "Please cover yourself. I may be old, but my fires have not given out."

"And I thought *I* was too old for *you*," Laurence joked, pulling on his breeches. "So what on earth brought you all the way here?"

"Beaumont, something most untoward happened yesterday. Sir Bernard Radcliff visited me at Merton."

"Good Christ." Laurence sat down beside him on the grass. "What did he want?"

Seward recounted the conversation. "I am certain that he is a lying rogue, but he is trapped like a fish in a barrel," he went on. "And we know there is some truth to his assertion that Pembroke is sniffing at your heels. I spoke with Falkland, and he has impressed upon His Majesty the need for action. Yet it is a delicate matter. His Majesty would still prefer to retain every possible ally he has in the House of Lords."

"He's fooling himself, in Pembroke's case."

"Wipe that sneer off your face, and listen. We are to meet – Falkland, you, Radcliff, and myself. His Majesty has agreed to pre-serve Radcliff from a traitor's death in exchange for his switch in loyalties, and also a list he has apparently made of Parliamentary agents. Then, under the Secretary of State's authority and safe conduct, you and he will travel to London and engage in negotiations with Pembroke."

"*Negotiations*? Pembroke should be brought to trial, and so should Radcliff! Is the King going to let Pembroke get away with plotting his death?"

"You and Radcliff must persuade him that the conspiracy is still-born, and that if he so much as dreams of any violence against His Majesty, or any of His Majesty's servants such as yourself, he is finished."

"Or I may be, if things go wrong. Radcliff could easily change his tune again, once we arrive in London."

"We have his letters, don't forget."

"True. But, as you said," Laurence reminded Seward, "he's a lying rogue."

V.

It was a still, sultry evening turning to dusk, the sky streaked with gold and rose in the west; and to the east, a few pinpoint stars glittered against the deepening blue. Radcliff could hear wood pigeons cooing in the trees and invisible animals stirring the hedgerows, and he could smell the sweet odour of leaves and damp sod beneath his horse's hooves. All this would be the same whether he lived or died, he thought. What self-important creatures men were.

He dismounted in Madam Musgrave's courtyard and gave the stable boy his reins. "Don't unsaddle him, Sam," he said. "I shan't be staying."

He walked along the stone path, through well-tended flowerbeds fragrant with the scent of roses and lavender and rosemary; and with distinct dread, he entered the house.

Madam Musgrave and Kate both leapt to their feet on seeing him. "Sir Bernard," Madam Musgrave exclaimed, "where have you been? Walter wrote to us that you had vanished from your troop to go to London. He is frantic with concern for you!"

"I know, I know," Radcliff said, assuming a carefree tone. "I shall catch up with him later – there's an appointment that I must first keep tonight, and then I ride for Oxford." The women exchanged consternated looks, suggesting to him that his bluster failed to convince them. Then he realised how he must appear: he had not had occasion to trim his beard or change his linen, and his clothes were hanging loose on him. He embraced Kate, thrilled to feel the swell of her stomach against him. "As you see, my dear, I am whole and hearty," he assured her.

"You do not seem hearty, sir," Kate said, rather fearfully.

"Aunt Musgrave," he hurried on, "I must beg your pardon – I should like a short time with my wife before I depart."

"Can you not even sup with us, sir?"

"I regret not. My dear, let's take a stroll outside."

He guided Kate off before Madam Musgrave could object, and they went along the same stone path that he had followed earlier, into the apple orchard beyond, where the trees were heavy with green fruit.

"Did you get back the letters that awful man stole from you?" she demanded at once.

"Oh yes – Mr. Beaumont and I have resolved that problem."

"Don't treat me like a child! Is your life in danger because of what he did?"

"I am no more at risk than I ever was – we *are* a country at war, my sweetheart! Although I do have some distressing news – my lawyer, Joshua Poole, passed away recently. But my documents, my will and so forth, are still at his chambers. I gave you the address –"

"You came to say goodbye. I won't see you again."

"My dearest, stop!" He seized her and kissed her. "Kate, please trust me. You have nothing to worry about."

But she did not look persuaded as they walked back to the house.

Madam Musgrave was waiting with a parcel wrapped in cloth. "A taste of our supper," she said, offering it to him. "And never again leave your wife so long without news of you, if you can possibly help it," she scolded, as they accompanied him to his horse. "It's not the only time you've been neglectful, sir."

He ignored this, saying, "Until soon, ladies. May God bless you." And he galloped off without turning back. When he had gone a little way, he hurled Madam Musgrave's package violently into the bushes.

At Faringdon, he left his horse outside the Cross Keys Inn, the place of his appointment, and walked into the taproom. Looking the picture of ease, Beaumont was sitting with his feet propped up on a bench, his shirt and doublet hanging open, and his hair tied back loosely. He was engrossed in reading a newssheet.

"Mr. Beaumont," Radcliff said, at which he glanced up and smiled. "We should talk elsewhere."

"Of course," he said, tossing aside the newssheet, and rose in a leisurely manner.

As they went out together into the courtyard, Radcliff studied his profile; the flare to his nostrils and the upward slant of his eyes and fine brows were reminiscent of a drawing Radcliff had once seen of some Oriental prince.

"Unbearably hot weather," Radcliff commented, trying to imitate Beaumont's relaxed air.

"I find it quite agreeable."

"Your Spanish blood must account for that."

"Blood's all the same, don't you think?"

They passed through the gates to the yard, and into the quiet country road beyond, where after a silence, Radcliff began, "I must admit, Dr. Seward has scarcely altered in these many years since I last met him."

"I doubt either of us will be as fortunate as he," Beaumont said, with a laugh.

"You don't expect we'll reach his age?"

"The odds aren't all that good. How I wish you'd never been robbed – in The Hague, I mean," Beaumont added. "It would have made life much less difficult for me."

"But you can't regret stealing my letters from the priest's hole." Radcliff halted, to face him. "Did my wife know that you had been in there?"

"Does it really matter now?" Beaumont grinned at him with sudden brilliance. "*I've* a question for *you*, Radcliff. Who was your favourite girl in Blackman Street?"

"What are you talking about?" Radcliff said sharply.

"Or at Simeon's house, then? I knew all the women – as in the Bible, you might say. Who did you prefer? Oh, I remember, it was Marie, wasn't it."

Radcliff's hands curled inadvertently into fists. "May we get to the point? Will you come with me to London?"

"I haven't decided yet. I don't believe in suicide."

"Is that what you think it would be?"

"Don't you want me dead?" Beaumont responded in a casual tone; he might have been asking Radcliff the time of day.

"My feelings are irrelevant," Radcliff said, his jaw clenched. "Part of my bargain with Lord Falkland is to ensure your safe return to him."

"Then I'll be most obliged to you. Let's talk about Pembroke," Beaumont went on, more seriously. "How could he hope to seize power with so few accomplices?"

"He had more than you were aware of, or I, probably. And then he did not require a large force if he could succeed in building his reputation as a peacemaker, even as he was –" Radcliff broke off.

"Plotting to murder the King. How did that sit with you?" Radcliff said nothing. "Even if he succeeded, there'd be no peace. I hear he can't even govern his own tongue. How could he govern a kingdom? You haven't answered me, by the way. How did *you* feel about regicide?"

"It was a necessary evil. And it was predicted."

"Ah yes, the horoscope. What did Pembroke promise you that would make it worth taking such a risk?"

"You would not understand. Your family circumstances are more blessed than mine."

Beaumont shook his head sceptically. "You weren't exactly starving."

"Look at me, Mr. Beaumont," Radcliff said, mastering an urge to draw out his sword and plunge it into Beaumont's guts. "I am a small landowner, not starving, but of modest means, and though gently born, unimportant. At forty, past the prime of my life, I find myself worse off for the increase in taxes than when I inherited at twenty-five. My only chance to rise has been through the condescension of my superiors. Men such as I cannot so much as piss in the wrong corner, lest we offend someone who might be useful to us at some future time. Now look at you. You scorn the pretensions of society and rank. When I said you were an honest man, in a way I meant it. You can afford to challenge convention, just as Pembroke can let loose any profanity he wishes. And you have friends in high places. Falkland, and Wilmot –"

"You had Pembroke, though all along you were prepared to sell him out if you had to. You've been hoist by your own petard. You should have betrayed him earlier."

"Where would that have got me? Again, I am not you. See how effortlessly you gained the confidence of the Secretary of State. Falkland gave the letters credence because of your father's name. He trusted you."

"And Pembroke trusted *you* because of your astrological skills. Is he really that superstitious?" Beaumont queried, as if it were an afterthought.

"I do not consider astrology a superstition. But yes, he is in other respects."

They were quiet for a while; then Beaumont said, "So you've been hunting about London for intelligence on Parliament's spies."

"I was lucky to have some useful connections in that regard. It's not to save myself, as I told Dr. Seward. I just want my wife to be able to raise our child without shrinking with shame at my memory."

"She won't shrink, Radcliff. She's not the sort."

Radcliff glared at him, livid. "What do you know about my wife?"

"No more than I ought to," Beaumont said, laughing again. "Now, Falkland is waiting for us. Shall we go to him?"

VI.

Stephens woke Falkland around midnight.

"I had that dream again, Stephens," Falkland said.

"Of Great Tew?"

"Yes. It is always so refreshing."

"My lord, Dr. Seward and Mr. Beaumont are here with Sir Bernard Radcliff."

Falkland sat up quickly, a sweat breaking over him; at long last, he and Radcliff would meet. "What does Radcliff look like, Stephens?"

"He has a grey aspect, my lord. He strikes me as a very sober man."

"And how is Mr. Beaumont with him?"

"Watching him as a fox might its quarry."

"Thank you, Stephens. Tell them that I shall join them directly."

Falkland had been sleeping dressed. He put on his boots, and tidied his hair before the looking glass, all the while thinking of that first day when Beaumont had come to him with the letters. "I pray I am not sending him to his death," he murmured to his own image, and walked out.

In the other chamber he found them all seated around the table. Radcliff and Seward made as if to rise, but Falkland motioned for them to stay where they were. Radcliff's expression was both dignified and respectful; how one could be deceived by it, Falkland thought.

He turned to Seward. "Doctor, is Sir Bernard Radcliff apprised of His Majesty's offer to him?"

"Yes, my Lord."

"And you too, Mr. Beaumont?"

"Yes," answered Beaumont, his eyes on Radcliff. "A ten-year sentence and a small fine. Not bad, for a would-be regicide."

Radcliff bit his lip but did not speak.

"Sir Bernard, the list, if you please," said Falkland. Radcliff produced a rolled document and placed it on the table. "Thank you. You may leave us." After Radcliff had gone, Falkland asked, "Are any of the names familiar to you, Mr. Beaumont?"

Without permission, Beaumont had picked up the list and was examining it. "No, though that means nothing."

"I must agree with you about Sir Bernard. It infuriates me that he should be so leniently treated."

"He may yet hang if he does not stick to the terms of the bargain," Seward put in. "Although His Majesty has given him every incentive to comply."

"Indeed he has," agreed Beaumont. "But I still don't trust Radcliff any further than I could throw him."

"While this mission has royal approval, Mr. Beaumont," Falkland said, "His Majesty has told me that any mistakes will be my responsibility."

"Isn't that always the way things are," Beaumont remarked, his voice full of contempt. "My lord, pray tell His Majesty that if there are any mistakes, they will be mine alone and you are not to blame. And if I don't return, you mustn't blame yourself, either, because I've chosen of my own accord what I'm about to do."

"Thank you, sir," murmured Falkland gravely; this was the man he had hesitated to trust.

"I should warn you, though – and His Majesty – that if Radcliff makes one false move, I'm going to kill him. Oh, and before I leave, I'd like to read over those coded letters again," said Beaumont, with a slight smile.

VII.

Having pondered all the dangers ahead, Laurence decided not to visit Isabella before setting out for London, although he swore to himself that if he did come back alive, he would never leave her again for as long as she wanted him.

He rode off with Radcliff the next day under a light rain, and they made fair progress. On the following morning, however, the heavens seemed to conspire against them. An unremitting downpour churned the roads into quagmires, they were soaked to the skin, and Radcliff's horse cast a shoe in the thick mud. When they stopped to find a blacksmith at an inn on the edge of Hounslow Heath, they were alarmed to encounter a party of Parliamentary soldiers jostling to be served beer, singing psalms as they quaffed their draughts. The men stared so at Laurence that he chose to wait in the stables for the blacksmith to finish.

He and Radcliff spoke infrequently, and when they did, his sole pleasure lay in continuing to goad the man into a silent rage. Sometimes he wished Radcliff would attack, so that he would be justified in killing him.

They took Laurence's old route as they neared the city by nightfall, stabling their horses with the Chelsea ostler. He wanted to steal a ride on one of the barges again, but Radcliff insisted that they should enter openly. "We'll take a boat at the nearest dock," he said, at which Laurence felt immediately nervous, and yet more suspicious of him.

When they reached the river, a crowd of wherrymen were waiting for custom. "Your destination, sirs?" asked a burly fellow, pushing himself forward.

"Whitehall," Radcliff told him. "How much?"

He named a sum that sounded cheap, until he explained that he had three more passengers going the same way. Radcliff argued to Laurence that they would be delayed, but Laurence quickly paid up the fare. The presence of others offered him a little security; one was a woman nursing her child.

The river stank, as always in high summer: a mixture of sewage, offal, rotting fish and animal carcasses, and the effluent of the tanneries. The night was cloudy, and after a while, as they sailed further from

the shore, everything grew dark. Once they were in open water Laurence
relaxed marginally, though he kept a grip on his pistols, and he was still
watching Radcliff, who sat perched at the edge of the small vessel.

"So, you must be looking forward to seeing your noble patron,"
Laurence remarked. "I wonder what he'll say when he finds out you've
betrayed him."

"My life won't be worth a damn," Radcliff whispered back harshly.
"Unlike you, I have no Secretary of State to protect me."

You have more than you deserve, as it is, Laurence nearly told him.

Radcliff lifted his hand as if to brush off a fly, and a second later
Laurence felt an enormous blow to the back of his own head. As he
tumbled into the bottom of the boat, he cursed not having trusted his
instinct. For that, he was about to die. There came another blow, to the
side of his jaw. Through the pain, he heard Radcliff shout, "Tie him up,
and attach the rope to that weight."

His pistols were wrenched out of his hands and his wrists bound
hastily in front. He was too stunned to resist. He heard a loud splash
and then sensed himself being rolled over the edge. At once he was
engulfed. The chill water shook him out of his stupor; he was sinking
fast. He must not panic, he urged himself, tugging at the rope around
his wrists. At last he managed to free one hand and then the other,
keeping well below the surface, knowing that Radcliff would wait to
make sure he had drowned. But after a while he was forced to raise his
head, gasping for air. He saw black all around except for the glimmer
of lights on either shore, a horribly long distance away. His waterlogged
clothes and boots were dragging him down again, and as he struggled
unsuccessfully to kick off the boots, he could not help swallowing gulps
of the foul river. His limbs were becoming leaden, his teeth chattered,
and he had started to give up hope when suddenly an even greater darkness burst out of the night like some primeval monster: a barge, bearing
straight for him. Either it would hit him, or it would rescue him. He

cried out, his voice so faint against the noise of swirling water that he despaired of anyone hearing him.

Yet gradually the barge altered course. "Fetch the line!" someone shouted.

The wet rope smacked Laurence hard in the face, but he caught it and clung on with both hands, and slowly he was brought in and fished out by a very amazed bargeman.

"Bless me if you aren't a strange catch!" the man exclaimed.

Laurence nodded, coughing up mouthfuls of the Thames. "What a drink," he said afterwards, spitting.

The man handed him a leather bottle. "Here's a better one."

Though he gagged at the coarse liquor, it stayed in its rightful place and revived him considerably. "Thank you for saving my life," he said, and reached out to clasp the man's hand. "Are you going upriver?"

"We are, sir. What the devil happened to you?"

"Someone tried to drown me," Laurence replied, accepting another swig from the bottle. "Can you set me down at Whitehall?"

"Aye, sir. Are you a Member of Parliament, perhaps?"

"No. That's not yet a drowning offence."

"Should be for some of 'em, sir," the man said ruefully.

The barge pulled in at the dock nearest to Whitehall. Laurence searched to see if he still had any money in his sodden pockets, which he did. The man protested that it was only his Christian duty to rescue souls in need, but he was not above taking some coin for it; and they said goodbye.

"Fuck you, Radcliff," Laurence muttered, as he staggered along the dock. Reeking and covered in slime, head aching from the blow, and with another bruise swelling his jaw, he was going to Pembroke's house.

When he arrived at the high walls that surrounded it, he was overcome by dizziness and had to lean against them for support as he felt his way to the main entrance. A liveried servant came quickly to demand his business, and a couple of guards bristled their weapons at him. "I am here on behalf of the Secretary of State," he said, his legs trembling with fatigue. "My name is Laurence Beaumont. I must see his lordship at once."

The servant admitted him with a revolted sniff, and ordered him to wait behind with the guards. Finally he was summoned, and accompanied by the guards he squelched along a corridor, past canvases and statues as refined in taste as those of his father, and into an elegant carpeted room, where two men stood before him.

"Mr. Beaumont, your lordship," he said to Pembroke, and bowed, deriving immense satisfaction from the horror on Radcliff's face.

Pembroke dismissed his guards, closed the door, and turned with infuriated surprise to Radcliff, then to Laurence. "Mr. Beaumont," he said, "did you come by some accident?"

"Oh no, my lord. It was such a warm night that Sir Bernard encouraged me to go for a dip in the Thames on our way here."

Pembroke smiled thinly. "I had been looking for you to thank you for the painting you had delivered to me."

"It was the only means I could think of to show you how badly you had misplaced your trust in Mr. Rose. He's been a thorn in your flesh for a while, if you'll forgive the tired metaphor."

Radcliff opened his mouth but Pembroke silenced him with a curt gesture. "Go on," he said to Laurence.

"He kept the correspondence that you'd ordered him to destroy."

"Which correspondence?"

"The most damaging to you, my lord, so he could sell you out if he decided he'd had enough."

"He is lying, my lord!" Radcliff shouted. "He is William Seward's accomplice."

"Which correspondence?" Pembroke repeated, in a frigid tone.

Laurence began to quote, word for word, Pembroke's letter about the King, and the hunting party at Wilton or wherever else was chosen for the assassination, and what would follow.

"What sort of magic is this?" Pembroke burst in.

"It's not magic, my lord," said Laurence. "In fact, the explanation is rather ordinary. As Sir Bernard can attest, he was robbed at a Dutch bawdy house by a friend of mine – robbed of your gold, his sword, and some letters. That's how I came to have them, and I found more, later, hidden away in a chest of his. All of the correspondence is now in His Majesty's possession. The sword I gave back to Sir Bernard, as you can see. And as for the money –" He dug from his pockets his few remaining coins and threw them at Pembroke's feet. "The rest is spent. My apologies." He sighed, suddenly exhausted. "Oh, and one last thing, my lord. His Majesty wishes you to know that in view of your past relations, he is inclined to treat you mercifully. He expects to hear from you soon. Good night to you both, gentlemen."

"Wait," cried Pembroke, and called out for his guards. "Detain him in one of the antechambers," he barked at them.

"My lord, I assure you, I've nothing more to say," Laurence objected, but the guards hustled him off, into a smaller adjoining room, and locked him in.

He slid down the door and knelt by it, listening. There came the sound of Radcliff's voice and Pembroke's arguing; then the voices subsided into whispers. He hauled himself to his feet and over to the window. It was a steep drop, but onto grass. Defenestration was becoming a regular habit, he thought, as he unfastened the casement and squeezed through. He hung for a second by the broad ledge before letting go and landing with a bump, rolling some way. Ahead was what appeared to be dense shrubbery. Crawling into the thick of it, he crouched and tried to catch his breath. Shouts issued from the open window. On all fours, he plunged further into the bushes, hoping to find the wall that surrounded Pembroke's house, yet he might as well have been blindfolded, for what he could discern in the dark. Recalling the thief Barlow's advice, he stood up and closed his eyes and stretched his hands out as he pressed forward. They met not stone, but wood, and he bashed his forehead against the branch of a tree. The shouting came nearer. He reached up and hoisted himself over the branch, edging along on his stomach until his feet encountered the girth of the trunk. By turning about and clinging to it, he could balance precariously and feel upwards for another branch thick enough to carry his weight. He got to a fork in which he could sit, propped against the trunk, and rest his shaking arms and wipe the blood from his brow. Lights were now approaching in the blackness, as though carried by invisible beings, to within a yard of his tree. "If you catch him, hold him fast: he's mine!" someone yelled out.

VIII.

"He's mine, you hear!" repeated Radcliff.

The guard nodded, and signalled to the men behind. "Where could he have got to, sir? Could he have scaled the wall yet?"

Radcliff lifted his torch, searching for some glimpse of Beaumont. He saw only the outline of branches and leaves creating sinister shapes above him. "I doubt that. He may have hurt himself when he jumped, and be hiding in the bushes. Spread out and keep looking. Well, get to it, men!" he said, as they hesitated.

"We're staying here," the guard said.

Radcliff felt a vague premonition; the torches were circling closer. "What in hell is wrong with you?" he demanded. They did not speak but edged nearer still. "Get after the prisoner, you fools!" he ordered. The same guard let out a low whistle, and the rest stepped forward unsheathing their swords. "By Jesus!" Radcliff exclaimed, unsheathing his. In the flickering light their faces took on beastly forms. Radcliff stared from one man to the next, in outrage: he was not an animal to be cornered and hunted down. "You bastards! You cowardly bastards – how many are you against one?" he screamed at them. "That yellow dog, Pembroke! Call him out to finish me himself!"

They advanced on him relentlessly, some of them dropping their torches, the better to manoeuvre their weapons. Radcliff could smell their sweat, and hear them grunting in anticipation. He took a thrust in the back, and a second blade pierced his thigh, causing him to stumble. He lifted his sword and began to lash out, but each time he left himself exposed in some part of his body, and they struck home again and again. He wounded a man and saw a spurt of blood; then he became maddened, not knowing where to turn. His arms were tiring, however, the energy leaking out of him. He could not see as well; the flames of the torches were now blurring before his eyes. The sword slipped from his hand, and he fell. A last thrust, fiercely delivered, made his stomach burn.

"We'll come for his body later," he heard the guard say. "Let's grab the other one."

There was a tramp of boots through undergrowth, then nothing but the rustling of boughs overheard. Shortly afterwards, Radcliff could detect a scrambling sound, then a light thud, and footsteps coming towards him. A hand lifted his head, while another went about his shoulders.

"Christ, they carved you up like a pig," said a familiar voice.

"Beaumont," he gasped. "Why are you still here?"

"I want the sword."

Radcliff struggled to focus, his wounds agonizing. "What for?" he hissed, blood gushing up between his teeth and bubbling out.

"Revenge," Beaumont answered flatly, as he unbuckled the belt attached to Radcliff's empty scabbard and slid it from his waist.

"On me?"

"A bit late for that, don't you think. Why did you try to kill me tonight?"

"B-because I've loathed you from the moment I set eyes on you." Radcliff was panting for air. "You had everything I ever wanted, and yet you had no respect for it."

"Hmm. Any last words for your wife?"

"T-tell her I wish I – I could have seen our child."

"You might have, if you'd played by the rules."

Radcliff tried to nod. "And tell Ingram I'm sorry."

Beaumont gave a little laugh. "Sorry? You're only sorry you got caught." He must have found the sword, for Radcliff heard a swishing noise as it was thrust back in its scabbard.

Radcliff felt for Beaumont's arm and gripped it with all the strength he had left. "Please, for the love of God, put that blade through me. End my suffering."

Beaumont did not speak, for what seemed an eternity. Then, very quietly, he whispered, "No."

CHAPTER TWENTY

I.

Laurence could barely recognise his old college: where previously few women were ever to be seen, Queen Henrietta Maria had established her entourage, packed into accommodations designed for half the number. Fashionable ladies and gentlemen milled about, playing at games or airing their lapdogs in the quadrangles, and there was a babble of chatter, the sound of someone playing a lute, and a heavy waft of perfume in the air.

He was weaving through the throngs of courtiers when a sharp blow stung him on the shins, and he looked down to see a young, blond dwarf, impeccably costumed, brandishing a diminutive walking cane.

"You could have knocked me over, sir!" cried the dwarf. "You shall apologise, or by my honour you'll pay the price."

"Very sorry indeed," said Laurence, scowling at him.

"Such riffraff they are letting in here these days!" the dwarf complained, as he stalked away.

Seward, fortunately, was at home. "Dear Beaumont, how relieved I am to see you!" he said, welcoming Laurence in. "I feared for your life all this time." Then he took a sniff. "What is that appalling smell?"

"The Thames," Laurence replied.

"Goodness! You must tell me all about your adventures, if we can hear a word over this infernal racket. Privileged as we are to house a royal guest, I cannot countenance the disorder that has ensued. Females in large numbers are more of a curse than any Biblical plague."

"I don't know about the women, but some dwarf just hit me with his walking stick."

Seward chuckled. "That would be Mr. Jeffrey Hudson, Her Majesty's little friend. She is devoted to him, and his pride is out of all proportion to his size."

"She likes her men as short as she is, doesn't she. Her husband's no exception."

"Now, now, Beaumont. Sit down. You look ill tempered."

"I am," said Laurence, pulling up a chair for himself. "I've just come from reporting to Falkland and the King. His Majesty said he was most dissatisfied with the way I left things in London."

"Why, what happened there?"

For the second time that day Laurence told his story, interrupted by many exclamations on Seward's part as he described how close he had come to a watery death.

"Radcliff was a treacherous knave," Seward commented, at the end.

"Pembroke's no better."

"Indeed not – you were fortunate to escape his clutches."

"Oh, but His Majesty is of a different view," said Laurence, not bothering to hide his disgust. "He suggested that before leaving, I should have discussed terms with Pembroke and secured his written promise to abandon the conspiracy. The King claimed that I had disappointed him yet *again*."

"Will he send you back to complete your mission?"

"I'm not sure he trusts me to make a success of it. But Pembroke is still a threat to *us*, Seward. Radcliff told him I was your associate, and being the sort of man he is, he'll come after us even if he gives up on his ambitions regarding the King. That's why I took this."

Laurence had Radcliff's sword wrapped in his cloak, and he now laid it on Seward's desk; there were bloodstains dried into the green leather of its scabbard, a lasting memorial of its owner. "Remember what you said about the Brotherhood of the Rosy Cross, that Pembroke had desecrated its symbols? And here they are on the blade – the same as on his paper."

Seward gazed down at the weapon, then frowned at Laurence. "Would you confront him with it?"

"It could be enough to convince him that he should leave us alone. Radcliff told me he was superstitious. And he may suspect that you taught Radcliff about the Brotherhood."

"It has nothing to do with superstition! He has a sword of Damocles hanging over his head. So you are going back whatever the King decides."

"I must. Ah well – Falkland and I will see His Majesty tomorrow, and I'll find out whether he's giving me another chance."

"Let's pray he does."

"Poor Falkland," Laurence remarked, with a sigh. "He needs all the support he can get, and he knows it. You should have seen his expression yesterday after we left the royal apartments."

"Your fealty to him does you credit. But, Beaumont, what might Radcliff have been planning to do that night, after he got rid of you? Would he still have betrayed Pembroke, or was he seeking to creep back into his master's good graces?"

"Who cares. He did a stupid thing and he paid dearly for it." Laurence rose and stretched. "Excuse me, Seward, I must be off. Would you look after the sword for me?"

"Yes, but where are you going?"

"Don't ask," Laurence said over his shoulder, as he walked out.

On the way to Isabella's house, he grew apprehensive: he had kept her waiting a very long time for news of him. Yet he was unprepared for her maid Lucy's terse greeting. "Mistress Savage cannot receive you, sir," she said.

"Is she sick?" Laurence asked anxiously.

"No, sir. She bade me tell you that she cannot receive you – ever."

"I understand why she may be upset, but I must talk to her."

"Mr. Beaumont, please go away."

"Has Digby forbidden her to see me?" Lucy shook her head. "What is it, then? There must be a reason," he said, more urgently. "I have to hear it, from her!"

"No, sir. Just go!" cried Lucy, and shut the door on him.

He banged on it for some time, but no one answered, so he climbed over a small gate to the side of the house and ran into the back garden; he and Isabella had often liked to sit out there in the early evenings, talking together, and the window of her bedchamber was just above. Increasingly desperate, he shouted up, "Isabella, please! Give me a chance to explain!" But the window remained closed, and the curtains drawn.

II.

Falkland opened his Bible at an unexpected book, the Song of Solomon. As he scanned the familiar verses, he thought of his wife, and to his surprise he felt a stirring in his body quite inappropriate to the circumstances, for he was about to accompany Beaumont again to the royal apartments. Although he shut the Bible quickly and tried to concentrate on more serious matters, the yearning for her did not pass until Stephens entered, followed by Beaumont. He was clean and freshly shaven, dressed in the plain black clothes he had worn to Hoare's trial, but Falkland caught the reek of alcohol on his breath almost immediately, and his eyes were bloodshot.

"Mr. Beaumont," Falkland said, "were you drinking with Dr. Seward last night?"

"No, I was alone."

"You seem out of sorts. Not bad news of your father, I trust?"

"No, my lord."

"Such a wet summer, most injurious to the health," Falkland said, to break Beaumont's taciturn silence, as they walked over to Christ Church. "Fever has laid low troops, townsfolk, and courtiers, without regard for social status."

"At least there's some justice in the world," Beaumont muttered, which made Falkland smile.

His Majesty was seated in an ornate armchair, a letter in his hand. He frowned at Beaumont, but addressed them with less reserve than he had the day before. "My lord, Mr. Beaumont," he said, "I have here a communication from my Lady d-d'Aubigny. She assures me that Mr. Beaumont did everything he could, under d-difficult circumstances, to ensure her security and that of Lady Sophia Murray, and that he quit the French Embassy in May on the Ambassador's expressed order."

Falkland saw Beaumont lower his eyes as if to check an impolite response; he must recognise that was as much of an apology as he could expect from the King.

"For this reason, sir," His Majesty continued, to Beaumont, "I shall overlook the mistakes you made in your n-negotiations with the Earl of Pembroke. I wish you to call upon him again in my name. Let him know that I should like to be able to count on his unswerving loyalty in my dealings with Parliament, as he pledged to me some time ago, or else the content of his letters shall be made public. And have him sign a document to that effect."

"Yes, Your Majesty," Beaumont said, his face impassive.

"My Lord Falkland will supervise the details of your journey. I thank you, gentlemen, and I shall await your lordship at Council tonight. We may have a fresh report of the present siege at Bristol. My nephew has high hopes that the city may be stormed tomorrow and victory will be his. It would be a magnificent prize, to control such a vital port," the King concluded, beaming at them.

So that you can bring in troops from Ireland, Falkland added to himself, *as your headstrong wife has always urged you to do*. "Let us pray it can be taken without too much loss of life," he said.

The King nodded graciously, and they were dismissed.

"My Lady d'Aubigny has come once more to your aid," Falkland observed, as he and Beaumont crossed the rain-soaked College lawn.

Beaumont seemed distracted, as if pondering another issue. "My lord, I'm not going to London. This time I'd like to meet Pembroke on his own territory, at Wilton. Can you arrange that for me?"

"Won't it be more dangerous?"

"He wouldn't dare touch the King's emissary," Beaumont said, with scathing irony. "Besides, I've never seen his house. My father says it's very splendid."

"I can send a guard with you – in fact, as many as you wish."

"Thank you, but I'd prefer to travel by myself. There is one thing you could get for me, however: a brace of pistols. I lost mine when Radcliff tried to drown me. They were French flintlocks."

"Yes, of course. I shall have them delivered to you at Merton." As they walked on, Falkland had an urge to confess to Beaumont his feelings of utter despair, in spite of the King's blithe optimism about taking Bristol. Instead he asked, "How long do you think this war will continue?"

Beaumont turned to look at him piercingly. "Do you want my honest opinion?" Falkland nodded. "For some years more."

Falkland swallowed, and nodded again. "Ah well, if Prince Rupert manages to occupy Bristol, it is likely that His Majesty and the Council of War may join him in the West Country. You might have to find me there. Although if Rupert fails, I could yet be where I am now."

"Knowing the Prince, I'll find you at Bristol," Beaumont said. "Good day, my lord."

III.

Pembroke listened to spurs clanking in time with the tread of feet coming nearer and nearer, and was reminded of a play he had seen in which an avenging ghost had appeared, to much the same sounds, and borne witness to his own murder. Then Pembroke forgot about the play, for here was the man who had told him of Radcliff's treachery. Beaumont bowed, regarding Pembroke with those transparent, feral eyes; were he cast for the stage he would make a perfect assassin. And, to Pembroke's amazement, he was wearing Radcliff's sword.

"Well, sir," Pembroke said, "you've balls, I must admit, to demand that I receive you here, though perhaps I should have expected something of the like, after your daring escape from my London house."

"Why, thank you, your lordship," Beaumont responded serenely.

"Let us make this brief. I gather that His Majesty is offering me terms. What are they?"

"His discretion in exchange for your cooperation."

As Beaumont explained, Pembroke felt as if the ground were opening beneath him into a gaping void. He became incensed that all his years of careful work should have come to this. "Mr. Beaumont, you were a soldier in the foreign war, were you not?" he asked, when Beaumont had finished. "You saw what hell it was. I wanted to spare our country from ruin."

"You wanted to rule it."

"With the support of a new Parliament. Charles Stuart has tried to rule without, as if by ignoring his people's grievances he could make them disappear. And look how he added to them. He sought to impose his bishops on us, his taxes, his duties on our ports. Over and over again, he has refused our peace initiatives and treated our Commissioners like so many criminals. Soon he will bring in Irish troops, even as he pretends to work towards a settlement. He is a Janus – two-faced! Should I trust his word?"

"I think you have no choice. And, after all, you *did* pledge yours."

Now more fascinated than afraid, Pembroke studied him. "How many links there were between you and Sir Bernard – first that bawdy house in The Hague, and then William Seward!"

"And Lady Radcliff. She's the sister of my closest friend."

"Unbelievable," Pembroke murmured.

"On that subject, I know you were protecting Radcliff's estate in Cambridgeshire. Is there a danger that it might be sequestrated upon his death? After all, he was posing as a Royalist – or rather, a *malignant*, which I believe is the current Parliamentary term for His Majesty's supporters."

"How much does Lady Radcliff know about my connection with her husband?"

"Nothing that could hurt you, as yet."

"If you keep it so, I shall ensure that she does not lose the property, though it is a mere few acres of marsh. Have we a bargain?"

"Yes, my lord."

"Sir Bernard said that she is exceptionally lovely. Is she?"

"In appearance, yes."

"Then she's bound to find herself another husband."

Beaumont's expression altered marginally, as if he had just registered in Pembroke a flaw of character for which he felt the utmost disdain. "What happened to the body?"

"It was given the same burial as he had hoped to give you." Beaumont nodded, his face now as relaxed as before. "What are you doing, sir?" Pembroke asked uneasily, as Beaumont started to unfasten Radcliff's sword.

Beaumont held it out to him. "This is for you."

"I *was* wondering . . . how did you get it?"

"I took it from him before he died."

"Ah, so you were watching when the end came."

"Yes. Not a pretty sight."

"Did he bequeath it to me?" Pembroke said, with a hint of mockery.

"No, my lord. You are to keep it as a constant reminder – from the Knights of the Rosy Cross." Pembroke started, his heart thumping in his chest. "Your alarm is entirely justified," Beaumont went on, "given how you have abused their symbols. They would never have sanctioned the murder of a king. And a Protestant king, at that."

"What – what have you to do with them?"

"If you think hard, my lord, you already have the answer." Beaumont smiled, flashing his even white teeth. "But let me make it easier for you. Why would Radcliff study so long with Dr. Seward? Not just to learn about the casting of horoscopes, surely. That's child's play, compared to the knowledge he desired."

"By Christ." Pembroke swallowed. "Is – is Seward an initiate?"

"As I said, think hard, and draw your own conclusion. It seems everyone is watching you, my lord, Parliament included – though you've less to fear from that quarter than from another, as I'm sure you must understand." Beaumont looked about, as if admiring the décor. "What a fine place you have. If I were you, I'd stay here and enjoy it. And hunt some four-legged game for a change."

"I might," whispered Pembroke. "I might at that."

IV.

"How did my husband die?" Kate asked Laurence, sitting down heavily on the bed and folding her hands beneath the expanse of her stomach. He felt suddenly sorry for her, as he noticed pieces of a baby's garment laid out upon the counterpane beside her, ready to be stitched.

"We had the misfortune to run into the city militia," he replied, thinking of Radcliff in the circle of flames, baited by Pembroke's guards. "They pursued us, and when we didn't stop they fired. He was killed outright. I had to flee for my own life, or else I would have tried to bring back his body."

"Why were you in London with him?"

"He wanted my assistance to get past the city defences. He must have confided in you what he was doing there."

Her eyes flickered from side to side; she probably knew no more than was in the letter that they had both read, he thought. "You are a spy, aren't you," she said, surprising him. "You stole his private corre-spondence. He gave me to believe that you had destroyed him. Though the next time I saw him – the last time, in fact – he said you had resolved that problem."

"Yes, we had."

"You're lying. He hated you, as doubtless you did him!"

"In our business, we can't always choose our bedfellows. My history with him isn't important any more, certainly not to you. I should tell you, however, that Parliament won't take it against you that he sided with the King. Your estate won't be touched."

"How can that be? Unless my husband *was* a traitor, after all."

"No, but the less you know of his activities, the safer for you," said Laurence, tempted to smile at the enormity of the understatement.

She glowered at him. "How smug and superior you men are, with all of your secrets."

He had to agree with her, though he made no sign of it. "I'm riding to Bristol, Lady Radcliff. Prince Rupert's forces occupied it some days ago. Ingram must be there, with his regiment. Would you like me to tell him about your husband?"

"Yes, thank you. And please let him know that I shall write to him soon." She picked up her sewing and began to fit the tiny pieces together, as if she were alone in the room.

"Good day to you, then," Laurence excused himself. As he shut the door behind him, he heard a muffled sob and nearly went back in, then thought the better of it.

Madam Musgrave stood waiting for him downstairs in the hall. "How is she, Mr. Beaumont?"

"As you might imagine."

"At least she has Sir Bernard's property. And thank God – or should I say, God willing – she will have a child to console her. I did not enjoy such fortune myself," Madam Musgrave commented, heaving a wistful sigh as they went together to sit by the fireplace, where she had laid out some refreshments. "In some twenty years of marriage, I took every potion in the herbals, I consulted wise women, I drank from holy wells, much as it went against my religion, and I wore rabbits' feet and God knows what other charms tucked inside my shift. All to no avail."

"Maybe the fault wasn't yours."

"That is what I would tell Mr. Musgrave whenever he expressed his disappointment in our childless state," she agreed, pouring him a glass of wine.

"Do you – do you think," he said hesitantly, "that a woman could conceive again, if she once was pregnant but had to – to get rid of it?"

"That would depend upon how the operation was performed, and the present state of her health. Have you some particular woman in mind?" Madam Musgrave inquired, her shrewd eyes fixed on him as she sipped from her own cup.

"What if it had been brutally done?" Laurence asked, avoiding both her gaze and her question.

"Poor creature," she murmured. "It might be harder for her, and more difficult for her to bring another babe to term. Nonetheless, one should not give up hope. What about you, Mr. Beaumont – have you sired any bastards, to your knowledge?"

"I'm afraid I have," he confessed, at which she laughed aloud.

"You should be glad that you have proof of your virility, unlike my late husband. You should get married, sir! You're of the right age, neither too young nor too old. If you wait any longer you might become one of those confirmed bachelors, riddled with pox and gout and bitter memories. Find yourself a wife – although from what Walter has told me, most women will be hard pressed to match the beauty and wit of your mother, Lady Beaumont."

Laurence almost choked on his wine as an image flew into his head of Isabella in his mother's little office, drawing up accounts for the estate.

"Dear me," Madam Musgrave said, laughing again. "You look as if the very words 'husband' and 'wife' signify to you lifelong slavery and sapped desire. You can ride into battle, you can endure being thrashed to a pulp, yet you cannot stick your finger in a ring! Where is your courage, sir? There are worse things than failure, and never to have tried is one of them." He blinked at her, simultaneously shocked and exhilarated, as though she had just drenched him with icy water. "And by the bye," she added, "you should speak with your father about Walter's inheritance. Since Kate is settled with Sir Bernard's property, I have no hesitation in granting Walter mine upon my decease. I want him to know that, and he may consider Faringdon as his own home as of now. I do look forward to meeting his future bride. Is Anne at all like you in character?"

"No," said Laurence, smiling. "In fact, she and Ingram are rather alike – both good, honest souls. They'll be very well matched." Then he asked if he could borrow a pen and some paper; and when he had finished writing, he sealed the missive and gave Sam some coins to have it delivered to an address in Oxford.

V.

At Bristol, Laurence went straight to Falkland's quarters and recounted his discourse with Pembroke, omitting any mention of the Knights of the Rosy Cross.

"How certain can we be of the Earl's promise?" Falkland inquired.

"I think he has every reason to keep it."

"Then the conspiracy is dead at last." Laurence nodded, struck by the thought that part of Khadija's prophecy had now been fulfilled. "Meanwhile, here all is faction, Mr. Beaumont, in spite of the Prince's triumph, or indeed because of it. Bristol was won at a terrible cost. The Cornish suffered grievous casualties, amongst them their finest officers. And as for the defenders, after they ran out of ammunition and surrendered, some were set upon by our side as they quit the city under truce. Prince Rupert had literally to beat his men off them. Yet Prince Maurice continues to enrage the local population with his indiscriminate plundering."

"The foreign way," Laurence remarked.

"Yes, and Rupert cannot rein him in. His Majesty seems unconcerned, and more sanguine than ever, since we now control the second greatest seaport in England. We also have four ships of the Navy," Falkland continued in a despondent tone, as though he were enumerating defeats rather than successes. "We have overrun Dorsetshire, and Prince Maurice is threatening to wreak more devastation on all the ports thereabouts, if they do not surrender to him. We have blocked the flow of goods and livestock to the capital. We hear of disputes in London, where the House of Lords is again seeking compromise with His Majesty. It would seem that we could finish this war within the year. In fact, Digby and others in Council were encouraging the King to march on the capital while Parliament is still reeling from our victories. But on Rupert's advice, he decided against such a course."

"He was right to do so: our armies are too dispersed," said Laurence.

"Exactly. He has settled on laying siege to Gloucester, to make a clean sweep of the west behind him. Our intelligence suggests that the city will not hold out for Parliament. The governor, Colonel Massey, has intimated that he will open the gates to us if His Majesty appears in person and bids him do so."

"Is this intelligence sound?"

"I would be more inclined to rely on it if it came from you," Falkland said, smiling sadly. "We shall soon see. I forgot to ask, did you approve of the pistols I sent you?"

"Yes, thank you, my lord. They're better than the ones I lost."

"That pleases me, very much. Now, sir, you look in need of sustenance. You should go and get yourself a hot supper."

"I shall, my lord," Laurence said, but instead he went in search of Ingram's troop.

The men were assembled for their rations in a straggling queue before the quartermaster. Each soldier received a small loaf of bread and a piece of cheese, and could hold his tankard under a barrel with the spout left constantly running, for a draught of precious ale. Scarcely a drop was wasted, since the quartermaster herded them through like cattle, and they went as docilely. Laurence was relieved not to be one of them. In the line he saw Ingram, who waved at him immediately and came over.

"Beaumont, you stranger! So we're all in Bristol now. Though we may be marching for Gloucester tomorrow."

"I know. Ingram, I have some news for you."

"Good or bad?" Ingram asked, nervously.

"Both. My sister Anne may be getting married soon." Ingram looked crestfallen. "You'll have to ask her first, of course," Laurence added, and relayed to his friend Madam Musgrave's proposition.

Ingram let out a whoop, and hugged him. "Bless Aunt Musgrave! But you said –"

"Yes, I have bad news, too." Laurence gave Ingram a similarly palatable version of Radcliff's death as he had to Kate, and he gauged from Ingram's reaction that it was not altogether unexpected.

"This spring I confronted him about his absences from the troop," Ingram said, in a low voice, and he told Laurence all that had passed between them. "As I hadn't heard from him again in so long, I knew I had to prepare myself for the worst. How tragic for Radcliff. And for Kate." He fell silent, examining Laurence. "You're keeping a great deal to yourself, aren't you. I suspect you know who he was serving." Laurence made no reply. "How is Kate?"

"Admirably composed, as always." Laurence swiftly changed the subject. "Will you take command of Radcliff's troop?"

"No. It will pass to Blunt or Fuller. I'm not cut out for an officer," Ingram admitted, flushing.

"Nor am I, thank God," said Laurence, at which he was pleased to see Ingram smile.

VI.

"What a pair of yokels," Digby complained to the King, as the two Parliamentary messengers turned abruptly and walked away. "Fancy them striding off without the slightest obeisance to Your Majesty!"

In an open show of strength, the Royalist troops had assembled before the city of Gloucester anticipating its immediate surrender, but it now seemed they were to be disappointed.

The King, on his tall horse, wore an affronted expression. "Governor Massey was merely playing for time, and had no thought of capitulating," he declared.

As you have played for time on many occasions, Digby was tempted to comment. "An outrage, Your Majesty," he said. "But if he is expecting help from my Lord Essex, he will have a long wait ahead of him." He was irritated, too: at this very moment they could be moving on London, as he had recommended, instead of parleying with uncouth rebels.

"My Lord Falkland," the King said, "what is your opinion?"

"If we must take Gloucester by force," Falkland said, "let us be merciful in the way we accomplish it. Those men's faces were already pinched with hunger."

"They shall have to start eating their orange cockades," Digby jested, though neither the King nor Falkland appeared to appreciate his witticism.

"At Council tonight, we must decide whether to lay siege to the city or storm it, as Prince Rupert will no doubt urge," His Majesty said. "My Lord Falkland, pray send out a message to all concerned. And we should move our formations to the outskirts."

"How I lament Colonel Massey's choice," Digby heard Falkland shout to him, over the splashing of hooves in the mud, while they retreated. "He could have spared the townsfolk much hardship."

"My dear Lucius," Digby shouted back, "Massey is a Presbyterian, and they are as known for their stubbornness as for their lack of humour. Aha, behold your unlikely guardian angel," he said next, of a rider approaching them.

"Why do you call him that?" snapped Falkland.

"Because he appears to me more diabolic than angelic." As Beaumont reined in his horse beside theirs, Digby asked, "What do you make of it all, Mr. Beaumont? The rebels say they will be at His Majesty's service as soon as they are informed of the fact by both Houses of Parliament."

"I think they're very brave to hold out on such short supplies," Beaumont replied.

"Do you. Oh well, a little fasting can be a healthy thing."

Beaumont fixed his gaze on Digby's stomach. "For some, perhaps. You sent for me, my lord," he said to Falkland.

"Yes. I wish us to talk in my quarters tonight, after Council. I fear it may prove to be a late night, gentlemen. And now I must attend to His Majesty's request," Falkland told them, and he galloped off.

"Mr. Beaumont," said Digby, "might we broach another issue, of import to us both?" Beaumont nodded, quietening his black stallion.

"I had predicted that you would behave badly towards Isabella, yet I kept my mouth shut about it, knowing she would tire of you in time. She is tired of you now, and I would prefer that you stop pestering her."

"With respect, my lord, she should tell me so, not you."

"Why would she want to see or speak to you again? You have mistreated her affections as a mistress by abandoning her for an unaccountable length of time, and you will never marry her, so let this be the end of it."

"I *will* marry her, if she so chooses," Beaumont said, looking straight at him.

"My dear sir," exclaimed Digby, genuinely flabbergasted, "even if you think yourself serious – and even were she interested in your offer – there is not the remotest possibility that you could carry through with it. Be honest with yourself, if not with me," he said, laughing, "you don't know what it is to love for any longer than your prick can stand." Beaumont smiled, but said nothing. "I suppose you expect Isabella is still burning with passion for you, though you would be quite wrong," Digby went on, trying to provoke some other reaction in him. "All your life you must have been spoiled for female company. Women are attracted to you as they are to some foreign dish they have not sampled before." He paused again, riled by Beaumont's lack of fire. "You may not know, but my father was Ambassador to the Spanish Court and I was born in Madrid. Although I am fluent in your mother's language, I left too young to remember much of the country. Yet I would hazard a guess that faces like yours must be ten a penny over there."

"As faces like yours are here, my lord," Beaumont said, with the same bland smile.

Digby had to chuckle. "*Touché*! Mr. Beaumont, I bear you no ill will, for you are merely one in the list of Isabella's conquests, and I cannot blame you for falling under her spell. I am eager for us to be friends. Don't let a temporary difference come between us. And I am most indebted to you for tending to my leg," he added. "If you were not born a nobleman, you could have made a great doctor."

"You're too generous, my lord," said Beaumont, and rode away leaving Digby puzzled as to who had got the better of whom.

VII.

After his exchange with Digby, Laurence wanted to howl out loud. While immune to Digby's spiteful personal jabs, he had been cut to the core on hearing that Isabella had given up on him once and for all. What a fool he had been not to see her before leaving for London and ask outright for her hand in marriage. He had indeed neglected her, and now it might be too late to mend his mistake; though he would have to try.

The Council of War dragged on into the morning, and it was not until afternoon that Laurence was summoned to Falkland's billet, a windowless cottage, hardly fit for a Secretary of State. The air was thick with smoke from the fireplace, where Stephens was turning some pigeons on a spit.

Laurence saw the terrible strain, more pronounced than ever, in Falkland's eyes. "Forgive my delay, Mr. Beaumont," he said. "As you might expect, there were divisions in Council as to how we should take Gloucester."

"What has His Majesty chosen to do?"

"We shall besiege it. Prince Rupert will supervise the laying of mines."

"How will he fire mines in this wet weather? They'll be flooded."

Falkland made no response to this; he was examining Laurence gravely. "Sir," he said, "but for you our King might still be in peril from the conspiracy. And in the affair of Colonel Hoare, you showed both valour and a devotion to me that I lack words to thank you for. I once offered to free you from my service, and you declined. Now I insist that you accept. I wish you to rejoin Lord Wilmot as soon as you can. He has orders to scout the area about Oxford, lest Parliament send any rescuing party to Essex's aid."

"I could be more helpful to you here."

"No, sir, you have more than fulfilled your obligations to me. You know how much I have always hated the business of espionage, and I would not willingly engage anyone I respected in it."

"I believe you, yet I think there's more to it than that." Falkland glanced aside, his expression so legible that Laurence needed no explanation. "You intend to fight in the siege."

"It is my duty."

"It's not duty that's driving you, my lord."

"Should I not face the same dangers as other men of my age, simply because I am one of the King's ministers?" demanded Falkland, his voice becoming shrill. "I have not yearned for peace out of a lack of courage. If anything I should be prepared to venture my person yet *more* readily than other men."

"I don't doubt your courage, my lord, but it would be a serious mistake to –"

"I did not ask for your advice, sir. Stephens, Mr. Beaumont is about to go. You may bring my plate after you have seen him out. Greet Wilmot for me when you see him," he told Laurence, "and God speed."

Outside, the sky had the colour of slate. Rain poured down, and the ground was slippery with mud. Laurence untethered his dripping horse and led it off, and as they trudged through the camp he apologised to it, not in English but in Spanish, for having stolen it from a sunny home and brought it to a damp hell. Why was hell portrayed as hot, he wondered, when this constant drizzle in half-darkness felt so much worse? He would give anything for a blast of sun on his skin.

What a vital distinction there was, he thought, for good Christians like Falkland, between the cowardly escape of suicide and embracing certain death in an honourable fight. Falkland might choose the latter and consider himself free of sin or dishonour, whereas in Spain Laurence had attempted both within the same day, unconcerned by belief in any Divine judgement. Even upon reflection, it would have made no difference to him if he had died by his own hand, or by that of a petty thief on the road to Cadiz. In the end, out of instinct, he had chosen to live; yet he could still remember vividly how it was to peer over the precipice, into nothingness, hungering to jump.

VIII.

That night, as the gypsies made camp, the women whisked Juana away, and since no one else said another word to Laurence, he watched from a distance as the men put up their threadbare tents and dug a fire pit in which they quickly conjured up a blaze. Soon the women brought out cooking pots and started to busy themselves with supper. Juana was not amongst them. Later, a boy brought him a bowl of stew for which he should have been grateful, but the mere smell made his gorge rise.

After their meal, the gypsies entertained themselves with songs, dirge-like melodies accompanied by flute and guitar, while Laurence distracted himself less happily, feeding the contents of his bowl to their yapping dogs. He was angry with Juana for abandoning him, yet he had to be patient: thus far, her people had treated him better than she had been served by most *gadje*.

When the music faded, the women scoured out their pots with sand and chased the children into the tents for the night. It was then that Pedro rose from the fireside and strode over to the place where Laurence was sitting.

"If I wake tomorrow and find you here," Pedro told him bluntly, "I am going to kill you."

Laurence stood up to his full height; the top of Pedro's head did not reach his shoulder. "Why should I deserve that?"

"For what you have done to our sister."

"I brought her back to you."

"But she is not the same."

"What the hell do you mean?" demanded Laurence, taking a step forward.

Pedro shouted a few words in his own tongue and half a dozen men ran over, armed with long knives and a decrepit-looking musket. Pedro grabbed the gun and trained it on Laurence. "I have changed my mind," he announced. "You will leave now."

"I want to talk to her."

"You will never see her again," Pedro spat back. "By all the saints, I'd like to blow a hole in you and fill it with my own shit." He gestured to the others, and all of them sloped away.

If they would not permit him to see Juana, Laurence thought furiously, they must be keeping her from him against her will. Retreating behind a pile of boulders, he charged his pistols and strapped on the Toledo sword; and he waited again, controlling the urge to rush down on the camp immediately and drag her off.

When even the dogs were quiet, he stole over to the women's tent, a mere canopy of cloth supported by sticks. Juana was sleeping curled up beside a younger girl, as she had often slept next to him. He pressed the nose of his pistol to her cheek and nudged her awake. She gave him a startled frown, yet came without a murmur, which reassured him, and she followed him to the lonely place where he had been sitting earlier.

"What did you tell them?" he asked in a whisper.

"That you forced me to be your mistress, in exchange for travelling with me," she replied, her eyes averted.

For an instant, he could not breathe; she might as well have thrust a knife into his flesh. "What need had you to say that?"

She touched her belly, lightly; and he recalled her in Granada, standing by the window. A visceral instinct swept over him: for the first time he wanted desperately to be a father; but more desperately, he wanted her. "In a few months," she said, "everyone would find out. And it was nearly the truth."

"I didn't force you, Juana. You know that very well."

"Oh no?" She assumed an exaggerated version of her mendicant's whine. "The kind gentleman may take her to Paris, and to Spain if it suits him. But he will desert her when she becomes too much of a burden. She will not fuck him, as most other women do, so she's not worth his trouble. Admit," she said in her own voice, "that you intended to leave me behind at the convent in Pamplona. I had to come and find you, and give my body to you, or else you would have shaken me off as a dog shakes off its fleas."

He shrank inwardly; she was not entirely wrong. "Then why did you swear afterwards that you would never leave me?"

"What could you expect? You were protecting me. And if I had to be sullied by a *gadje*, you were above the rest: handsome, and honourable in your own fashion."

"*Sullied*? Is *that* what you felt?"

She hesitated, her mouth trembling. "I was ashamed, because I liked it. Even in Granada, I liked it. As I liked you."

"So come with me! I promise I'll do anything I can for you – you and our child."

"No. I belong here."

"But I love you," he protested, making a start towards her.

She cowered back, as if he might hurt her. "Monsieur, you are a fool. You cannot love whoever you wish."

"Did you never love me?"

"Never. Now you must go. It is only because I told Pedro how you saved my life that he has not taken yours tonight." She gave a quick sob. "We did not create this world, Monsieur, but we must abide by its rules. For my people you are *marime*!"

"And the child? Is it polluted, too?"

"The child is *mine*," she said, crossing her arms over her stomach.

He took off the Toledo sword, and from his saddlebag withdrew the stolen purse, and tossed them at her. "As are these."

"I don't want them. They will bring me bad luck." She bowed her head, turning away. "Goodbye, Monsieur. Our journey together is finished."

She ran for the camp, and he knew that it was truly finished between them.

He heard the dogs barking; in a short time, the men would also wake. A vengeful idea flashed into his mind, and he went to where the horses were tethered. Taking the saddle off his own weary mount, he threw it across the back of Pedro's stallion and fastened its girth. Shouts were already echoing from the tents as he led the beast over to his isolated place, strapped the sword to his saddle and stuck his pistols in their holsters. The purse he stuffed back into his saddlebag; if she had no interest in it, he was not about to leave it for Pedro. Gathering up his bag and slinging it over the pommel, he heard more angry cries. Then an ill-aimed shot cracked over his head, frightening the horse, which reared violently. As it plunged down again, he hoisted himself into the saddle and dug spurs into its sides.

He did not recall how he arrived at the coast or how long it had taken him, though he must have ridden at breakneck speed, for the stallion's coat was flecked with foam. To the east, the sun was piercing through a bed of thin clouds that would burn off with the heat of day. Dismounting, he looked down at the jagged rocks and tide below, and then out over the sea, watching the gulls soar and swoop amongst the crashing waves. What next, he thought: he was unmanned, cut adrift with nowhere to go and no will to preserve himself. He had even come to the very end of Spain.

From his saddle, he took one of the pistols with which he had dispatched so many men. Kneeling down in the dirt, he thrust the barrel deep into his mouth, but gagged at the oily taste. Applying it instead to his temple he cocked it, reflecting on the absurdity of fate: after struggling to survive countless dangers these past six years, he was choosing to die by his own hand.

He depressed the trigger slightly, all that was needed, though in the final moment his hand must have jerked aside, for the ball blasted past his ear, deafening him. Numbly he rose, pulled the other pistol from the saddle and cocked it, to try again. Yet he found himself transfixed by the sight of Cadiz on the far horizon, a haze of walls and turrets; and he fired the second shot, aimlessly, into the lightening sky.

IX.

"May it p-please God that our supplies of ammunition arrive in time from Oxford," His Majesty, said, as the meeting of Council drew to a close. "And sleep well, gentlemen, for tomorrow we do battle."

Falkland stood to bow with the rest of them, and the King departed for his quarters. At once, the arguments began.

"What sheer incompetence to let Essex slip through and relieve Gloucester," Digby exclaimed, to the obvious outrage of Prince Rupert and Wilmot. "Afterwards our intelligence was a shambles," he went on, eyeing Falkland, "deceiving us that he would head north, when all the while he intended to plod home to London. And despite His Royal Highness' noble efforts to prevent him," he concluded, "he managed to march his army all the way past Hungerford through hostile territory."

"We made Newbury too hot for him last night," Rupert growled, glaring back at Digby. "And we've blocked the London road. We have the advantage of him, my lord, and we'll prove it to him in the morning." With this he marched out, followed by Boy.

"Temper, temper," Digby murmured, gazing after him.

"I didn't notice you amongst our ranks, while we were trying to intercept the enemy," Wilmot sneered. "What important work kept you away, my lord – were you penning some lines for your newssheet?"

"My dear Lord Wilmot, how on earth do you think I got these? Not from an exploding quill!" Digby was indicating the powder burns on his cheek, still red and raw, that Falkland knew he had sustained in an earlier skirmish with the enemy.

"Gentlemen," Falkland told them, "I shall allow you to continue this scintillating debate without me. I am going to bed."

"My lord," said Wilmot, "may we walk out together?" Falkland nodded, although he had no taste for any company tonight. "Why did you enlist with Byron's regiment?" Wilmot asked, when they were alone. "If you must take part in the action, join me, as you did at Edgehill. You'll be safer, my lord. I hear that you've been rather reckless in exposing yourself to fire ever since the siege at Gloucester."

"Thank you, but I have made my plans." Falkland stopped, seeing a tall figure in the distance who appeared to be waiting for them. "Did Mr. Beaumont prompt you to ask?"

"Yes, he did," admitted Wilmot.

"He has been avoiding me, I think, for the past three weeks. I'm afraid I was sharp with him when we last spoke."

"Oh, I wouldn't put it down to that, my lord. He's in the most maudlin state because his lover has rejected him. Digby told me all about it."

"Who is she?"

"Isabella Savage. They had a brief dalliance in Oxford last June, and now she won't have anything to do with him."

Falkland thought of that day at Oxford Castle when Mistress Savage had bent down to touch Beaumont's chest, as if to raise him from the dead. "What went wrong between them?"

"You can't win with women like her," said Wilmot, with an air of authority. "Once they have power over you, they get bored and move on to make some other conquest. I'm amazed that Beaumont shouldn't have foreseen it."

Falkland beckoned for him to come to them. The alteration in him was marked: even in the gloom of night, Falkland could detect how thin his face had become, a shadow of beard on his chin and upper lip, and yet darker circles about his eyes. He glanced at Wilmot, who quickly excused himself, reminding Falkland, "My invitation stands. We're bivouacked near Rupert's Horse."

"God be with you tomorrow," Falkland responded.

"And you too."

"How are you, my lord?" Beaumont asked, after Wilmot had gone.

"Better than you, it appears."

Beaumont gave a shrug, more resigned than indifferent. "My lord, I won't offer you my advice, as I know you've had enough of it, but I just had to – to say to you, you will be careful tomorrow?"

"We shall all have to be careful."

He sighed, a short, frustrated breath, as though Falkland were purposely misunderstanding him. "You can't stop this war, but rather than sacrifice yourself, consider what you value that the war can't change: your family, your friendships, your ideals."

"You surprise me, sir. I did not imagine you such a philosopher."

"I don't love wisdom." He smiled, with a hint of his old spirit. "I like life, even though it's kicked me in the teeth a few times." Then his smile disappeared, and he regarded Falkland with acute concern. "My lord, you believe you compromised yourself, that you lost your integrity. It's not true. His Majesty compromised you, as he has so many of his servants in the past, and there'll be others to come. Remember your wife and children. They may be worth dying for. His Majesty's cause is not."

"Treasonous words, Mr. Beaumont – good that only I can hear you," Falkland commented, attempting humour.

"I only hope that you listen." He smiled at Falkland again, more weakly. "Forgive me, my lord – I *am* giving you advice, after all."

Falkland did not know what to say. They were quiet, still looking at each other. Then on impulse he reached up, being so much shorter, to embrace Beaumont. "I thank you, sir," he whispered, releasing him. "Good night."

"Good night, my lord," said Beaumont, in a hoarse, muffled voice.

Falkland watched him go, his lanky form graceful in contrast to his actions, for he was sniffing and wiping his eyes and nose on his sleeve like a beaten schoolboy.

Before bedding down, Falkland wrote a letter to his wife in which he professed his love for her, and for his sons. When he had finished, he asked Stephens to set out a fresh shirt for the morning, as he had each night since the failed siege of Gloucester. Then he prayed, and settled down to catch what sleep he could. Tired as he was, he drowsed; and he seemed to be floating over his property at Tew. He soared effortlessly over trees and soft, rolling meadows, where sheep grazed, all bathed in golden sunlight. His house was spread out like an architect's design below him, and he could almost brush the rooftops. He hovered, catching the scent of wood smoke from the chimneys, and wanted to descend and peer through the window, hoping for a glimpse of Lettice at her needlework, or of the boys playing. Yet he could not stop. On he went, over more countryside elegiac its beauty, the patched fields marked out by dry-stone walls; and there were great abbeys, with cathedral spires rising up towards him; and the sound of chanting, as of the monks that used to inhabit them. He was aware of an immense peace and happiness, now untroubled by the desire to direct his flight. But he was snatched, and pulled downwards; and as he woke to someone calling his name, he knew that although he had had that dream many times, never before had he understood what it signified.

"My lord," Stephens said, "Byron has been ordered to attack the enemy flank, on the hills outside Newbury. Early this morning Essex moved up and stole the high ground from us. He has a couple of field pieces up there and has already opened fire on our men down on the plain."

Falkland rose hastily, unbuttoned his doublet for Stephens to remove it, pulled off his soiled shirt and drew on the clean linen, enjoying its crispness next to his skin. The Rector of Newbury had arrived to give him communion, and as he took the sacrament, he felt within himself that same profound peace and solemn joy. Trumpets were sounding all about the camp, and drums beating. He went out to find his horse saddled, and his pistols primed. He mounted, gave instructions to Stephens about the letter, and cantered over to the place where Byron's Horse had started to assemble. They were to accompany a regiment of foot led by Byron's uncle, and would proceed uphill, along a lane lined with tall hedgerows, to challenge those of Essex's troops already positioned there. Byron was in a black mood, annoyed that this area had not been scouted and occupied earlier. They might have a difficult task ahead of them, he warned Falkland, because the thick hedgerows would give the enemy cover from which to fire, while they themselves would have little room to manoeuvre.

They set off, their scouts ahead on horseback, then the ranks of foot, and lastly two regiments of horse. As they toiled up the incline, Falkland could not see over the wall of green on either side, lush from the wet summer. The men appeared uneasy, glancing about and murmuring to each other. Shots rang out, and the foot began to cave and scatter, some seeking cover behind a grassy bank, yelling for the horse to come to their defence. The horse was still protected by a shoulder of hill, and Byron gave the command to advance, to reconnoitre.

Falkland pushed to the front, beside Byron. He saw that their line of advance was almost completely blocked by a hedge, save for a gap so narrow that only one horseman could press through at a time.

"Widen the gap!" Byron shouted.

In the same second, Falkland heard the whiz of a ball near his ear, and Byron's horse screamed, blood pouring from its neck. Byron leapt off before it could fall and crush him, and the wounded beast tumbled into the ditch and lay, still screaming and quivering in agony, on its side.

Falkland could not bear the noise any longer. He looked from Byron to the gap in the hedge, cocked his pistol and charged.

X.

Laurence surfaced slowly from a drunken sleep, to pounding at the door. "Who's there?" he called out.

"A messenger from the Secretary of State, for Mr. Beaumont."

He sat up in bed, rousing the woman whom he had forgotten was beside him, the sister of Wilmot's latest mistress. As she yawned lazily, he wished that he could make her disappear with the morning light, which was not flattering to her after so much liquor and so few hours' rest; nor probably to him, he reminded himself, as he slid out and searched for his breeches on the floor. Then he stopped: Falkland was dead, so whose messenger was this?

The night after the battle of Newbury, Falkland had been missing from Byron's regiment. Prince Rupert had written to the Earl of Essex asking if he had been taken prisoner, and learnt that he must be amongst the fallen. His body was eventually found, so mangled and disfigured that it could only be identified by a mole on his throat. Laurence had felt sick when he heard, and for the whole week since he thought constantly of Falkland, tormented by the idea that there might have been something more that he could have said to prevent such a senseless loss. Against Prince Rupert's counsel, the King had subsequently withdrawn most of his forces to Oxford. Deeply grieved by the death of Falkland, and those of others who had perished in the muddy lanes and fields, His Majesty was unwilling to re-engage with Essex and suffer further casualties. Although harried by Rupert's Horse, Essex had marched his army back to London, and a hero's welcome. Meanwhile, Wilmot had taken charge of Laurence, knowing how much Falkland's death had devastated him. He kept him occupied scouting the Oxford environs by day, after which they would drink away most evenings in town.

Still fastening his breeches, Laurence opened the door to a liveried servant. "Who *is* the Secretary of State?" he inquired.

"My Lord Digby, sir."

"Since when?"

"The appointment was made yesterday. He wishes an audience with you," the man replied, smirking; he had caught a glimpse of the woman.

Laurence shut the door and went to put on the rest of his clothes.

Upon arrival at the Secretary of State's quarters, he bowed to Digby, who was humming a tune as he perused some documents. "Ah, Mr. Beaumont!" he cried, looking up. "My servant was able to ferret you out!"

"Congratulations on your appointment, my lord," Laurence said.

"It was not entirely my choice, but Her Majesty urged me to accept." Of course she would, Laurence thought: she resented the influence of Prince Rupert over her husband, and Rupert was no ally of Digby's. "May I offer you some hair of the dog that so evidently bit you?" Digby asked, waving for Laurence to take a seat.

"No, thank you."

"Very well, then." Digby began again in a more efficient tone. "I know how you must mourn my predecessor, and I also know how well you served him. I should like you to continue in the service of the Secretary of State, as my chief agent. Amongst Lord Falkland's papers, I have inherited a curious list that he received from a Sir

Bernard Radcliff, with whom I gather you were acquainted. It merits investigation – by you." Laurence remained silent, waiting for Digby to speak his piece. "Unlike Falkland, I have a great enthusiasm for your profession, sir. I have always had my own agents here and there, and they will be at your disposal. I can give you all the latitude you require. There will be no lectures from me on the evils of dissimulation, nor shall I issue any moral rebukes. Do you grasp my meaning?"

"You would give me a free hand."

"How we understand each other!"

There was a pause, during which Laurence regretted that he had not taken advantage of Digby's other offer: he could have used a glass of wine. "My lord," he said, "Lord Falkland released me from my duties early in August. Since then, as you're aware, I've been serving with Wilmot – excuse me, with Lord Wilmot – and I don't intend to leave him."

"Has he seduced you so easily with liquor and women?"

"No. It's my wish."

"So you categorically refuse?"

"I do."

"You might reconsider, in time."

"I won't. Is that all, my lord?"

Digby hesitated, shuffling the papers before him. "Isabella wants to see you. *Not* to renew your former friendship but in order to return to you something you gave her. A necklace, I believe."

"She should have given it to you to return."

"As I told her, but you know women – once they have an idea in their heads, they are as immoveable as mountains. There's a banquet tonight, at Merton. She will be in attendance. Do spruce yourself up for the occasion."

"What an excellent idea, my lord," Laurence said.

All the city bathhouses were shut, clean water being in short supply although the drainage ditches were overflowing from the heavy rains. He had to wash and shave in Seward's rooms, while Seward mocked him for accepting the invitation. "Not your style, Beaumont, these frivolous Court events. Why are you bothering?"

"Oh, politics," he said, shrugging.

He decided to arrive late. Isabella would guess where to find him if she had not seen him at table, for since the day had been dry and the evening was cloudless, torches had been set up to mark a path into the gardens beyond the College terrace so that the courtiers could filter out after their repast to take fresh air; and there was a special pavilion for the royal family where musicians were playing viols and assorted wind instruments. He waited, skulking in the shadows, until he saw groups of people begin to emerge from the brightness of the hall. Finally she appeared on Digby's arm, the unwanted necklace about her throat. Laurence edged closer and concealed himself behind a wall.

"You owe me five pounds, Digby," she was saying; she did not look in the least unhappy.

"How disappointing – I thought it a sure bet that he would come," said Digby. "Are you unwell, my dear?"

"I feel indigested, after that revolting goose we ate."

"I hope it is not your quartain sickness. You always say that your food tastes odd when it comes over you."

"I have no fever. But would you bring me a glass of spirits to settle my stomach?"

"At once," Digby told her, with a sweet affection that Laurence had not heard from him before. "Wait here on this bench."

Digby returned towards the hall, stopping occasionally to bow or exchange a greeting, while she sat staring ahead, motionless. Laurence crept out and sat beside her, though not too close.

She turned to look at him, a fierce glitter in her eyes, as brilliant as the jewels round her neck. "I knew you were here."

"You lost faith in me, didn't you," he said.

"Why wouldn't I? In a whole month while you were supposedly with your father, all that I received from you was a single, most unsatisfactory letter."

"If I had time I could tell you what kept me away, but in part it was because of what I had to do for Falkland. When I came back to your house, you refused to see me. And I did write to you again, after that."

"Another literary masterpiece," she said scornfully.

"I know, I've got no talent for expressing my feelings on paper," he confessed.

She seemed temporarily mollified; then her face hardened again. "Such fun you must be having with Wilmot. Digby says he's quite the bawd. And Oxford is a gentleman's paradise nowadays."

"You know none of that means a thing to me!" he retorted.

She rose abruptly, picked up her skirts, and rushed off into the darkness.

He followed and grabbed her by the shoulder, twisting her around. "I love you, Isabella, but I can't go on loving in vain! If there's no hope, then for God's sake say so."

She was fumbling to unclasp her necklace, and when it came free she attempted to throw at him. He stayed her hand; she was panting, as though she had run a great distance.

"Will you marry me?" he asked, tightening his grip as she tried to pull away from him.

"What a question! Or are you being deliberately cruel?"

"If you'll have me, I'm yours – and no one else's."

She was frowning at him with the same hostile mistrust. Unable to contain himself, he seized her and kissed her, almost roughly at first, until she relaxed against him and opened her mouth to his; and they stayed locked together for some time.

Then she tilted back her head and whispered, "Help me with this necklace, Beaumont." She held it about her throat and turned for him to fasten it, which he did with trembling fingers. "Digby's back," she said next, peering towards the terrace. "I must go to him. Call at my house tomorrow, and I promise I shall receive you – warmly."

He kissed her again before releasing her, and she walked slowly up to the terrace, a hand over her mouth, as though nauseated.

Digby held out a little glass to her as she came closer. "My dear, where were you?" Laurence heard him ask.

"I went into the bushes – I thought I was about to be sick. I can't drink it, Digby," she added, refusing the glass. "Just take me home. I want an early night."

"Yes, yes," Digby said, squinting for a second in Laurence's direction, and gave her his arm; and the two of them were swallowed by the crowd.

Still bursting with ungovernable energy, Laurence retreated to pace the streets around the College and run over in his mind every word of his conversation with Isabella. After an hour or so of this, he knew that he absolutely could not wait until the next day to see her.

He sped towards her house, but as he was approaching her door, someone seized his collar, and a cold object was rammed against his temple. "Hello there, Mr. Beaumont," said a voice.

"Hello, Captain Milne," said Laurence.

"Did you think I'd forgotten about that night you cheated me?"

There were four or five others in the shadows, two of whom Laurence knew from the Blue Boar: the card players, Ruskell and Pickett. "What are you doing here?" he demanded of Milne, remembering that Digby had paid the man to leave her alone. "And who told you I would be –"

"We're going out to the fields, sir, to settle our dispute like gentlemen. If you object, however, I'll put a ball in your skull right now. We brought you a sword in case you weren't wearing one, as I see you're not."

"Most considerate of you," Laurence said, as they marched him off at gunpoint. He felt aghast at the terrible irony of the situation: Milne could not know what an inept opponent he was.

A low fog hung about the meadows down by the river. The grass was pooled with water after all the rain, and their boots sank deeply into it as they walked. Bad terrain for a duel, Laurence thought, not that he had much chance on the driest of ground.

Milne tossed him the sword. "Put up your blade." Laurence shook his head. "Or would you prefer a round of *primero*?" Milne asked snidely.

"Can't you get it up?" Ruskell jeered.

Laurence had to raise the weapon. It was not the same as riding into battle, where confusion, smoke, and an enemy's nerves could hide his poor swordsmanship, and as he had been warned, Milne was agile and skilful. They parried and feinted for a bit, to much comment from their audience, the clash of steel ringing out in the quiet of night. Then Milne wounded him on his sword arm.

"All your breeding and you handle your rapier worse than any ploughman," Milne taunted him, dancing about, apparently unimpeded by the soggy turf. "Come at me! Come at me!" The blood from Laurence's cut made his grip slippery, and he was slower than Milne, breathing hard. "Are you as clumsy with your cock?" Milne persisted. "All show and no action, aren't you!"

Laurence managed to dodge a few more thrusts, but Milne delivered a serious slash to his shoulder, the blade entering and withdrawing like a shaft of flame. From Milne's expression, nearly demented with pleasure, he knew that the man would kill him, and the thought of dying such a ridiculous death infuriated him. As Milne paused, guard momentarily down, no doubt preparing to utter another insult, Laurence jerked up his sword, intending to point it at Milne's throat and demand an end to the fight. Yet he was too clumsy, after all: instead he caught Milne on the side of the neck. Blood shot out as if from a fountain.

Milne exclaimed aloud, dropping his sword, and fell. Laurence tossed aside his, also, and went down on his knees, clapping both hands to the wound. Milne's body had started to judder. As for the friends, they were running away, melting into the fog. The flow of blood gradually stopped spraying in Laurence's face, and pulsed more dully through his fingers. Wincing with pain, he stripped off his doublet and pressed it to Milne's neck, knowing as he did so that the man was past help and that he himself had to disappear.

He rose and pulled the drenched garment over his good arm, buttoning it to form a makeshift sling. Dawn began to break as he retraced his steps to Isabella's house, and hammered on the door with his free hand.

"Who is it?" said Lucy, from within.

"Lucy, let me in," he yelled, and this time she did. She gave a shriek on seeing him.

"What's the matter, Lucy?" Isabella called, from upstairs.

"It's Mr. Beaumont and he's – he's almost dead!"

"No I'm not," said Laurence, as Isabella hurried down.

"Oh my God, Beaumont, who did this to you?" She drew him in and lowered him into a chair. "Where are you hurt?" Helping him off with his doublet, she tore away his shirt to view the wounds: a gash on his right arm, below the muscle of his shoulder, and in the shoulder itself a wider, more profound incision. "You've lost so much blood!"

"Most of it isn't mine. Bring bandages, and hot water. And a needle and some strong thread. I could do with some liquor, too."

When she and Lucy returned, she went to work immediately, washing away the blood with a cloth that became redder each time she applied it. "With whom did you fight?"

"Milne."

"That can't be! Digby sent him off."

"Apparently not far enough. He was waiting for me outside your house."

"I hope you served him as well as he did you."

"I killed him."

"Oh no! Beaumont, that's dreadful!"

"I can assure you, it wasn't my intention," he said, taking a swig of liquor.

"I am not sorry for *him*, I am worried for *you*! Did anyone witness the fight?"

"About half a dozen of his friends."

"Dear Jesus! All of Oxford must know by now. Should I bandage you?"

He shook his head, with difficulty since the pain was now spreading upwards from his shoulder. "The cuts have to be stitched."

"I'll send Lucy for a surgeon."

"You can sew, can't you?"

"I can try," she said bravely, but as she began, she was shaking and overly tentative. He had to guide her, insisting that she dig the needle further in and pull the thread tighter. By the end, she seemed about to faint.

"You did very well," he said, kissing her on the cheek. "Now for the bandages." This she was accomplishing more speedily, when they heard loud noises outside.

"Open up, Mistress Savage!" came a stern order. "Open now, or we shall break down the door."

"What should I do?" Lucy gasped.

"Nothing for it but to answer," Laurence said, nearly laughing at the hopelessness of it all, and on Isabella's command Lucy opened, to a troop of soldiers.

"Mr. Beaumont," one of them said, "you are under arrest for the murder of Captain Milne."

"Can't you see he is wounded?" Isabella cried, as they hauled him out of the chair. "Let him be!" Then Laurence heard another voice at the entrance, and he realised instantly what trap had been set for him that night, though he could see from Isabella's face that she did not yet understand.

The Secretary of State strolled in, with the air of a guest invited to a surprise party thrown for his benefit. "Isabella, my darling, I must apologise for my sudden entrance! Release her and sit him down," he told the men. "How grievously are you hurt?" he inquired of Laurence.

"Not as grievously as Milne. You were behind this, weren't you, my lord."

Isabella moved nearer to Laurence, as if to shield him. "Digby, that can't be true!"

"You may wait outside," Digby commanded the soldiers. When they had left, he beamed at Isabella. "You *do* owe me that five pounds. I knew Mr. Beaumont would show himself at the banquet – though sneakily, so as not to encounter me – and I gave you both what I believed was sufficient time in the dark to rediscover your fondness for each other. I also anticipated that after such a prolonged drought, Mr. Beaumont would seek to refresh his thirst for you as soon as possible, and in a more private location. And Captain Milne, who I'm sure we all considered ultimately dispensable, was overjoyed to accept the errand on which I sent him. He had been yearning to exact vengeance, though I hear from his friends it was a far closer thing than I had predicted, and I *am* sorry about that," he said to Laurence. "Sir, you have committed a crime punishable by death. A tribulation for you, though not for our gallant Captain Milne."

"You were not above duelling yourself in the past," Isabella told him angrily.

"And got myself imprisoned for it once, as a young man. But I did not kill my opponent – indeed, I disarmed him. And we were not at war, as we are now, when sterner measures are required to stamp out such unruly behaviour."

"Digby, you will not allow him to suffer for this."

"It is the law, Isabella. Do you think me above the law?"

"You *are* the Secretary of State!"

"My dear, you tear at my heartstrings! How can I oppose the arrows of Cupid, when even the gods are impotent against them? But the truth is," he went on to Laurence, beaming again, "I told His Majesty about your refusing my offer of employment, and he thought it most ill-advised that I should lack such a good man to assist me. So here we are. You need a favour, which I admit I have the power to grant, if you will only be persuaded to revoke your decision. No need to answer straight away. I shall come tomorrow to see how the patient is faring," he said to Isabella. "Nurse him well. Oh – there's a guard on the house, just in case. Mr. Beaumont is precious to both of us now." And he bowed to them and sauntered out.

XI.

On the following day, which had turned sunny and hot for the end of September, Laurence was sitting in the back garden reading an issue of *Mercurius Aulicus* when Digby appeared. "Entertained by the product of my genius?" he asked.

"Somewhat more than I was yesterday," Laurence said, with a smile.

"Always a joker! One of the many things I like about you, sir. Well, have you reviewed your options?"

"I don't believe you gave me any, as I could have told you then."

"How are your cuts?"

"Sore, but tolerable."

"Then it would not tire you, to receive some company?"

Again he gave Laurence no alternative, for Isabella had emerged from the house with Prince Charles and Dr. Earle.

"Don't disturb yourself, Mr. Beaumont," the Prince said, as Laurence was about to rise. "You know," he added, grinning, "we never finished our discussion of Thucydides – do you remember?"

"Yes, Your Highness," Laurence replied.

"I hope we can do so, at some future date." The Prince appraised Isabella with his large, dark eyes. "Madam, may we speak alone with him?"

"Certainly," she said, and left them.

"Dr. Earle has explained what you accomplished for my father and for me, in the matter of the conspiracy," the Prince said to Laurence. "I must thank you. My father was also delighted to hear that you have accepted to work with our new Secretary of State." Laurence gave Digby a sideways glance but said nothing. "How enchanting Mistress Savage is," the Prince observed next. "I should not mind being wounded if I could have a woman such as her ministering to *my* every need."

Earle shot him a reproving look and turned to Laurence. "Mr. Beaumont, I confess I am still mourning the death of my Lord Falkland. England has lost one of her greatest and fairest minds, and I a dear friend."

"He was a better man than most," Laurence said, with another glance at Digby, who had moved a few paces away with the Prince, as though uninterested in any enumeration of Falkland's virtues; he and the boy were now engaged in some private chat, both of them laughing.

"He was the best of men," Earle agreed. "He could not act ignobly, and it cost him the ultimate sacrifice." Then he bent forward, to whisper in Laurence's ear, "His Majesty showed me the regicides' letters, and explained why he always doubted they could succeed. He wanted you to know, because he was aware of your impatience with him on the whole issue." Laurence frowned, about to interrupt. "You see," Earle hurried on, "his father King James was a strong believer in sorcery, and lived most of his life in fear of assassination – this last being understandable, given the circumstances of his mother's life and death. For these reasons he kept from record the true hour of his children's birth, so that no one could attempt an accurate prediction of their future."

Laurence shook his head, astonished. "But what about Radcliff's horoscope?"

"It was in error, His Majesty said. He even confided in me the correct hour of his delivery, which he had from Lady Ochiltrie, who looked after him in Scotland until his second year."

"Good God," Laurence murmured.

Digby and the Prince were returning, at which Earle straightened quickly. "Now, Your Highness, we must go back to our Aristotle."

The Prince pulled a face. "He is such a dry study, don't you think, Mr. Beaumont?"

Laurence had to laugh, though he was still stunned by Earle's news. "Yes indeed, he used to put me to sleep."

"I shall be visiting our friend Dr. Seward soon, Mr. Beaumont," Earle said. "Should I tell him where he might find you?"

"I suspect he knows, but please do." Laurence hesitated. "And could you also tell him what you just told me? I think it would be important to him to know that, too."

"I shall, sir," Earle said, and took the Prince's arm.

"Goodbye, Mr. Beaumont, and Lord Digby," the Prince called back as he and Earle departed.

To Laurence's annoyance, Digby stayed, plucking an apple from his pocket and munching on it pensively. "Isabella refuses to talk to me," he said. "She does not appreciate reasons of state, a typical feminine weakness to which I thought her immune. Could you help her to accept the necessity of my ploy?"

"I have accepted to serve you, my lord, but only in an official capacity," answered Laurence. "I wouldn't dream of interfering in your relations with Isabella, as I trust you won't in mine with her."

"Goodness me, I can foresee that you will be very prickly to handle."

"As they say, be careful what you wish for."

Digby took another bite of his apple. "As to *what they say*, you might be amused to hear the silliest piece of gossip that is circulating these days about Lord Falkland. People are whispering that he did not charge bravely into musket fire because he was tormented to distraction by our current woes, but because he was stricken with grief at the death of a certain lady at Court – a Mistress Moray, is her name – with whom he had been madly in love!" He started to giggle. "Can you believe it!"

For a moment, Laurence was too enraged to speak. "Are you trying on purpose to lower my opinion of you, my lord?" he demanded, staring straight at Digby. "If so, you're succeeding admirably." Digby blushed, and looked away. "And if I ever catch anyone repeating that vile slander," Laurence went on, "I swear, I shan't be responsible for my actions."

Digby cleared his throat a little nervously. "I must beg your pardon," he said in a quiet voice, at last meeting Laurence's gaze. "That *was* unworthy of me, and I stand corrected." They were both silent; then he tossed aside his apple core and added cheerfully, "Oh well, I shall expect you to report for duty as soon as you are able. Sir Bernard Radcliff's list awaits. Good day to you, sir."

Over the next few days, Digby left Laurence and Isabella alone. They spent the time at their leisure, not rising from bed until late afternoon. In the evenings they often played chess, at which Isabella excelled, or simply talked. Both of them were reticent on certain subjects, however: he about his work for Falkland, and she about her past. But he was in no rush: with her he felt complete, and he derived as much satisfaction from their conversations as from their nights together.

Towards the end of the week, as they were drinking sack in the parlour, Lucy announced another visitor, much to their surprise: Lady Beaumont.

Isabella got up at once. "I should retire."

"Please don't," Laurence insisted.

Lady Beaumont entered, followed by Geoffrey, holding her cloak. Laurence was immediately irritated, as she surveyed Isabella with far less enthusiasm than Prince Charles had shown. "Mistress Savage," she said, after Laurence had introduced them, "Are you attending to my son in his convalescence?"

"I am endeavouring to, your ladyship," Isabella responded politely.

Lady Beaumont gave her a bleak smile. "How kind."

"I was about to see to our supper. Would you do us the honour of sharing it tonight?"

"I thank you, but no."

"Pray excuse me, then," Isabella said, and she curtseyed and disappeared.

"She has a rare beauty," Lady Beaumont commented to Laurence.

"Yes, she has. How is my father?"

"Almost fully in possession of his normal strength and faculties. He wished to undertake this journey with me, yet I considered it wiser for him to stay at Chipping Campden. I heard of the fevers in town and did not want him exposed to them." Laurence waited for her to continue; she seemed flustered, speaking more rapidly than usual. "Thomas came home to see him at last, with happy news. He has been granted a commission in Prince Rupert's Lifeguard."

"Oh, that's very good. And Elizabeth? How is she?"

"Strong," said Lady Beaumont, her expression softening. "We are proud of her."

"Tell me, does my father know that I'm to be employed again by the Secretary of State?"

"Yes, Lord Digby wrote to inform us. He is full of praise for you, Laurence, particularly since you risked your life to protect him." Laurence squinted at her, baffled. "Don't pretend such modesty! He told us how you were wounded in a duel with some rogue who tried to attack him in the street. Hence his obtaining the King's mercy for you, in the death of that despicable man." More genius on Digby's part, Laurence thought, and why contradict it? "Even if we are not altogether pleased at what you will be doing for him," she went on, "we are reconciled to it, nonetheless, by a certain debt we owe his father, the Earl of Bristol."

"What debt is that?"

"The Earl, or Sir John Digby as he was then, had been appointed Ambassador to the Court of Spain in 1611, the same year that your father was making his tour of the continent. Sir John knew my family by reputation as one of the oldest and noblest in Seville, and gave your father an introduction to us." She paused, a discernible flush rising in her cheeks. "And that is how I met my husband."

"Then the Earl of Bristol can take credit for both his son's entry into the world *and* mine, if rather more indirectly in my case."

"I suppose he can. Laurence, I do hope you are feeling better, because Her Majesty the Queen has requested that we join her and his lordship at a masque she has organized for the Court tomorrow. There are some . . . presentations that she wishes to make, that might interest you."

"Ah," he said; so his mother had come to field the possibility of another betrothal. "I'm sorry, but I must refuse."

"There is no harm in your going out a little in society."

"Thank you, but I have here all the society I want."

Lady Beaumont pursed her lips, scanning the parlour as though it were some insalubrious hovel. "Could not my Lord Digby find you other accommodation?"

"I doubt it, Oxford is so overcrowded," Laurence replied, smiling at her.

Lady Beaumont signalled to Geoffrey to bring her cloak. "I am lodged for the next week near Her Majesty's quarters in Merton," she said, in a tight voice. "You may call on me there, if you choose. Good day to you, Laurence, and please bid Mistress Savage farewell from me, since I do not expect to see her ever again."

He accompanied his mother out, with a wink at Geoffrey, and then poured himself a much needed glass of sack. Of course, he reflected, the Queen would gladly oblige his mother by selecting those young ladies amongst her retinue who might be suitable brides for Lord Beaumont's heir. And Laurence could not go out in society with Isabella, for although the Queen was reputedly less censorious about illicit liaisons than her husband, it was more acceptable at Court to commit adultery in private than to be an unmarried couple living openly in sin. Her Majesty probably enjoyed interfering in matters of love as much as she most certainly did in matters of state; on that last score, she was as much of a danger to the nation as her husband.

Laurence sat down and stared into the depths of his glass, swirling about the amber liquid. Pembroke had not been so wrong in the end: there would be no peace while the present monarch reigned. And if the regicide had succeeded, would that have been such a tragedy? Falkland's death was more tragic to Laurence than the King's could ever be. He recalled his moment of victory in the priest's hole when he had exulted over the letters and the freedom they might buy him. How wrong he had been.

He closed his eyes, and as though one memory had triggered another, an image flashed before him, of Khadija leading him through the mysterious rooms of the Alhambra Palace. He felt the stem of his glass snap in his hand; suddenly the whole of Khadija's prophecy had returned to him with stunning clarity. Leaping up, he tossed aside the broken glass and ran to find Isabella in the kitchen.

"Come," he said, grabbing her by the arm.

"Where are you taking me?" she asked.

"Upstairs."

"Oh not now, Beaumont – we are just about to eat," she protested, laughing, as he led her into the bedchamber.

"It can wait." He sat her down on the bed beside him, and faced her directly. "Isabella, let's get married at once. Why not? We can do it tomorrow, if you agree."

"You impetuous creature!" She gave him a tender smile, running her fingers through his hair. "Must we fight everyone? That is what our marriage would entail."

"Are you afraid to fight? You have the name of a queen, a great queen. You can't be afraid."

"Indeed I can be, after meeting her ladyship your mother! I felt quite naked beneath her scrutiny."

"Then she saw you at your best," Laurence said, gazing into her eyes.

At this, she became grave. "Beaumont, with you I'll always be afraid. You are not the sort of man to lead a quiet life. If I did not love you so much, I should believe myself foolish to share it with you."

"I'll take care of us."

"First practise your duelling skills. Speaking of which, Prince Charles asked me how you acquired this scar on your mouth," she remarked, touching it. "He wondered if it was from another duel. I said I didn't know, and that all your scars are a map of your past, about which I have much to learn."

"As I do about yours."

"You cannot see my scars," she said, with a shade of melancholy. "Yet they are there."

"They may not be as bad as you think."

"*That* would be wishful thinking, my friend. No, we must accept that we have an uncertain future ahead of us, and enjoy the day. So I shall concede to you in only one respect," she added, pulling him closer.

"Which is?" he asked, though he was beginning to have some idea.

She smiled again, languorously, and told him, "Our supper can wait."

EPILOGUE
Oxford, October, 1643

S eward had arranged everything on his desk: clean sheets of paper, a freshly cut quill, and a pot of his favourite ink. Before starting work, he decided to prepare his pipe. He reached for a jar from the cupboard, and shook out from it a small, moist pellet: the last of Beaumont's hashish, which he had been saving especially for just such an occasion. He heated and crumbled the drug, added a pinch of tobacco, and with a silent thanks to the old Moor of Cadiz, lit the pipe. Then, almost fearfully, he withdrew from his gown the brief note he had made after dining with Earle in College, and began to consult his dog-eared book of astrological tables.

Under the influence of the drug, his hand no longer trembled as he copied down various figures in separate columns. On a new sheet he drew a square, and traced inside it the dimensions of a horoscope. "Twelve spaces in all, for the cabal of twelve houses," he mumbled to himself. "And in the spaces, I shall fill in the figures." He did so carefully, checking them each time. At length, pausing to relight his pipe, which had gone cold, he inspected the result.

When he finished, it was dawn. Collecting his papers together, he stored them safely away in between the pages of a large tome, put on his cloak, and slipped out. Although Beaumont had never liked early mornings and would complain about being roused from his bed, Seward could not wait to inform him: King Charles was to die not in the summer of the coming year but on the thirtieth of January, six years hence. Radcliff had predicted rightly, however, that the King would come to a violent end. Yet it was beyond even Seward's occult skills to foretell who would cut him down.

The End

HISTORICAL NOTE

As a keen student of history, particularly that of the English Civil War, I made a deliberate effort to remain faithful to written accounts from and about the period, sometimes even using the recorded words of my non-fictional characters. The protracted peace negotiations between King and Parliament, the complex rivalries within the King's camp, the confusing course of battles and skirmishes, and the failed Royalist uprising in London have been represented as accurately as possible, though the truth is often hard to identify well over three hundred and fifty years after the events. While my sources are too numerous to list here, I would like to acknowledge my great debt to C. V. Wedgwood's *The King's Peace* and *The King's War*, as well as to S. R. Gardiner's classic *History of the Great Civil War* and H. C. B. Rogers' *Battles and Generals of the Civil Wars*.

I have, however, taken some creative liberties with history. The Earl of Pembroke did indeed pledge a secret oath of fealty to King Charles, but the plot to regicide was entirely my invention and I must apologise to the Earl's living descendants for casting any fictional cloud over his good name. On another issue, contemporaries of Lord Falkland and historians writing later about his death have differed as to why he plunged into enemy fire at the battle of Newbury: had the bloody turmoil of war driven him to utter despair, or was he simply overeager to share the perils of combat with his fellow troops? I chose to lean towards the view of his dear friend, Edward Hyde, the Earl of Clarendon, as expressed in *The Great Rebellion*. Along with many other figures involved in the events of the war, Hyde is absent from *The Best of Men*; for purposes of brevity and clarity, I could not include them all.

In the story, I treated as factual the existence of the Brotherhood of the Rosy Cross, which has been the subject of much controversy ever since the first appearance of the mysterious German romance *The Chemical Wedding of Christian Rosencreutz* in 1616 (for the Rosicrucian and Hermetic influences on seventeenth century thought and politics, I relied heavily on the fascinating work of Frances A. Yates, *The Rosicrucian Enlightenment*). On a final point, I am not sure whether the exact time of King Charles' birth was ever set down, but his father's belief in witchcraft and fear of assassination are both well documented, so it is not inconceivable – no pun intended – that he might have sought to protect his children by hiding such vital details from the curious astrologers of his age.

MAIN HISTORICAL CHARACTERS

Charles Stuart, King of England, 1600–49

Henrietta Maria, his wife, 1609–69

Charles Stuart, Prince of Wales, 1630–85: heir to the throne; restored as Charles II in 1660.

Prince Rupert, 1619–82: son of King Charles' sister, Elizabeth of Bohemia; Commander in Chief of His Majesty's Horse during the first years of the Civil War.

Lady Catharine d'Aubigny, née Howard; married Lord George d'Aubigny, King Charles' cousin in 1638; widowed in 1642.

Lucius Cary, Viscount Falkland, 1610–43: principal Secretary of State 1642–43; friend of John Earle; seat at Great Tew, Oxfordshire.

Lettice Cary: Lord Falkland's wife; mother of his two sons.

Henry Wilmot, 1612–58: Commissioner General of the King's Horse; created Baron Adderbury in 1643; created first Earl of Rochester in 1652; father to the infamous poet.

Lord George Digby, 1612–77: married Anne Russell in 1640; created Baron Digby in 1641; succeeded Falkland as Secretary of State in 1643.

Dr. John Earle, 1601?–65: former chaplain to the Earl of Pembroke; tutor to Prince Charles, along with Thomas Hobbes, the philosopher.

Philip Herbert, 1584–1650: became fourth Earl of Pembroke, 1630, on the death of the third Earl, his brother, William; seat at Wilton House, Wiltshire.

Edmund Waller, 1606–87: Member of Parliament and friend of Falkland; exiled in 1643 by Parliament for his part in the Royalist plot; reconciled with Cromwell in 1651; reconciled with Charles II in 1660.

ACKNOWLEDGEMENTS

I want to thank all the people who offered me inspiration and support, many of whom were kind enough to read or listen to various versions of the story as it developed over the years. I am especially grateful to Jennifer Roblin for her incisive criticism, her equally mordant wit, and her profoundly sensitive understanding of my fictional and non-fictional characters; to my agent, Sam Hiyate, for his enthusiasm and professional acumen; to Jennifer Lambert, who first championed publication of the book; to my wonderful and eternally patient editor, Lara Hinchberger, and the team at McClelland and Stewart; to Stephen Walker, for encouraging me early on to pursue this project; and to Caro Soles and her writers' group, who helped me to stay with it. I am tremendously grateful to Dan Franklin at Jonathan Cape for returning Laurence Beaumont to his native land. Finally, I owe an enormous thanks to my family, to my familiars Daisy and Lupin, and to my very best of men, Oscar (Ousseynou) Thiaw.